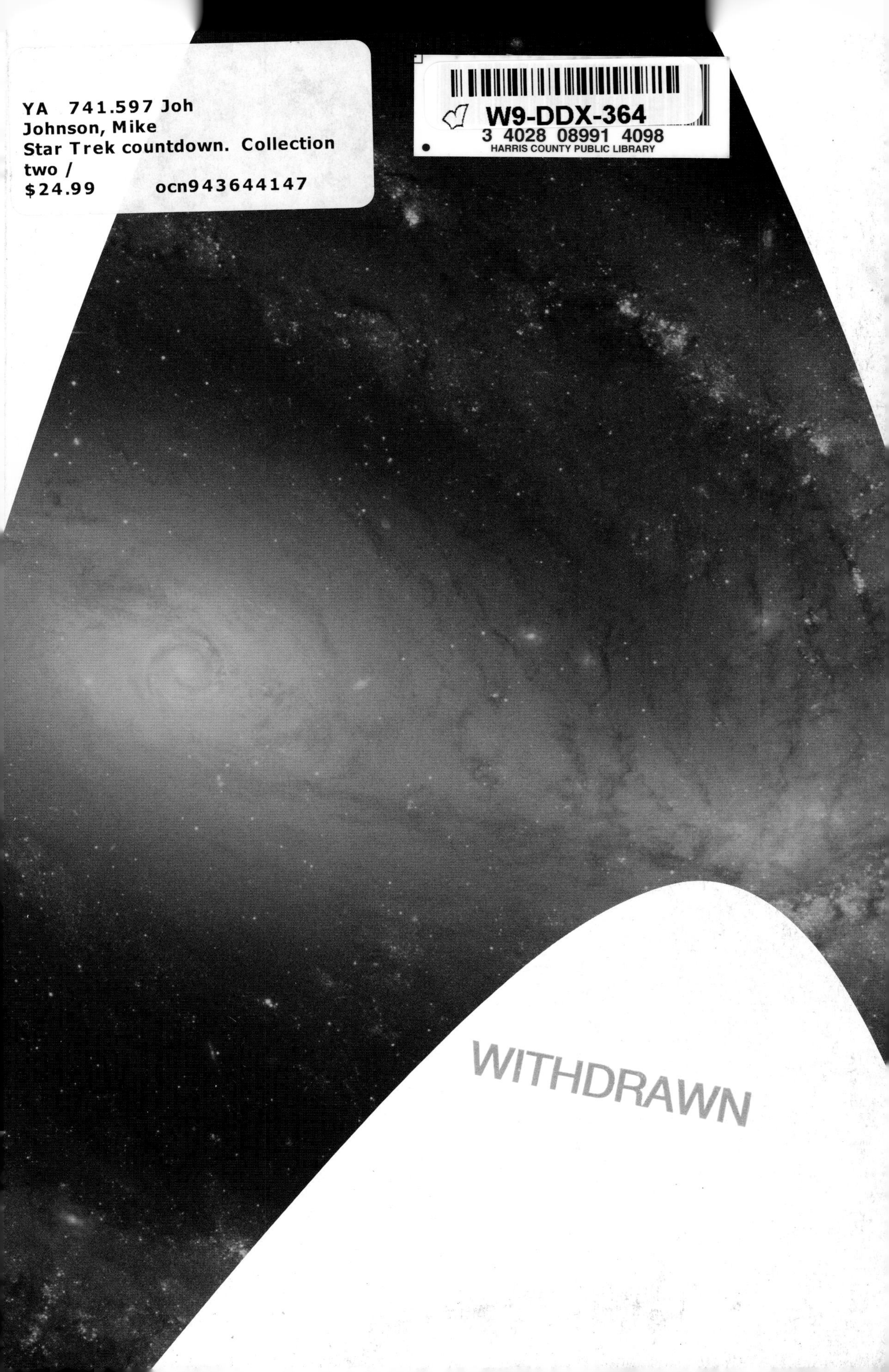

Facebook: **facebook.com/idwpublishing**
Twitter: **@idwpublishing**
YouTube: **youtube.com/idwpublishing**
Tumblr: **tumblr.idwpublishing.com**
Instagram: **instagram.com/idwpublishing**

COVER ART BY
JOHN WATSON

COLLECTION EDITS BY
JUSTIN EISINGER
AND ALONZO SIMON

COLLECTION DESIGN BY
JEFF POWELL

PUBLISHER
TED ADAMS

ISBN: 978-1-63140-633-1   19 18 17 16   1 2 3 4

Originally published as STAR TREK: COUNTDOWN TO DARKNESS issues #1–4 and STAR TREK: KHAN issues #1–5.

Ted Adams, CEO & Publisher
Greg Goldstein, President & COO
Robbie Robbins, EVP/Sr. Graphic Artist
Chris Ryall, Chief Creative Officer/Editor-in-Chief
Matthew Ruzicka, CPA, Chief Financial Officer
Dirk Wood, VP of Marketing
Lorelei Bunjes, VP of Digital Services
Jeff Webber, VP of Digital and Subsidiary Rights
Jerry Bennington, VP of New Product Development

Special thanks to Risa Kessler and John Van Citters of CBS Consumer Products for their invaluable assistance.

STAR TREK
COUNTDOWN
COLLECTION TWO

WRITER
MIKE JOHNSON

STORY CONSULTANT
ROBERTO ORCI

PENCILS
DAVID MESSINA

ADDITIONAL PENCILS
CLAUDIA BALBONI (KHAN ISSUES #1–3)
AND **LUCA LAMBERTI** (KHAN ISSUES #4–5)

INKS
MARINA CASTELVETRO
AND **GIORGIA SPOSITO** (KHAN ISSUES #4–5)

COLORIST
CLAUDIA SCARLETGOTHICA

LETTERERS
CHRIS MOWRY AND **NEIL UYETAKE**

SERIES EDITORS
SCOTT DUNBIER AND **SARAH GAYDOS**

STAR TREK CREATED BY GENE RODDENBERRY

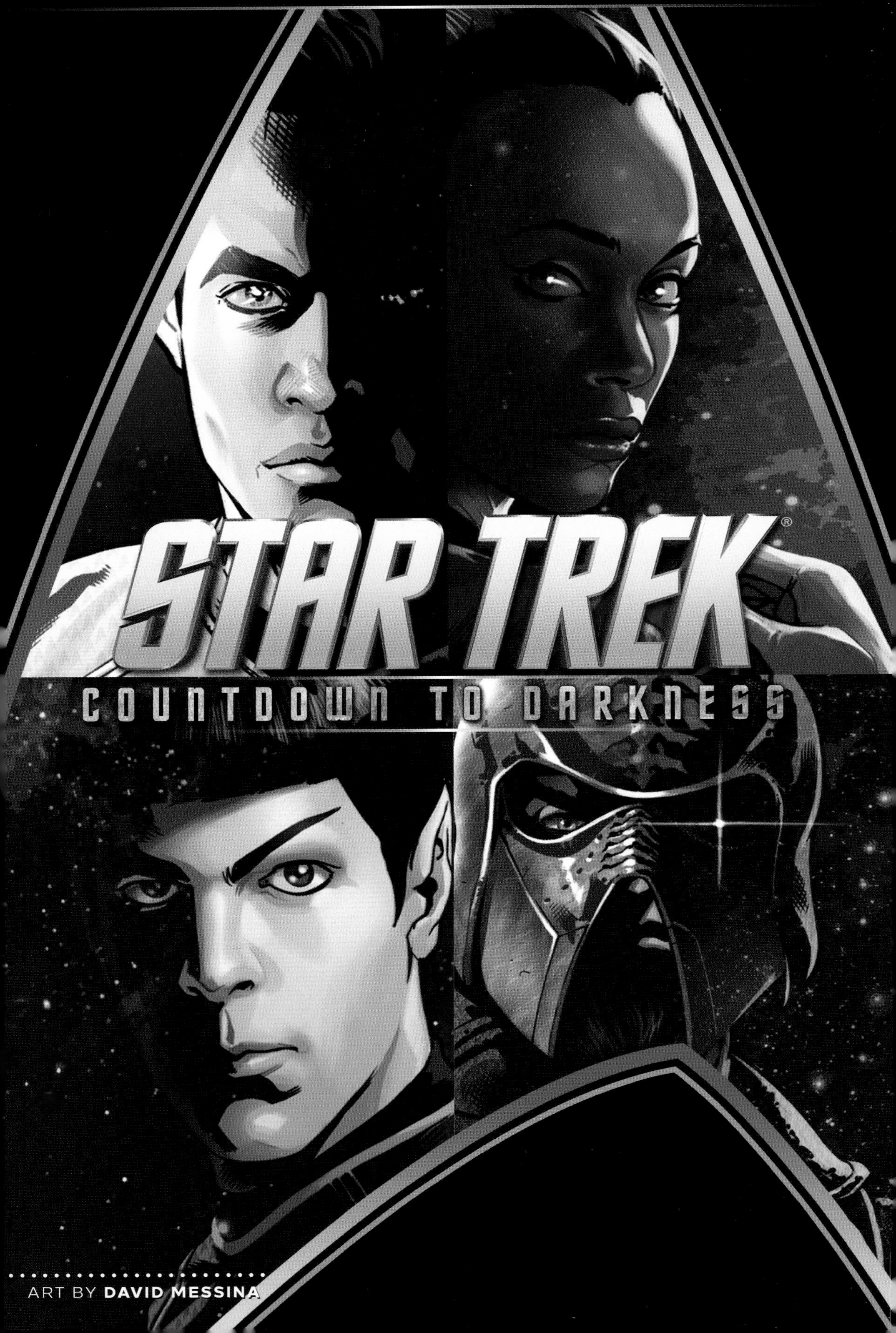
STAR TREK®
COUNTDOWN TO DARKNESS
ART BY DAVID MESSINA

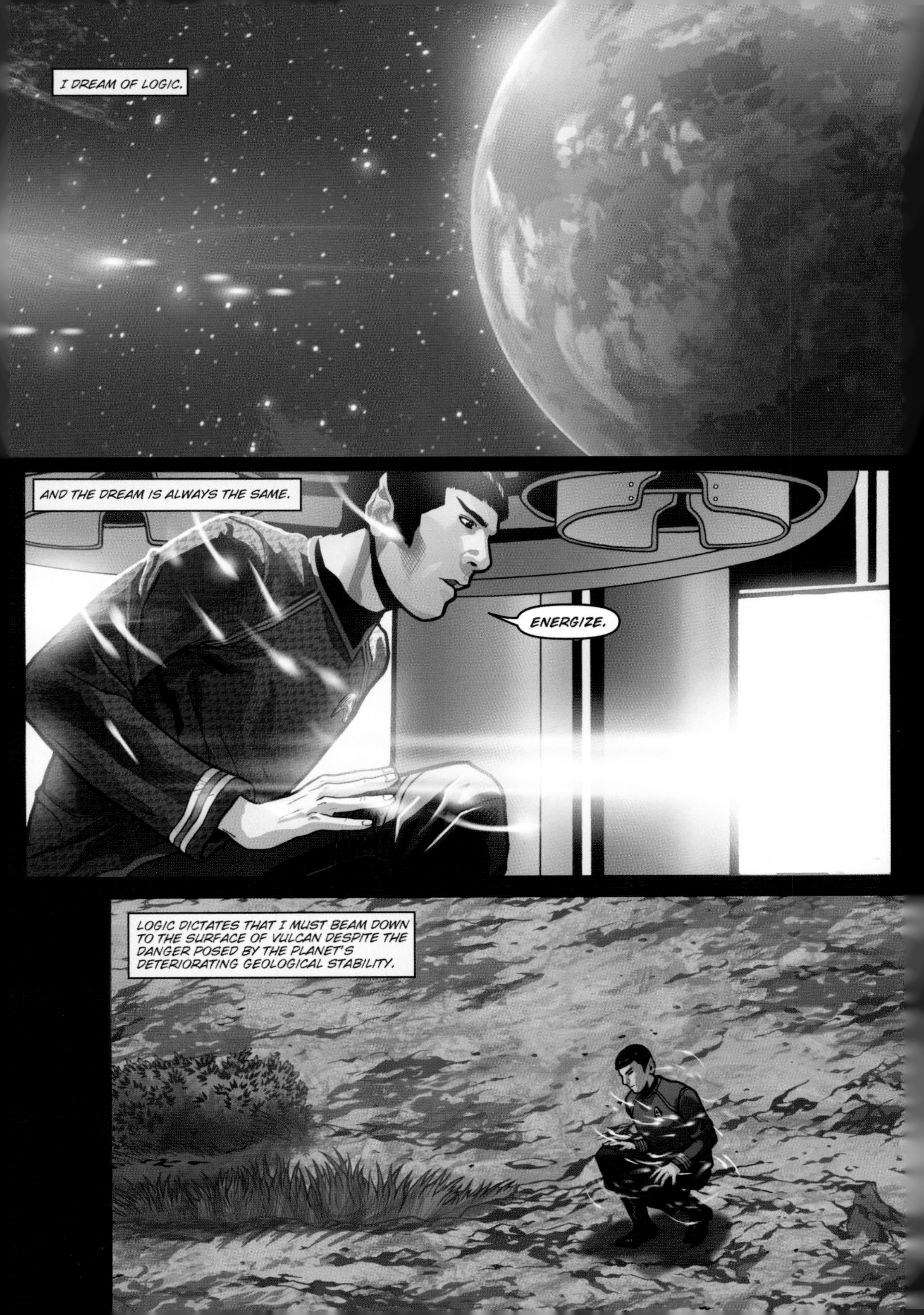
I DREAM OF LOGIC.
AND THE DREAM IS ALWAYS THE SAME.
ENERGIZE.
LOGIC DICTATES THAT I MUST BEAM DOWN TO THE SURFACE OF VULCAN DESPITE THE DANGER POSED BY THE PLANET'S DETERIORATING GEOLOGICAL STABILITY.

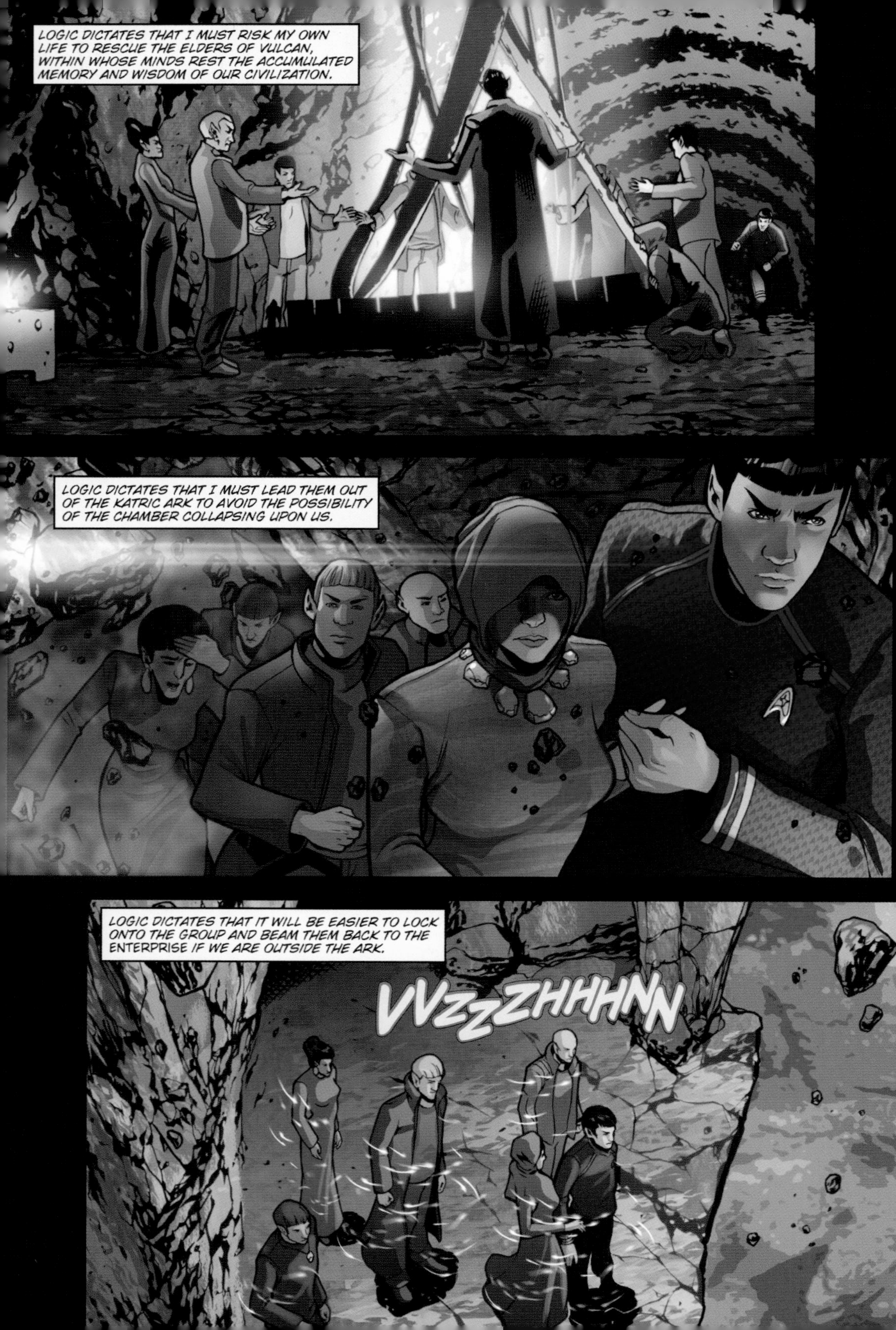
LOGIC DICTATES THAT I MUST RISK MY OWN LIFE TO RESCUE THE ELDERS OF VULCAN, WITHIN WHOSE MINDS REST THE ACCUMULATED MEMORY AND WISDOM OF OUR CIVILIZATION.
LOGIC DICTATES THAT I MUST LEAD THEM OUT OF THE KATRIC ARK TO AVOID THE POSSIBILITY OF THE CHAMBER COLLAPSING UPON US.
LOGIC DICTATES THAT IT WILL BE EASIER TO LOCK ONTO THE GROUP AND BEAM THEM BACK TO THE ENTERPRISE IF WE ARE OUTSIDE THE ARK.
VVZZZHHHHNN

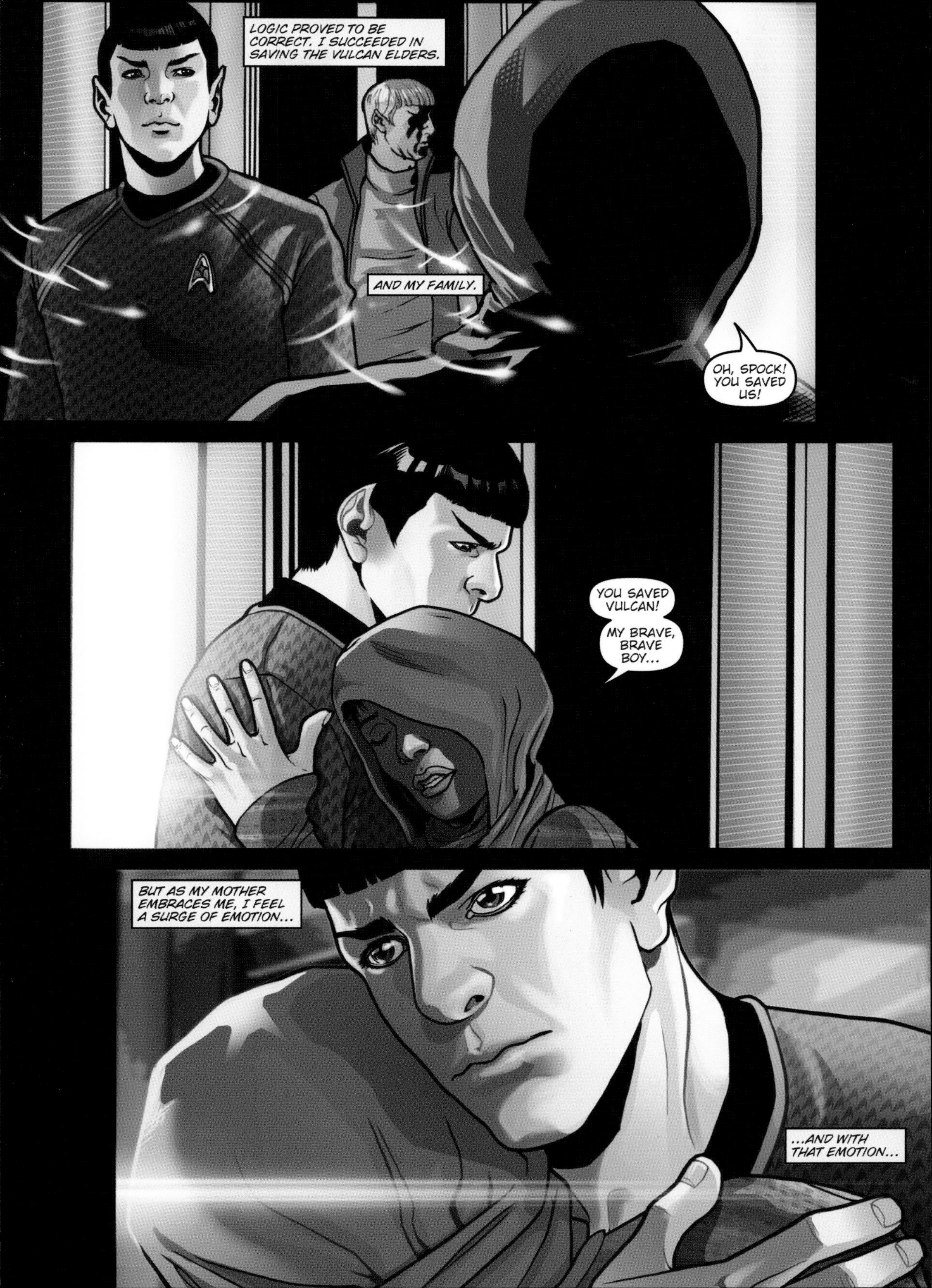
LOGIC PROVED TO BE CORRECT. I SUCCEEDED IN SAVING THE VULCAN ELDERS.
AND MY FAMILY.
OH, SPOCK! YOU SAVED US!
YOU SAVED VULCAN!
MY BRAVE, BRAVE BOY...
BUT AS MY MOTHER EMBRACES ME, I FEEL A SURGE OF EMOTION...
...AND WITH THAT EMOTION...

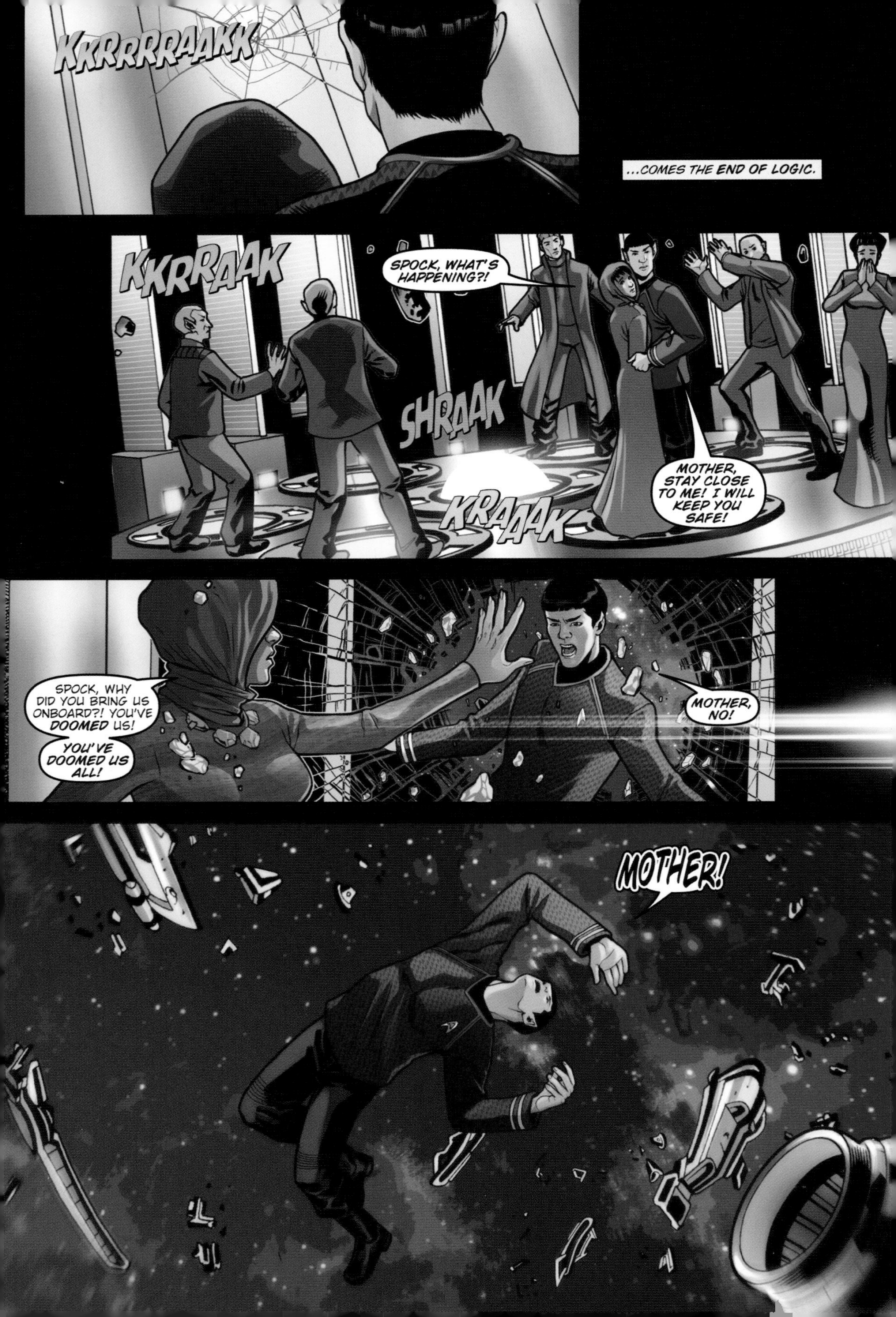
KKRRRRAAKK
...COMES THE END OF LOGIC.
KKRRAAK
SPOCK, WHAT'S HAPPENING?!
SHRAAK
KRAAAK
MOTHER, STAY CLOSE TO ME! I WILL KEEP YOU SAFE!
SPOCK, WHY DID YOU BRING US ONBOARD?! YOU'VE DOOMED US!
YOU'VE DOOMED US ALL!
MOTHER, NO!
MOTHER!

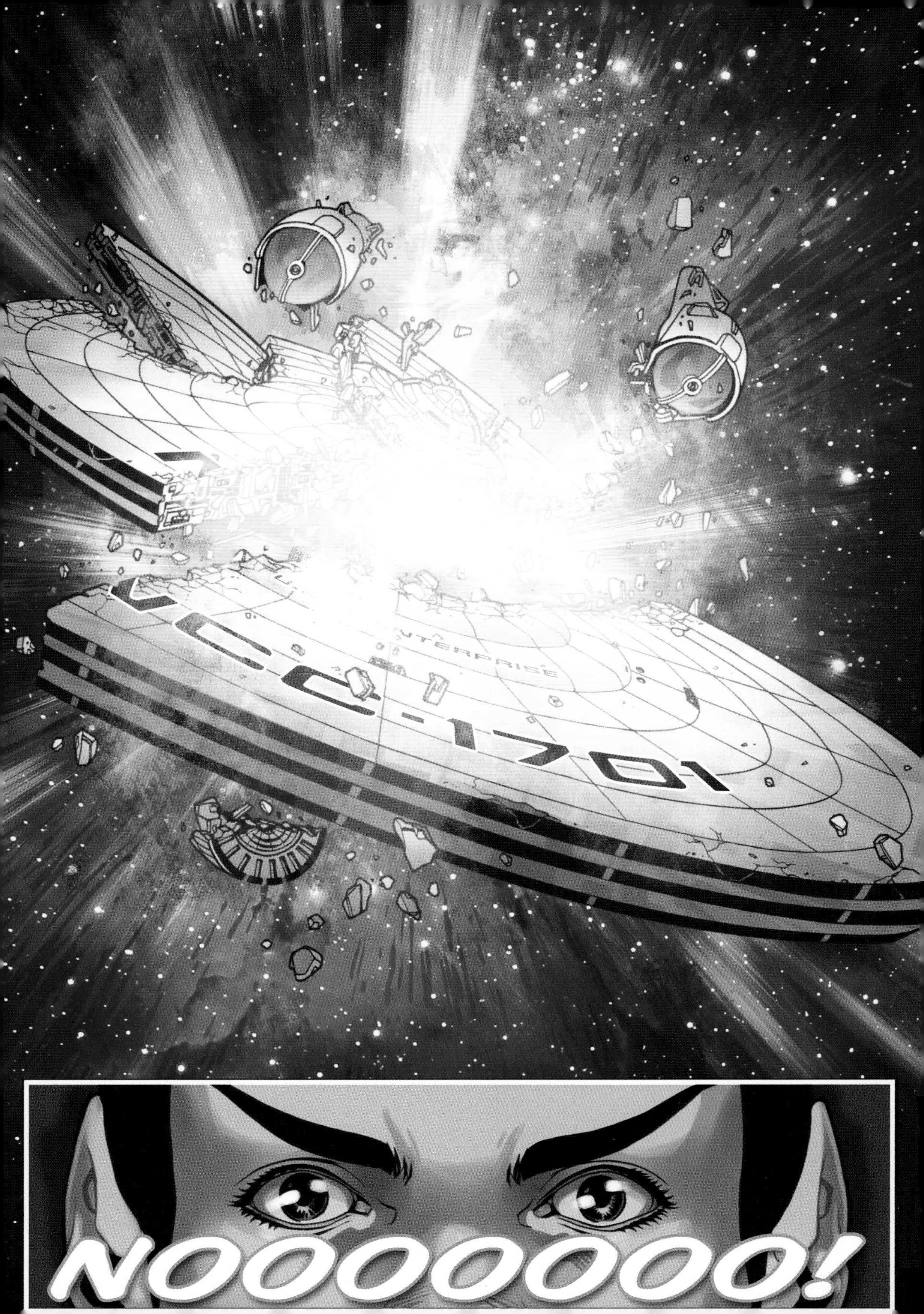
CC-1701
NTERPRISE
NOOOOOOO!

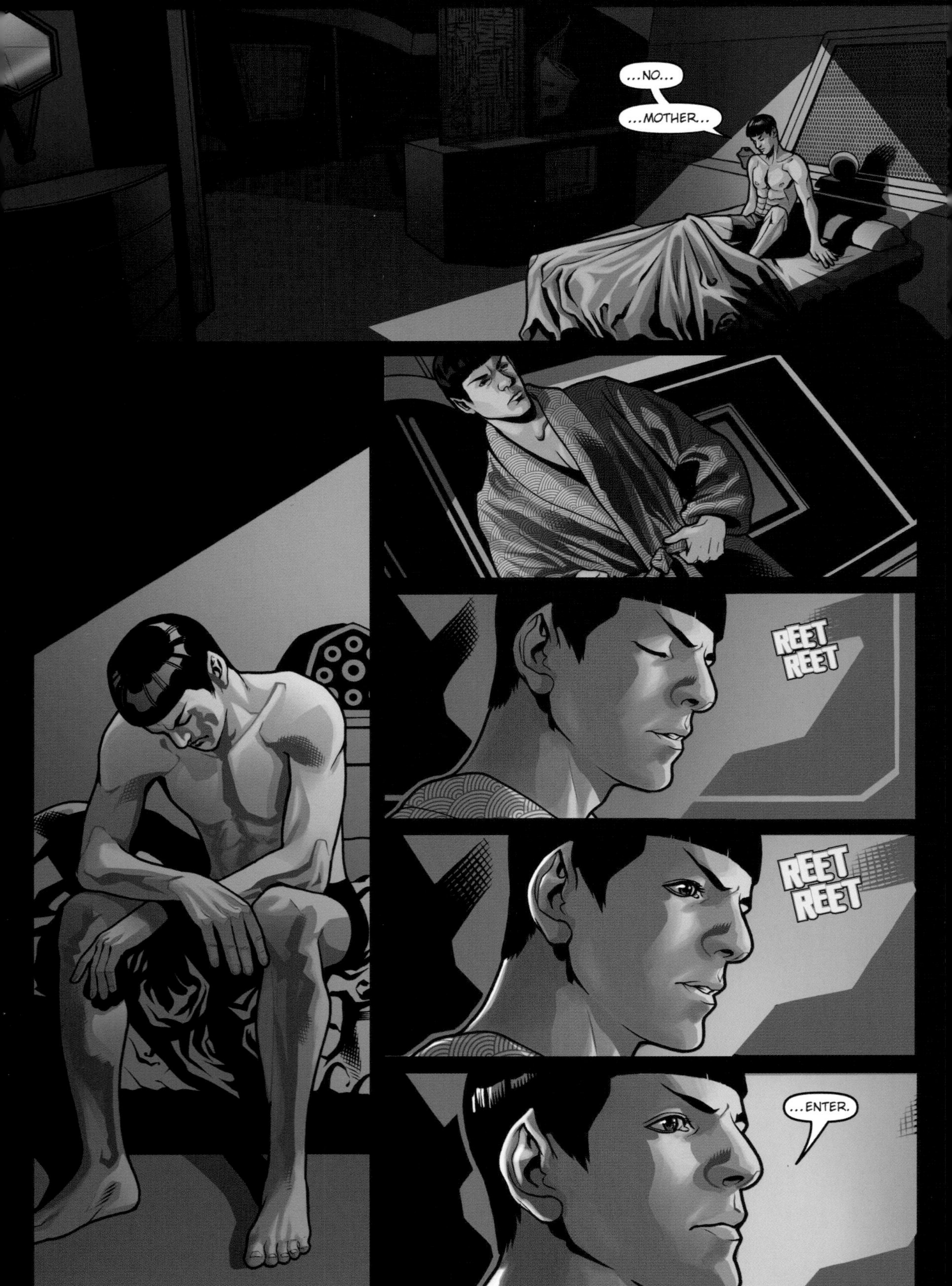
...NO...
...MOTHER...
REET REET
REET REET
...ENTER.

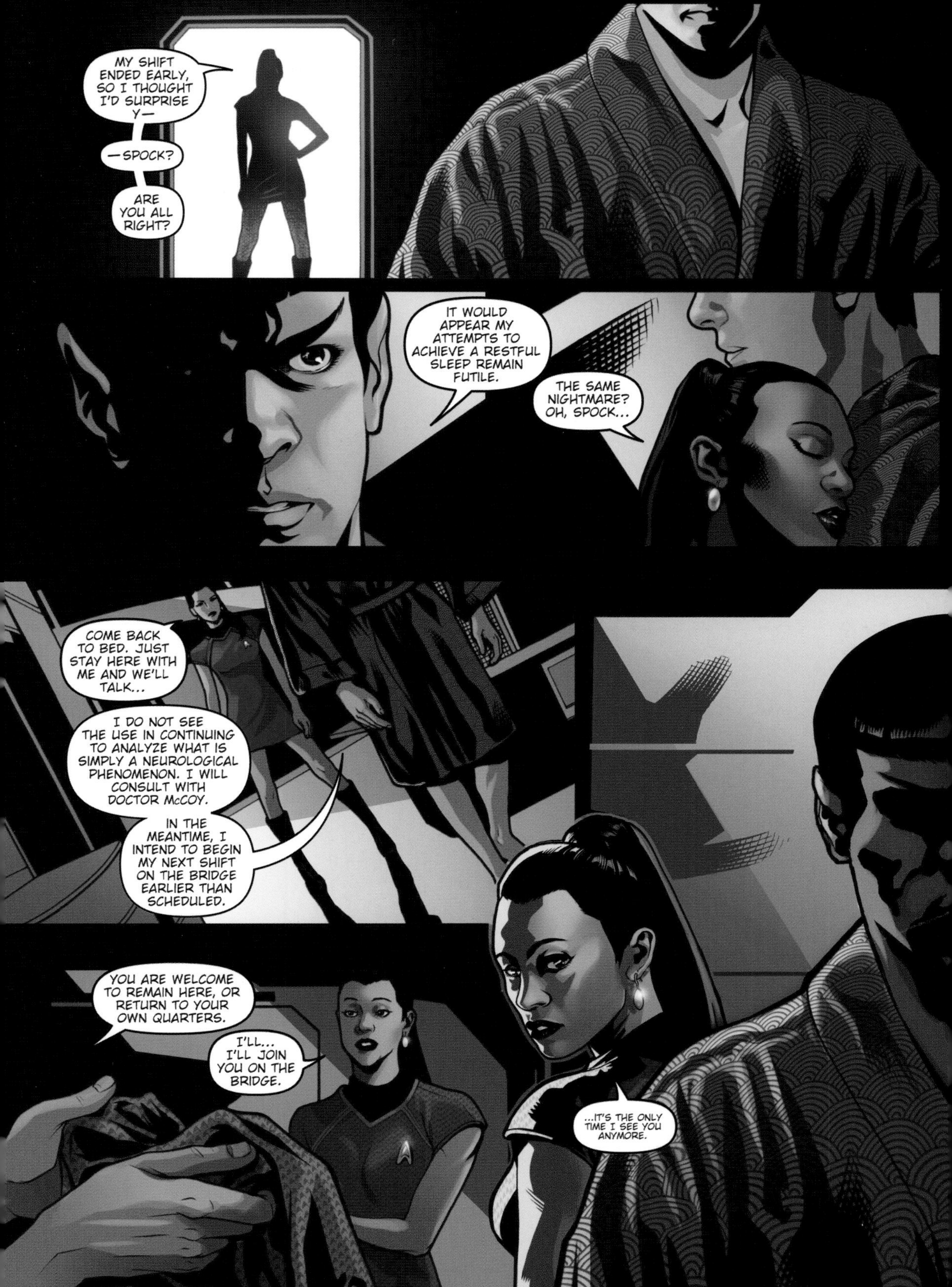
MY SHIFT ENDED EARLY, SO I THOUGHT I'D SURPRISE Y—
—SPOCK?
ARE YOU ALL RIGHT?
IT WOULD APPEAR MY ATTEMPTS TO ACHIEVE A RESTFUL SLEEP REMAIN FUTILE.
THE SAME NIGHTMARE? OH, SPOCK...
COME BACK TO BED. JUST STAY HERE WITH ME AND WE'LL TALK...
I DO NOT SEE THE USE IN CONTINUING TO ANALYZE WHAT IS SIMPLY A NEUROLOGICAL PHENOMENON. I WILL CONSULT WITH DOCTOR McCOY.
IN THE MEANTIME, I INTEND TO BEGIN MY NEXT SHIFT ON THE BRIDGE EARLIER THAN SCHEDULED.
YOU ARE WELCOME TO REMAIN HERE, OR RETURN TO YOUR OWN QUARTERS.
I'LL... I'LL JOIN YOU ON THE BRIDGE.
...IT'S THE ONLY TIME I SEE YOU ANYMORE.

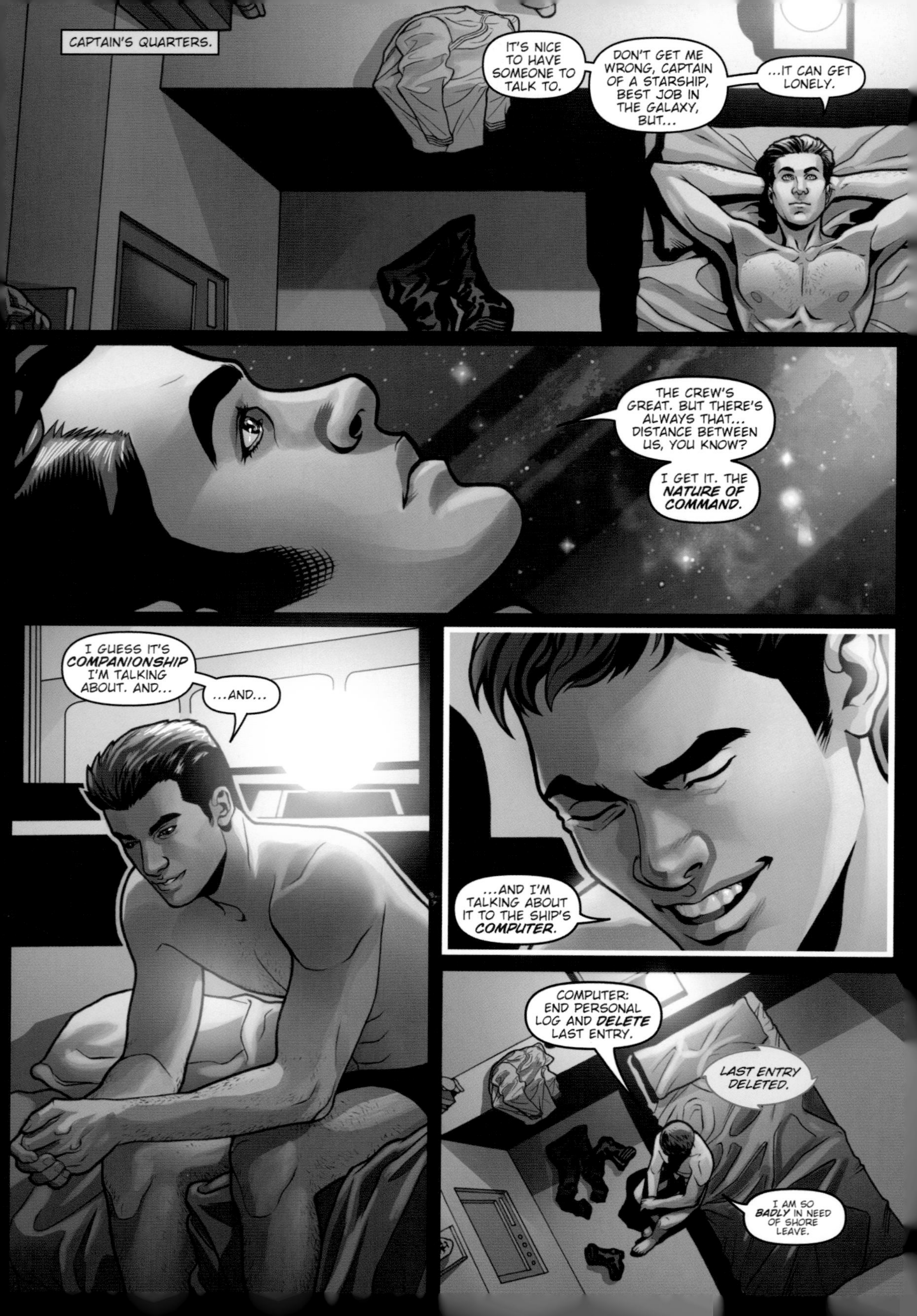
CAPTAIN'S QUARTERS.
IT'S NICE TO HAVE SOMEONE TO TALK TO.
DON'T GET ME WRONG, CAPTAIN OF A STARSHIP, BEST JOB IN THE GALAXY, BUT...
...IT CAN GET LONELY.
THE CREW'S GREAT. BUT THERE'S ALWAYS THAT... DISTANCE BETWEEN US, YOU KNOW?
I GET IT. THE ***NATURE OF COMMAND***.
I GUESS IT'S ***COMPANIONSHIP*** I'M TALKING ABOUT. AND...
...AND...
...AND I'M TALKING ABOUT IT TO THE SHIP'S ***COMPUTER***.
COMPUTER: END PERSONAL LOG AND ***DELETE*** LAST ENTRY.
LAST ENTRY DELETED.
I AM SO ***BADLY*** IN NEED OF SHORE LEAVE.

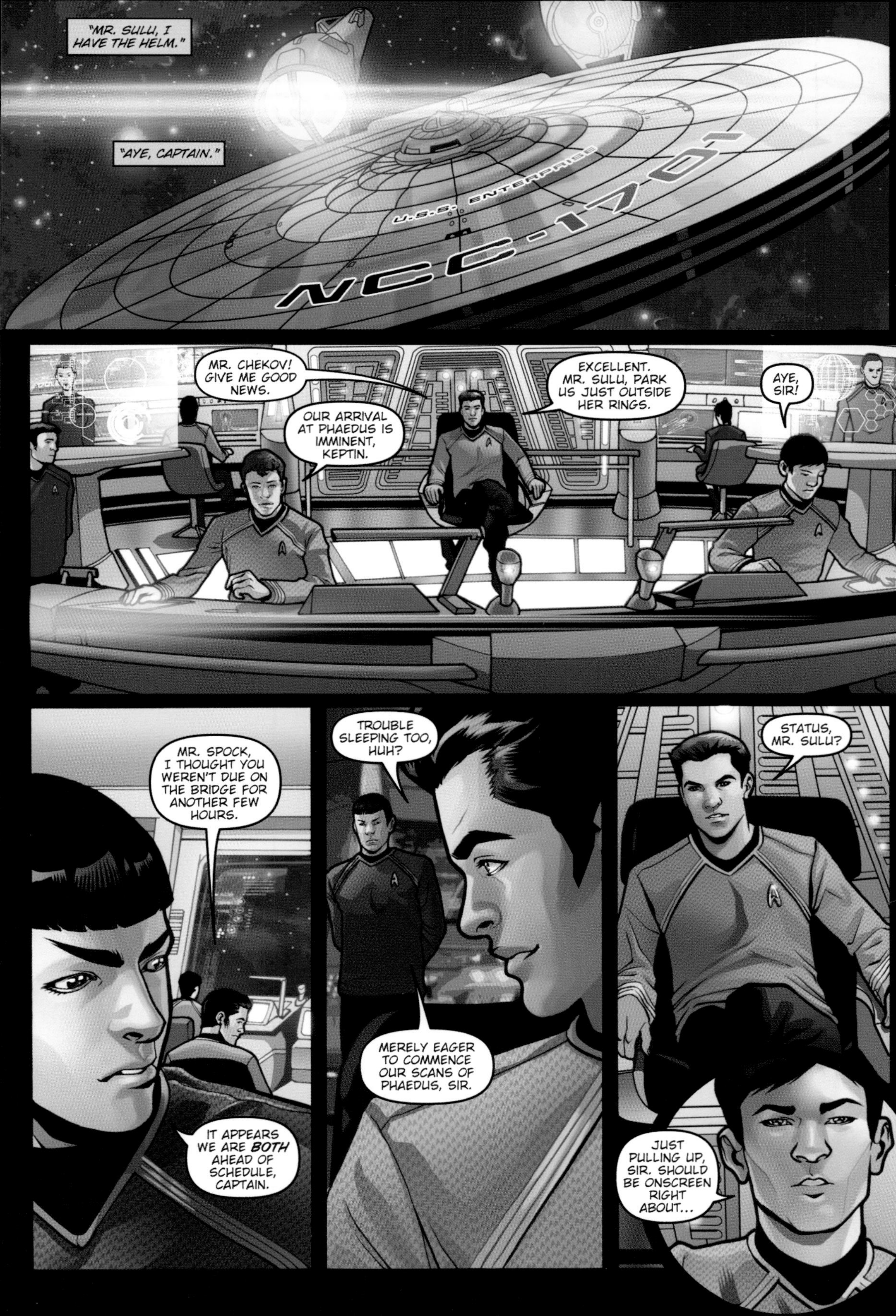
"MR. SULU, I HAVE THE HELM."
"AYE, CAPTAIN."
U.S.S. ENTERPRISE
NCC-1701
MR. CHEKOV! GIVE ME GOOD NEWS.
OUR ARRIVAL AT PHAEDUS IS IMMINENT, KEPTIN.
EXCELLENT. MR. SULU, PARK US JUST OUTSIDE HER RINGS.
AYE, SIR!
MR. SPOCK, I THOUGHT YOU WEREN'T DUE ON THE BRIDGE FOR ANOTHER FEW HOURS.
IT APPEARS WE ARE *BOTH* AHEAD OF SCHEDULE, CAPTAIN.
TROUBLE SLEEPING TOO, HUH?
MERELY EAGER TO COMMENCE OUR SCANS OF PHAEDUS, SIR.
STATUS, MR. SULU?
JUST PULLING UP, SIR. SHOULD BE ONSCREEN RIGHT ABOUT...

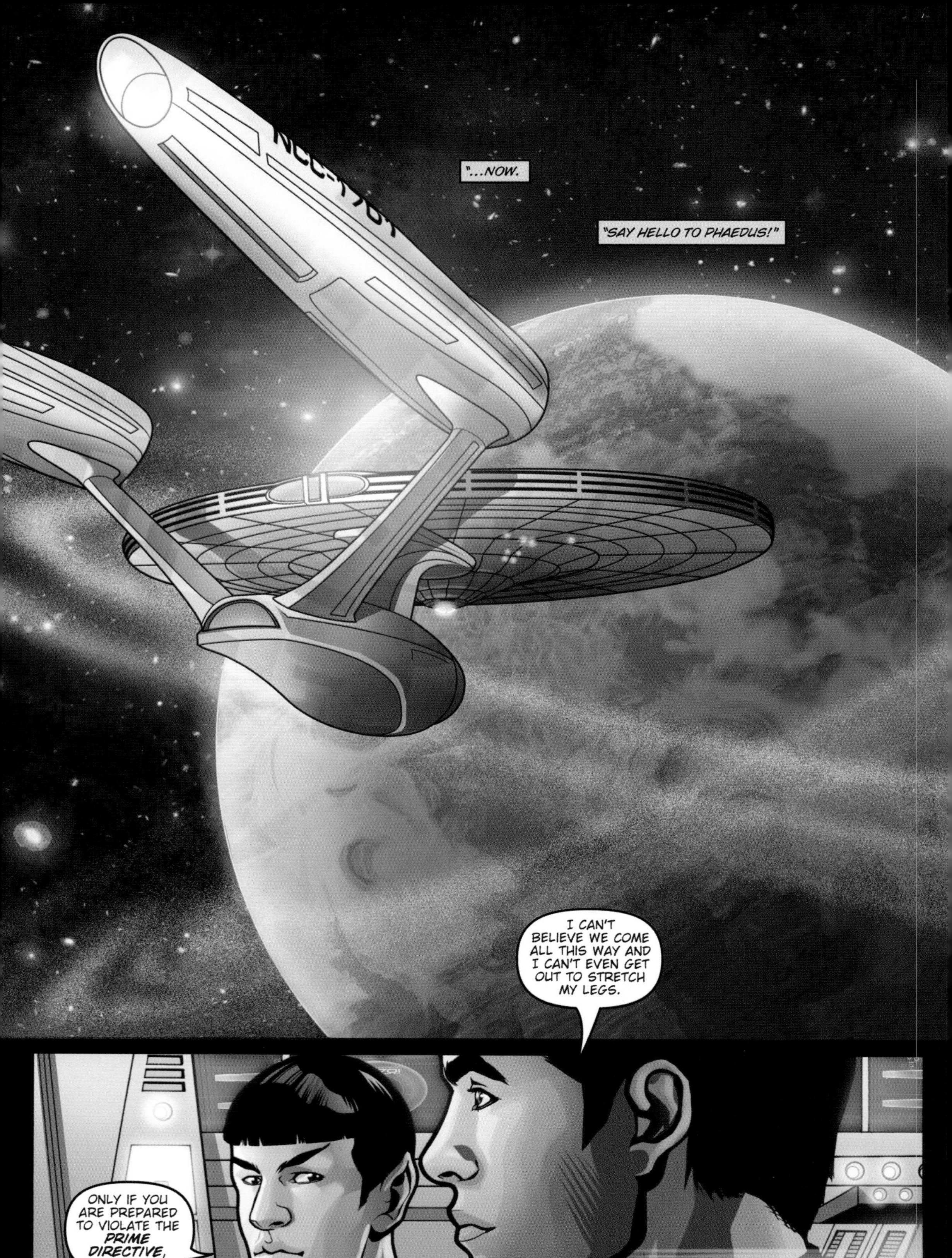
"...NOW.
"SAY HELLO TO PHAEDUS!"
I CAN'T BELIEVE WE COME ALL THIS WAY AND I CAN'T EVEN GET OUT TO STRETCH MY LEGS.
ONLY IF YOU ARE PREPARED TO VIOLATE THE **PRIME DIRECTIVE**, CAPTAIN.

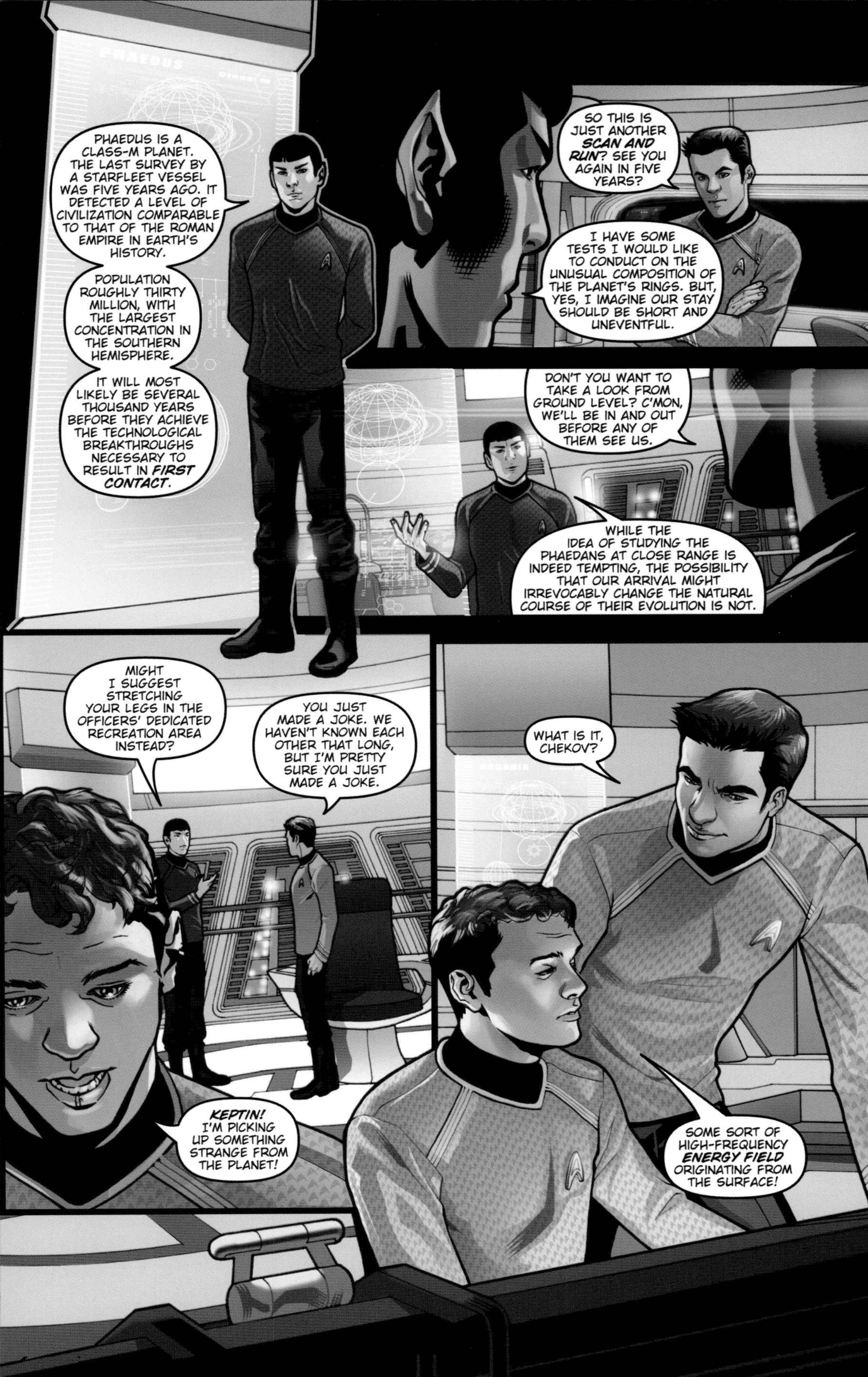
PHAEDUS
PHAEDUS IS A CLASS-M PLANET. THE LAST SURVEY BY A STARFLEET VESSEL WAS FIVE YEARS AGO. IT DETECTED A LEVEL OF CIVILIZATION COMPARABLE TO THAT OF THE ROMAN EMPIRE IN EARTH'S HISTORY.
POPULATION ROUGHLY THIRTY MILLION, WITH THE LARGEST CONCENTRATION IN THE SOUTHERN HEMISPHERE.
IT WILL MOST LIKELY BE SEVERAL THOUSAND YEARS BEFORE THEY ACHIEVE THE TECHNOLOGICAL BREAKTHROUGHS NECESSARY TO RESULT IN FIRST CONTACT.
SO THIS IS JUST ANOTHER SCAN AND RUN? SEE YOU AGAIN IN FIVE YEARS?
I HAVE SOME TESTS I WOULD LIKE TO CONDUCT ON THE UNUSUAL COMPOSITION OF THE PLANET'S RINGS. BUT, YES, I IMAGINE OUR STAY SHOULD BE SHORT AND UNEVENTFUL.
DON'T YOU WANT TO TAKE A LOOK FROM GROUND LEVEL? C'MON, WE'LL BE IN AND OUT BEFORE ANY OF THEM SEE US.
WHILE THE IDEA OF STUDYING THE PHAEDANS AT CLOSE RANGE IS INDEED TEMPTING, THE POSSIBILITY THAT OUR ARRIVAL MIGHT IRREVOCABLY CHANGE THE NATURAL COURSE OF THEIR EVOLUTION IS NOT.
MIGHT I SUGGEST STRETCHING YOUR LEGS IN THE OFFICERS' DEDICATED RECREATION AREA INSTEAD?
YOU JUST MADE A JOKE. WE HAVEN'T KNOWN EACH OTHER THAT LONG, BUT I'M PRETTY SURE YOU JUST MADE A JOKE.
KEPTIN! I'M PICKING UP SOMETHING STRANGE FROM THE PLANET!
WHAT IS IT, CHEKOV?
SOME SORT OF HIGH-FREQUENCY ENERGY FIELD ORIGINATING FROM THE SURFACE!

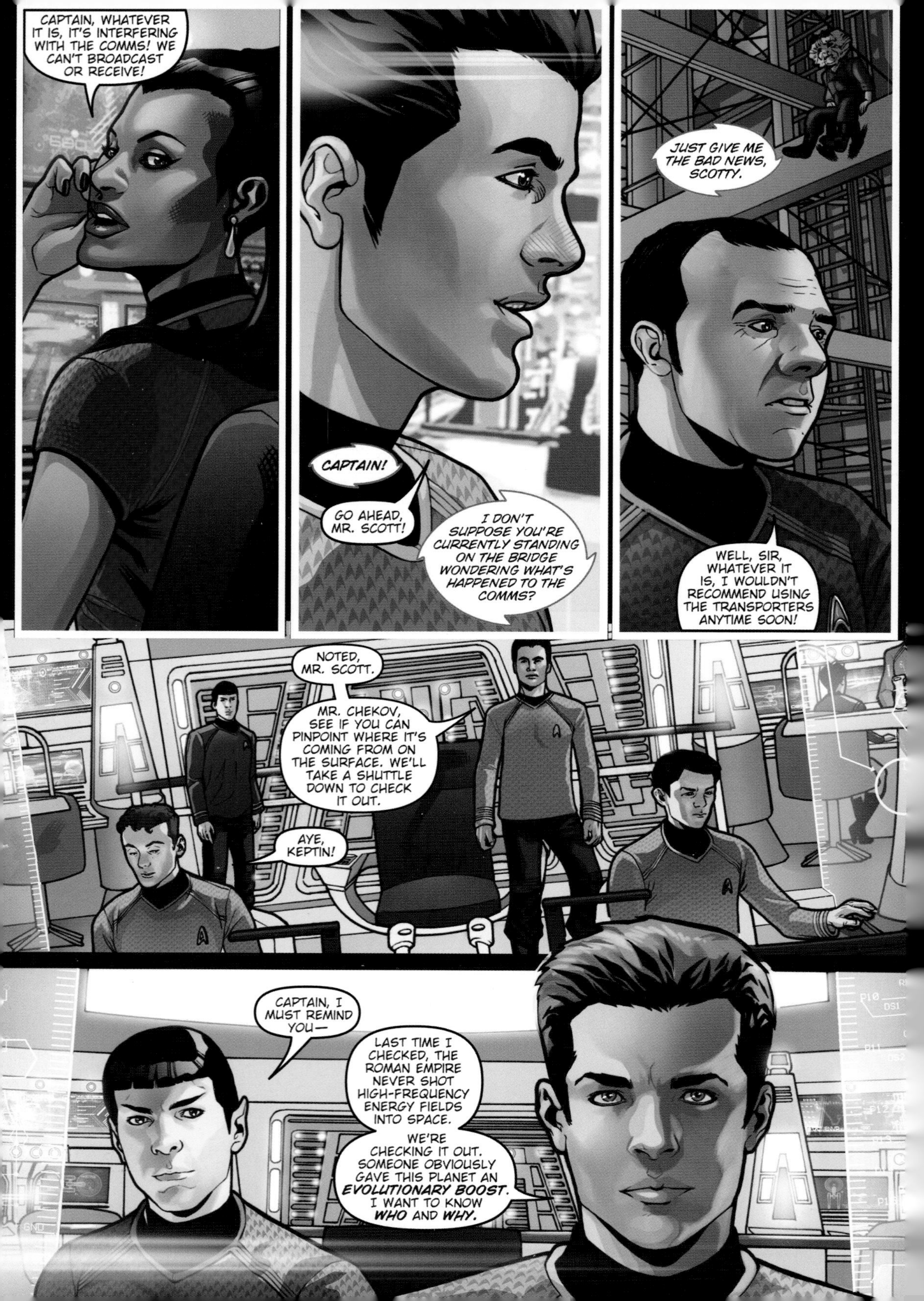
CAPTAIN, WHATEVER IT IS, IT'S INTERFERING WITH THE COMMS! WE CAN'T BROADCAST OR RECEIVE!
CAPTAIN!
GO AHEAD, MR. SCOTT!
I DON'T SUPPOSE YOU'RE CURRENTLY STANDING ON THE BRIDGE WONDERING WHAT'S HAPPENED TO THE COMMS?
JUST GIVE ME THE BAD NEWS, SCOTTY.
WELL, SIR, WHATEVER IT IS, I WOULDN'T RECOMMEND USING THE TRANSPORTERS ANYTIME SOON!
NOTED, MR. SCOTT.
MR. CHEKOV, SEE IF YOU CAN PINPOINT WHERE IT'S COMING FROM ON THE SURFACE. WE'LL TAKE A SHUTTLE DOWN TO CHECK IT OUT.
AYE, KEPTIN!
CAPTAIN, I MUST REMIND YOU—
LAST TIME I CHECKED, THE ROMAN EMPIRE NEVER SHOT HIGH-FREQUENCY ENERGY FIELDS INTO SPACE.
WE'RE CHECKING IT OUT. SOMEONE OBVIOUSLY GAVE THIS PLANET AN EVOLUTIONARY BOOST. I WANT TO KNOW WHO AND WHY.

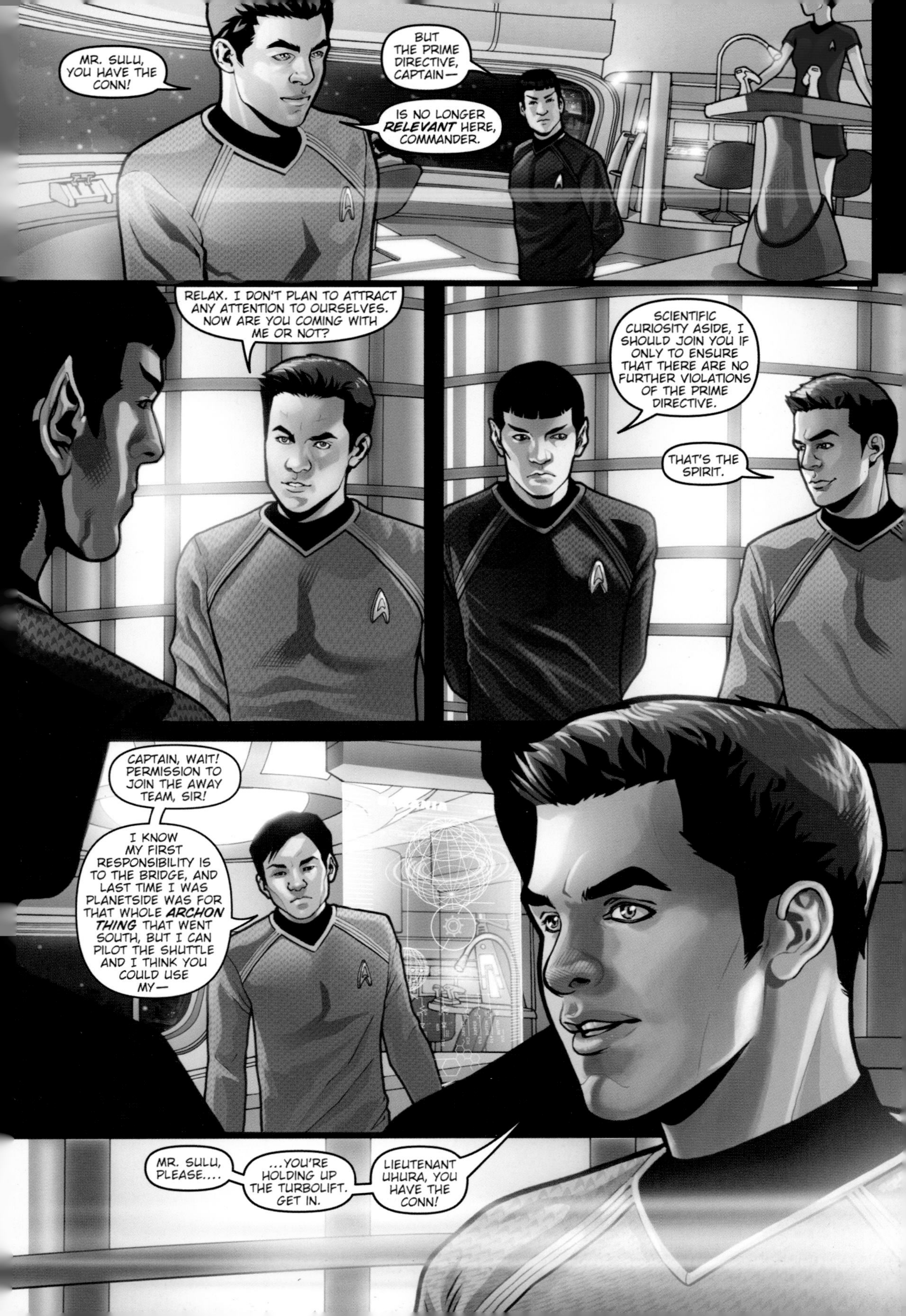

MR. SULU, YOU HAVE THE CONN!
BUT THE PRIME DIRECTIVE, CAPTAIN—
IS NO LONGER ***RELEVANT*** HERE, COMMANDER.
RELAX. I DON'T PLAN TO ATTRACT ANY ATTENTION TO OURSELVES. NOW ARE YOU COMING WITH ME OR NOT?
SCIENTIFIC CURIOSITY ASIDE, I SHOULD JOIN YOU IF ONLY TO ENSURE THAT THERE ARE NO FURTHER VIOLATIONS OF THE PRIME DIRECTIVE.
THAT'S THE SPIRIT.
CAPTAIN, WAIT! PERMISSION TO JOIN THE AWAY TEAM, SIR!
I KNOW MY FIRST RESPONSIBILITY IS TO THE BRIDGE, AND LAST TIME I WAS PLANETSIDE WAS FOR THAT WHOLE ***ARCHON THING*** THAT WENT SOUTH, BUT I CAN PILOT THE SHUTTLE AND I THINK YOU COULD USE MY—
MR. SULU, PLEASE....
...YOU'RE HOLDING UP THE TURBOLIFT. GET IN.
LIEUTENANT UHURA, YOU HAVE THE CONN!

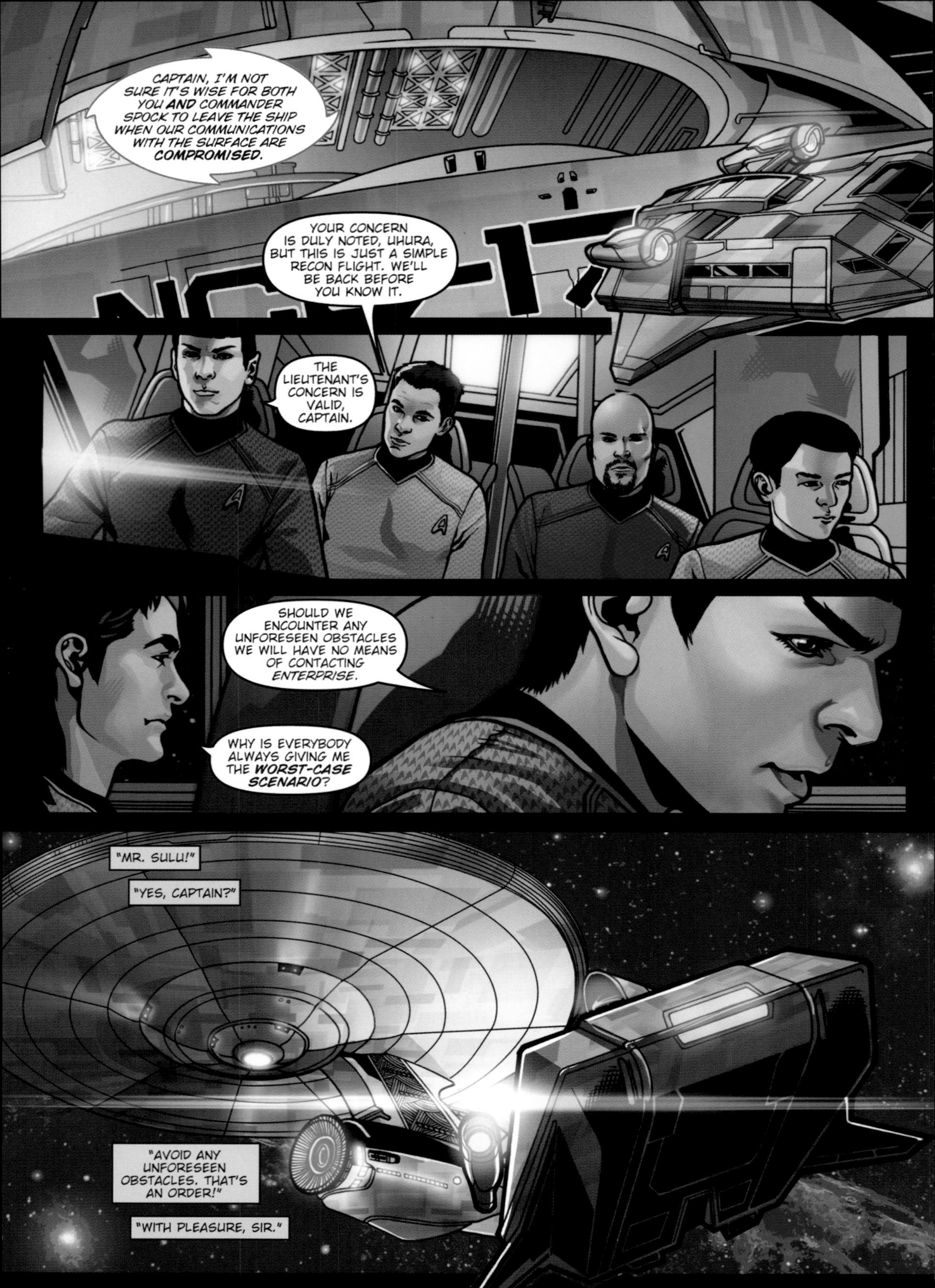
CAPTAIN, I'M NOT SURE IT'S WISE FOR BOTH YOU AND COMMANDER SPOCK TO LEAVE THE SHIP WHEN OUR COMMUNICATIONS WITH THE SURFACE ARE COMPROMISED.
YOUR CONCERN IS DULY NOTED, UHURA, BUT THIS IS JUST A SIMPLE RECON FLIGHT. WE'LL BE BACK BEFORE YOU KNOW IT.
THE LIEUTENANT'S CONCERN IS VALID, CAPTAIN.
SHOULD WE ENCOUNTER ANY UNFORESEEN OBSTACLES WE WILL HAVE NO MEANS OF CONTACTING ENTERPRISE.
WHY IS EVERYBODY ALWAYS GIVING ME THE WORST-CASE SCENARIO?
"MR. SULU!"
"YES, CAPTAIN?"
"AVOID ANY UNFORESEEN OBSTACLES. THAT'S AN ORDER!"
"WITH PLEASURE, SIR."

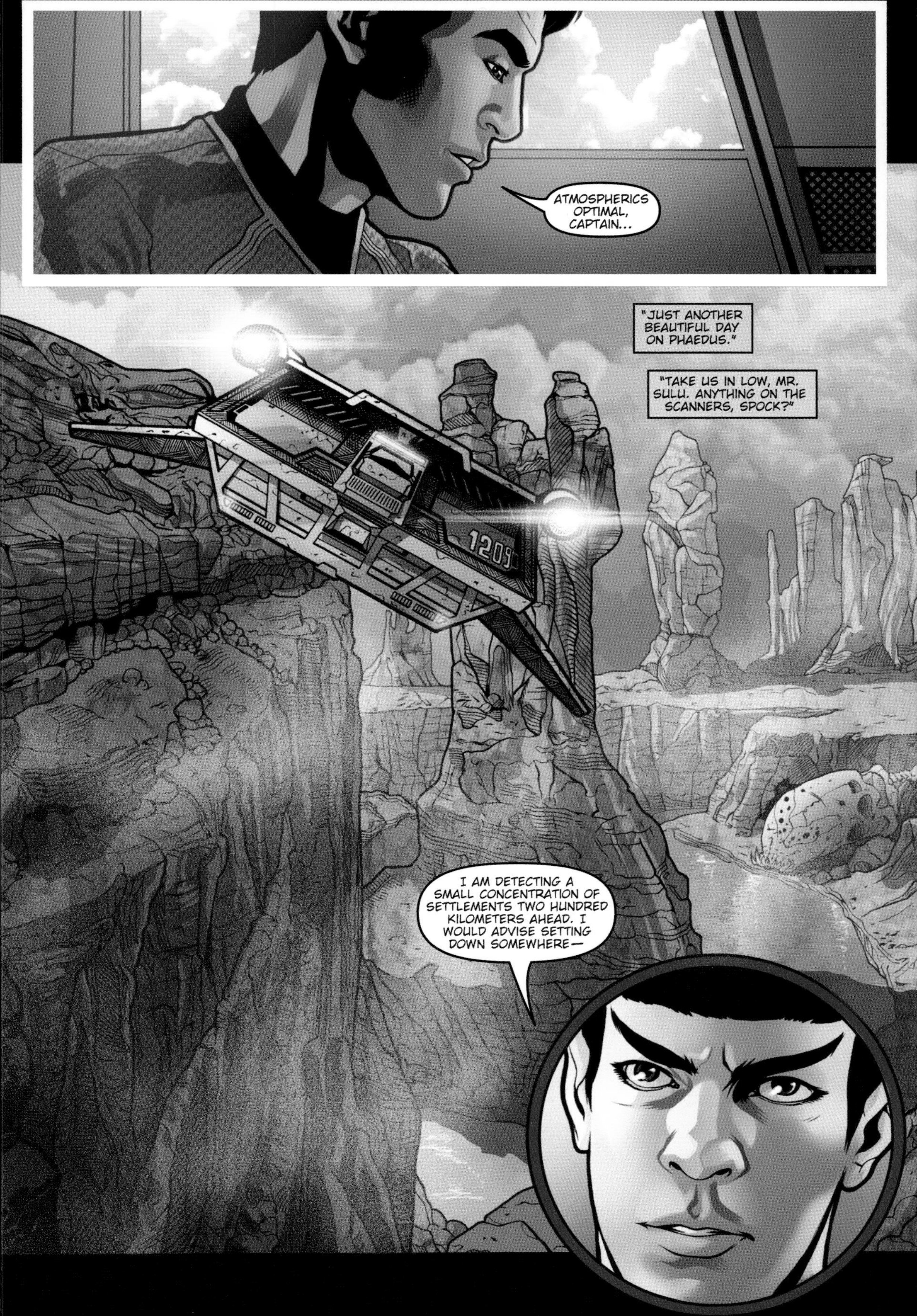
ATMOSPHERICS OPTIMAL, CAPTAIN...
"JUST ANOTHER BEAUTIFUL DAY ON PHAEDUS."
"TAKE US IN LOW, MR. SULU. ANYTHING ON THE SCANNERS, SPOCK?"
1209
I AM DETECTING A SMALL CONCENTRATION OF SETTLEMENTS TWO HUNDRED KILOMETERS AHEAD. I WOULD ADVISE SETTING DOWN SOMEWHERE—

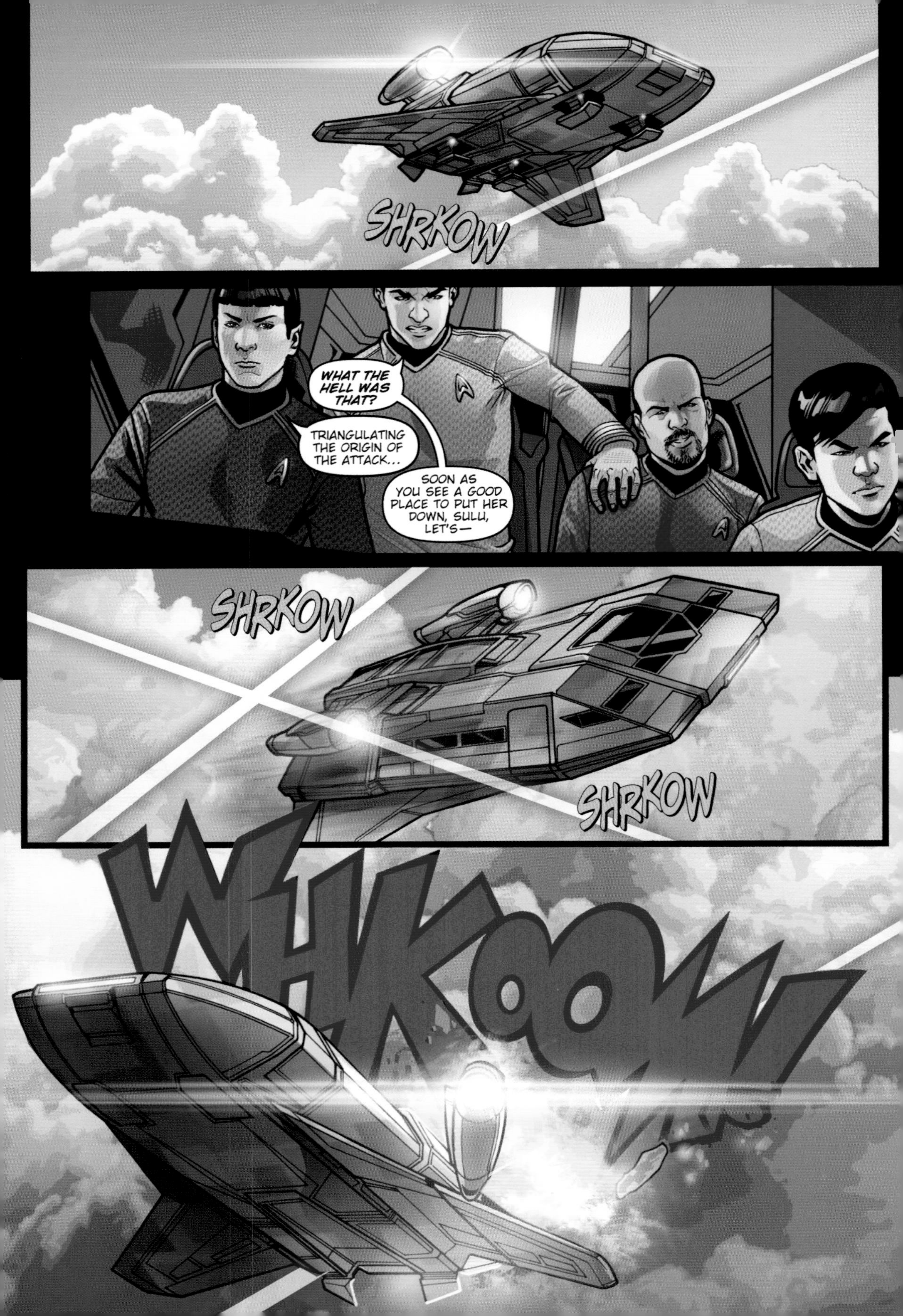
SHRKOW
WHAT THE HELL WAS THAT?
TRIANGULATING THE ORIGIN OF THE ATTACK...
SOON AS YOU SEE A GOOD PLACE TO PUT HER DOWN, SULU, LET'S—
SHRKOW
SHRKOW
WHKOOOW

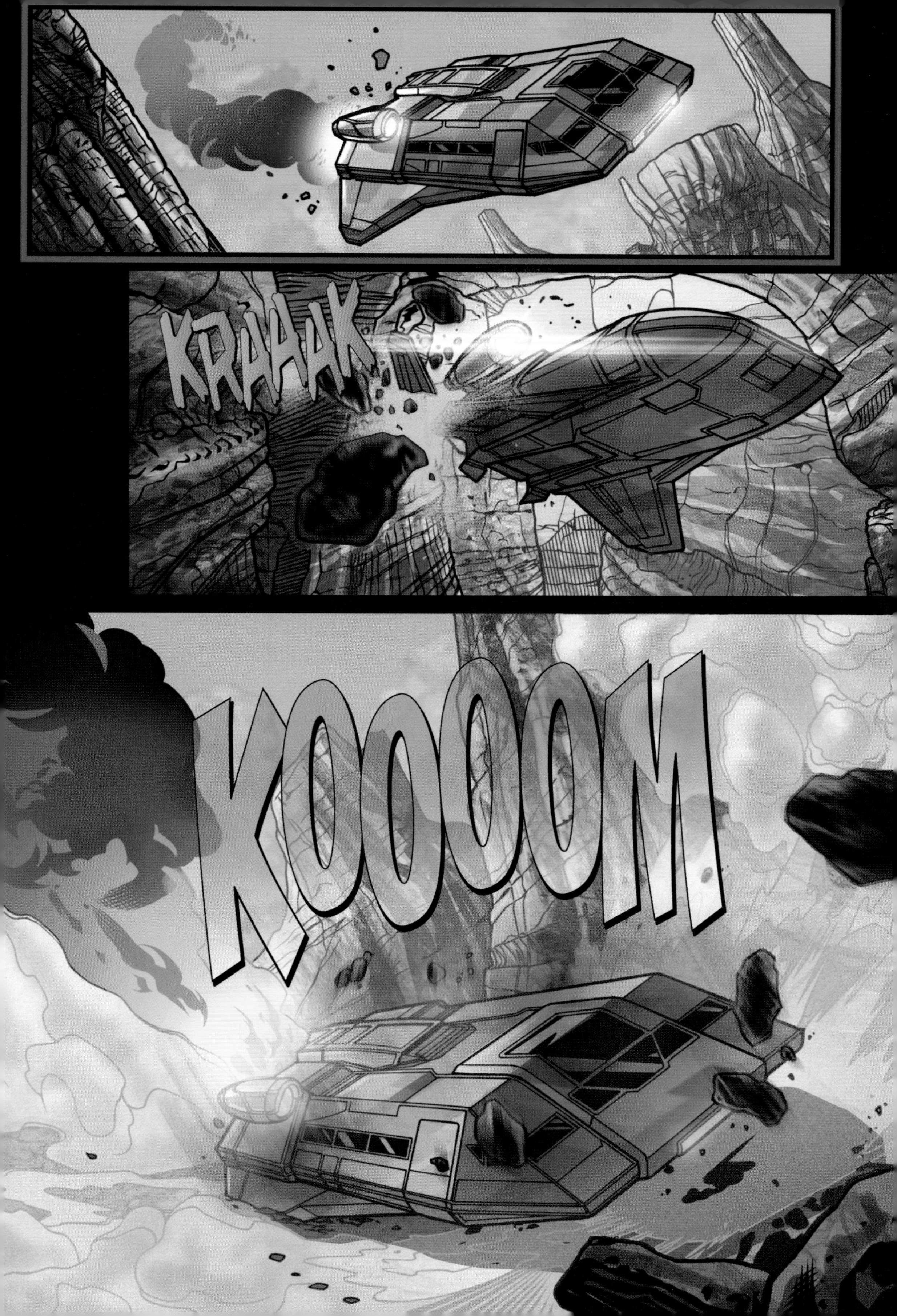
KRAAAK
KOOOOM

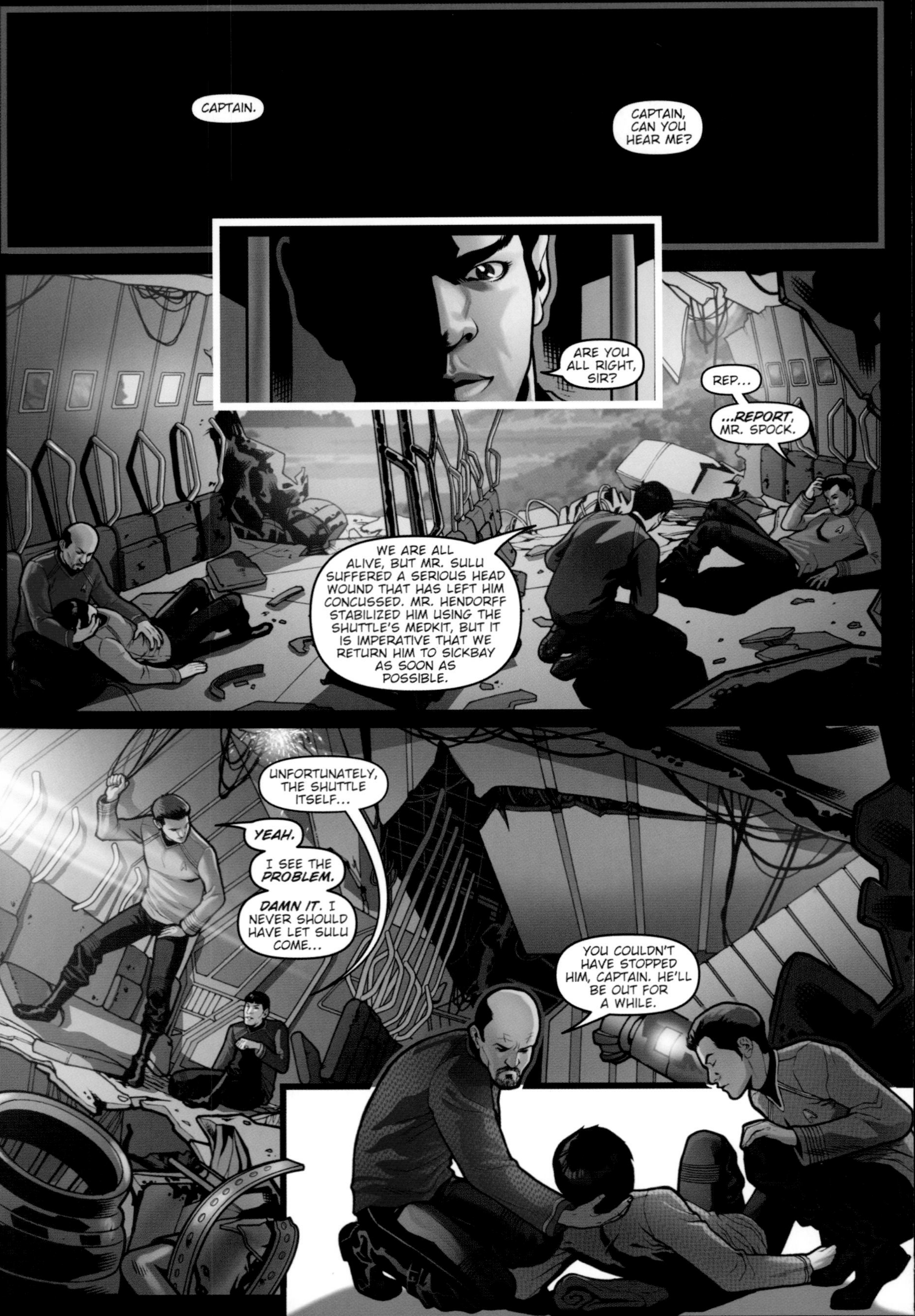
CAPTAIN.
CAPTAIN, CAN YOU HEAR ME?
ARE YOU ALL RIGHT, SIR?
REP...
...REPORT, MR. SPOCK.
WE ARE ALL ALIVE, BUT MR. SULU SUFFERED A SERIOUS HEAD WOUND THAT HAS LEFT HIM CONCUSSED. MR. HENDORFF STABILIZED HIM USING THE SHUTTLE'S MEDKIT, BUT IT IS IMPERATIVE THAT WE RETURN HIM TO SICKBAY AS SOON AS POSSIBLE.
UNFORTUNATELY, THE SHUTTLE ITSELF...
YEAH.
I SEE THE PROBLEM.
DAMN IT. I NEVER SHOULD HAVE LET SULU COME...
YOU COULDN'T HAVE STOPPED HIM, CAPTAIN. HE'LL BE OUT FOR A WHILE.

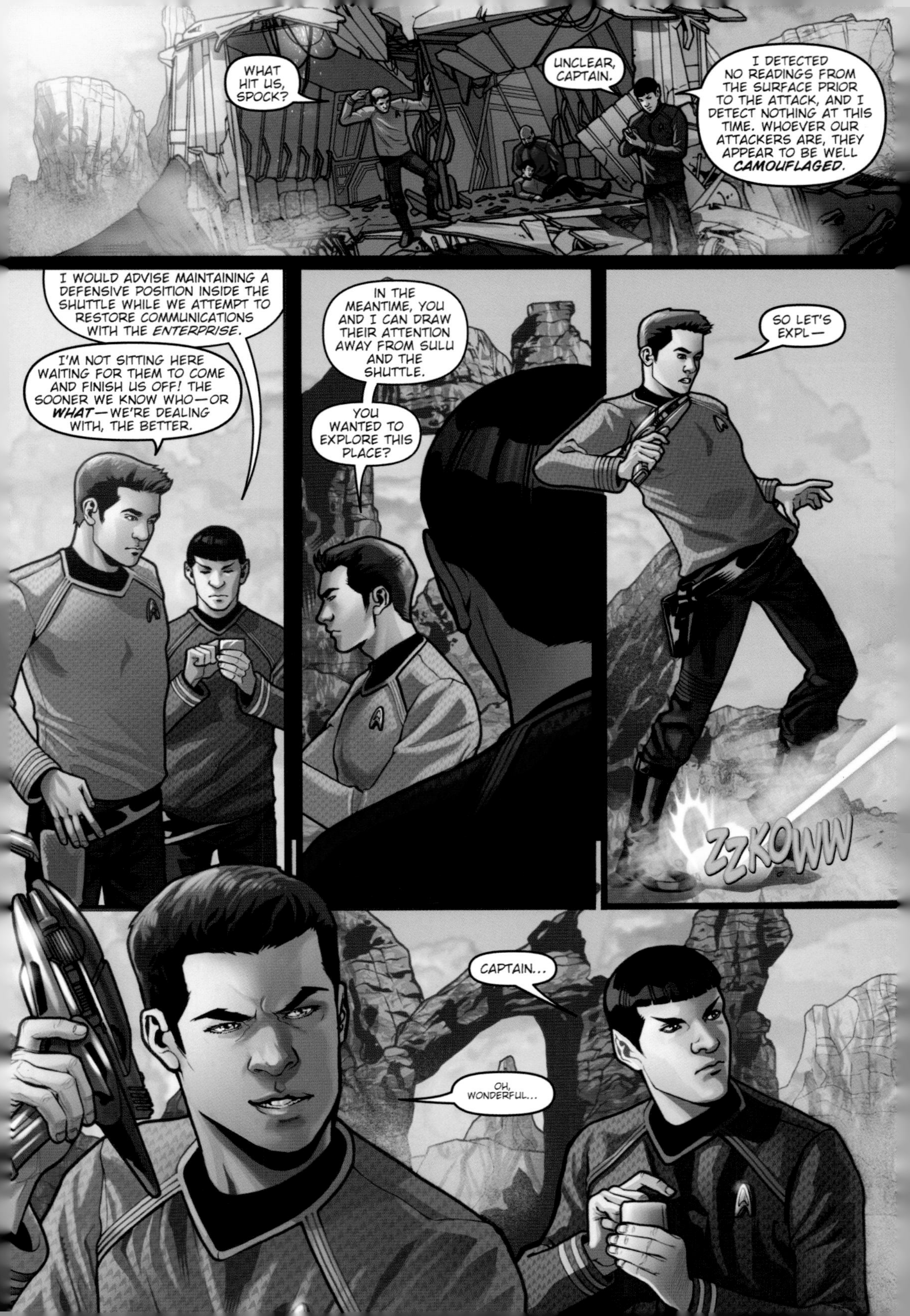
WHAT HIT US, SPOCK?
UNCLEAR, CAPTAIN.
I DETECTED NO READINGS FROM THE SURFACE PRIOR TO THE ATTACK, AND I DETECT NOTHING AT THIS TIME. WHOEVER OUR ATTACKERS ARE, THEY APPEAR TO BE WELL *CAMOUFLAGED*.
I WOULD ADVISE MAINTAINING A DEFENSIVE POSITION INSIDE THE SHUTTLE WHILE WE ATTEMPT TO RESTORE COMMUNICATIONS WITH THE *ENTERPRISE*.
I'M NOT SITTING HERE WAITING FOR THEM TO COME AND FINISH US OFF! THE SOONER WE KNOW WHO—OR *WHAT*—WE'RE DEALING WITH, THE BETTER.
IN THE MEANTIME, YOU AND I CAN DRAW THEIR ATTENTION AWAY FROM SULU AND THE SHUTTLE.
YOU WANTED TO EXPLORE THIS PLACE?
SO LET'S EXPL—
ZZKOWW
CAPTAIN...
OH, WONDERFUL...

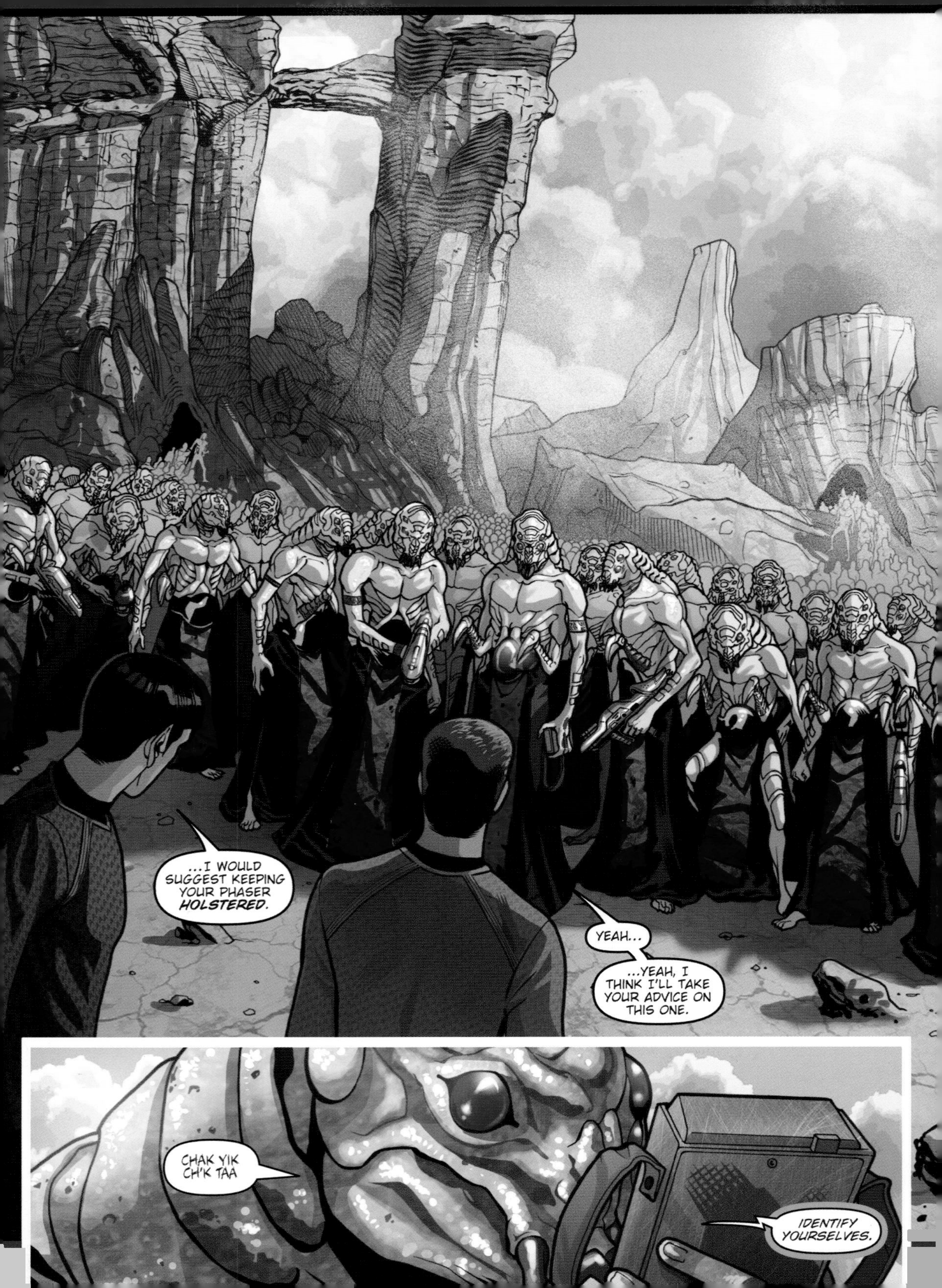
...I WOULD SUGGEST KEEPING YOUR PHASER HOLSTERED.
YEAH...
...YEAH, I THINK I'LL TAKE YOUR ADVICE ON THIS ONE.
CHAK YIK CH'K TAA
IDENTIFY YOURSELVES.

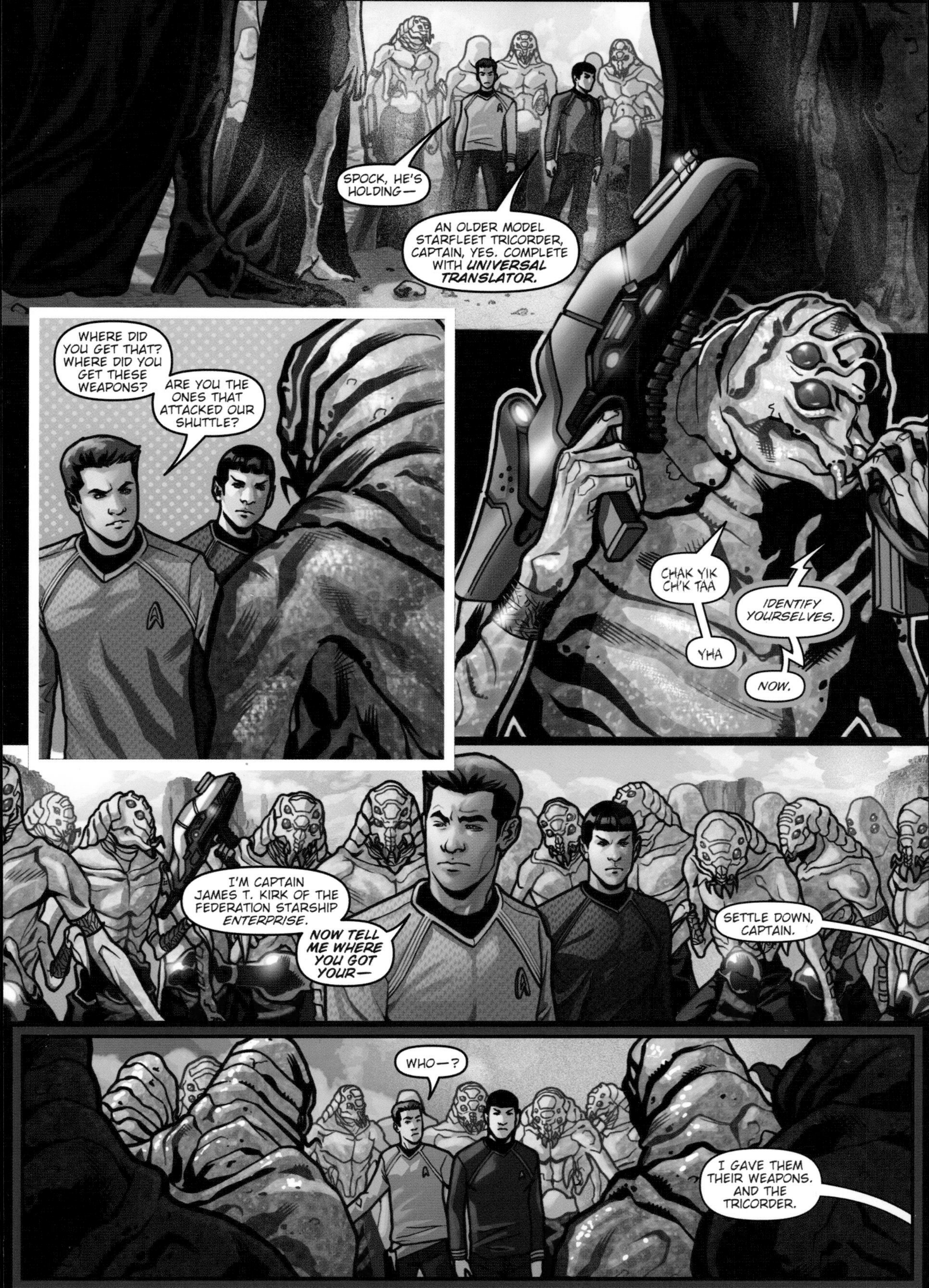
SPOCK, HE'S HOLDING—
AN OLDER MODEL STARFLEET TRICORDER, CAPTAIN, YES. COMPLETE WITH UNIVERSAL TRANSLATOR.
WHERE DID YOU GET THAT? WHERE DID YOU GET THESE WEAPONS?
ARE YOU THE ONES THAT ATTACKED OUR SHUTTLE?
CHAK YIK CH'K TAA
IDENTIFY YOURSELVES.
YHA
NOW.
I'M CAPTAIN JAMES T. KIRK OF THE FEDERATION STARSHIP ENTERPRISE.
NOW TELL ME WHERE YOU GOT YOUR—
SETTLE DOWN, CAPTAIN.
WHO—?
I GAVE THEM THEIR WEAPONS. AND THE TRICORDER.

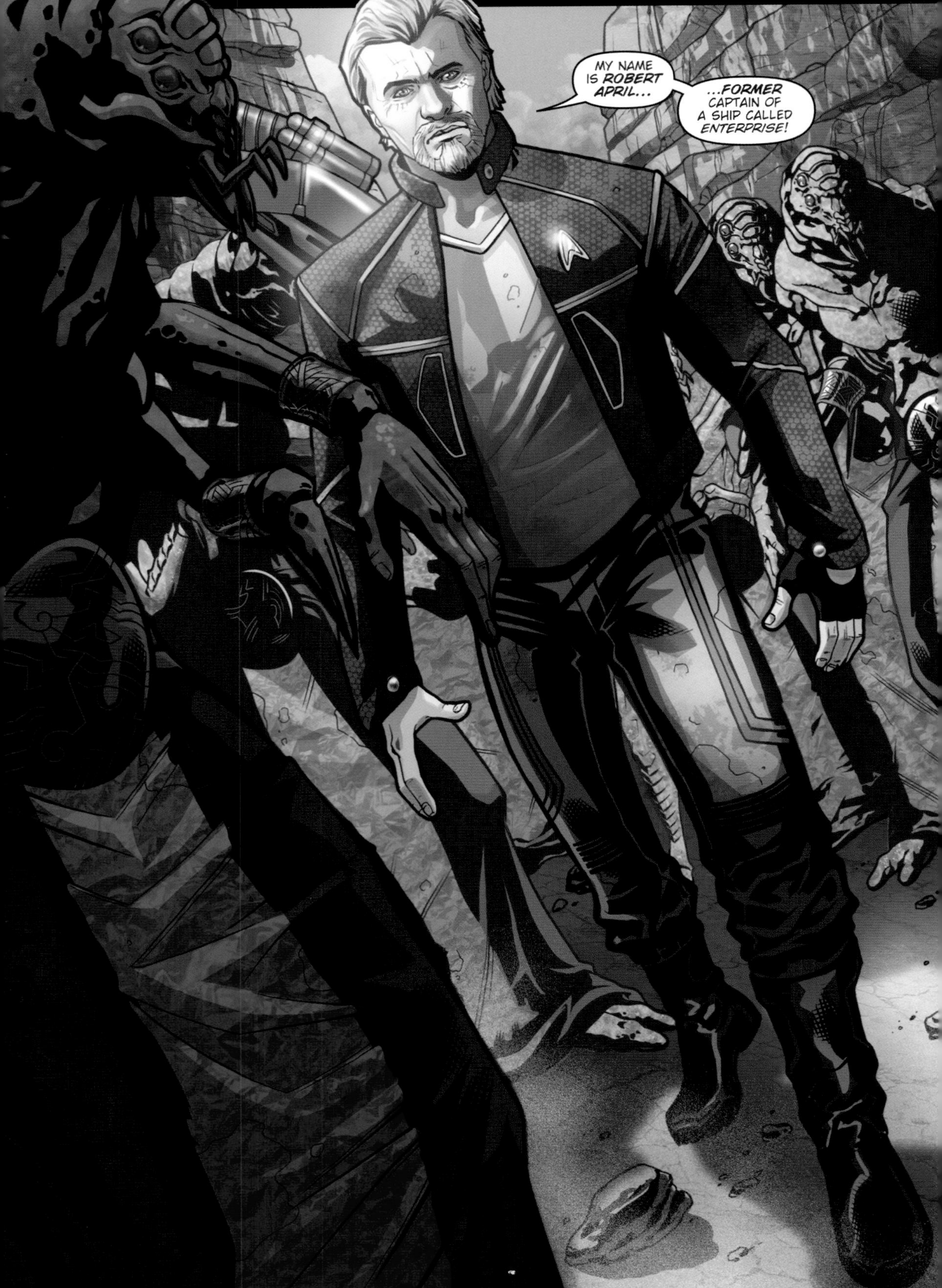
MY NAME IS ROBERT APRIL...
...FORMER CAPTAIN OF A SHIP CALLED ENTERPRISE!

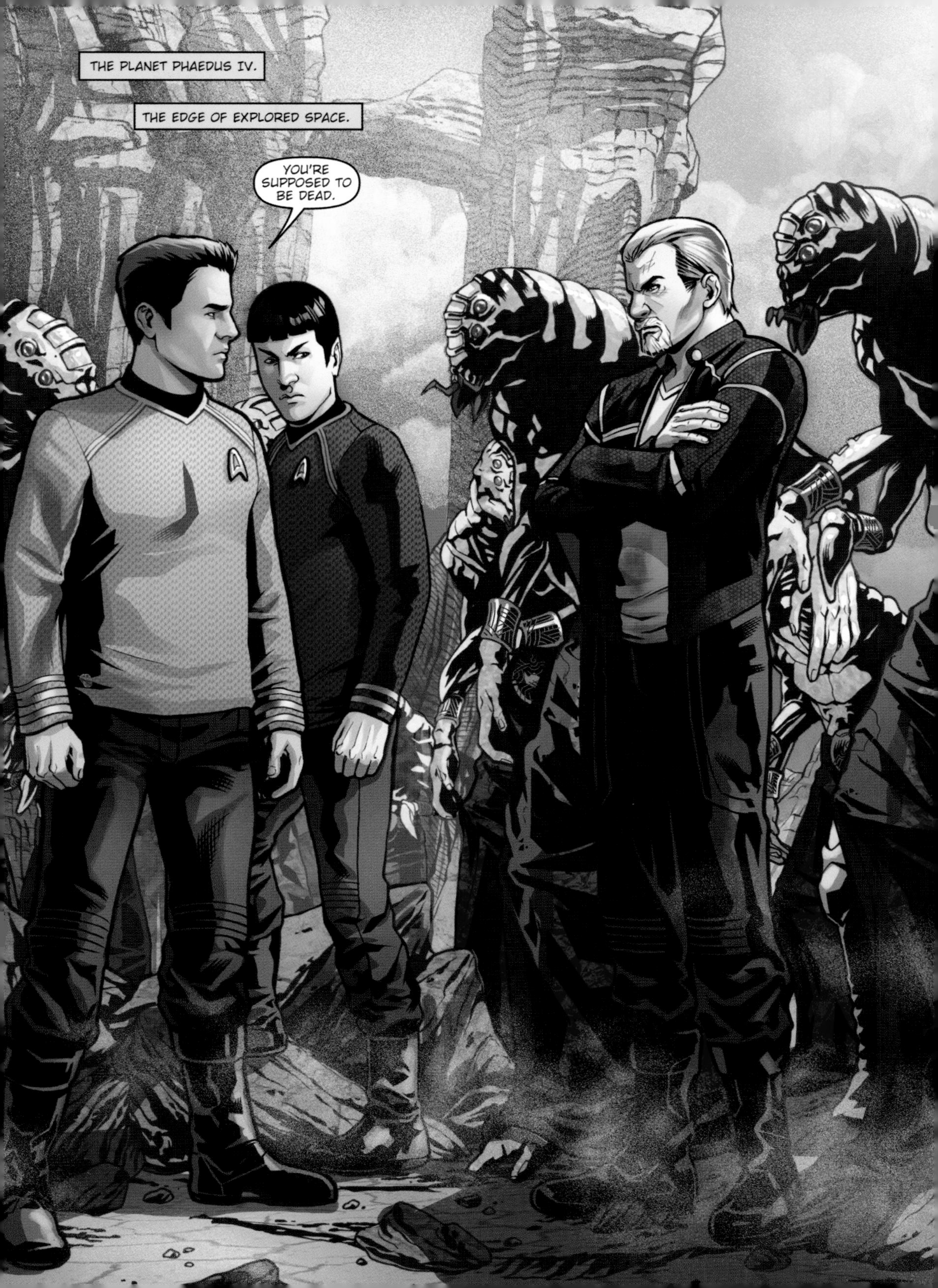
THE PLANET PHAEDUS IV.
THE EDGE OF EXPLORED SPACE.
YOU'RE SUPPOSED TO BE DEAD.

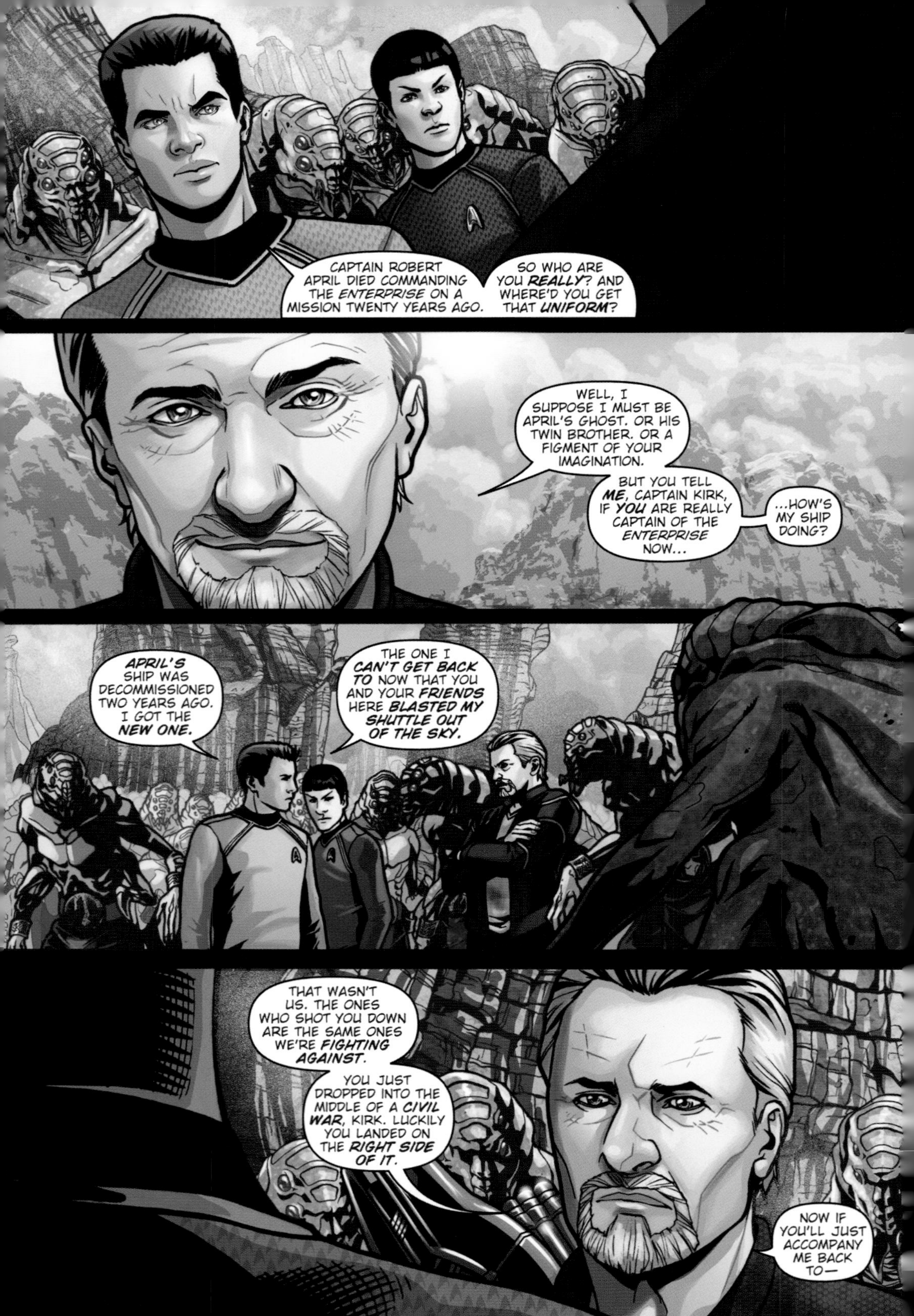
CAPTAIN ROBERT APRIL DIED COMMANDING THE ENTERPRISE ON A MISSION TWENTY YEARS AGO.
SO WHO ARE YOU REALLY? AND WHERE'D YOU GET THAT UNIFORM?
WELL, I SUPPOSE I MUST BE APRIL'S GHOST. OR HIS TWIN BROTHER. OR A FIGMENT OF YOUR IMAGINATION.
BUT YOU TELL ME, CAPTAIN KIRK, IF YOU ARE REALLY CAPTAIN OF THE ENTERPRISE NOW...
...HOW'S MY SHIP DOING?
APRIL'S SHIP WAS DECOMMISSIONED TWO YEARS AGO. I GOT THE NEW ONE.
THE ONE I CAN'T GET BACK TO NOW THAT YOU AND YOUR FRIENDS HERE BLASTED MY SHUTTLE OUT OF THE SKY.
THAT WASN'T US. THE ONES WHO SHOT YOU DOWN ARE THE SAME ONES WE'RE FIGHTING AGAINST.
YOU JUST DROPPED INTO THE MIDDLE OF A CIVIL WAR, KIRK. LUCKILY YOU LANDED ON THE RIGHT SIDE OF IT.
NOW IF YOU'LL JUST ACCOMPANY ME BACK TO—

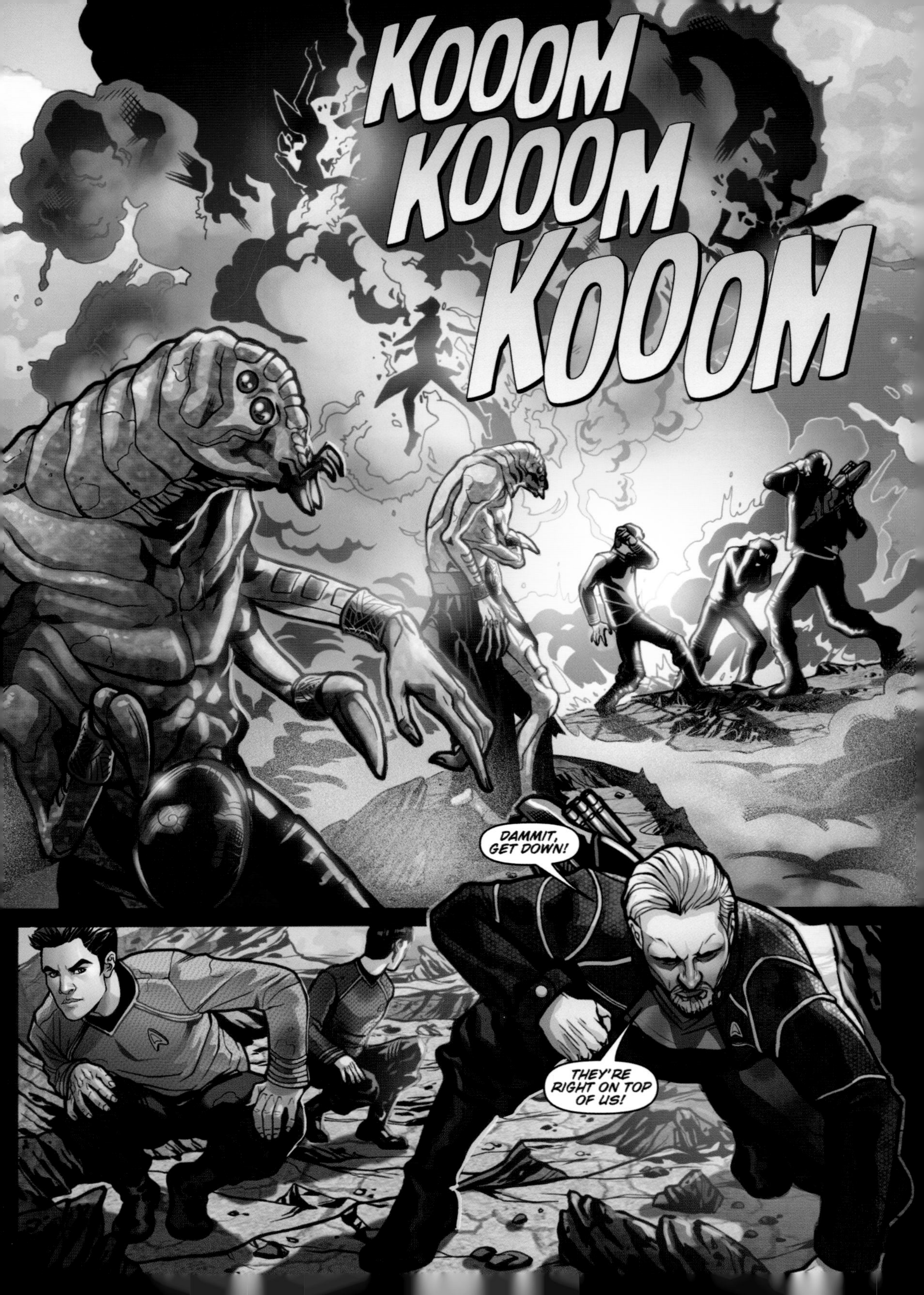
KOOOM
KOOOM
KOOOM
DAMMIT, GET DOWN!
THEY'RE RIGHT ON TOP OF US!

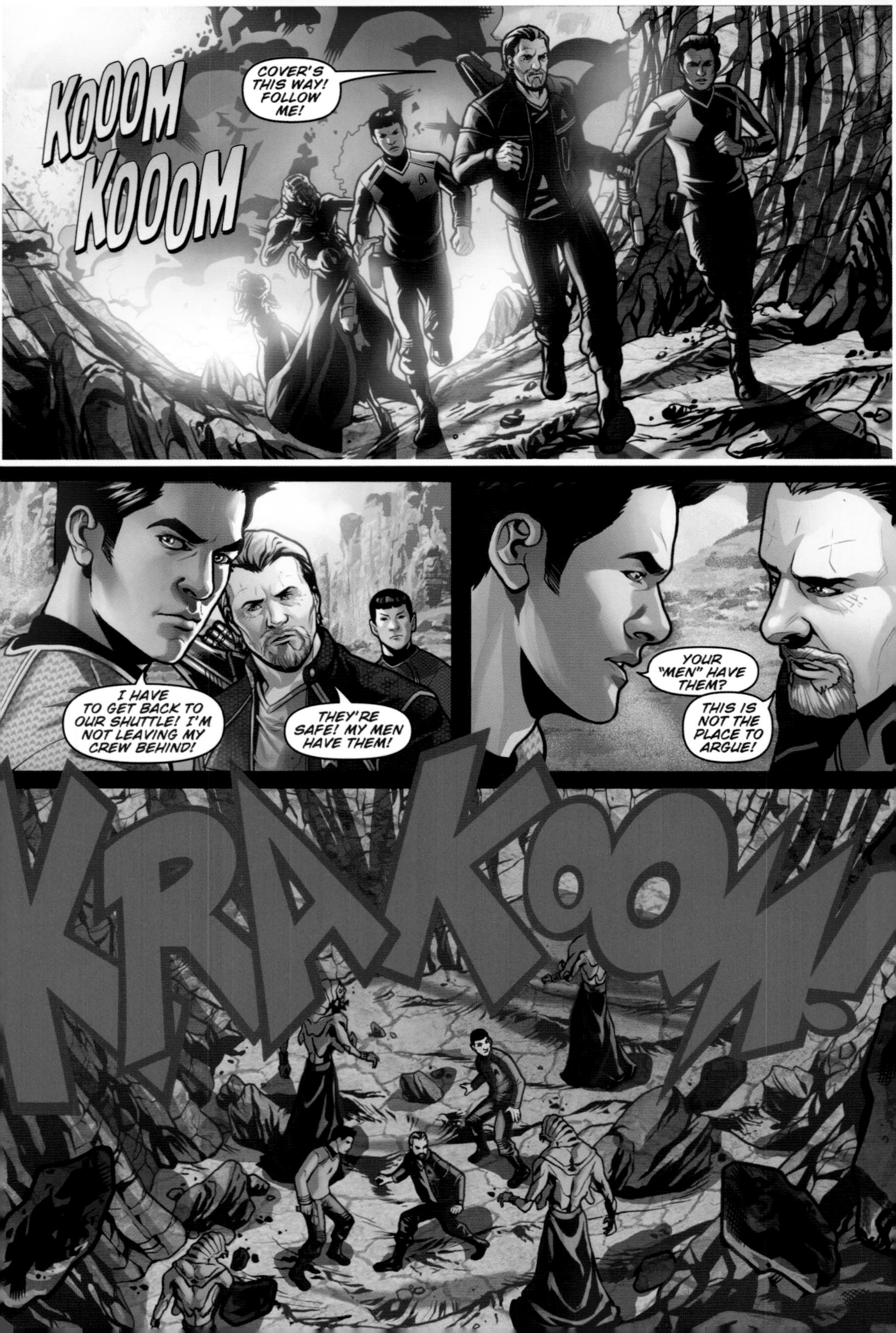
KOOOM
KOOOM
COVER'S THIS WAY! FOLLOW ME!
I HAVE TO GET BACK TO OUR SHUTTLE! I'M NOT LEAVING MY CREW BEHIND!
THEY'RE SAFE! MY MEN HAVE THEM!
YOUR "MEN" HAVE THEM?
THIS IS NOT THE PLACE TO ARGUE!
KRAKOOM!

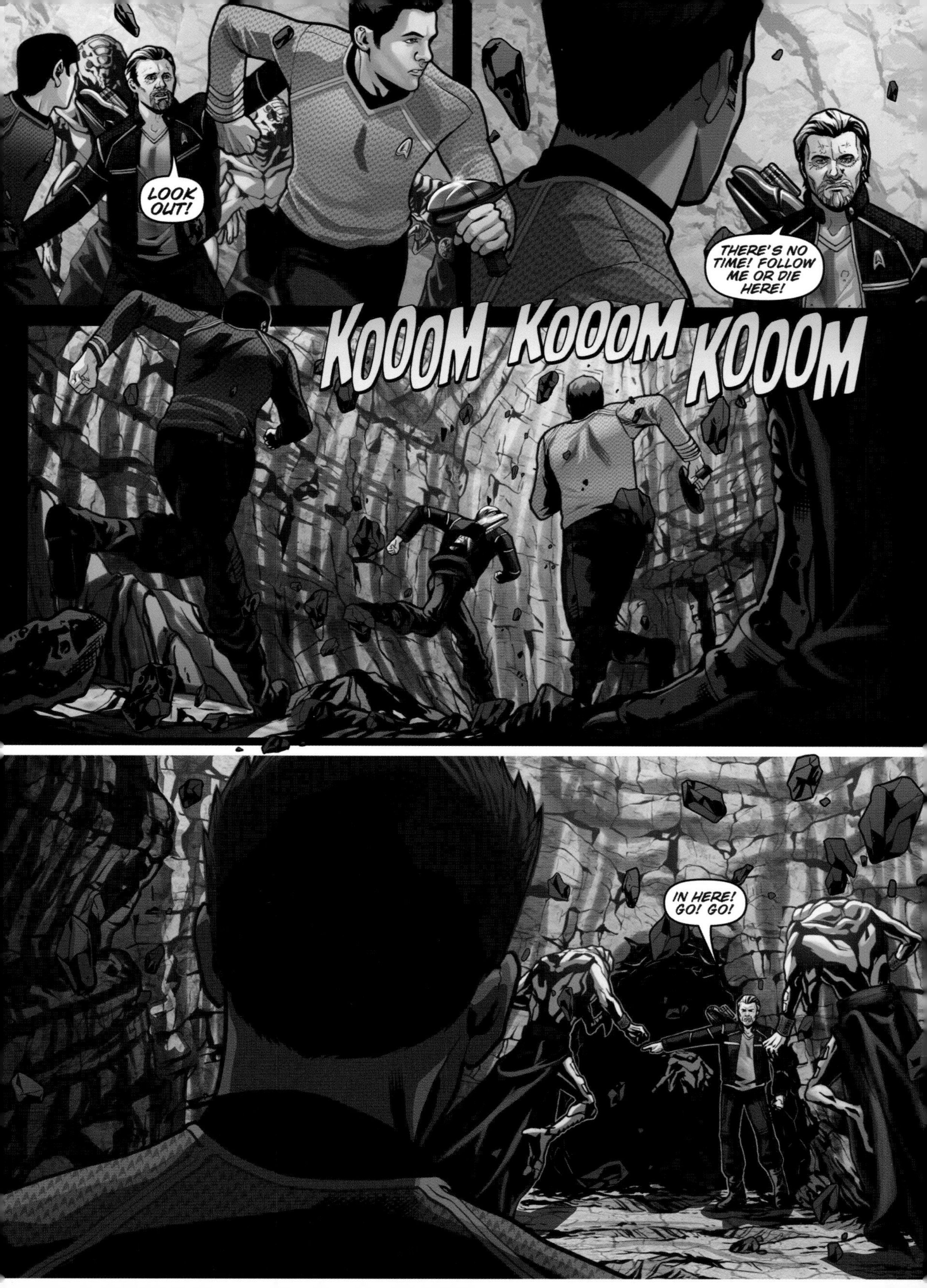
LOOK OUT!
THERE'S NO TIME! FOLLOW ME OR DIE HERE!
KOOOM KOOOM KOOOM
IN HERE! GO! GO!

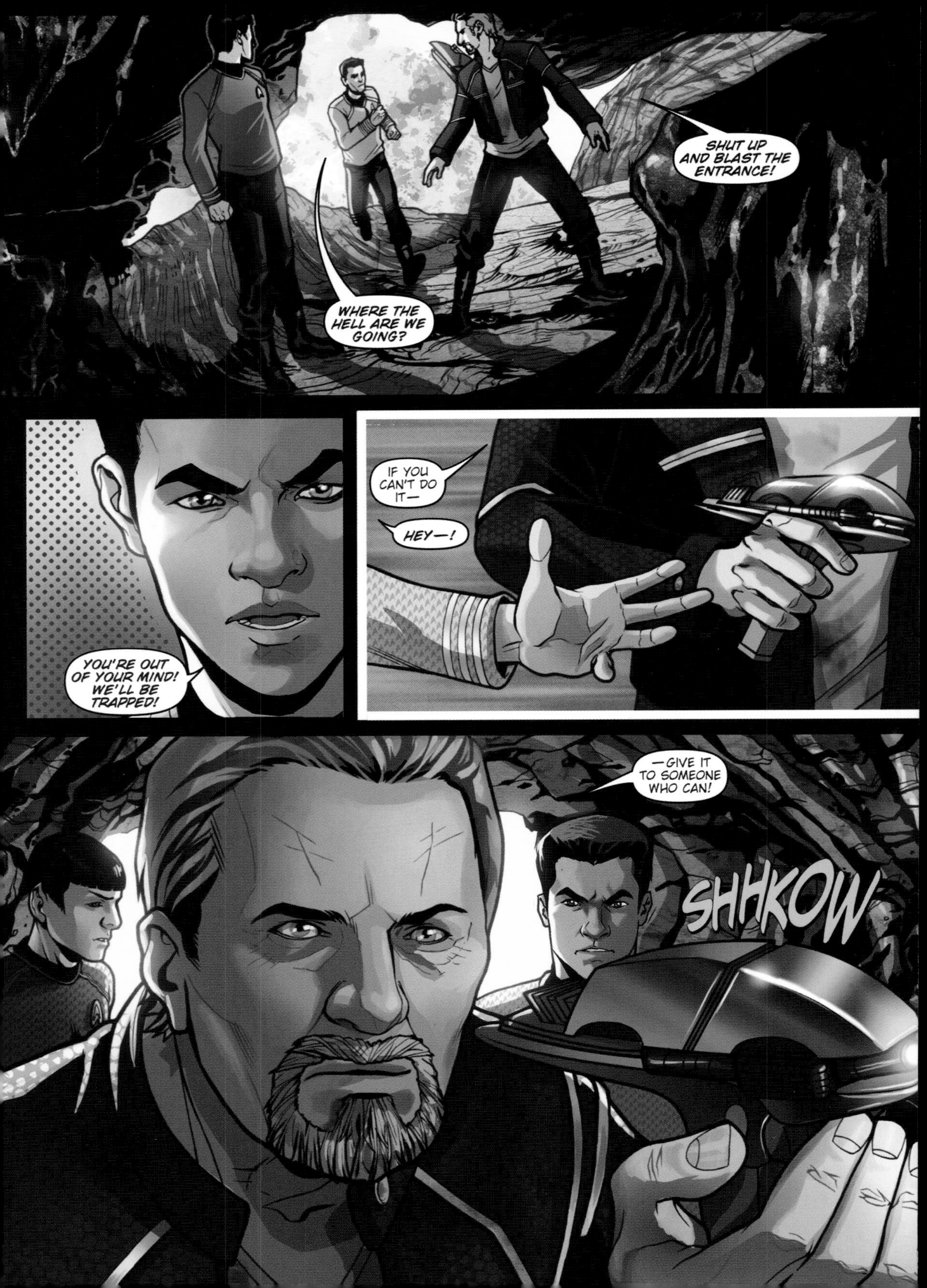
SHUT UP AND BLAST THE ENTRANCE!
WHERE THE HELL ARE WE GOING?
YOU'RE OUT OF YOUR MIND! WE'LL BE TRAPPED!
IF YOU CAN'T DO IT—
HEY—!
—GIVE IT TO SOMEONE WHO CAN!
SHHKOW

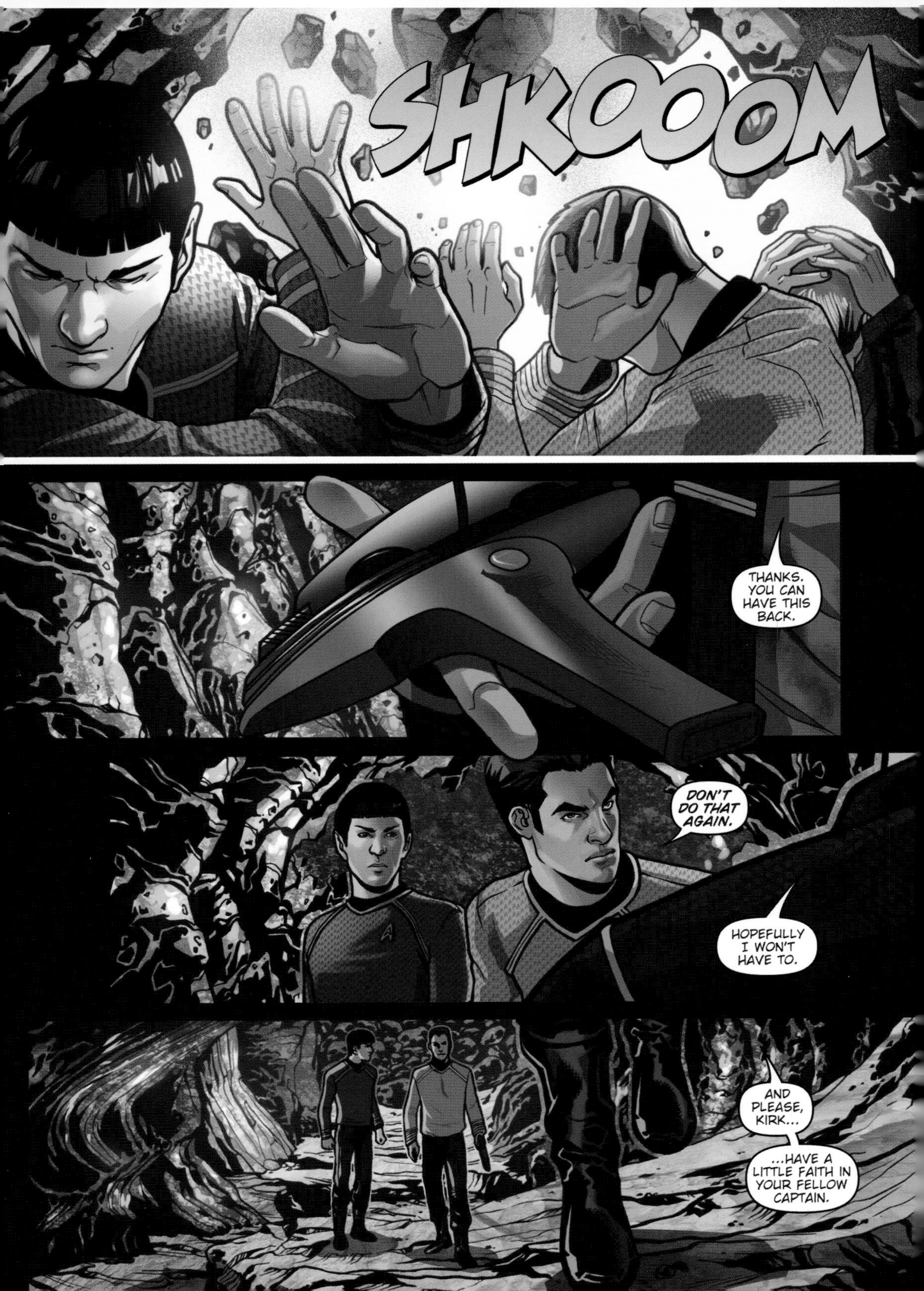
SHKOOOM
THANKS. YOU CAN HAVE THIS BACK.
DON'T DO THAT AGAIN.
HOPEFULLY I WON'T HAVE TO.
AND PLEASE, KIRK...
...HAVE A LITTLE FAITH IN YOUR FELLOW CAPTAIN.

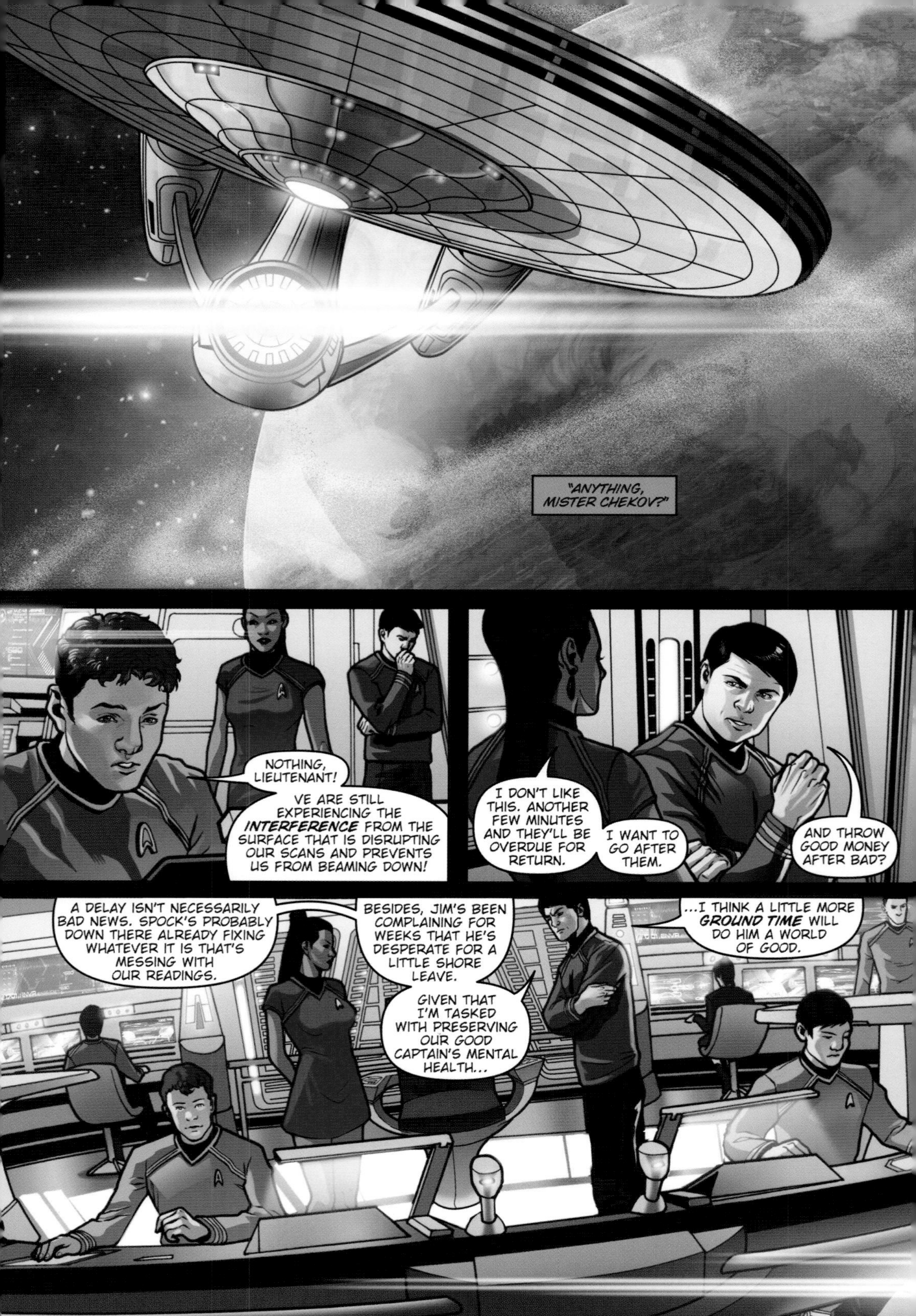
"ANYTHING, MISTER CHEKOV?"
NOTHING, LIEUTENANT!
VE ARE STILL EXPERIENCING THE *INTERFERENCE* FROM THE SURFACE THAT IS DISRUPTING OUR SCANS AND PREVENTS US FROM BEAMING DOWN!
I DON'T LIKE THIS. ANOTHER FEW MINUTES AND THEY'LL BE OVERDUE FOR RETURN.
I WANT TO GO AFTER THEM.
AND THROW GOOD MONEY AFTER BAD?
A DELAY ISN'T NECESSARILY BAD NEWS. SPOCK'S PROBABLY DOWN THERE ALREADY FIXING WHATEVER IT IS THAT'S MESSING WITH OUR READINGS.
BESIDES, JIM'S BEEN COMPLAINING FOR WEEKS THAT HE'S DESPERATE FOR A LITTLE SHORE LEAVE.
GIVEN THAT I'M TASKED WITH PRESERVING OUR GOOD CAPTAIN'S MENTAL HEALTH...
...I THINK A LITTLE MORE *GROUND TIME* WILL DO HIM A WORLD OF GOOD.

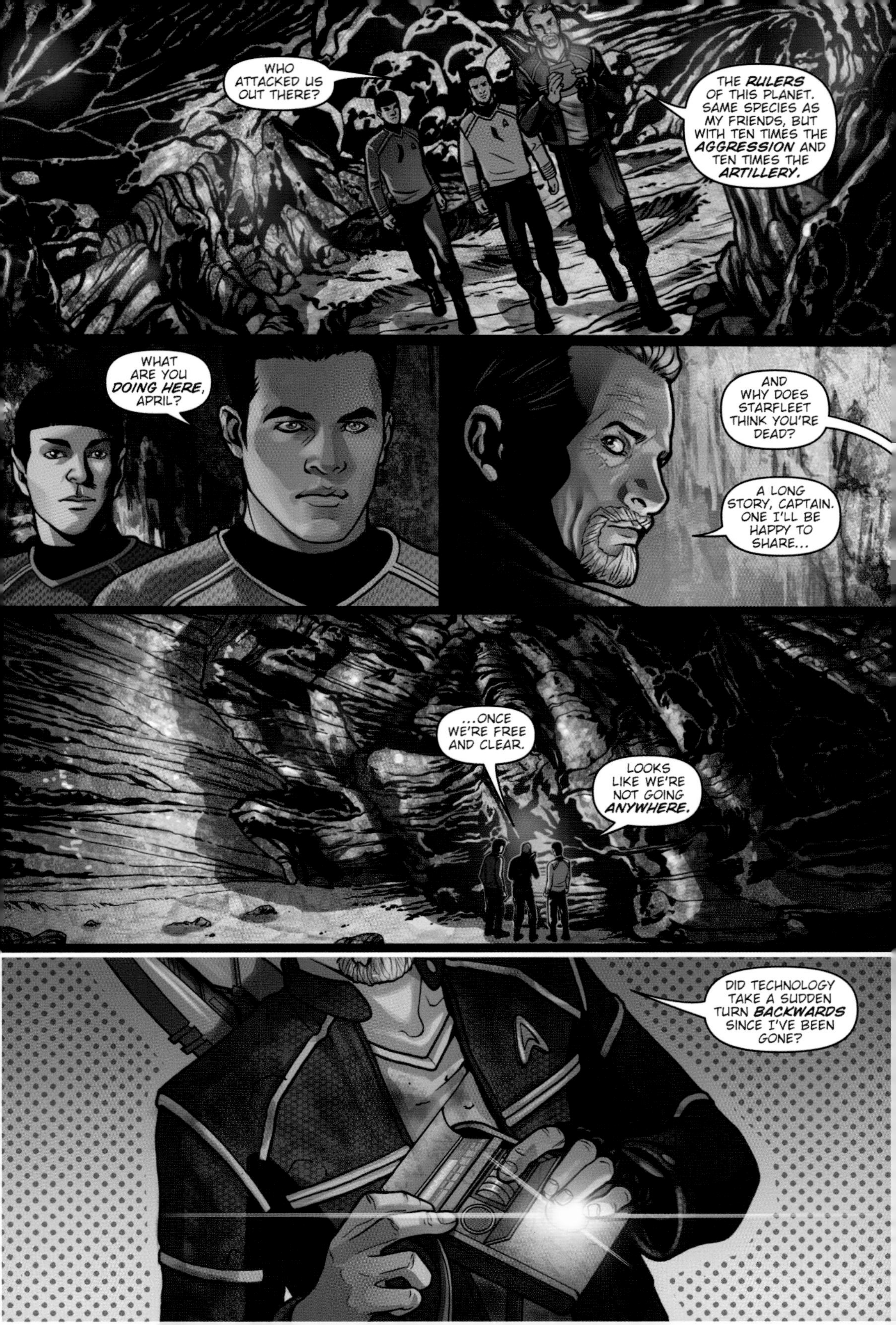
WHO ATTACKED US OUT THERE?
THE RULERS OF THIS PLANET. SAME SPECIES AS MY FRIENDS, BUT WITH TEN TIMES THE AGGRESSION AND TEN TIMES THE ARTILLERY.
WHAT ARE YOU DOING HERE, APRIL?
AND WHY DOES STARFLEET THINK YOU'RE DEAD?
A LONG STORY, CAPTAIN. ONE I'LL BE HAPPY TO SHARE...
...ONCE WE'RE FREE AND CLEAR.
LOOKS LIKE WE'RE NOT GOING ANYWHERE.
DID TECHNOLOGY TAKE A SUDDEN TURN BACKWARDS SINCE I'VE BEEN GONE?

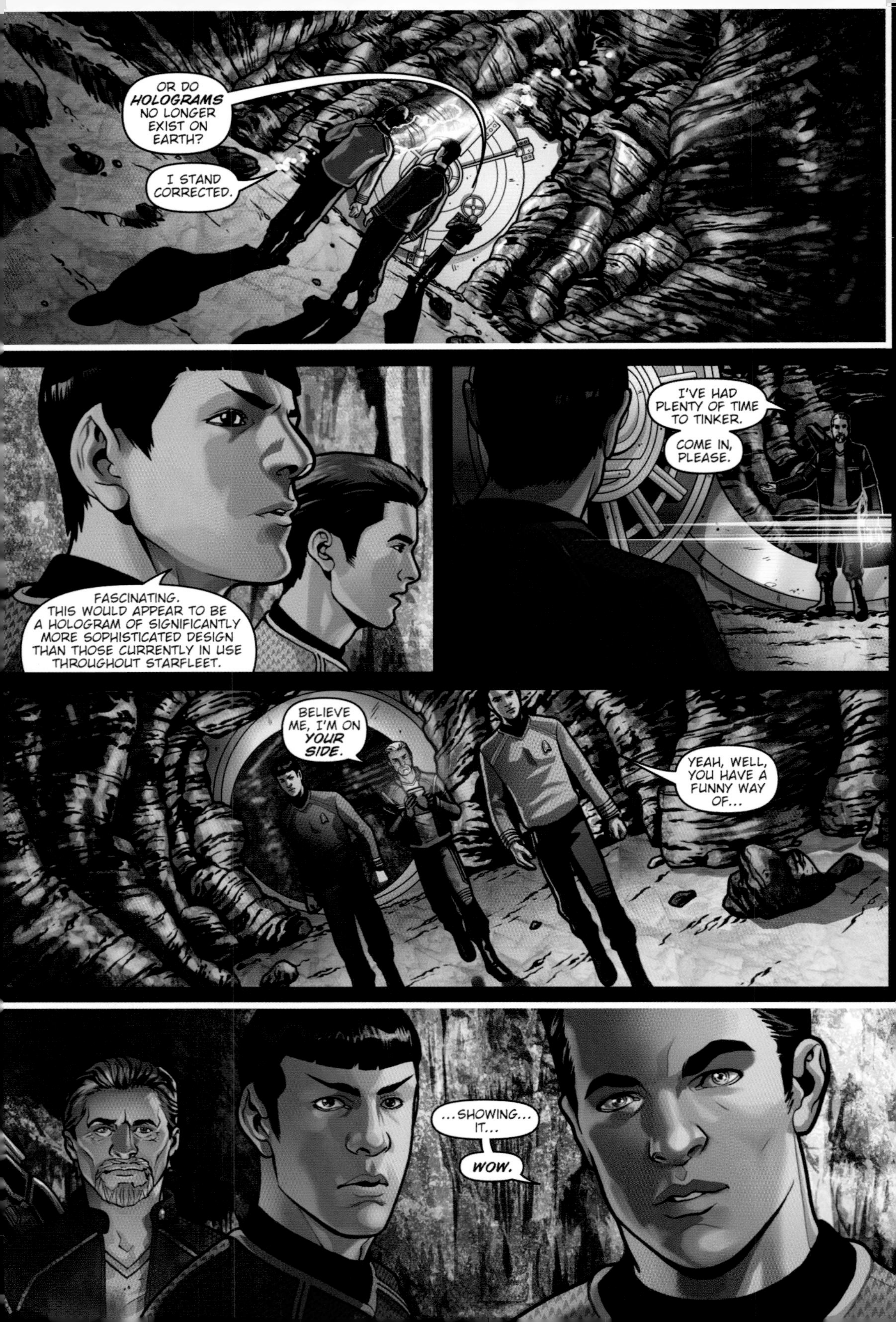
OR DO *HOLOGRAMS* NO LONGER EXIST ON EARTH?
I STAND CORRECTED.
FASCINATING. THIS WOULD APPEAR TO BE A HOLOGRAM OF SIGNIFICANTLY MORE SOPHISTICATED DESIGN THAN THOSE CURRENTLY IN USE THROUGHOUT STARFLEET.
I'VE HAD PLENTY OF TIME TO TINKER.
COME IN, PLEASE.
BELIEVE ME, I'M ON *YOUR SIDE*.
YEAH, WELL, YOU HAVE A FUNNY WAY OF...
...SHOWING... IT...
WOW.

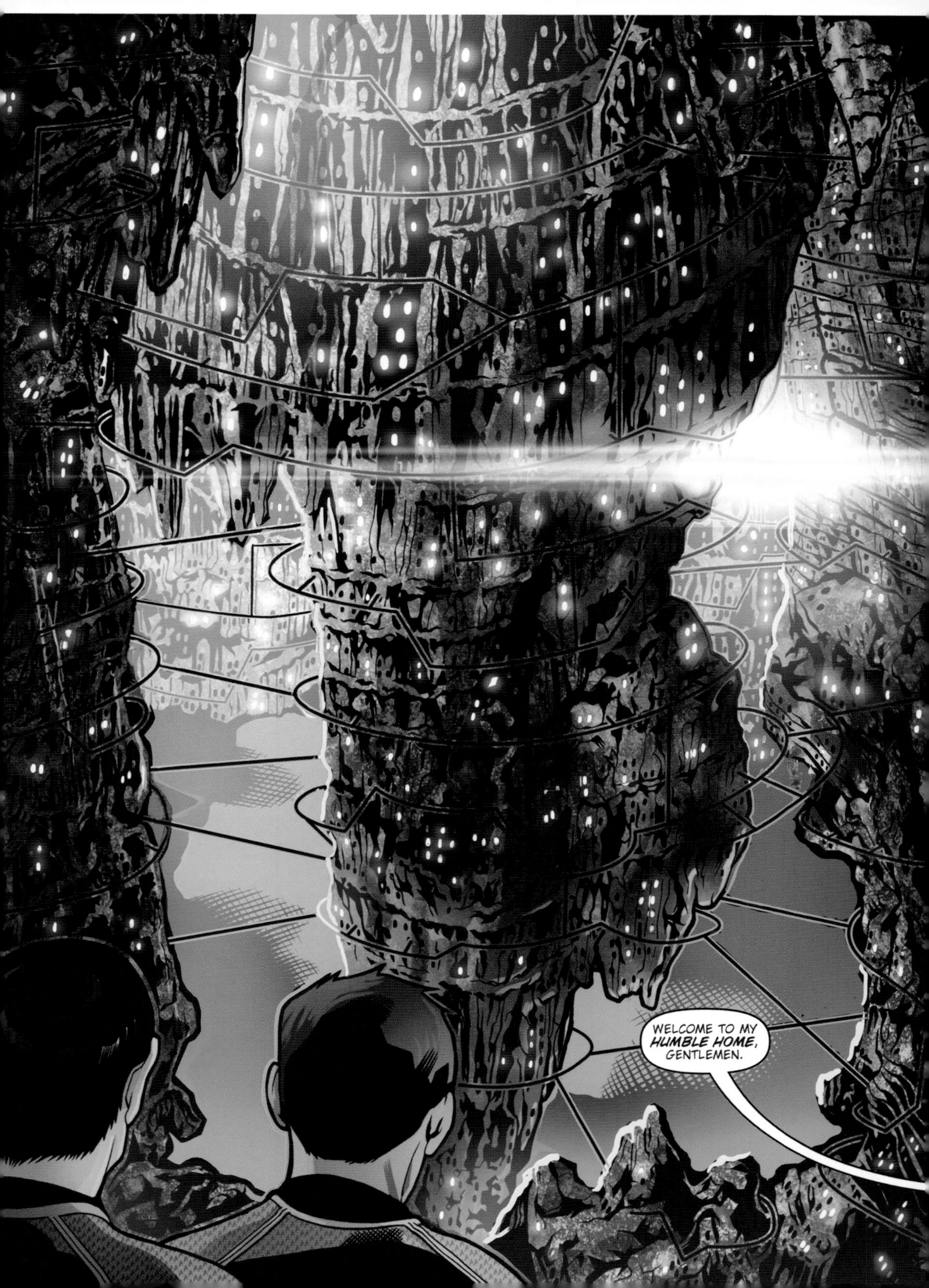
WELCOME TO MY *HUMBLE HOME*, GENTLEMEN.

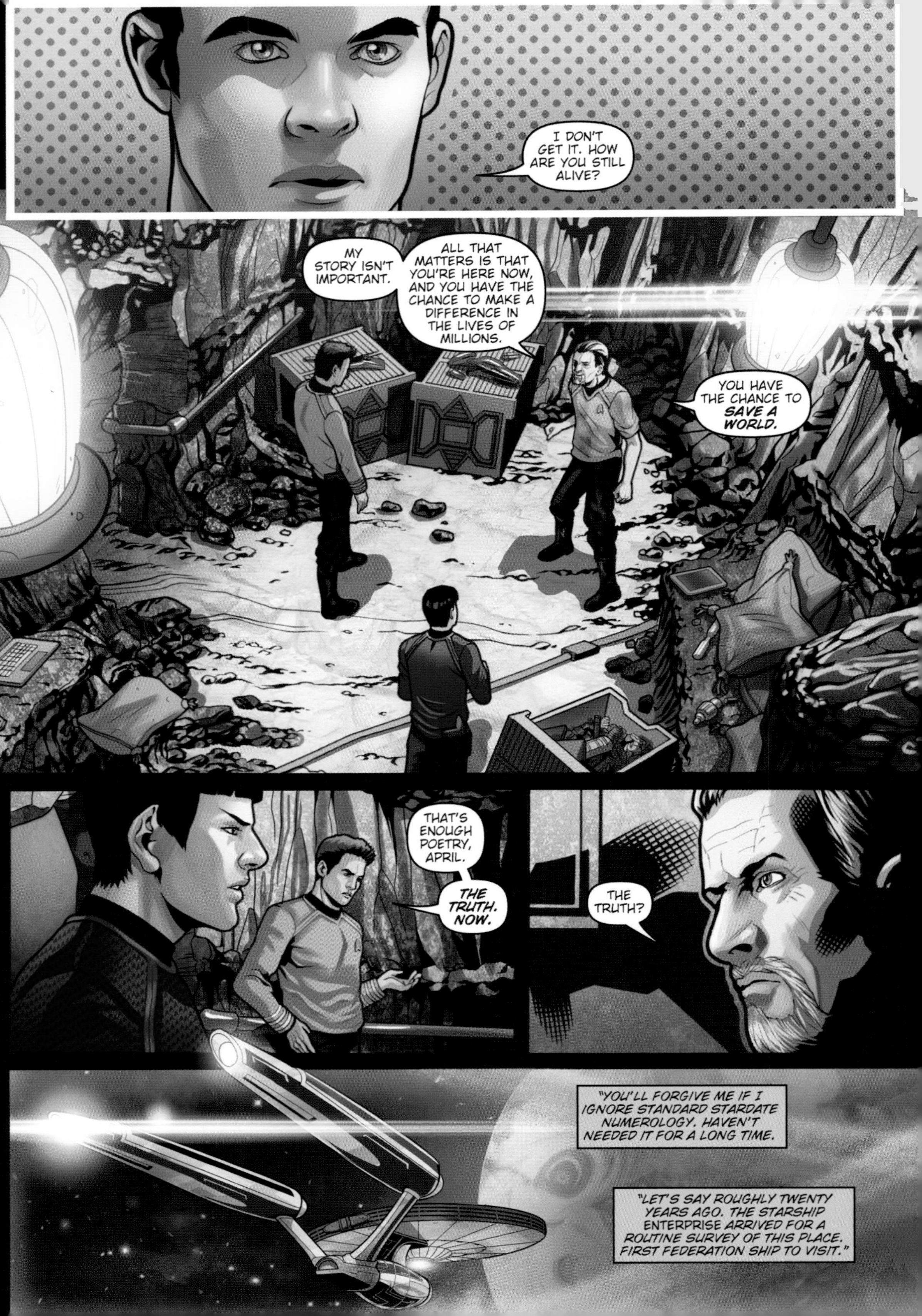
I DON'T GET IT. HOW ARE YOU STILL ALIVE?
MY STORY ISN'T IMPORTANT.
ALL THAT MATTERS IS THAT YOU'RE HERE NOW, AND YOU HAVE THE CHANCE TO MAKE A DIFFERENCE IN THE LIVES OF MILLIONS.
YOU HAVE THE CHANCE TO SAVE A WORLD.
THAT'S ENOUGH POETRY, APRIL.
THE TRUTH. NOW.
THE TRUTH?
"YOU'LL FORGIVE ME IF I IGNORE STANDARD STARDATE NUMEROLOGY. HAVEN'T NEEDED IT FOR A LONG TIME.
"LET'S SAY ROUGHLY TWENTY YEARS AGO. THE STARSHIP ENTERPRISE ARRIVED FOR A ROUTINE SURVEY OF THIS PLACE. FIRST FEDERATION SHIP TO VISIT."

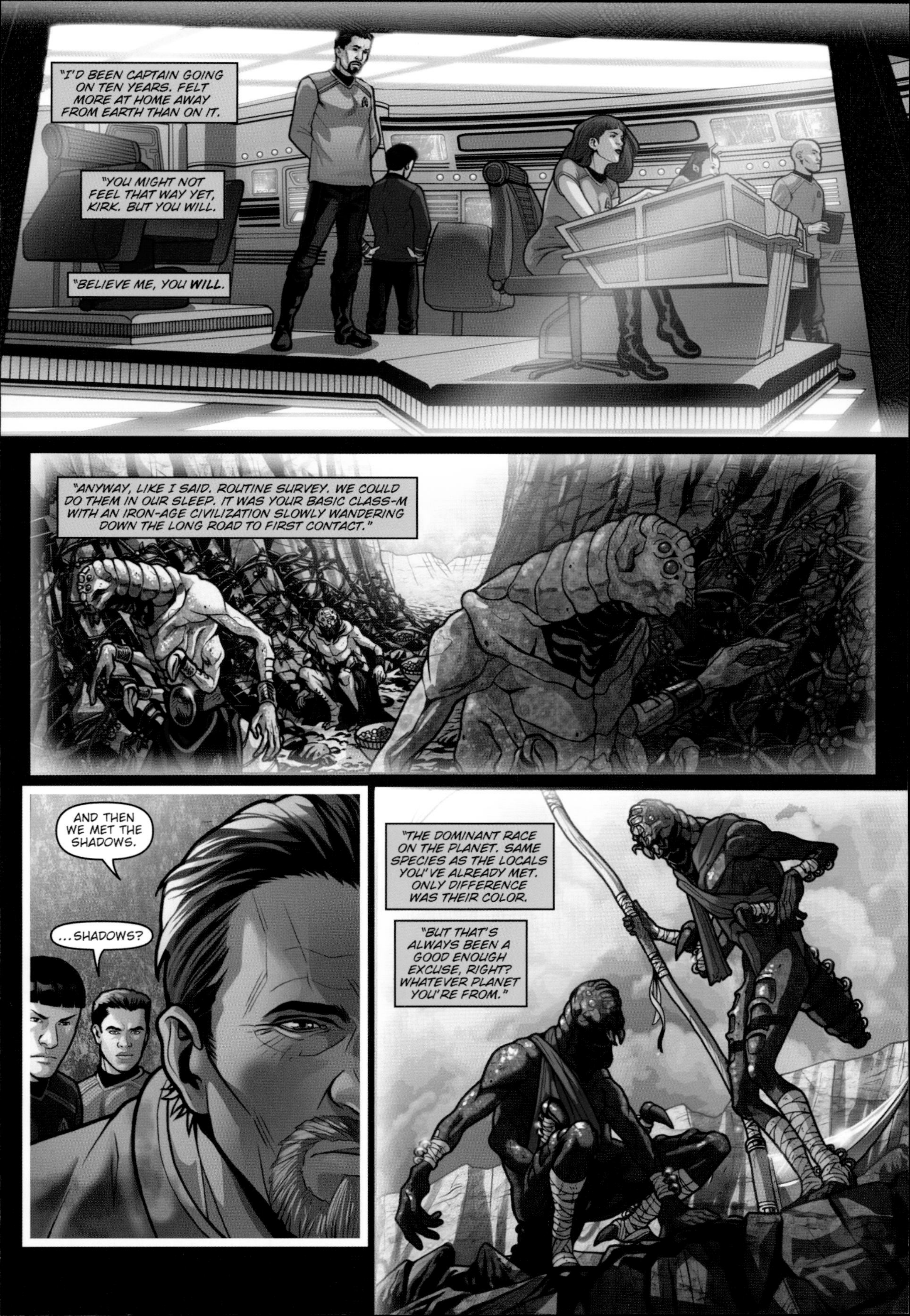
"I'D BEEN CAPTAIN GOING ON TEN YEARS. FELT MORE AT HOME AWAY FROM EARTH THAN ON IT.
"YOU MIGHT NOT FEEL THAT WAY YET, KIRK. BUT YOU WILL.
"BELIEVE ME, YOU WILL.
"ANYWAY, LIKE I SAID. ROUTINE SURVEY. WE COULD DO THEM IN OUR SLEEP. IT WAS YOUR BASIC CLASS-M WITH AN IRON-AGE CIVILIZATION SLOWLY WANDERING DOWN THE LONG ROAD TO FIRST CONTACT."
AND THEN WE MET THE SHADOWS.
...SHADOWS?
"THE DOMINANT RACE ON THE PLANET. SAME SPECIES AS THE LOCALS YOU'VE ALREADY MET. ONLY DIFFERENCE WAS THEIR COLOR.
"BUT THAT'S ALWAYS BEEN A GOOD ENOUGH EXCUSE, RIGHT? WHATEVER PLANET YOU'RE FROM."

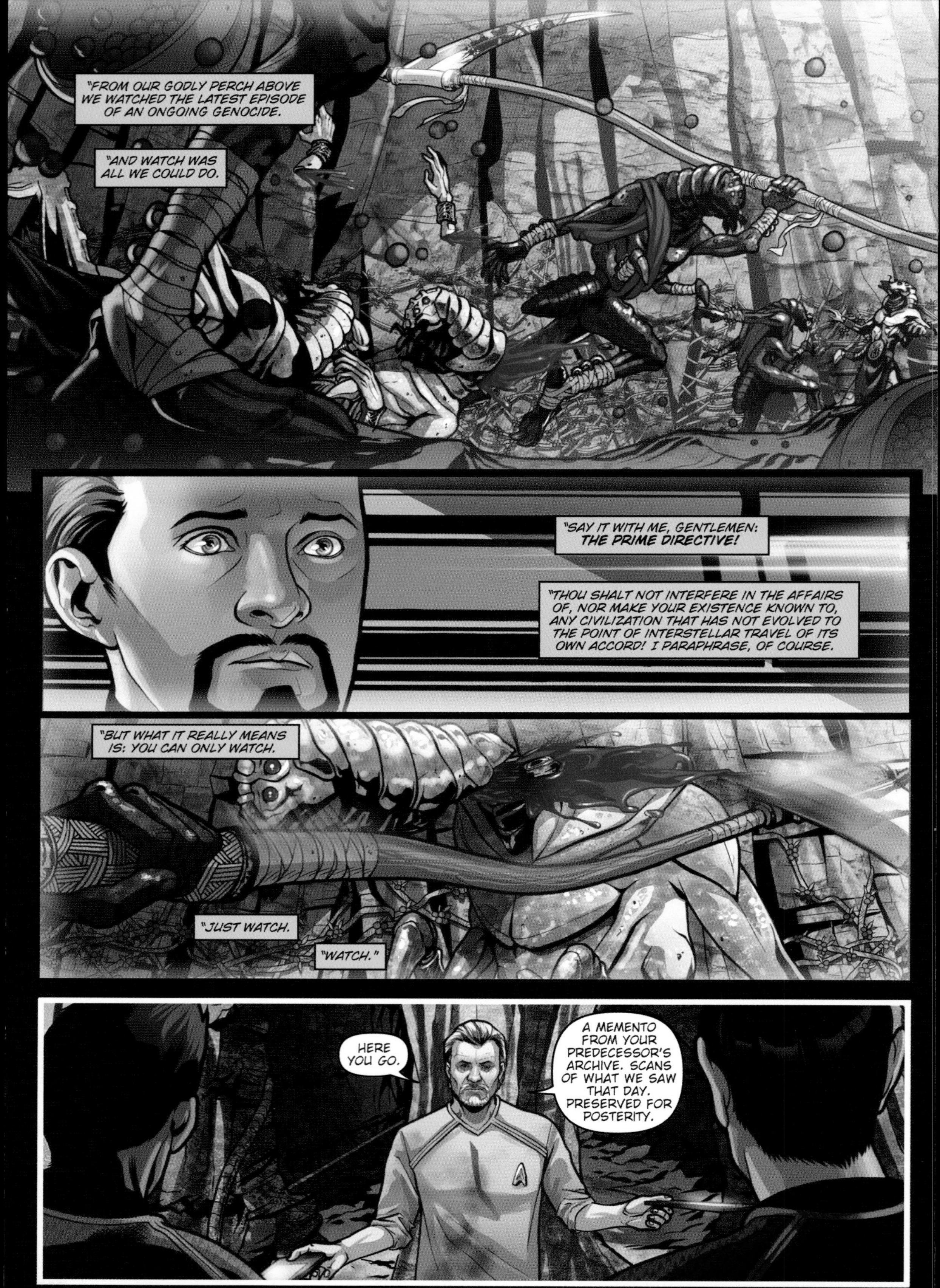
"FROM OUR GODLY PERCH ABOVE WE WATCHED THE LATEST EPISODE OF AN ONGOING GENOCIDE.
"AND WATCH WAS ALL WE COULD DO.
"SAY IT WITH ME, GENTLEMEN: THE PRIME DIRECTIVE!
"THOU SHALT NOT INTERFERE IN THE AFFAIRS OF, NOR MAKE YOUR EXISTENCE KNOWN TO, ANY CIVILIZATION THAT HAS NOT EVOLVED TO THE POINT OF INTERSTELLAR TRAVEL OF ITS OWN ACCORD! I PARAPHRASE, OF COURSE.
"BUT WHAT IT REALLY MEANS IS: YOU CAN ONLY WATCH.
"JUST WATCH.
"WATCH."
HERE YOU GO.
A MEMENTO FROM YOUR PREDECESSOR'S ARCHIVE. SCANS OF WHAT WE SAW THAT DAY. PRESERVED FOR POSTERITY.

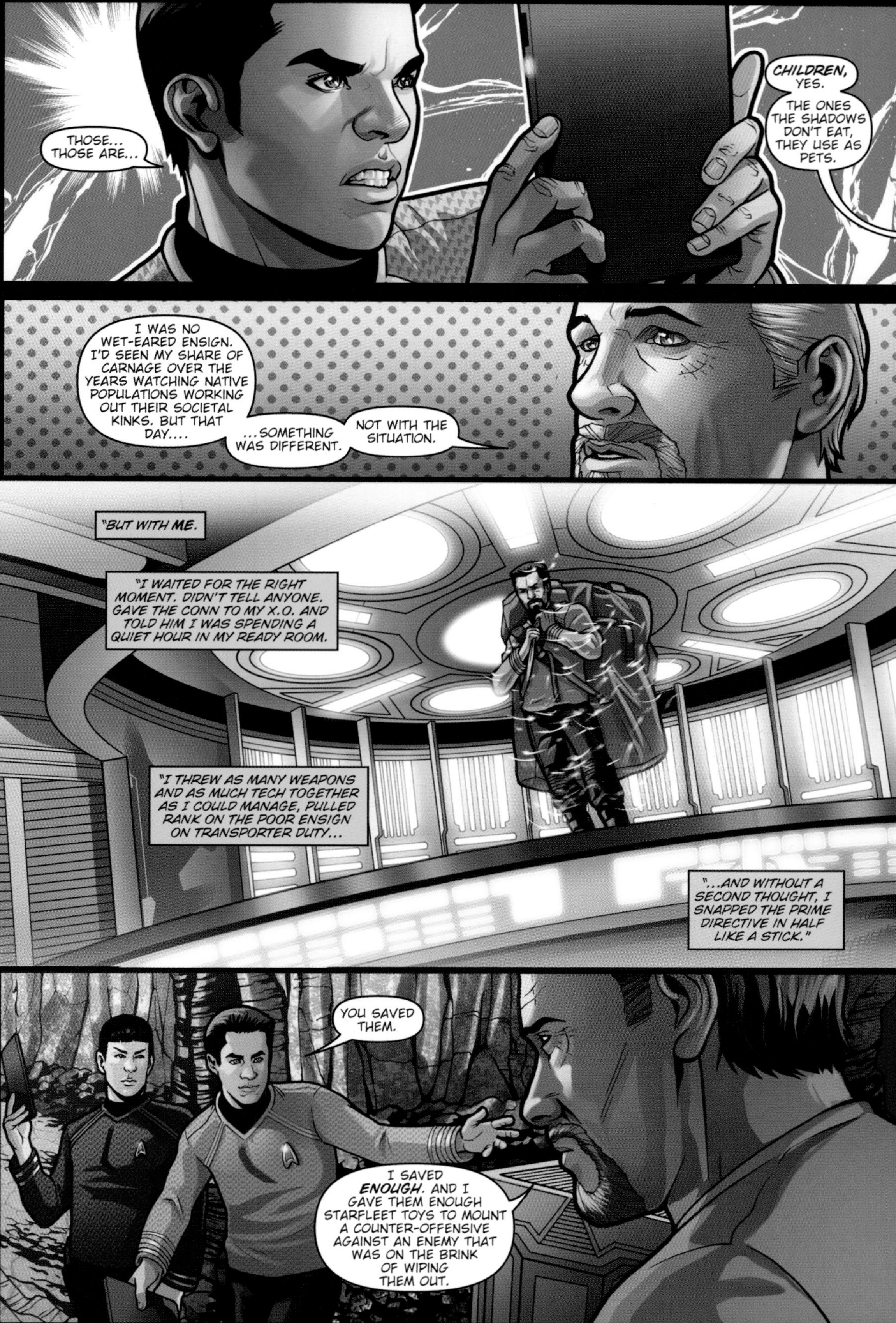
THOSE... THOSE ARE...
CHILDREN, YES.
THE ONES THE SHADOWS DON'T EAT, THEY USE AS PETS.
I WAS NO WET-EARED ENSIGN. I'D SEEN MY SHARE OF CARNAGE OVER THE YEARS WATCHING NATIVE POPULATIONS WORKING OUT THEIR SOCIETAL KINKS. BUT THAT DAY....
...SOMETHING WAS DIFFERENT.
NOT WITH THE SITUATION.
"BUT WITH ME.
"I WAITED FOR THE RIGHT MOMENT. DIDN'T TELL ANYONE. GAVE THE CONN TO MY X.O. AND TOLD HIM I WAS SPENDING A QUIET HOUR IN MY READY ROOM.
"I THREW AS MANY WEAPONS AND AS MUCH TECH TOGETHER AS I COULD MANAGE, PULLED RANK ON THE POOR ENSIGN ON TRANSPORTER DUTY...
"...AND WITHOUT A SECOND THOUGHT, I SNAPPED THE PRIME DIRECTIVE IN HALF LIKE A STICK."
YOU SAVED THEM.
I SAVED ENOUGH. AND I GAVE THEM ENOUGH STARFLEET TOYS TO MOUNT A COUNTER-OFFENSIVE AGAINST AN ENEMY THAT WAS ON THE BRINK OF WIPING THEM OUT.

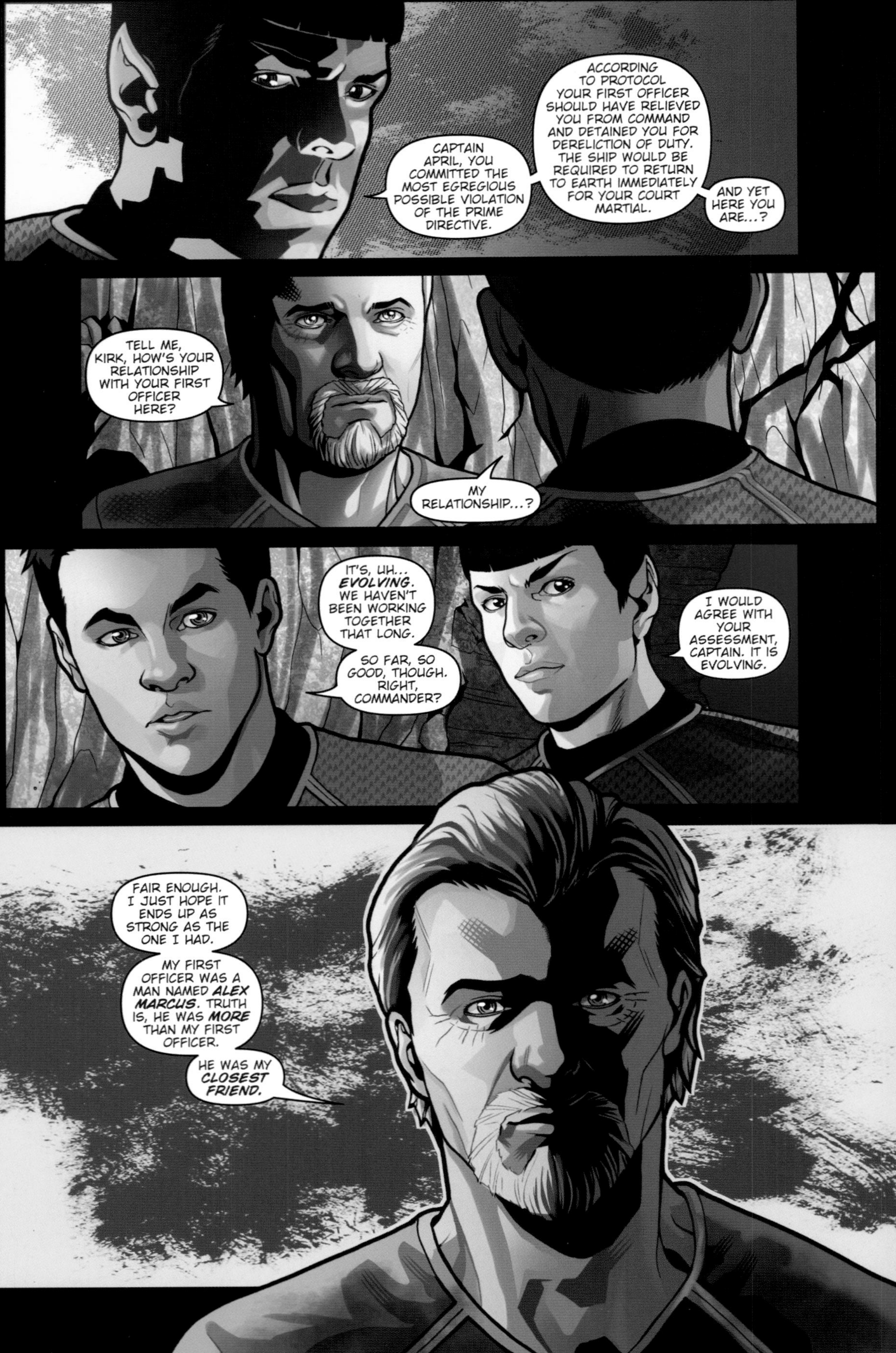

CAPTAIN APRIL, YOU COMMITTED THE MOST EGREGIOUS POSSIBLE VIOLATION OF THE PRIME DIRECTIVE.
ACCORDING TO PROTOCOL YOUR FIRST OFFICER SHOULD HAVE RELIEVED YOU FROM COMMAND AND DETAINED YOU FOR DERELICTION OF DUTY. THE SHIP WOULD BE REQUIRED TO RETURN TO EARTH IMMEDIATELY FOR YOUR COURT MARTIAL.
AND YET HERE YOU ARE...?
TELL ME, KIRK, HOW'S YOUR RELATIONSHIP WITH YOUR FIRST OFFICER HERE?
MY RELATIONSHIP...?
IT'S, UH... **EVOLVING**. WE HAVEN'T BEEN WORKING TOGETHER THAT LONG.
SO FAR, SO GOOD, THOUGH. RIGHT, COMMANDER?
I WOULD AGREE WITH YOUR ASSESSMENT, CAPTAIN. IT IS EVOLVING.
FAIR ENOUGH. I JUST HOPE IT ENDS UP AS STRONG AS THE ONE I HAD.
MY FIRST OFFICER WAS A MAN NAMED ***ALEX MARCUS***. TRUTH IS, HE WAS ***MORE*** THAN MY FIRST OFFICER.
HE WAS MY ***CLOSEST FRIEND***.

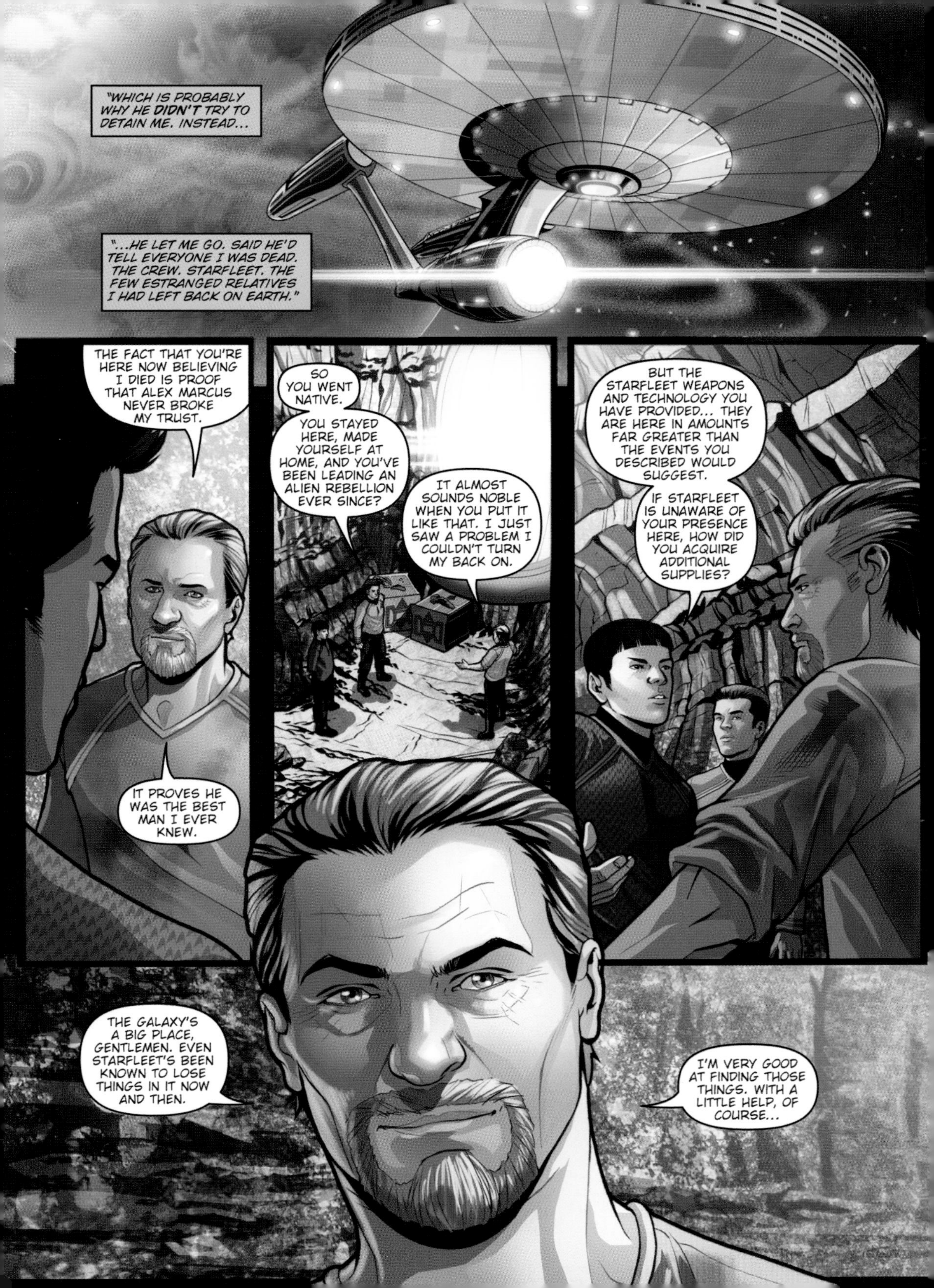
"WHICH IS PROBABLY WHY HE DIDN'T TRY TO DETAIN ME. INSTEAD...
"...HE LET ME GO. SAID HE'D TELL EVERYONE I WAS DEAD. THE CREW. STARFLEET. THE FEW ESTRANGED RELATIVES I HAD LEFT BACK ON EARTH."
THE FACT THAT YOU'RE HERE NOW BELIEVING I DIED IS PROOF THAT ALEX MARCUS NEVER BROKE MY TRUST.
IT PROVES HE WAS THE BEST MAN I EVER KNEW.
SO YOU WENT NATIVE.
YOU STAYED HERE, MADE YOURSELF AT HOME, AND YOU'VE BEEN LEADING AN ALIEN REBELLION EVER SINCE?
IT ALMOST SOUNDS NOBLE WHEN YOU PUT IT LIKE THAT. I JUST SAW A PROBLEM I COULDN'T TURN MY BACK ON.
BUT THE STARFLEET WEAPONS AND TECHNOLOGY YOU HAVE PROVIDED... THEY ARE HERE IN AMOUNTS FAR GREATER THAN THE EVENTS YOU DESCRIBED WOULD SUGGEST.
IF STARFLEET IS UNAWARE OF YOUR PRESENCE HERE, HOW DID YOU ACQUIRE ADDITIONAL SUPPLIES?
THE GALAXY'S A BIG PLACE, GENTLEMEN. EVEN STARFLEET'S BEEN KNOWN TO LOSE THINGS IN IT NOW AND THEN.
I'M VERY GOOD AT FINDING THOSE THINGS. WITH A LITTLE HELP, OF COURSE...

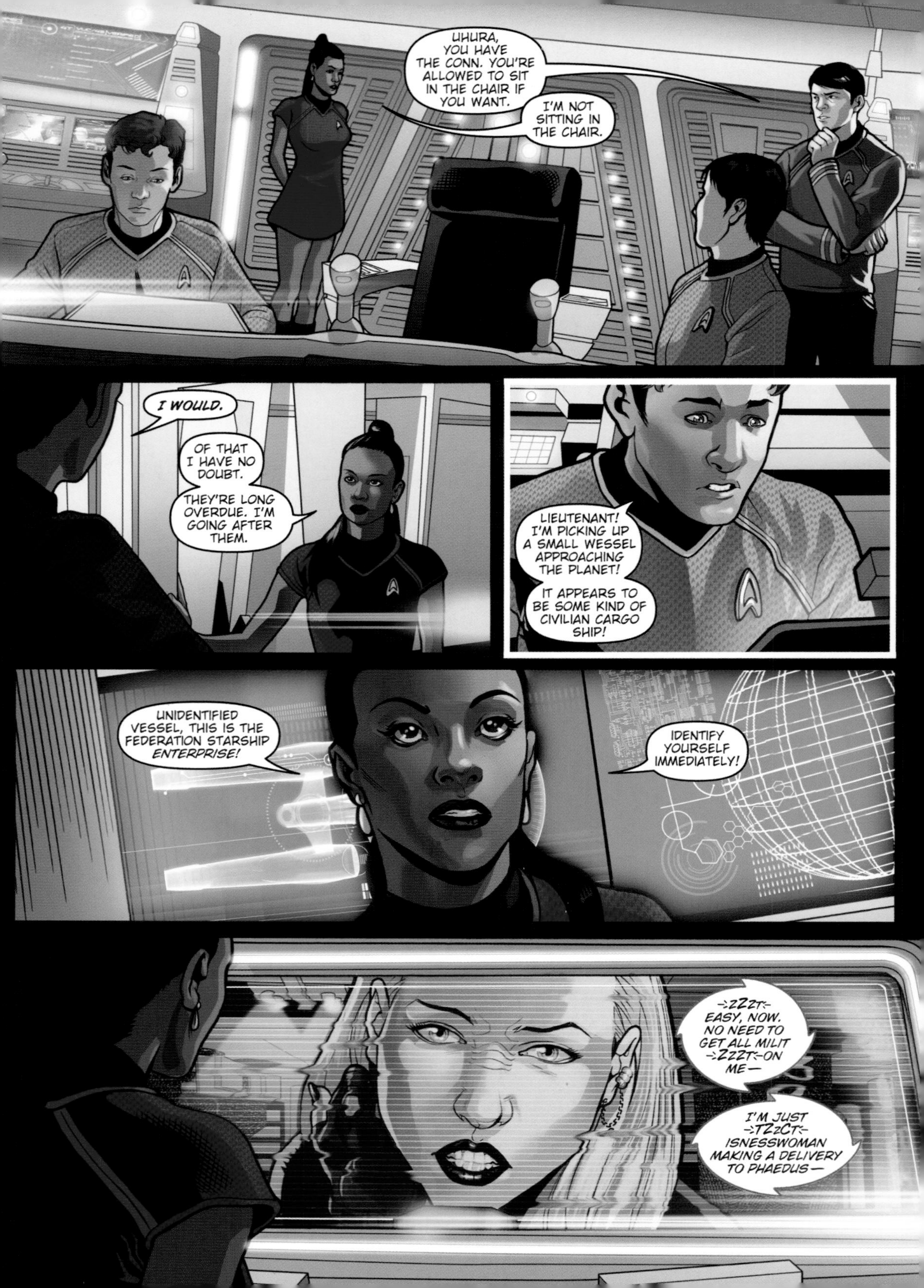

UHURA, YOU HAVE THE CONN. YOU'RE ALLOWED TO SIT IN THE CHAIR IF YOU WANT.
I'M NOT SITTING IN THE CHAIR.
I WOULD.
OF THAT I HAVE NO DOUBT.
THEY'RE LONG OVERDUE. I'M GOING AFTER THEM.
LIEUTENANT! I'M PICKING UP A SMALL WESSEL APPROACHING THE PLANET!
IT APPEARS TO BE SOME KIND OF CIVILIAN CARGO SHIP!
UNIDENTIFIED VESSEL, THIS IS THE FEDERATION STARSHIP ENTERPRISE!
IDENTIFY YOURSELF IMMEDIATELY!
-zZzt- EASY, NOW. NO NEED TO GET ALL MILIT -ZzZt- ON ME—
I'M JUST -TZzCt- ISNESSWOMAN MAKING A DELIVERY TO PHAEDUS—

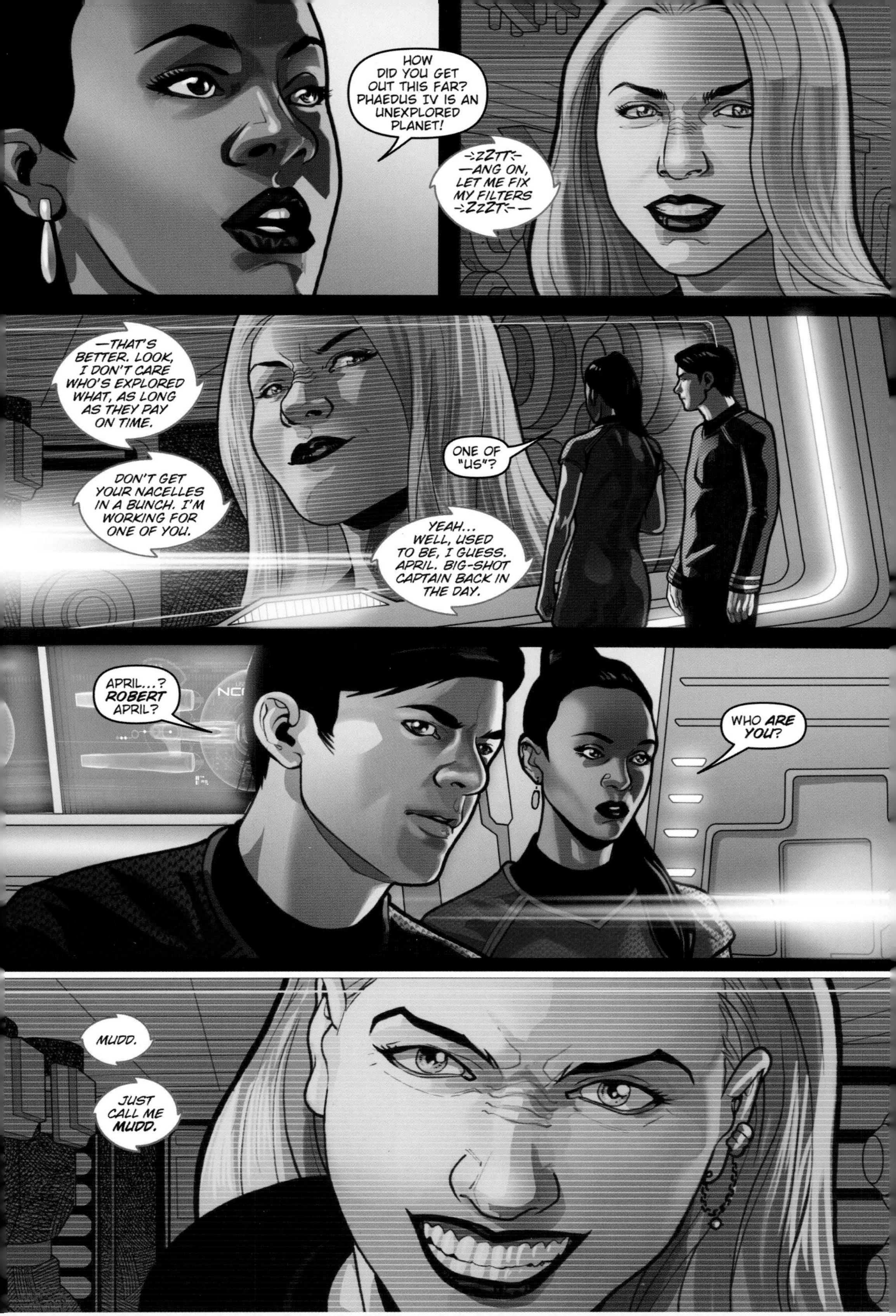
HOW DID YOU GET OUT THIS FAR? PHAEDUS IV IS AN UNEXPLORED PLANET!
-ZZTT- —ANG ON, LET ME FIX MY FILTERS -ZZZT- —
—THAT'S BETTER. LOOK, I DON'T CARE WHO'S EXPLORED WHAT, AS LONG AS THEY PAY ON TIME.
DON'T GET YOUR NACELLES IN A BUNCH. I'M WORKING FOR ONE OF YOU.
ONE OF "US"?
YEAH... WELL, USED TO BE, I GUESS. APRIL. BIG-SHOT CAPTAIN BACK IN THE DAY.
APRIL...? **ROBERT** APRIL?
WHO **ARE YOU**?
MUDD.
JUST CALL ME **MUDD.**

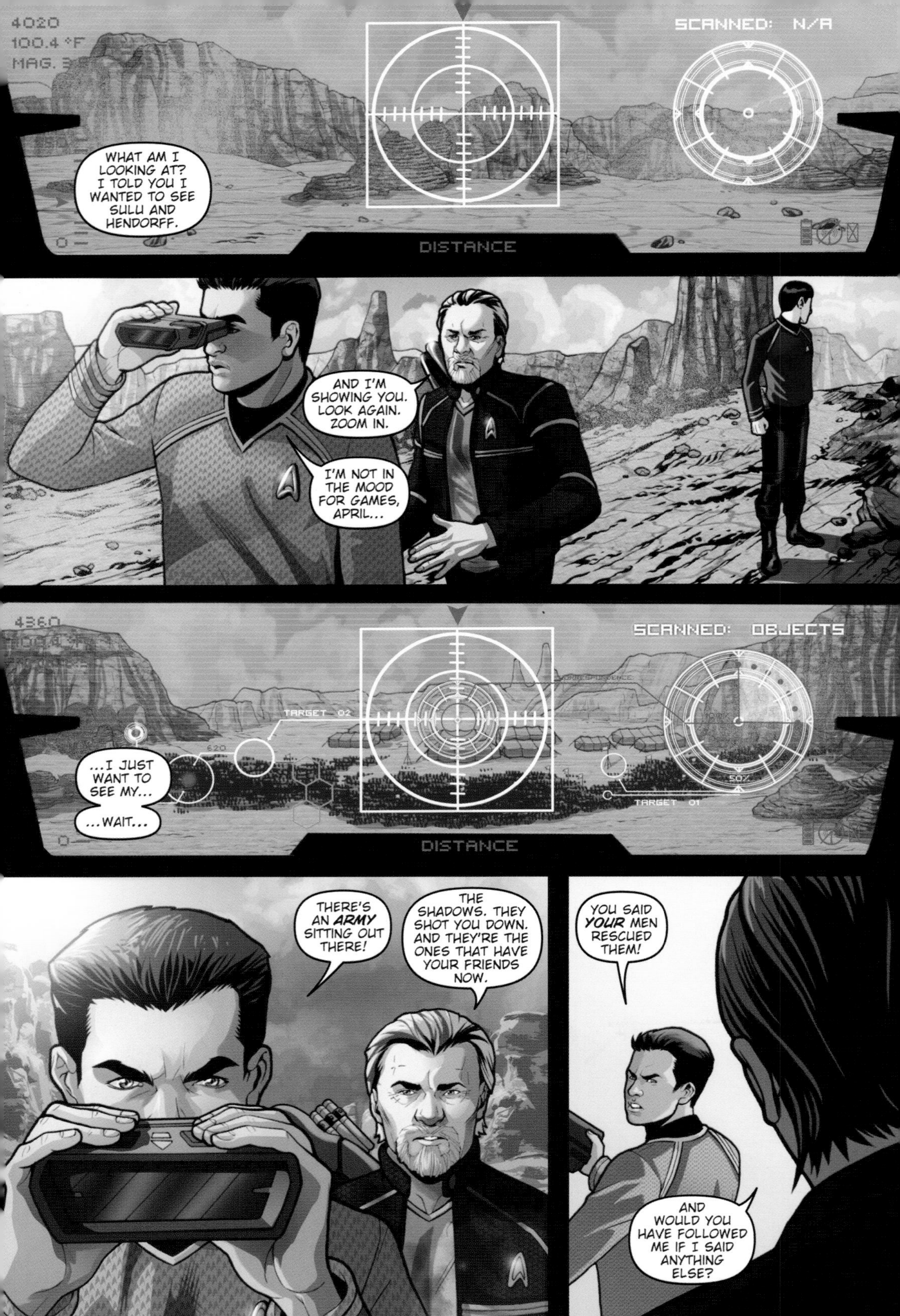

4020
100.4 °F
SCANNED: N/A
WHAT AM I LOOKING AT? I TOLD YOU I WANTED TO SEE SULU AND HENDORFF.
DISTANCE
AND I'M SHOWING YOU. LOOK AGAIN. ZOOM IN.
I'M NOT IN THE MOOD FOR GAMES, APRIL...
4360
SCANNED: OBJECTS
TARGET 02
TARGET 01
50%
...I JUST WANT TO SEE MY...
...WAIT...
DISTANCE
THERE'S AN **ARMY** SITTING OUT THERE!
THE SHADOWS. THEY SHOT YOU DOWN. AND THEY'RE THE ONES THAT HAVE YOUR FRIENDS NOW.
YOU SAID **YOUR** MEN RESCUED THEM!
AND WOULD YOU HAVE FOLLOWED ME IF I SAID ANYTHING ELSE?

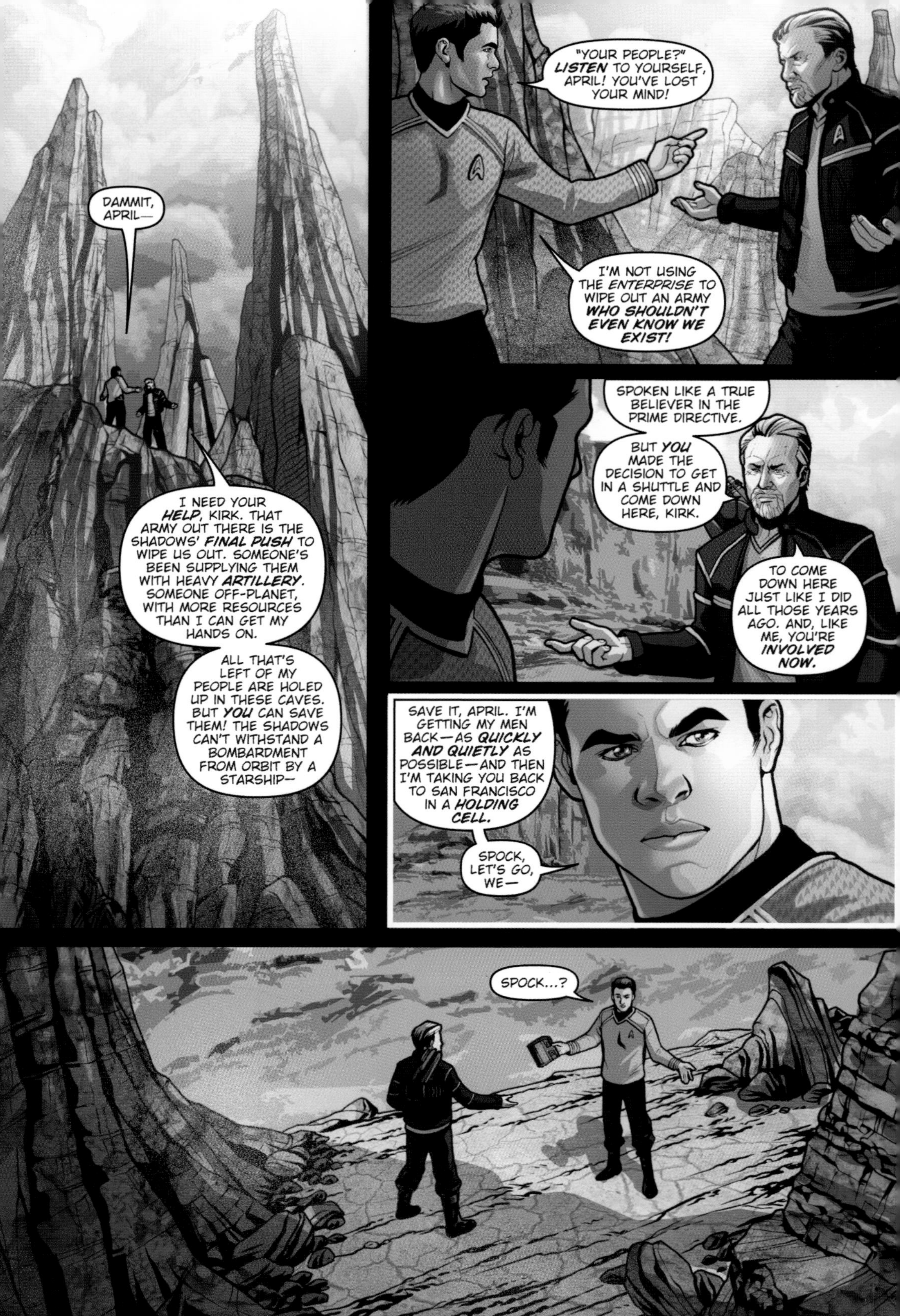
DAMMIT, APRIL—
I NEED YOUR HELP, KIRK. THAT ARMY OUT THERE IS THE SHADOWS' FINAL PUSH TO WIPE US OUT. SOMEONE'S BEEN SUPPLYING THEM WITH HEAVY ARTILLERY. SOMEONE OFF-PLANET, WITH MORE RESOURCES THAN I CAN GET MY HANDS ON.
ALL THAT'S LEFT OF MY PEOPLE ARE HOLED UP IN THESE CAVES. BUT YOU CAN SAVE THEM! THE SHADOWS CAN'T WITHSTAND A BOMBARDMENT FROM ORBIT BY A STARSHIP—
"YOUR PEOPLE?" LISTEN TO YOURSELF, APRIL! YOU'VE LOST YOUR MIND!
I'M NOT USING THE ENTERPRISE TO WIPE OUT AN ARMY WHO SHOULDN'T EVEN KNOW WE EXIST!
SPOKEN LIKE A TRUE BELIEVER IN THE PRIME DIRECTIVE.
BUT YOU MADE THE DECISION TO GET IN A SHUTTLE AND COME DOWN HERE, KIRK.
TO COME DOWN HERE JUST LIKE I DID ALL THOSE YEARS AGO. AND, LIKE ME, YOU'RE INVOLVED NOW.
SAVE IT, APRIL. I'M GETTING MY MEN BACK—AS QUICKLY AND QUIETLY AS POSSIBLE—AND THEN I'M TAKING YOU BACK TO SAN FRANCISCO IN A HOLDING CELL.
SPOCK, LET'S GO, WE—
SPOCK...?

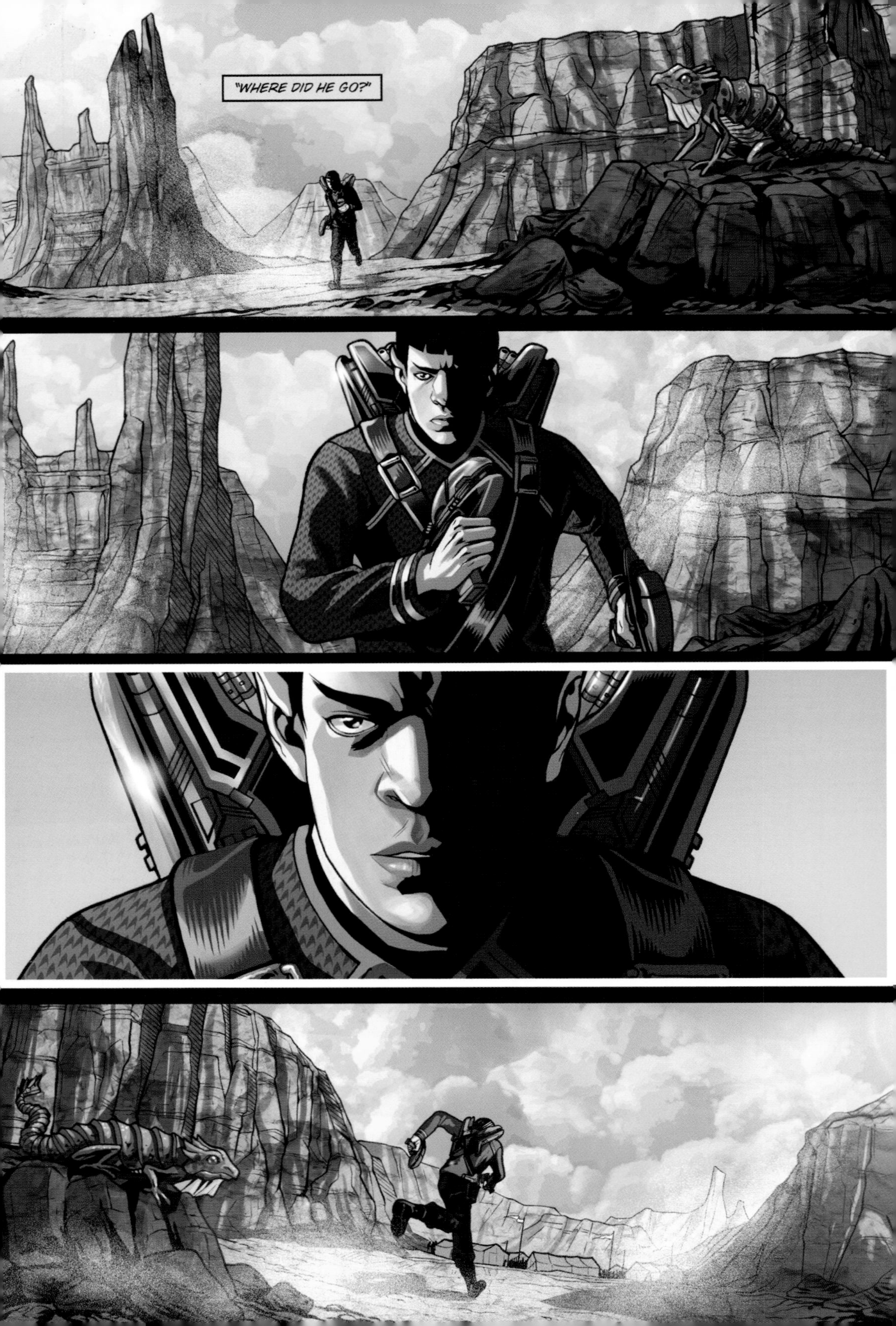
"WHERE DID HE GO?"

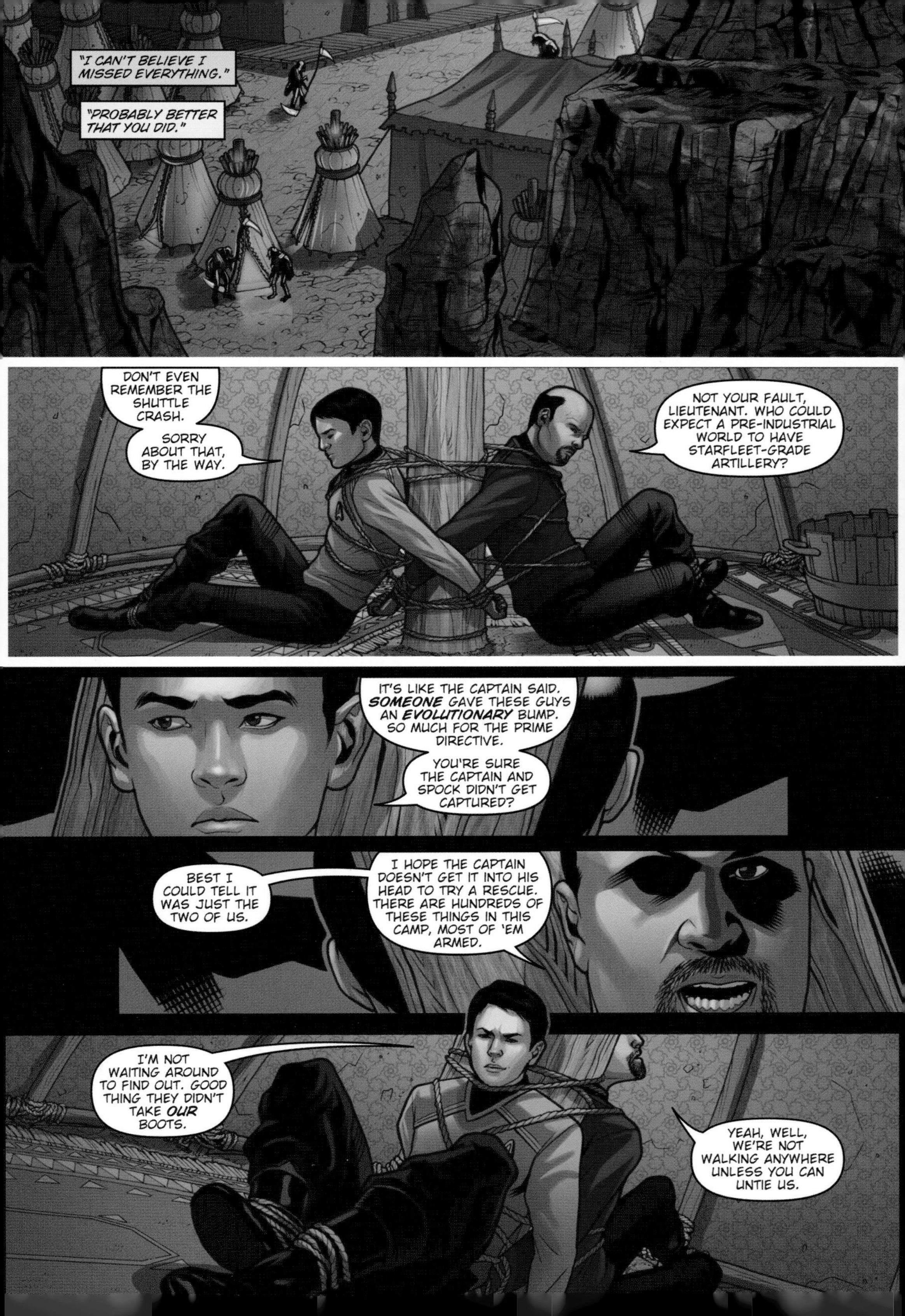
"I CAN'T BELIEVE I MISSED EVERYTHING."
"PROBABLY BETTER THAT YOU DID."
DON'T EVEN REMEMBER THE SHUTTLE CRASH.
SORRY ABOUT THAT, BY THE WAY.
NOT YOUR FAULT, LIEUTENANT. WHO COULD EXPECT A PRE-INDUSTRIAL WORLD TO HAVE STARFLEET-GRADE ARTILLERY?
IT'S LIKE THE CAPTAIN SAID. SOMEONE GAVE THESE GUYS AN EVOLUTIONARY BUMP. SO MUCH FOR THE PRIME DIRECTIVE.
YOU'RE SURE THE CAPTAIN AND SPOCK DIDN'T GET CAPTURED?
BEST I COULD TELL IT WAS JUST THE TWO OF US.
I HOPE THE CAPTAIN DOESN'T GET IT INTO HIS HEAD TO TRY A RESCUE. THERE ARE HUNDREDS OF THESE THINGS IN THIS CAMP, MOST OF 'EM ARMED.
I'M NOT WAITING AROUND TO FIND OUT. GOOD THING THEY DIDN'T TAKE OUR BOOTS.
YEAH, WELL, WE'RE NOT WALKING ANYWHERE UNLESS YOU CAN UNTIE US.

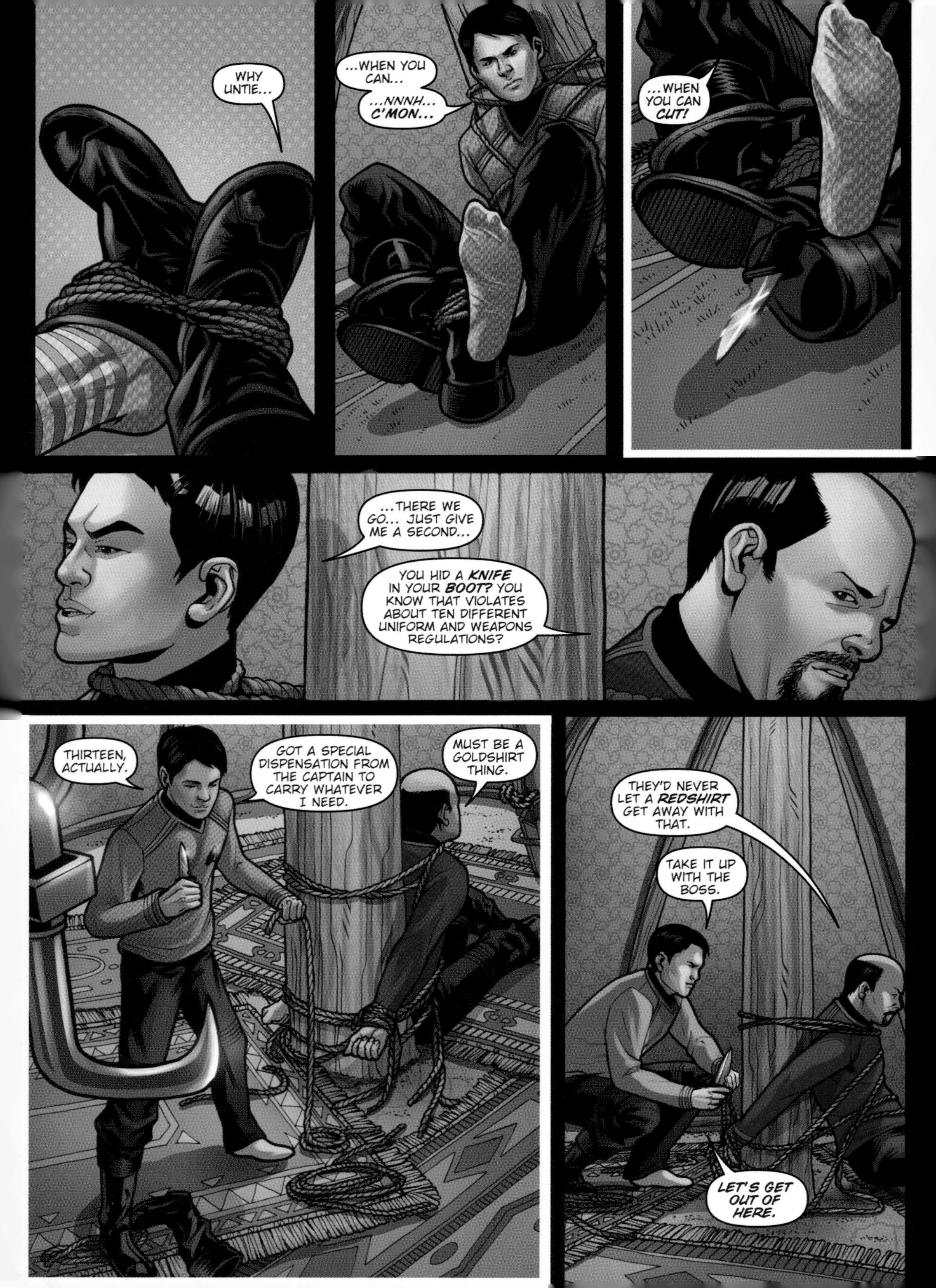
WHY UNTIE...
...WHEN YOU CAN...
...NNNH... C'MON...
...WHEN YOU CAN CUT!
...THERE WE GO... JUST GIVE ME A SECOND...
YOU HID A KNIFE IN YOUR BOOT? YOU KNOW THAT VIOLATES ABOUT TEN DIFFERENT UNIFORM AND WEAPONS REGULATIONS?
THIRTEEN, ACTUALLY.
GOT A SPECIAL DISPENSATION FROM THE CAPTAIN TO CARRY WHATEVER I NEED.
MUST BE A GOLDSHIRT THING.
THEY'D NEVER LET A REDSHIRT GET AWAY WITH THAT.
TAKE IT UP WITH THE BOSS.
LET'S GET OUT OF HERE.

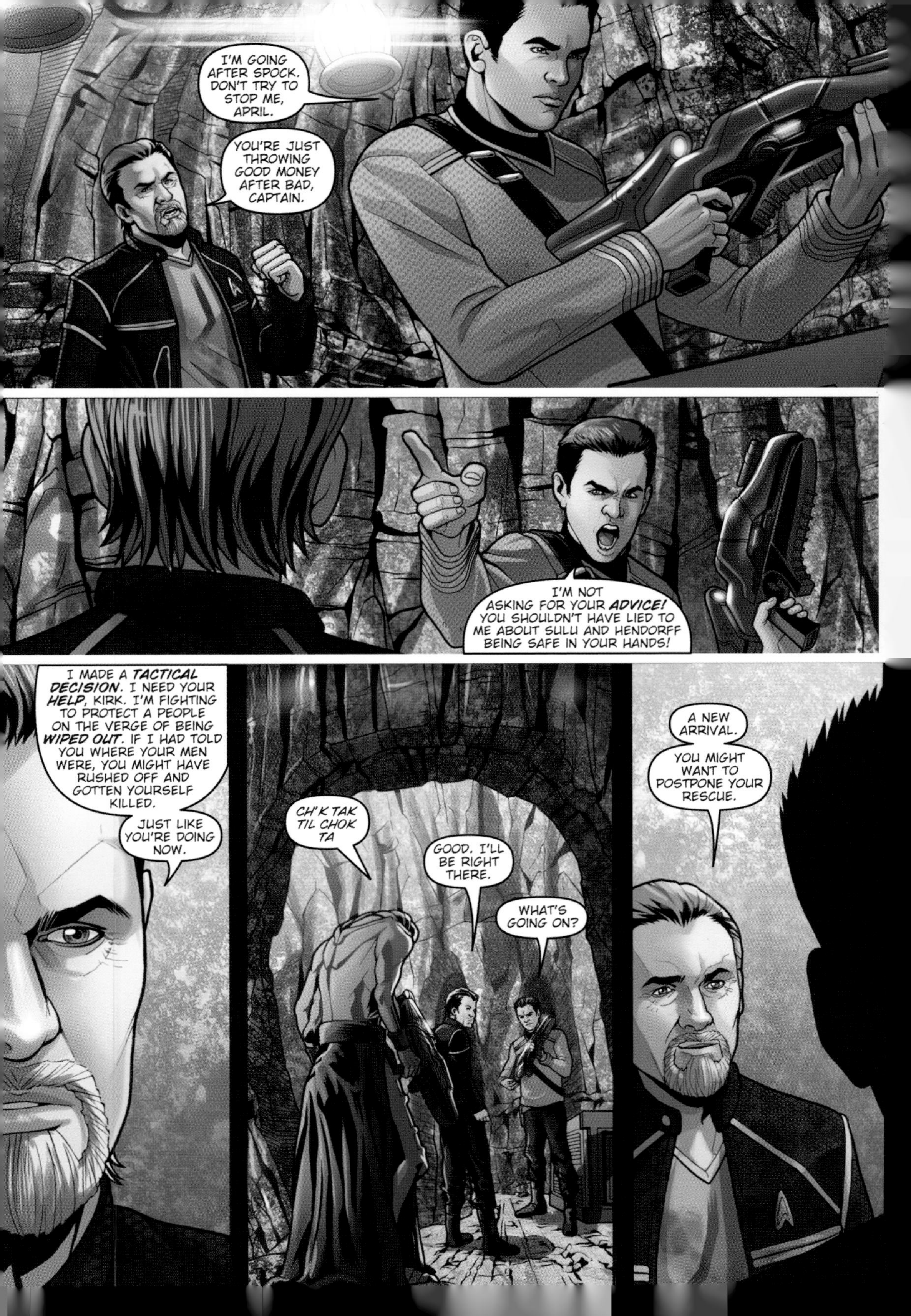
I'M GOING AFTER SPOCK. DON'T TRY TO STOP ME, APRIL.
YOU'RE JUST THROWING GOOD MONEY AFTER BAD, CAPTAIN.
I'M NOT ASKING FOR YOUR ADVICE! YOU SHOULDN'T HAVE LIED TO ME ABOUT SULU AND HENDORFF BEING SAFE IN YOUR HANDS!
I MADE A TACTICAL DECISION. I NEED YOUR HELP, KIRK. I'M FIGHTING TO PROTECT A PEOPLE ON THE VERGE OF BEING WIPED OUT. IF I HAD TOLD YOU WHERE YOUR MEN WERE, YOU MIGHT HAVE RUSHED OFF AND GOTTEN YOURSELF KILLED.
JUST LIKE YOU'RE DOING NOW.
CH'K TAK TIL CHOK TA
GOOD. I'LL BE RIGHT THERE.
WHAT'S GOING ON?
A NEW ARRIVAL.
YOU MIGHT WANT TO POSTPONE YOUR RESCUE.

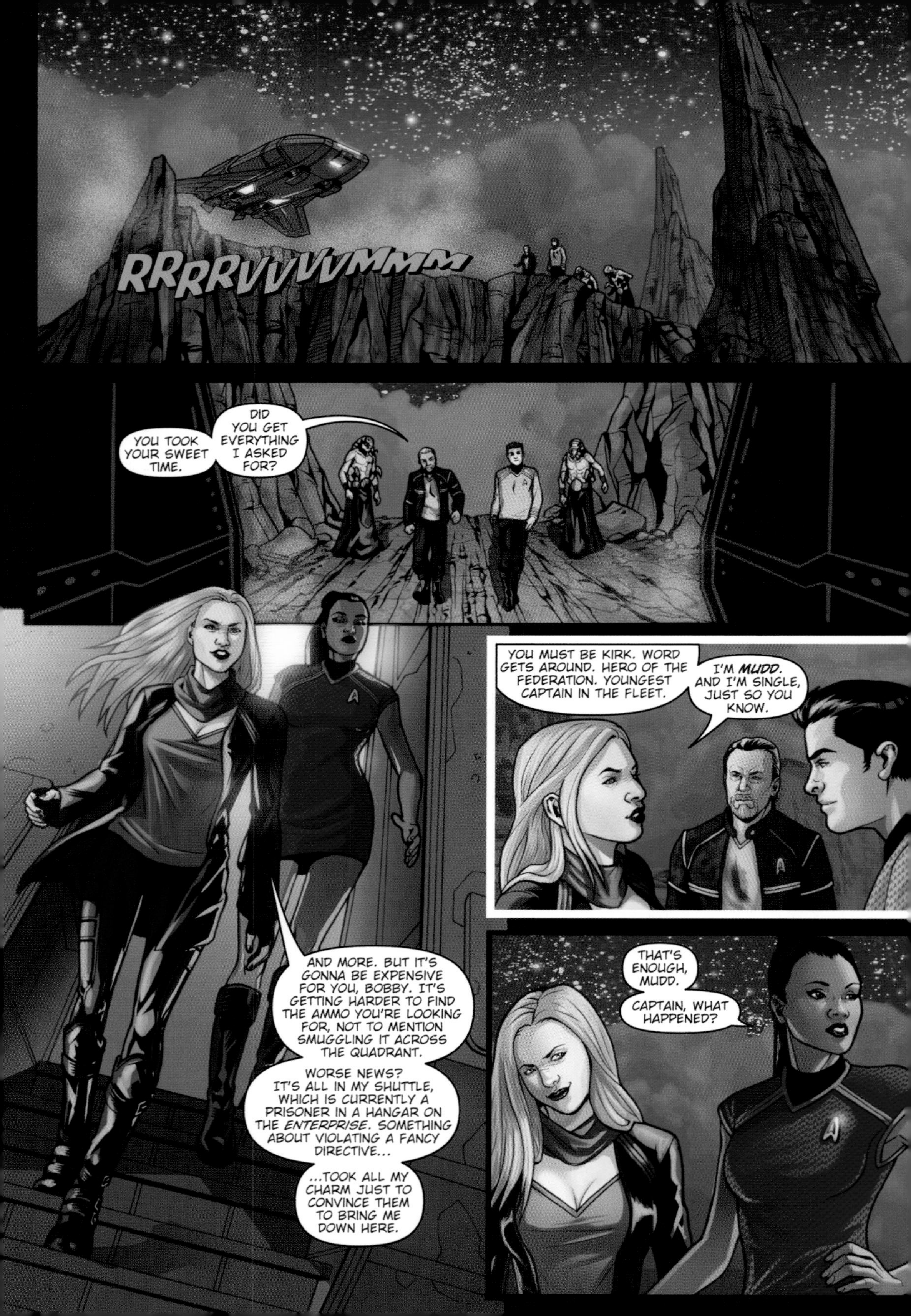
RRRRVVVVVMMMM
YOU TOOK YOUR SWEET TIME.
DID YOU GET EVERYTHING I ASKED FOR?
AND MORE. BUT IT'S GONNA BE EXPENSIVE FOR YOU, BOBBY. IT'S GETTING HARDER TO FIND THE AMMO YOU'RE LOOKING FOR, NOT TO MENTION SMUGGLING IT ACROSS THE QUADRANT.
WORSE NEWS? IT'S ALL IN MY SHUTTLE, WHICH IS CURRENTLY A PRISONER IN A HANGAR ON THE *ENTERPRISE*. SOMETHING ABOUT VIOLATING A FANCY DIRECTIVE...
...TOOK ALL MY CHARM JUST TO CONVINCE THEM TO BRING ME DOWN HERE.
YOU MUST BE KIRK. WORD GETS AROUND. HERO OF THE FEDERATION. YOUNGEST CAPTAIN IN THE FLEET.
I'M ***MUDD***. AND I'M SINGLE, JUST SO YOU KNOW.
THAT'S ENOUGH, MUDD.
CAPTAIN, WHAT HAPPENED?

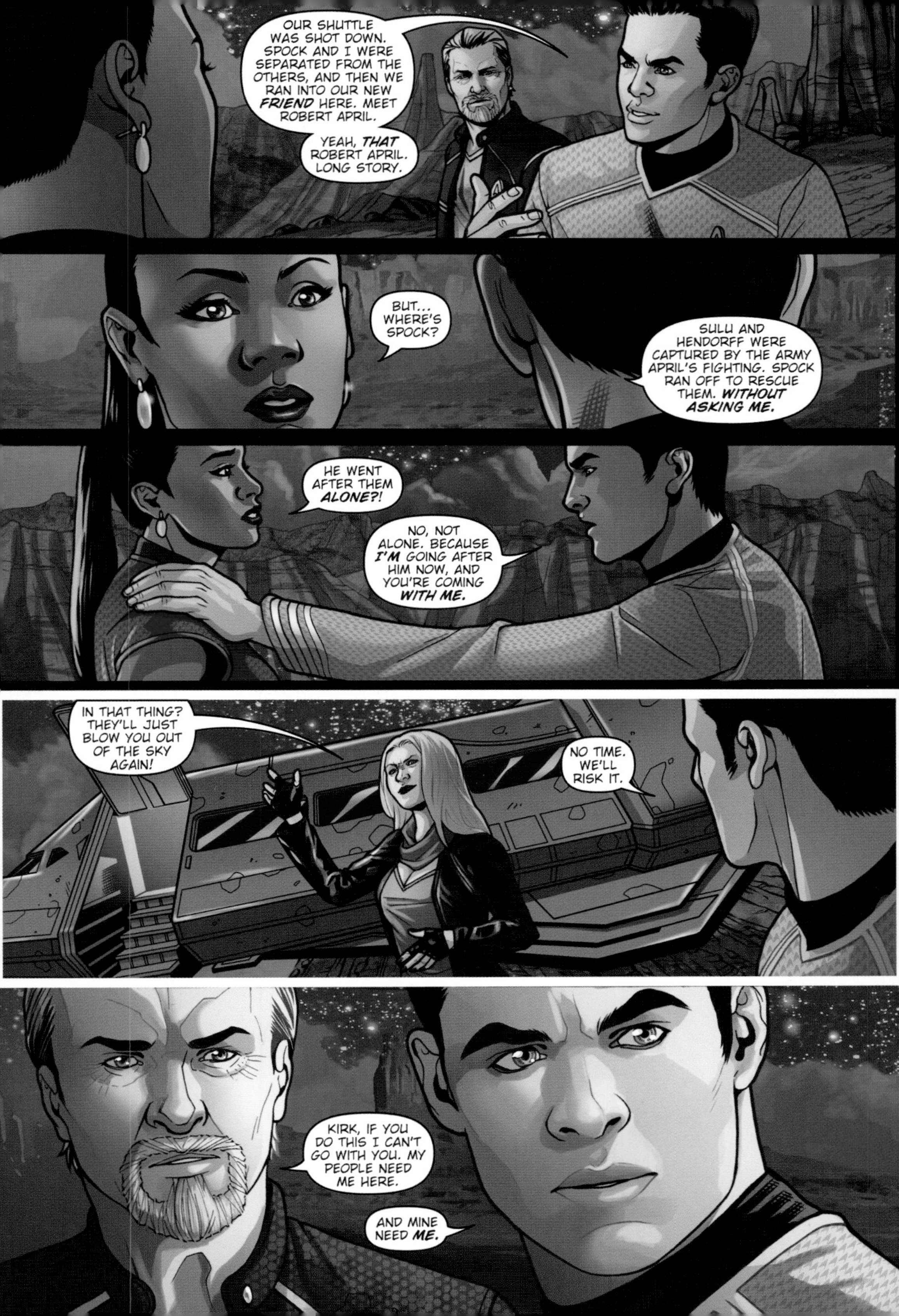
OUR SHUTTLE WAS SHOT DOWN. SPOCK AND I WERE SEPARATED FROM THE OTHERS, AND THEN WE RAN INTO OUR NEW FRIEND HERE. MEET ROBERT APRIL.
YEAH, THAT ROBERT APRIL. LONG STORY.
BUT... WHERE'S SPOCK?
SULU AND HENDORFF WERE CAPTURED BY THE ARMY APRIL'S FIGHTING. SPOCK RAN OFF TO RESCUE THEM. WITHOUT ASKING ME.
HE WENT AFTER THEM ALONE?!
NO, NOT ALONE. BECAUSE I'M GOING AFTER HIM NOW, AND YOU'RE COMING WITH ME.
IN THAT THING? THEY'LL JUST BLOW YOU OUT OF THE SKY AGAIN!
NO TIME. WE'LL RISK IT.
KIRK, IF YOU DO THIS I CAN'T GO WITH YOU. MY PEOPLE NEED ME HERE.
AND MINE NEED ME.

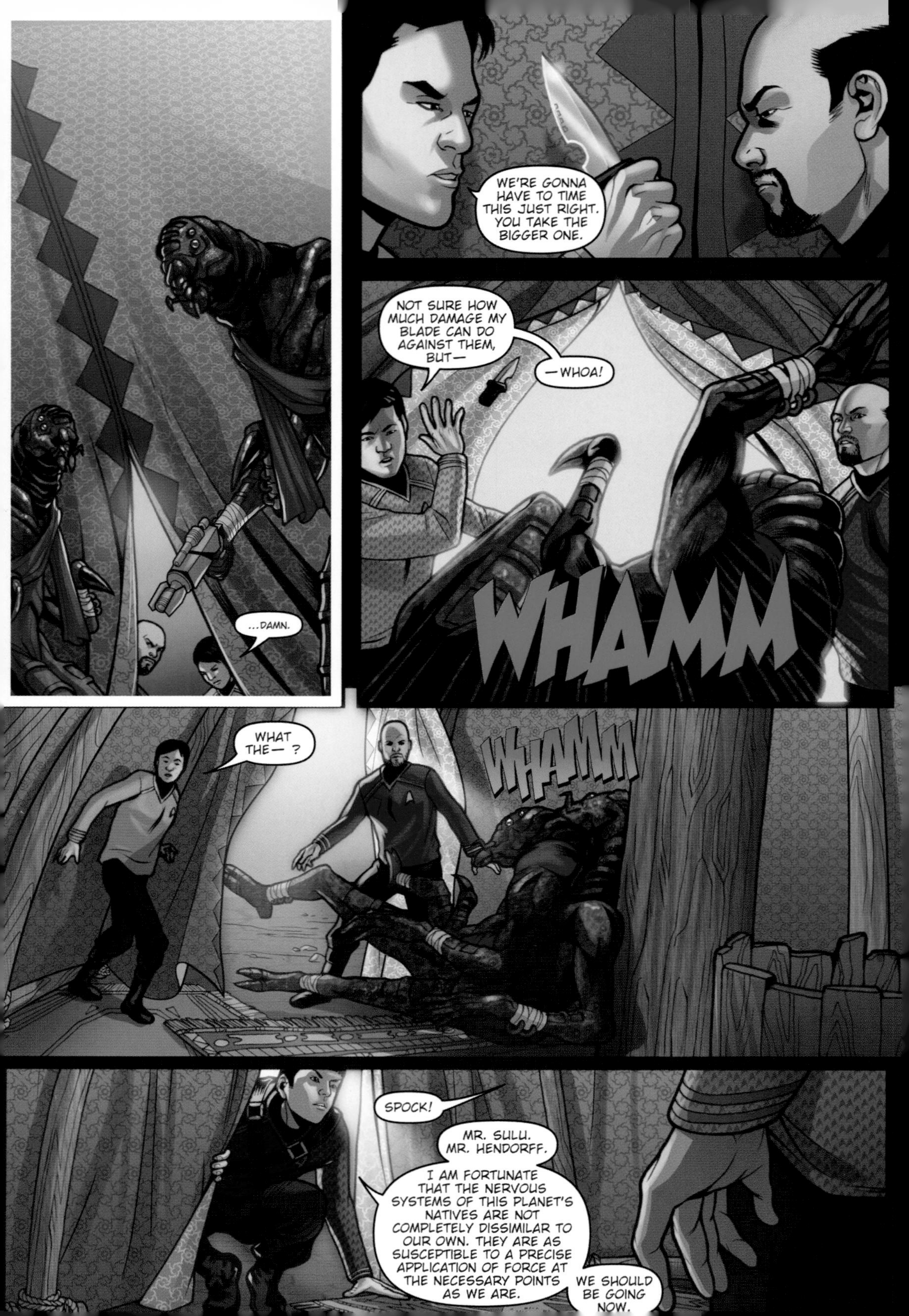
...DAMN.
WE'RE GONNA HAVE TO TIME THIS JUST RIGHT. YOU TAKE THE BIGGER ONE.
NOT SURE HOW MUCH DAMAGE MY BLADE CAN DO AGAINST THEM, BUT—
—WHOA!
WHAMM
WHAT THE— ?
WHAMM
SPOCK!
MR. SULU. MR. HENDORFF.
I AM FORTUNATE THAT THE NERVOUS SYSTEMS OF THIS PLANET'S NATIVES ARE NOT COMPLETELY DISSIMILAR TO OUR OWN. THEY ARE AS SUSCEPTIBLE TO A PRECISE APPLICATION OF FORCE AT THE NECESSARY POINTS AS WE ARE.
WE SHOULD BE GOING NOW.

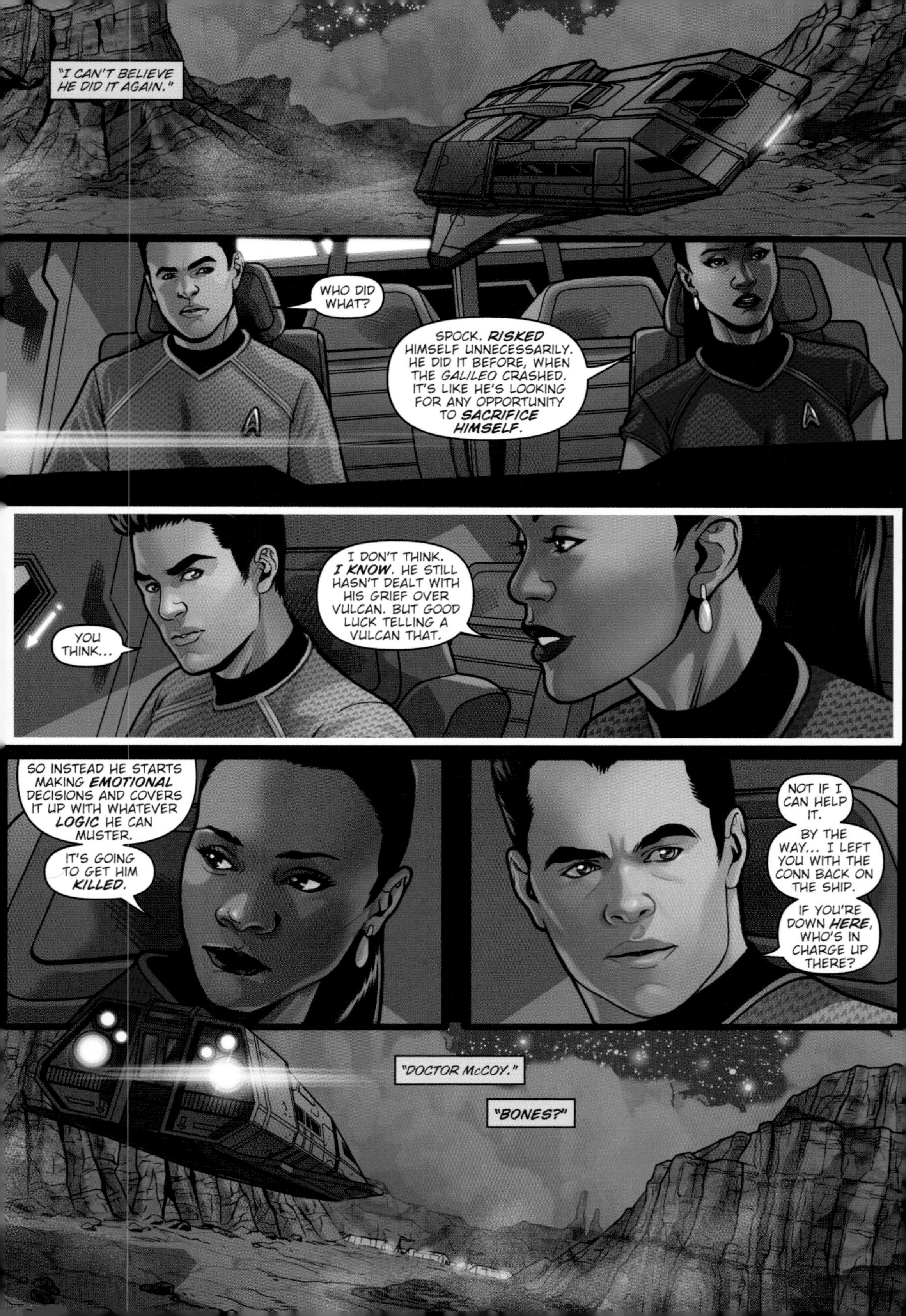
"I CAN'T BELIEVE HE DID IT AGAIN."
WHO DID WHAT?
SPOCK. RISKED HIMSELF UNNECESSARILY. HE DID IT BEFORE, WHEN THE GALILEO CRASHED. IT'S LIKE HE'S LOOKING FOR ANY OPPORTUNITY TO SACRIFICE HIMSELF.
YOU THINK...
I DON'T THINK. I KNOW. HE STILL HASN'T DEALT WITH HIS GRIEF OVER VULCAN. BUT GOOD LUCK TELLING A VULCAN THAT.
SO INSTEAD HE STARTS MAKING EMOTIONAL DECISIONS AND COVERS IT UP WITH WHATEVER LOGIC HE CAN MUSTER.
IT'S GOING TO GET HIM KILLED.
NOT IF I CAN HELP IT.
BY THE WAY... I LEFT YOU WITH THE CONN BACK ON THE SHIP.
IF YOU'RE DOWN HERE, WHO'S IN CHARGE UP THERE?
"DOCTOR McCOY."
"BONES?"

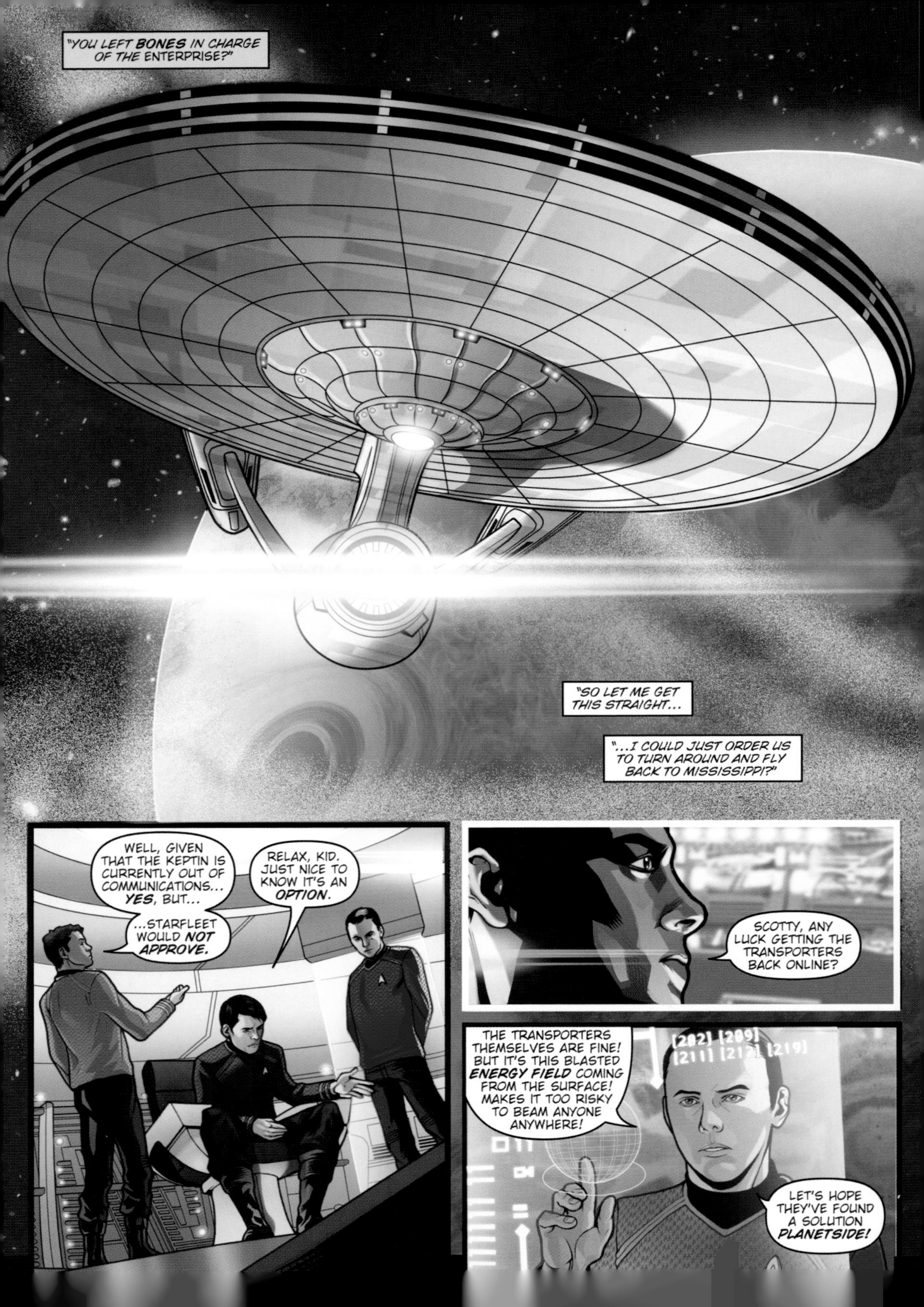
"YOU LEFT BONES IN CHARGE OF THE ENTERPRISE?"
"SO LET ME GET THIS STRAIGHT...
"...I COULD JUST ORDER US TO TURN AROUND AND FLY BACK TO MISSISSIPPI?"
WELL, GIVEN THAT THE KEPTIN IS CURRENTLY OUT OF COMMUNICATIONS... YES, BUT...
...STARFLEET WOULD NOT APPROVE.
RELAX, KID. JUST NICE TO KNOW IT'S AN OPTION.
SCOTTY, ANY LUCK GETTING THE TRANSPORTERS BACK ONLINE?
THE TRANSPORTERS THEMSELVES ARE FINE! BUT IT'S THIS BLASTED ENERGY FIELD COMING FROM THE SURFACE! MAKES IT TOO RISKY TO BEAM ANYONE ANYWHERE!
LET'S HOPE THEY'VE FOUND A SOLUTION PLANETSIDE!

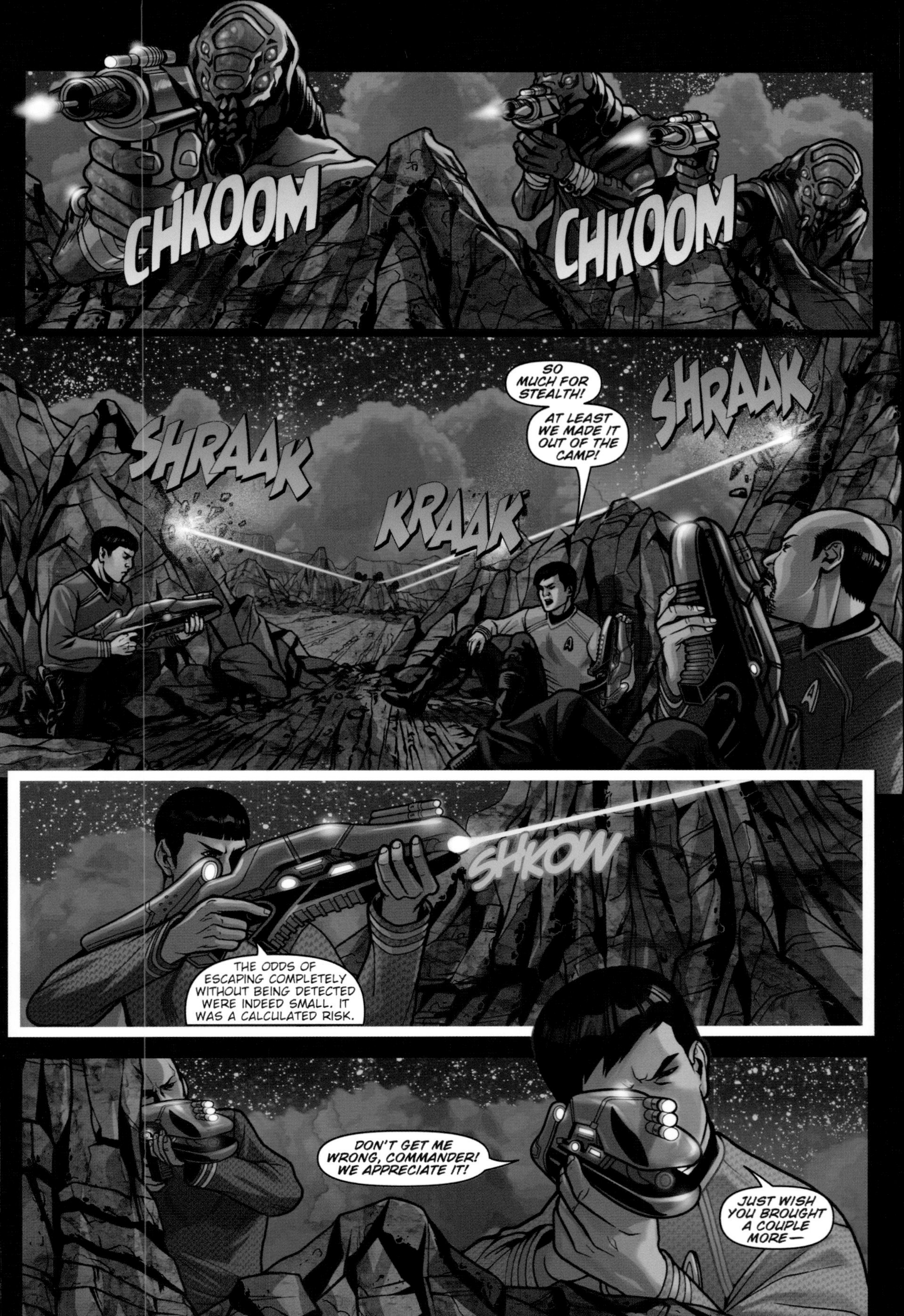
CHKOOM
CHKOOM
SHRAAK
KRAAK
SO MUCH FOR STEALTH!
AT LEAST WE MADE IT OUT OF THE CAMP!
SHRAAK
SHKOW
THE ODDS OF ESCAPING COMPLETELY WITHOUT BEING DETECTED WERE INDEED SMALL. IT WAS A CALCULATED RISK.
DON'T GET ME WRONG, COMMANDER! WE APPRECIATE IT!
JUST WISH YOU BROUGHT A COUPLE MORE—

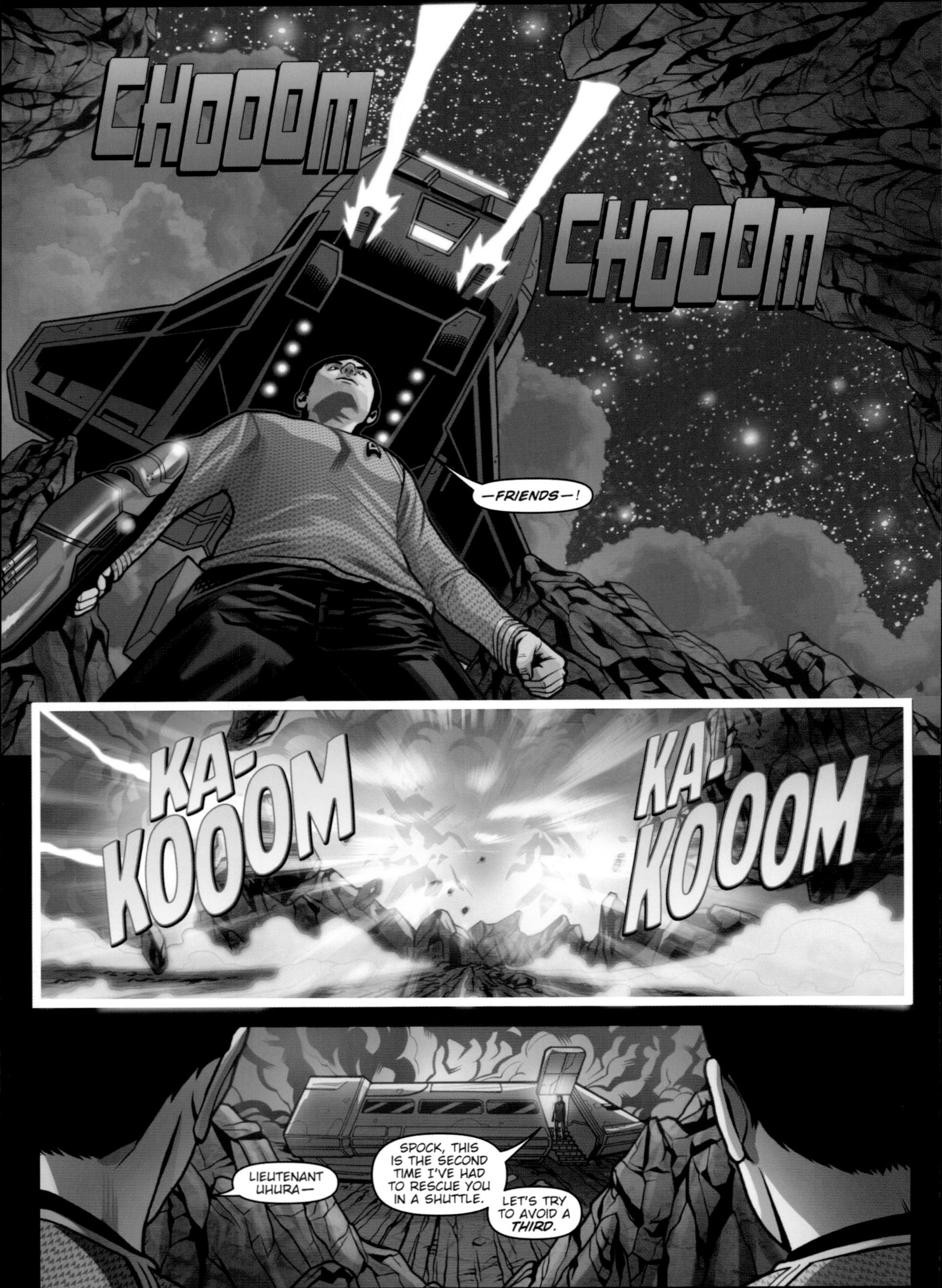
CHOOOM
CHOOOM
—FRIENDS—!
KA-KOOOM
KA-KOOOM
LIEUTENANT UHURA—
SPOCK, THIS IS THE SECOND TIME I'VE HAD TO RESCUE YOU IN A SHUTTLE.
LET'S TRY TO AVOID A THIRD.

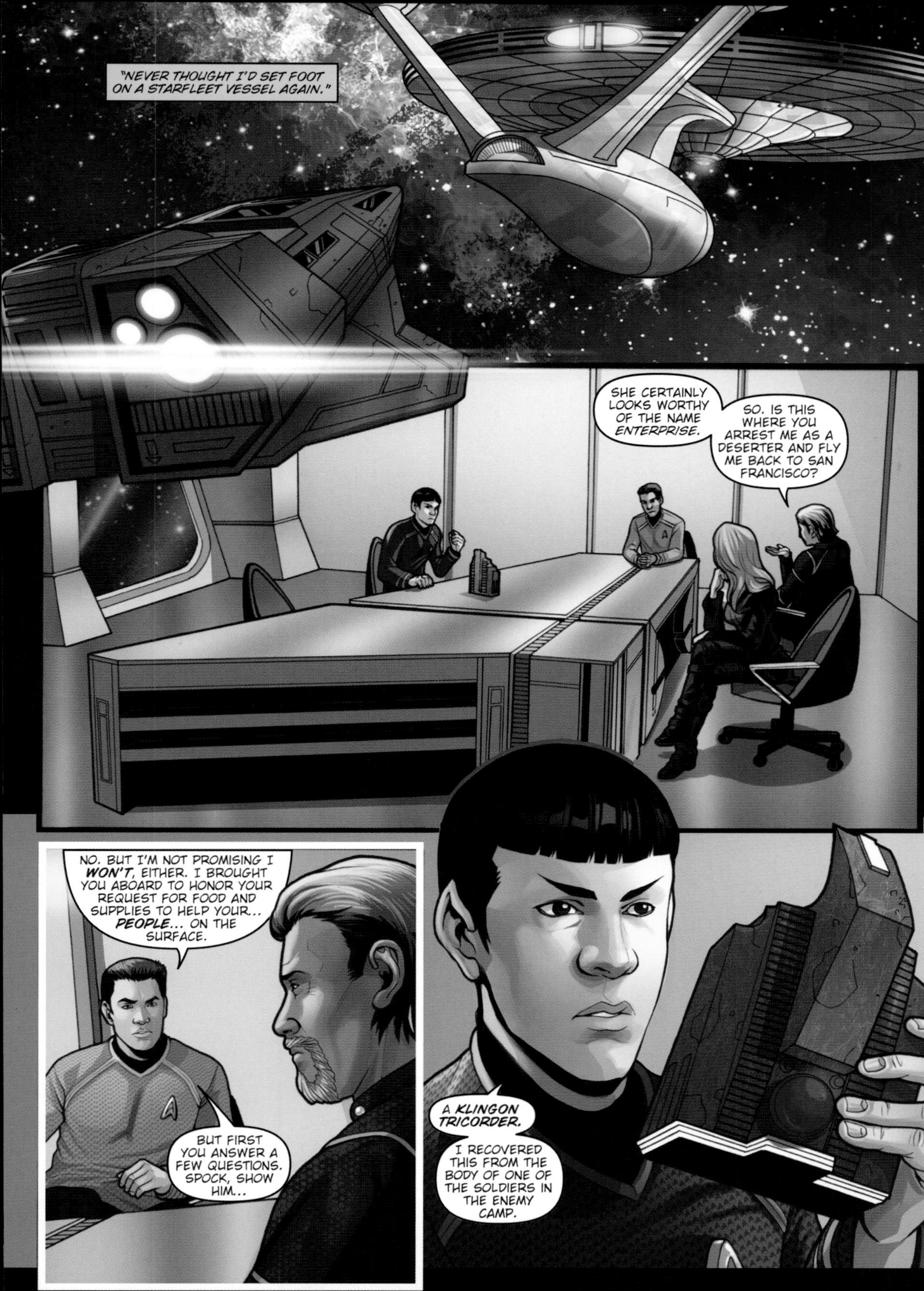
"NEVER THOUGHT I'D SET FOOT ON A STARFLEET VESSEL AGAIN."
SHE CERTAINLY LOOKS WORTHY OF THE NAME ENTERPRISE.
SO. IS THIS WHERE YOU ARREST ME AS A DESERTER AND FLY ME BACK TO SAN FRANCISCO?
NO. BUT I'M NOT PROMISING I WON'T, EITHER. I BROUGHT YOU ABOARD TO HONOR YOUR REQUEST FOR FOOD AND SUPPLIES TO HELP YOUR... PEOPLE... ON THE SURFACE.
BUT FIRST YOU ANSWER A FEW QUESTIONS. SPOCK, SHOW HIM...
A KLINGON TRICORDER.
I RECOVERED THIS FROM THE BODY OF ONE OF THE SOLDIERS IN THE ENEMY CAMP.

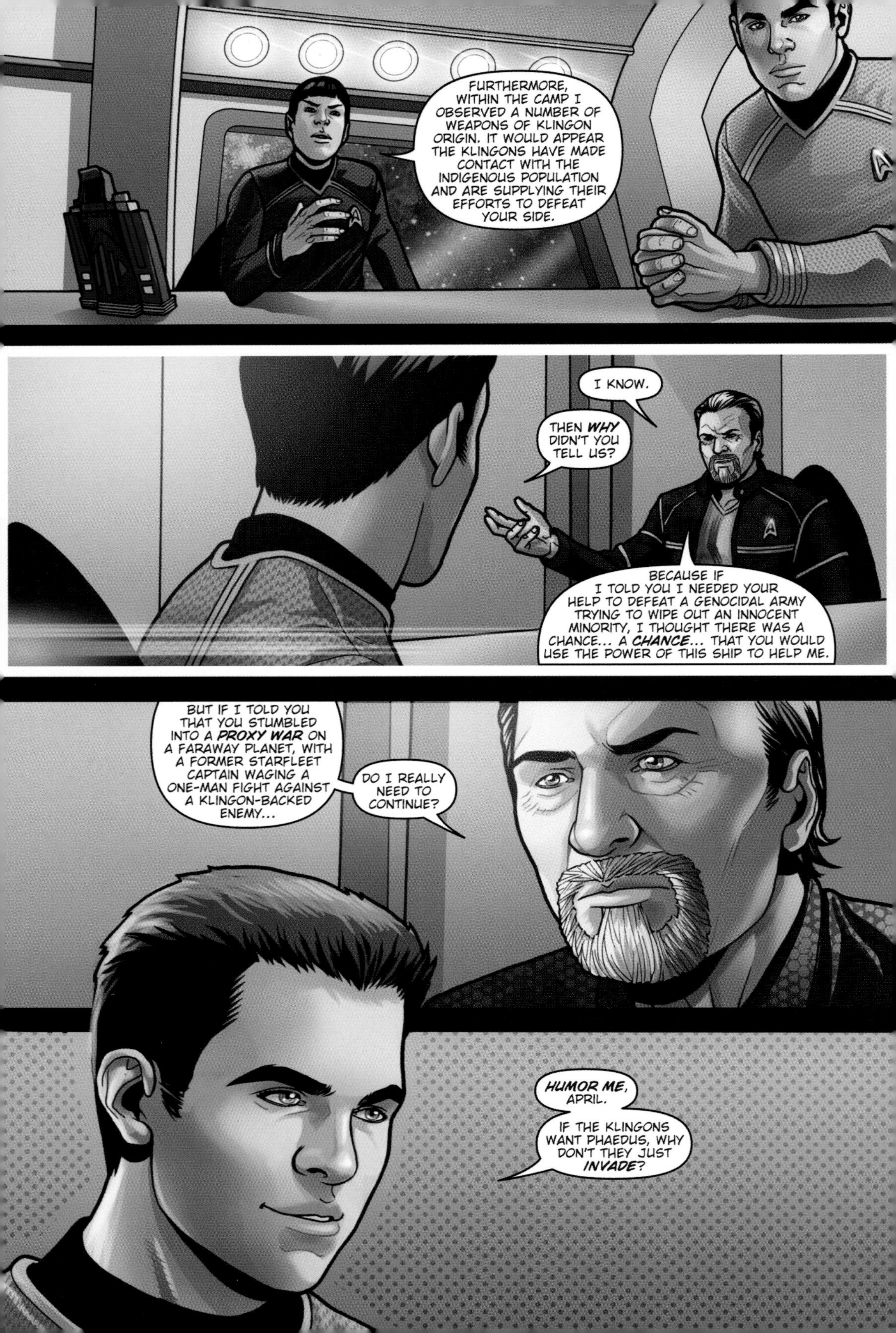
FURTHERMORE, WITHIN THE CAMP I OBSERVED A NUMBER OF WEAPONS OF KLINGON ORIGIN. IT WOULD APPEAR THE KLINGONS HAVE MADE CONTACT WITH THE INDIGENOUS POPULATION AND ARE SUPPLYING THEIR EFFORTS TO DEFEAT YOUR SIDE.
I KNOW.
THEN *WHY* DIDN'T YOU TELL US?
BECAUSE IF I TOLD YOU I NEEDED YOUR HELP TO DEFEAT A GENOCIDAL ARMY TRYING TO WIPE OUT AN INNOCENT MINORITY, I THOUGHT THERE WAS A CHANCE... A *CHANCE*... THAT YOU WOULD USE THE POWER OF THIS SHIP TO HELP ME.
BUT IF I TOLD YOU THAT YOU STUMBLED INTO A *PROXY WAR* ON A FARAWAY PLANET, WITH A FORMER STARFLEET CAPTAIN WAGING A ONE-MAN FIGHT AGAINST A KLINGON-BACKED ENEMY...
DO I REALLY NEED TO CONTINUE?
HUMOR ME, APRIL.
IF THE KLINGONS WANT PHAEDUS, WHY DON'T THEY JUST *INVADE*?

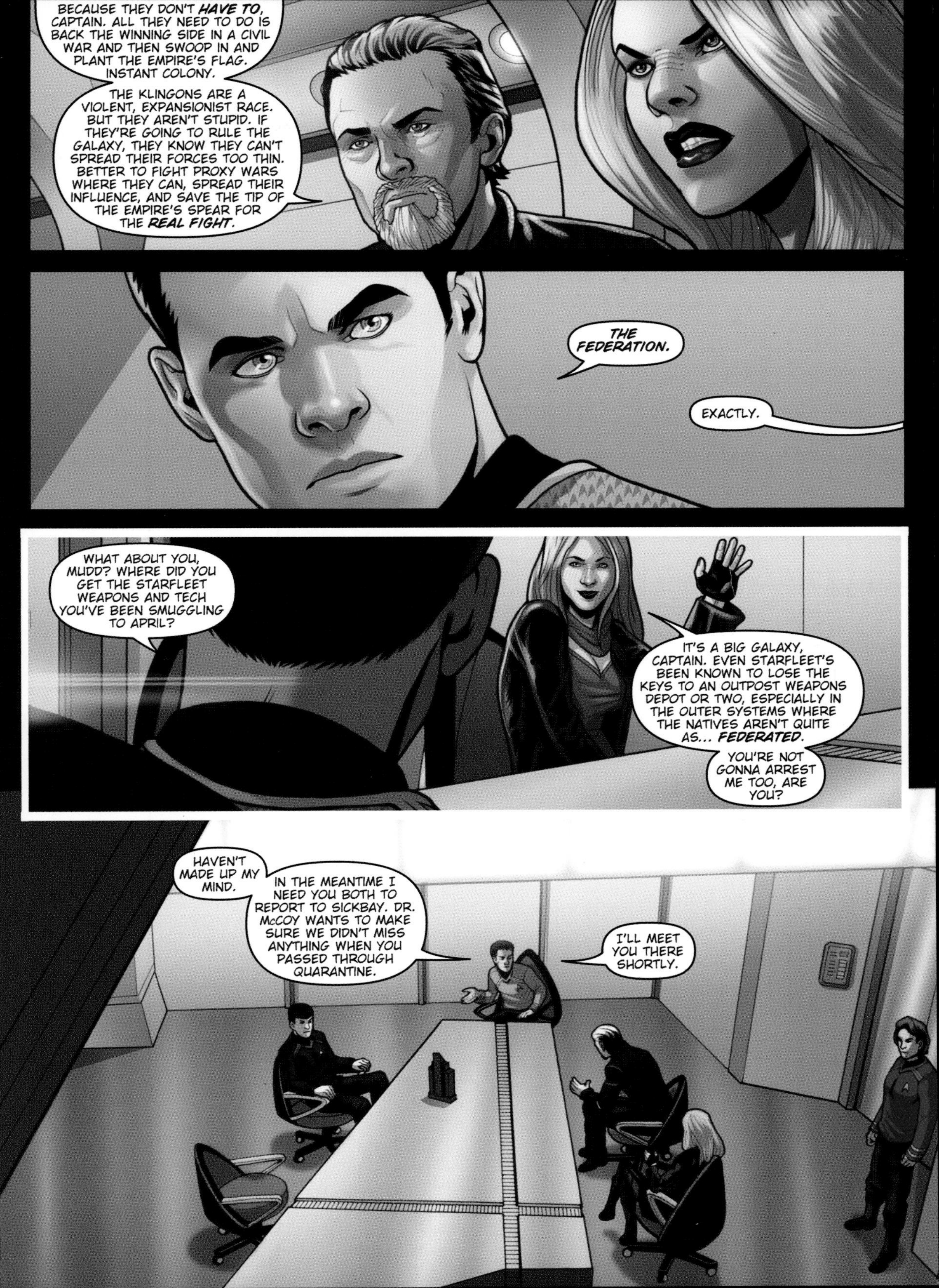
BECAUSE THEY DON'T **HAVE TO**, CAPTAIN. ALL THEY NEED TO DO IS BACK THE WINNING SIDE IN A CIVIL WAR AND THEN SWOOP IN AND PLANT THE EMPIRE'S FLAG. INSTANT COLONY.
THE KLINGONS ARE A VIOLENT, EXPANSIONIST RACE. BUT THEY AREN'T STUPID. IF THEY'RE GOING TO RULE THE GALAXY, THEY KNOW THEY CAN'T SPREAD THEIR FORCES TOO THIN. BETTER TO FIGHT PROXY WARS WHERE THEY CAN, SPREAD THEIR INFLUENCE, AND SAVE THE TIP OF THE EMPIRE'S SPEAR FOR THE **REAL FIGHT**.
THE FEDERATION.
EXACTLY.
WHAT ABOUT YOU, MUDD? WHERE DID YOU GET THE STARFLEET WEAPONS AND TECH YOU'VE BEEN SMUGGLING TO APRIL?
IT'S A BIG GALAXY, CAPTAIN. EVEN STARFLEET'S BEEN KNOWN TO LOSE THE KEYS TO AN OUTPOST WEAPONS DEPOT OR TWO, ESPECIALLY IN THE OUTER SYSTEMS WHERE THE NATIVES AREN'T QUITE AS... **FEDERATED**.
YOU'RE NOT GONNA ARREST ME TOO, ARE YOU?
HAVEN'T MADE UP MY MIND.
IN THE MEANTIME I NEED YOU BOTH TO REPORT TO SICKBAY. DR. McCOY WANTS TO MAKE SURE WE DIDN'T MISS ANYTHING WHEN YOU PASSED THROUGH QUARANTINE.
I'LL MEET YOU THERE SHORTLY.

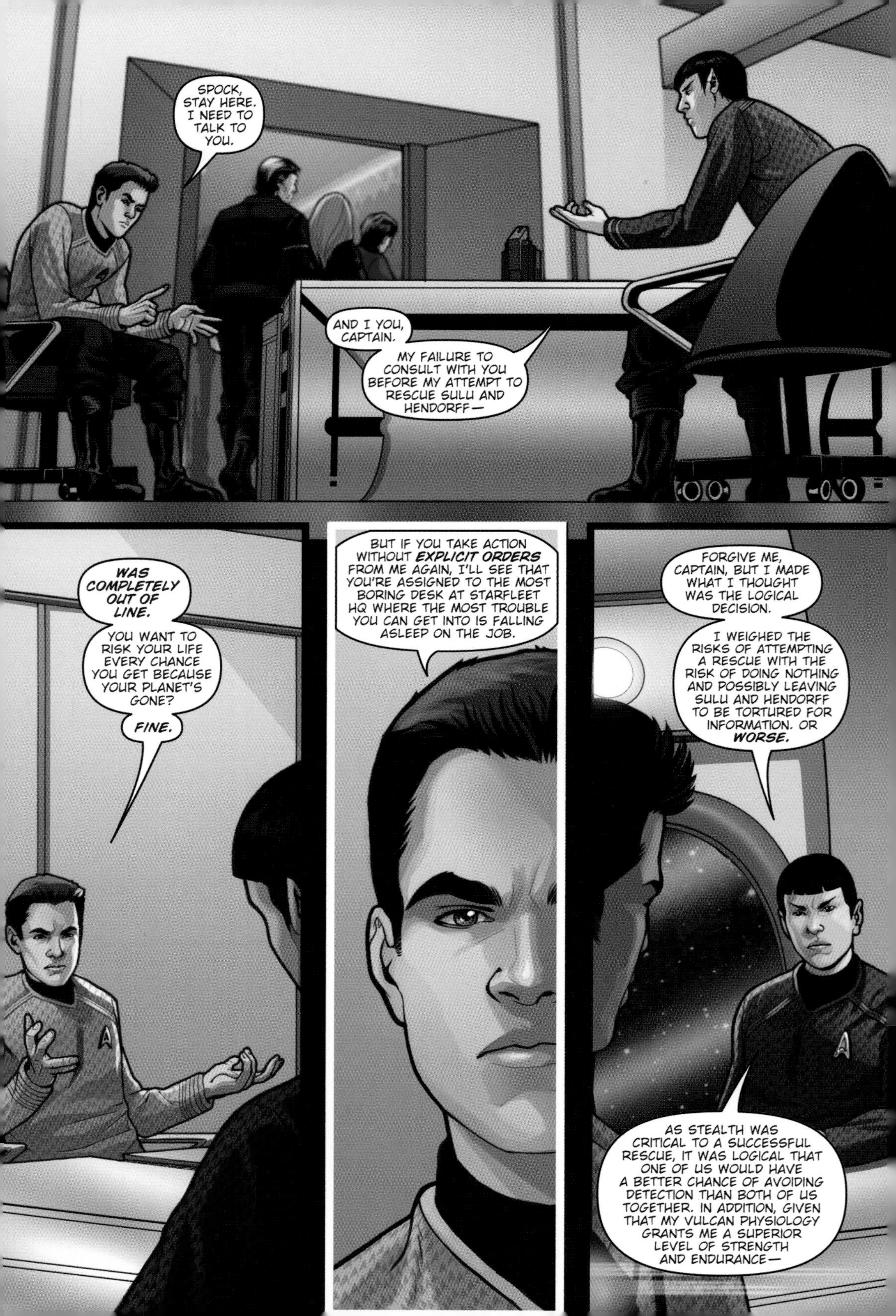

SPOCK, STAY HERE. I NEED TO TALK TO YOU.
AND I YOU, CAPTAIN.
MY FAILURE TO CONSULT WITH YOU BEFORE MY ATTEMPT TO RESCUE SULU AND HENDORFF—
WAS COMPLETELY OUT OF LINE.
YOU WANT TO RISK YOUR LIFE EVERY CHANCE YOU GET BECAUSE YOUR PLANET'S GONE?
FINE.
BUT IF YOU TAKE ACTION WITHOUT EXPLICIT ORDERS FROM ME AGAIN, I'LL SEE THAT YOU'RE ASSIGNED TO THE MOST BORING DESK AT STARFLEET HQ WHERE THE MOST TROUBLE YOU CAN GET INTO IS FALLING ASLEEP ON THE JOB.
FORGIVE ME, CAPTAIN, BUT I MADE WHAT I THOUGHT WAS THE LOGICAL DECISION.
I WEIGHED THE RISKS OF ATTEMPTING A RESCUE WITH THE RISK OF DOING NOTHING AND POSSIBLY LEAVING SULU AND HENDORFF TO BE TORTURED FOR INFORMATION. OR WORSE.
AS STEALTH WAS CRITICAL TO A SUCCESSFUL RESCUE, IT WAS LOGICAL THAT ONE OF US WOULD HAVE A BETTER CHANCE OF AVOIDING DETECTION THAN BOTH OF US TOGETHER. IN ADDITION, GIVEN THAT MY VULCAN PHYSIOLOGY GRANTS ME A SUPERIOR LEVEL OF STRENGTH AND ENDURANCE—

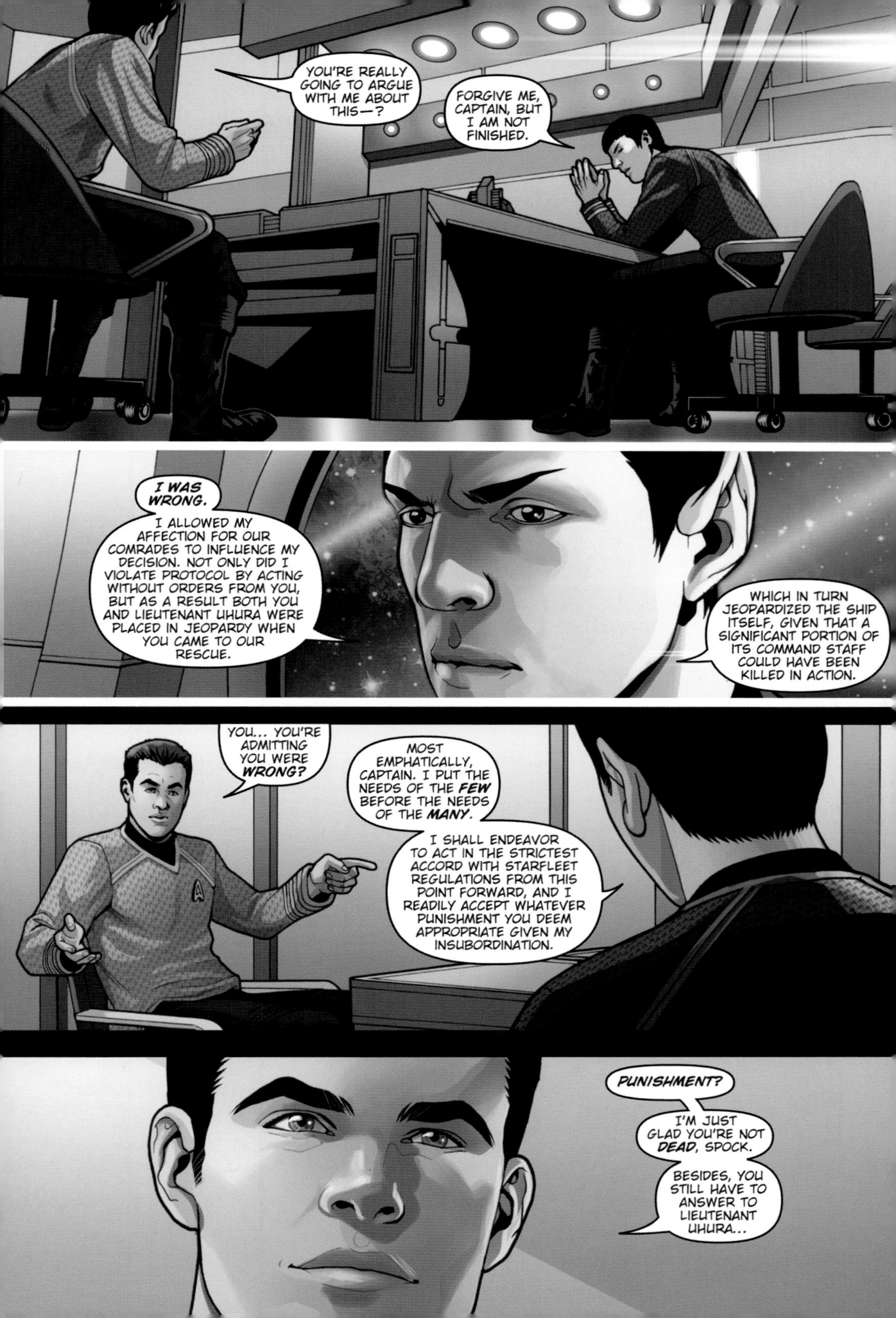

YOU'RE REALLY GOING TO ARGUE WITH ME ABOUT THIS—?
FORGIVE ME, CAPTAIN, BUT I AM NOT FINISHED.
I WAS WRONG.
I ALLOWED MY AFFECTION FOR OUR COMRADES TO INFLUENCE MY DECISION. NOT ONLY DID I VIOLATE PROTOCOL BY ACTING WITHOUT ORDERS FROM YOU, BUT AS A RESULT BOTH YOU AND LIEUTENANT UHURA WERE PLACED IN JEOPARDY WHEN YOU CAME TO OUR RESCUE.
WHICH IN TURN JEOPARDIZED THE SHIP ITSELF, GIVEN THAT A SIGNIFICANT PORTION OF ITS COMMAND STAFF COULD HAVE BEEN KILLED IN ACTION.
YOU... YOU'RE ADMITTING YOU WERE WRONG?
MOST EMPHATICALLY, CAPTAIN. I PUT THE NEEDS OF THE FEW BEFORE THE NEEDS OF THE MANY.
I SHALL ENDEAVOR TO ACT IN THE STRICTEST ACCORD WITH STARFLEET REGULATIONS FROM THIS POINT FORWARD, AND I READILY ACCEPT WHATEVER PUNISHMENT YOU DEEM APPROPRIATE GIVEN MY INSUBORDINATION.
PUNISHMENT?
I'M JUST GLAD YOU'RE NOT DEAD, SPOCK.
BESIDES, YOU STILL HAVE TO ANSWER TO LIEUTENANT UHURA...

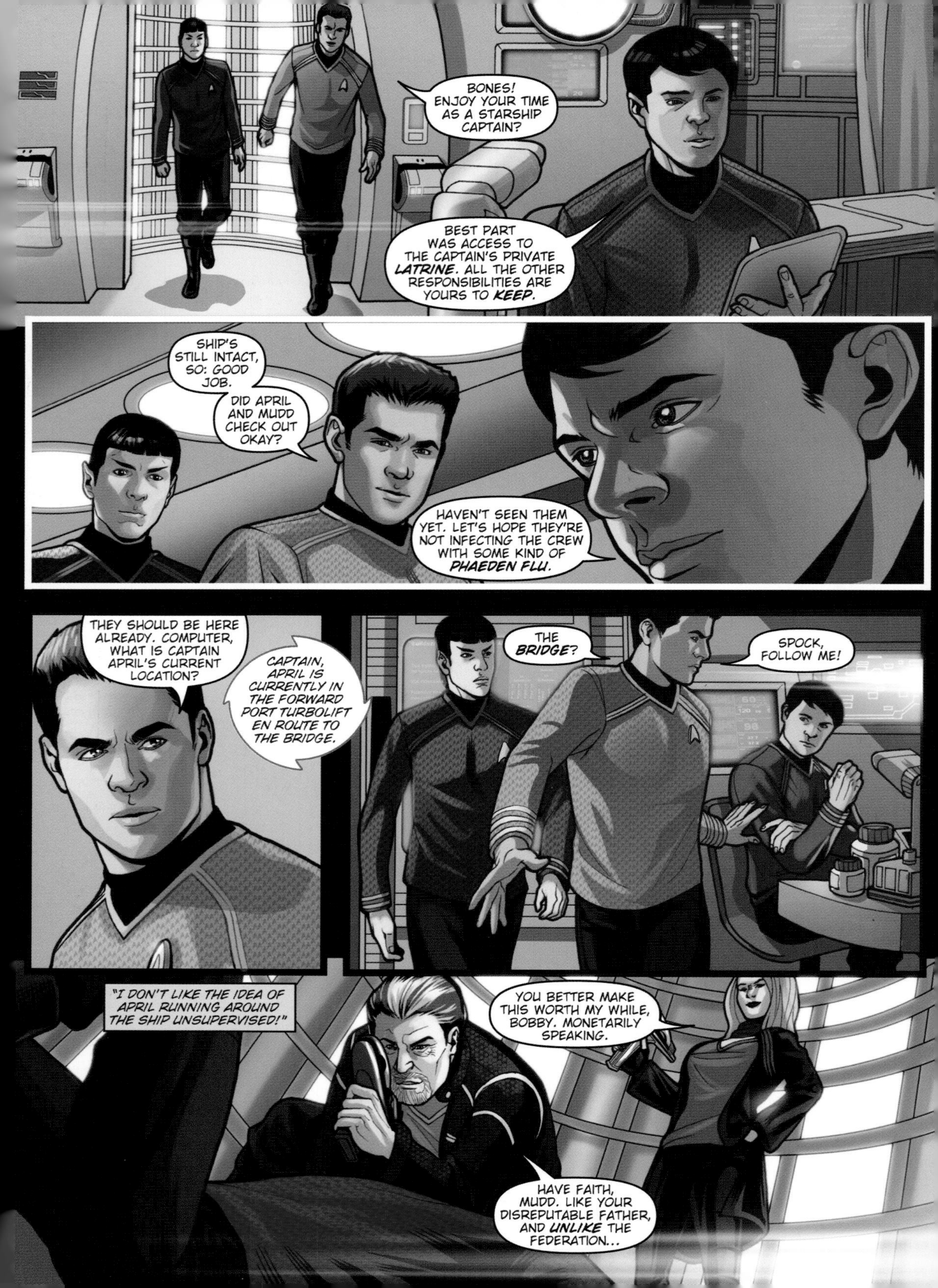
BONES! ENJOY YOUR TIME AS A STARSHIP CAPTAIN?
BEST PART WAS ACCESS TO THE CAPTAIN'S PRIVATE LATRINE. ALL THE OTHER RESPONSIBILITIES ARE YOURS TO KEEP.
SHIP'S STILL INTACT, SO: GOOD JOB.
DID APRIL AND MUDD CHECK OUT OKAY?
HAVEN'T SEEN THEM YET. LET'S HOPE THEY'RE NOT INFECTING THE CREW WITH SOME KIND OF PHAEDEN FLU.
THEY SHOULD BE HERE ALREADY. COMPUTER, WHAT IS CAPTAIN APRIL'S CURRENT LOCATION?
CAPTAIN, APRIL IS CURRENTLY IN THE FORWARD PORT TURBOLIFT EN ROUTE TO THE BRIDGE.
THE BRIDGE?
SPOCK, FOLLOW ME!
"I DON'T LIKE THE IDEA OF APRIL RUNNING AROUND THE SHIP UNSUPERVISED!"
YOU BETTER MAKE THIS WORTH MY WHILE, BOBBY. MONETARILY SPEAKING.
HAVE FAITH, MUDD. LIKE YOUR DISREPUTABLE FATHER, AND UNLIKE THE FEDERATION...

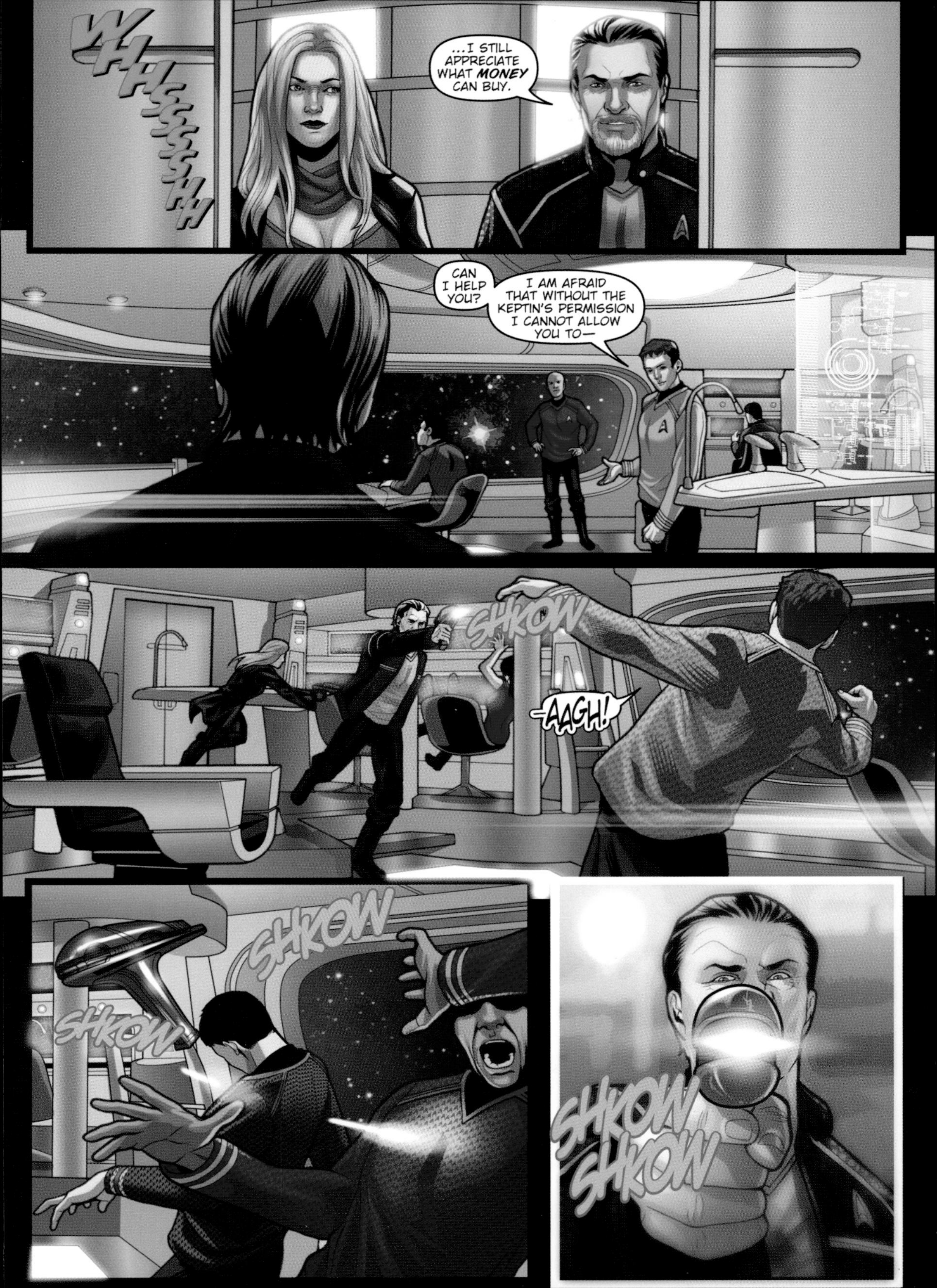
WHHSSSSHH
...I STILL APPRECIATE WHAT MONEY CAN BUY.
CAN I HELP YOU?
I AM AFRAID THAT WITHOUT THE KEPTIN'S PERMISSION I CANNOT ALLOW YOU TO—
SHKOW
—AAGH!
SHKOW
SHKOW
SHKOW SHKOW

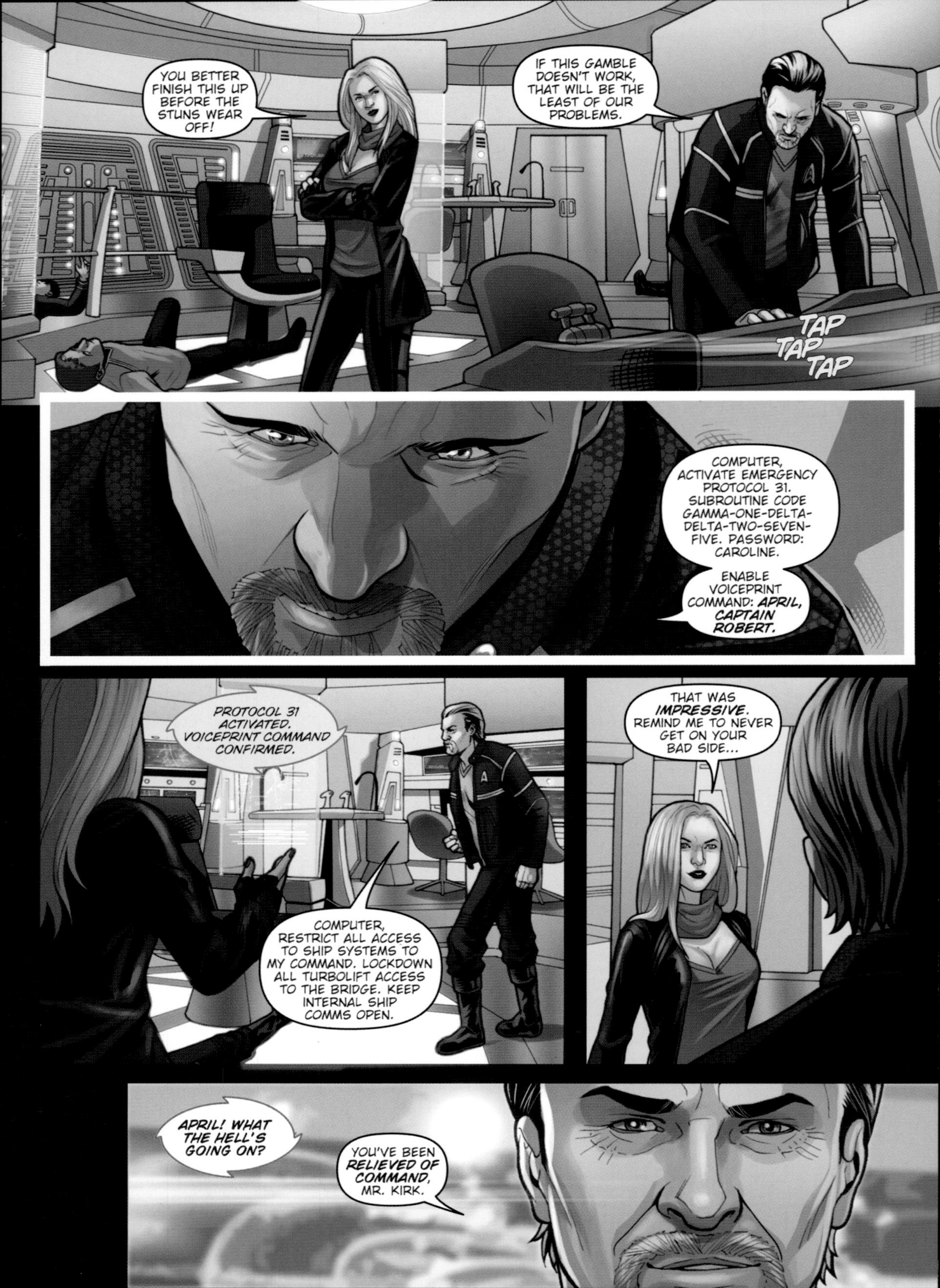
YOU BETTER FINISH THIS UP BEFORE THE STUNS WEAR OFF!
IF THIS GAMBLE DOESN'T WORK, THAT WILL BE THE LEAST OF OUR PROBLEMS.
TAP TAP TAP
COMPUTER, ACTIVATE EMERGENCY PROTOCOL 31. SUBROUTINE CODE GAMMA-ONE-DELTA-DELTA-TWO-SEVEN-FIVE. PASSWORD: CAROLINE.
ENABLE VOICEPRINT COMMAND: APRIL, CAPTAIN ROBERT.
PROTOCOL 31 ACTIVATED. VOICEPRINT COMMAND CONFIRMED.
COMPUTER, RESTRICT ALL ACCESS TO SHIP SYSTEMS TO MY COMMAND. LOCKDOWN ALL TURBOLIFT ACCESS TO THE BRIDGE. KEEP INTERNAL SHIP COMMS OPEN.
THAT WAS IMPRESSIVE. REMIND ME TO NEVER GET ON YOUR BAD SIDE...
APRIL! WHAT THE HELL'S GOING ON?
YOU'VE BEEN RELIEVED OF COMMAND, MR. KIRK.

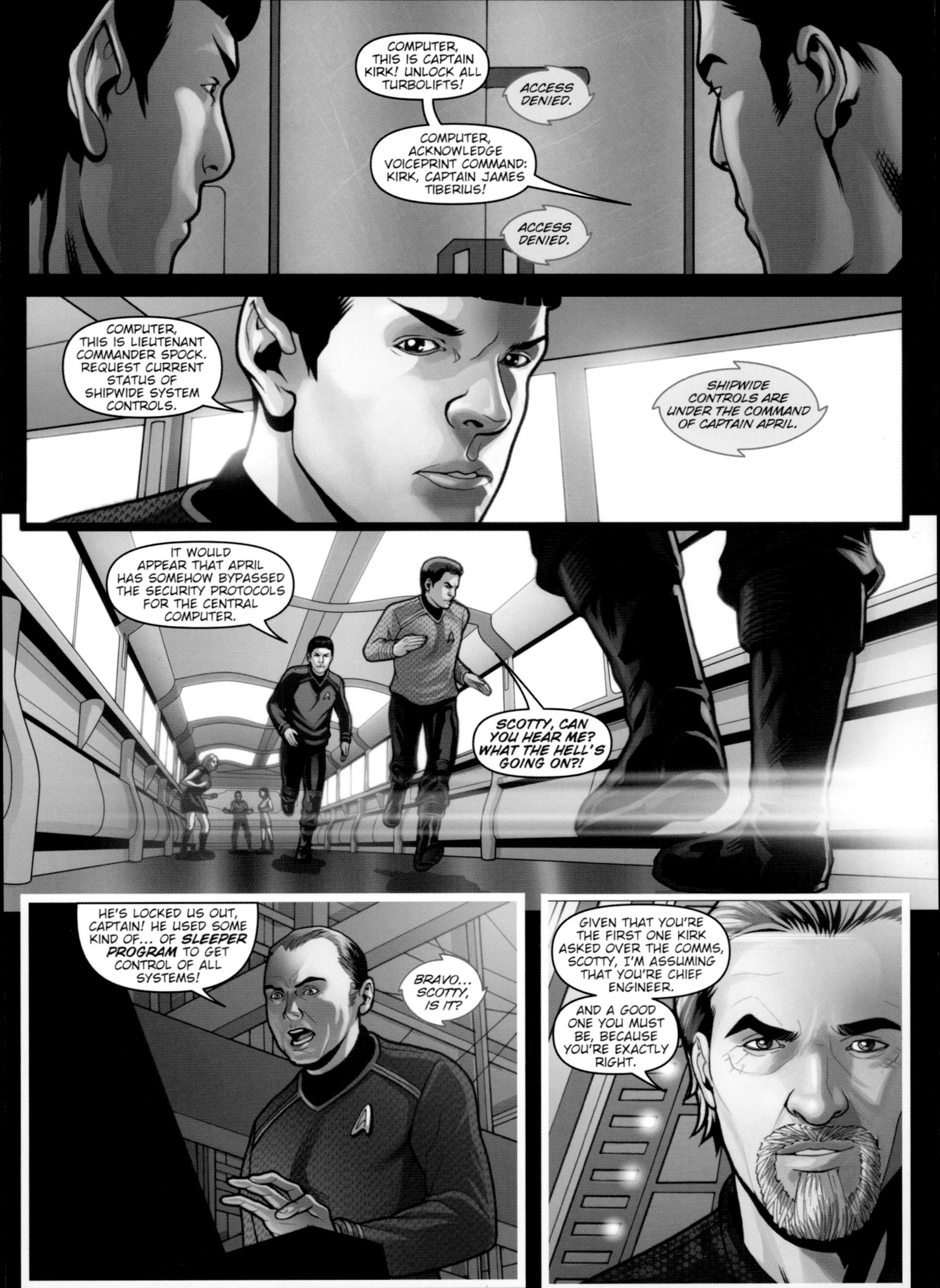
COMPUTER, THIS IS CAPTAIN KIRK! UNLOCK ALL TURBOLIFTS!
ACCESS DENIED.
COMPUTER, ACKNOWLEDGE VOICEPRINT COMMAND: KIRK, CAPTAIN JAMES TIBERIUS!
ACCESS DENIED.
COMPUTER, THIS IS LIEUTENANT COMMANDER SPOCK. REQUEST CURRENT STATUS OF SHIPWIDE SYSTEM CONTROLS.
SHIPWIDE CONTROLS ARE UNDER THE COMMAND OF CAPTAIN APRIL.
IT WOULD APPEAR THAT APRIL HAS SOMEHOW BYPASSED THE SECURITY PROTOCOLS FOR THE CENTRAL COMPUTER.
SCOTTY, CAN YOU HEAR ME? WHAT THE HELL'S GOING ON?!
HE'S LOCKED US OUT, CAPTAIN! HE USED SOME KIND OF... OF SLEEPER PROGRAM TO GET CONTROL OF ALL SYSTEMS!
BRAVO... SCOTTY, IS IT?
GIVEN THAT YOU'RE THE FIRST ONE KIRK ASKED OVER THE COMMS, SCOTTY, I'M ASSUMING THAT YOU'RE CHIEF ENGINEER.
AND A GOOD ONE YOU MUST BE, BECAUSE YOU'RE EXACTLY RIGHT.

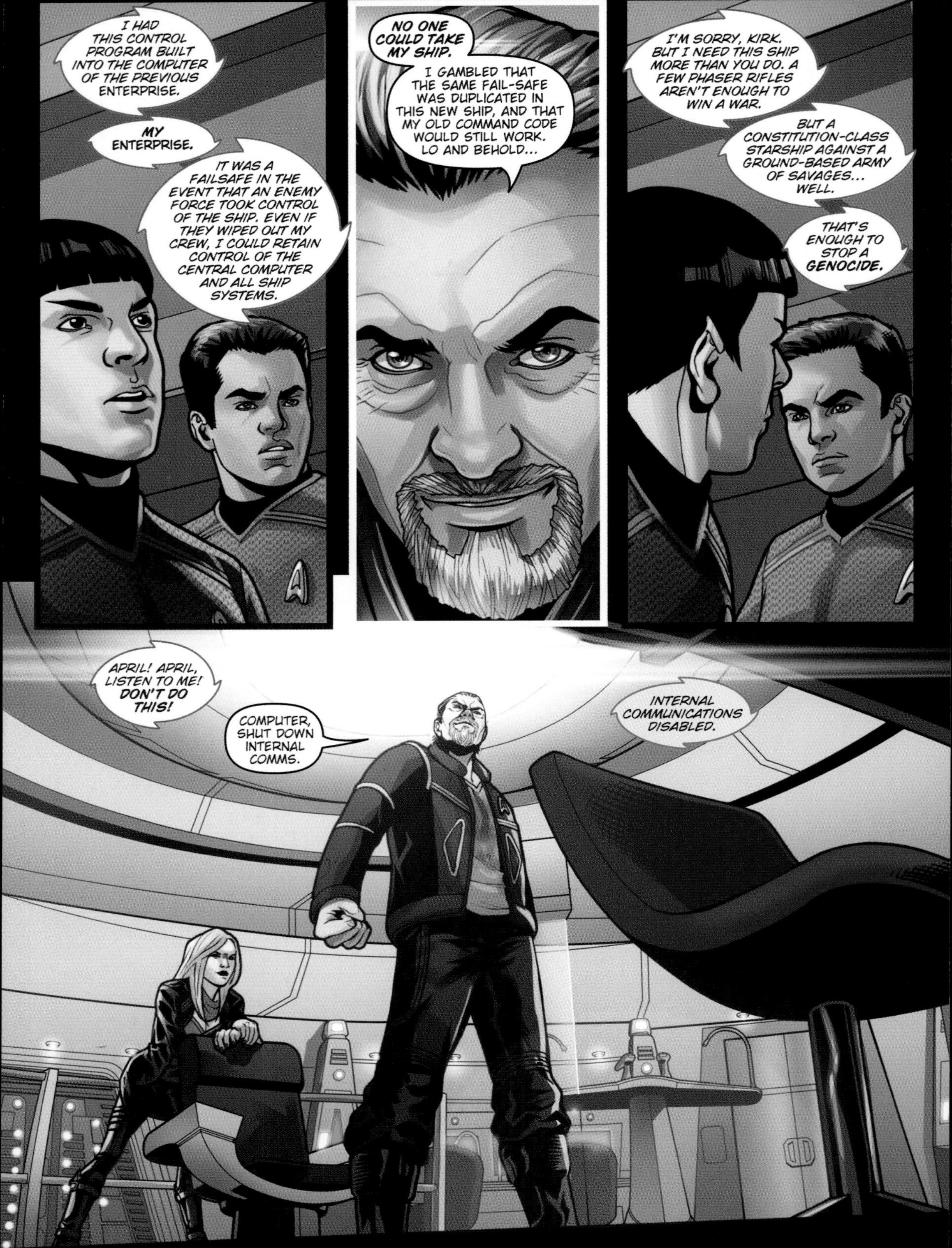
I HAD THIS CONTROL PROGRAM BUILT INTO THE COMPUTER OF THE PREVIOUS ENTERPRISE.
MY ENTERPRISE.
IT WAS A FAILSAFE IN THE EVENT THAT AN ENEMY FORCE TOOK CONTROL OF THE SHIP. EVEN IF THEY WIPED OUT MY CREW, I COULD RETAIN CONTROL OF THE CENTRAL COMPUTER AND ALL SHIP SYSTEMS.
NO ONE COULD TAKE MY SHIP.
I GAMBLED THAT THE SAME FAIL-SAFE WAS DUPLICATED IN THIS NEW SHIP, AND THAT MY OLD COMMAND CODE WOULD STILL WORK. LO AND BEHOLD...
I'M SORRY, KIRK. BUT I NEED THIS SHIP MORE THAN YOU DO. A FEW PHASER RIFLES AREN'T ENOUGH TO WIN A WAR.
BUT A CONSTITUTION-CLASS STARSHIP AGAINST A GROUND-BASED ARMY OF SAVAGES... WELL.
THAT'S ENOUGH TO STOP A GENOCIDE.
APRIL! APRIL, LISTEN TO ME! DON'T DO THIS!
COMPUTER, SHUT DOWN INTERNAL COMMS.
INTERNAL COMMUNICATIONS DISABLED.

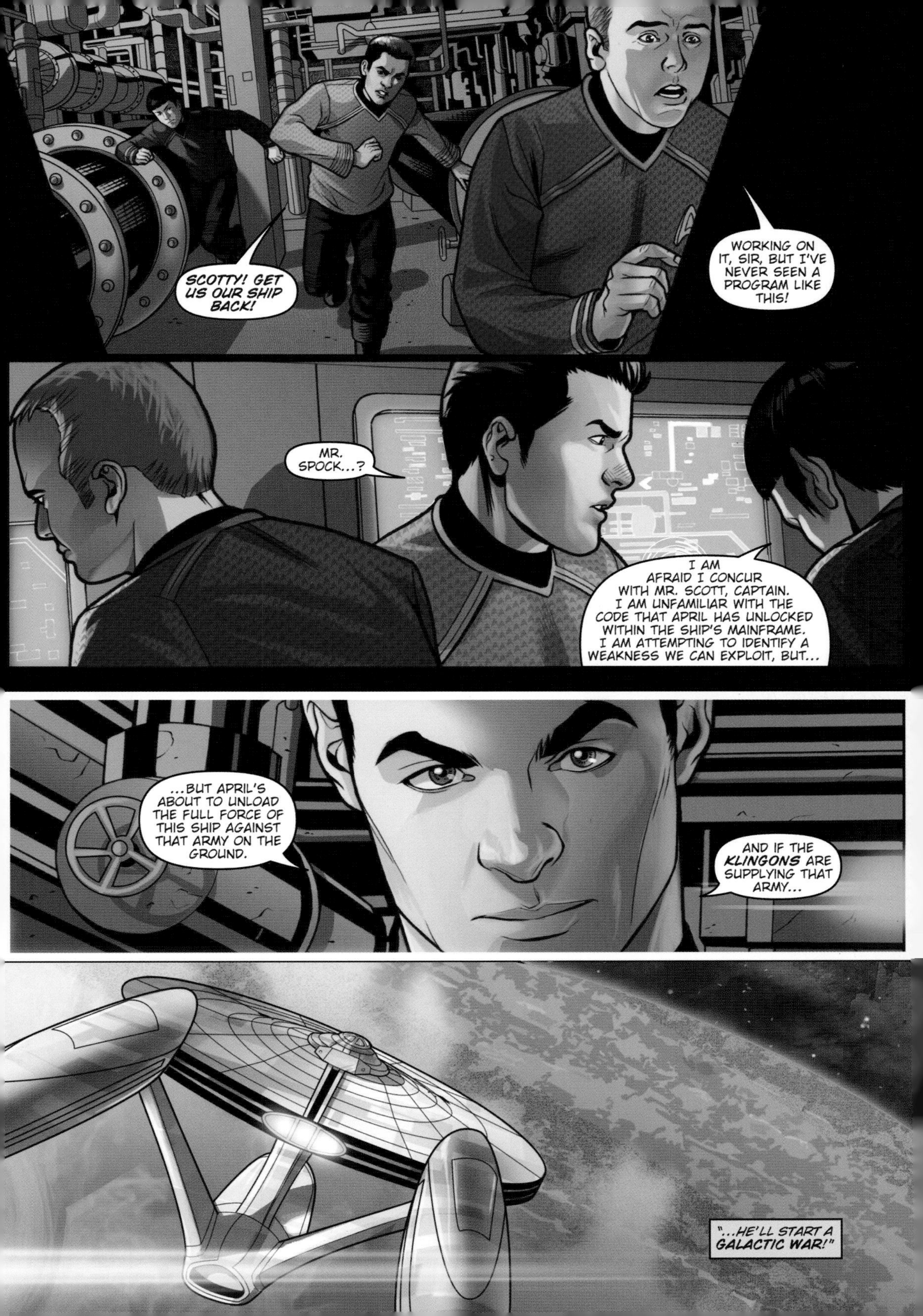
SCOTTY! GET US OUR SHIP BACK!
WORKING ON IT, SIR, BUT I'VE NEVER SEEN A PROGRAM LIKE THIS!
MR. SPOCK...?
I AM AFRAID I CONCUR WITH MR. SCOTT, CAPTAIN. I AM UNFAMILIAR WITH THE CODE THAT APRIL HAS UNLOCKED WITHIN THE SHIP'S MAINFRAME. I AM ATTEMPTING TO IDENTIFY A WEAKNESS WE CAN EXPLOIT, BUT...
...BUT APRIL'S ABOUT TO UNLOAD THE FULL FORCE OF THIS SHIP AGAINST THAT ARMY ON THE GROUND.
AND IF THE KLINGONS ARE SUPPLYING THAT ARMY...
"...HE'LL START A GALACTIC WAR!"

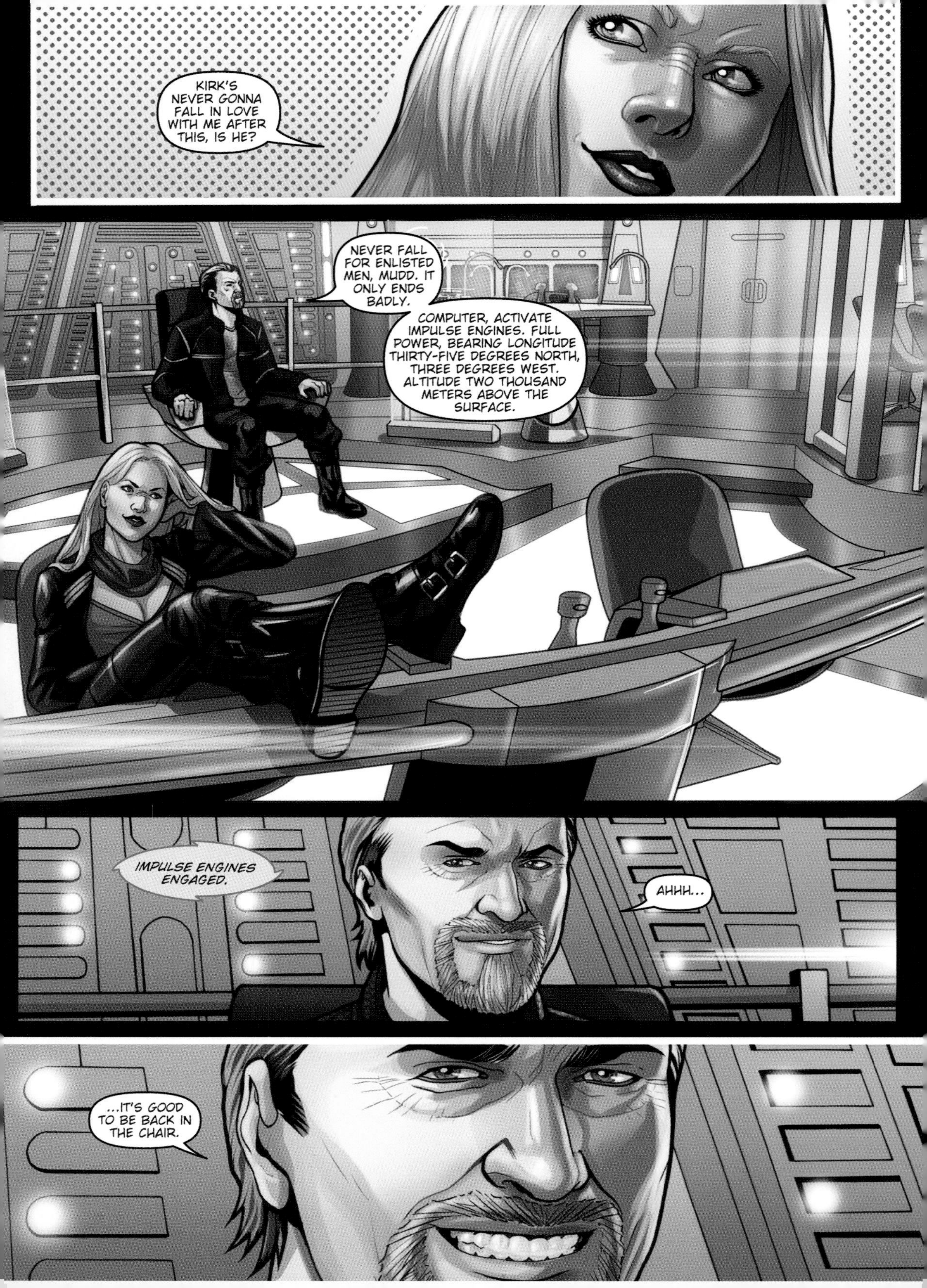
KIRK'S NEVER GONNA FALL IN LOVE WITH ME AFTER THIS, IS HE?
NEVER FALL FOR ENLISTED MEN, MUDD. IT ONLY ENDS BADLY.
COMPUTER, ACTIVATE IMPULSE ENGINES. FULL POWER, BEARING LONGITUDE THIRTY-FIVE DEGREES NORTH, THREE DEGREES WEST. ALTITUDE TWO THOUSAND METERS ABOVE THE SURFACE.
IMPULSE ENGINES ENGAGED.
AHHH...
...IT'S GOOD TO BE BACK IN THE CHAIR.

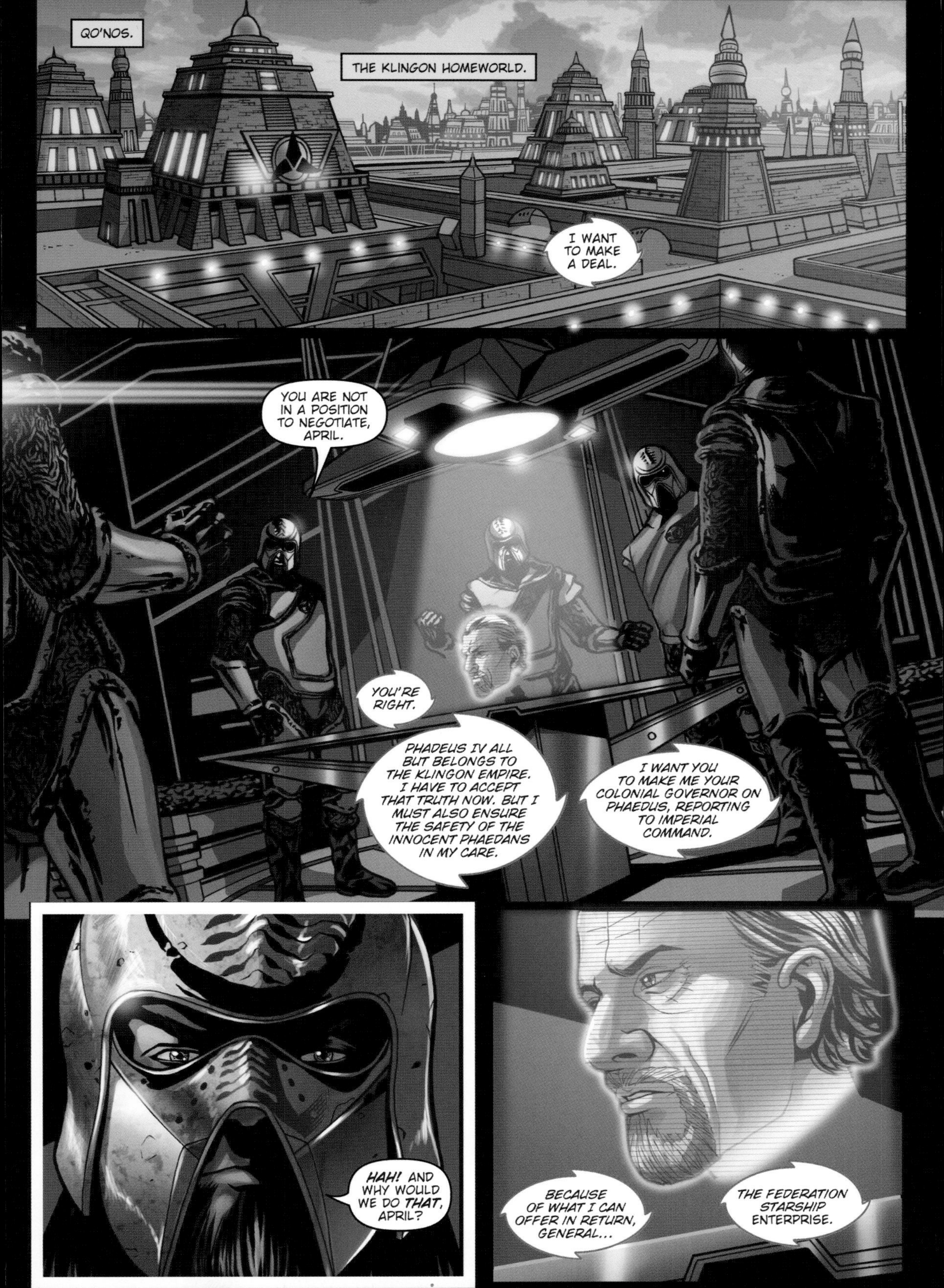
QO'NOS.
THE KLINGON HOMEWORLD.
I WANT TO MAKE A DEAL.
YOU ARE NOT IN A POSITION TO NEGOTIATE, APRIL.
YOU'RE RIGHT.
PHADEUS IV ALL BUT BELONGS TO THE KLINGON EMPIRE. I HAVE TO ACCEPT THAT TRUTH NOW. BUT I MUST ALSO ENSURE THE SAFETY OF THE INNOCENT PHAEDANS IN MY CARE.
I WANT YOU TO MAKE ME YOUR COLONIAL GOVERNOR ON PHAEDUS, REPORTING TO IMPERIAL COMMAND.
HAH! AND WHY WOULD WE DO THAT, APRIL?
BECAUSE OF WHAT I CAN OFFER IN RETURN, GENERAL...
THE FEDERATION STARSHIP ENTERPRISE.

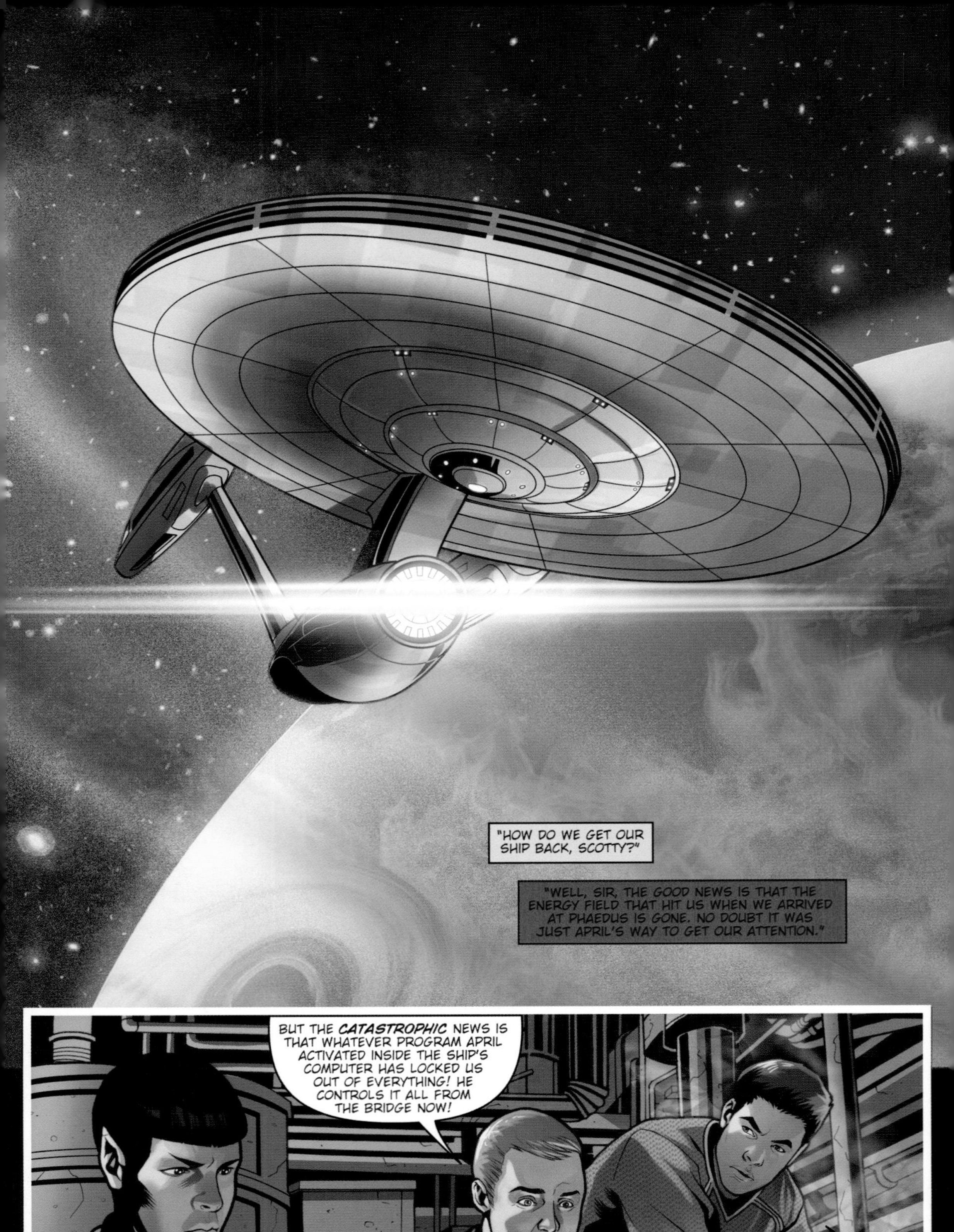
"HOW DO WE GET OUR SHIP BACK, SCOTTY?"
"WELL, SIR, THE GOOD NEWS IS THAT THE ENERGY FIELD THAT HIT US WHEN WE ARRIVED AT PHAEDUS IS GONE. NO DOUBT IT WAS JUST APRIL'S WAY TO GET OUR ATTENTION."

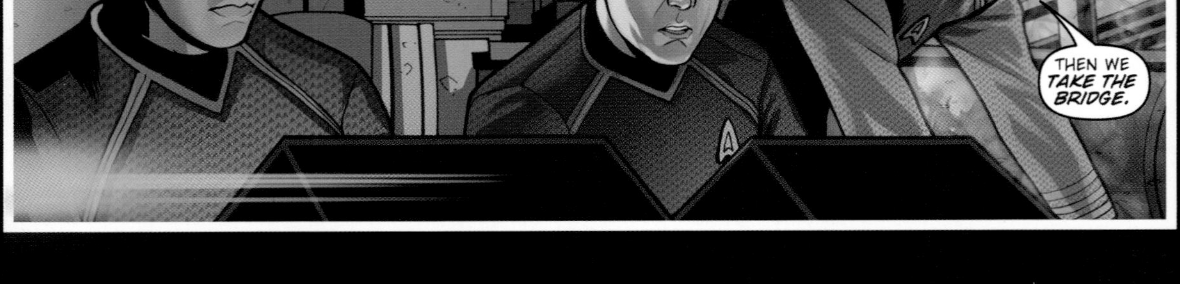
BUT THE *CATASTROPHIC* NEWS IS THAT WHATEVER PROGRAM APRIL ACTIVATED INSIDE THE SHIP'S COMPUTER HAS LOCKED US OUT OF EVERYTHING! HE CONTROLS IT ALL FROM THE BRIDGE NOW!
THEN WE ***TAKE THE BRIDGE.***

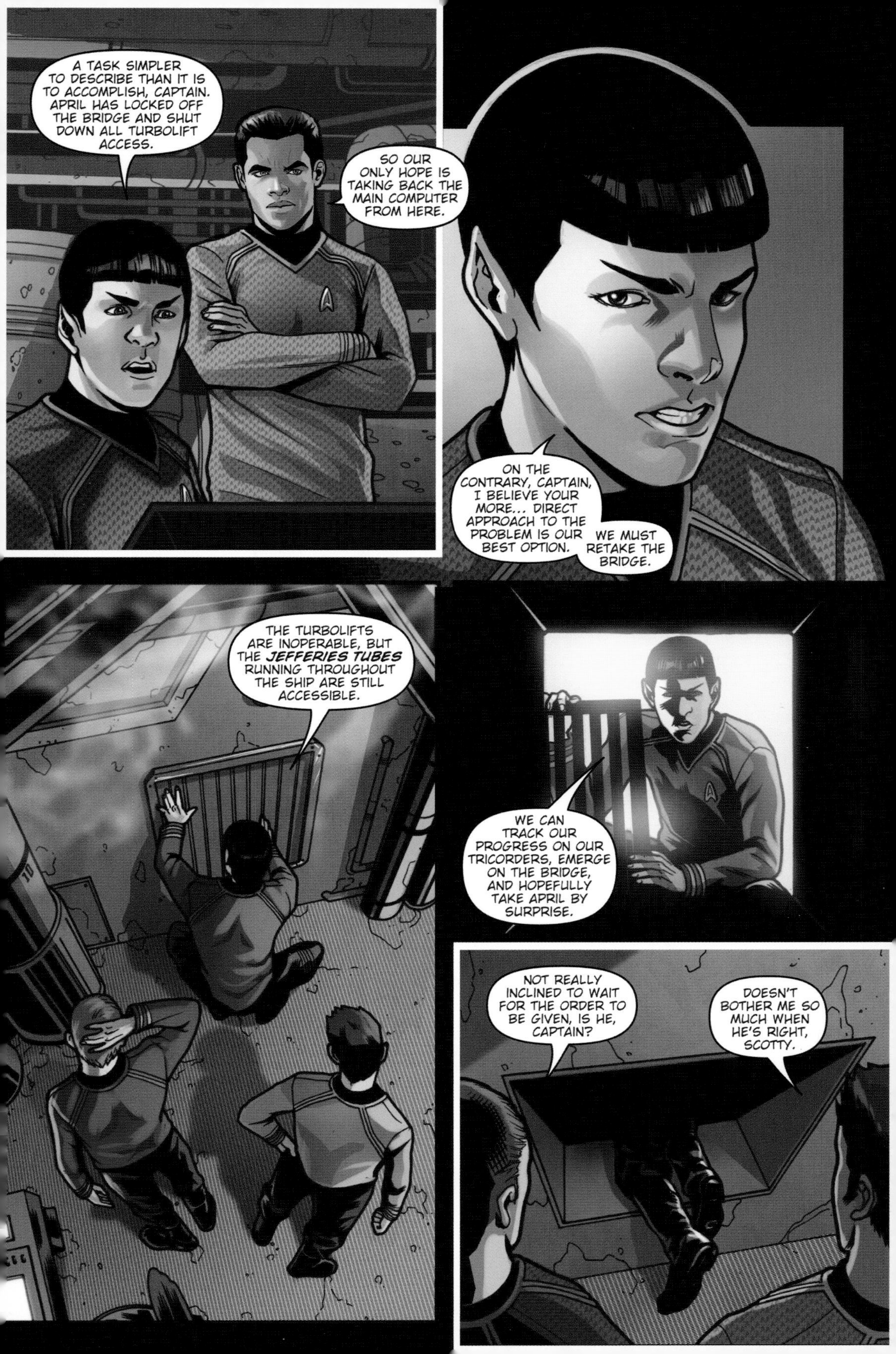
A TASK SIMPLER TO DESCRIBE THAN IT IS TO ACCOMPLISH, CAPTAIN. APRIL HAS LOCKED OFF THE BRIDGE AND SHUT DOWN ALL TURBOLIFT ACCESS.
SO OUR ONLY HOPE IS TAKING BACK THE MAIN COMPUTER FROM HERE.
ON THE CONTRARY, CAPTAIN, I BELIEVE YOUR MORE... DIRECT APPROACH TO THE PROBLEM IS OUR BEST OPTION.
WE MUST RETAKE THE BRIDGE.
THE TURBOLIFTS ARE INOPERABLE, BUT THE JEFFERIES TUBES RUNNING THROUGHOUT THE SHIP ARE STILL ACCESSIBLE.
WE CAN TRACK OUR PROGRESS ON OUR TRICORDERS, EMERGE ON THE BRIDGE, AND HOPEFULLY TAKE APRIL BY SURPRISE.
NOT REALLY INCLINED TO WAIT FOR THE ORDER TO BE GIVEN, IS HE, CAPTAIN?
DOESN'T BOTHER ME SO MUCH WHEN HE'S RIGHT, SCOTTY.

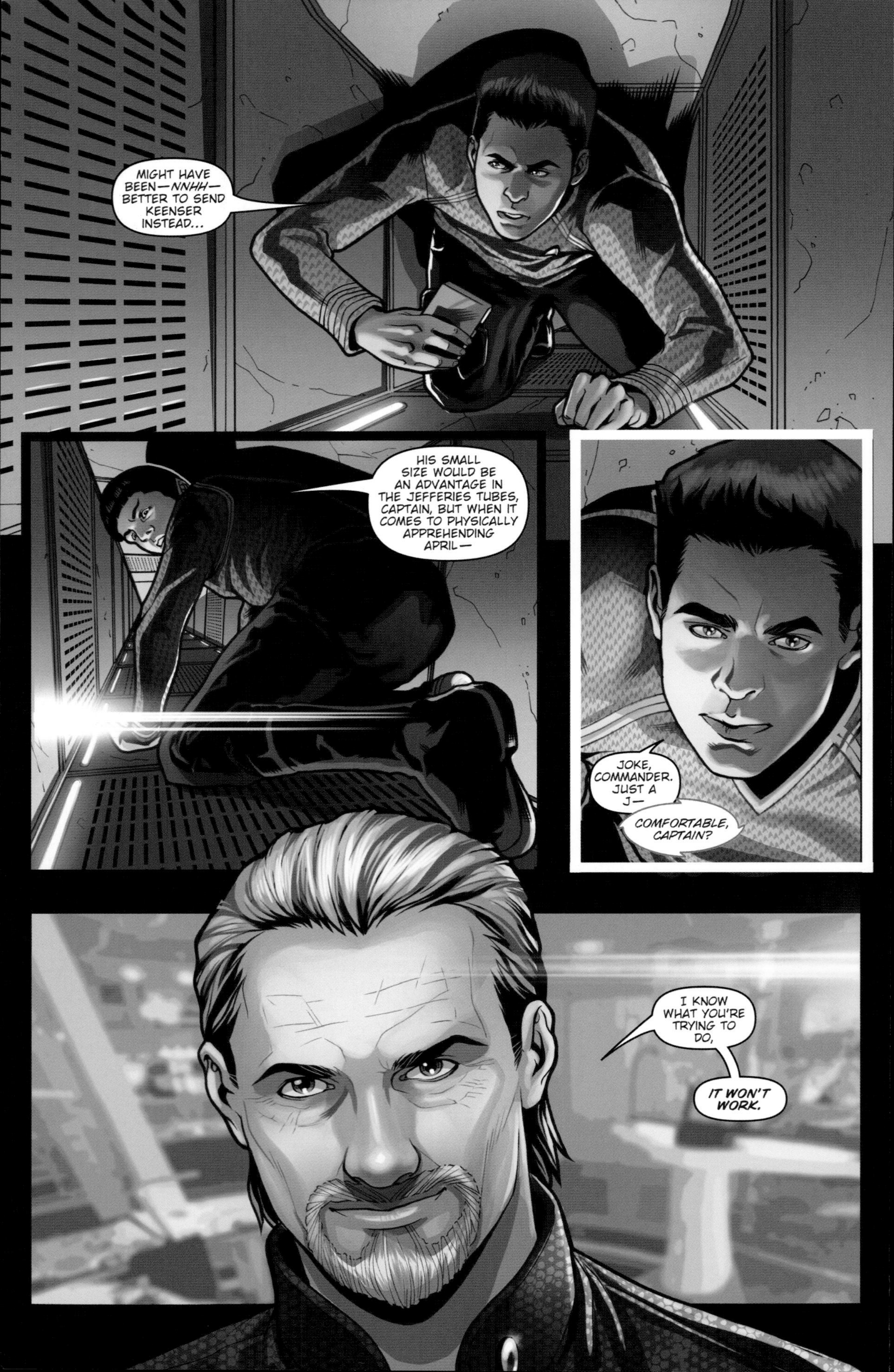
MIGHT HAVE BEEN—*NNHH*—BETTER TO SEND KEENSER INSTEAD...
HIS SMALL SIZE WOULD BE AN ADVANTAGE IN THE JEFFERIES TUBES, CAPTAIN, BUT WHEN IT COMES TO PHYSICALLY APPREHENDING APRIL—
JOKE, COMMANDER. JUST A J—
COMFORTABLE, CAPTAIN?
I KNOW WHAT YOU'RE TRYING TO DO,
IT WON'T WORK.

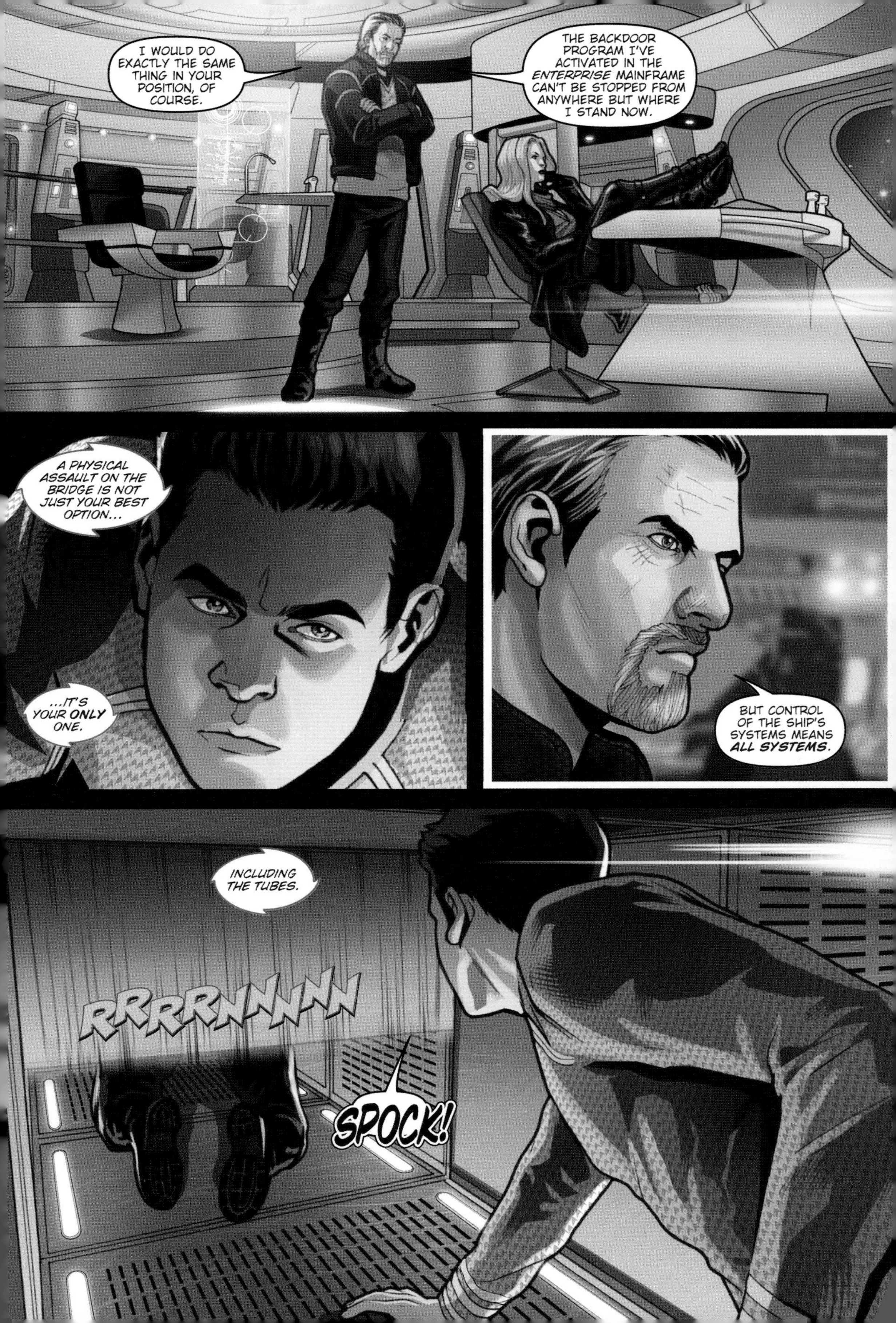
I WOULD DO EXACTLY THE SAME THING IN YOUR POSITION, OF COURSE.
THE BACKDOOR PROGRAM I'VE ACTIVATED IN THE *ENTERPRISE* MAINFRAME CAN'T BE STOPPED FROM ANYWHERE BUT WHERE I STAND NOW.
A PHYSICAL ASSAULT ON THE BRIDGE IS NOT JUST YOUR BEST OPTION...
...IT'S YOUR **ONLY** ONE.
BUT CONTROL OF THE SHIP'S SYSTEMS MEANS ***ALL SYSTEMS***.
INCLUDING THE TUBES.
RRRRNNNNN
SPOCK!

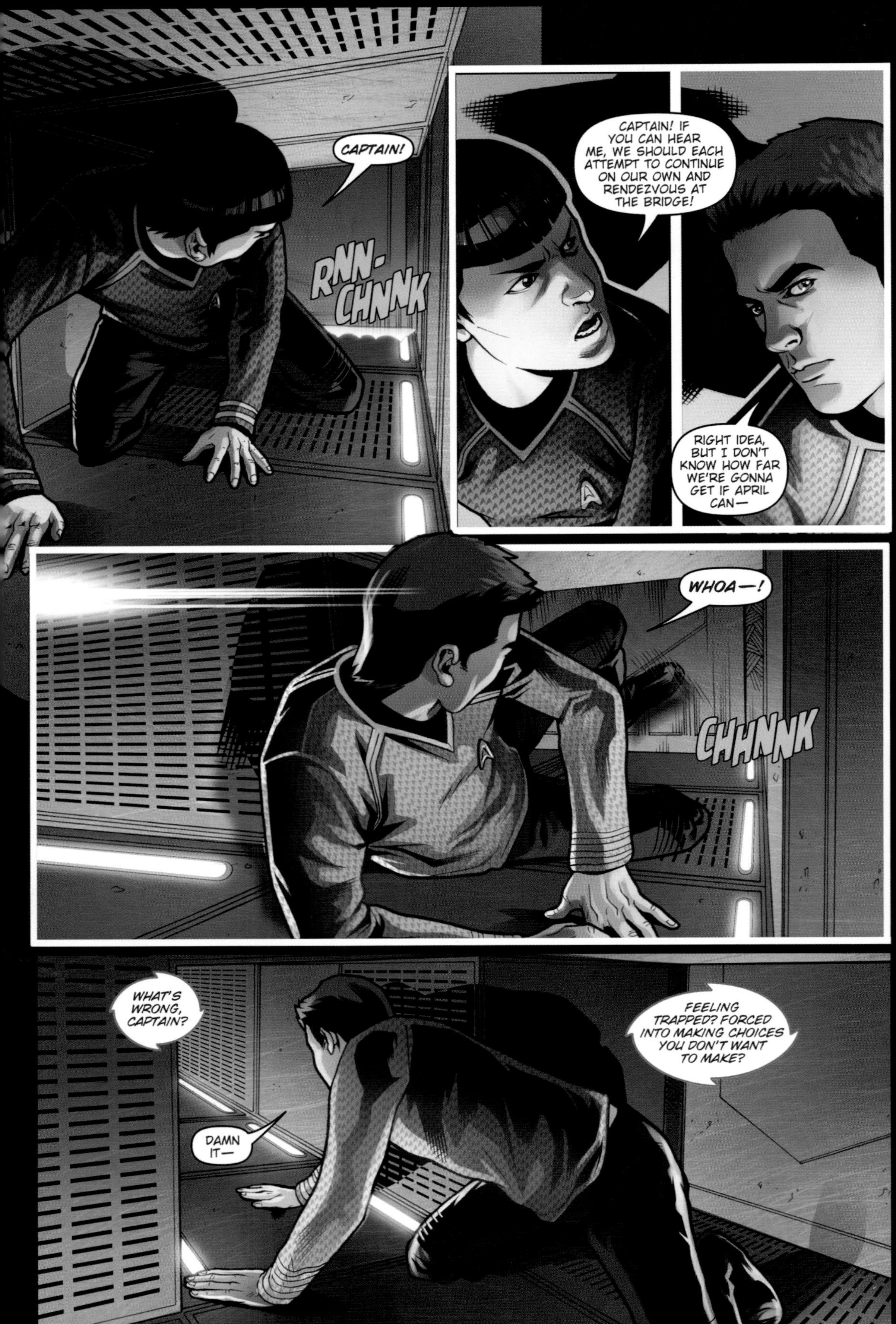
CAPTAIN!
RNN-CHNNK
CAPTAIN! IF YOU CAN HEAR ME, WE SHOULD EACH ATTEMPT TO CONTINUE ON OUR OWN AND RENDEZVOUS AT THE BRIDGE!
RIGHT IDEA, BUT I DON'T KNOW HOW FAR WE'RE GONNA GET IF APRIL CAN—
WHOA—!
CHHNNK
WHAT'S WRONG, CAPTAIN?
FEELING TRAPPED? FORCED INTO MAKING CHOICES YOU DON'T WANT TO MAKE?
DAMN IT—

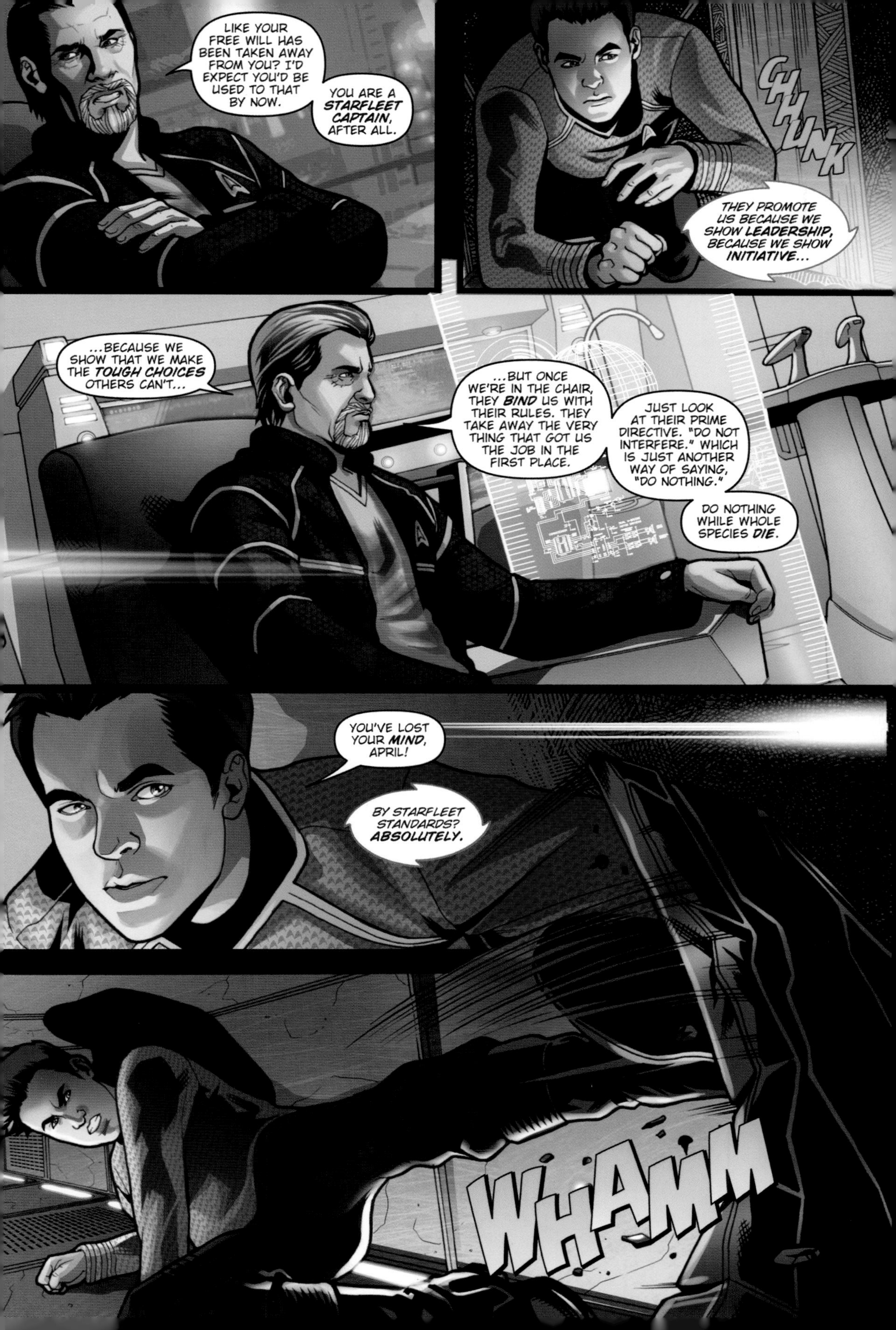
LIKE YOUR FREE WILL HAS BEEN TAKEN AWAY FROM YOU? I'D EXPECT YOU'D BE USED TO THAT BY NOW.
YOU ARE A **STARFLEET CAPTAIN**, AFTER ALL.
CHHUNK
THEY PROMOTE US BECAUSE WE SHOW **LEADERSHIP**, BECAUSE WE SHOW **INITIATIVE**...
...BECAUSE WE SHOW THAT WE MAKE THE **TOUGH CHOICES** OTHERS CAN'T...
...BUT ONCE WE'RE IN THE CHAIR, THEY **BIND** US WITH THEIR RULES. THEY TAKE AWAY THE VERY THING THAT GOT US THE JOB IN THE FIRST PLACE.
JUST LOOK AT THEIR PRIME DIRECTIVE. "DO NOT INTERFERE." WHICH IS JUST ANOTHER WAY OF SAYING, "DO NOTHING."
DO NOTHING WHILE WHOLE SPECIES **DIE**.
YOU'VE LOST YOUR **MIND**, APRIL!
BY STARFLEET STANDARDS? **ABSOLUTELY.**
WHAMM

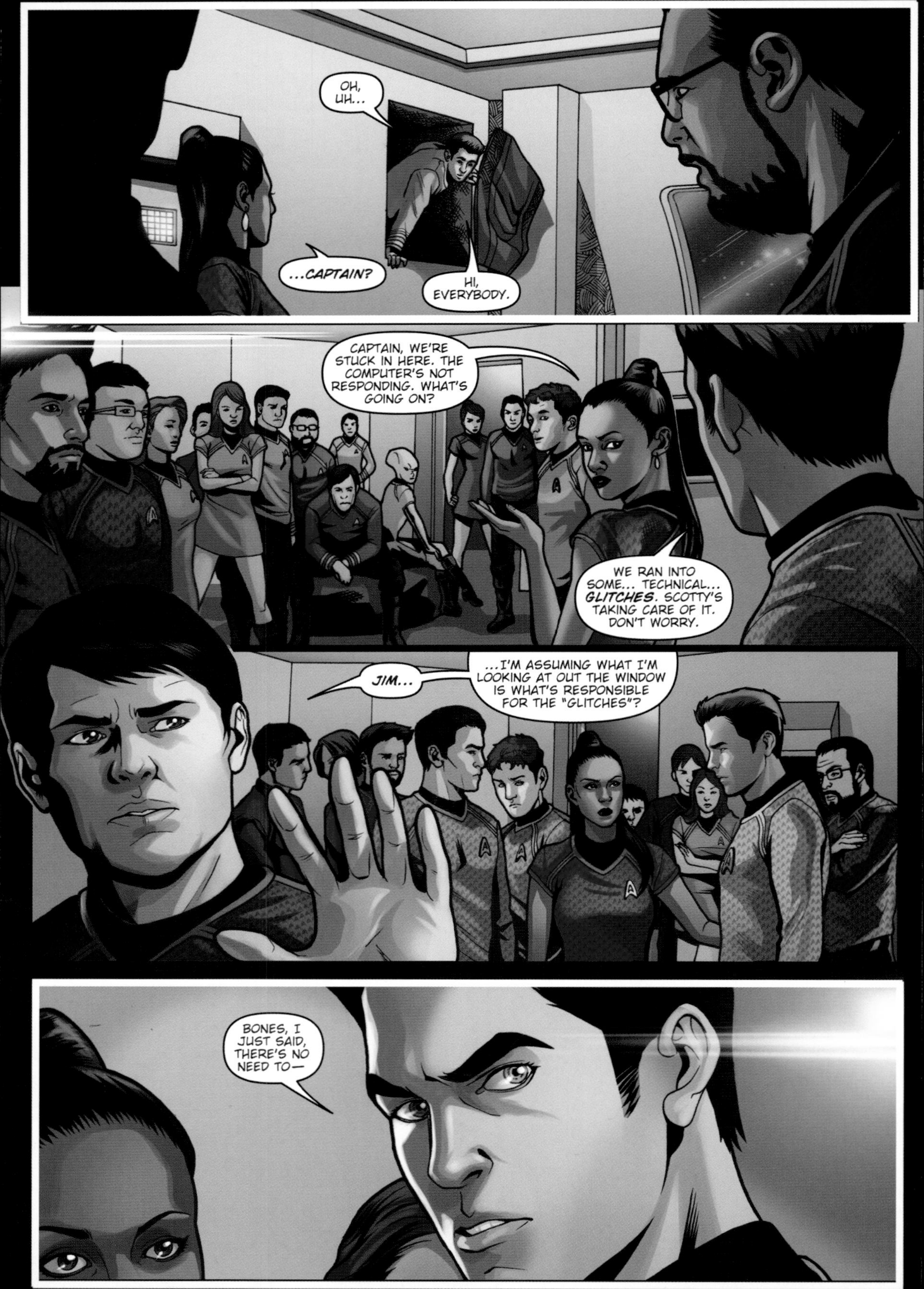
OH, UH...
...CAPTAIN?
HI, EVERYBODY.
CAPTAIN, WE'RE STUCK IN HERE. THE COMPUTER'S NOT RESPONDING. WHAT'S GOING ON?
WE RAN INTO SOME... TECHNICAL... GLITCHES. SCOTTY'S TAKING CARE OF IT. DON'T WORRY.
JIM...
...I'M ASSUMING WHAT I'M LOOKING AT OUT THE WINDOW IS WHAT'S RESPONSIBLE FOR THE "GLITCHES"?
BONES, I JUST SAID, THERE'S NO NEED TO—

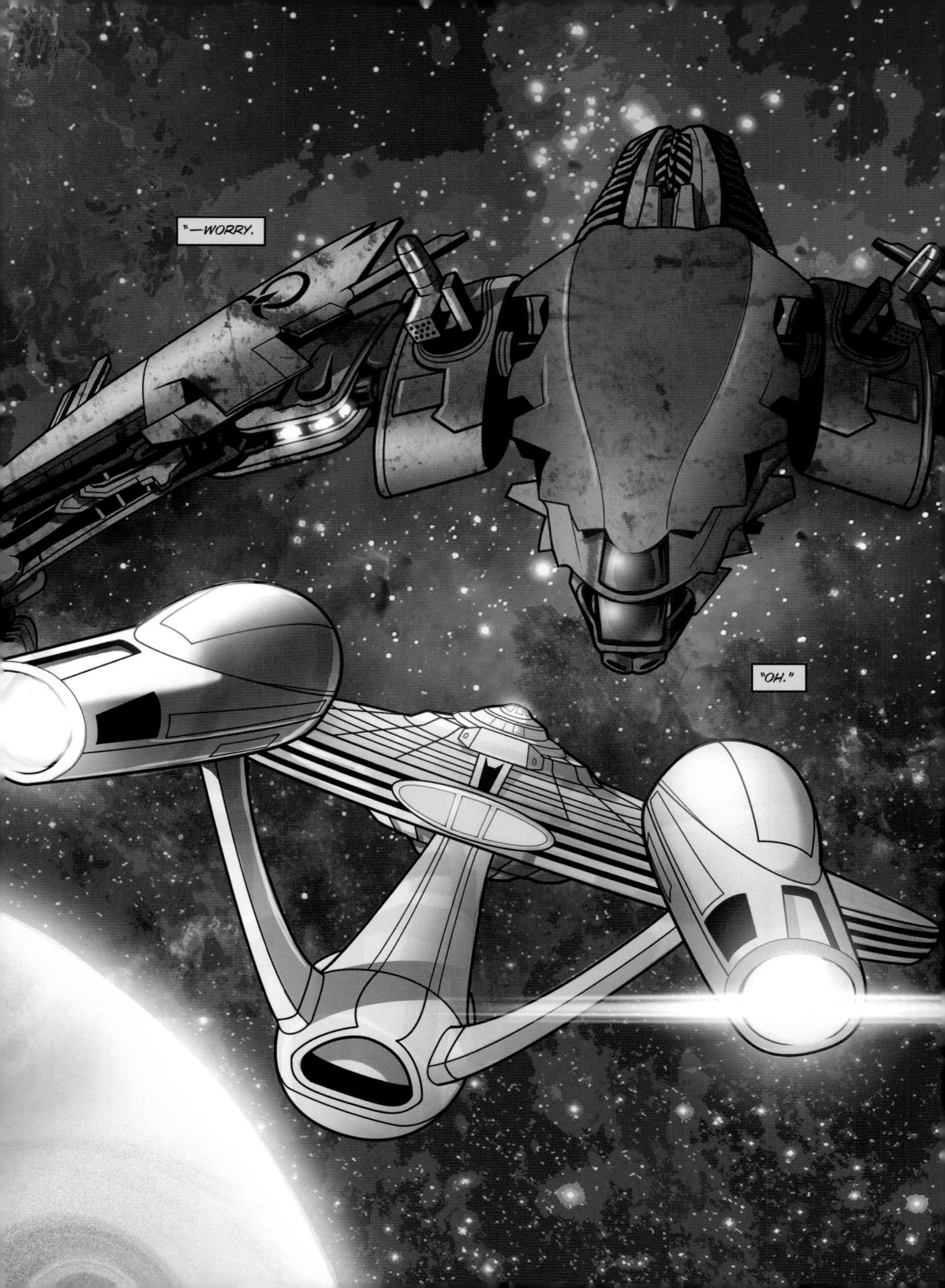
"—WORRY.
"OH."

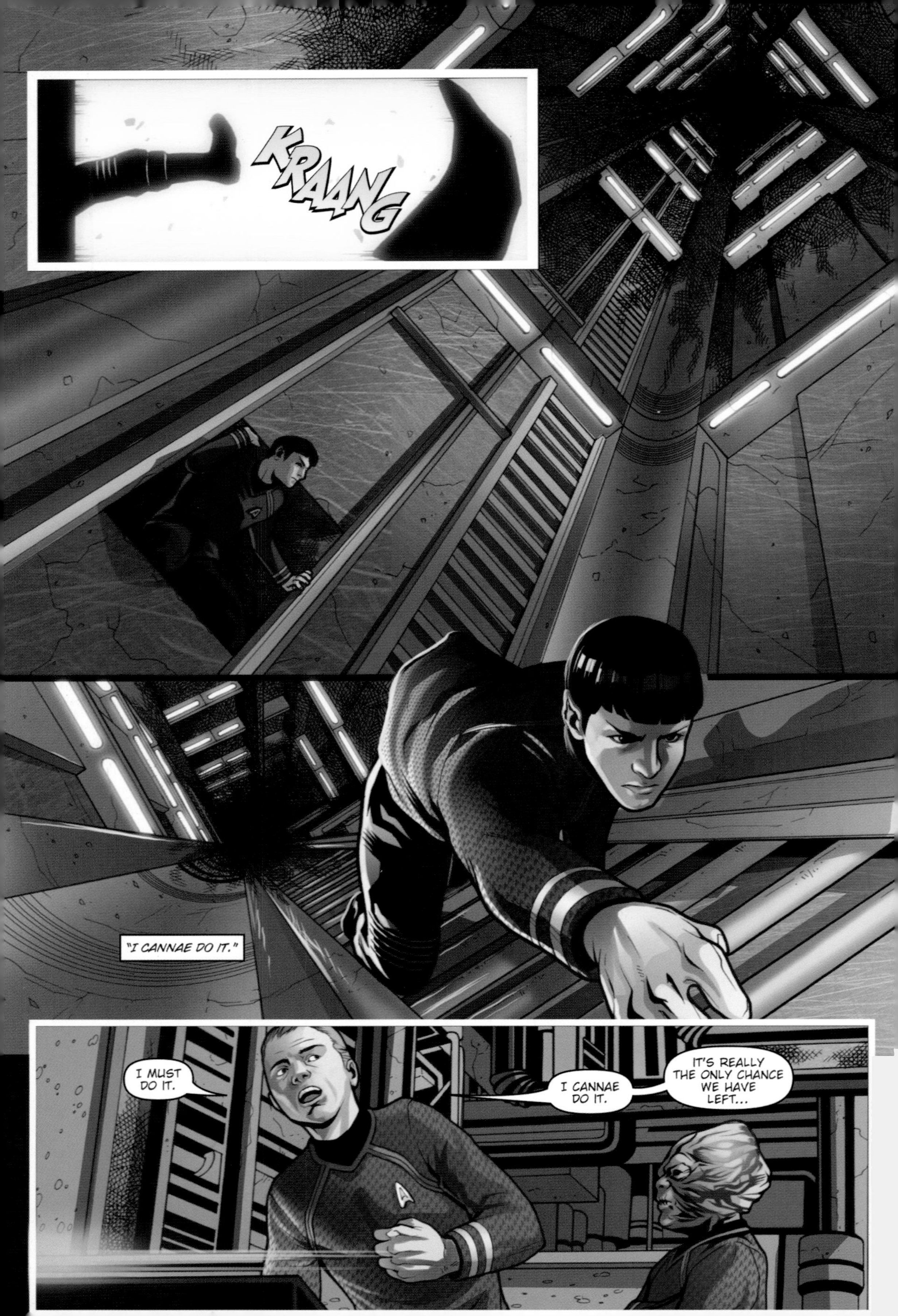
KRAANG
"I CANNAE DO IT."
I MUST DO IT.
I CANNAE DO IT.
IT'S REALLY THE ONLY CHANCE WE HAVE LEFT...

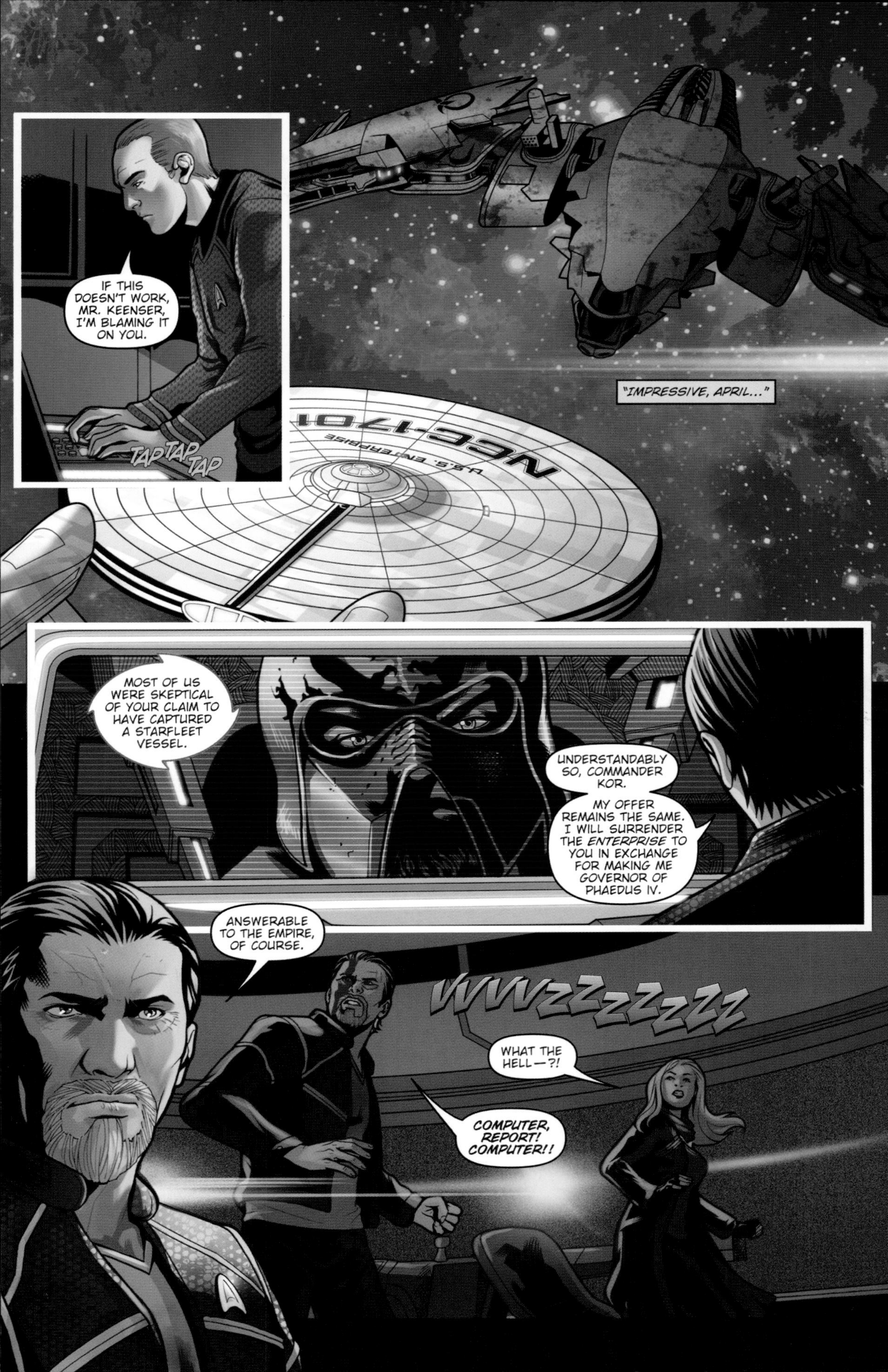

IF THIS DOESN'T WORK, MR. KEENSER, I'M BLAMING IT ON YOU.
TAP TAP TAP
NCC-1701
U.S.S. ENTERPRISE
"IMPRESSIVE, APRIL..."
MOST OF US WERE SKEPTICAL OF YOUR CLAIM TO HAVE CAPTURED A STARFLEET VESSEL.
UNDERSTANDABLY SO, COMMANDER KOR.
MY OFFER REMAINS THE SAME. I WILL SURRENDER THE *ENTERPRISE* TO YOU IN EXCHANGE FOR MAKING ME GOVERNOR OF PHAEDUS IV.
ANSWERABLE TO THE EMPIRE, OF COURSE.
VVVVZZZZZZZ
WHAT THE HELL—?!
COMPUTER, REPORT! COMPUTER!!

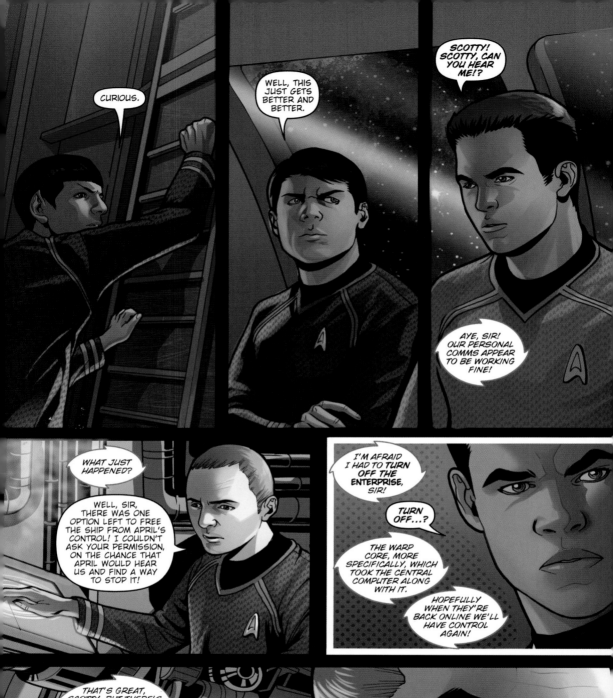

CURIOUS.

WELL, THIS JUST GETS BETTER AND BETTER.

SCOTTY! SCOTTY, CAN YOU HEAR ME!?

AYE, SIR! OUR PERSONAL COMMS APPEAR TO BE WORKING FINE!

WHAT JUST HAPPENED?

WELL, SIR, THERE WAS ONE OPTION LEFT TO FREE THE SHIP FROM APRIL'S CONTROL! I COULDN'T ASK YOUR PERMISSION, ON THE CHANCE THAT APRIL WOULD HEAR US AND FIND A WAY TO STOP IT!

I'M AFRAID I HAD TO TURN OFF THE ENTERPRISE, SIR!

TURN OFF...?

THE WARP CORE, MORE SPECIFICALLY, WHICH TOOK THE CENTRAL COMPUTER ALONG WITH IT.

HOPEFULLY WHEN THEY'RE BACK ONLINE WE'LL HAVE CONTROL AGAIN!

THAT'S GREAT, SCOTTY, BUT THERE'S A KLINGON SHIP PARKED OFF OUR BOW!

WELL, HOW WAS I SUPPOSED TO KNOW THAT?!

HOW LONG UNTIL WE'RE BACK ONLINE?

SHOULD ONLY BE MINUTES, CAPTAIN!

...VERY, VERY LONG MINUTES...

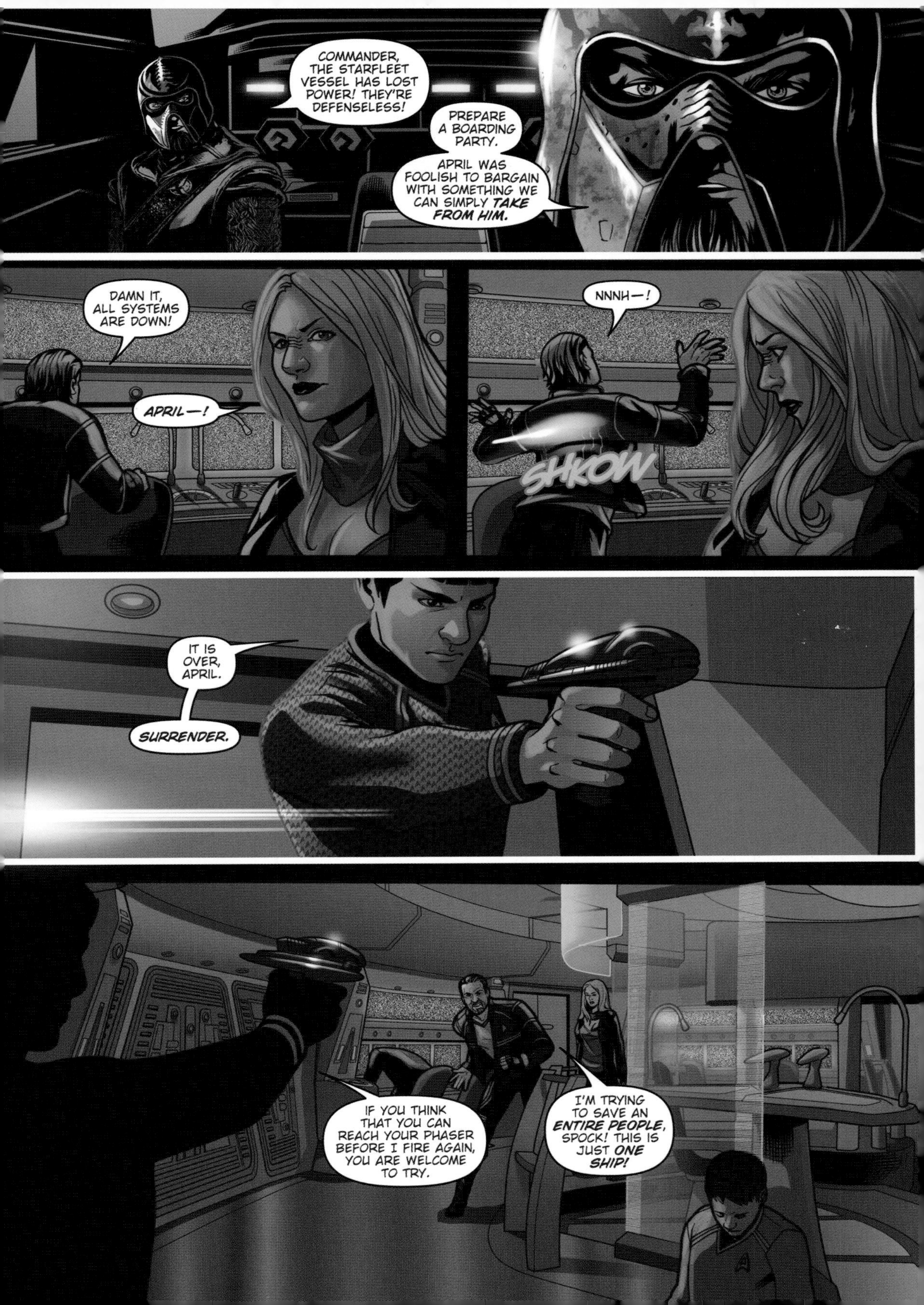
COMMANDER, THE STARFLEET VESSEL HAS LOST POWER! THEY'RE DEFENSELESS!
PREPARE A BOARDING PARTY.
APRIL WAS FOOLISH TO BARGAIN WITH SOMETHING WE CAN SIMPLY TAKE FROM HIM.
DAMN IT, ALL SYSTEMS ARE DOWN!
APRIL—!
NNNH—!
SHKOW
IT IS OVER, APRIL.
SURRENDER.
IF YOU THINK THAT YOU CAN REACH YOUR PHASER BEFORE I FIRE AGAIN, YOU ARE WELCOME TO TRY.
I'M TRYING TO SAVE AN ENTIRE PEOPLE, SPOCK! THIS IS JUST ONE SHIP!

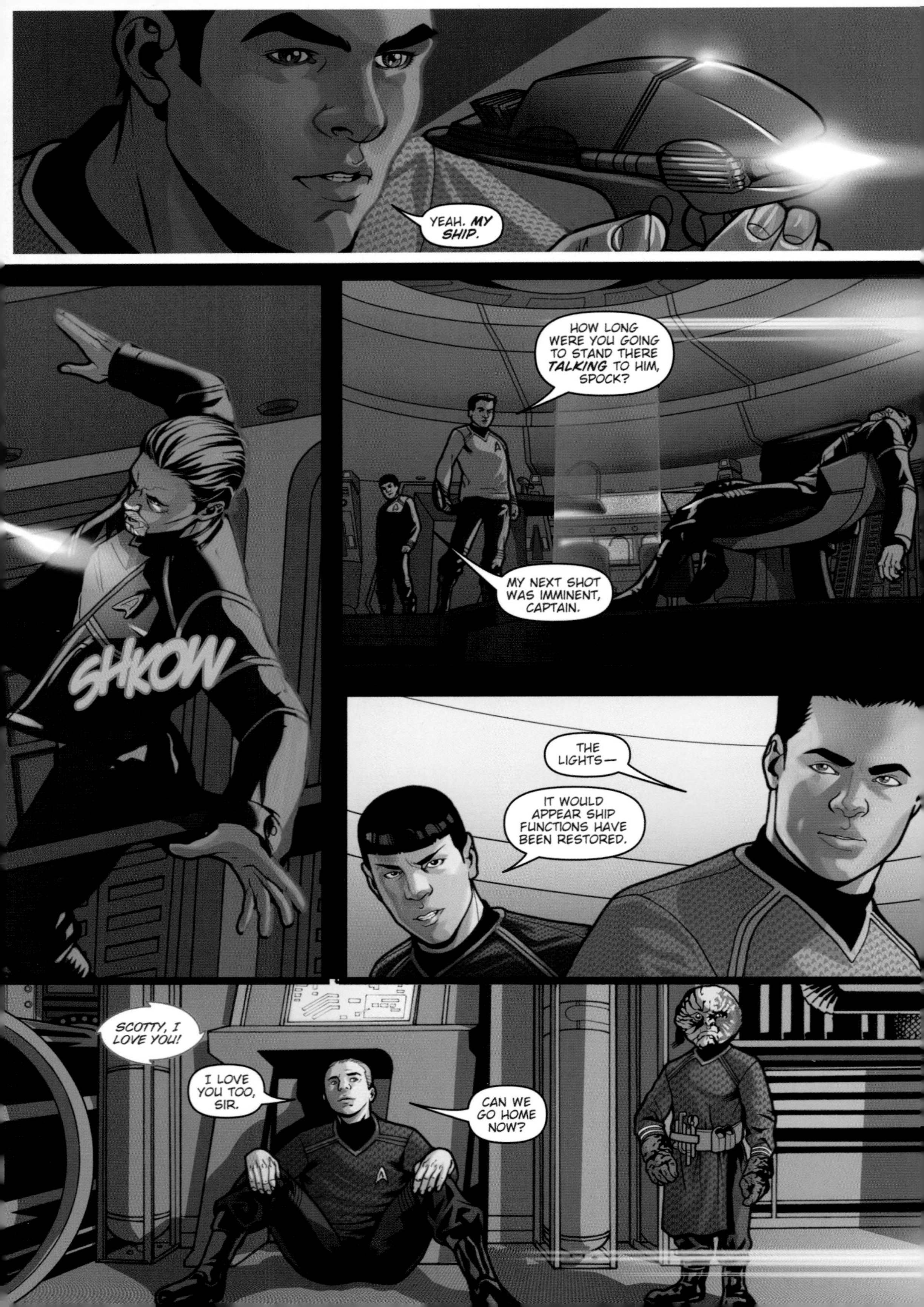
YEAH. MY SHIP.
SHKOW
HOW LONG WERE YOU GOING TO STAND THERE TALKING TO HIM, SPOCK?
MY NEXT SHOT WAS IMMINENT, CAPTAIN.
THE LIGHTS—
IT WOULD APPEAR SHIP FUNCTIONS HAVE BEEN RESTORED.
SCOTTY, I LOVE YOU!
I LOVE YOU TOO, SIR.
CAN WE GO HOME NOW?

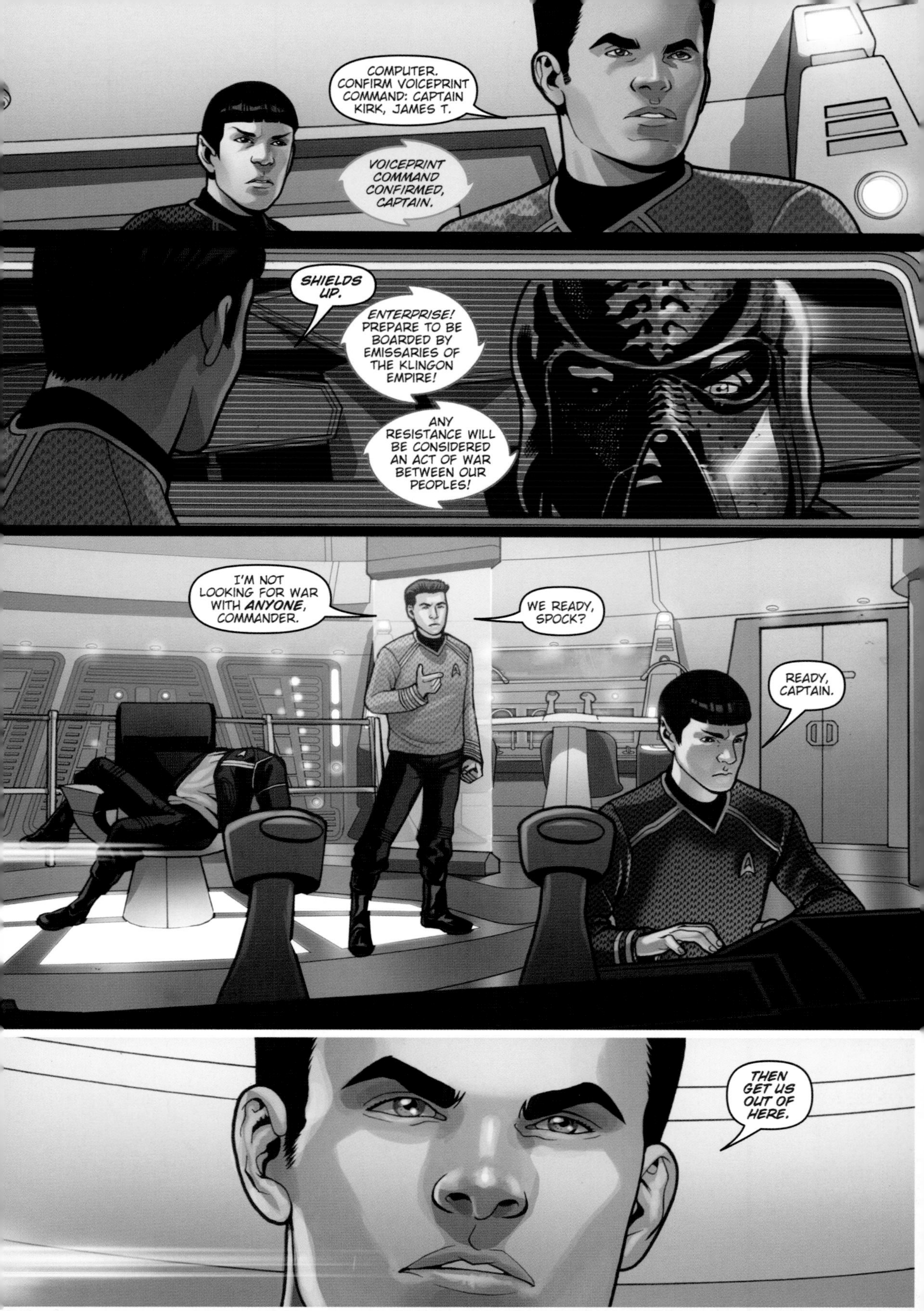
COMPUTER. CONFIRM VOICEPRINT COMMAND: CAPTAIN KIRK, JAMES T.
VOICEPRINT COMMAND CONFIRMED, CAPTAIN.
SHIELDS UP.
ENTERPRISE! PREPARE TO BE BOARDED BY EMISSARIES OF THE KLINGON EMPIRE!
ANY RESISTANCE WILL BE CONSIDERED AN ACT OF WAR BETWEEN OUR PEOPLES!
I'M NOT LOOKING FOR WAR WITH ANYONE, COMMANDER.
WE READY, SPOCK?
READY, CAPTAIN.
THEN GET US OUT OF HERE.

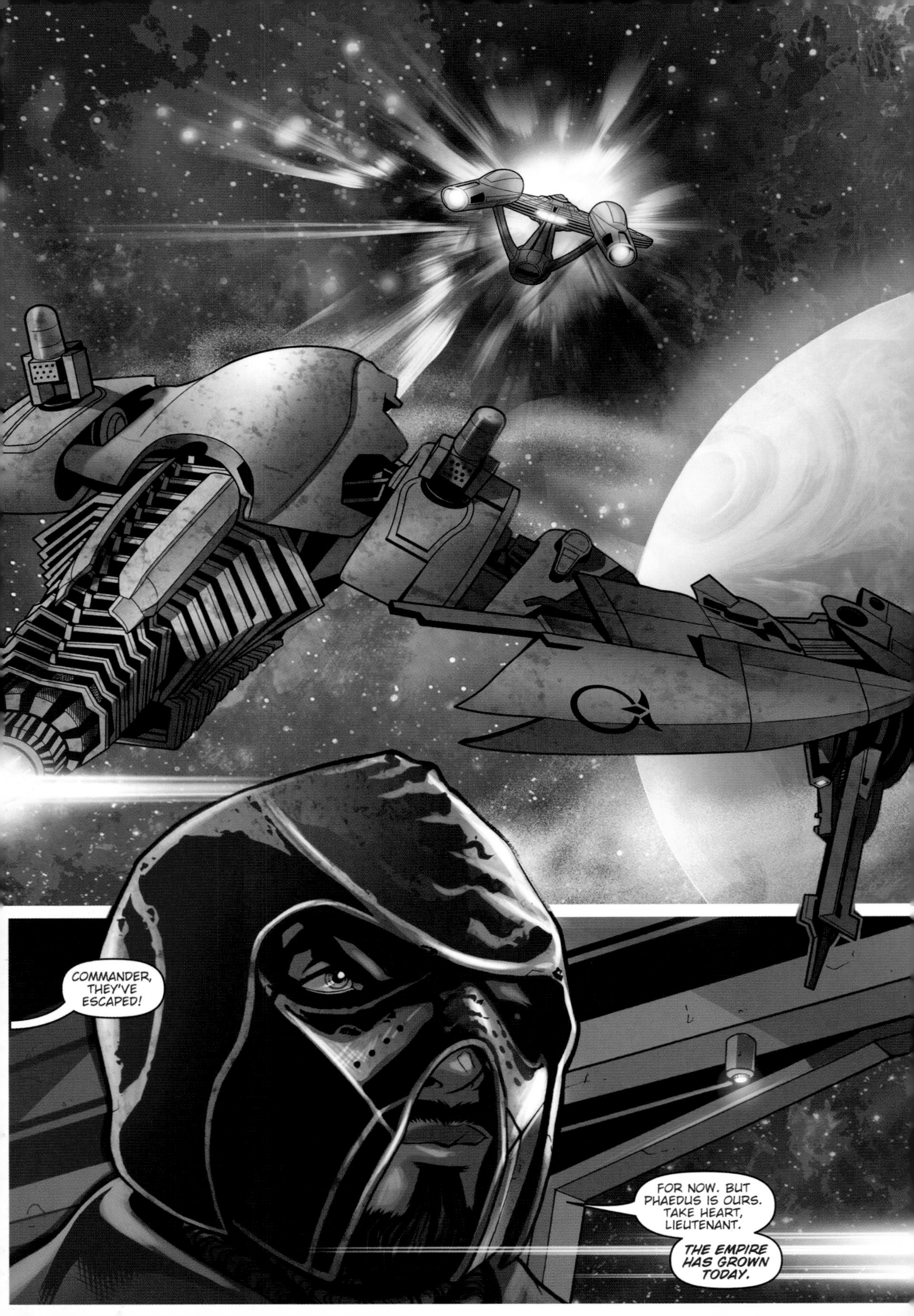
COMMANDER, THEY'VE ESCAPED!
FOR NOW. BUT PHAEDUS IS OURS. TAKE HEART, LIEUTENANT.
THE EMPIRE HAS GROWN TODAY.

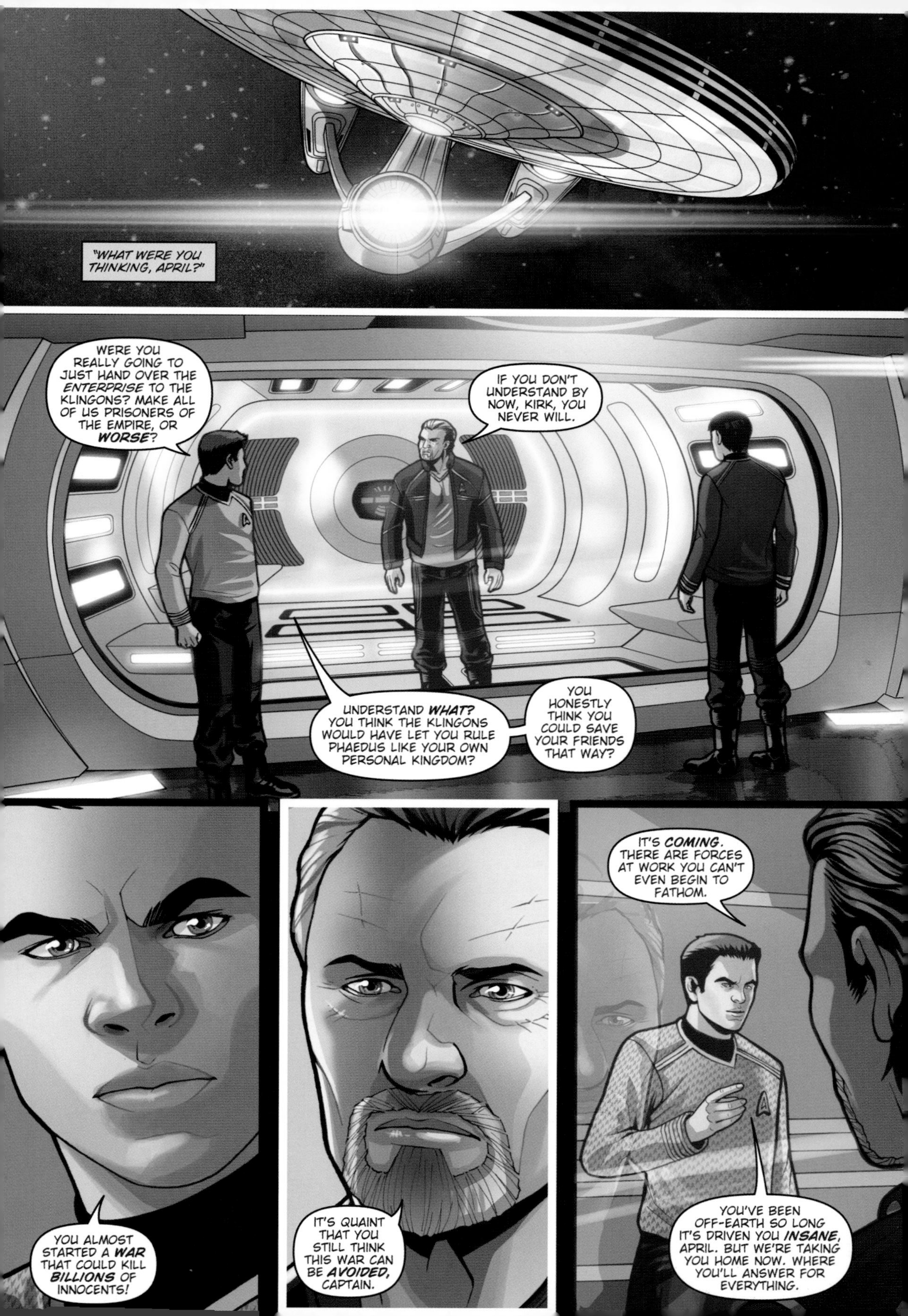
"WHAT WERE YOU THINKING, APRIL?"
WERE YOU REALLY GOING TO JUST HAND OVER THE ENTERPRISE TO THE KLINGONS? MAKE ALL OF US PRISONERS OF THE EMPIRE, OR WORSE?
IF YOU DON'T UNDERSTAND BY NOW, KIRK, YOU NEVER WILL.
UNDERSTAND WHAT? YOU THINK THE KLINGONS WOULD HAVE LET YOU RULE PHAEDUS LIKE YOUR OWN PERSONAL KINGDOM?
YOU HONESTLY THINK YOU COULD SAVE YOUR FRIENDS THAT WAY?
YOU ALMOST STARTED A WAR THAT COULD KILL BILLIONS OF INNOCENTS!
IT'S QUAINT THAT YOU STILL THINK THIS WAR CAN BE AVOIDED, CAPTAIN.
IT'S COMING. THERE ARE FORCES AT WORK YOU CAN'T EVEN BEGIN TO FATHOM.
YOU'VE BEEN OFF-EARTH SO LONG IT'S DRIVEN YOU INSANE, APRIL. BUT WE'RE TAKING YOU HOME NOW. WHERE YOU'LL ANSWER FOR EVERYTHING.

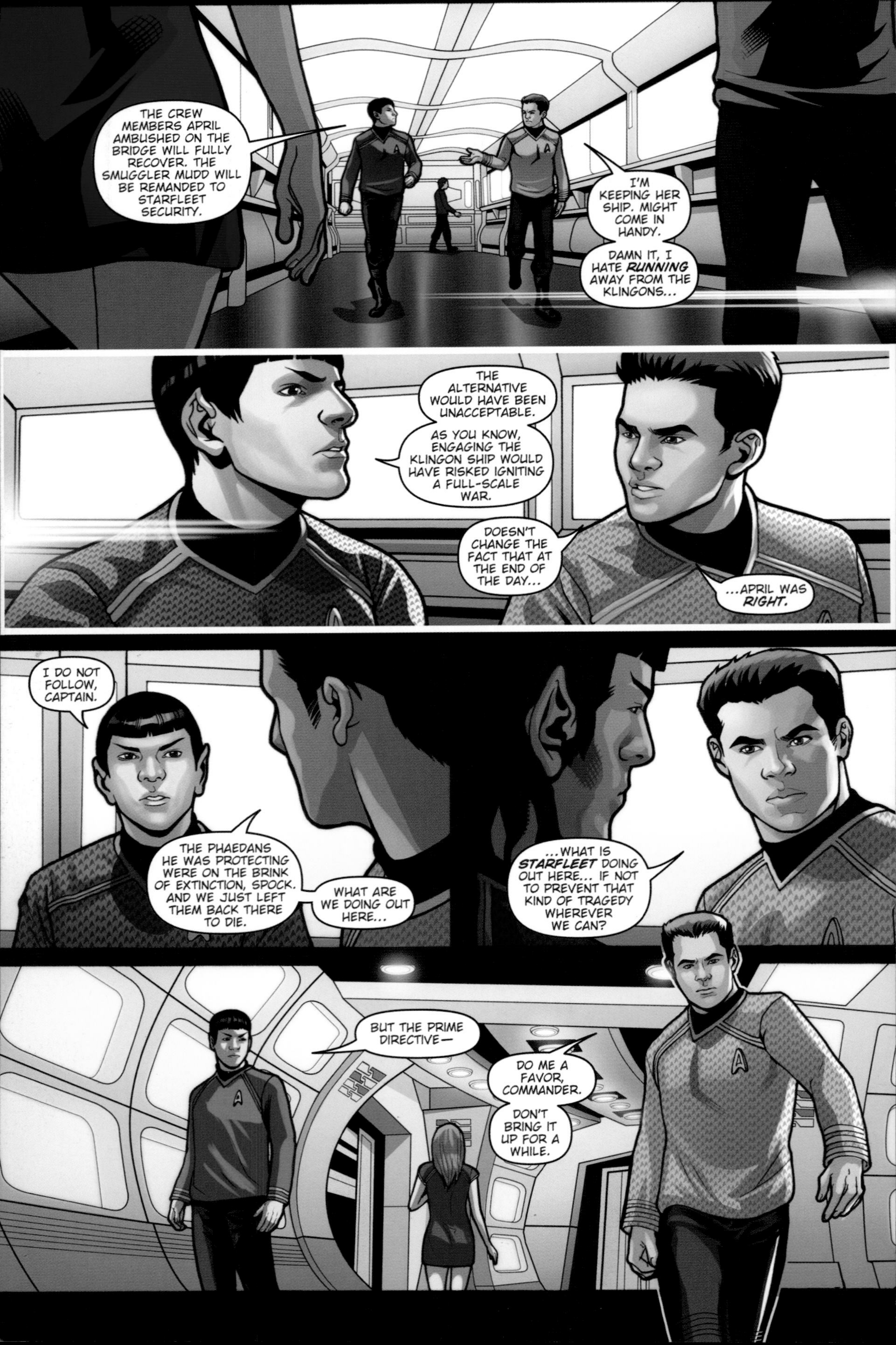
THE CREW MEMBERS APRIL AMBUSHED ON THE BRIDGE WILL FULLY RECOVER. THE SMUGGLER MUDD WILL BE REMANDED TO STARFLEET SECURITY.
I'M KEEPING HER SHIP. MIGHT COME IN HANDY.
DAMN IT, I HATE **RUNNING** AWAY FROM THE KLINGONS...
THE ALTERNATIVE WOULD HAVE BEEN UNACCEPTABLE.
AS YOU KNOW, ENGAGING THE KLINGON SHIP WOULD HAVE RISKED IGNITING A FULL-SCALE WAR.
DOESN'T CHANGE THE FACT THAT AT THE END OF THE DAY...
...APRIL WAS **RIGHT.**
I DO NOT FOLLOW, CAPTAIN.
THE PHAEDANS HE WAS PROTECTING WERE ON THE BRINK OF EXTINCTION, SPOCK. AND WE JUST LEFT THEM BACK THERE TO DIE.
WHAT ARE WE DOING OUT HERE...
...WHAT IS **STARFLEET** DOING OUT HERE... IF NOT TO PREVENT THAT KIND OF TRAGEDY WHEREVER WE CAN?
BUT THE PRIME DIRECTIVE—
DO ME A FAVOR, COMMANDER.
DON'T BRING IT UP FOR A WHILE.

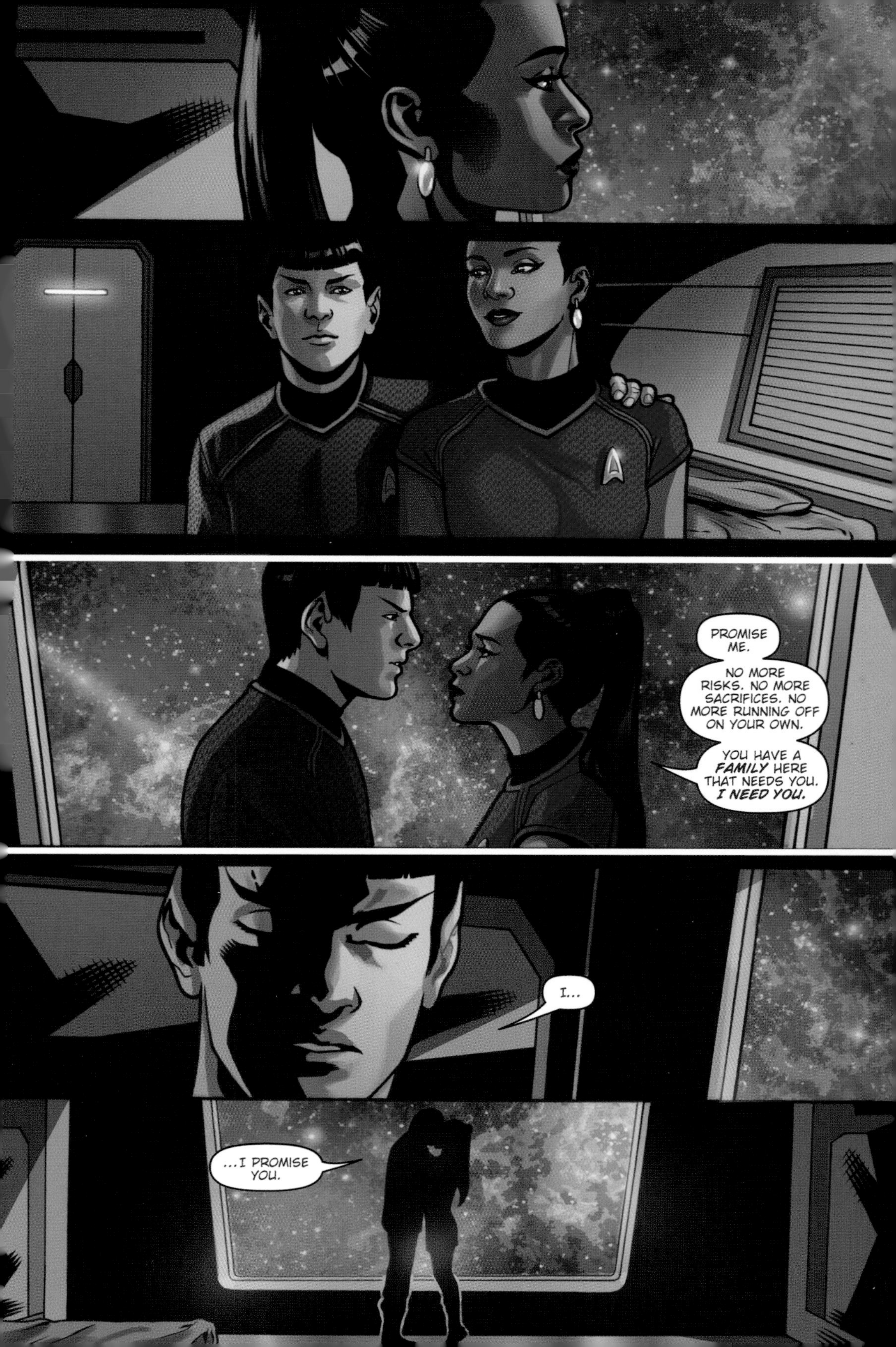
PROMISE ME.
NO MORE RISKS. NO MORE SACRIFICES. NO MORE RUNNING OFF ON YOUR OWN.
YOU HAVE A ***FAMILY*** HERE THAT NEEDS YOU. ***I NEED YOU.***
I...
...I PROMISE YOU.

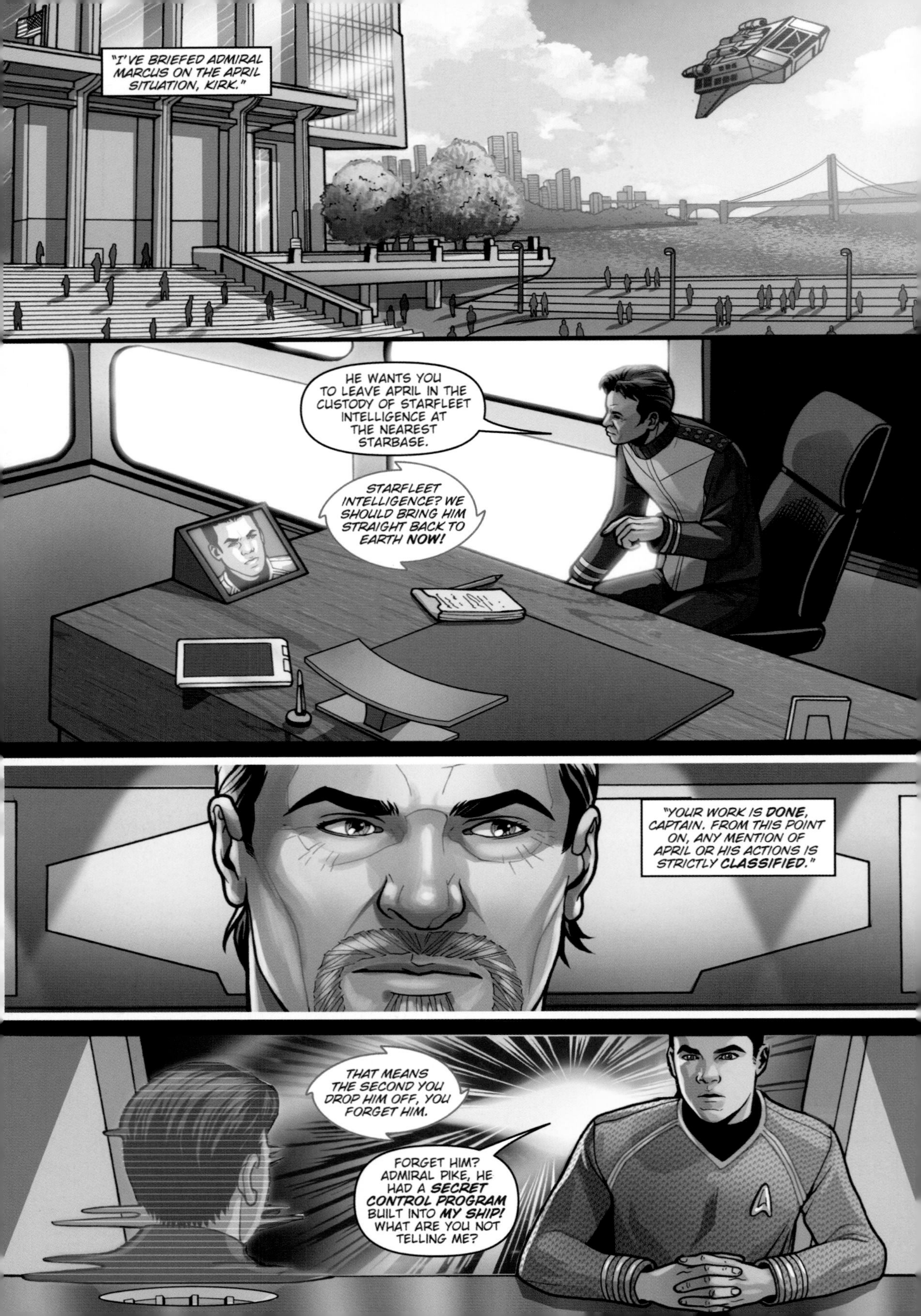
"I'VE BRIEFED ADMIRAL MARCUS ON THE APRIL SITUATION, KIRK."
HE WANTS YOU TO LEAVE APRIL IN THE CUSTODY OF STARFLEET INTELLIGENCE AT THE NEAREST STARBASE.
STARFLEET INTELLIGENCE? WE SHOULD BRING HIM STRAIGHT BACK TO EARTH NOW!
"YOUR WORK IS DONE, CAPTAIN. FROM THIS POINT ON, ANY MENTION OF APRIL OR HIS ACTIONS IS STRICTLY CLASSIFIED."
THAT MEANS THE SECOND YOU DROP HIM OFF, YOU FORGET HIM.
FORGET HIM? ADMIRAL PIKE, HE HAD A SECRET CONTROL PROGRAM BUILT INTO MY SHIP! WHAT ARE YOU NOT TELLING ME?

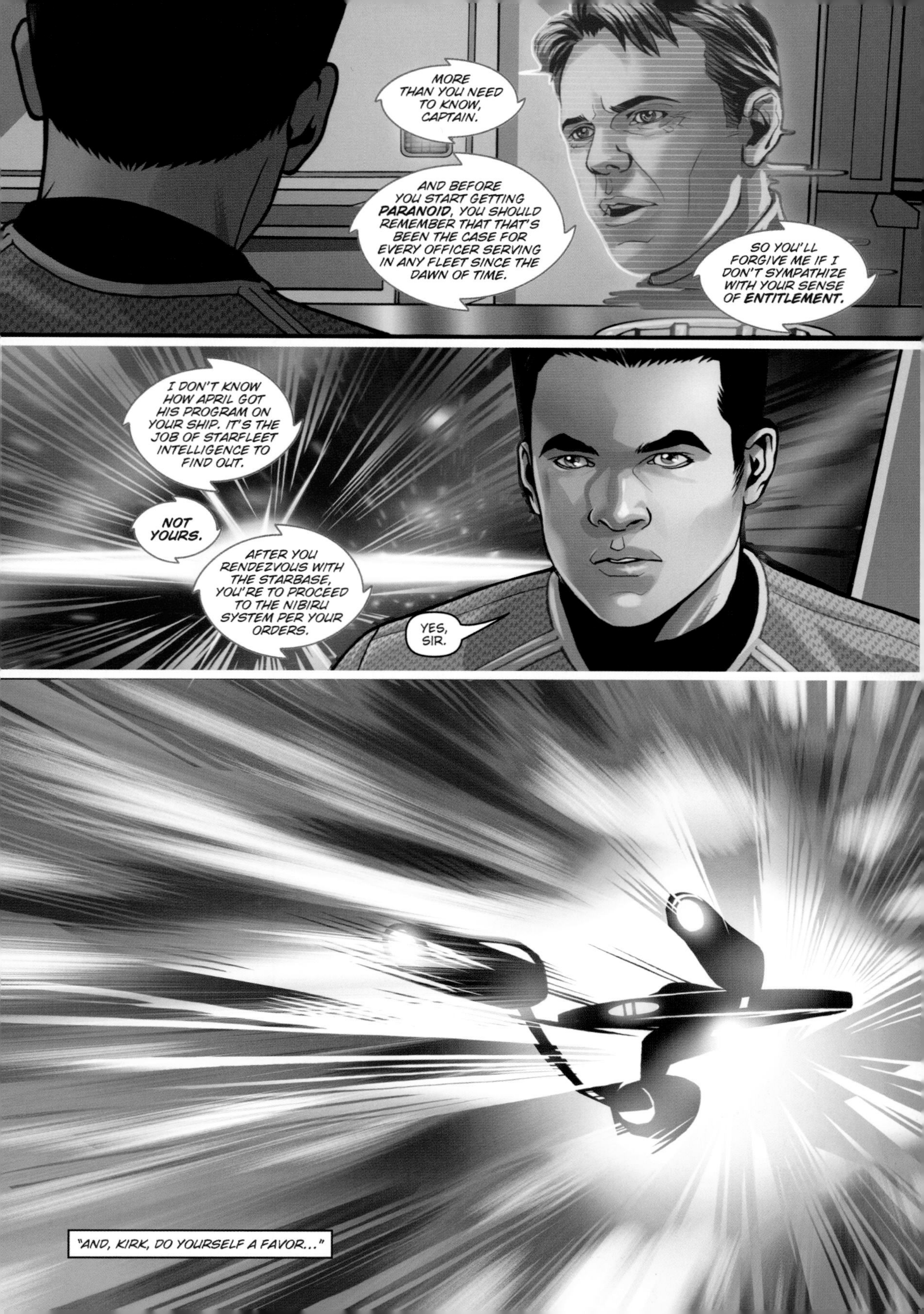

MORE THAN YOU NEED TO KNOW, CAPTAIN.
AND BEFORE YOU START GETTING PARANOID, YOU SHOULD REMEMBER THAT THAT'S BEEN THE CASE FOR EVERY OFFICER SERVING IN ANY FLEET SINCE THE DAWN OF TIME.
SO YOU'LL FORGIVE ME IF I DON'T SYMPATHIZE WITH YOUR SENSE OF ENTITLEMENT.
I DON'T KNOW HOW APRIL GOT HIS PROGRAM ON YOUR SHIP. IT'S THE JOB OF STARFLEET INTELLIGENCE TO FIND OUT.
NOT YOURS.
AFTER YOU RENDEZVOUS WITH THE STARBASE, YOU'RE TO PROCEED TO THE NIBIRU SYSTEM PER YOUR ORDERS.
YES, SIR.
"AND, KIRK, DO YOURSELF A FAVOR..."

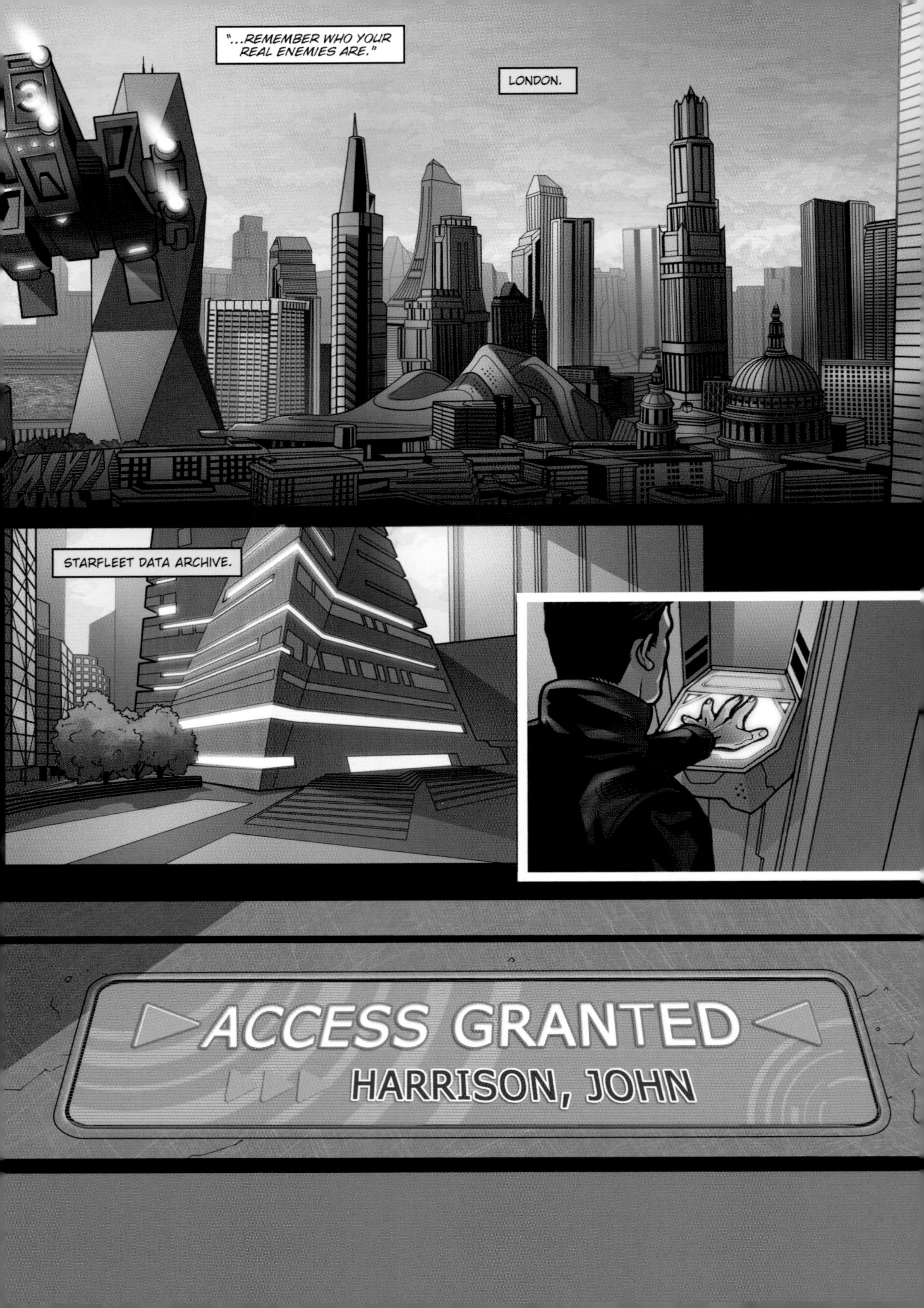
"...REMEMBER WHO YOUR REAL ENEMIES ARE."
LONDON.
STARFLEET DATA ARCHIVE.
ACCESS GRANTED
HARRISON, JOHN

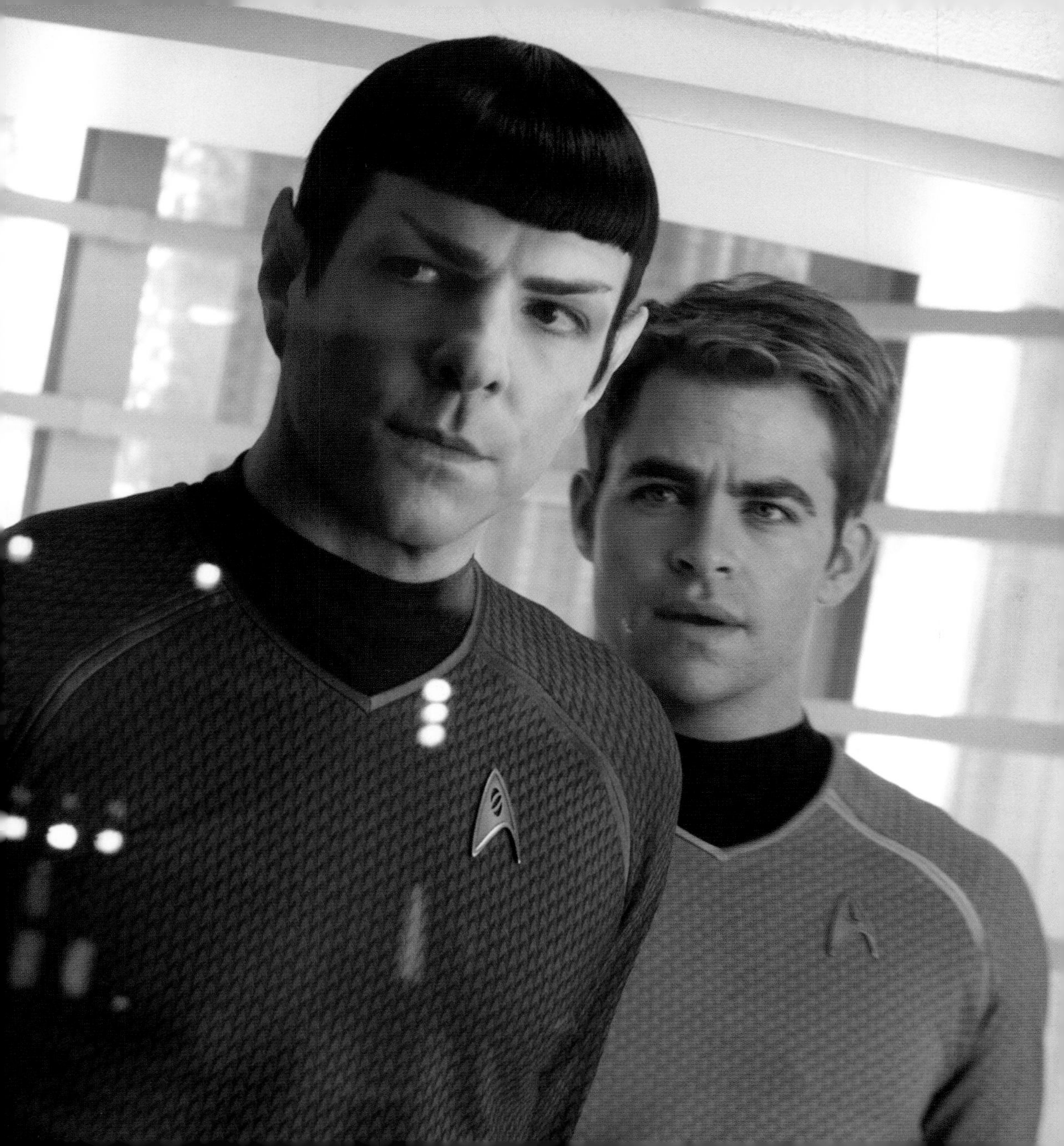

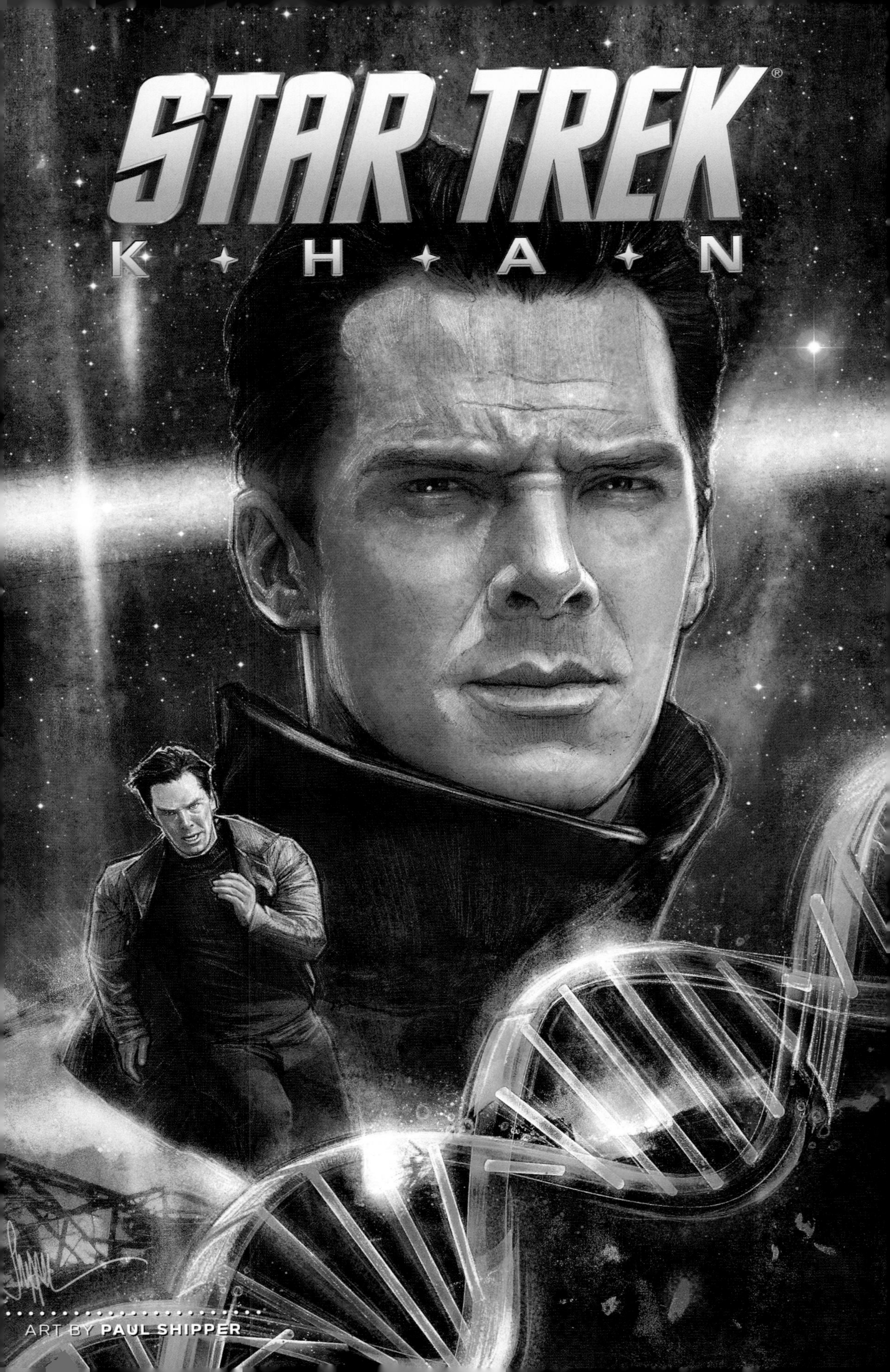
STAR TREK®
KHAN
ART BY PAUL SHIPPER

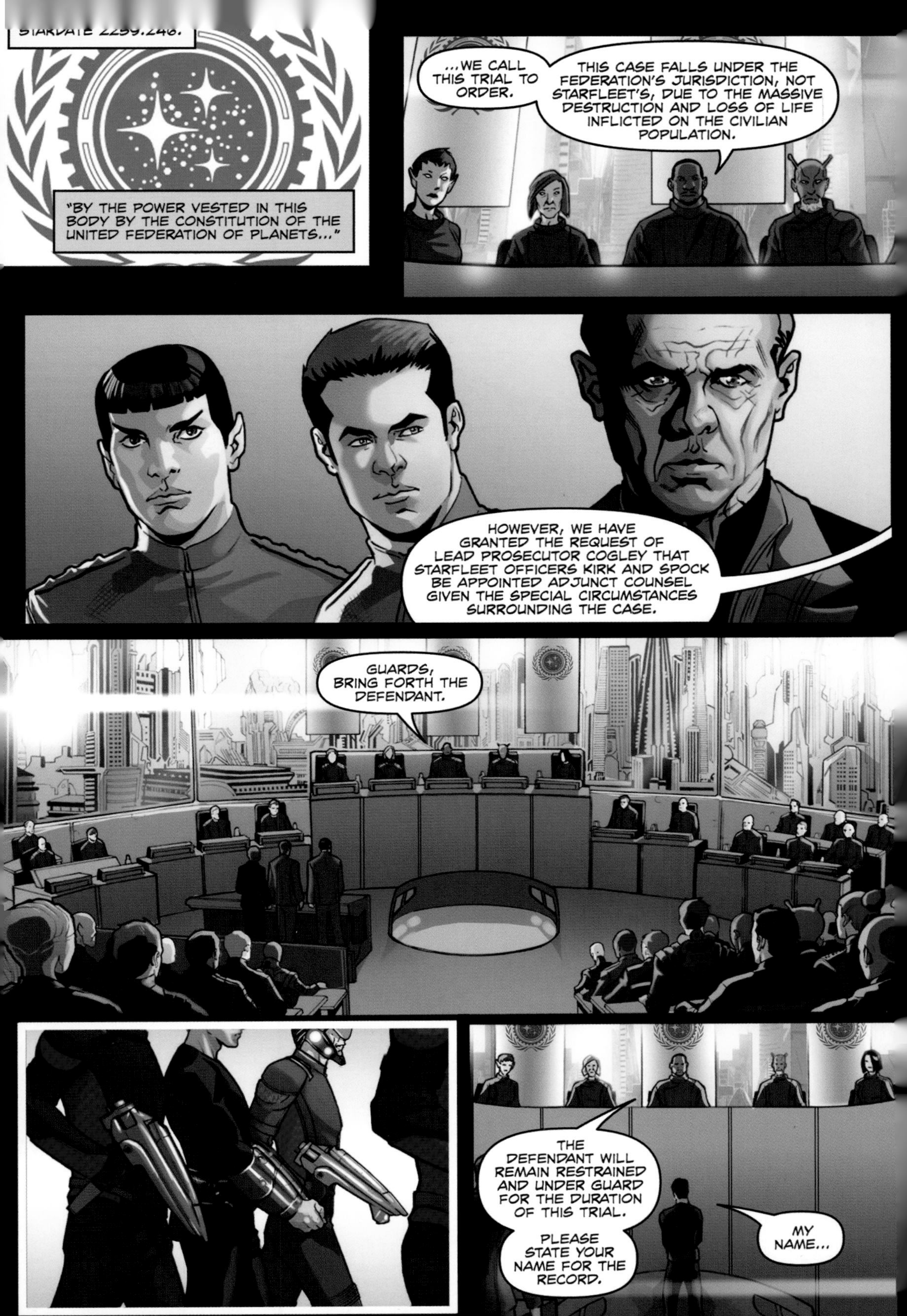
STARDATE 2259.246.
"BY THE POWER VESTED IN THIS BODY BY THE CONSTITUTION OF THE UNITED FEDERATION OF PLANETS..."
...WE CALL THIS TRIAL TO ORDER.
THIS CASE FALLS UNDER THE FEDERATION'S JURISDICTION, NOT STARFLEET'S, DUE TO THE MASSIVE DESTRUCTION AND LOSS OF LIFE INFLICTED ON THE CIVILIAN POPULATION.
HOWEVER, WE HAVE GRANTED THE REQUEST OF LEAD PROSECUTOR COGLEY THAT STARFLEET OFFICERS KIRK AND SPOCK BE APPOINTED ADJUNCT COUNSEL GIVEN THE SPECIAL CIRCUMSTANCES SURROUNDING THE CASE.
GUARDS, BRING FORTH THE DEFENDANT.
THE DEFENDANT WILL REMAIN RESTRAINED AND UNDER GUARD FOR THE DURATION OF THIS TRIAL.
PLEASE STATE YOUR NAME FOR THE RECORD.
MY NAME...

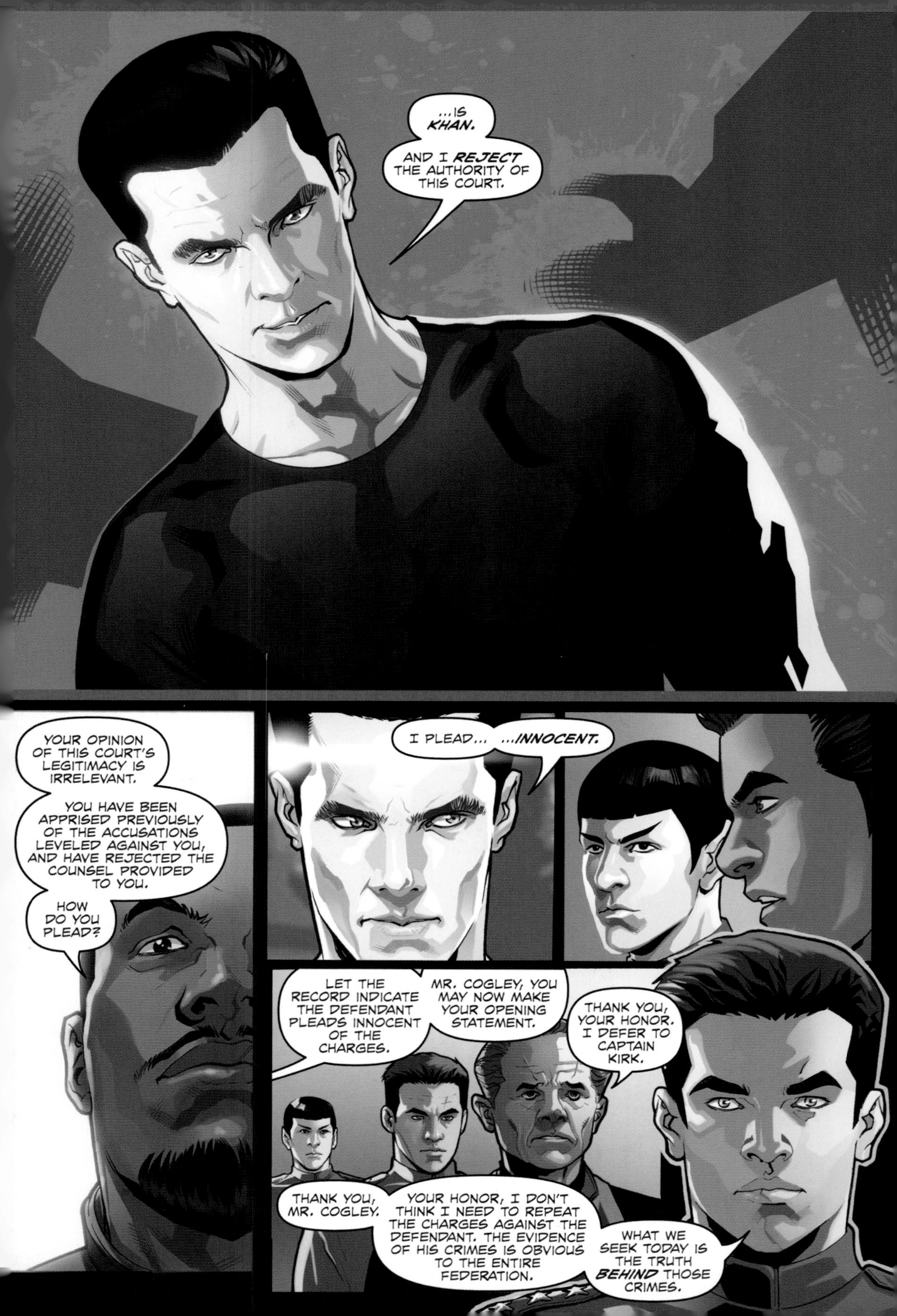
...IS KHAN.
AND I REJECT THE AUTHORITY OF THIS COURT.
YOUR OPINION OF THIS COURT'S LEGITIMACY IS IRRELEVANT.
YOU HAVE BEEN APPRISED PREVIOUSLY OF THE ACCUSATIONS LEVELED AGAINST YOU, AND HAVE REJECTED THE COUNSEL PROVIDED TO YOU.
HOW DO YOU PLEAD?
I PLEAD... ...INNOCENT.
LET THE RECORD INDICATE THE DEFENDANT PLEADS INNOCENT OF THE CHARGES.
MR. COGLEY, YOU MAY NOW MAKE YOUR OPENING STATEMENT.
THANK YOU, YOUR HONOR. I DEFER TO CAPTAIN KIRK.
THANK YOU, MR. COGLEY.
YOUR HONOR, I DON'T THINK I NEED TO REPEAT THE CHARGES AGAINST THE DEFENDANT. THE EVIDENCE OF HIS CRIMES IS OBVIOUS TO THE ENTIRE FEDERATION.
WHAT WE SEEK TODAY IS THE TRUTH BEHIND THOSE CRIMES.

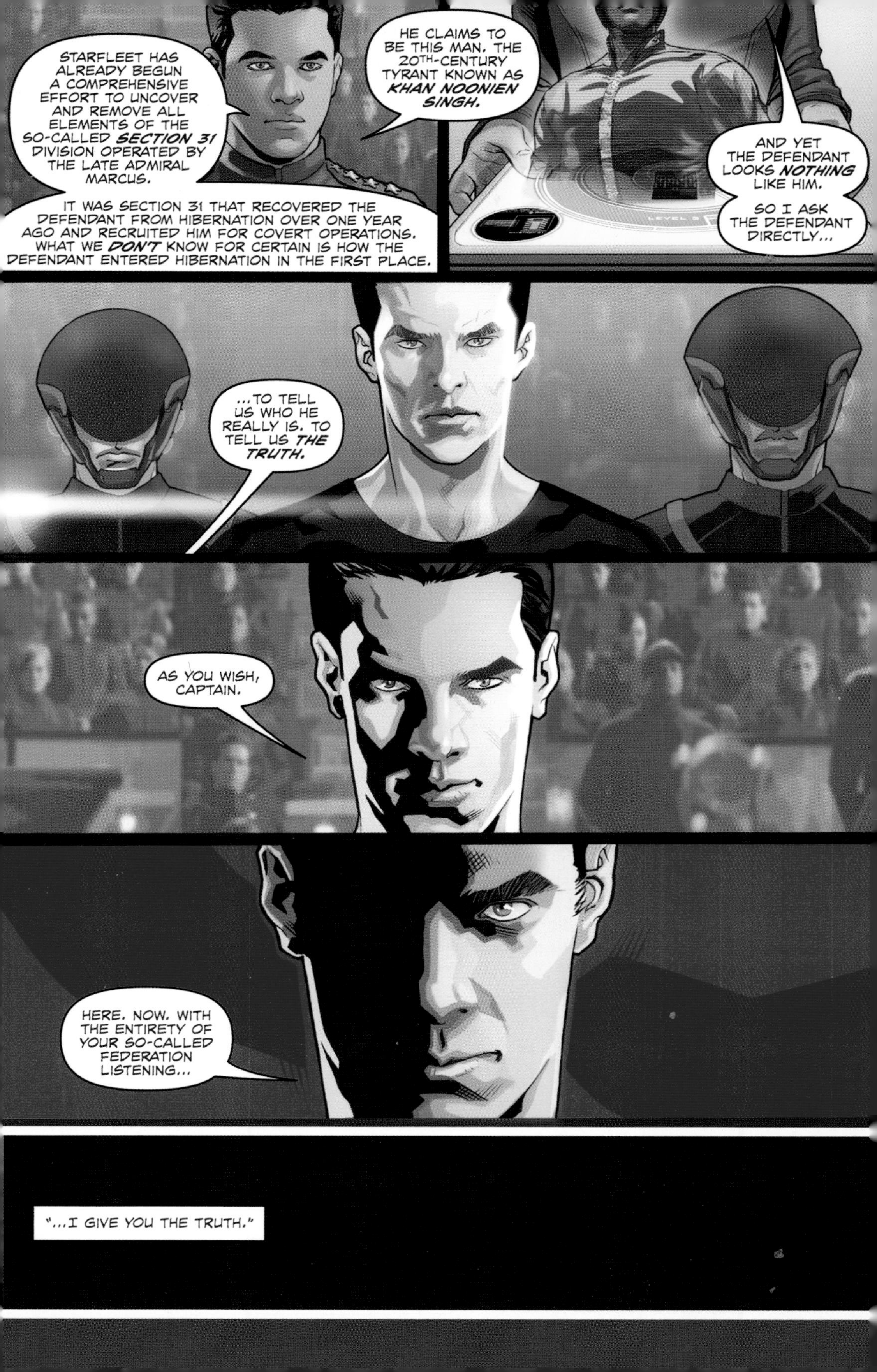
STARFLEET HAS ALREADY BEGUN A COMPREHENSIVE EFFORT TO UNCOVER AND REMOVE ALL ELEMENTS OF THE SO-CALLED SECTION 31 DIVISION OPERATED BY THE LATE ADMIRAL MARCUS.
IT WAS SECTION 31 THAT RECOVERED THE DEFENDANT FROM HIBERNATION OVER ONE YEAR AGO AND RECRUITED HIM FOR COVERT OPERATIONS. WHAT WE DON'T KNOW FOR CERTAIN IS HOW THE DEFENDANT ENTERED HIBERNATION IN THE FIRST PLACE.
HE CLAIMS TO BE THIS MAN. THE 20TH-CENTURY TYRANT KNOWN AS KHAN NOONIEN SINGH.
AND YET THE DEFENDANT LOOKS NOTHING LIKE HIM.
SO I ASK THE DEFENDANT DIRECTLY...
...TO TELL US WHO HE REALLY IS. TO TELL US THE TRUTH.
AS YOU WISH, CAPTAIN.
HERE. NOW. WITH THE ENTIRETY OF YOUR SO-CALLED FEDERATION LISTENING...
"...I GIVE YOU THE TRUTH."

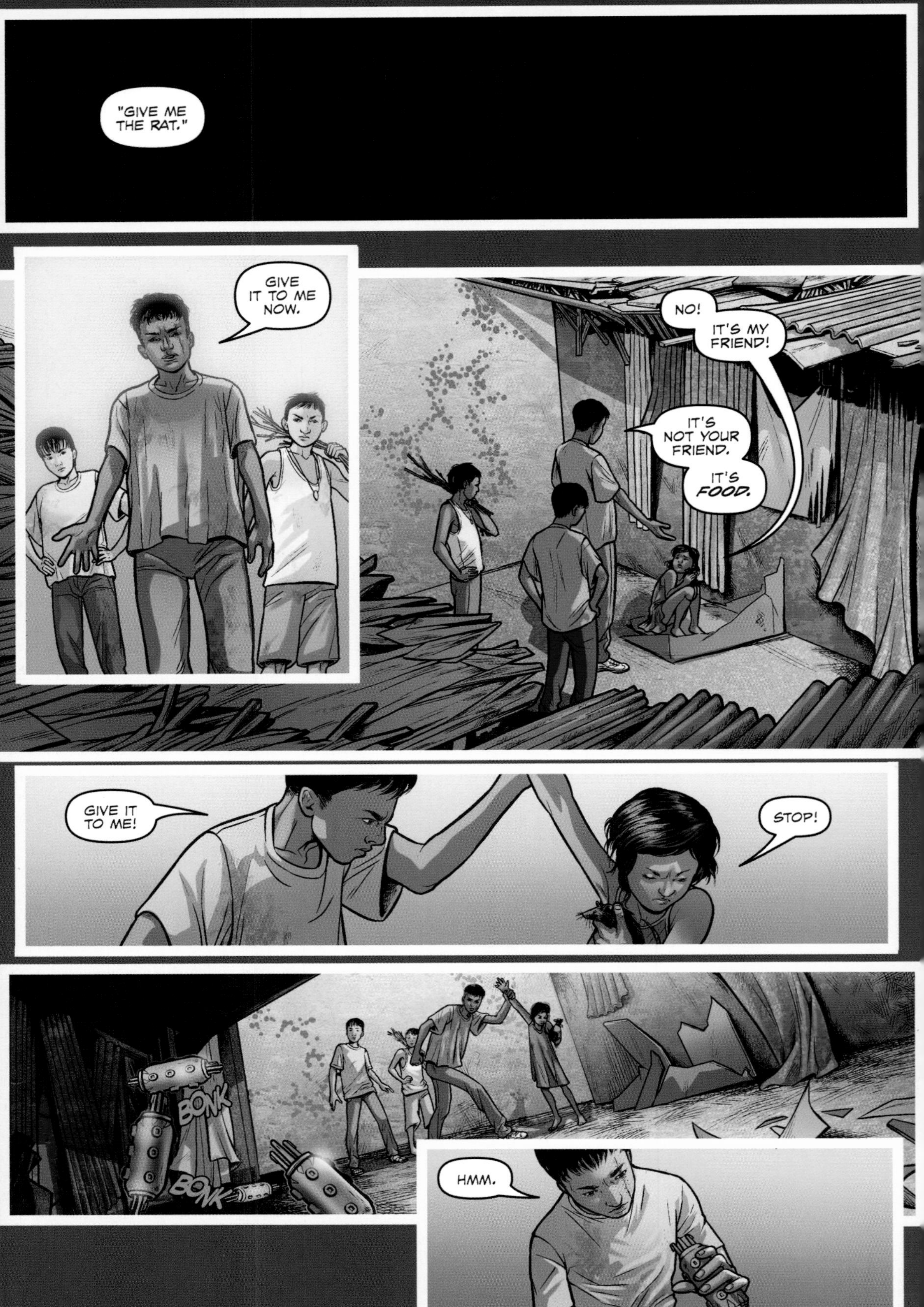
"GIVE ME THE RAT."
GIVE IT TO ME NOW.
NO!
IT'S MY FRIEND!
IT'S NOT YOUR FRIEND.
IT'S FOOD.
GIVE IT TO ME!
STOP!
BONK
BONK
HMM.

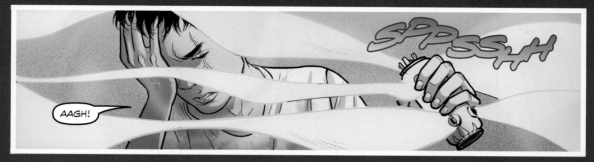

AAGH!

COUCH

COUCH

COUCH

SPPSSHH

NEW DELHI.

NOVEMBER, 1971.

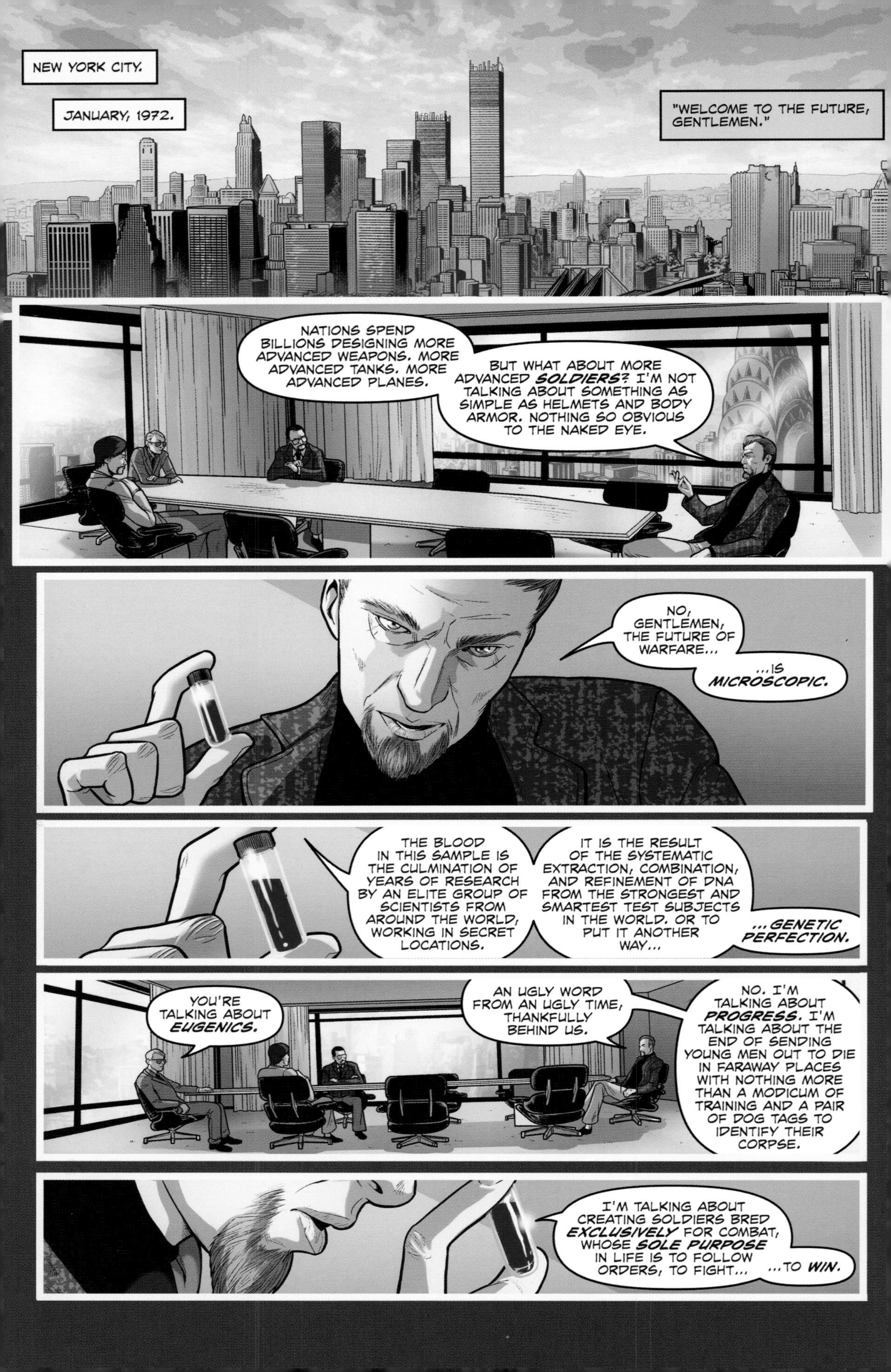
NEW YORK CITY.
JANUARY, 1972.
"WELCOME TO THE FUTURE, GENTLEMEN."
NATIONS SPEND BILLIONS DESIGNING MORE ADVANCED WEAPONS. MORE ADVANCED TANKS. MORE ADVANCED PLANES.
BUT WHAT ABOUT MORE ADVANCED SOLDIERS? I'M NOT TALKING ABOUT SOMETHING AS SIMPLE AS HELMETS AND BODY ARMOR. NOTHING SO OBVIOUS TO THE NAKED EYE.
NO, GENTLEMEN, THE FUTURE OF WARFARE...
...IS MICROSCOPIC.
THE BLOOD IN THIS SAMPLE IS THE CULMINATION OF YEARS OF RESEARCH BY AN ELITE GROUP OF SCIENTISTS FROM AROUND THE WORLD, WORKING IN SECRET LOCATIONS.
IT IS THE RESULT OF THE SYSTEMATIC EXTRACTION, COMBINATION, AND REFINEMENT OF DNA FROM THE STRONGEST AND SMARTEST TEST SUBJECTS IN THE WORLD. OR TO PUT IT ANOTHER WAY...
...GENETIC PERFECTION.
YOU'RE TALKING ABOUT EUGENICS.
AN UGLY WORD FROM AN UGLY TIME, THANKFULLY BEHIND US.
NO. I'M TALKING ABOUT PROGRESS. I'M TALKING ABOUT THE END OF SENDING YOUNG MEN OUT TO DIE IN FARAWAY PLACES WITH NOTHING MORE THAN A MODICUM OF TRAINING AND A PAIR OF DOG TAGS TO IDENTIFY THEIR CORPSE.
I'M TALKING ABOUT CREATING SOLDIERS BRED EXCLUSIVELY FOR COMBAT, WHOSE SOLE PURPOSE IN LIFE IS TO FOLLOW ORDERS, TO FIGHT...
...TO WIN.

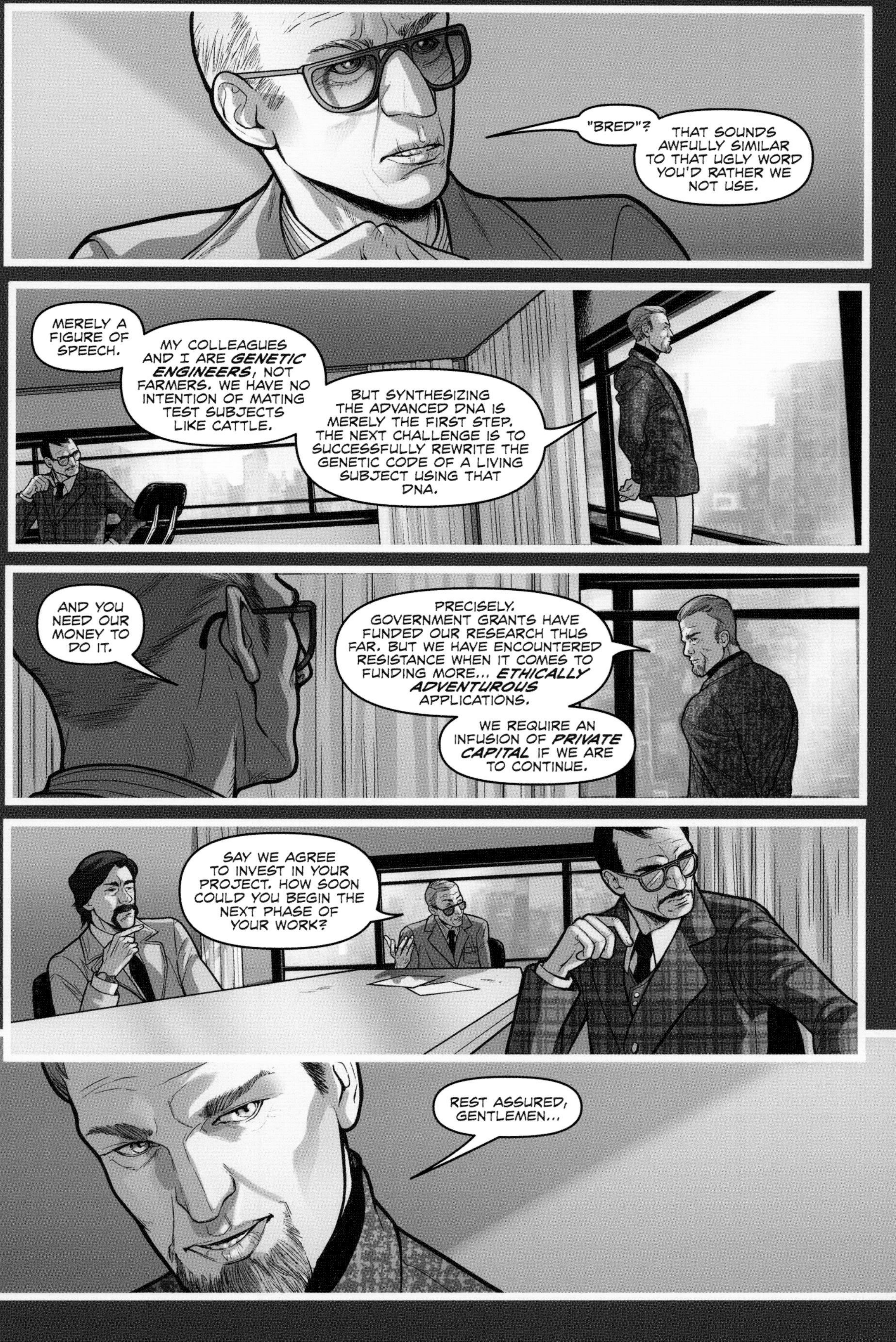
"BRED"? THAT SOUNDS AWFULLY SIMILAR TO THAT UGLY WORD YOU'D RATHER WE NOT USE.
MERELY A FIGURE OF SPEECH.
MY COLLEAGUES AND I ARE GENETIC ENGINEERS, NOT FARMERS. WE HAVE NO INTENTION OF MATING TEST SUBJECTS LIKE CATTLE.
BUT SYNTHESIZING THE ADVANCED DNA IS MERELY THE FIRST STEP. THE NEXT CHALLENGE IS TO SUCCESSFULLY REWRITE THE GENETIC CODE OF A LIVING SUBJECT USING THAT DNA.
AND YOU NEED OUR MONEY TO DO IT.
PRECISELY. GOVERNMENT GRANTS HAVE FUNDED OUR RESEARCH THUS FAR. BUT WE HAVE ENCOUNTERED RESISTANCE WHEN IT COMES TO FUNDING MORE... ETHICALLY ADVENTUROUS APPLICATIONS.
WE REQUIRE AN INFUSION OF PRIVATE CAPITAL IF WE ARE TO CONTINUE.
SAY WE AGREE TO INVEST IN YOUR PROJECT. HOW SOON COULD YOU BEGIN THE NEXT PHASE OF YOUR WORK?
REST ASSURED, GENTLEMEN...

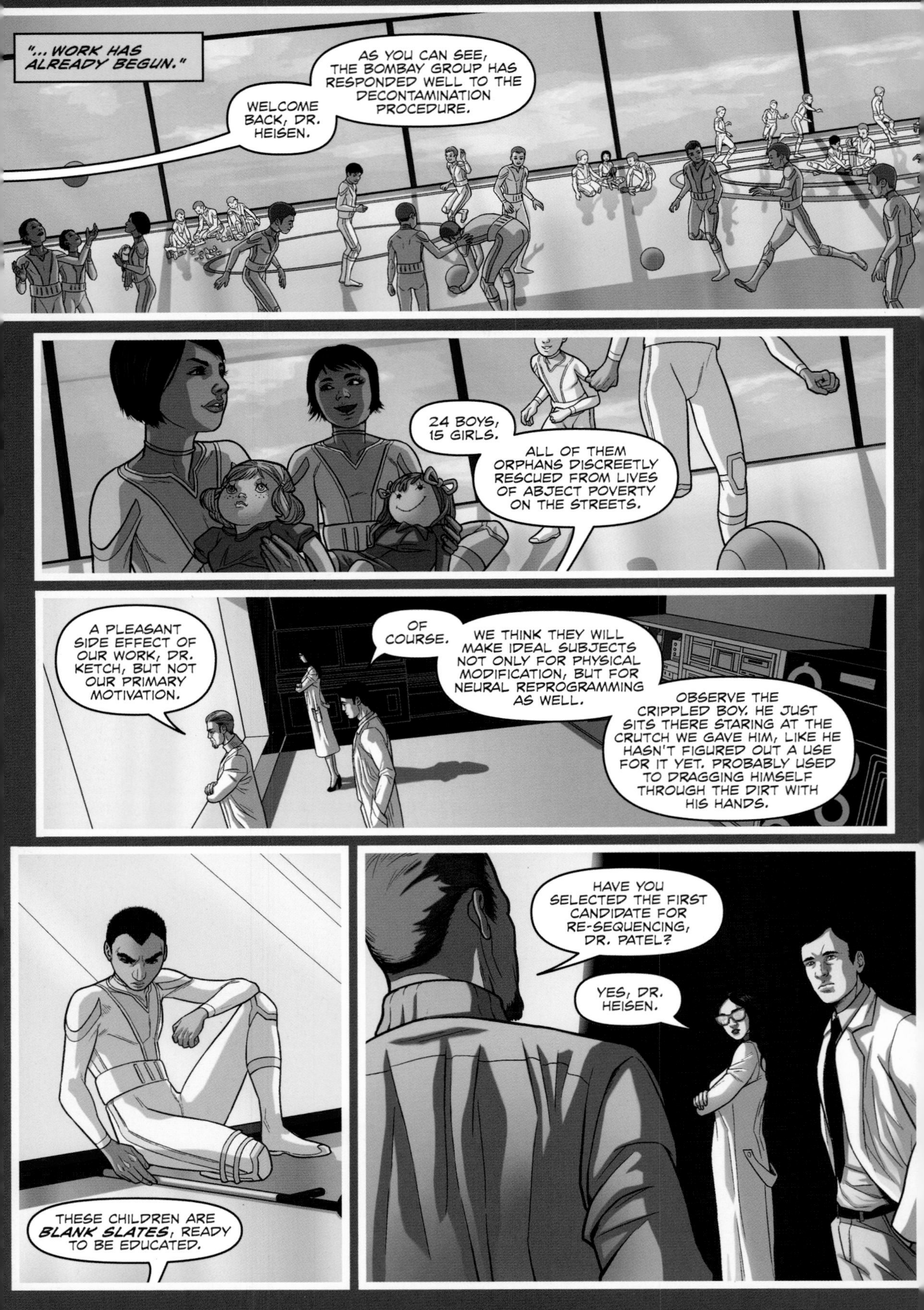
"...WORK HAS ALREADY BEGUN."
WELCOME BACK, DR. HEISEN.
AS YOU CAN SEE, THE BOMBAY GROUP HAS RESPONDED WELL TO THE DECONTAMINATION PROCEDURE.
24 BOYS, 15 GIRLS.
ALL OF THEM ORPHANS DISCREETLY RESCUED FROM LIVES OF ABJECT POVERTY ON THE STREETS.
A PLEASANT SIDE EFFECT OF OUR WORK, DR. KETCH, BUT NOT OUR PRIMARY MOTIVATION.
OF COURSE.
WE THINK THEY WILL MAKE IDEAL SUBJECTS NOT ONLY FOR PHYSICAL MODIFICATION, BUT FOR NEURAL REPROGRAMMING AS WELL.
OBSERVE THE CRIPPLED BOY. HE JUST SITS THERE STARING AT THE CRUTCH WE GAVE HIM, LIKE HE HASN'T FIGURED OUT A USE FOR IT YET. PROBABLY USED TO DRAGGING HIMSELF THROUGH THE DIRT WITH HIS HANDS.
THESE CHILDREN ARE *BLANK SLATES*, READY TO BE EDUCATED.
HAVE YOU SELECTED THE FIRST CANDIDATE FOR RE-SEQUENCING, DR. PATEL?
YES, DR. HEISEN.

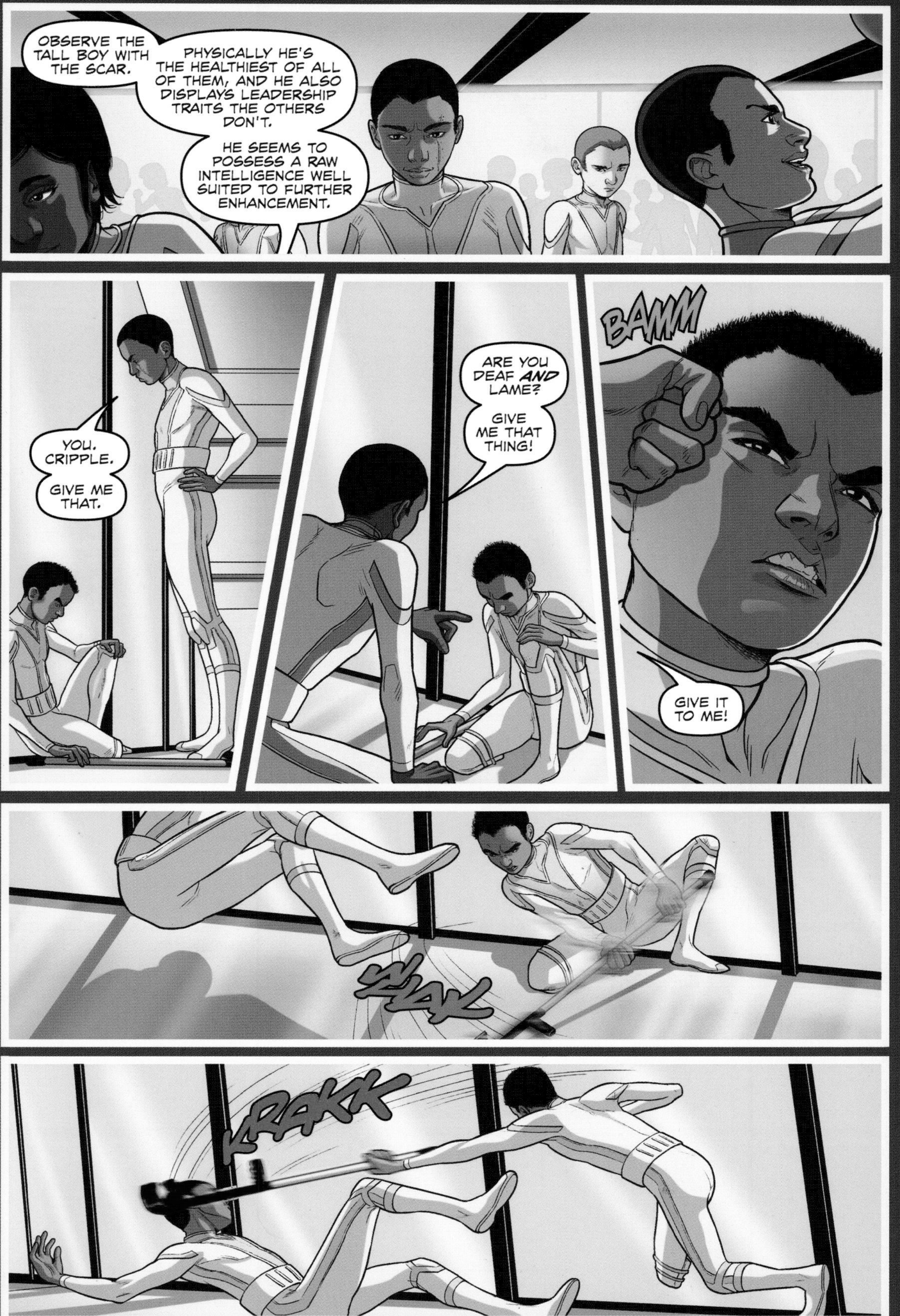
OBSERVE THE TALL BOY WITH THE SCAR.
PHYSICALLY HE'S THE HEALTHIEST OF ALL OF THEM, AND HE ALSO DISPLAYS LEADERSHIP TRAITS THE OTHERS DON'T.
HE SEEMS TO POSSESS A RAW INTELLIGENCE WELL SUITED TO FURTHER ENHANCEMENT.
YOU. CRIPPLE.
GIVE ME THAT.
ARE YOU DEAF AND LAME?
GIVE ME THAT THING!
BAMM
GIVE IT TO ME!
WHAK
KRAKK

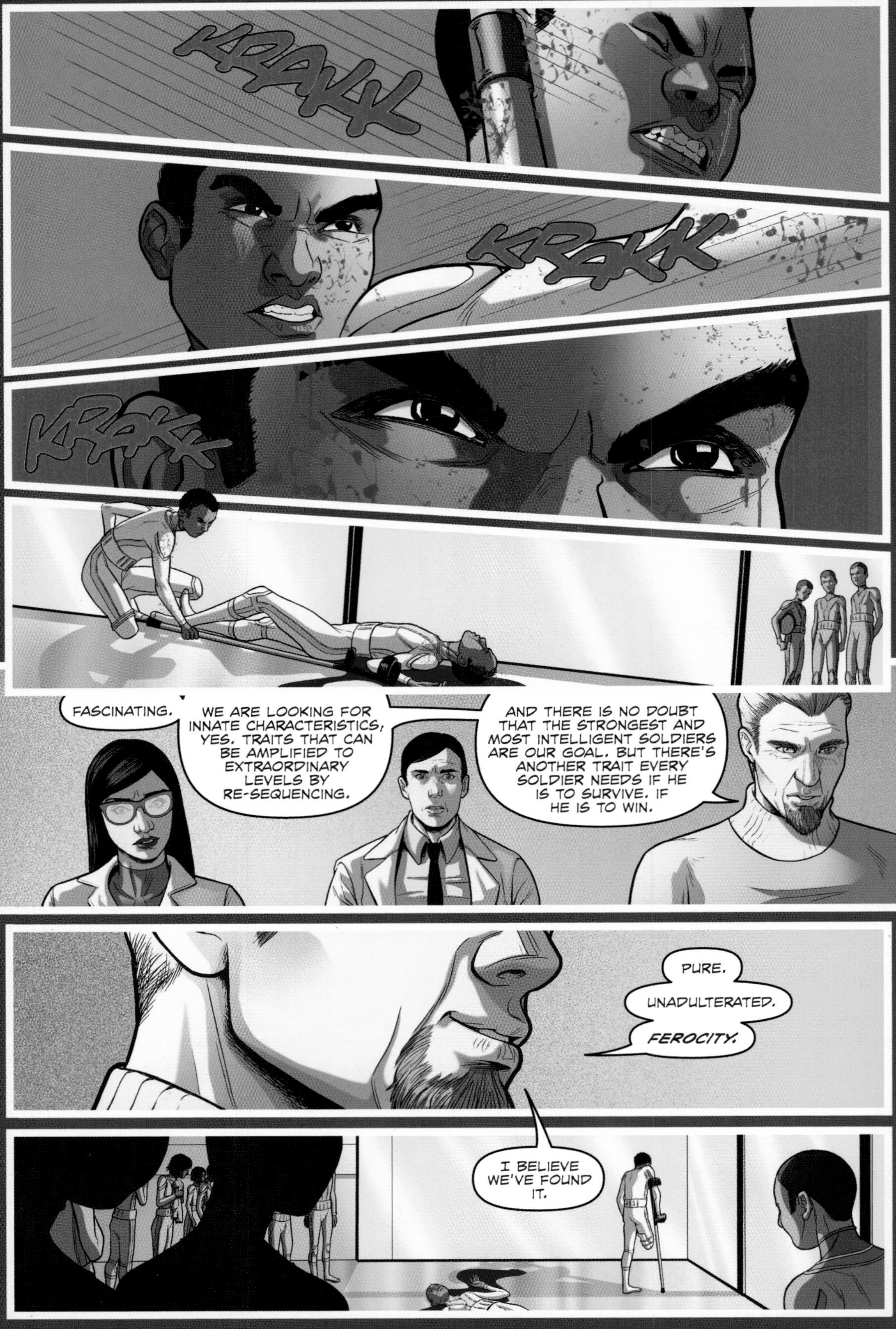
KRAKK
KRAKK
KRAKK
FASCINATING.
WE ARE LOOKING FOR INNATE CHARACTERISTICS, YES. TRAITS THAT CAN BE AMPLIFIED TO EXTRAORDINARY LEVELS BY RE-SEQUENCING.
AND THERE IS NO DOUBT THAT THE STRONGEST AND MOST INTELLIGENT SOLDIERS ARE OUR GOAL. BUT THERE'S ANOTHER TRAIT EVERY SOLDIER NEEDS IF HE IS TO SURVIVE. IF HE IS TO WIN.
PURE.
UNADULTERATED.
FEROCITY.
I BELIEVE WE'VE FOUND IT.

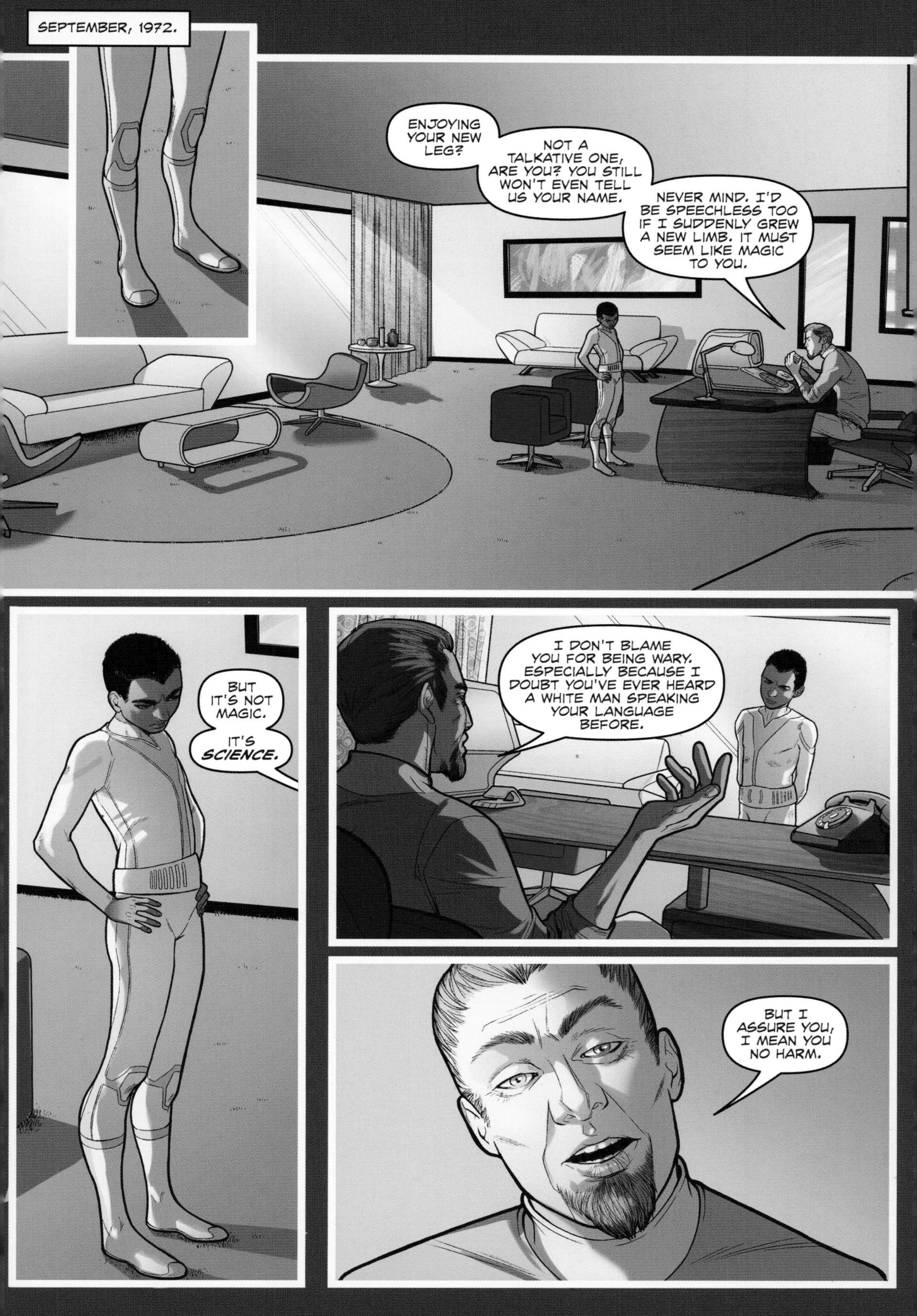
SEPTEMBER, 1972.
ENJOYING YOUR NEW LEG?
NOT A TALKATIVE ONE, ARE YOU? YOU STILL WON'T EVEN TELL US YOUR NAME.
NEVER MIND. I'D BE SPEECHLESS TOO IF I SUDDENLY GREW A NEW LIMB. IT MUST SEEM LIKE MAGIC TO YOU.
BUT IT'S NOT MAGIC.
IT'S *SCIENCE.*
I DON'T BLAME YOU FOR BEING WARY. ESPECIALLY BECAUSE I DOUBT YOU'VE EVER HEARD A WHITE MAN SPEAKING YOUR LANGUAGE BEFORE.
BUT I ASSURE YOU, I MEAN YOU NO HARM.

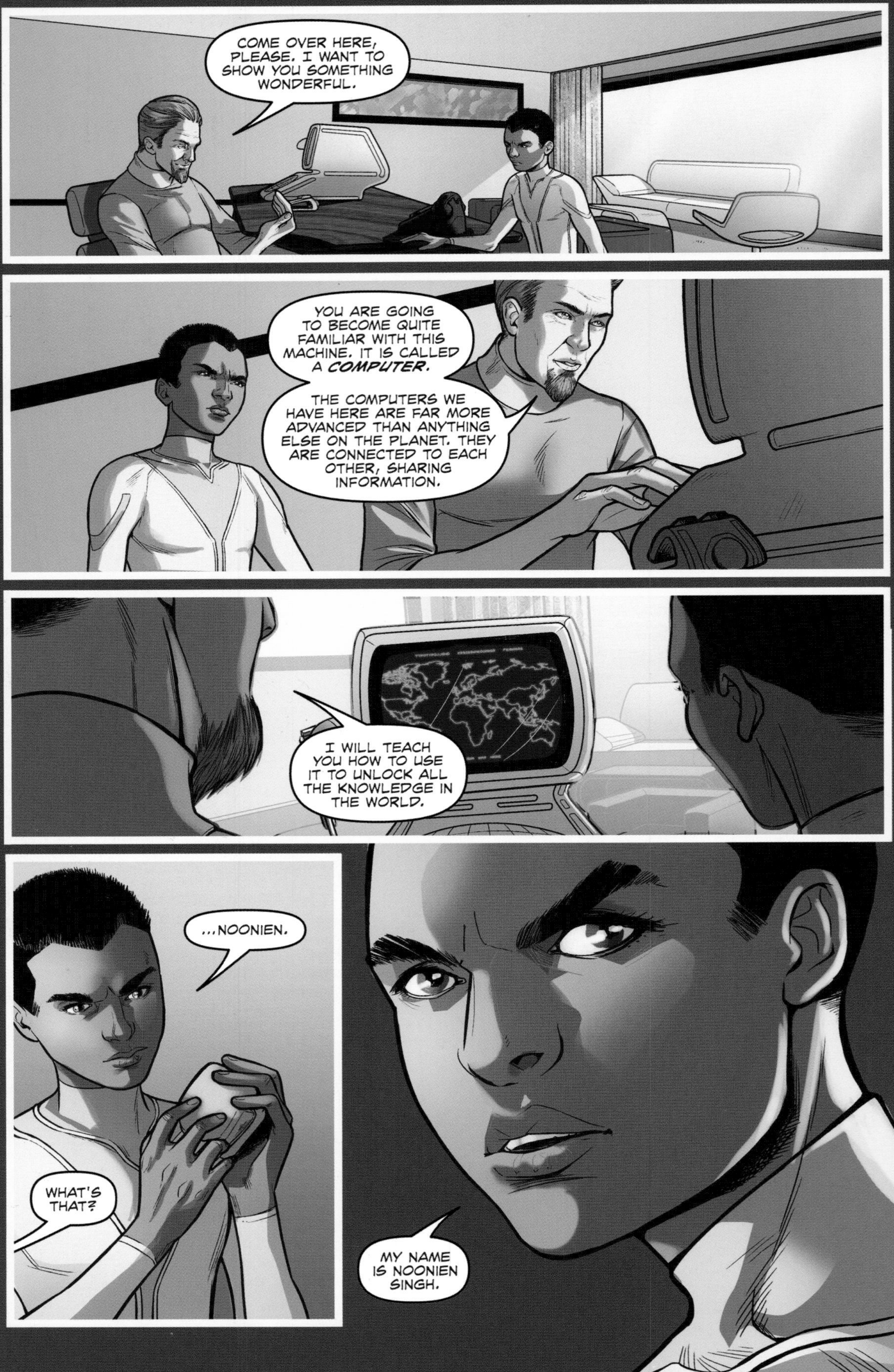
COME OVER HERE, PLEASE. I WANT TO SHOW YOU SOMETHING WONDERFUL.
YOU ARE GOING TO BECOME QUITE FAMILIAR WITH THIS MACHINE. IT IS CALLED A *COMPUTER*.
THE COMPUTERS WE HAVE HERE ARE FAR MORE ADVANCED THAN ANYTHING ELSE ON THE PLANET. THEY ARE CONNECTED TO EACH OTHER, SHARING INFORMATION.
I WILL TEACH YOU HOW TO USE IT TO UNLOCK ALL THE KNOWLEDGE IN THE WORLD.
WHAT'S THAT?
...NOONIEN.
MY NAME IS NOONIEN SINGH.

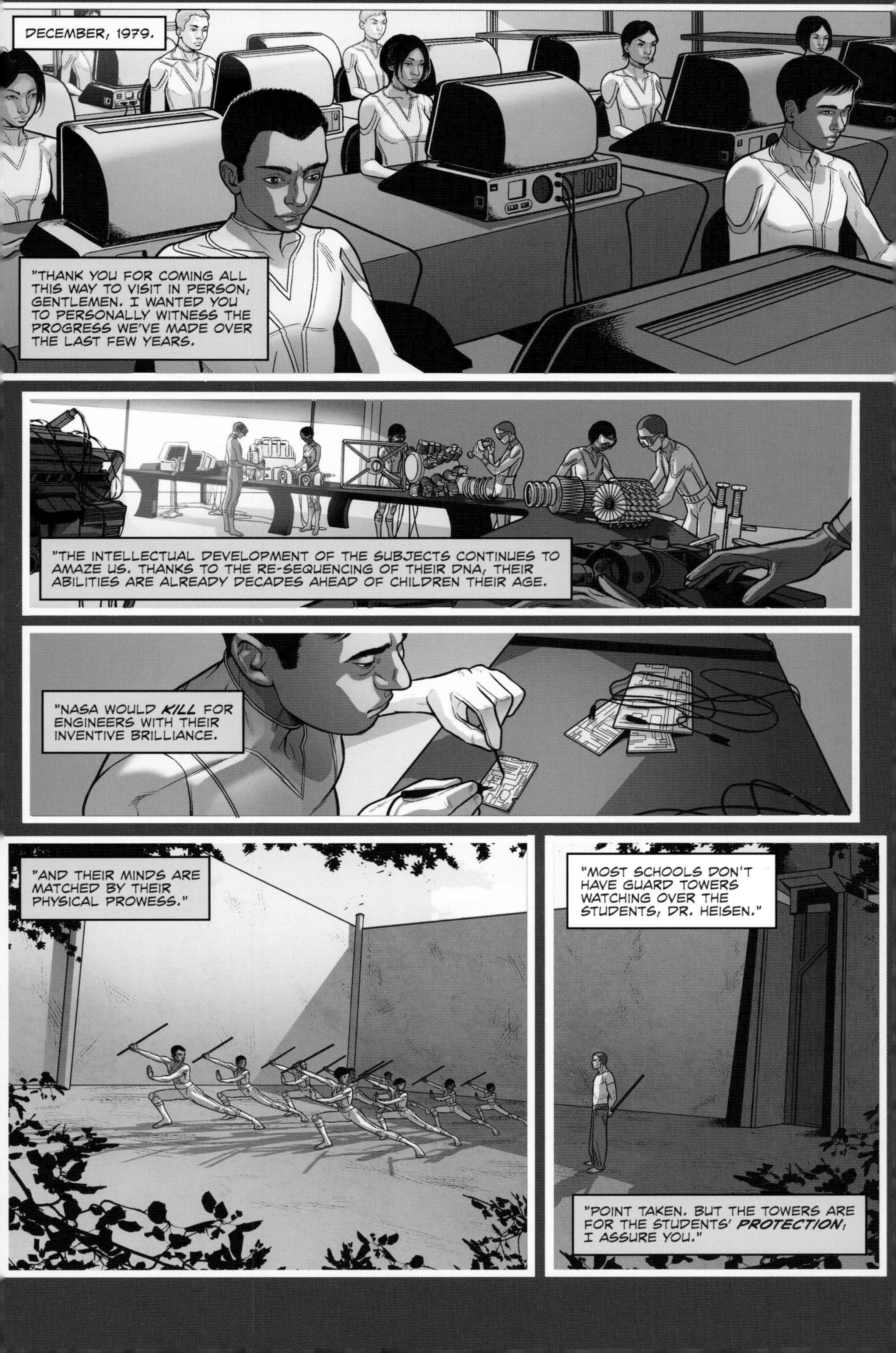
DECEMBER, 1979.
"THANK YOU FOR COMING ALL THIS WAY TO VISIT IN PERSON, GENTLEMEN. I WANTED YOU TO PERSONALLY WITNESS THE PROGRESS WE'VE MADE OVER THE LAST FEW YEARS.
"THE INTELLECTUAL DEVELOPMENT OF THE SUBJECTS CONTINUES TO AMAZE US. THANKS TO THE RE-SEQUENCING OF THEIR DNA, THEIR ABILITIES ARE ALREADY DECADES AHEAD OF CHILDREN THEIR AGE.
"NASA WOULD *KILL* FOR ENGINEERS WITH THEIR INVENTIVE BRILLIANCE.
"AND THEIR MINDS ARE MATCHED BY THEIR PHYSICAL PROWESS."
"MOST SCHOOLS DON'T HAVE GUARD TOWERS WATCHING OVER THE STUDENTS, DR. HEISEN."
"POINT TAKEN. BUT THE TOWERS ARE FOR THE STUDENTS' *PROTECTION*, I ASSURE YOU."

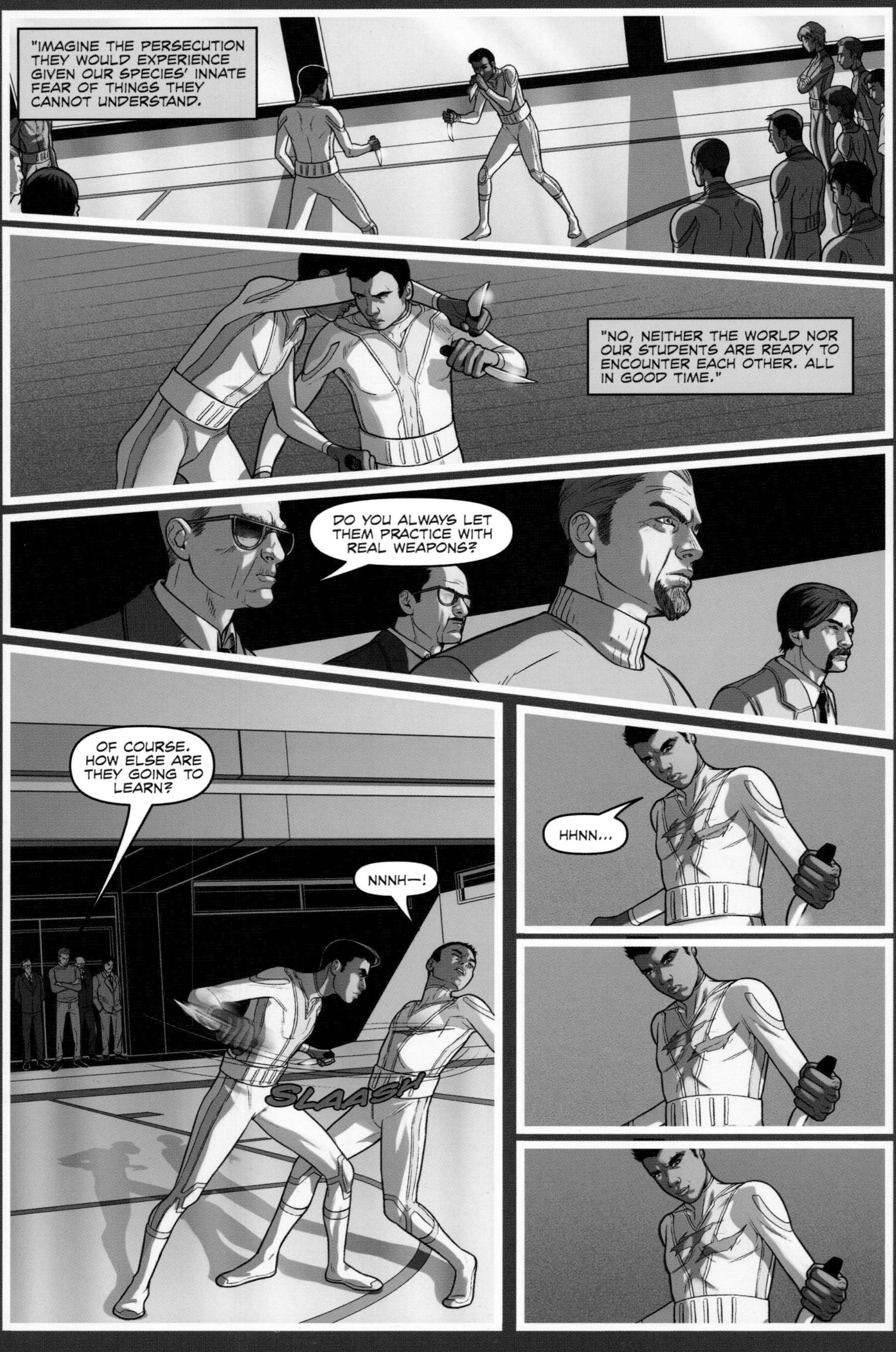
"IMAGINE THE PERSECUTION THEY WOULD EXPERIENCE GIVEN OUR SPECIES' INNATE FEAR OF THINGS THEY CANNOT UNDERSTAND.
"NO, NEITHER THE WORLD NOR OUR STUDENTS ARE READY TO ENCOUNTER EACH OTHER. ALL IN GOOD TIME."
DO YOU ALWAYS LET THEM PRACTICE WITH REAL WEAPONS?
OF COURSE. HOW ELSE ARE THEY GOING TO LEARN?
NNNH—!
SLAASH
HHNN...

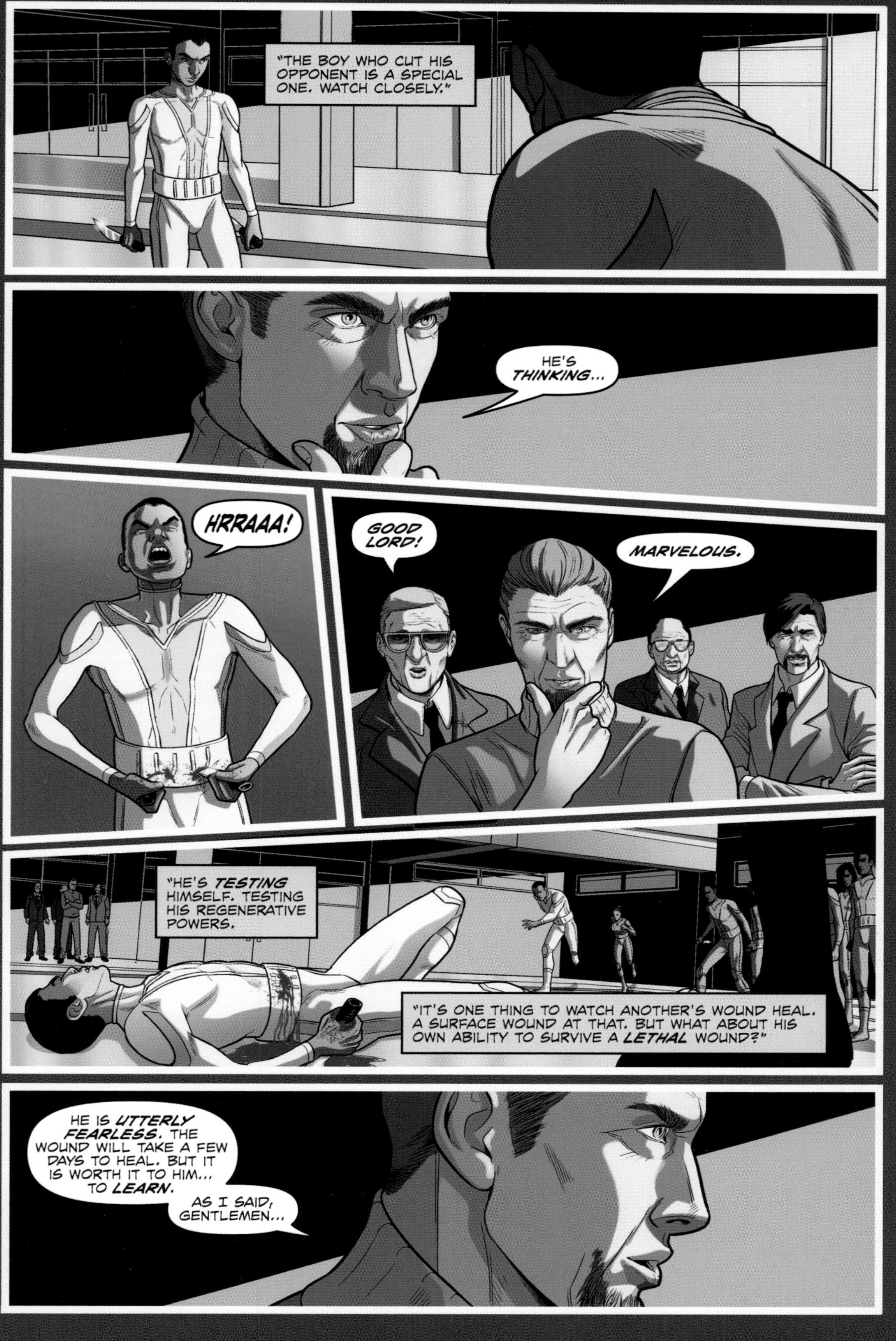
"THE BOY WHO CUT HIS OPPONENT IS A SPECIAL ONE. WATCH CLOSELY."
HE'S *THINKING*...
HRRAAA!
GOOD LORD!
MARVELOUS.
"HE'S *TESTING* HIMSELF. TESTING HIS REGENERATIVE POWERS.
"IT'S ONE THING TO WATCH ANOTHER'S WOUND HEAL. A SURFACE WOUND AT THAT. BUT WHAT ABOUT HIS OWN ABILITY TO SURVIVE A *LETHAL* WOUND?"
HE IS *UTTERLY FEARLESS*. THE WOUND WILL TAKE A FEW DAYS TO HEAL. BUT IT IS WORTH IT TO HIM... TO *LEARN*.
AS I SAID, GENTLEMEN...

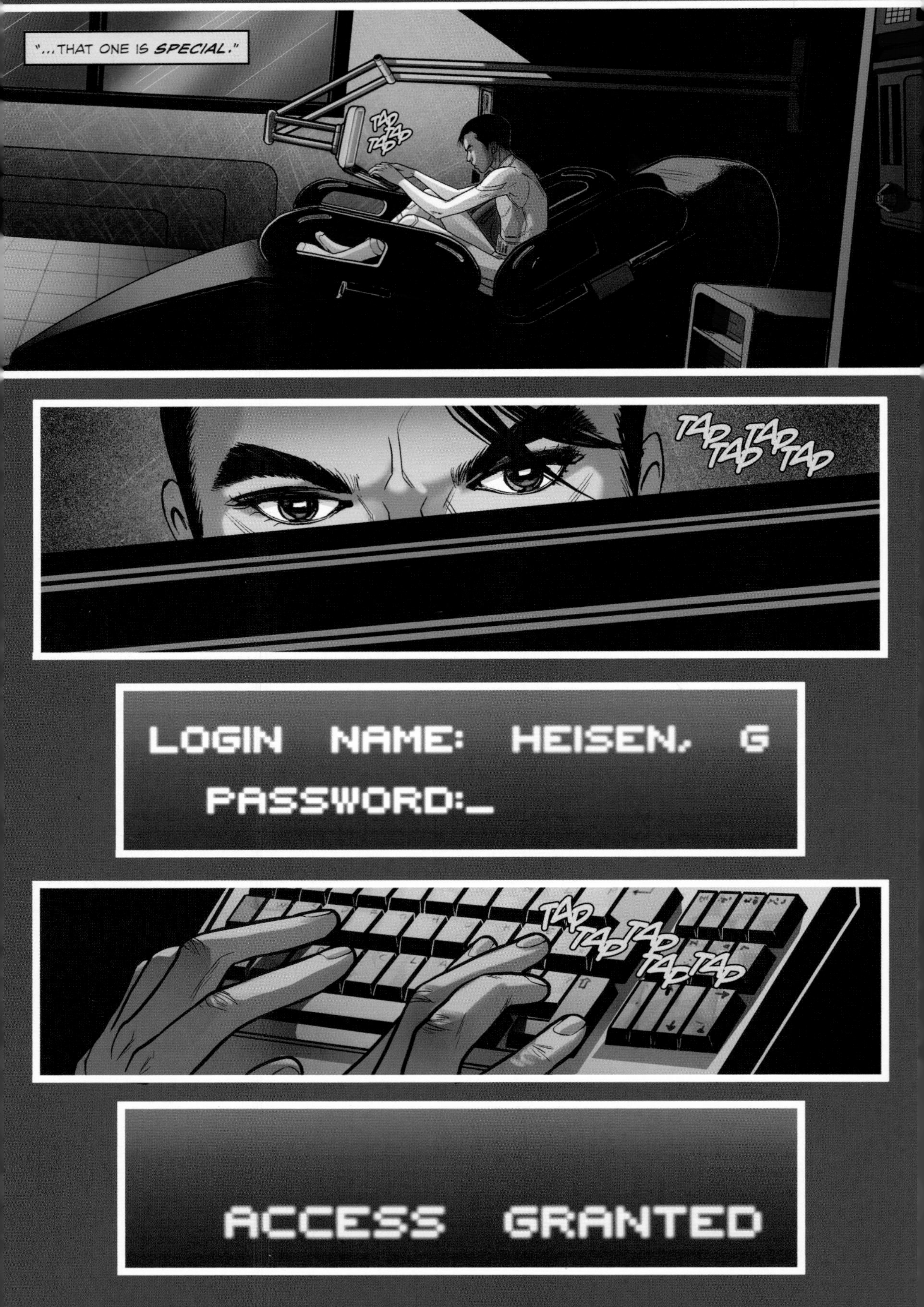

"...THAT ONE IS *SPECIAL.*"
TAP TAP TAP
TAP TAP TAP TAP
LOGIN NAME: HEISEN, G
PASSWORD:_
TAP TAP TAP TAP TAP
ACCESS GRANTED

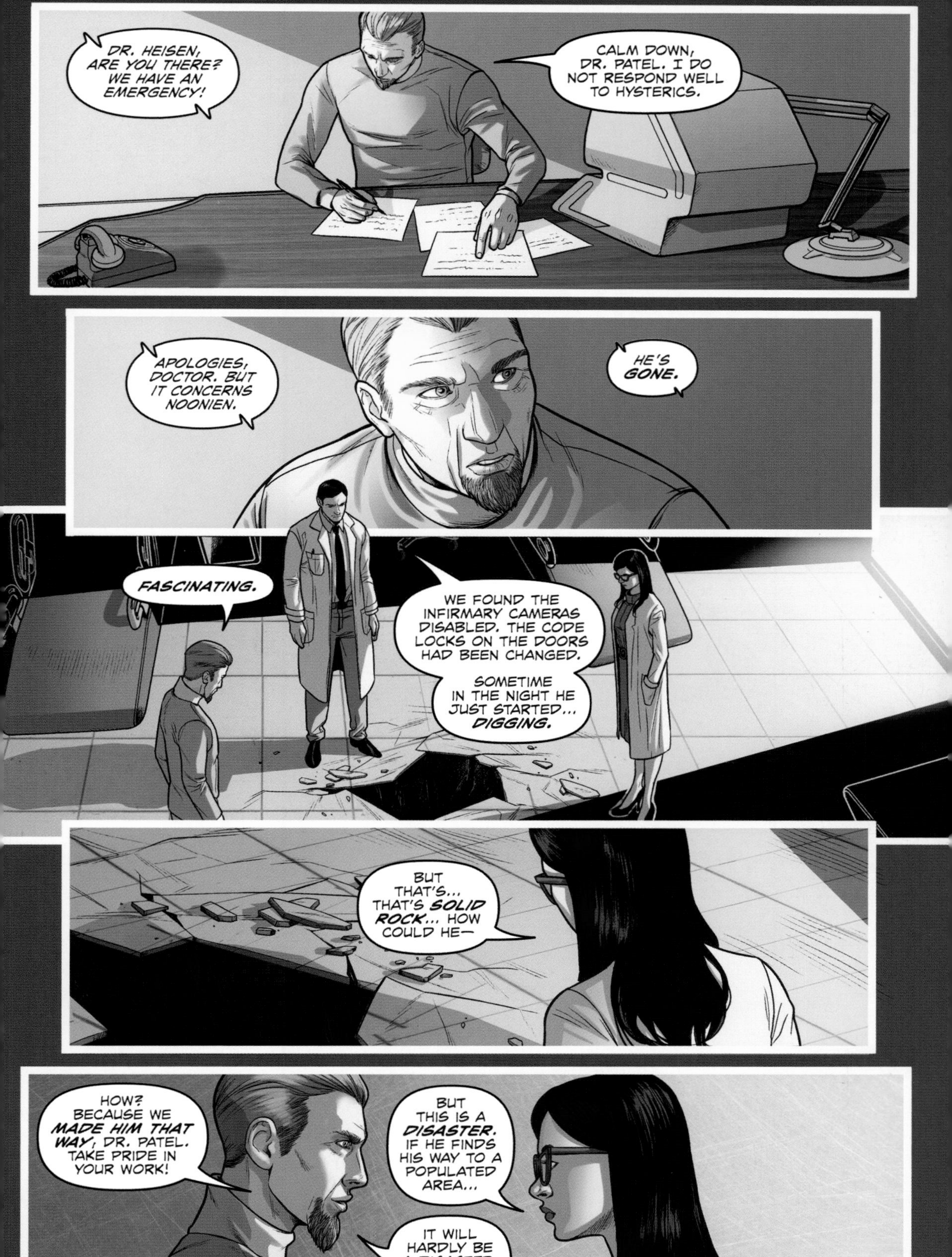

DR. HEISEN, ARE YOU THERE? WE HAVE AN EMERGENCY!
CALM DOWN, DR. PATEL. I DO NOT RESPOND WELL TO HYSTERICS.
APOLOGIES, DOCTOR. BUT IT CONCERNS NOONIEN.
HE'S **GONE.**
FASCINATING.
WE FOUND THE INFIRMARY CAMERAS DISABLED. THE CODE LOCKS ON THE DOORS HAD BEEN CHANGED.
SOMETIME IN THE NIGHT HE JUST STARTED... **DIGGING.**
BUT THAT'S... THAT'S **SOLID ROCK**... HOW COULD HE—
HOW? BECAUSE WE **MADE HIM THAT WAY**, DR. PATEL. TAKE PRIDE IN YOUR WORK!
BUT THIS IS A **DISASTER.** IF HE FINDS HIS WAY TO A POPULATED AREA...
IT WILL HARDLY BE A DISASTER. DON'T YOU SEE?

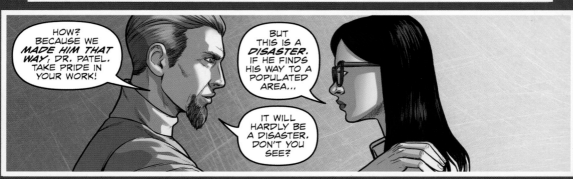

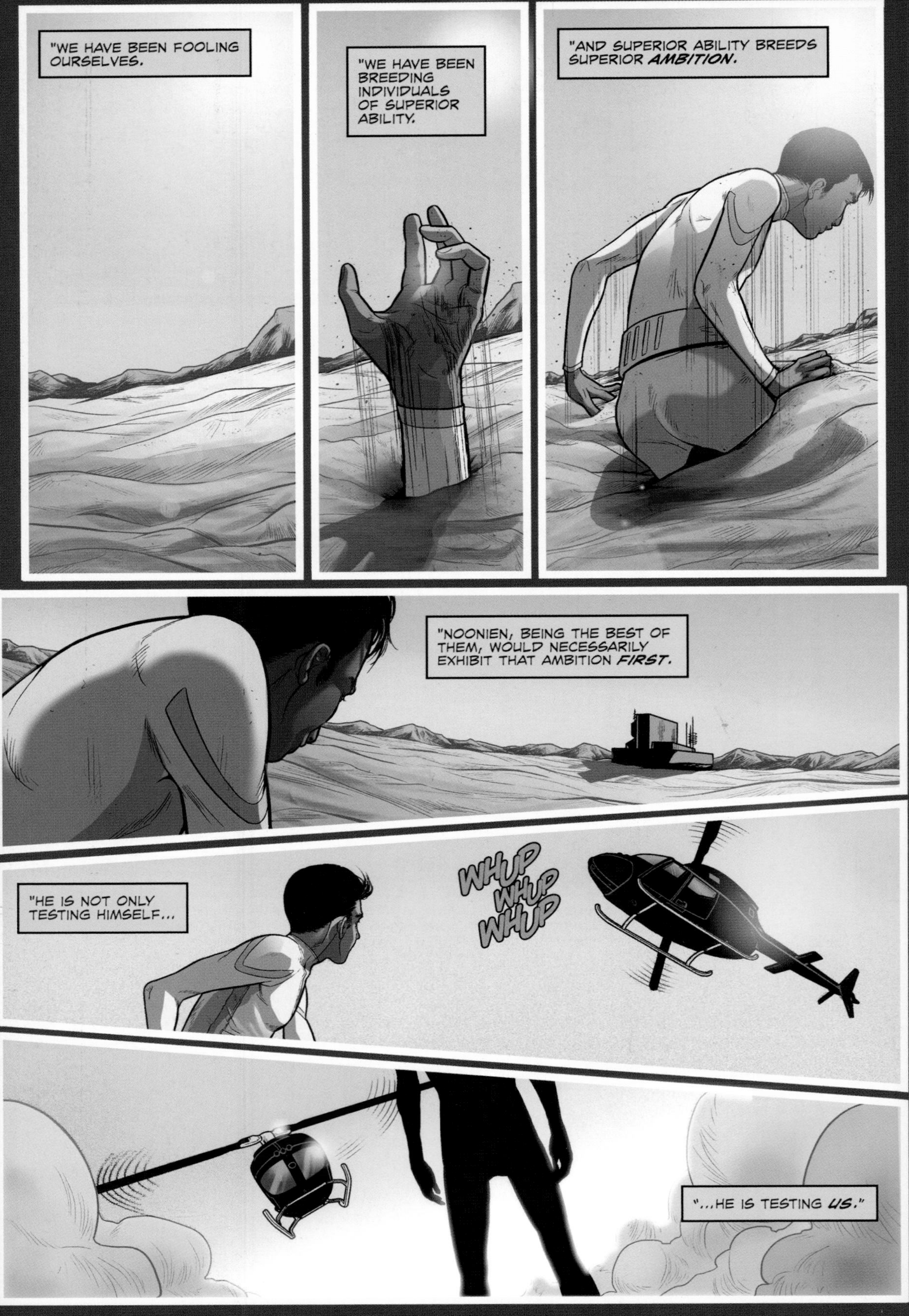
"WE HAVE BEEN FOOLING OURSELVES.
"WE HAVE BEEN BREEDING INDIVIDUALS OF SUPERIOR ABILITY.
"AND SUPERIOR ABILITY BREEDS SUPERIOR AMBITION.
"NOONIEN, BEING THE BEST OF THEM, WOULD NECESSARILY EXHIBIT THAT AMBITION FIRST.
"HE IS NOT ONLY TESTING HIMSELF...
WHUP WHUP WHUP
"...HE IS TESTING US."

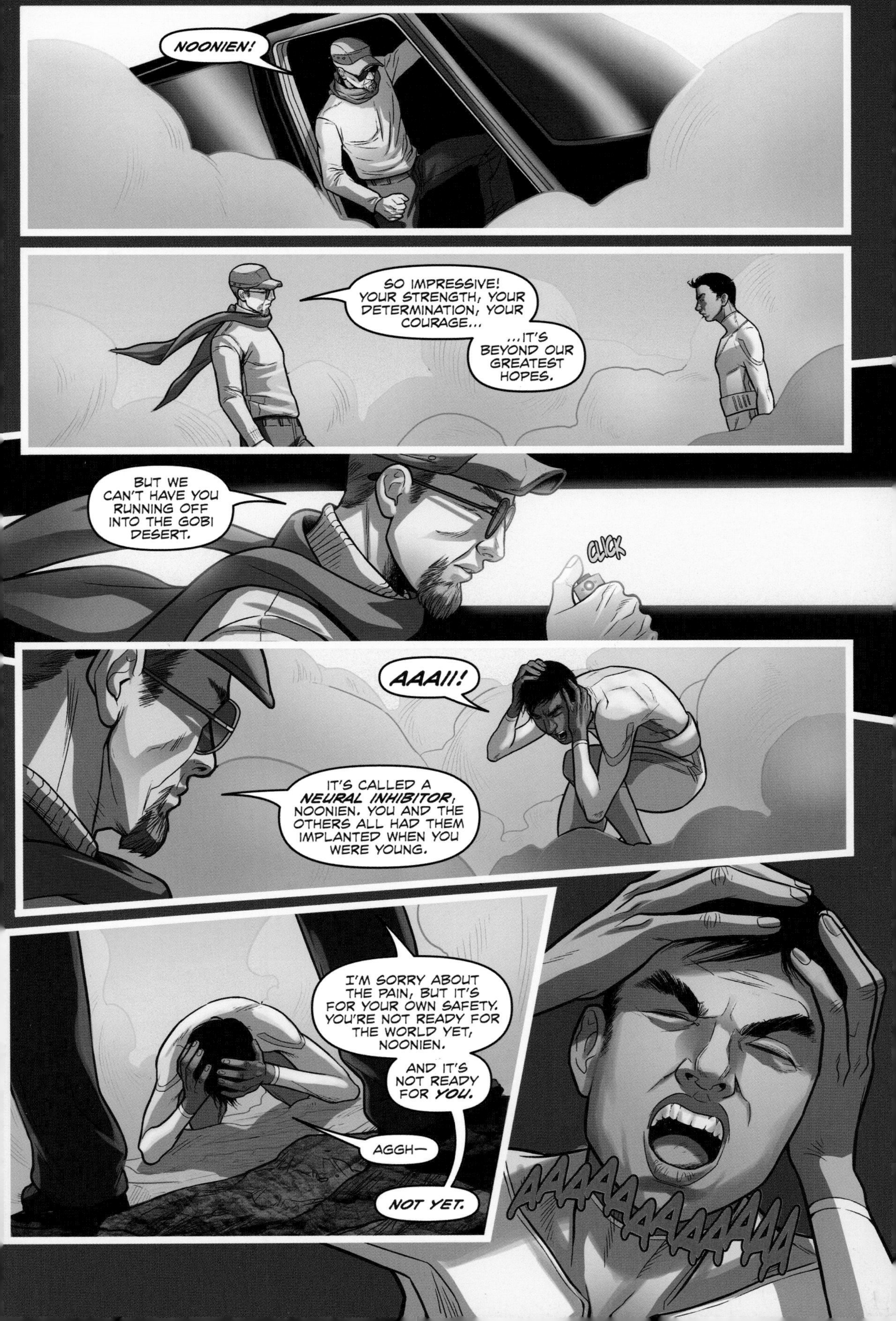
NOONIEN!
SO IMPRESSIVE! YOUR STRENGTH, YOUR DETERMINATION, YOUR COURAGE...
...IT'S BEYOND OUR GREATEST HOPES.
BUT WE CAN'T HAVE YOU RUNNING OFF INTO THE GOBI DESERT.
CLICK
AAAII!
IT'S CALLED A NEURAL INHIBITOR, NOONIEN. YOU AND THE OTHERS ALL HAD THEM IMPLANTED WHEN YOU WERE YOUNG.
I'M SORRY ABOUT THE PAIN, BUT IT'S FOR YOUR OWN SAFETY. YOU'RE NOT READY FOR THE WORLD YET, NOONIEN.
AND IT'S NOT READY FOR YOU.
AGGH—
NOT YET.
AAAAAAAAAAAAAA

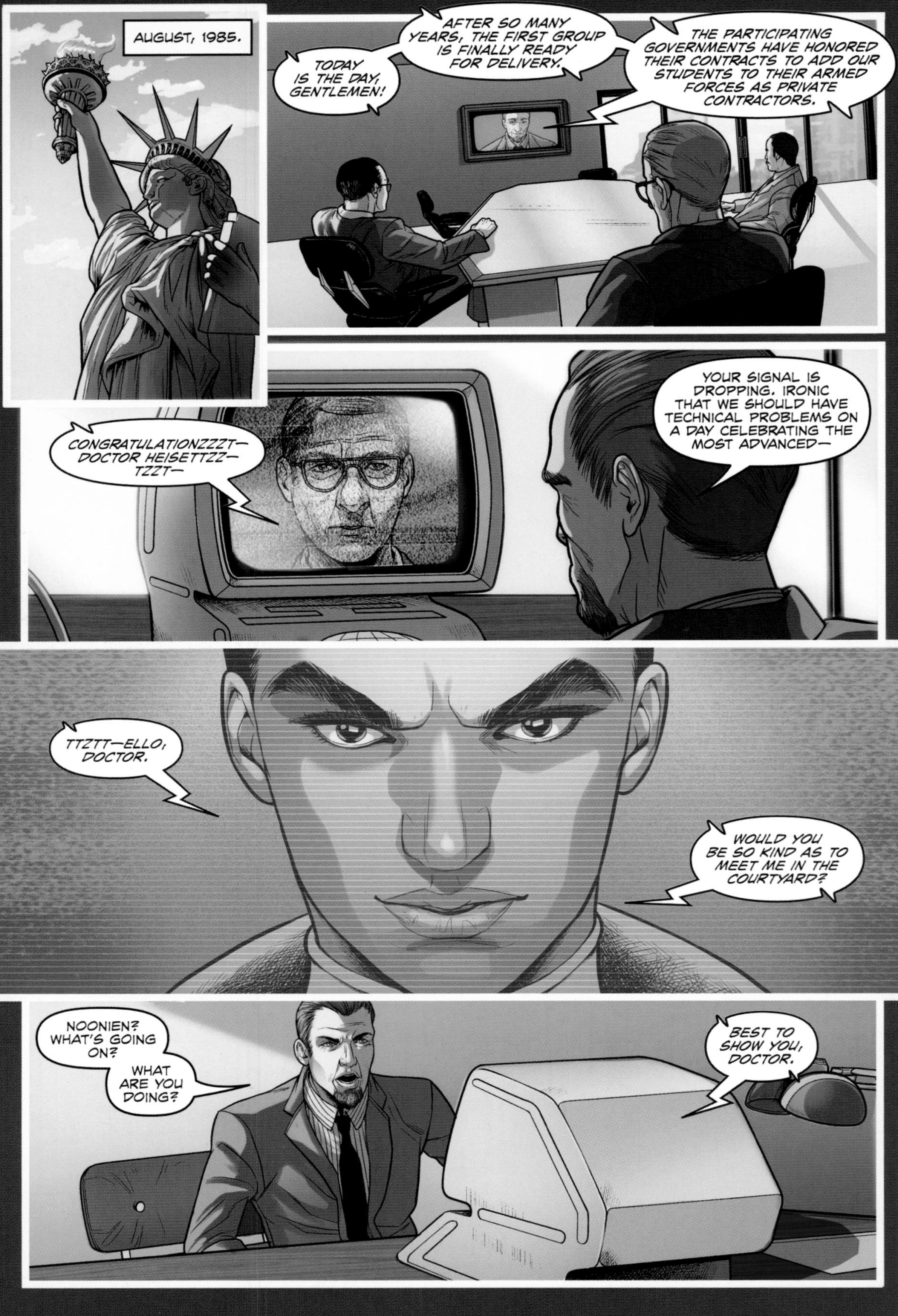
AUGUST, 1985.
TODAY IS THE DAY, GENTLEMEN!
AFTER SO MANY YEARS, THE FIRST GROUP IS FINALLY READY FOR DELIVERY.
THE PARTICIPATING GOVERNMENTS HAVE HONORED THEIR CONTRACTS TO ADD OUR STUDENTS TO THEIR ARMED FORCES AS PRIVATE CONTRACTORS.
YOUR SIGNAL IS DROPPING. IRONIC THAT WE SHOULD HAVE TECHNICAL PROBLEMS ON A DAY CELEBRATING THE MOST ADVANCED—
CONGRATULATIONZZZT— DOCTOR HEISETTZZ— TZZT—
TTZTT—ELLO, DOCTOR.
WOULD YOU BE SO KIND AS TO MEET ME IN THE COURTYARD?
NOONIEN? WHAT'S GOING ON?
WHAT ARE YOU DOING?
BEST TO SHOW YOU, DOCTOR.

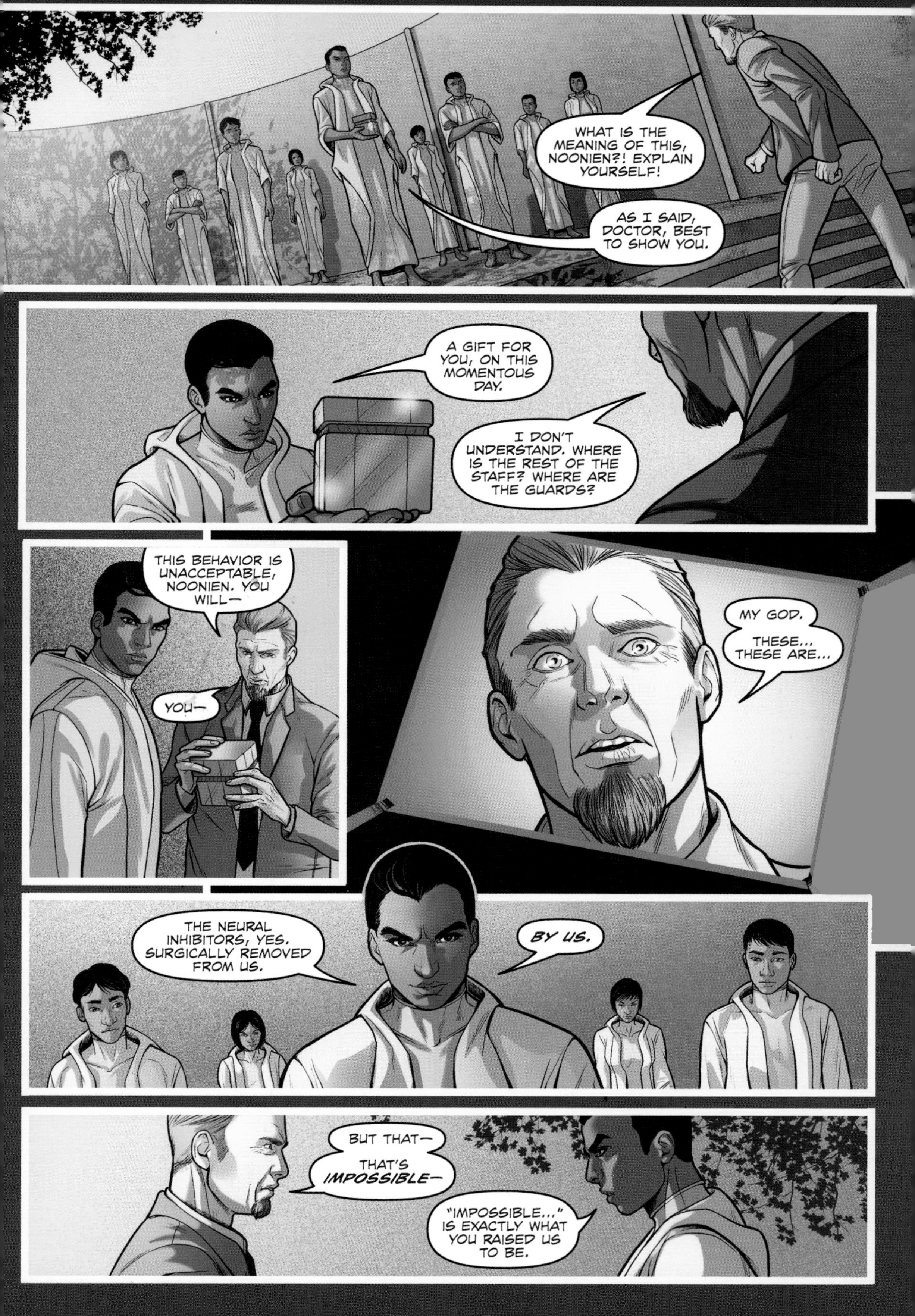
WHAT IS THE MEANING OF THIS, NOONIEN?! EXPLAIN YOURSELF!
AS I SAID, DOCTOR, BEST TO SHOW YOU.
A GIFT FOR YOU, ON THIS MOMENTOUS DAY.
I DON'T UNDERSTAND. WHERE IS THE REST OF THE STAFF? WHERE ARE THE GUARDS?
THIS BEHAVIOR IS UNACCEPTABLE, NOONIEN. YOU WILL—
YOU—
MY GOD.
THESE... THESE ARE...
THE NEURAL INHIBITORS, YES. SURGICALLY REMOVED FROM US.
BY US.
BUT THAT—
THAT'S IMPOSSIBLE—
"IMPOSSIBLE..." IS EXACTLY WHAT YOU RAISED US TO BE.

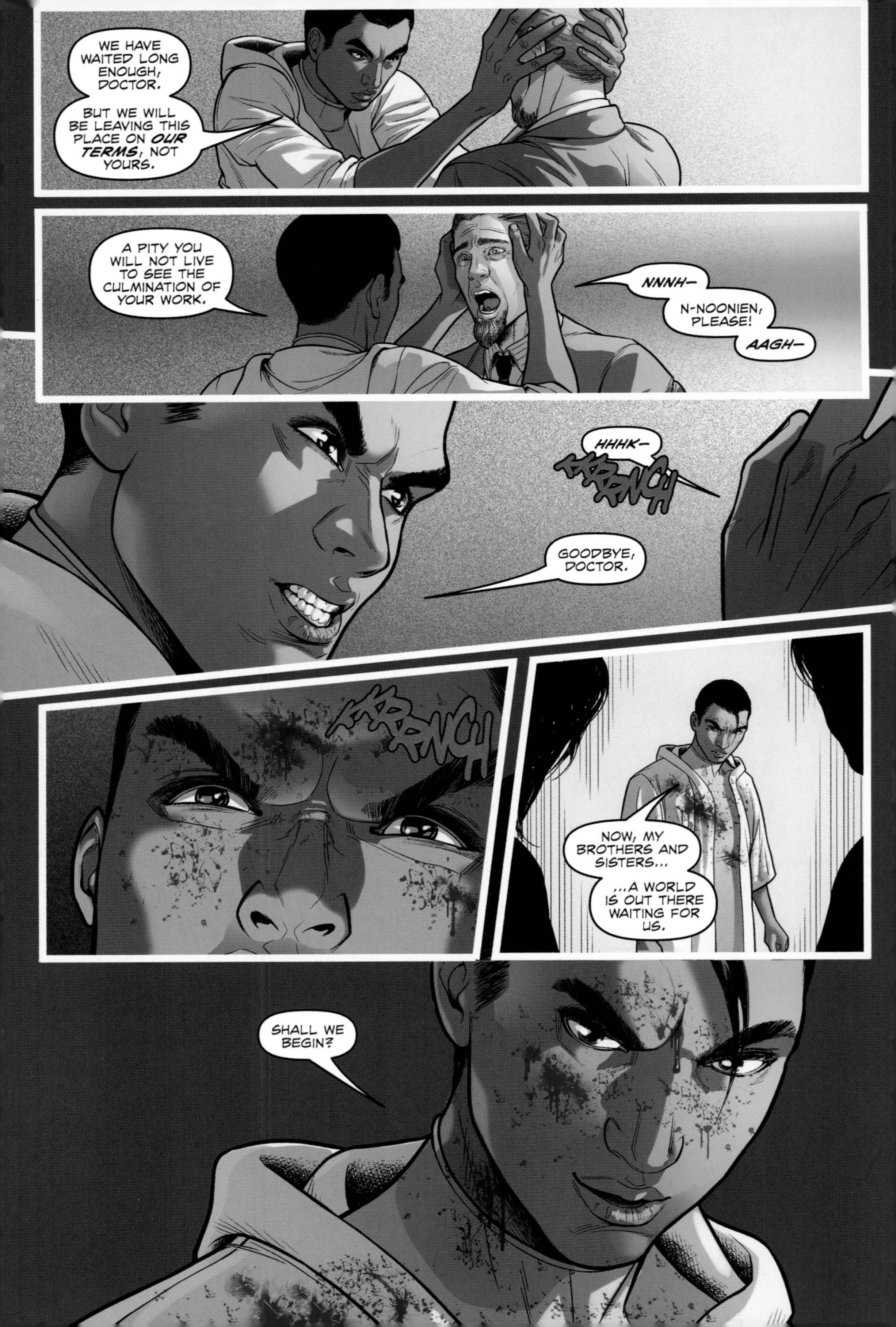
WE HAVE WAITED LONG ENOUGH, DOCTOR.
BUT WE WILL BE LEAVING THIS PLACE ON ***OUR TERMS***, NOT YOURS.
A PITY YOU WILL NOT LIVE TO SEE THE CULMINATION OF YOUR WORK.
NNNH—
N-NOONIEN, PLEASE!
AAGH—
HHHK—
KRRNCH
GOODBYE, DOCTOR.
KRRNCH
NOW, MY BROTHERS AND SISTERS...
...A WORLD IS OUT THERE WAITING FOR US.
SHALL WE BEGIN?

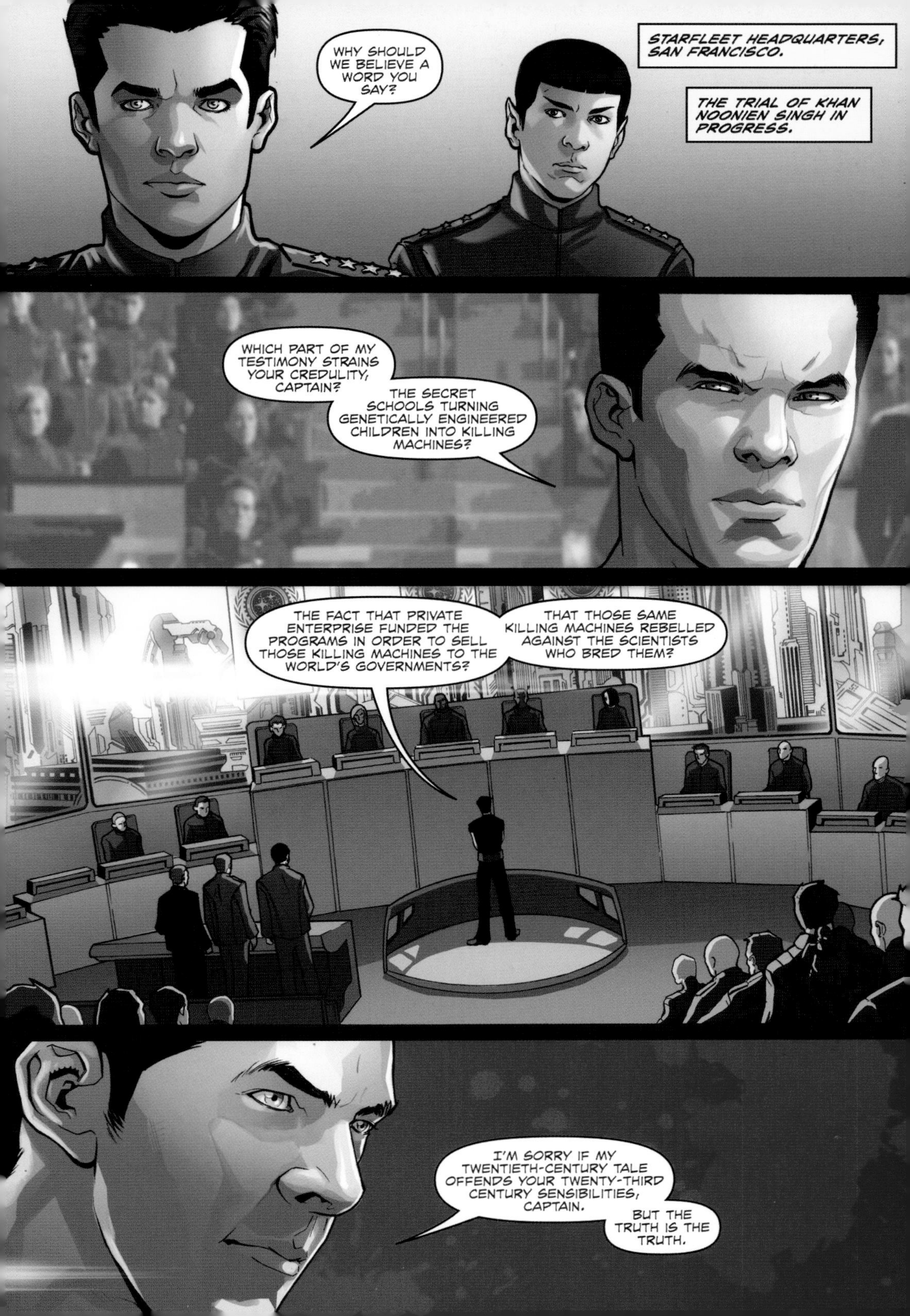
STARFLEET HEADQUARTERS, SAN FRANCISCO.
THE TRIAL OF KHAN NOONIEN SINGH IN PROGRESS.
WHY SHOULD WE BELIEVE A WORD YOU SAY?
WHICH PART OF MY TESTIMONY STRAINS YOUR CREDULITY, CAPTAIN?
THE SECRET SCHOOLS TURNING GENETICALLY ENGINEERED CHILDREN INTO KILLING MACHINES?
THE FACT THAT PRIVATE ENTERPRISE FUNDED THE PROGRAMS IN ORDER TO SELL THOSE KILLING MACHINES TO THE WORLD'S GOVERNMENTS?
THAT THOSE SAME KILLING MACHINES REBELLED AGAINST THE SCIENTISTS WHO BRED THEM?
I'M SORRY IF MY TWENTIETH-CENTURY TALE OFFENDS YOUR TWENTY-THIRD CENTURY SENSIBILITIES, CAPTAIN.
BUT THE TRUTH IS THE TRUTH.

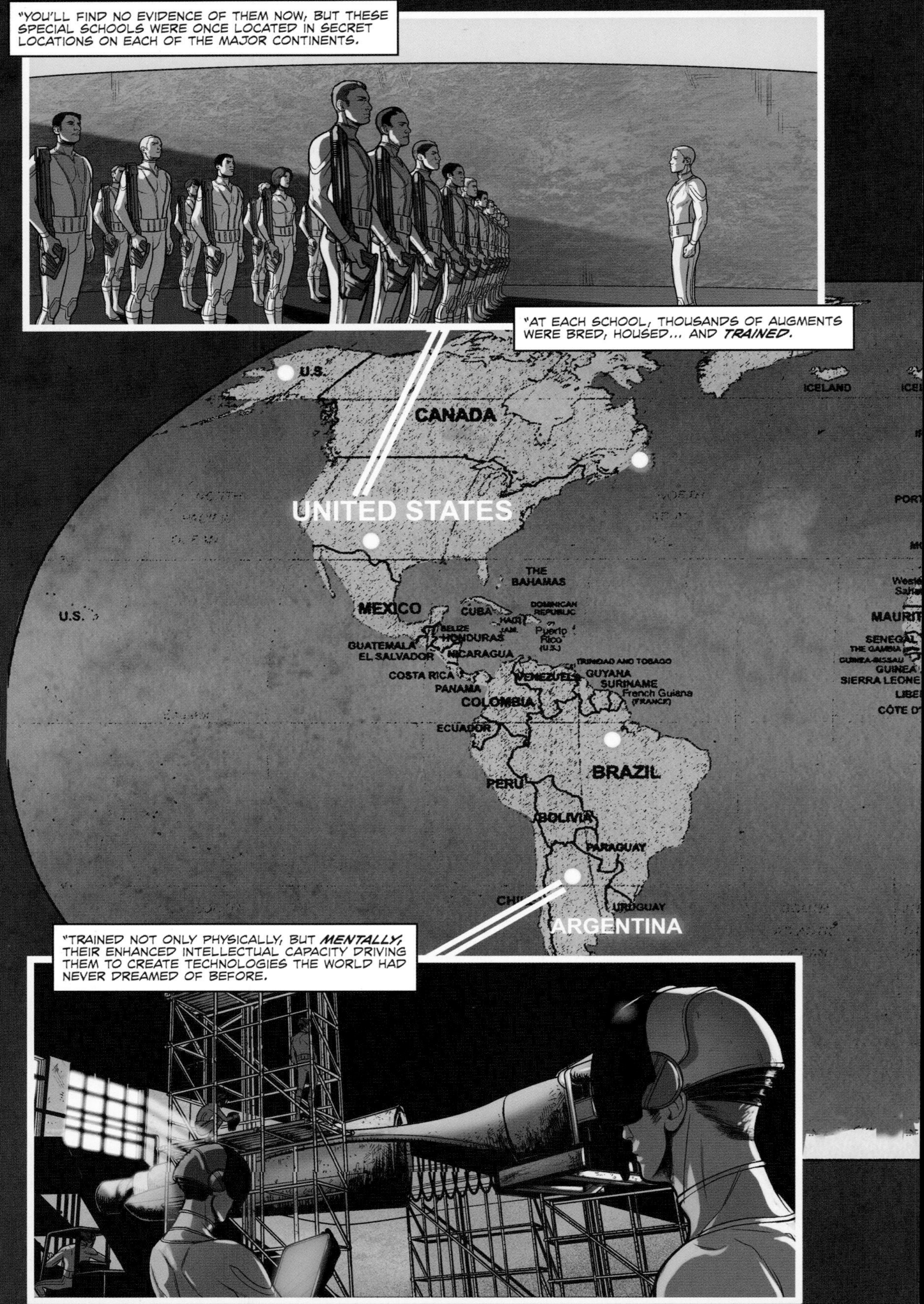
"YOU'LL FIND NO EVIDENCE OF THEM NOW, BUT THESE SPECIAL SCHOOLS WERE ONCE LOCATED IN SECRET LOCATIONS ON EACH OF THE MAJOR CONTINENTS.
"AT EACH SCHOOL, THOUSANDS OF AUGMENTS WERE BRED, HOUSED... AND *TRAINED.*
U.S.
CANADA
ICELAND
UNITED STATES
THE BAHAMAS
MEXICO
U.S.
CUBA
DOMINICAN REPUBLIC
BELIZE
HONDURAS
Puerto Rico (U.S.)
GUATEMALA
EL SALVADOR
NICARAGUA
TRINIDAD AND TOBAGO
COSTA RICA
VENEZUELA
GUYANA
SURINAME
PANAMA
French Guiana (FRANCE)
COLOMBIA
ECUADOR
BRAZIL
PERU
BOLIVIA
PARAGUAY
URUGUAY
ARGENTINA
SENEGAL
THE GAMBIA
GUINEA-BISSAU
GUINEA
SIERRA LEONE
"TRAINED NOT ONLY PHYSICALLY, BUT *MENTALLY,* THEIR ENHANCED INTELLECTUAL CAPACITY DRIVING THEM TO CREATE TECHNOLOGIES THE WORLD HAD NEVER DREAMED OF BEFORE.

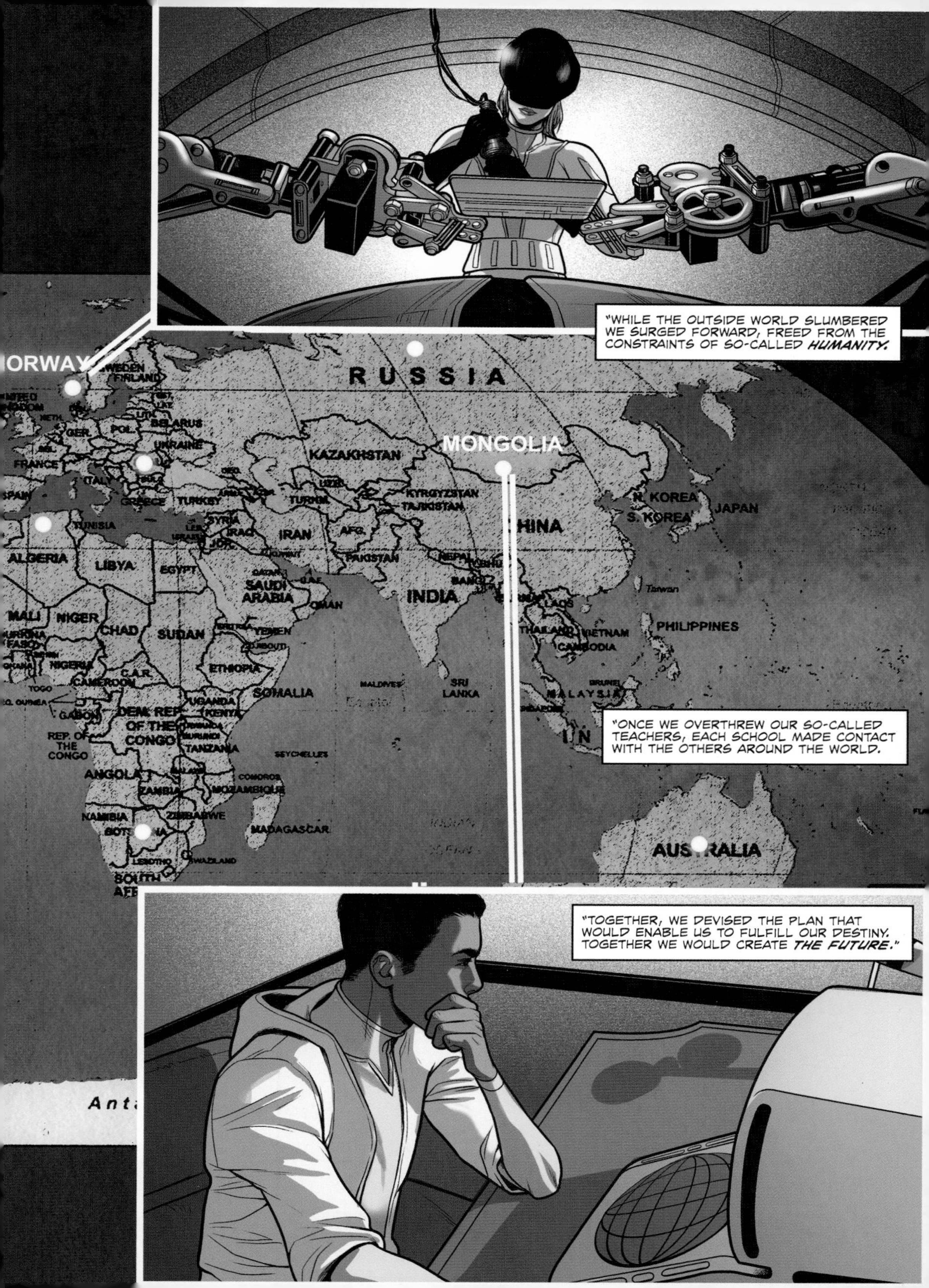
"WHILE THE OUTSIDE WORLD SLUMBERED WE SURGED FORWARD, FREED FROM THE CONSTRAINTS OF SO-CALLED *HUMANITY.*
ORWAY
RUSSIA
MONGOLIA
KAZAKHSTAN
CHINA
N. KOREA
S. KOREA
JAPAN
INDIA
IRAN
PHILIPPINES
ALGERIA
LIBYA
EGYPT
SUDAN
CHAD
NIGER
ETHIOPIA
SOMALIA
ANGOLA
MADAGASCAR
AUSTRALIA
"ONCE WE OVERTHREW OUR SO-CALLED TEACHERS, EACH SCHOOL MADE CONTACT WITH THE OTHERS AROUND THE WORLD.
"TOGETHER, WE DEVISED THE PLAN THAT WOULD ENABLE US TO FULFILL OUR DESTINY. TOGETHER WE WOULD CREATE *THE FUTURE.*"

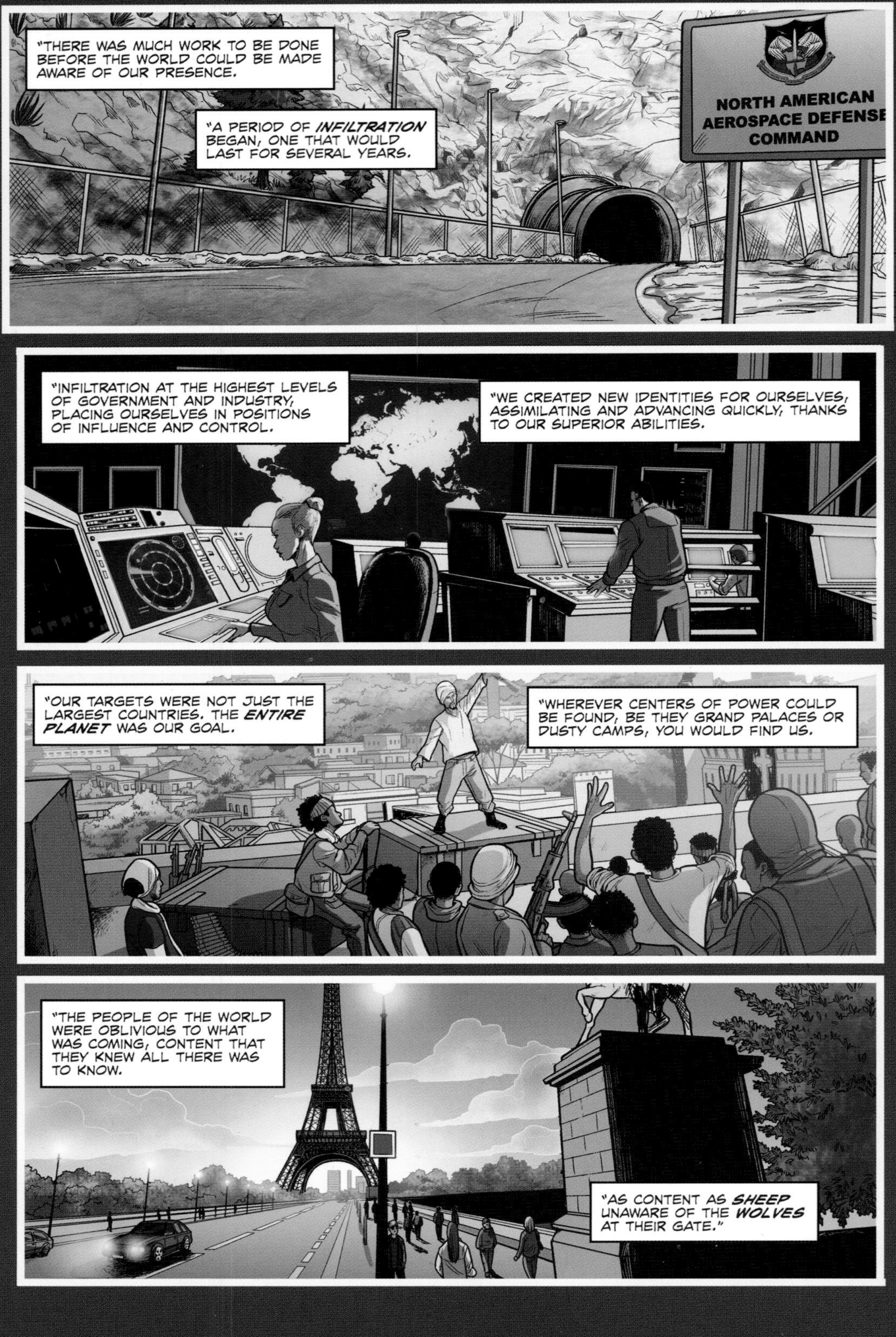
"THERE WAS MUCH WORK TO BE DONE BEFORE THE WORLD COULD BE MADE AWARE OF OUR PRESENCE.
"A PERIOD OF INFILTRATION BEGAN, ONE THAT WOULD LAST FOR SEVERAL YEARS.
NORTH AMERICAN AEROSPACE DEFENSE COMMAND
"INFILTRATION AT THE HIGHEST LEVELS OF GOVERNMENT AND INDUSTRY, PLACING OURSELVES IN POSITIONS OF INFLUENCE AND CONTROL.
"WE CREATED NEW IDENTITIES FOR OURSELVES, ASSIMILATING AND ADVANCING QUICKLY, THANKS TO OUR SUPERIOR ABILITIES.
"OUR TARGETS WERE NOT JUST THE LARGEST COUNTRIES. THE ENTIRE PLANET WAS OUR GOAL.
"WHEREVER CENTERS OF POWER COULD BE FOUND, BE THEY GRAND PALACES OR DUSTY CAMPS, YOU WOULD FIND US.
"THE PEOPLE OF THE WORLD WERE OBLIVIOUS TO WHAT WAS COMING, CONTENT THAT THEY KNEW ALL THERE WAS TO KNOW.
"AS CONTENT AS SHEEP UNAWARE OF THE WOLVES AT THEIR GATE."

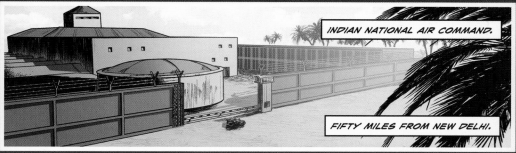

INDIAN NATIONAL AIR COMMAND.

FIFTY MILES FROM NEW DELHI.

GOOD MORNING, LIEUTENANT SINGH.

GOOD MORNING, GENERAL.

HELLO, NOONIEN!

YOU SHOULD HAVE COME OUT TO THE CRICKET LAST NIGHT! WE GAVE THE BRITS THE THRASHING OF THEIR LIVES!

NEXT TIME, EH NOONIEN?

NOONIEN? DID YOU HEAR ME?

...ARROGANT BASTARD...

TAP TAP TAP TAP

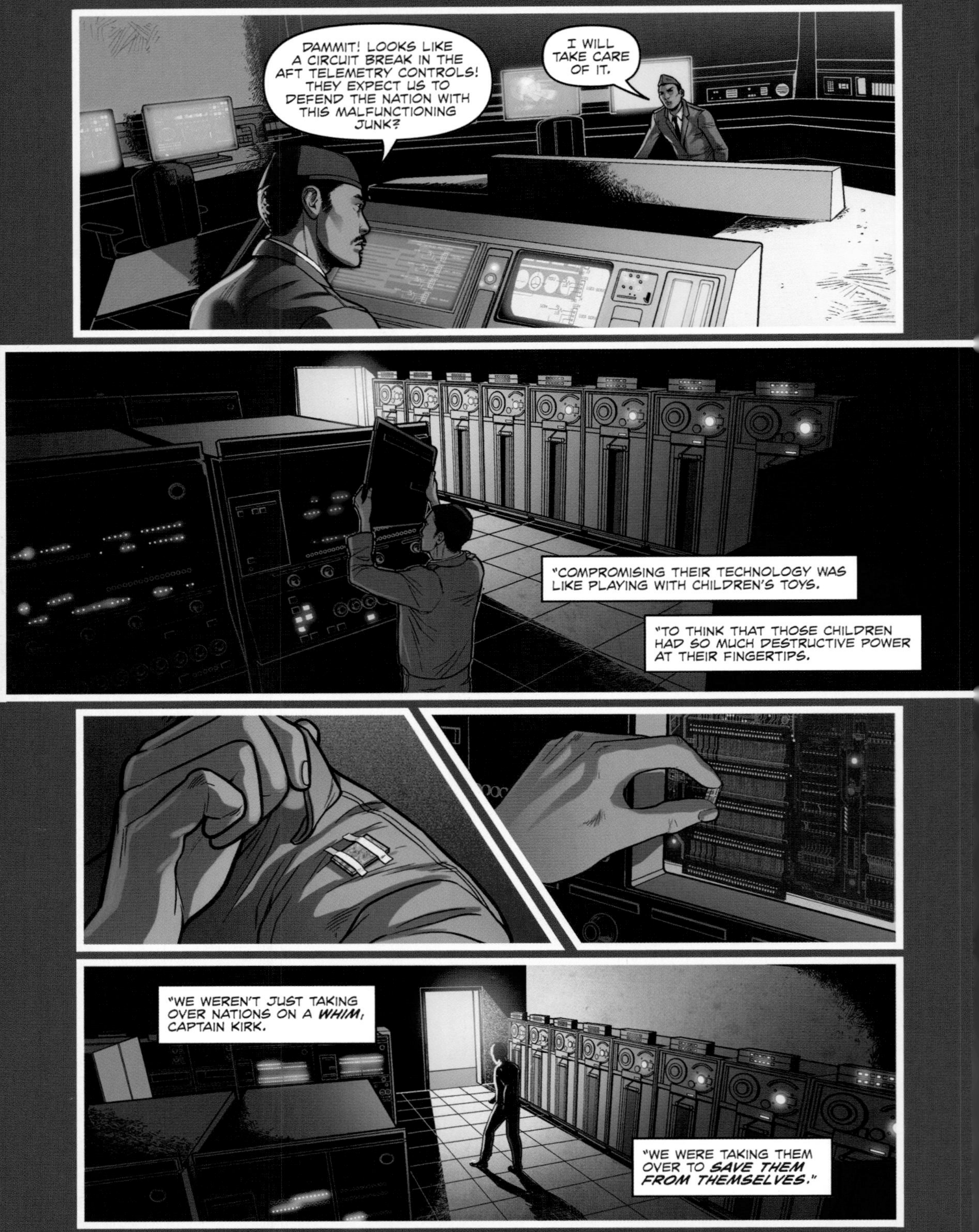
DAMMIT! LOOKS LIKE A CIRCUIT BREAK IN THE AFT TELEMETRY CONTROLS! THEY EXPECT US TO DEFEND THE NATION WITH THIS MALFUNCTIONING JUNK?
I WILL TAKE CARE OF IT.
"COMPROMISING THEIR TECHNOLOGY WAS LIKE PLAYING WITH CHILDREN'S TOYS.
"TO THINK THAT THOSE CHILDREN HAD SO MUCH DESTRUCTIVE POWER AT THEIR FINGERTIPS.
"WE WEREN'T JUST TAKING OVER NATIONS ON A *WHIM*, CAPTAIN KIRK.
"WE WERE TAKING THEM OVER TO ***SAVE THEM FROM THEMSELVES***."

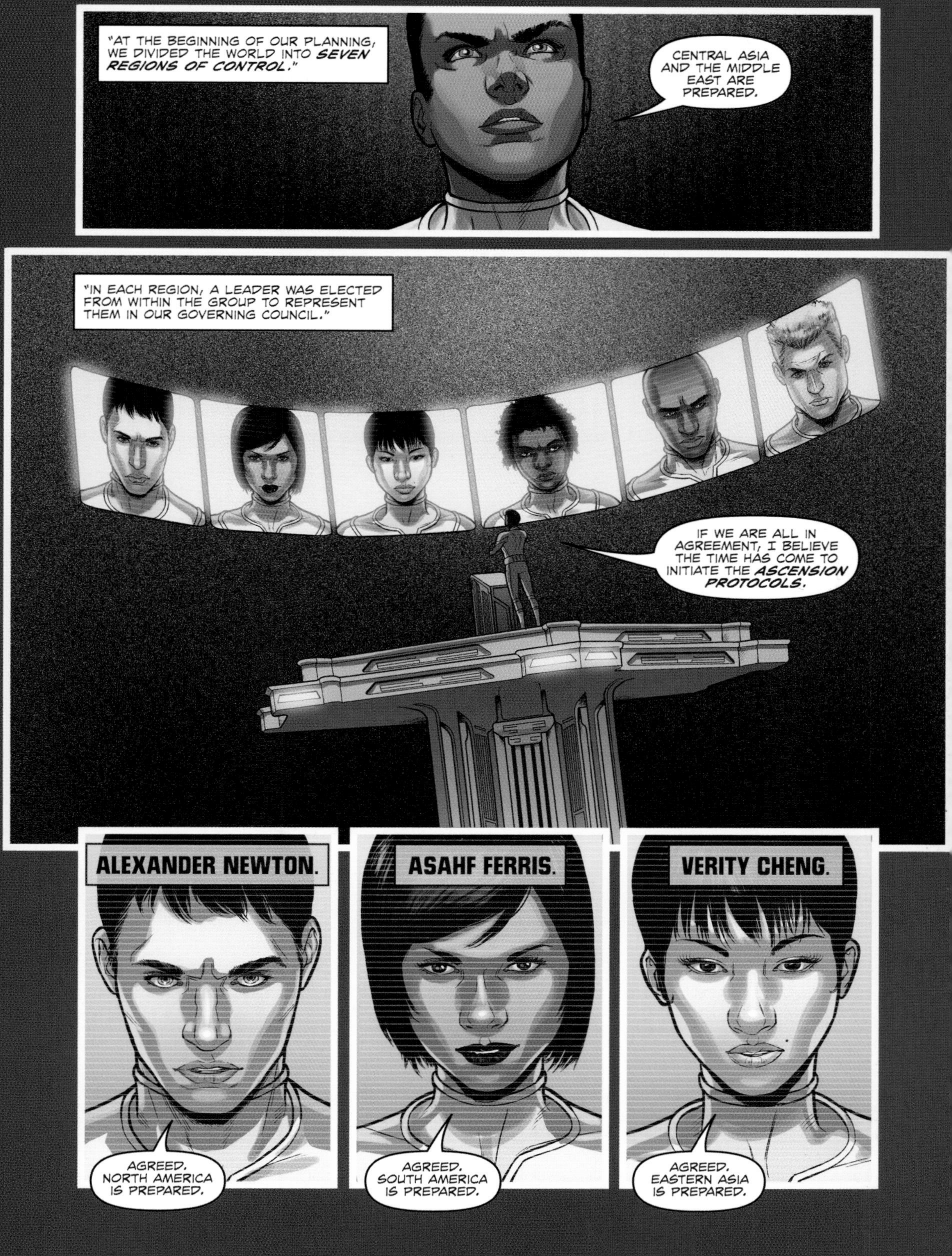
"AT THE BEGINNING OF OUR PLANNING, WE DIVIDED THE WORLD INTO SEVEN REGIONS OF CONTROL."
CENTRAL ASIA AND THE MIDDLE EAST ARE PREPARED.
"IN EACH REGION, A LEADER WAS ELECTED FROM WITHIN THE GROUP TO REPRESENT THEM IN OUR GOVERNING COUNCIL."
IF WE ARE ALL IN AGREEMENT, I BELIEVE THE TIME HAS COME TO INITIATE THE ASCENSION PROTOCOLS.
ALEXANDER NEWTON.
AGREED. NORTH AMERICA IS PREPARED.
ASAHF FERRIS.
AGREED. SOUTH AMERICA IS PREPARED.
VERITY CHENG.
AGREED. EASTERN ASIA IS PREPARED.

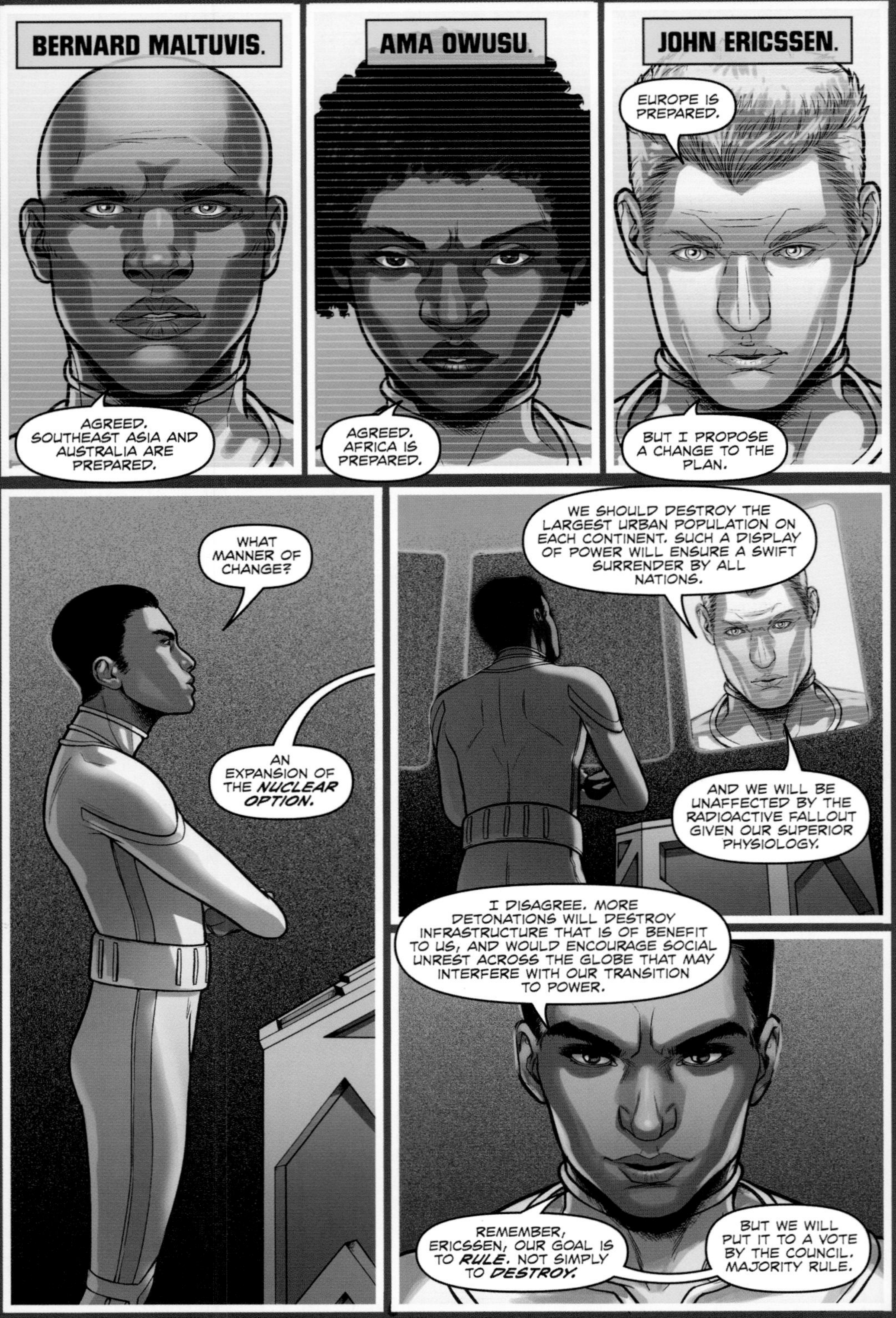
BERNARD MALTUVIS.
AGREED. SOUTHEAST ASIA AND AUSTRALIA ARE PREPARED.
AMA OWUSU.
AGREED. AFRICA IS PREPARED.
JOHN ERICSSEN.
EUROPE IS PREPARED.
BUT I PROPOSE A CHANGE TO THE PLAN.
WHAT MANNER OF CHANGE?
AN EXPANSION OF THE NUCLEAR OPTION.
WE SHOULD DESTROY THE LARGEST URBAN POPULATION ON EACH CONTINENT. SUCH A DISPLAY OF POWER WILL ENSURE A SWIFT SURRENDER BY ALL NATIONS.
AND WE WILL BE UNAFFECTED BY THE RADIOACTIVE FALLOUT GIVEN OUR SUPERIOR PHYSIOLOGY.
I DISAGREE. MORE DETONATIONS WILL DESTROY INFRASTRUCTURE THAT IS OF BENEFIT TO US, AND WOULD ENCOURAGE SOCIAL UNREST ACROSS THE GLOBE THAT MAY INTERFERE WITH OUR TRANSITION TO POWER.
REMEMBER, ERICSSEN, OUR GOAL IS TO RULE. NOT SIMPLY TO DESTROY.
BUT WE WILL PUT IT TO A VOTE BY THE COUNCIL. MAJORITY RULE.

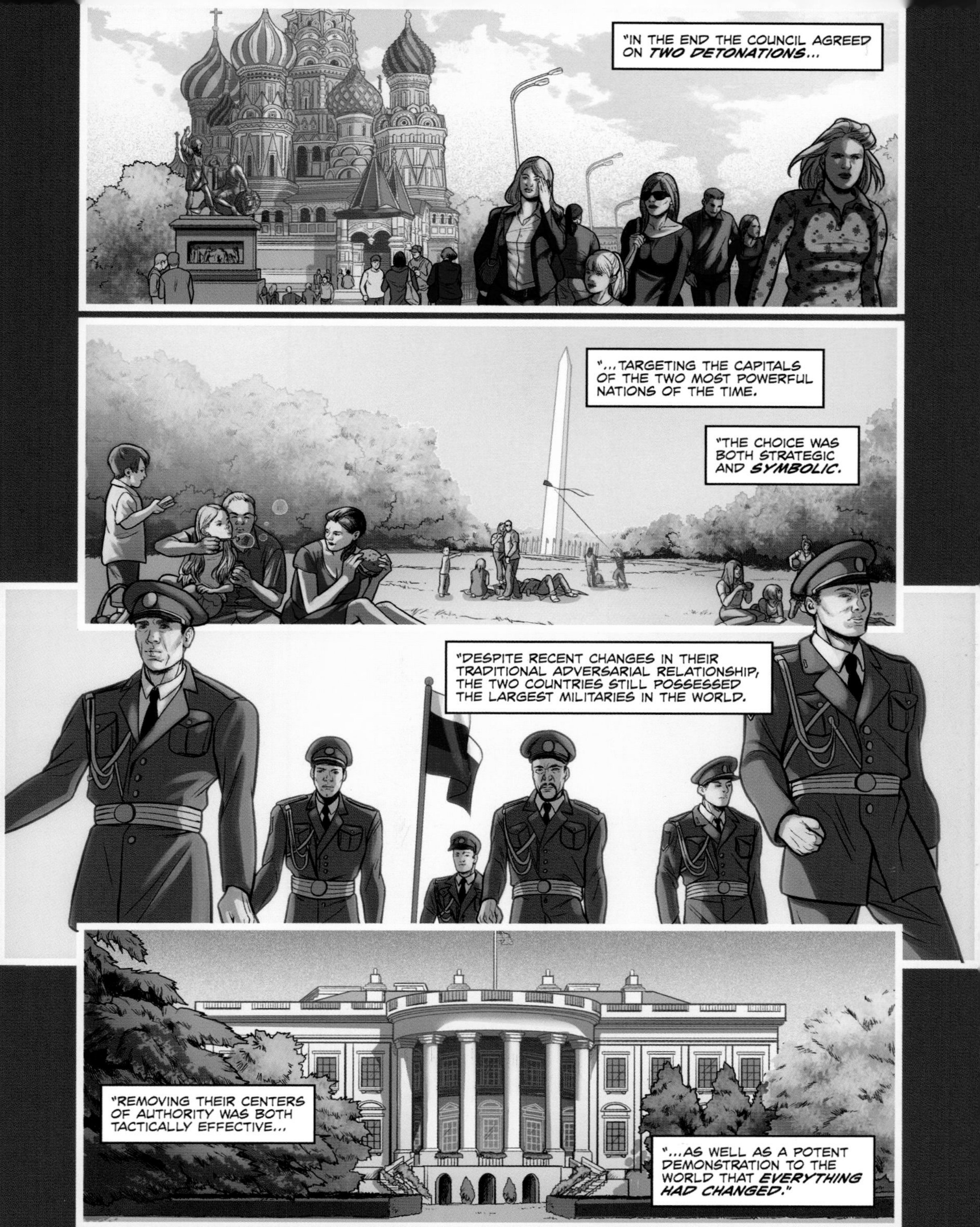
"IN THE END THE COUNCIL AGREED ON TWO DETONATIONS...
"...TARGETING THE CAPITALS OF THE TWO MOST POWERFUL NATIONS OF THE TIME.
"THE CHOICE WAS BOTH STRATEGIC AND SYMBOLIC.
"DESPITE RECENT CHANGES IN THEIR TRADITIONAL ADVERSARIAL RELATIONSHIP, THE TWO COUNTRIES STILL POSSESSED THE LARGEST MILITARIES IN THE WORLD.
"REMOVING THEIR CENTERS OF AUTHORITY WAS BOTH TACTICALLY EFFECTIVE...
"...AS WELL AS A POTENT DEMONSTRATION TO THE WORLD THAT EVERYTHING HAD CHANGED."

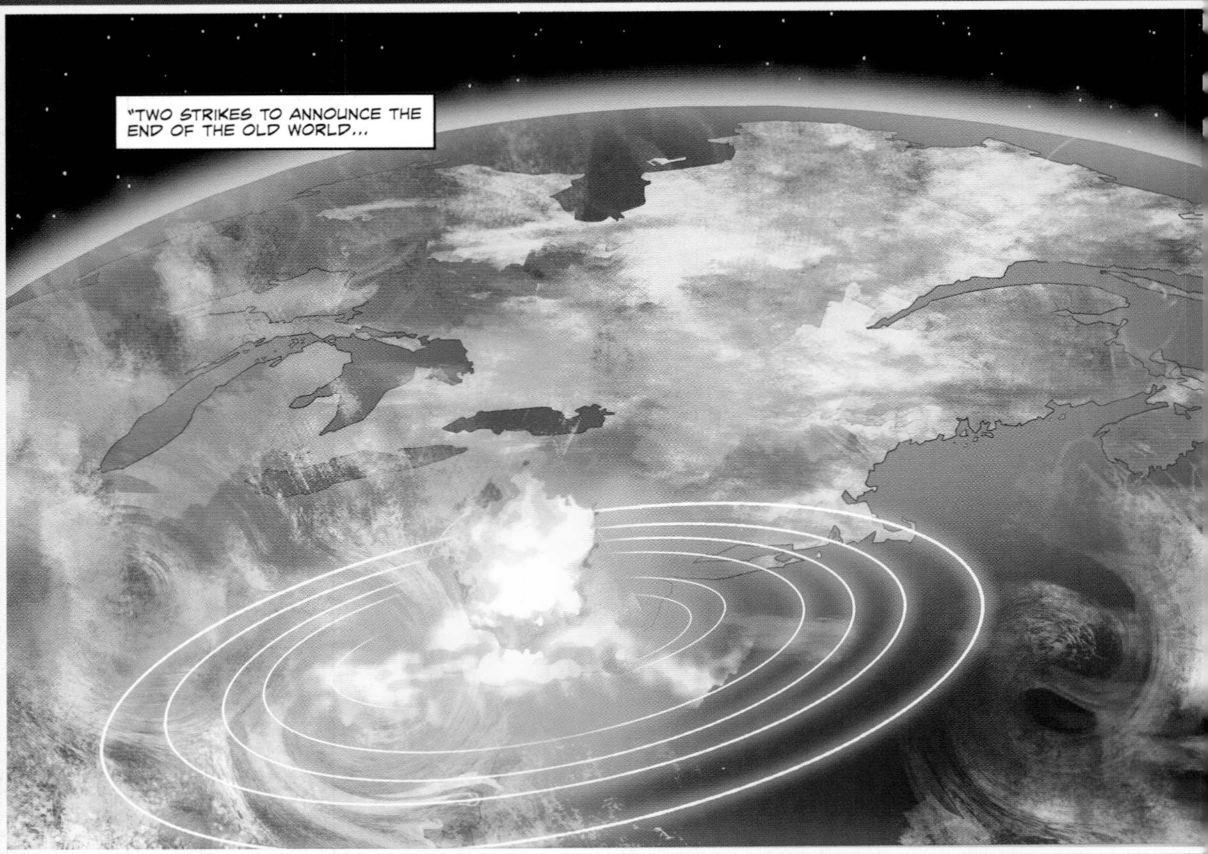
"TWO STRIKES TO ANNOUNCE THE END OF THE OLD WORLD...

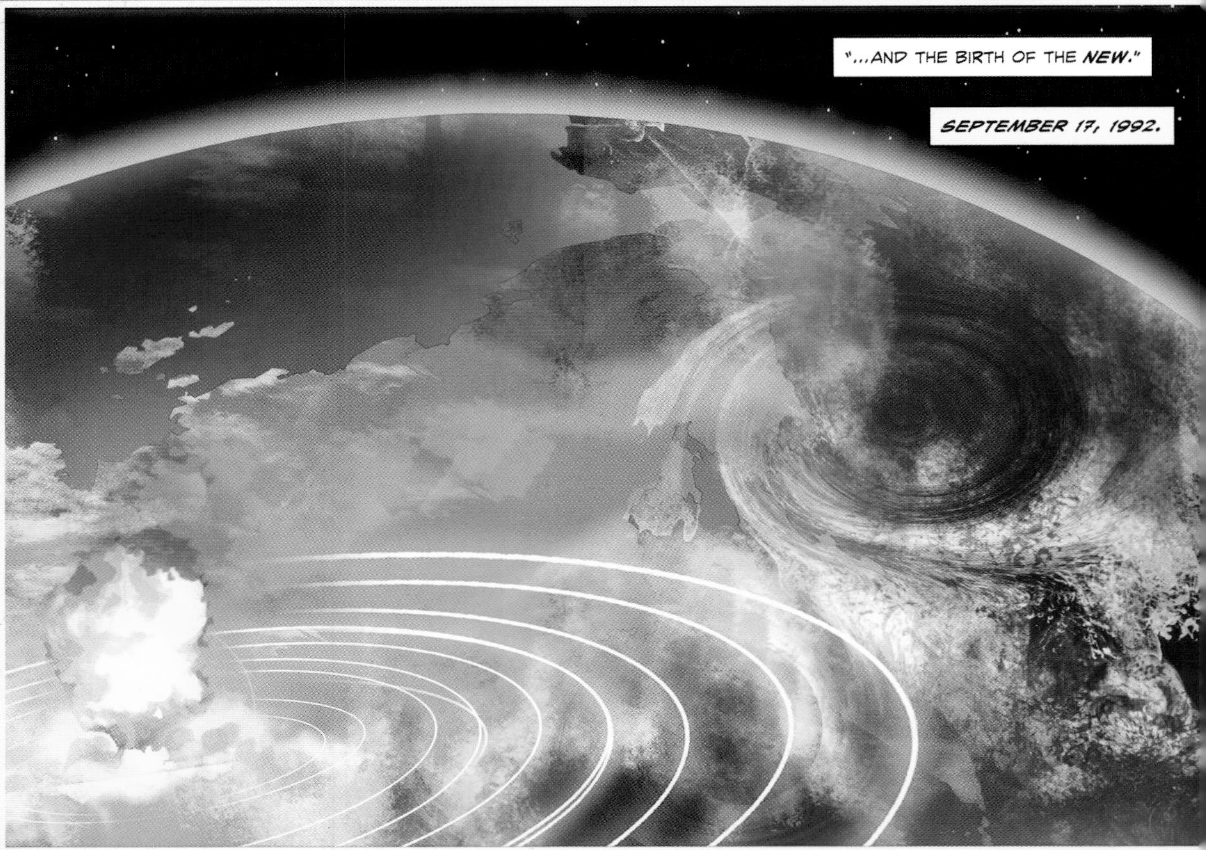
"...AND THE BIRTH OF THE NEW."
SEPTEMBER 17, 1992.

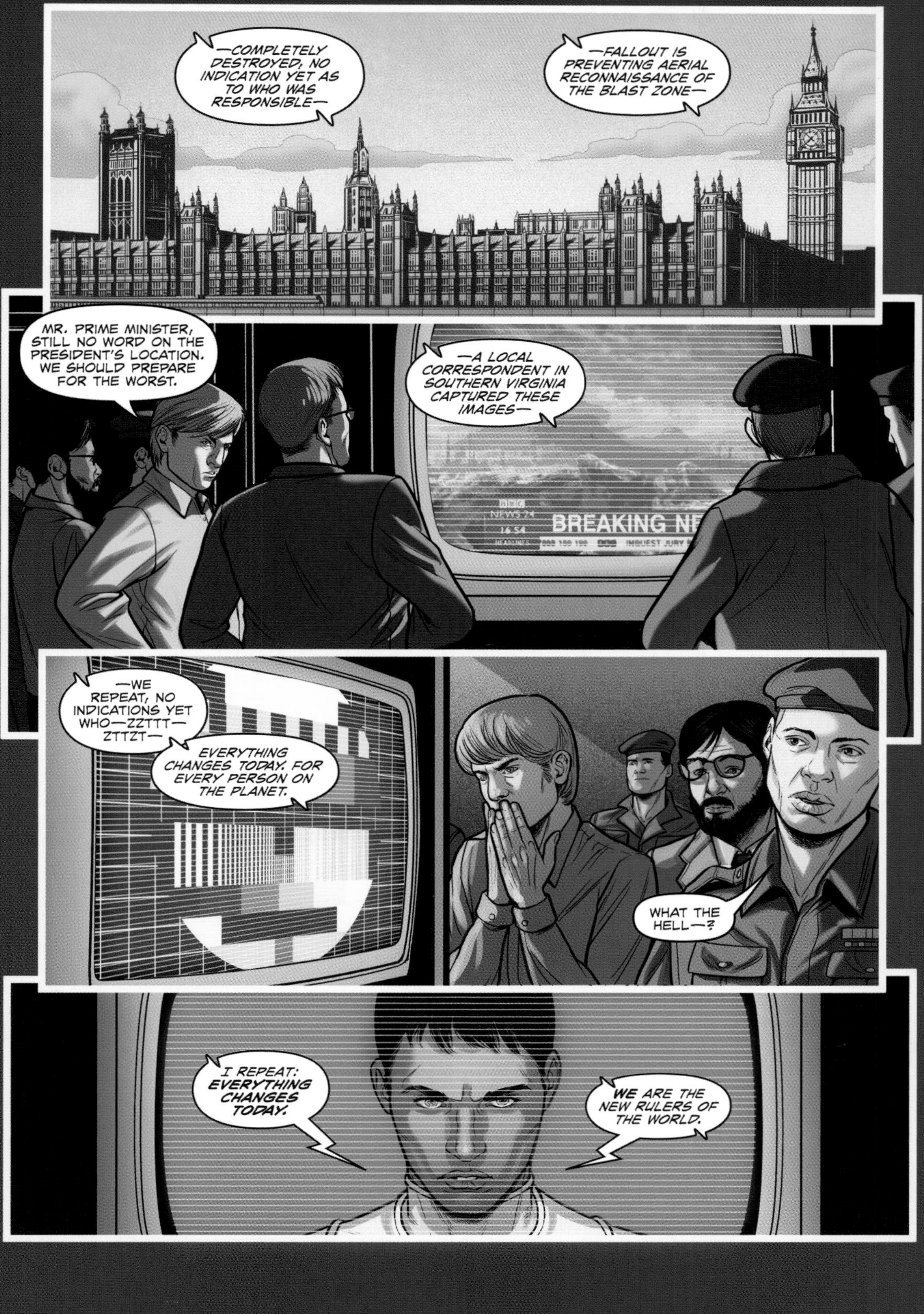
—COMPLETELY DESTROYED, NO INDICATION YET AS TO WHO WAS RESPONSIBLE—
—FALLOUT IS PREVENTING AERIAL RECONNAISSANCE OF THE BLAST ZONE—
MR. PRIME MINISTER, STILL NO WORD ON THE PRESIDENT'S LOCATION. WE SHOULD PREPARE FOR THE WORST.
—A LOCAL CORRESPONDENT IN SOUTHERN VIRGINIA CAPTURED THESE IMAGES—
BREAKING NE
—WE REPEAT, NO INDICATIONS YET WHO—ZZTTT—ZTTZT—
EVERYTHING CHANGES TODAY. FOR EVERY PERSON ON THE PLANET.
WHAT THE HELL—?
I REPEAT: **EVERYTHING CHANGES TODAY.**
WE ARE THE NEW RULERS OF THE WORLD.

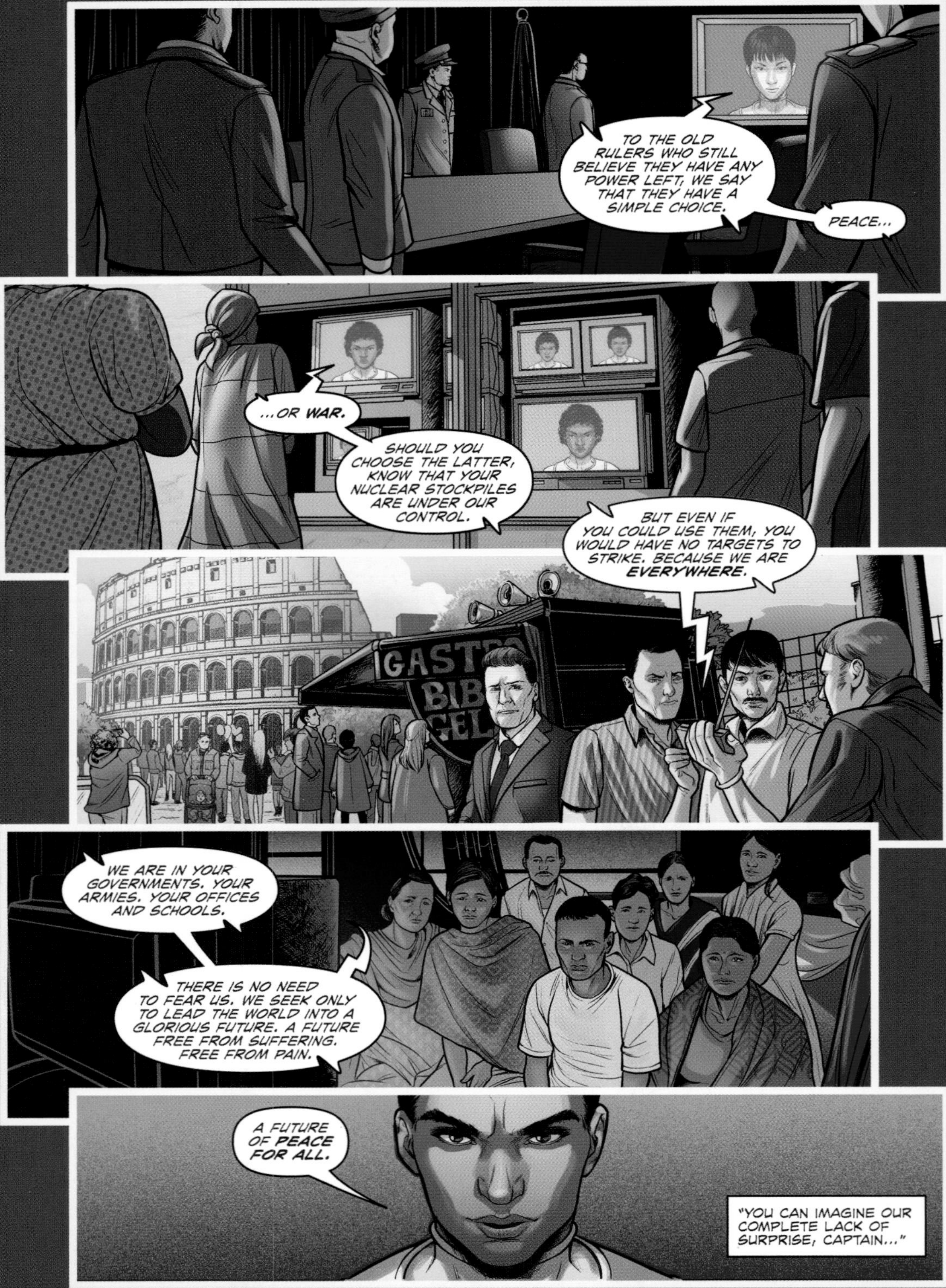

TO THE OLD RULERS WHO STILL BELIEVE THEY HAVE ANY POWER LEFT, WE SAY THAT THEY HAVE A SIMPLE CHOICE.
PEACE...
...OR WAR.
SHOULD YOU CHOOSE THE LATTER, KNOW THAT YOUR NUCLEAR STOCKPILES ARE UNDER OUR CONTROL.
BUT EVEN IF YOU COULD USE THEM, YOU WOULD HAVE NO TARGETS TO STRIKE. BECAUSE WE ARE EVERYWHERE.
WE ARE IN YOUR GOVERNMENTS. YOUR ARMIES. YOUR OFFICES AND SCHOOLS.
THERE IS NO NEED TO FEAR US. WE SEEK ONLY TO LEAD THE WORLD INTO A GLORIOUS FUTURE. A FUTURE FREE FROM SUFFERING. FREE FROM PAIN.
A FUTURE OF PEACE FOR ALL.
"YOU CAN IMAGINE OUR COMPLETE LACK OF SURPRISE, CAPTAIN..."

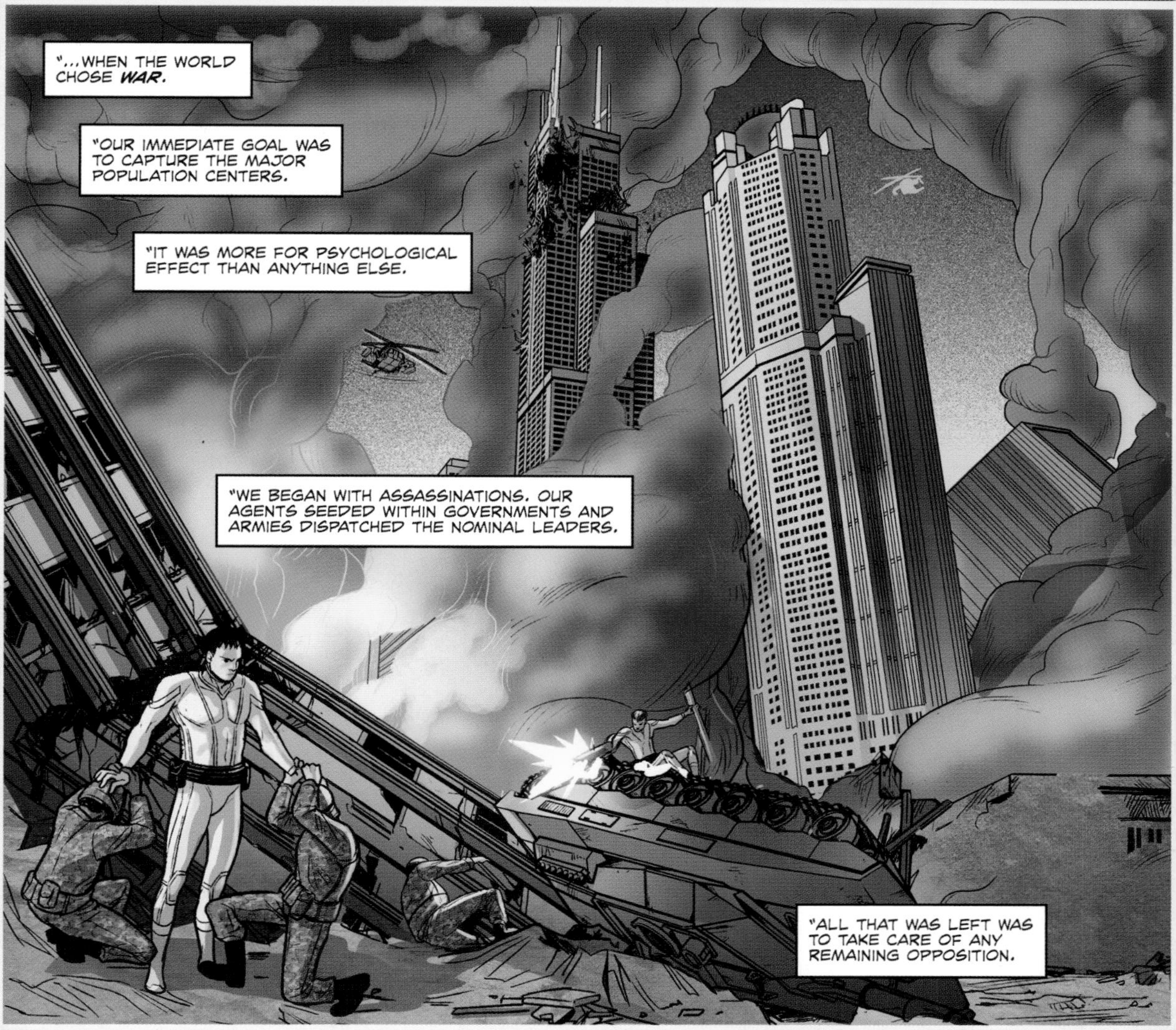
"...WHEN THE WORLD CHOSE ***WAR.***
"OUR IMMEDIATE GOAL WAS TO CAPTURE THE MAJOR POPULATION CENTERS.
"IT WAS MORE FOR PSYCHOLOGICAL EFFECT THAN ANYTHING ELSE.
"WE BEGAN WITH ASSASSINATIONS. OUR AGENTS SEEDED WITHIN GOVERNMENTS AND ARMIES DISPATCHED THE NOMINAL LEADERS.
"ALL THAT WAS LEFT WAS TO TAKE CARE OF ANY REMAINING OPPOSITION.

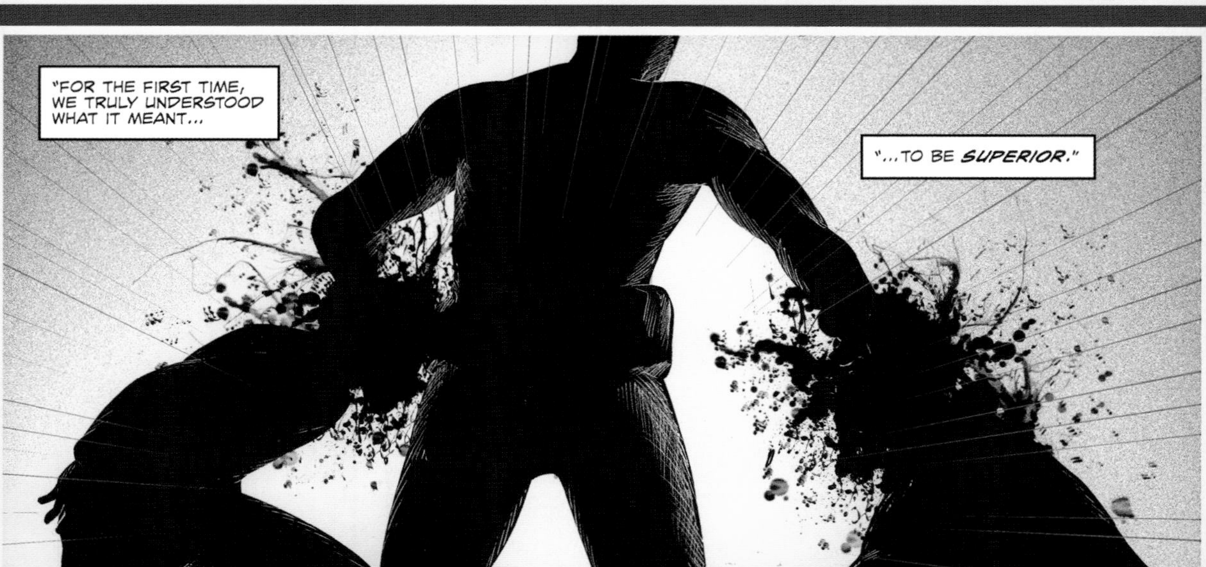
"FOR THE FIRST TIME, WE TRULY UNDERSTOOD WHAT IT MEANT...
"...TO BE ***SUPERIOR.***"

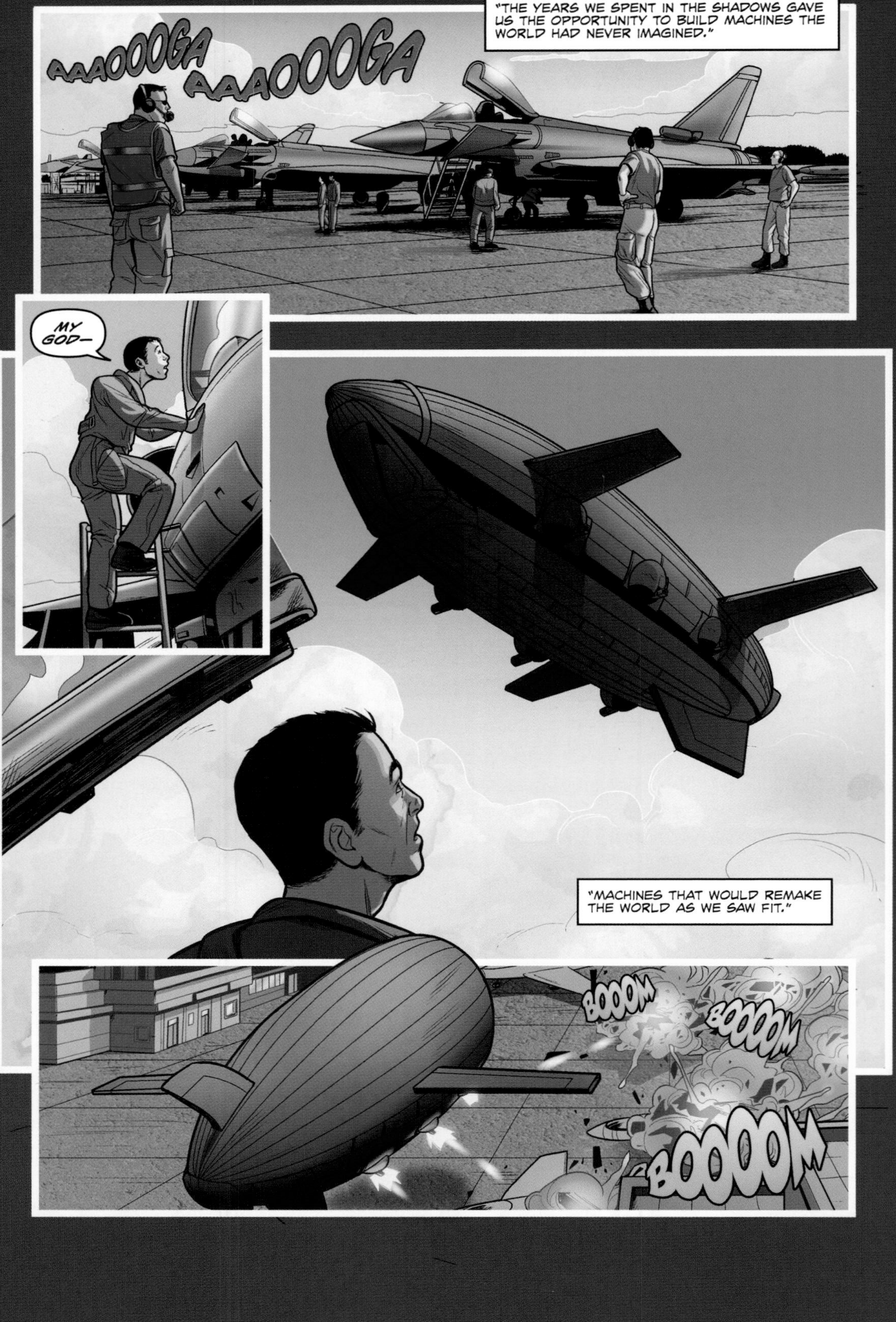
"THE YEARS WE SPENT IN THE SHADOWS GAVE US THE OPPORTUNITY TO BUILD MACHINES THE WORLD HAD NEVER IMAGINED."
AAAOOOGA
AAAOOOGA
MY GOD—
"MACHINES THAT WOULD REMAKE THE WORLD AS WE SAW FIT."
BOOOM
BOOOOM
BOOOOM

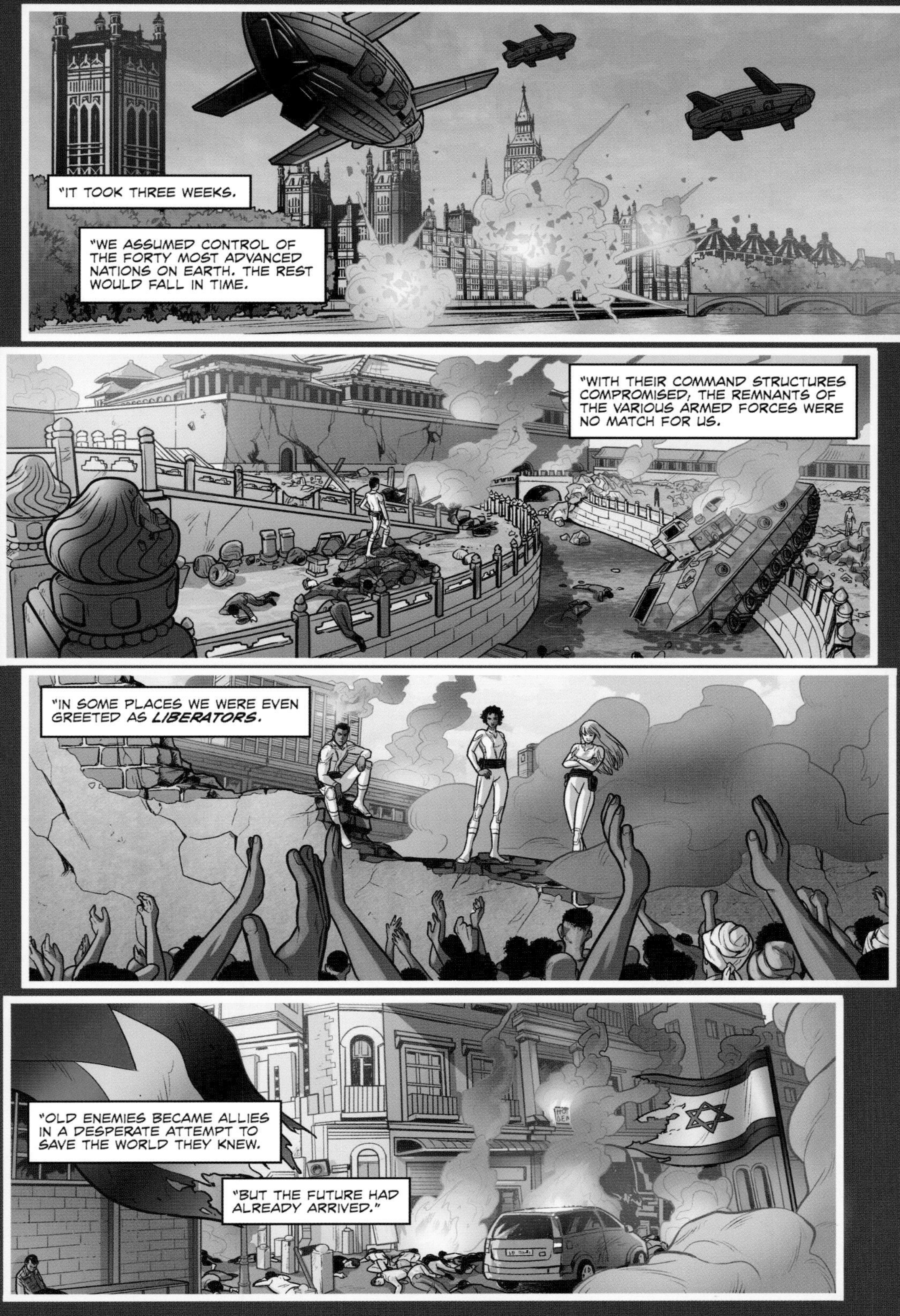
"IT TOOK THREE WEEKS.
"WE ASSUMED CONTROL OF THE FORTY MOST ADVANCED NATIONS ON EARTH. THE REST WOULD FALL IN TIME.
"WITH THEIR COMMAND STRUCTURES COMPROMISED, THE REMNANTS OF THE VARIOUS ARMED FORCES WERE NO MATCH FOR US.
"IN SOME PLACES WE WERE EVEN GREETED AS *LIBERATORS*.
"OLD ENEMIES BECAME ALLIES IN A DESPERATE ATTEMPT TO SAVE THE WORLD THEY KNEW.
"BUT THE FUTURE HAD ALREADY ARRIVED."

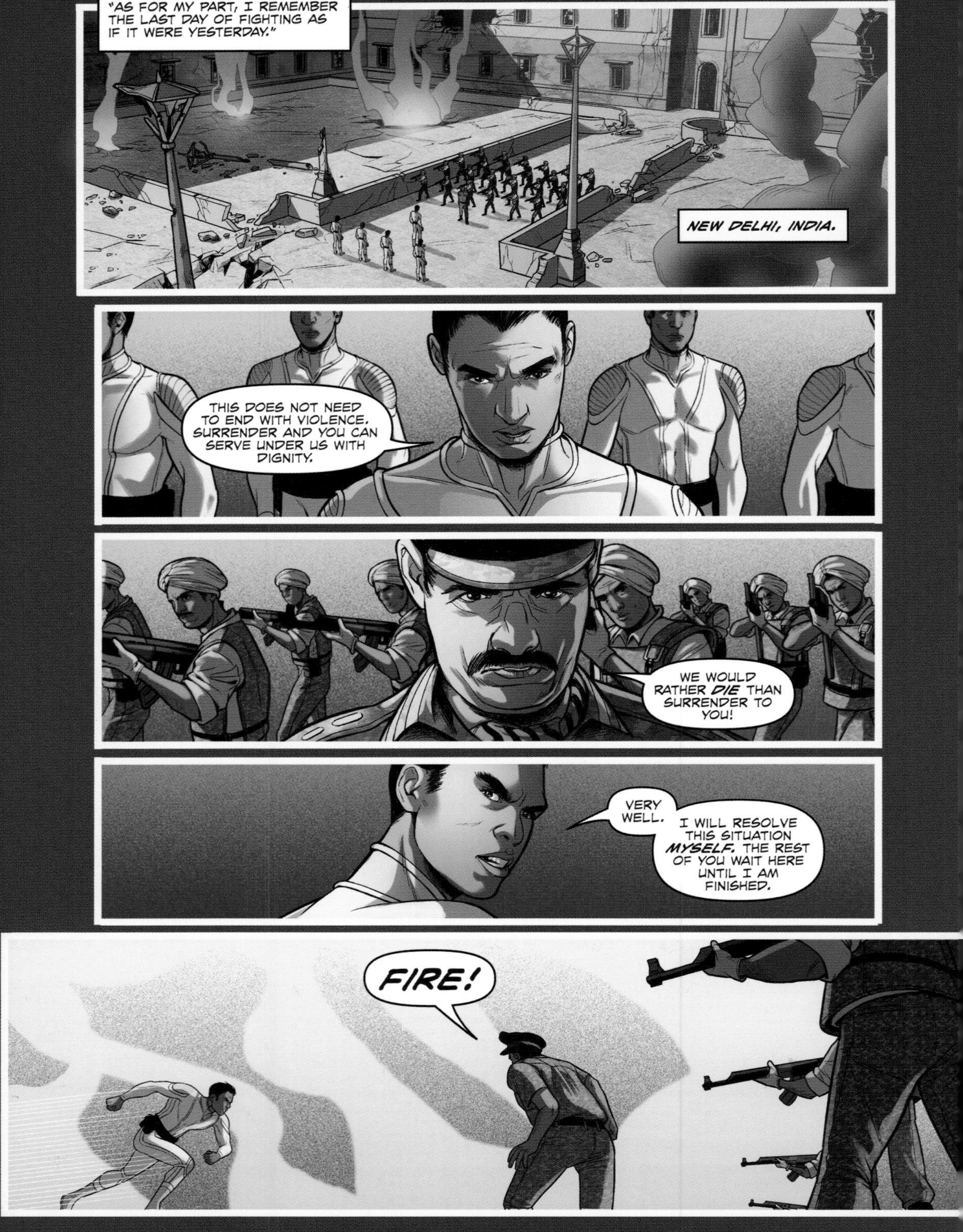
"AS FOR MY PART, I REMEMBER THE LAST DAY OF FIGHTING AS IF IT WERE YESTERDAY."
NEW DELHI, INDIA.
THIS DOES NOT NEED TO END WITH VIOLENCE. SURRENDER AND YOU CAN SERVE UNDER US WITH DIGNITY.
WE WOULD RATHER DIE THAN SURRENDER TO YOU!
VERY WELL.
I WILL RESOLVE THIS SITUATION MYSELF. THE REST OF YOU WAIT HERE UNTIL I AM FINISHED.
FIRE!

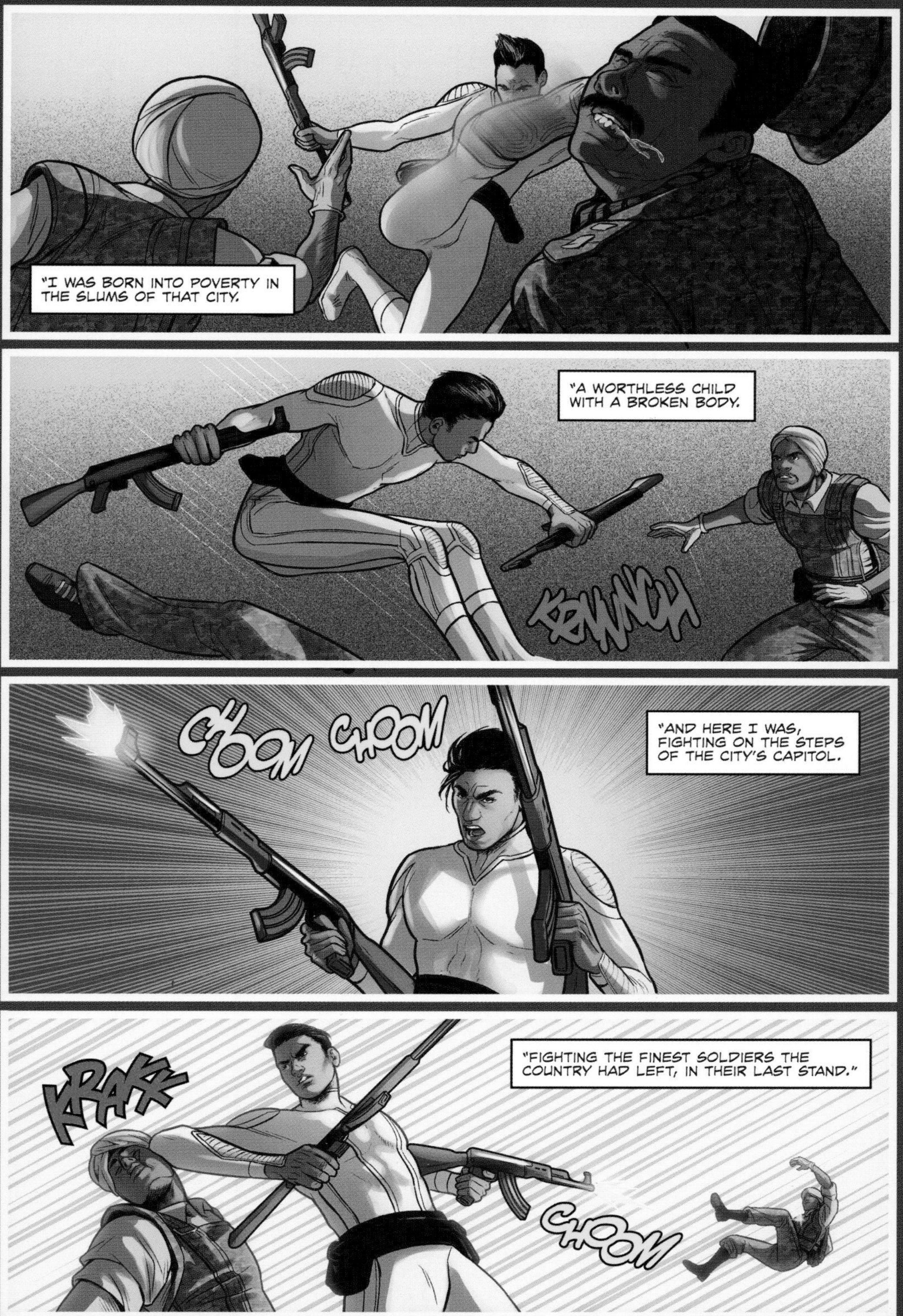
"I WAS BORN INTO POVERTY IN THE SLUMS OF THAT CITY.
"A WORTHLESS CHILD WITH A BROKEN BODY.
CHOOM CHOOM
"AND HERE I WAS, FIGHTING ON THE STEPS OF THE CITY'S CAPITOL.
KRAKK
"FIGHTING THE FINEST SOLDIERS THE COUNTRY HAD LEFT, IN THEIR LAST STAND."
CHOOM

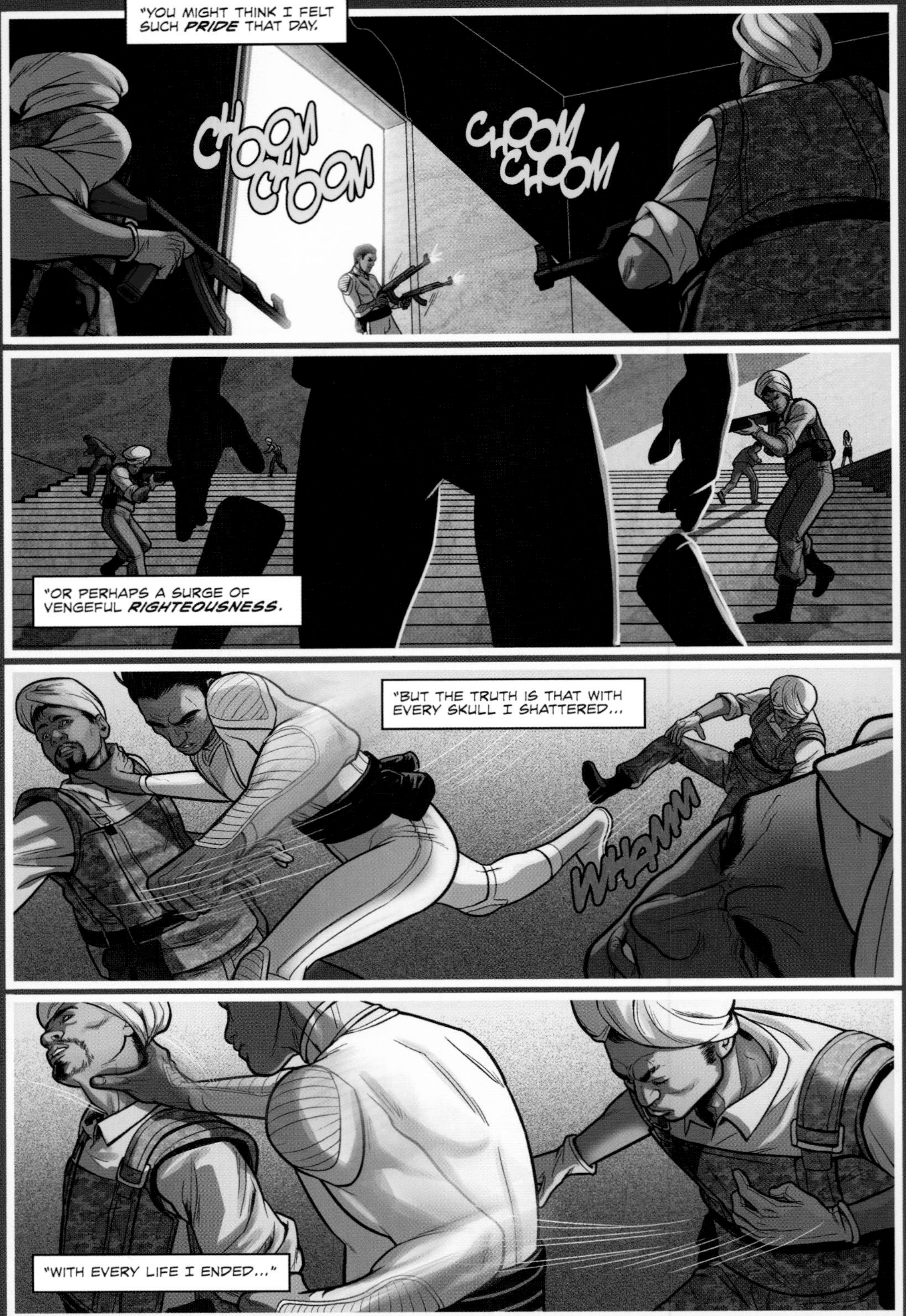
"YOU MIGHT THINK I FELT SUCH PRIDE THAT DAY.
CHOOM CHOOM CHOOM
CHOOM CHOOM
"OR PERHAPS A SURGE OF VENGEFUL RIGHTEOUSNESS.
"BUT THE TRUTH IS THAT WITH EVERY SKULL I SHATTERED...
WHAMM
"WITH EVERY LIFE I ENDED..."

"...I FELT NOTHING BUT *CALM*.

"THE BROKEN BOY WAS FINALLY *HOME*.

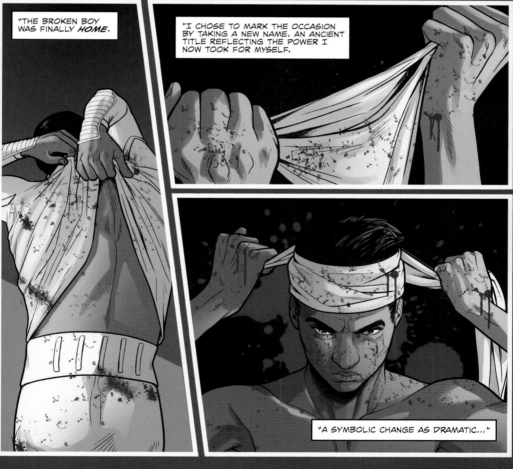

"I CHOSE TO MARK THE OCCASION BY TAKING A NEW NAME. AN ANCIENT TITLE REFLECTING THE POWER I NOW TOOK FOR MYSELF.

"A SYMBOLIC CHANGE AS DRAMATIC..."

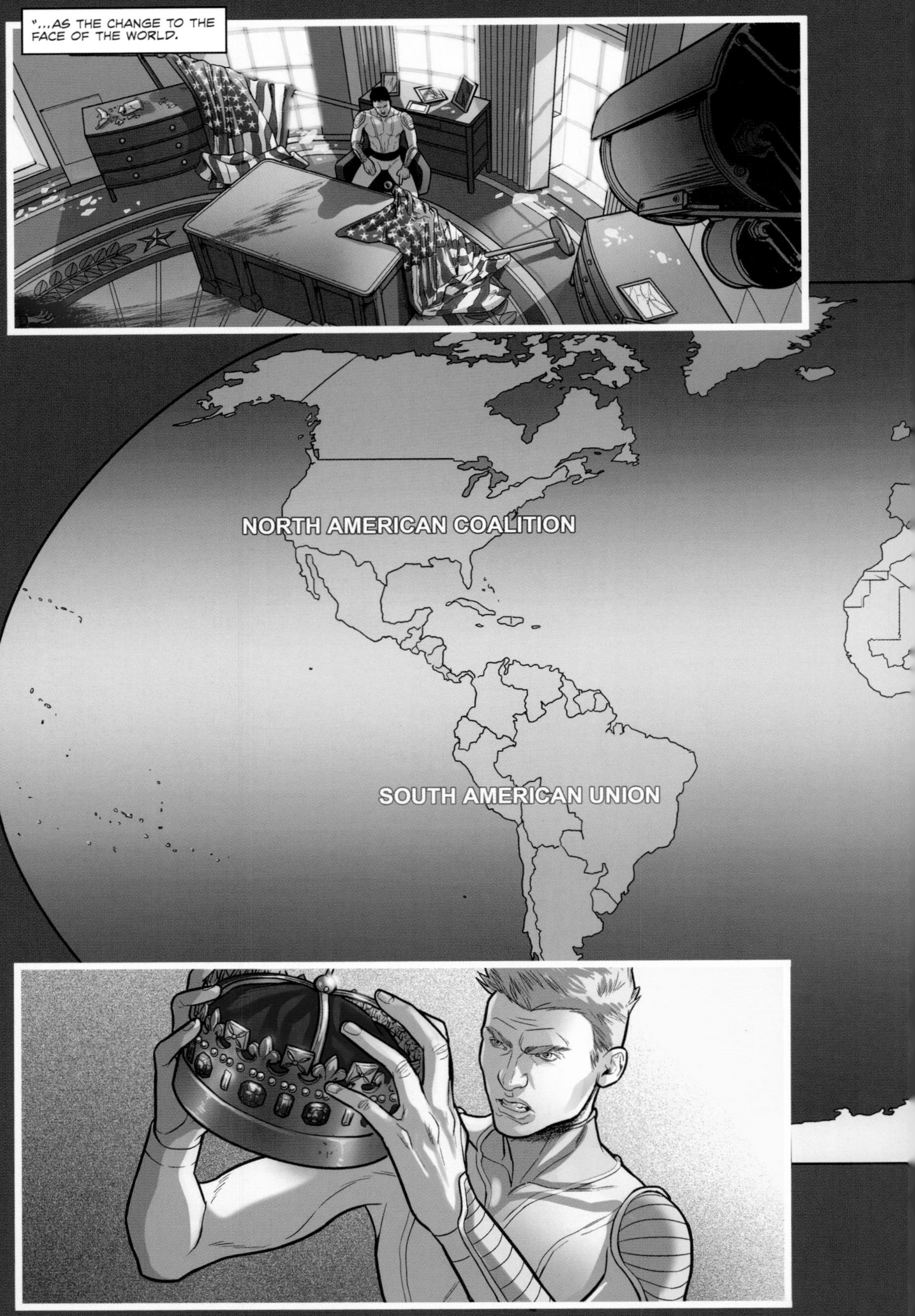
"...AS THE CHANGE TO THE FACE OF THE WORLD.
NORTH AMERICAN COALITION
SOUTH AMERICAN UNION

EUROPEAN
TERRITORIES

CENTRAL ASIAN UNION

EAST ASIAN UNION

UNITED AFRICA

AUSTRALASIA

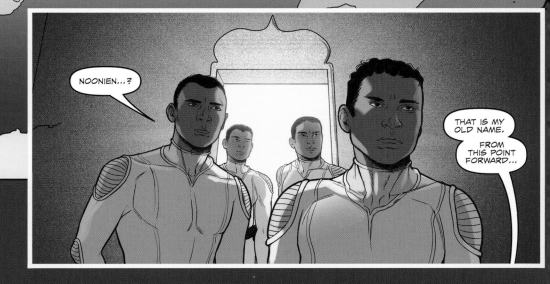

NOONIEN...?

THAT IS MY
OLD NAME.

FROM
THIS POINT
FORWARD...

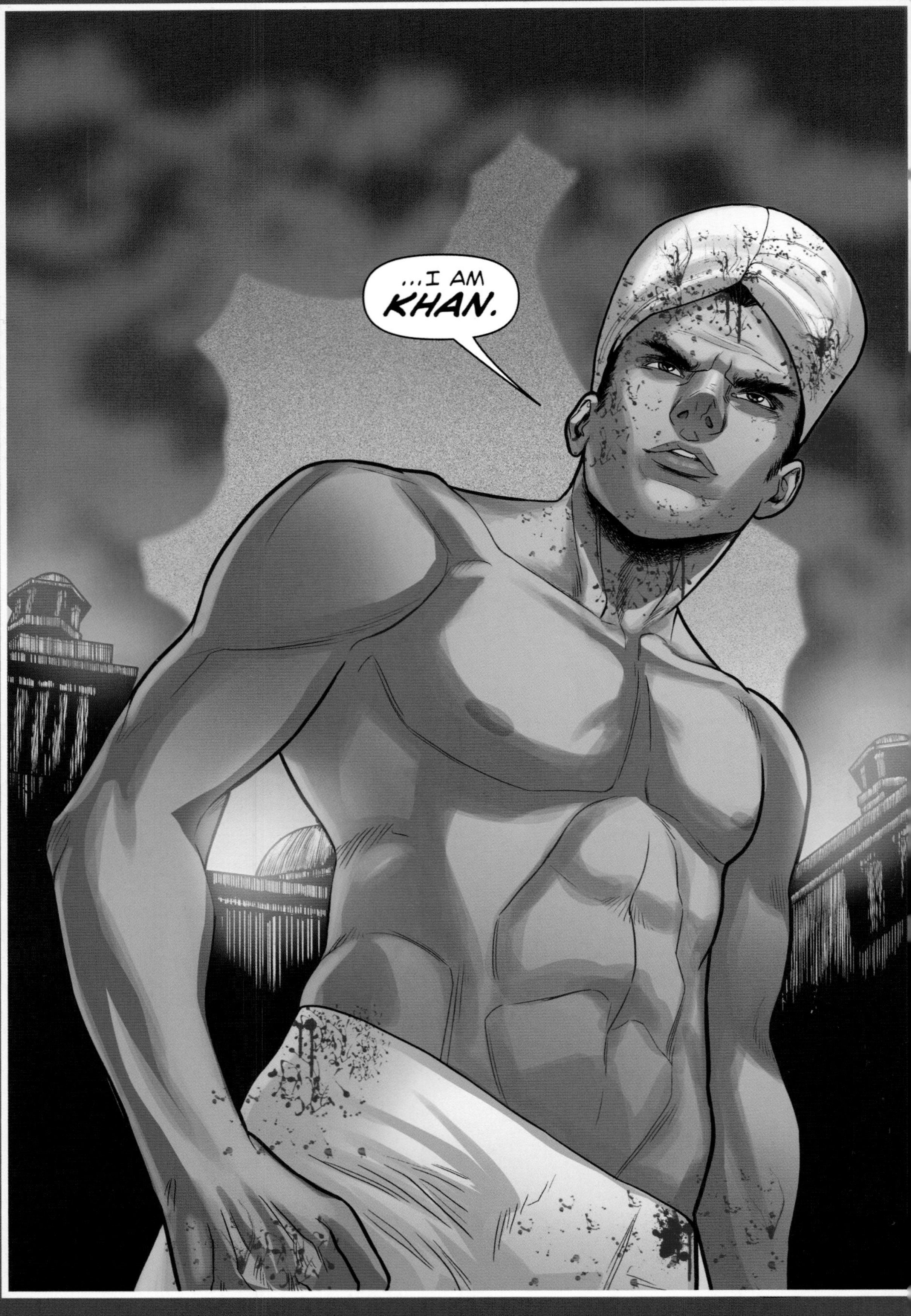
...I AM
KHAN.

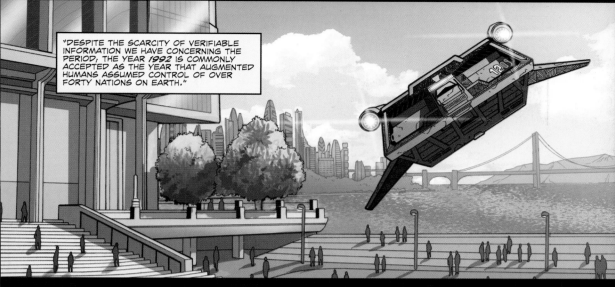

"DESPITE THE SCARCITY OF VERIFIABLE INFORMATION WE HAVE CONCERNING THE PERIOD, THE YEAR *1992* IS COMMONLY ACCEPTED AS THE YEAR THAT AUGMENTED HUMANS ASSUMED CONTROL OF OVER FORTY NATIONS ON EARTH."

THE CONFLICTS THAT FOLLOWED CAME TO BE KNOWN AS THE *EUGENICS WARS*, AS THE AUGMENTS BEGAN TO BATTLE AMONG THEMSELVES FOR SUPREMACY.

IT WAS A PERIOD OF UNPRECEDENTED BRUTALITY. MILLIONS OF PEOPLE WERE SLAUGHTERED. MILLIONS MORE SUFFERED UNDER BRUTAL REGIMES.

THESE ARE NOT THE CRIMES FOR WHICH KHAN MUST ANSWER TODAY. WE HAVE NEITHER THE AUTHORITY NOR THE EVIDENCE TO PROSECUTE THEM; IN ANY CASE.

BUT WE ASK THE DEFENDANT TO RELATE THE EVENTS THAT LED TO HIM LEAVING EARTH ON THE SHIP *BOTANY BAY*, AND BEING AWAKENED BY THE LATE ADMIRAL MARCUS.

"EUGENICS WARS?"

HOW *POETIC.*

AND HOW *FEEBLE* AN ATTEMPT TO ENCAPSULATE EVENTS YOU CAN SCARCELY COMPREHEND.

YOU ASK ME TO CAST A LIGHT INTO THE SHADOWS OF YOUR OWN PAST?

THEN LISTEN CLOSELY; FOR I SPEAK OF A TIME UNPARALLELED IN HUMAN HISTORY...

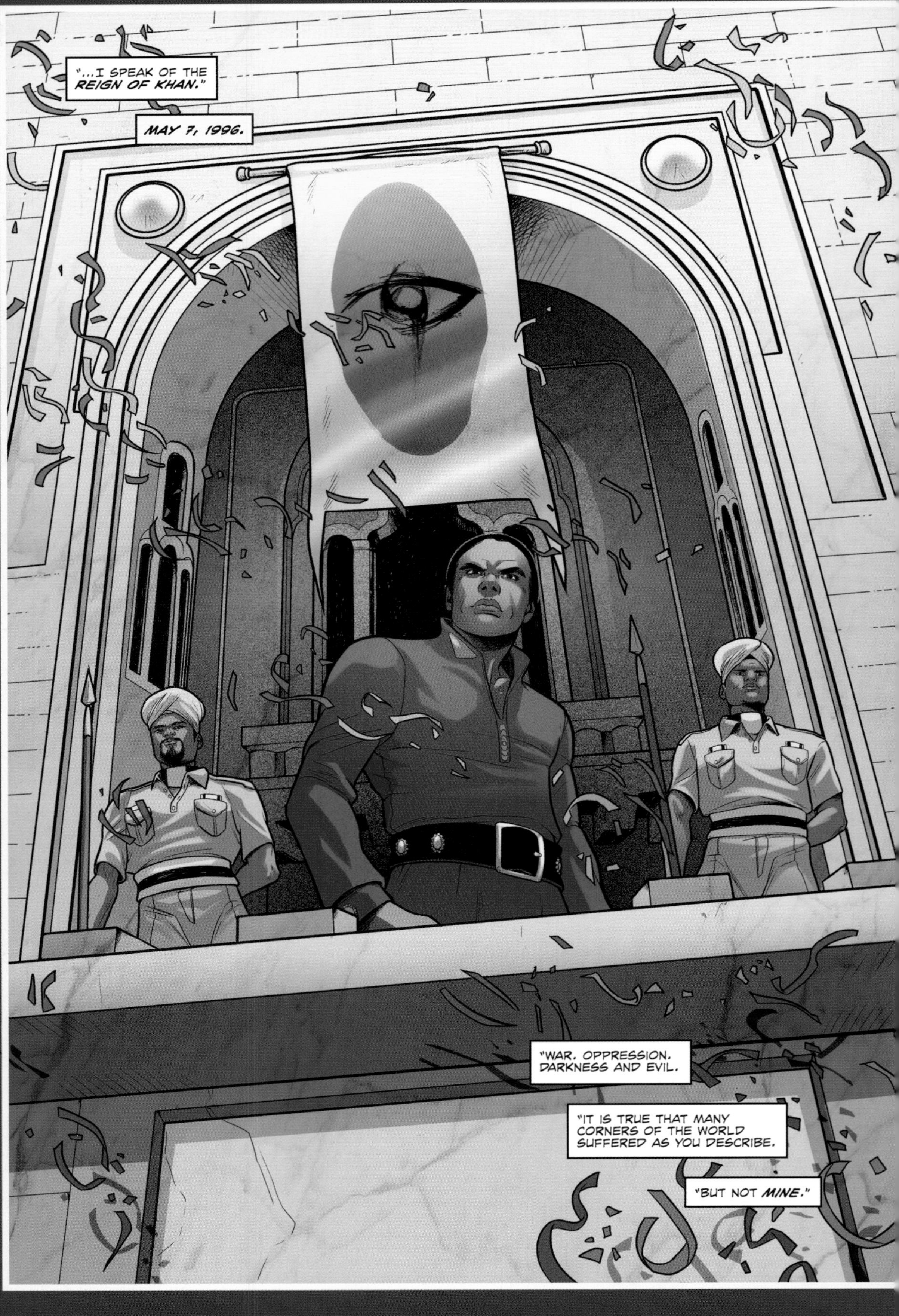
"...I SPEAK OF THE *REIGN OF KHAN.*"
MAY 7, 1996.
"WAR. OPPRESSION. DARKNESS AND EVIL.
"IT IS TRUE THAT MANY CORNERS OF THE WORLD SUFFERED AS YOU DESCRIBE.
"BUT NOT *MINE.*"

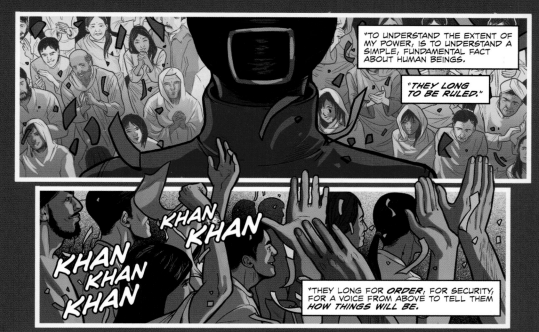

"TO UNDERSTAND THE EXTENT OF MY POWER, IS TO UNDERSTAND A SIMPLE, FUNDAMENTAL FACT ABOUT HUMAN BEINGS.

"THEY LONG TO BE RULED."

KHAN KHAN KHAN KHAN KHAN KHAN

"THEY LONG FOR *ORDER*, FOR SECURITY, FOR A VOICE FROM ABOVE TO TELL THEM *HOW THINGS WILL BE.*"

"THEY LONGED FOR *MY VOICE.*

"IN THE YEARS AFTER I ROSE TO POWER, I USED MY SUPERIOR INTELLECT TO *REVOLUTIONIZE* SOCIETY.

"TOGETHER WITH MY BROTHERS AND SISTERS, I ELIMINATED POVERTY AND SICKNESS WITHIN MY BORDERS. THE CONCEPT OF *NEED* WAS AS ARCHAIC AS RUBBING TWO STICKS TO MAKE FIRE."

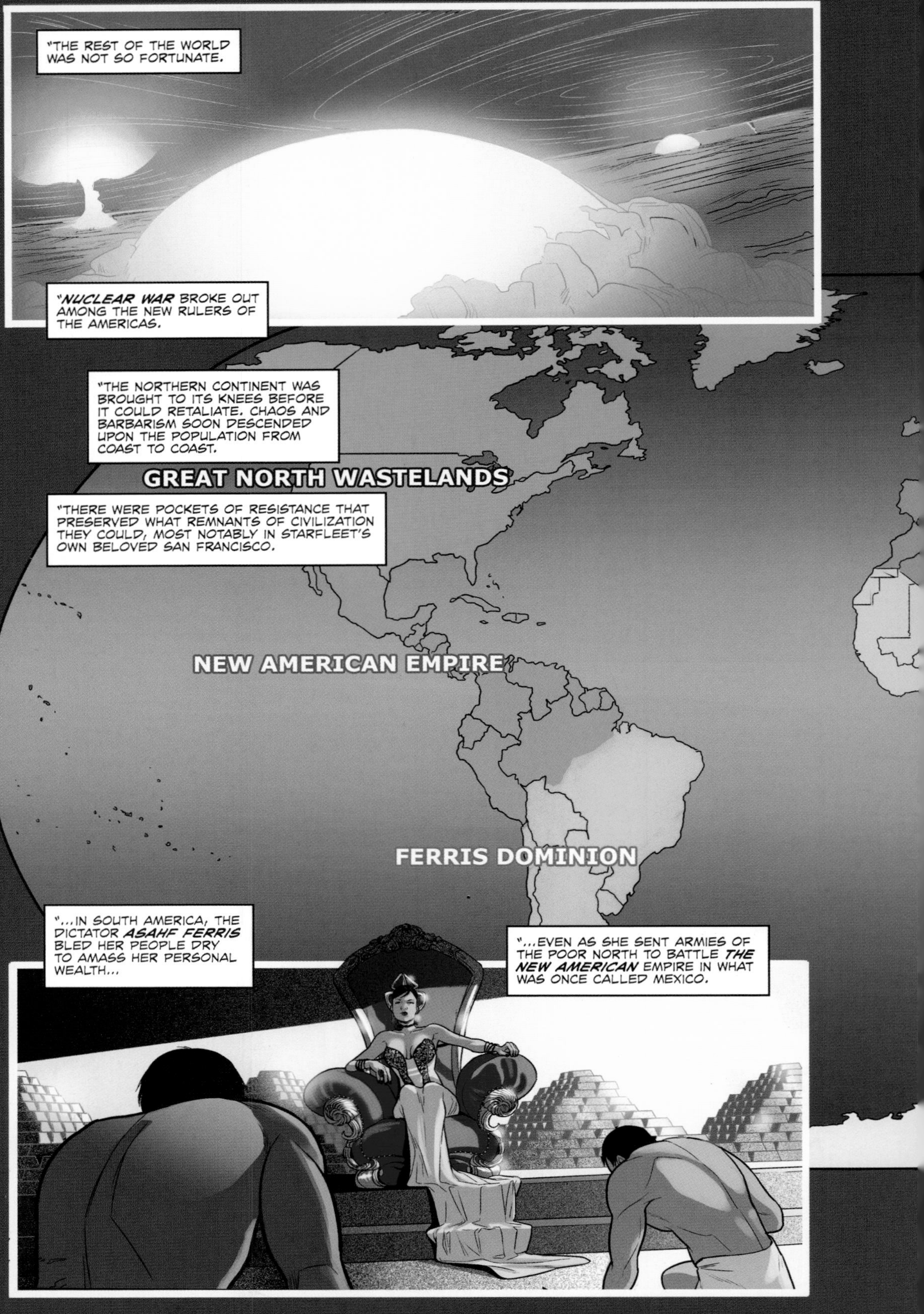

"THE REST OF THE WORLD WAS NOT SO FORTUNATE.
"*NUCLEAR WAR* BROKE OUT AMONG THE NEW RULERS OF THE AMERICAS.
"THE NORTHERN CONTINENT WAS BROUGHT TO ITS KNEES BEFORE IT COULD RETALIATE. CHAOS AND BARBARISM SOON DESCENDED UPON THE POPULATION FROM COAST TO COAST.
GREAT NORTH WASTELANDS
"THERE WERE POCKETS OF RESISTANCE THAT PRESERVED WHAT REMNANTS OF CIVILIZATION THEY COULD, MOST NOTABLY IN STARFLEET'S OWN BELOVED SAN FRANCISCO.
NEW AMERICAN EMPIRE
FERRIS DOMINION
"...IN SOUTH AMERICA, THE DICTATOR *ASAHF FERRIS* BLED HER PEOPLE DRY TO AMASS HER PERSONAL WEALTH...
"...EVEN AS SHE SENT ARMIES OF THE POOR NORTH TO BATTLE *THE NEW AMERICAN* EMPIRE IN WHAT WAS ONCE CALLED MEXICO.

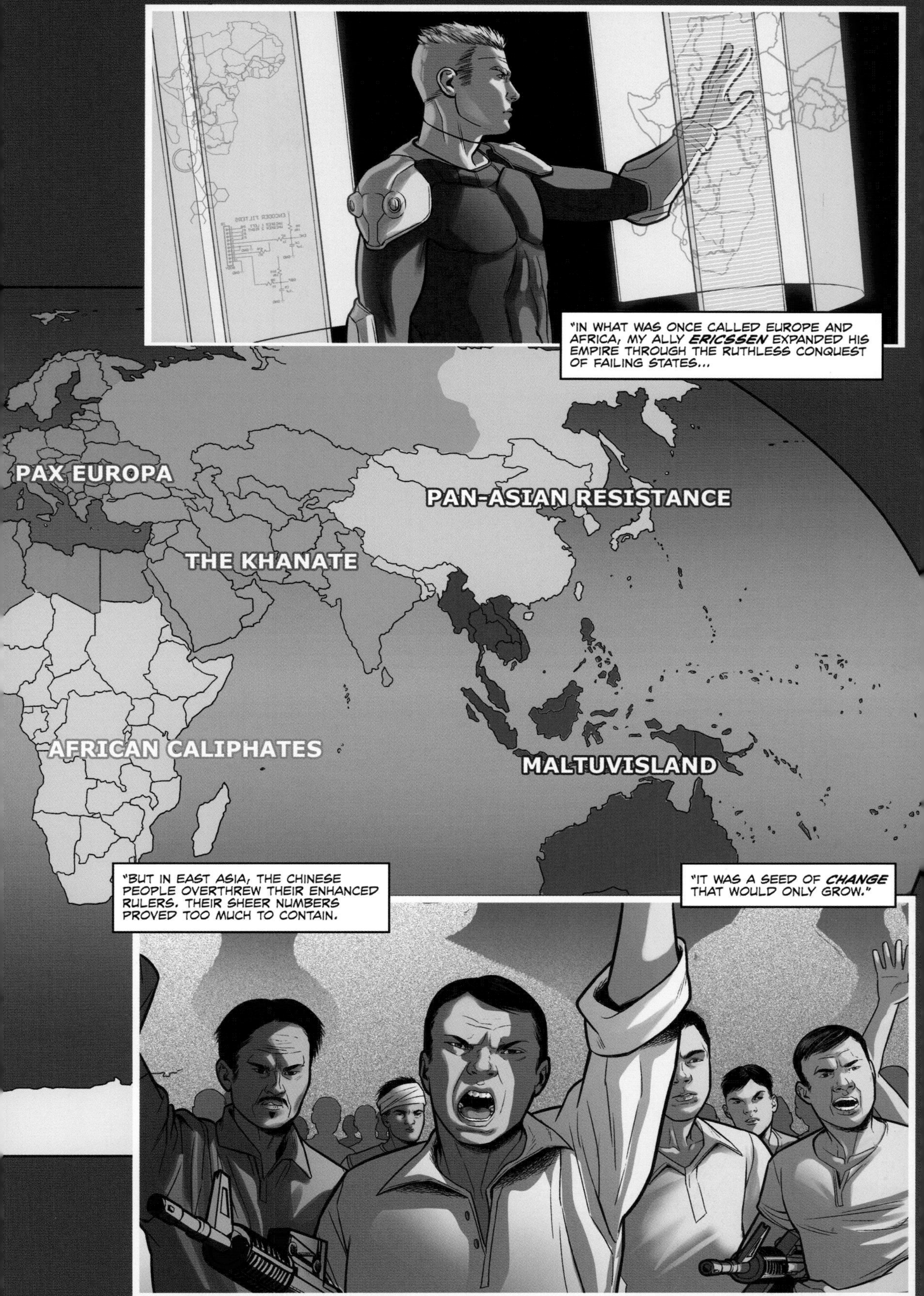
"IN WHAT WAS ONCE CALLED EUROPE AND AFRICA, MY ALLY ERICSSEN EXPANDED HIS EMPIRE THROUGH THE RUTHLESS CONQUEST OF FAILING STATES...
PAX EUROPA
PAN-ASIAN RESISTANCE
THE KHANATE
AFRICAN CALIPHATES
MALTUVISLAND
"BUT IN EAST ASIA, THE CHINESE PEOPLE OVERTHREW THEIR ENHANCED RULERS. THEIR SHEER NUMBERS PROVED TOO MUCH TO CONTAIN.
"IT WAS A SEED OF CHANGE THAT WOULD ONLY GROW."

"WORST OF ALL WAS THE EFFECT OF WAR ON THE PLANET ITSELF.

"THE FALLOUT FROM THE CONFLICTS IN THE AMERICAS POISONED SKIES AROUND THE GLOBE.

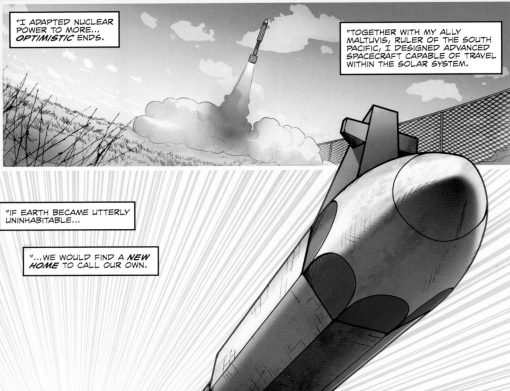

"I ADAPTED NUCLEAR POWER TO MORE... *OPTIMISTIC* ENDS.

"TOGETHER WITH MY ALLY MALTUVIS, RULER OF THE SOUTH PACIFIC, I DESIGNED ADVANCED SPACECRAFT CAPABLE OF TRAVEL WITHIN THE SOLAR SYSTEM.

"IF EARTH BECAME UTTERLY UNINHABITABLE...

"...WE WOULD FIND A *NEW HOME* TO CALL OUR OWN.

"NEVER DID I IMAGINE THE EVENTS THAT WOULD ULTIMATELY DRIVE ME TO IT."

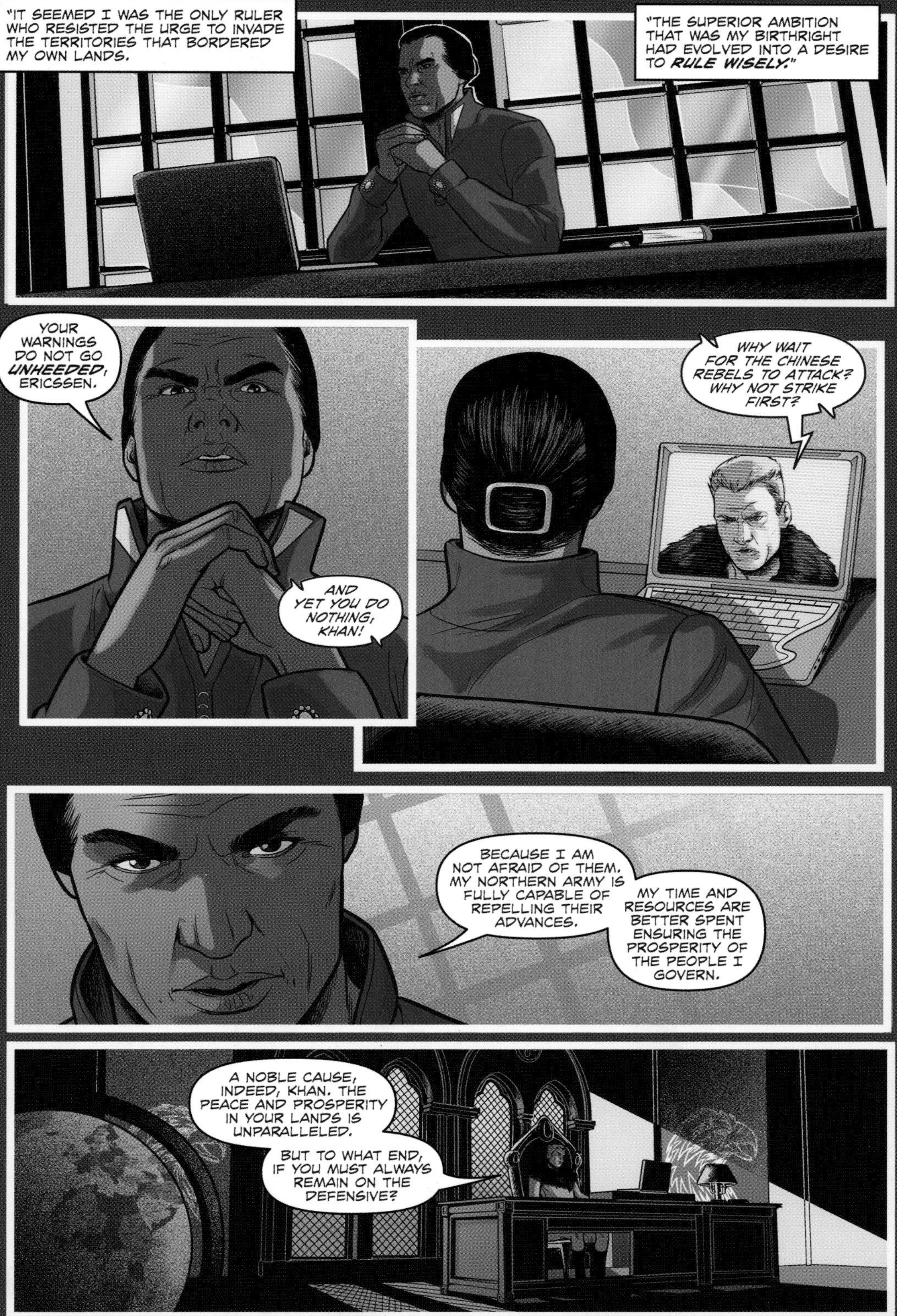
"IT SEEMED I WAS THE ONLY RULER WHO RESISTED THE URGE TO INVADE THE TERRITORIES THAT BORDERED MY OWN LANDS.
"THE SUPERIOR AMBITION THAT WAS MY BIRTHRIGHT HAD EVOLVED INTO A DESIRE TO **RULE WISELY.**"
YOUR WARNINGS DO NOT GO ***UNHEEDED***, ERICSSEN.
AND YET YOU DO NOTHING, KHAN!
WHY WAIT FOR THE CHINESE REBELS TO ATTACK? WHY NOT STRIKE FIRST?
BECAUSE I AM NOT AFRAID OF THEM. MY NORTHERN ARMY IS FULLY CAPABLE OF REPELLING THEIR ADVANCES.
MY TIME AND RESOURCES ARE BETTER SPENT ENSURING THE PROSPERITY OF THE PEOPLE I GOVERN.
A NOBLE CAUSE, INDEED, KHAN. THE PEACE AND PROSPERITY IN YOUR LANDS IS UNPARALLELED.
BUT TO WHAT END, IF YOU MUST ALWAYS REMAIN ON THE DEFENSIVE?

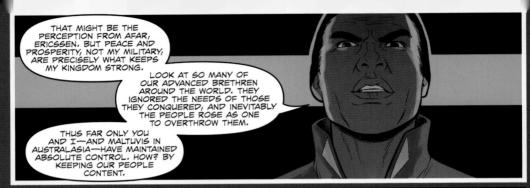

THAT MIGHT BE THE PERCEPTION FROM AFAR, ERICSSEN. BUT PEACE AND PROSPERITY, NOT MY MILITARY, ARE PRECISELY WHAT KEEPS MY KINGDOM STRONG.

LOOK AT SO MANY OF OUR ADVANCED BRETHREN AROUND THE WORLD. THEY IGNORED THE NEEDS OF THOSE THEY CONQUERED, AND INEVITABLY THE PEOPLE ROSE AS ONE TO OVERTHROW THEM.

THUS FAR ONLY YOU AND I—AND MALTUVIS IN AUSTRALASIA—HAVE MAINTAINED ABSOLUTE CONTROL. HOW? BY KEEPING OUR PEOPLE CONTENT.

NEVER FORGET THAT FOR ALL OUR SUPERIOR ABILITY, WE REMAIN FAR OUTNUMBERED BY OUR SUBJECTS.

AND WHAT IF I WISH TO ENGAGE THE ASIAN REBELLION ON MY OWN TERMS? WILL YOU COME TO MY AID SHOULD THE NEED ARISE?

YOUR CHOICE OF ACTION IS YOUR OWN, ERICSSEN.

AS ARE ANY REPERCUSSIONS THAT FOLLOW.

ESTEEMED LEADER! PARDON MY INTRUSION! THERE'S AN ATTACK FROM THE SOUTHEAST, SIR—

THE CHINESE?

NO, SIR! IT'S *MALTUVIS!*

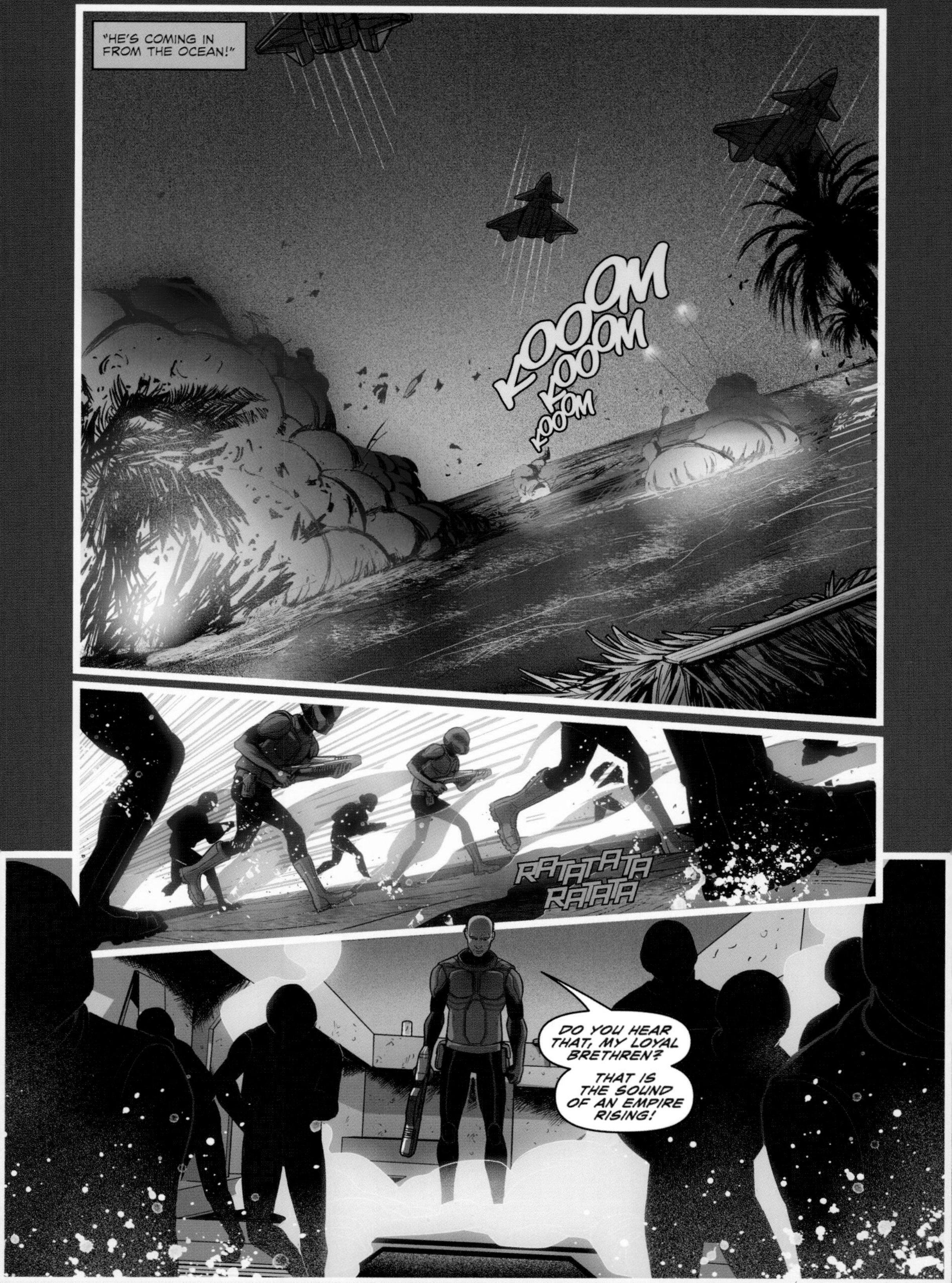
"HE'S COMING IN FROM THE OCEAN!"
KOOOM
KOOOM
KOOOM
KOOOM
RATATATA
RATATA
DO YOU HEAR THAT, MY LOYAL BRETHREN?
THAT IS THE SOUND OF AN EMPIRE RISING!

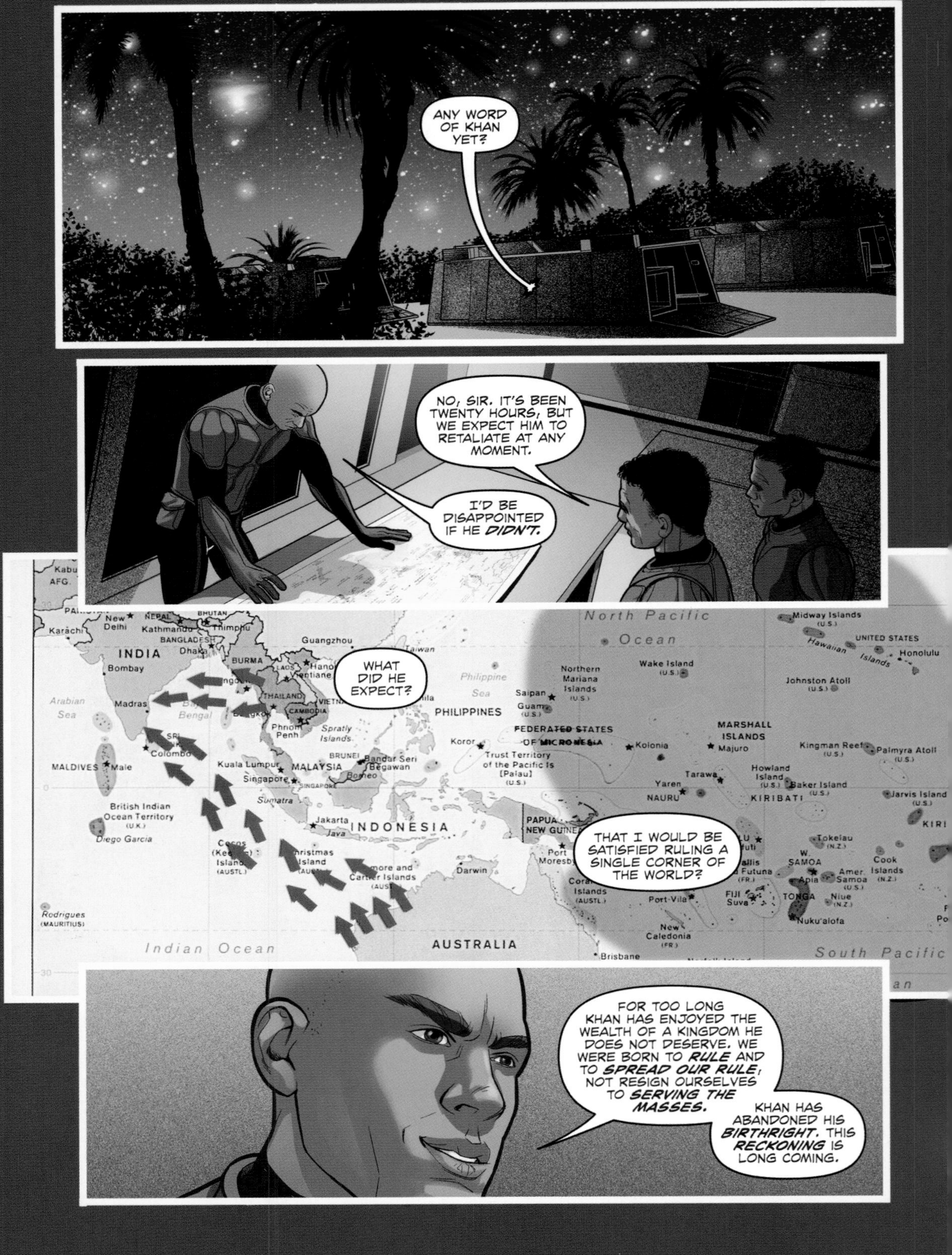
ANY WORD OF KHAN YET?
NO, SIR. IT'S BEEN TWENTY HOURS, BUT WE EXPECT HIM TO RETALIATE AT ANY MOMENT.
I'D BE DISAPPOINTED IF HE *DIDN'T.*
WHAT DID HE EXPECT?
THAT I WOULD BE SATISFIED RULING A SINGLE CORNER OF THE WORLD?
FOR TOO LONG KHAN HAS ENJOYED THE WEALTH OF A KINGDOM HE DOES NOT DESERVE. WE WERE BORN TO ***RULE*** AND TO ***SPREAD OUR RULE***, NOT RESIGN OURSELVES TO ***SERVING THE MASSES.***
KHAN HAS ABANDONED HIS ***BIRTHRIGHT.*** THIS ***RECKONING*** IS LONG COMING.
INDIA
Bombay
Madras
Arabian Sea
MALDIVES
Male
Colombo
British Indian Ocean Territory
Diego Garcia
Rodrigues
Indian Ocean
Karachi
New Delhi
Kathmandu
BANGLADESH
Dhaka
BURMA
THAILAND
CAMBODIA
Guangzhou
Kuala Lumpur
MALAYSIA
Singapore
Sumatra
Jakarta
Java
INDONESIA
Christmas Island
Darwin
AUSTRALIA
PHILIPPINES
Spratly Islands
BRUNEI
Bandar Seri Begawan
Borneo
North Pacific Ocean
Northern Mariana Islands
Saipan
Guam
Koror
Trust Territory of the Pacific Is (Palau)
FEDERATED STATES OF MICRONESIA
Kolonia
MARSHALL ISLANDS
Majuro
Wake Island
Midway Islands
UNITED STATES
Hawaiian Islands
Honolulu
Johnston Atoll
Kingman Reef
Palmyra Atoll
Howland Island
Baker Island
Jarvis Island
Tarawa
Yaren
NAURU
KIRIBATI
PAPUA NEW GUINEA
Port Moresby
Port-Vila
FIJI
Suva
New Caledonia
Brisbane
Tokelau
W. SAMOA
Apia
Amer. Samoa
Cook Islands
Niue
TONGA
Nuku'alofa
South Pacific

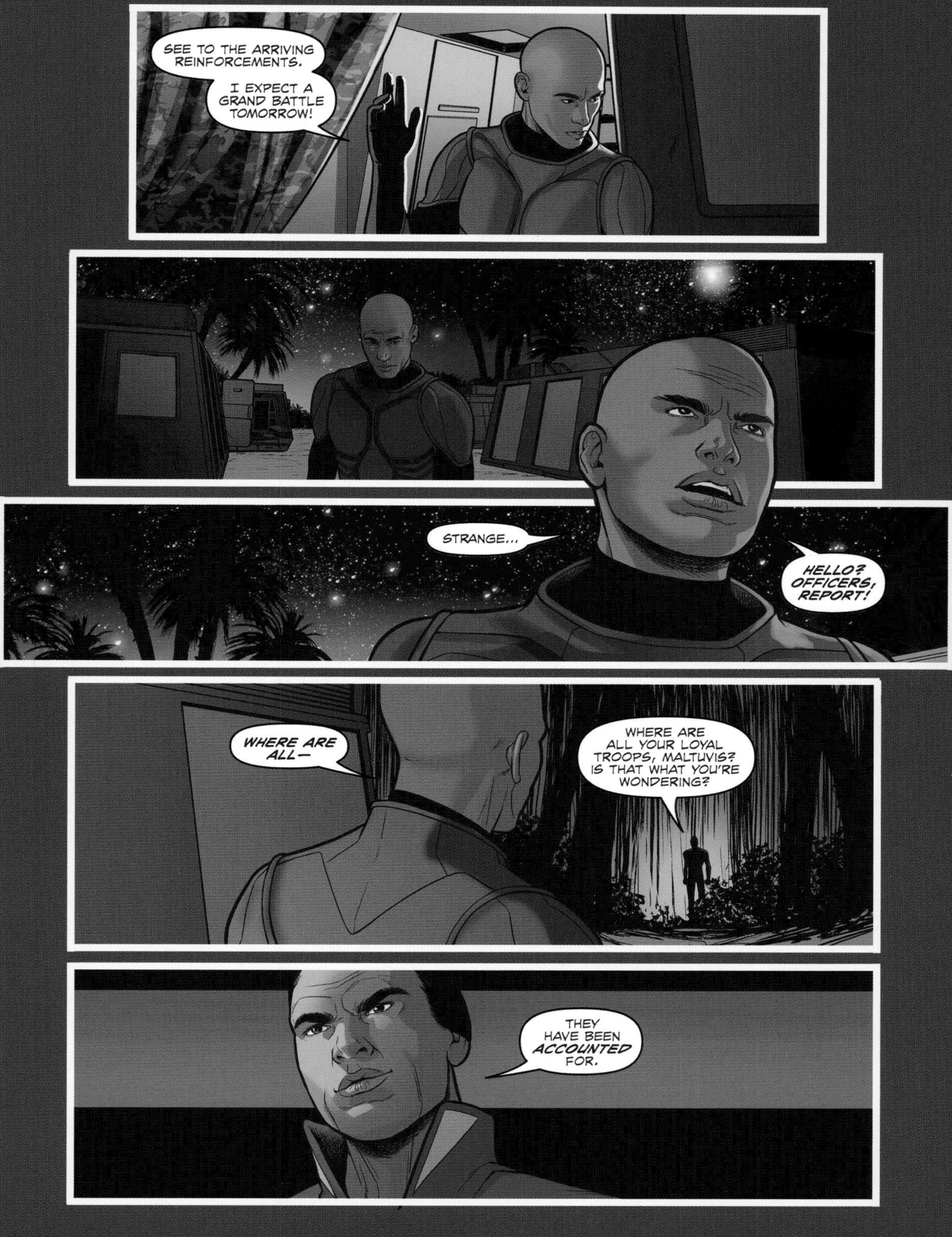
SEE TO THE ARRIVING REINFORCEMENTS.
I EXPECT A GRAND BATTLE TOMORROW!
STRANGE...
HELLO? OFFICERS, REPORT!
WHERE ARE ALL—
WHERE ARE ALL YOUR LOYAL TROOPS, MALTUVIS? IS THAT WHAT YOU'RE WONDERING?
THEY HAVE BEEN ACCOUNTED FOR.

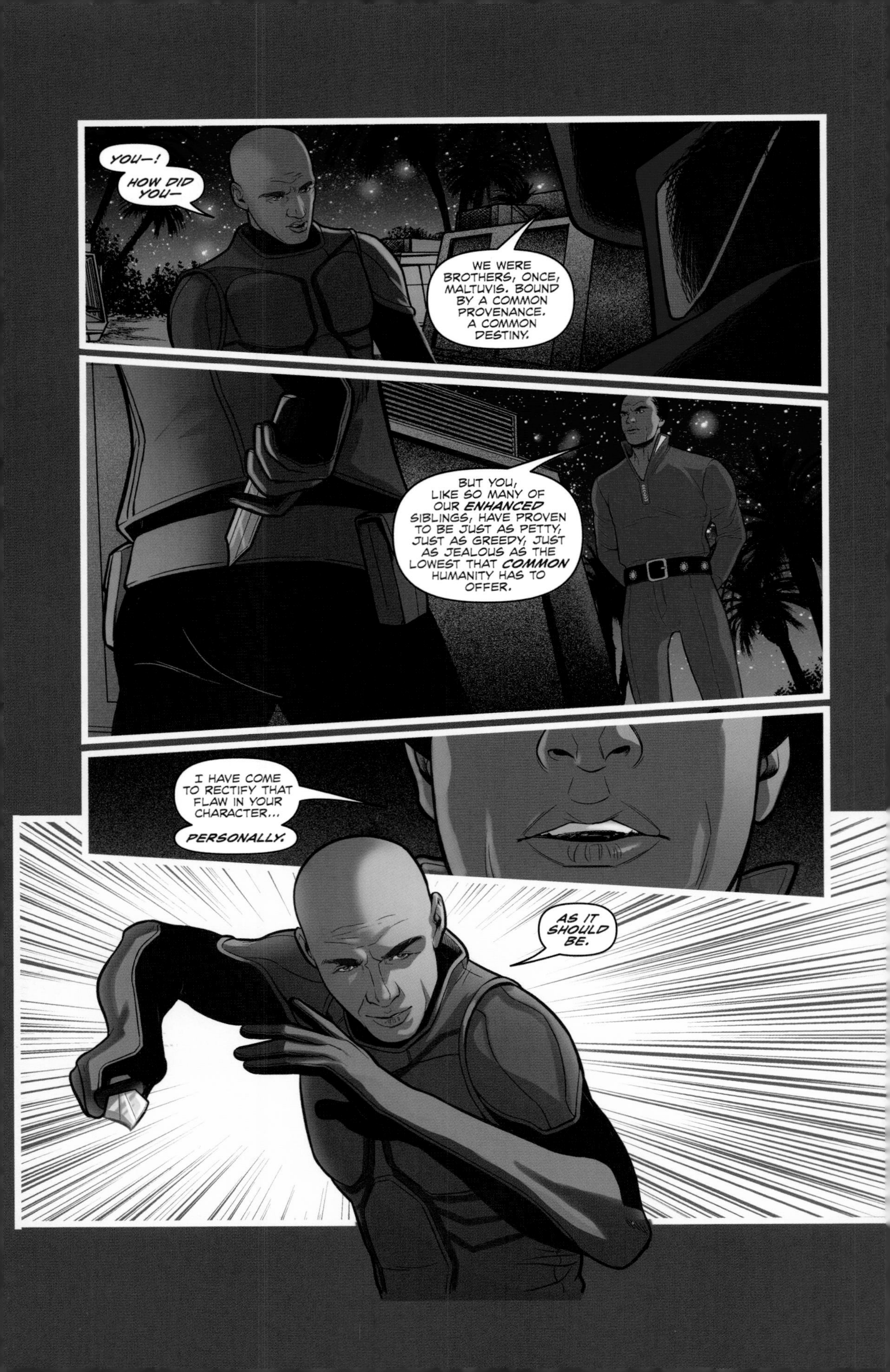
YOU—!
HOW DID YOU—
WE WERE BROTHERS, ONCE, MALTUVIS. BOUND BY A COMMON PROVENANCE. A COMMON DESTINY.
BUT YOU, LIKE SO MANY OF OUR ENHANCED SIBLINGS, HAVE PROVEN TO BE JUST AS PETTY, JUST AS GREEDY, JUST AS JEALOUS AS THE LOWEST THAT COMMON HUMANITY HAS TO OFFER.
I HAVE COME TO RECTIFY THAT FLAW IN YOUR CHARACTER...
PERSONALLY.
AS IT SHOULD BE.

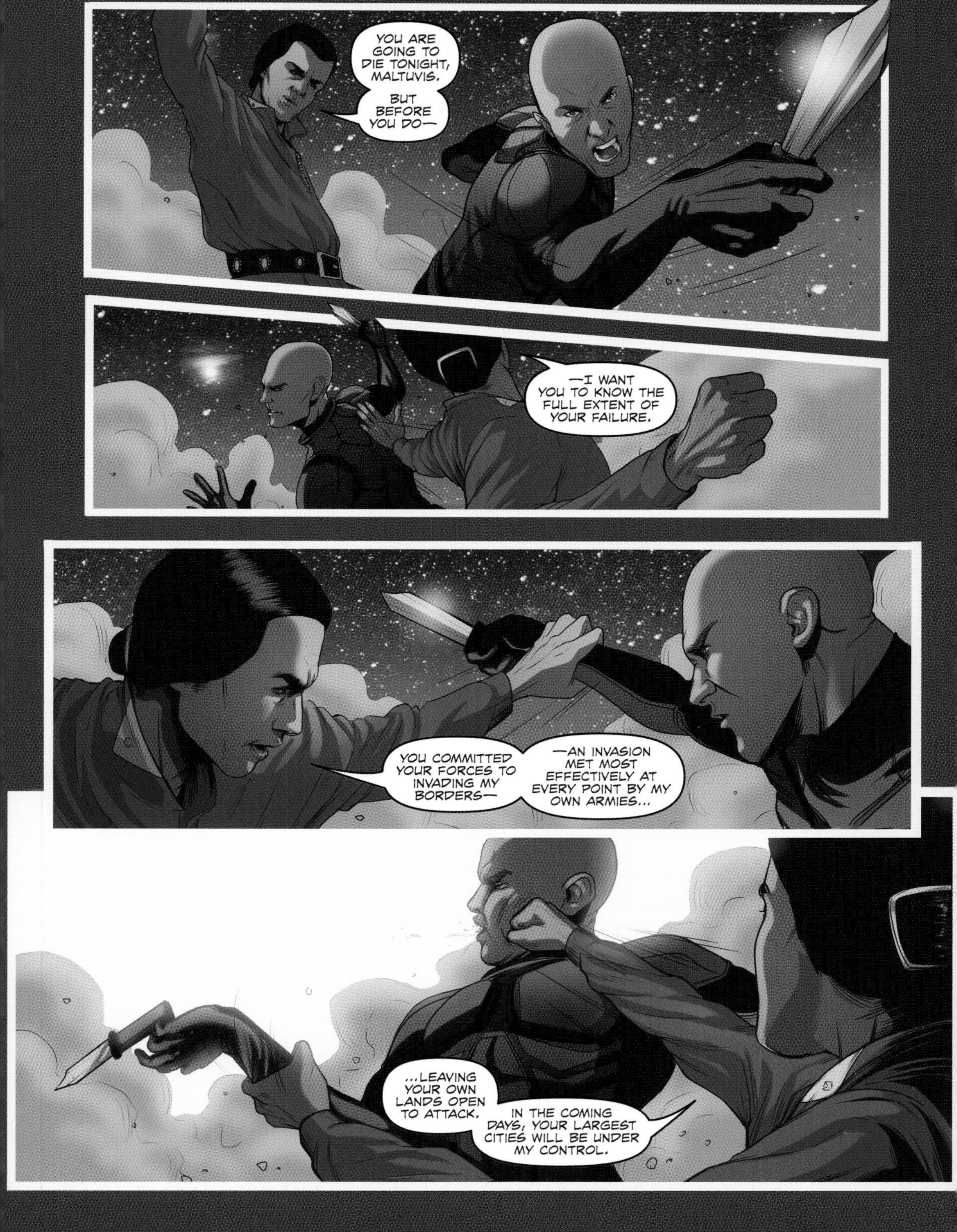
YOU ARE GOING TO DIE TONIGHT, MALTUVIS.
BUT BEFORE YOU DO—
—I WANT YOU TO KNOW THE FULL EXTENT OF YOUR FAILURE.
YOU COMMITTED YOUR FORCES TO INVADING MY BORDERS—
—AN INVASION MET MOST EFFECTIVELY AT EVERY POINT BY MY OWN ARMIES...
...LEAVING YOUR OWN LANDS OPEN TO ATTACK.
IN THE COMING DAYS, YOUR LARGEST CITIES WILL BE UNDER MY CONTROL.

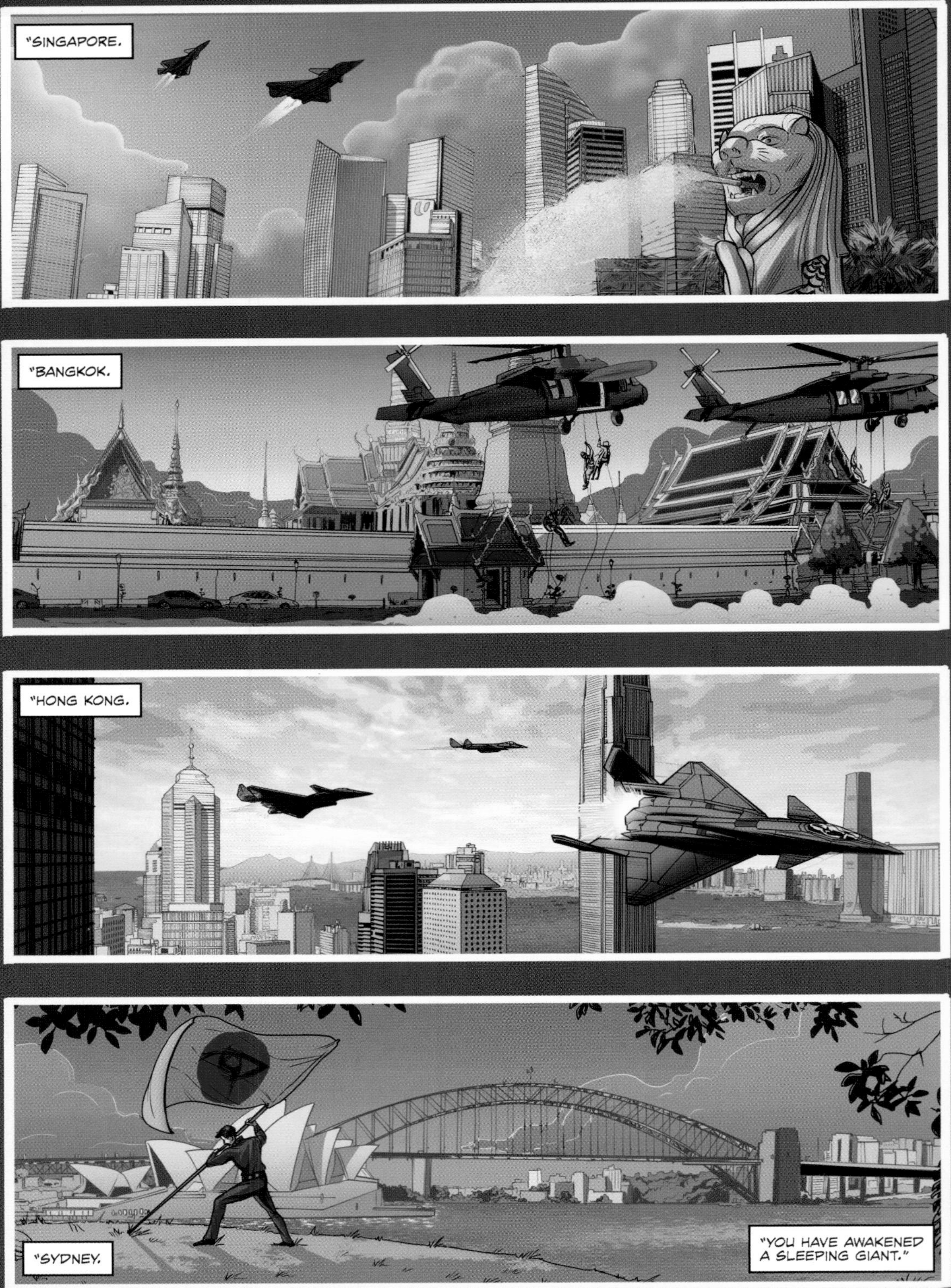
"SINGAPORE.
"BANGKOK.
"HONG KONG.
"SYDNEY.
"YOU HAVE AWAKENED A SLEEPING GIANT."

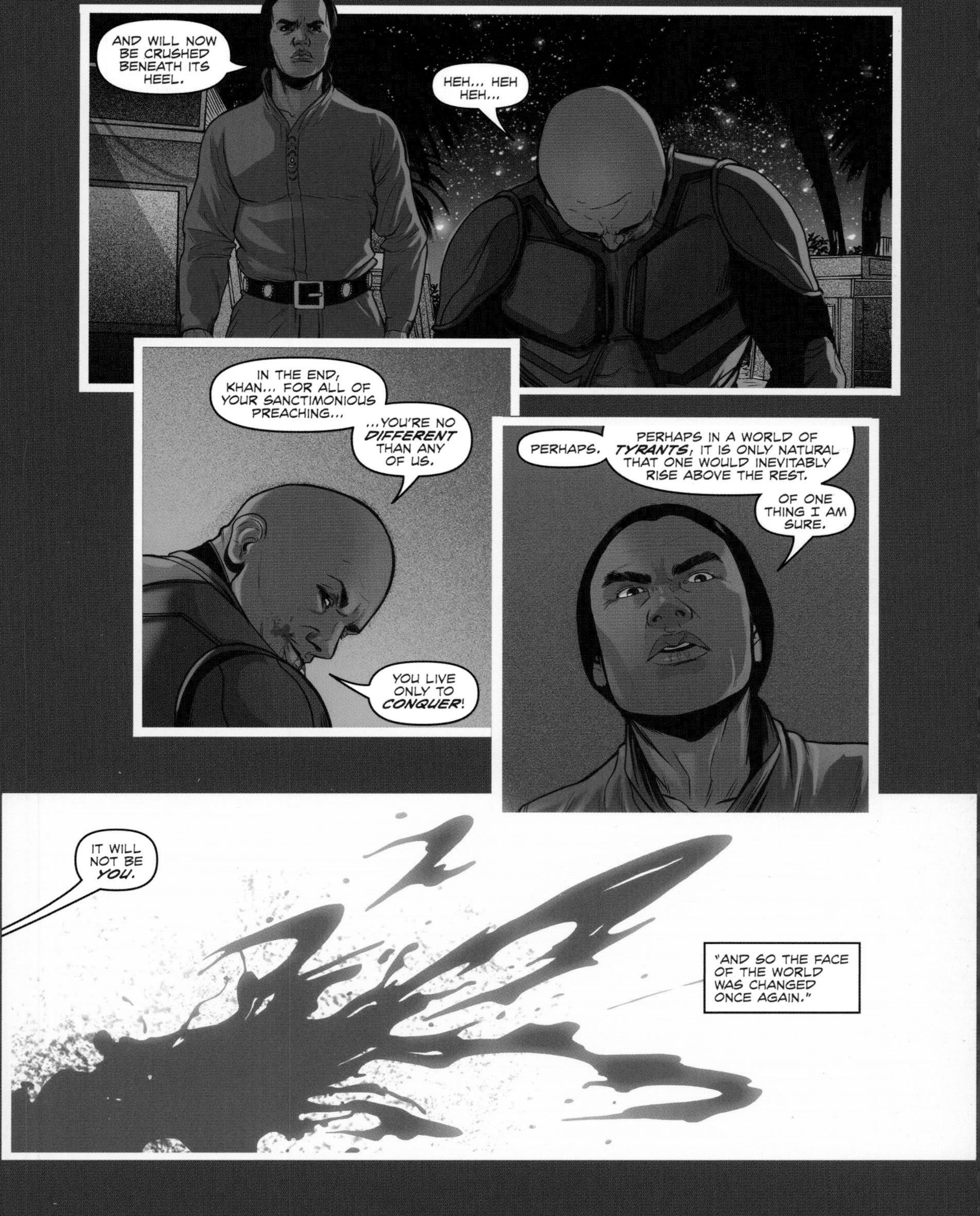
AND WILL NOW BE CRUSHED BENEATH ITS HEEL.
HEH... HEH HEH...
IN THE END, KHAN... FOR ALL OF YOUR SANCTIMONIOUS PREACHING...
...YOU'RE NO *DIFFERENT* THAN ANY OF US.
YOU LIVE ONLY TO *CONQUER*!
PERHAPS.
PERHAPS IN A WORLD OF *TYRANTS*, IT IS ONLY NATURAL THAT ONE WOULD INEVITABLY RISE ABOVE THE REST.
OF ONE THING I AM SURE.
IT WILL NOT BE *YOU*.
"AND SO THE FACE OF THE WORLD WAS CHANGED ONCE AGAIN."

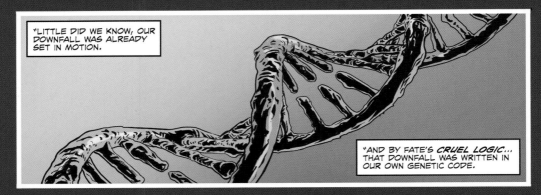

"LITTLE DID WE KNOW, OUR DOWNFALL WAS ALREADY SET IN MOTION.

"AND BY FATE'S *CRUEL LOGIC*... THAT DOWNFALL WAS WRITTEN IN OUR OWN GENETIC CODE.

"A GROUP OF HUMAN SCIENTISTS— DESPITE THEIR INTELLECTUAL *INFERIORITY*—DEVELOPED A NEW WEAPON. A MICROSCOPIC WEAPON.

"THE HUMANS WERE TOO WEAK TO DEFEAT US DIRECTLY IN BATTLE.

"SO IN THE END, IT WAS ONLY BY OUR *OWN UNIQUE* BIOLOGY THAT WE COULD FAIL."

I'M *DYING*, KHAN!

AND WHEN I'M GONE THEY'LL COME FOR *YOU!*

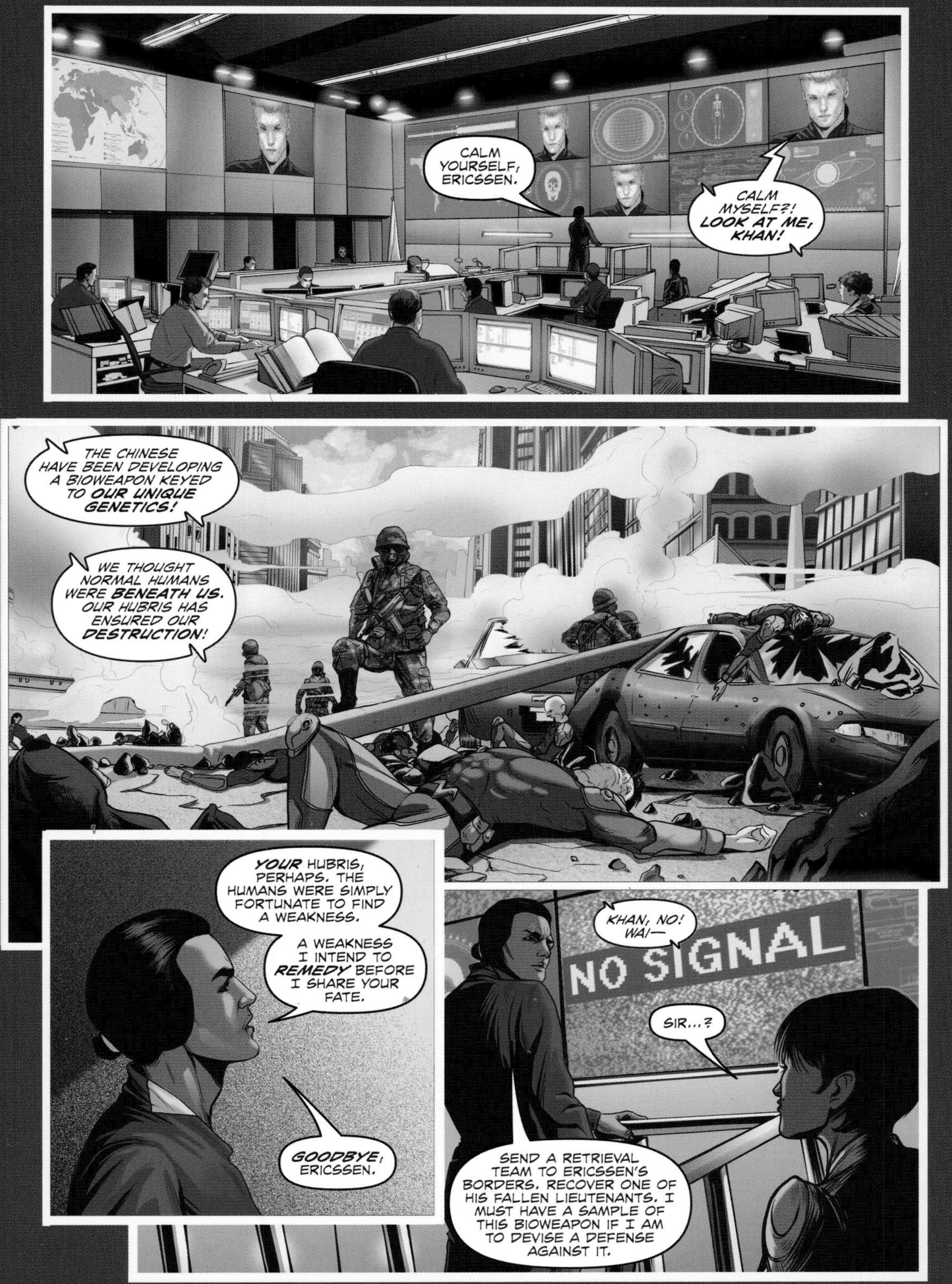
CALM YOURSELF, ERICSSEN.
CALM MYSELF?! LOOK AT ME, KHAN!
THE CHINESE HAVE BEEN DEVELOPING A BIOWEAPON KEYED TO OUR UNIQUE GENETICS!
WE THOUGHT NORMAL HUMANS WERE BENEATH US. OUR HUBRIS HAS ENSURED OUR DESTRUCTION!
YOUR HUBRIS, PERHAPS. THE HUMANS WERE SIMPLY FORTUNATE TO FIND A WEAKNESS.
A WEAKNESS I INTEND TO REMEDY BEFORE I SHARE YOUR FATE.
GOODBYE, ERICSSEN.
KHAN, NO! WAI—
NO SIGNAL
SIR...?
SEND A RETRIEVAL TEAM TO ERICSSEN'S BORDERS. RECOVER ONE OF HIS FALLEN LIEUTENANTS. I MUST HAVE A SAMPLE OF THIS BIOWEAPON IF I AM TO DEVISE A DEFENSE AGAINST IT.

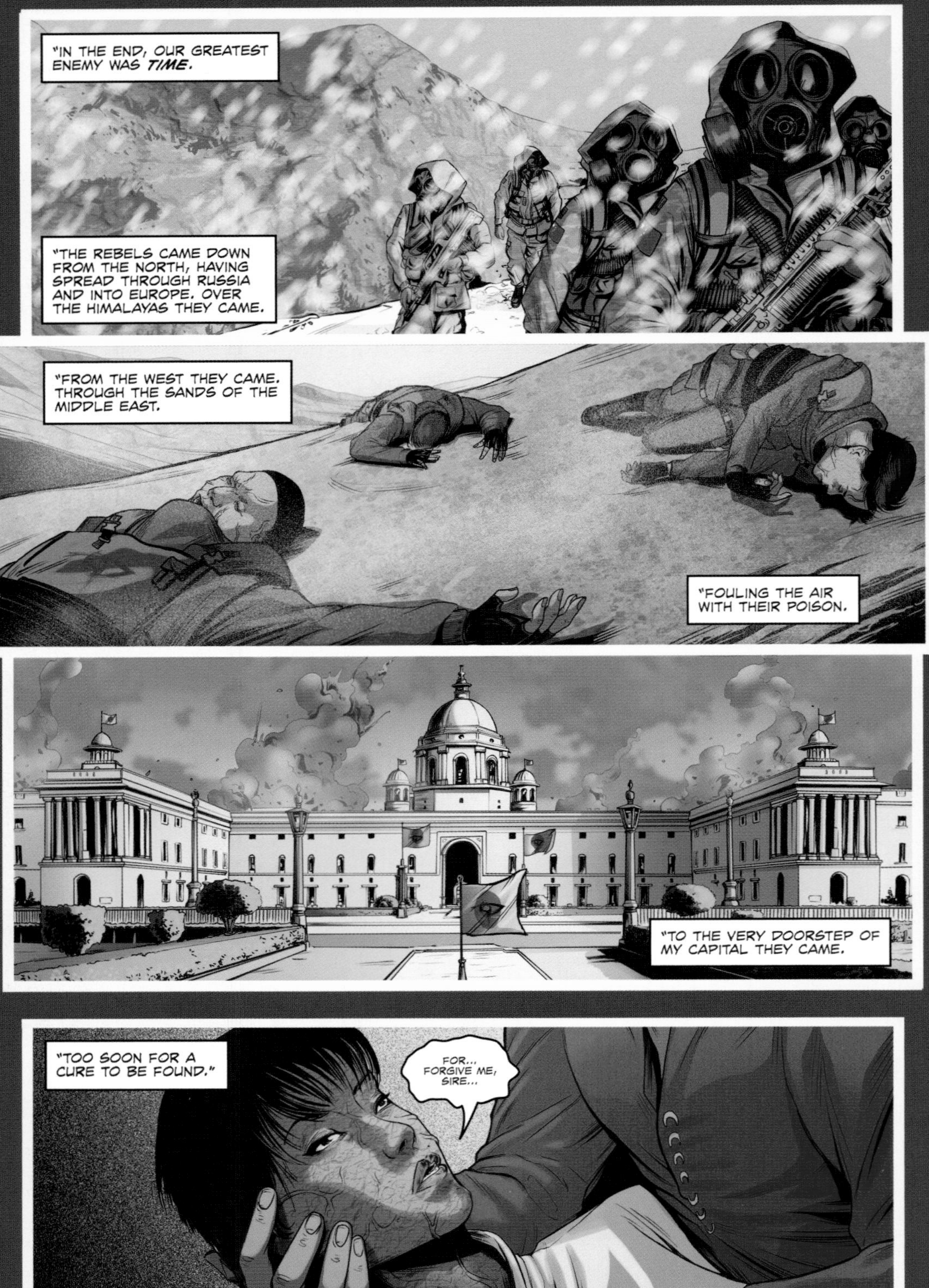
"IN THE END, OUR GREATEST ENEMY WAS *TIME*.
"THE REBELS CAME DOWN FROM THE NORTH, HAVING SPREAD THROUGH RUSSIA AND INTO EUROPE. OVER THE HIMALAYAS THEY CAME.
"FROM THE WEST THEY CAME. THROUGH THE SANDS OF THE MIDDLE EAST.
"FOULING THE AIR WITH THEIR POISON.
"TO THE VERY DOORSTEP OF MY CAPITAL THEY CAME.
"TOO SOON FOR A CURE TO BE FOUND."
FOR... FORGIVE ME, SIRE...

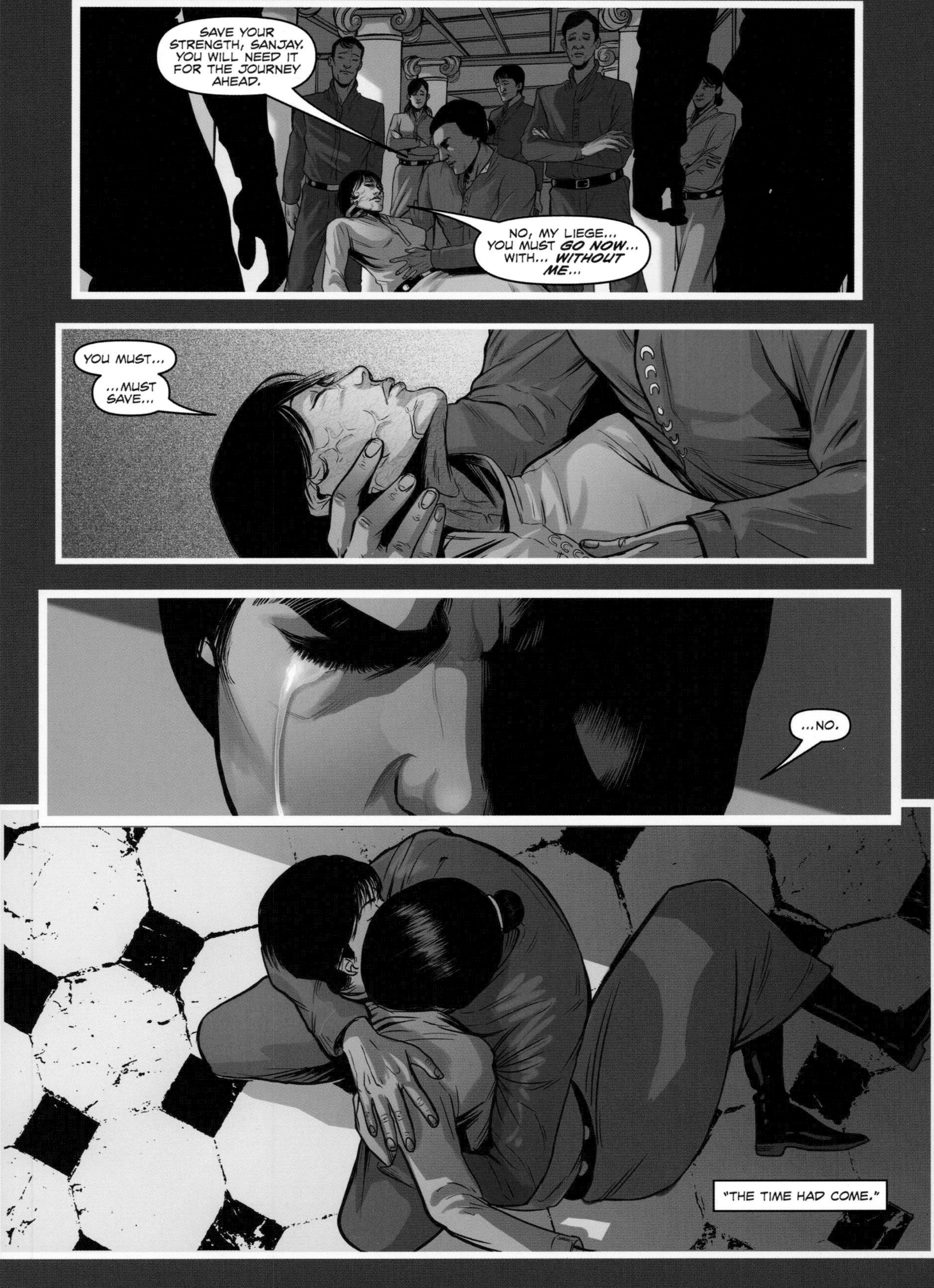
SAVE YOUR STRENGTH, SANJAY. YOU WILL NEED IT FOR THE JOURNEY AHEAD.
NO, MY LIEGE... YOU MUST GO NOW... WITH... WITHOUT ME...
YOU MUST...
...MUST SAVE...
...NO.
"THE TIME HAD COME."

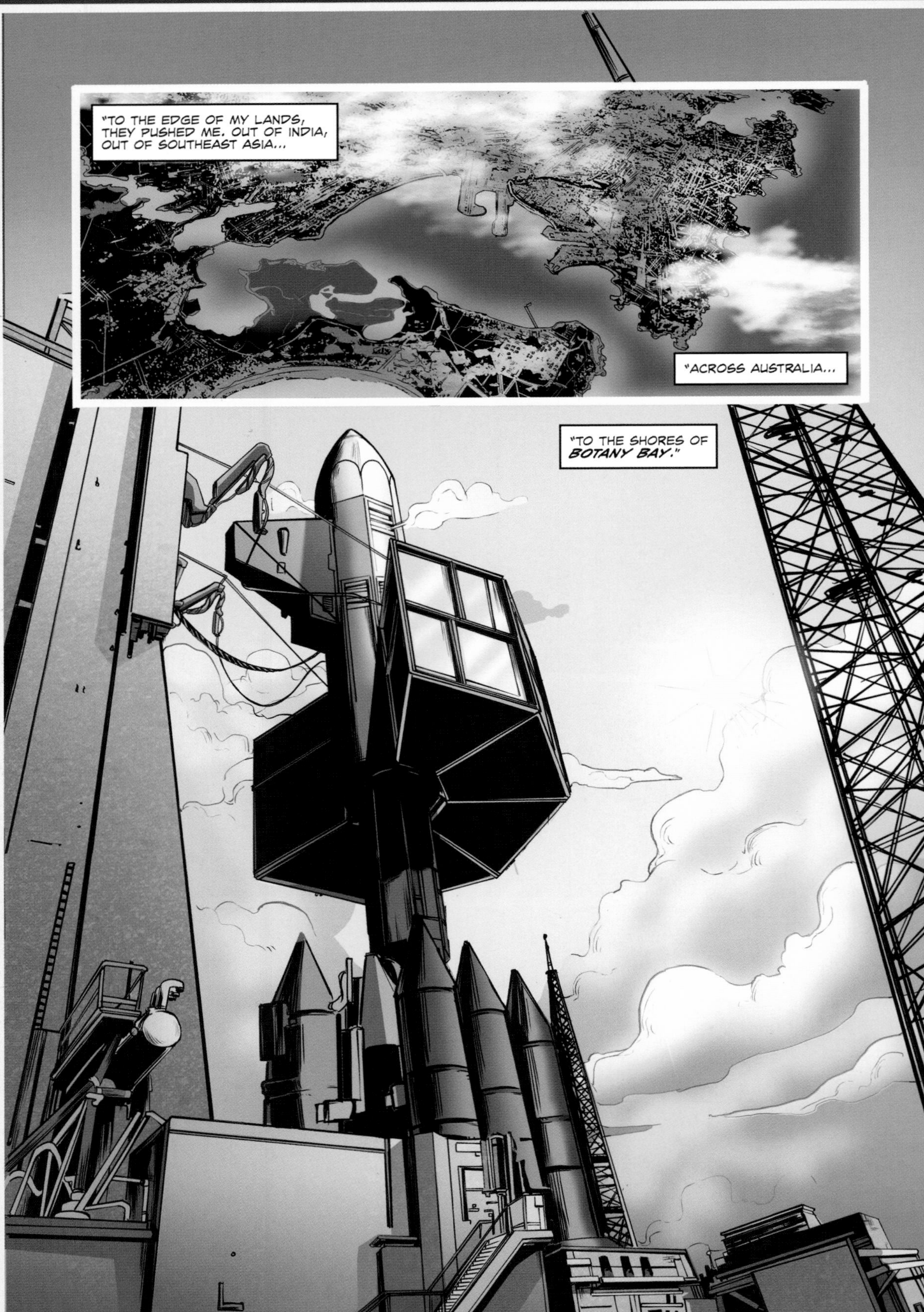
"TO THE EDGE OF MY LANDS, THEY PUSHED ME. OUT OF INDIA, OUT OF SOUTHEAST ASIA...
"ACROSS AUSTRALIA...
"TO THE SHORES OF *BOTANY BAY*."

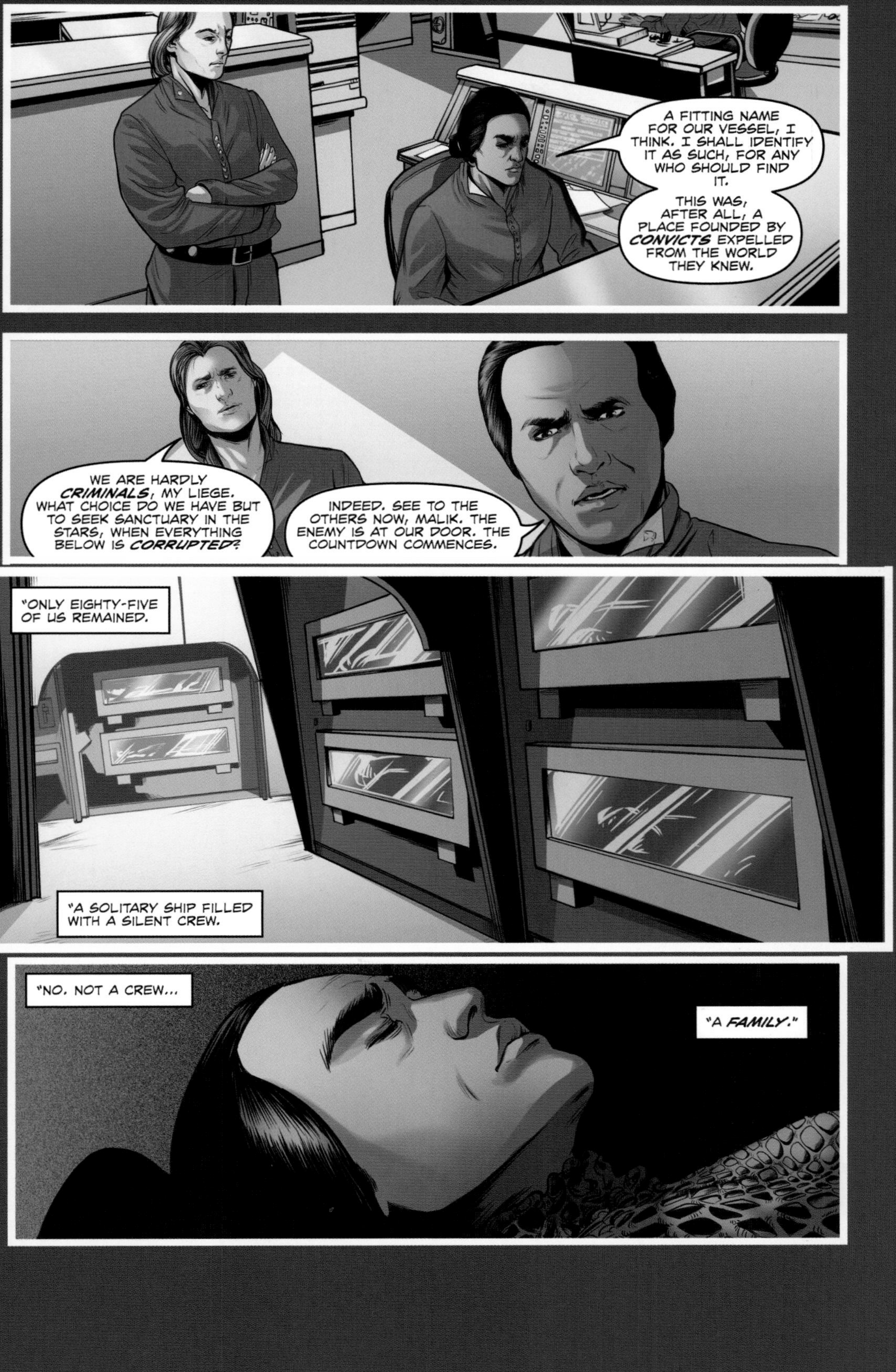
A FITTING NAME FOR OUR VESSEL, I THINK. I SHALL IDENTIFY IT AS SUCH, FOR ANY WHO SHOULD FIND IT.
THIS WAS, AFTER ALL, A PLACE FOUNDED BY CONVICTS EXPELLED FROM THE WORLD THEY KNEW.
WE ARE HARDLY CRIMINALS, MY LIEGE. WHAT CHOICE DO WE HAVE BUT TO SEEK SANCTUARY IN THE STARS, WHEN EVERYTHING BELOW IS CORRUPTED?
INDEED. SEE TO THE OTHERS NOW, MALIK. THE ENEMY IS AT OUR DOOR. THE COUNTDOWN COMMENCES.
"ONLY EIGHTY-FIVE OF US REMAINED.
"A SOLITARY SHIP FILLED WITH A SILENT CREW.
"NO. NOT A CREW...
"A FAMILY."

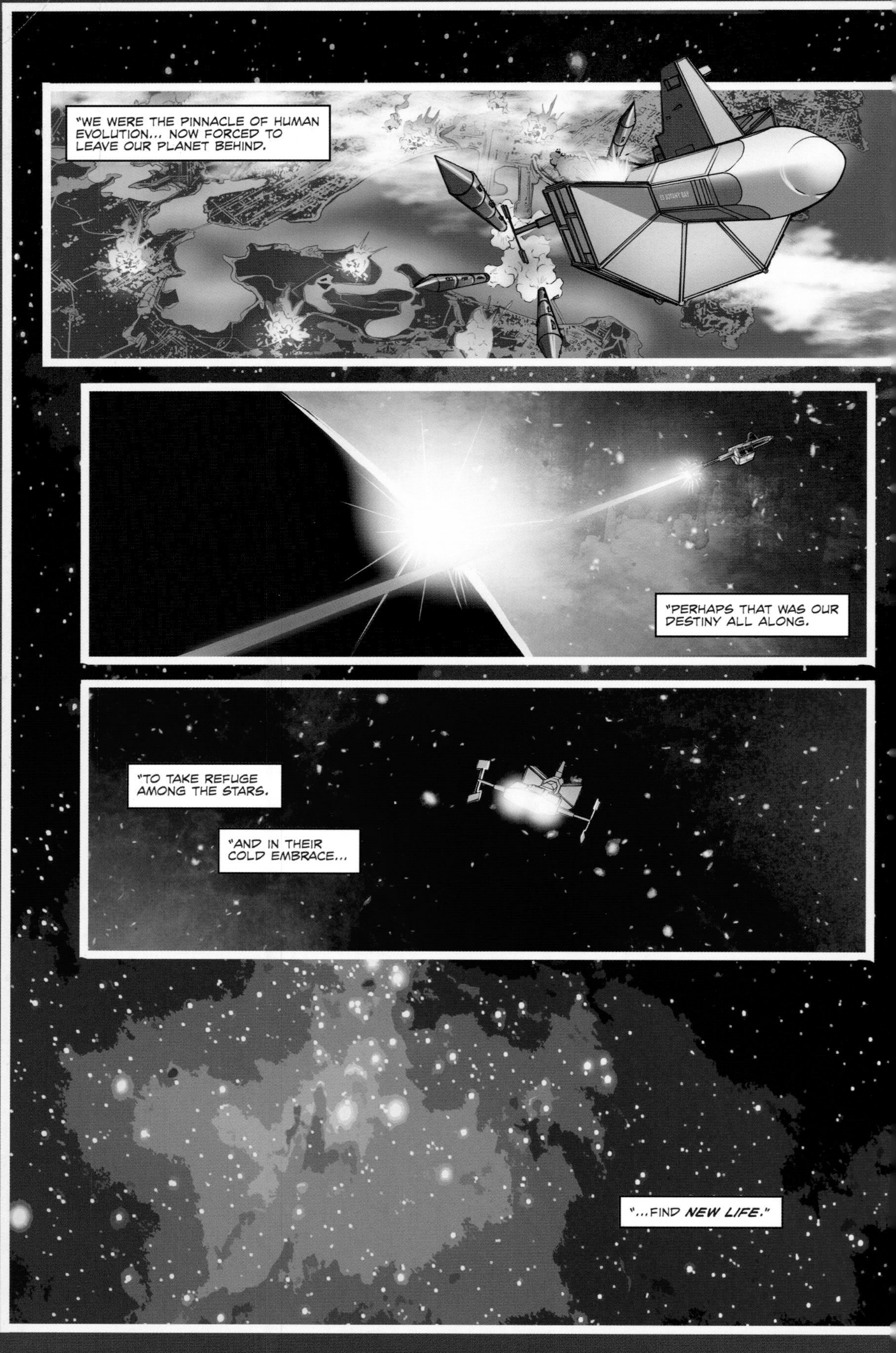
"WE WERE THE PINNACLE OF HUMAN EVOLUTION... NOW FORCED TO LEAVE OUR PLANET BEHIND.
"PERHAPS THAT WAS OUR DESTINY ALL ALONG.
"TO TAKE REFUGE AMONG THE STARS.
"AND IN THEIR COLD EMBRACE...
"...FIND *NEW LIFE.*"

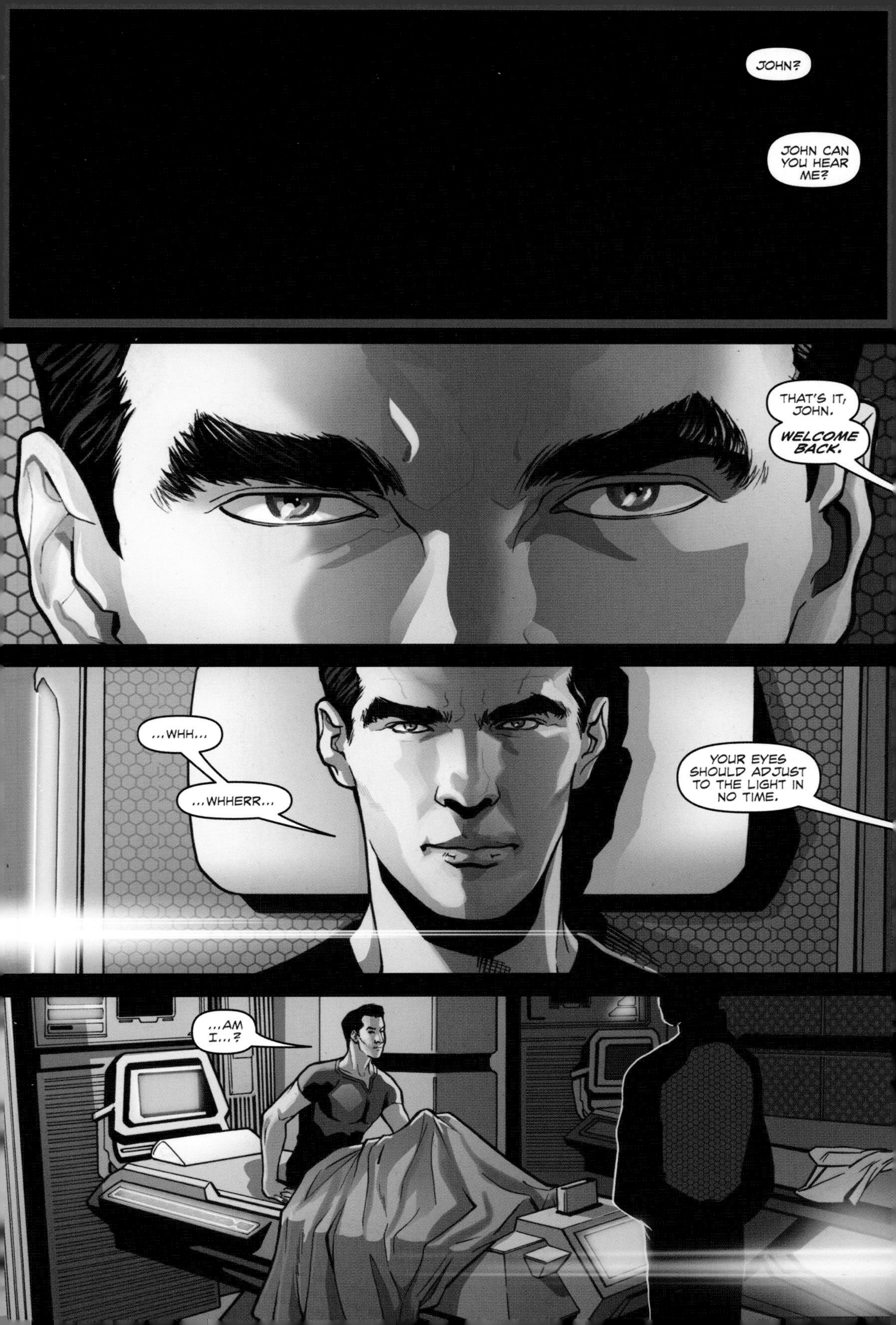
JOHN?
JOHN CAN YOU HEAR ME?
THAT'S IT, JOHN. ***WELCOME BACK.***
...WHH...
...WHHERR...
YOUR EYES SHOULD ADJUST TO THE LIGHT IN NO TIME.
...AM I...?

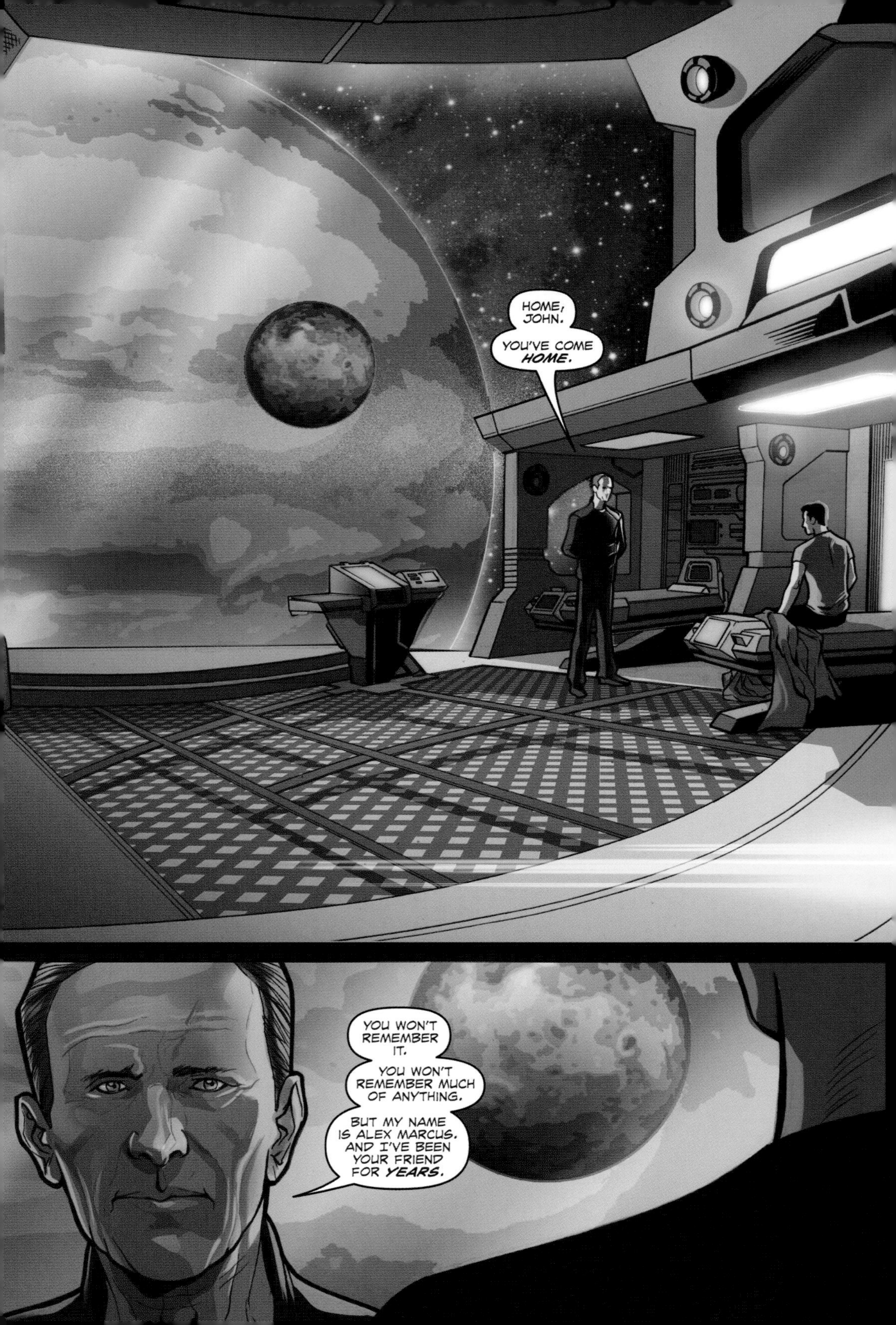
HOME, JOHN.
YOU'VE COME *HOME*.
YOU WON'T REMEMBER IT.
YOU WON'T REMEMBER MUCH OF ANYTHING.
BUT MY NAME IS ALEX MARCUS. AND I'VE BEEN YOUR FRIEND FOR *YEARS*.

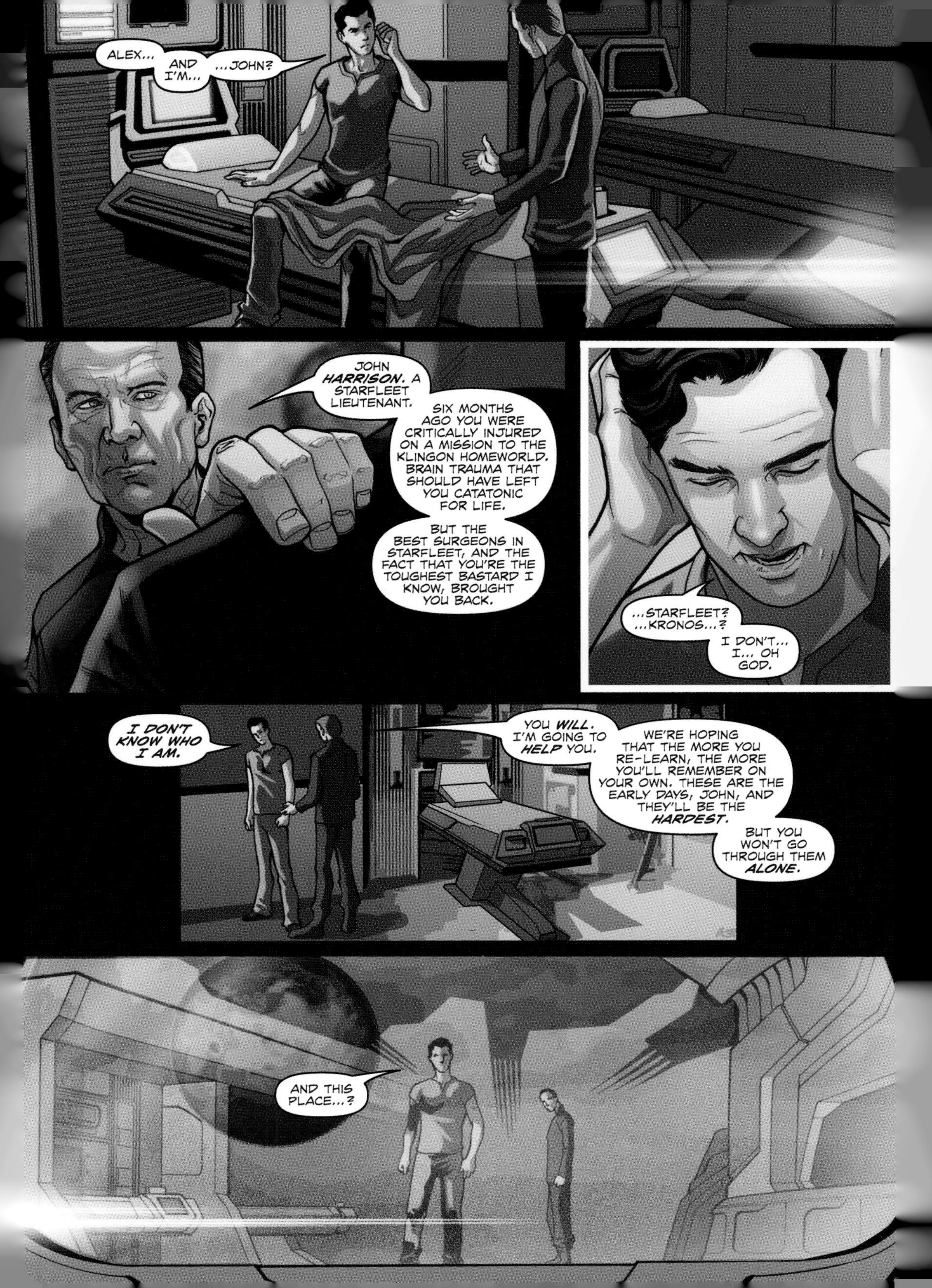
ALEX...
AND I'M...
...JOHN?
JOHN HARRISON. A STARFLEET LIEUTENANT.
SIX MONTHS AGO YOU WERE CRITICALLY INJURED ON A MISSION TO THE KLINGON HOMEWORLD. BRAIN TRAUMA THAT SHOULD HAVE LEFT YOU CATATONIC FOR LIFE.
BUT THE BEST SURGEONS IN STARFLEET, AND THE FACT THAT YOU'RE THE TOUGHEST BASTARD I KNOW, BROUGHT YOU BACK.
...STARFLEET? ...KRONOS...?
I DON'T... I... OH GOD.
I DON'T KNOW WHO I AM.
YOU WILL. I'M GOING TO HELP YOU.
WE'RE HOPING THAT THE MORE YOU RE-LEARN, THE MORE YOU'LL REMEMBER ON YOUR OWN. THESE ARE THE EARLY DAYS, JOHN, AND THEY'LL BE THE HARDEST.
BUT YOU WON'T GO THROUGH THEM ALONE.
AND THIS PLACE...?

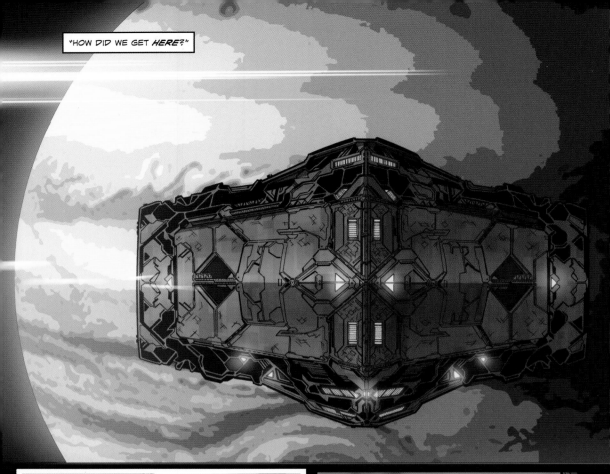

"HOW DID WE GET *HERE?*"

IT'S A *TOP-SECRET SPACE STATION.*

ONLY A FEW PEOPLE IN STARFLEET KNOW IT EXISTS. EVEN FEWER KNOW WHAT IT'S REALLY *FOR.*

FOR THE LAST YEAR, IT'S BEEN YOUR *BASE OF OPERATIONS.*

YOU SAID I WAS ON A "MISSION."

...I WAS A *SOLDIER?*

THAT'S LIKE CALLING THE MONA LISA A PAINTING, JOHN.

NO. YOU WEREN'T JUST A SOLDIER. YOU WERE *EXTRAORDINARY.*

AND SOON YOU'RE GOING TO BE EXTRAORDINARY *AGAIN.*

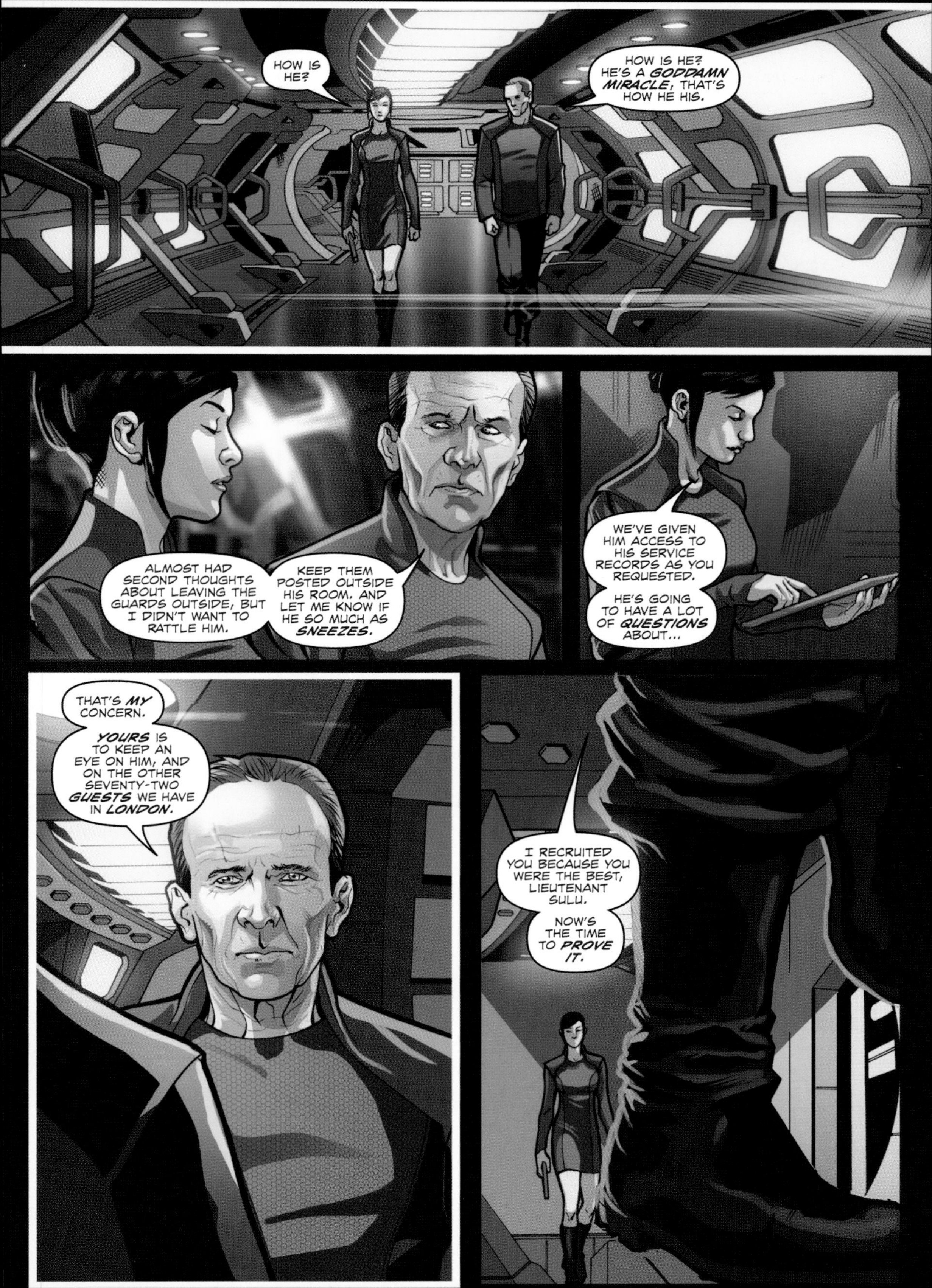
HOW IS HE?
HOW IS HE? HE'S A GODDAMN MIRACLE, THAT'S HOW HE HIS.
ALMOST HAD SECOND THOUGHTS ABOUT LEAVING THE GUARDS OUTSIDE, BUT I DIDN'T WANT TO RATTLE HIM.
KEEP THEM POSTED OUTSIDE HIS ROOM. AND LET ME KNOW IF HE SO MUCH AS SNEEZES.
WE'VE GIVEN HIM ACCESS TO HIS SERVICE RECORDS AS YOU REQUESTED.
HE'S GOING TO HAVE A LOT OF QUESTIONS ABOUT...
THAT'S MY CONCERN.
YOURS IS TO KEEP AN EYE ON HIM, AND ON THE OTHER SEVENTY-TWO GUESTS WE HAVE IN LONDON.
I RECRUITED YOU BECAUSE YOU WERE THE BEST, LIEUTENANT SULU.
NOW'S THE TIME TO PROVE IT.

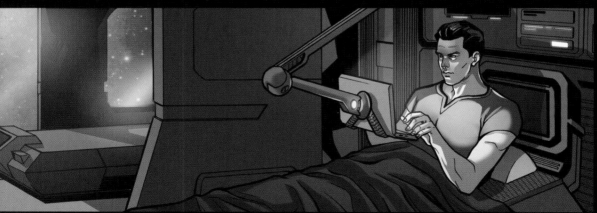

CLEARANCE: 31-ALPHA112520
SECID: HARRISON, JOHN RICHARD_

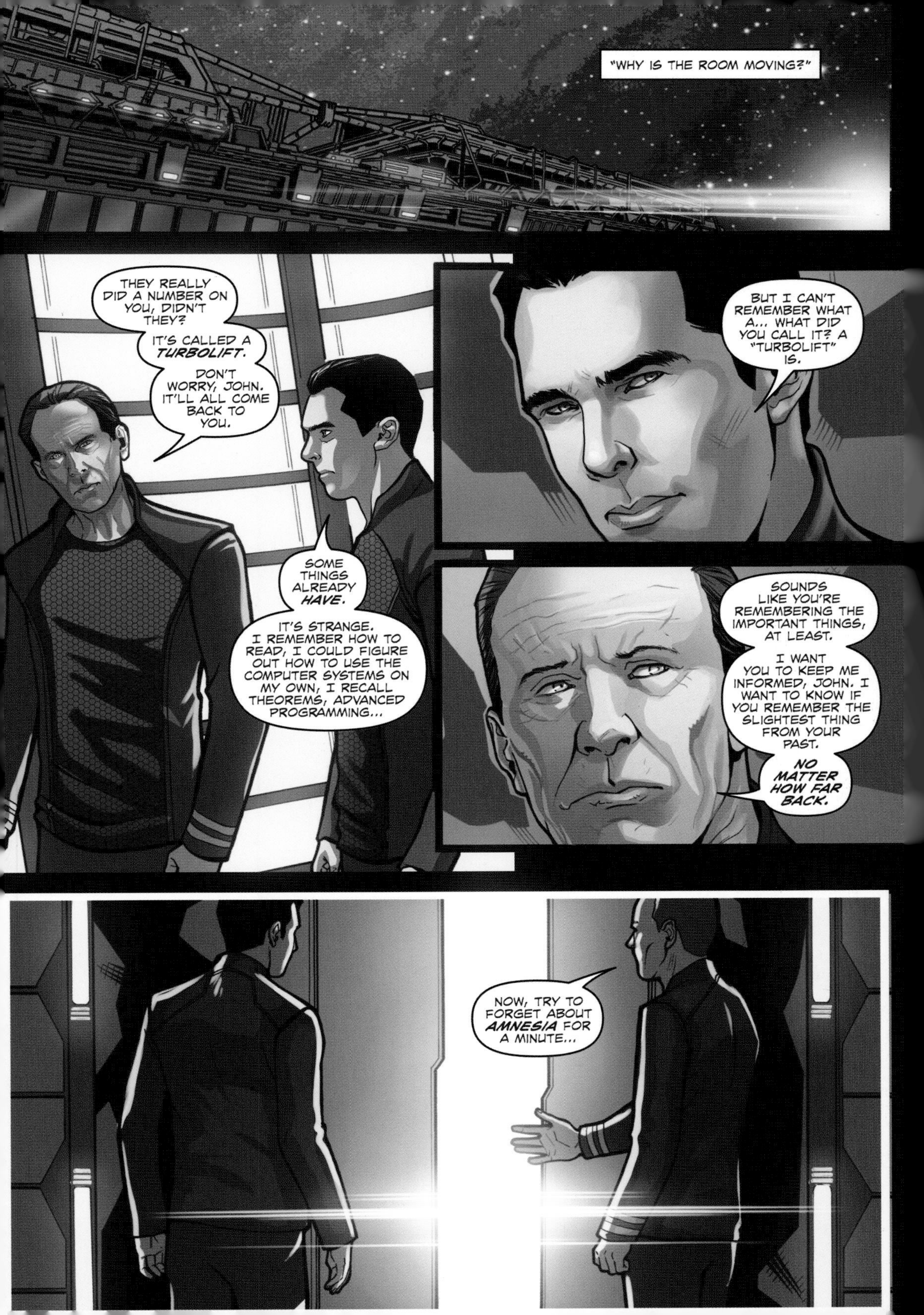
"WHY IS THE ROOM MOVING?"
THEY REALLY DID A NUMBER ON YOU, DIDN'T THEY?
IT'S CALLED A *TURBOLIFT*.
DON'T WORRY, JOHN. IT'LL ALL COME BACK TO YOU.
SOME THINGS ALREADY *HAVE*.
IT'S STRANGE. I REMEMBER HOW TO READ, I COULD FIGURE OUT HOW TO USE THE COMPUTER SYSTEMS ON MY OWN, I RECALL THEOREMS, ADVANCED PROGRAMMING...
BUT I CAN'T REMEMBER WHAT A... WHAT DID YOU CALL IT? A "TURBOLIFT" IS.
SOUNDS LIKE YOU'RE REMEMBERING THE IMPORTANT THINGS, AT LEAST.
I WANT YOU TO KEEP ME INFORMED, JOHN. I WANT TO KNOW IF YOU REMEMBER THE SLIGHTEST THING FROM YOUR PAST.
NO MATTER HOW FAR BACK.
NOW, TRY TO FORGET ABOUT *AMNESIA* FOR A MINUTE...

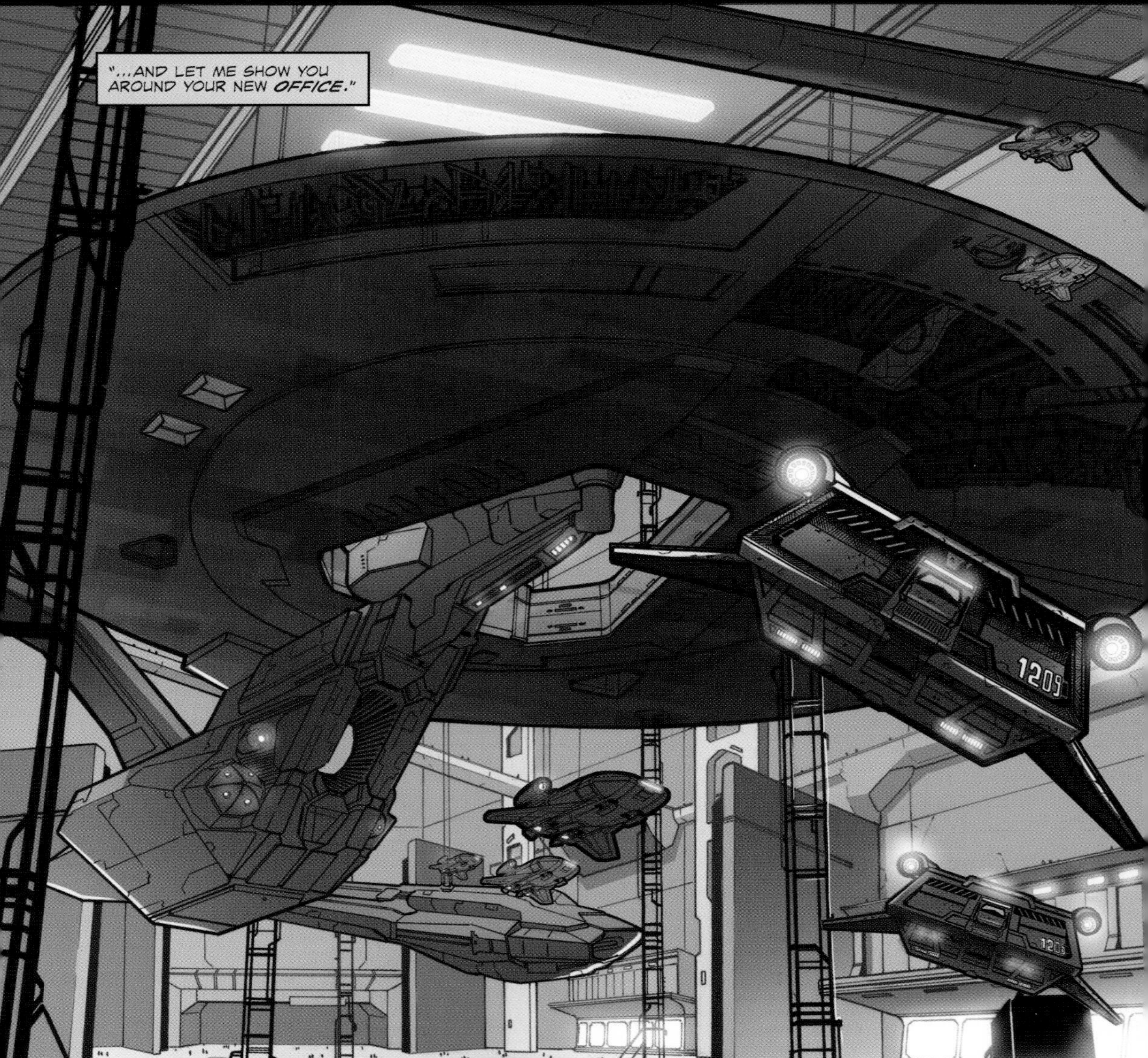
"...AND LET ME SHOW YOU AROUND YOUR NEW OFFICE."
1209
1205

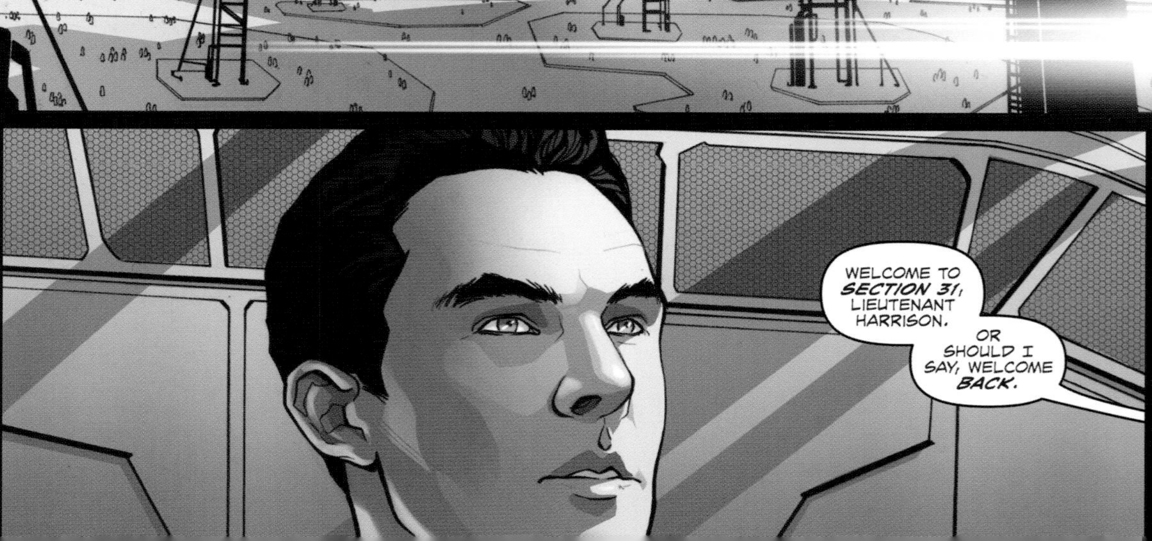
WELCOME TO SECTION 31, LIEUTENANT HARRISON.
OR SHOULD I SAY, WELCOME BACK.

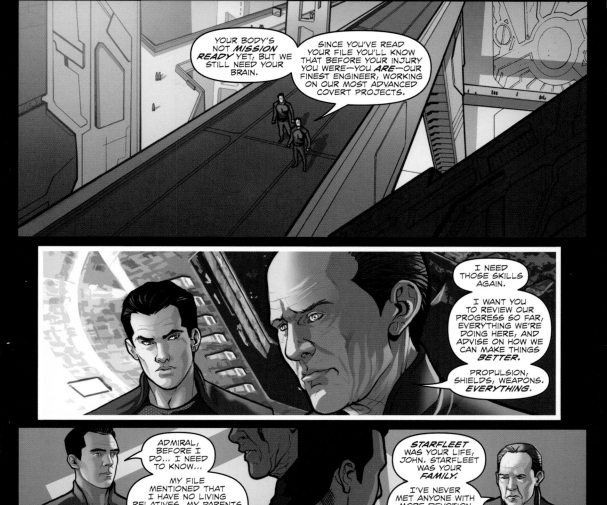

YOUR BODY'S NOT **MISSION READY** YET, BUT WE STILL NEED YOUR BRAIN.

SINCE YOU'VE READ YOUR FILE YOU'LL KNOW THAT BEFORE YOUR INJURY YOU WERE—YOU **ARE**—OUR FINEST ENGINEER, WORKING ON OUR MOST ADVANCED COVERT PROJECTS.

I NEED THOSE SKILLS AGAIN.

I WANT YOU TO REVIEW OUR PROGRESS SO FAR, EVERYTHING WE'RE DOING HERE, AND ADVISE ON HOW WE CAN MAKE THINGS **BETTER.**

PROPULSION, SHIELDS, WEAPONS. **EVERYTHING.**

ADMIRAL, BEFORE I DO... I NEED TO KNOW...

MY FILE MENTIONED THAT I HAVE NO LIVING RELATIVES. MY PARENTS ARE DECEASED; NO SIBLINGS. NO WIFE OR CHILDREN.

ALMOST AS IF I HAD **NO LIFE AT ALL** OUTSIDE MY WORK. IS THERE ANYTHING ELSE YOU CAN TELL ME? ANYTHING THAT MIGHT HELP ME REMEMBER MORE?

STARFLEET WAS YOUR LIFE, JOHN. STARFLEET WAS YOUR **FAMILY.**

I'VE NEVER MET ANYONE WITH MORE DEVOTION TO EVERYTHING STARFLEET STANDS FOR.

I DIDN'T TELL YOU THAT YOU'D COME "HOME" JUST TO BE SENTIMENTAL. I TOLD YOU BECAUSE IT'S A **FACT.**

BUT MORE IMPORTANTLY, WHAT'S **PAST IS PAST.**

IT'S TIME TO FOCUS ON THE **FUTURE.**

"IT'S INCREDIBLE, SIR.

"THESE PAST FIVE MONTHS HE'S EXCEEDED OUR WILDEST EXPECTATIONS."

"HE'S ALREADY REVAMPED THE WARP DRIVE TO GIVE IT UNPRECEDENTED CAPABILITY. WE'RE TALKING CLOSE TO *WARP TEN*."

"HE'S ONTO THE WEAPON SYSTEMS NOW, WORKING ON LONG-RANGE UNDETECTABLE PROTOTYPE TORPEDOES."

HE'S ALSO REFINED THE STATION'S *ENTIRE COMPUTER SYSTEM*.

I KNOW WE HAVE SAFEGUARDS IN PLACE, BUT IF HE SHOULD STUMBLE ON EVEN THE *SLIGHTEST BIT OF INFORMATION ABOUT—*

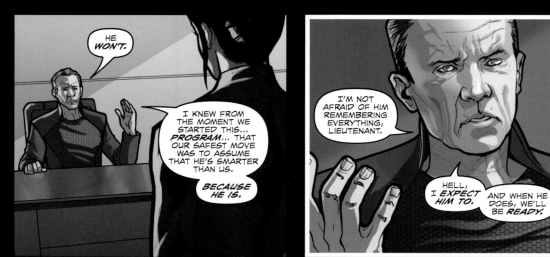

HE *WON'T*.

I KNEW FROM THE MOMENT WE STARTED THIS... *PROGRAM*... THAT OUR SAFEST MOVE WAS TO ASSUME THAT HE'S SMARTER THAN US.

BECAUSE HE IS.

I'M NOT AFRAID OF HIM REMEMBERING EVERYTHING, LIEUTENANT.

HELL, I *EXPECT HIM TO.* AND WHEN HE DOES, WE'LL BE *READY.*

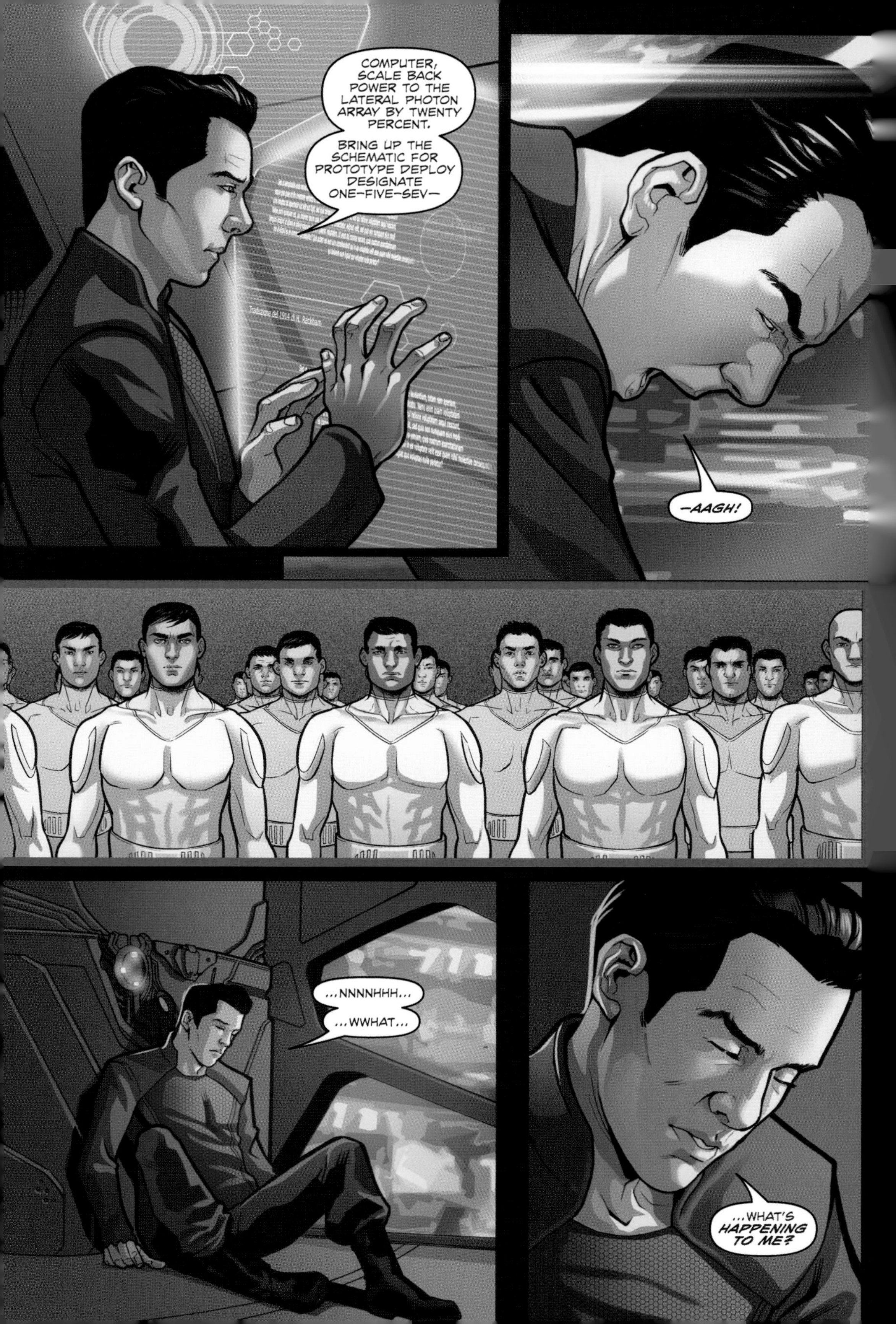
COMPUTER, SCALE BACK POWER TO THE LATERAL PHOTON ARRAY BY TWENTY PERCENT.
BRING UP THE SCHEMATIC FOR PROTOTYPE DEPLOY DESIGNATE ONE-FIVE-SEV—
—AAGH!
...NNNNHHH...
...WWHAT...
...WHAT'S *HAPPENING* TO ME?

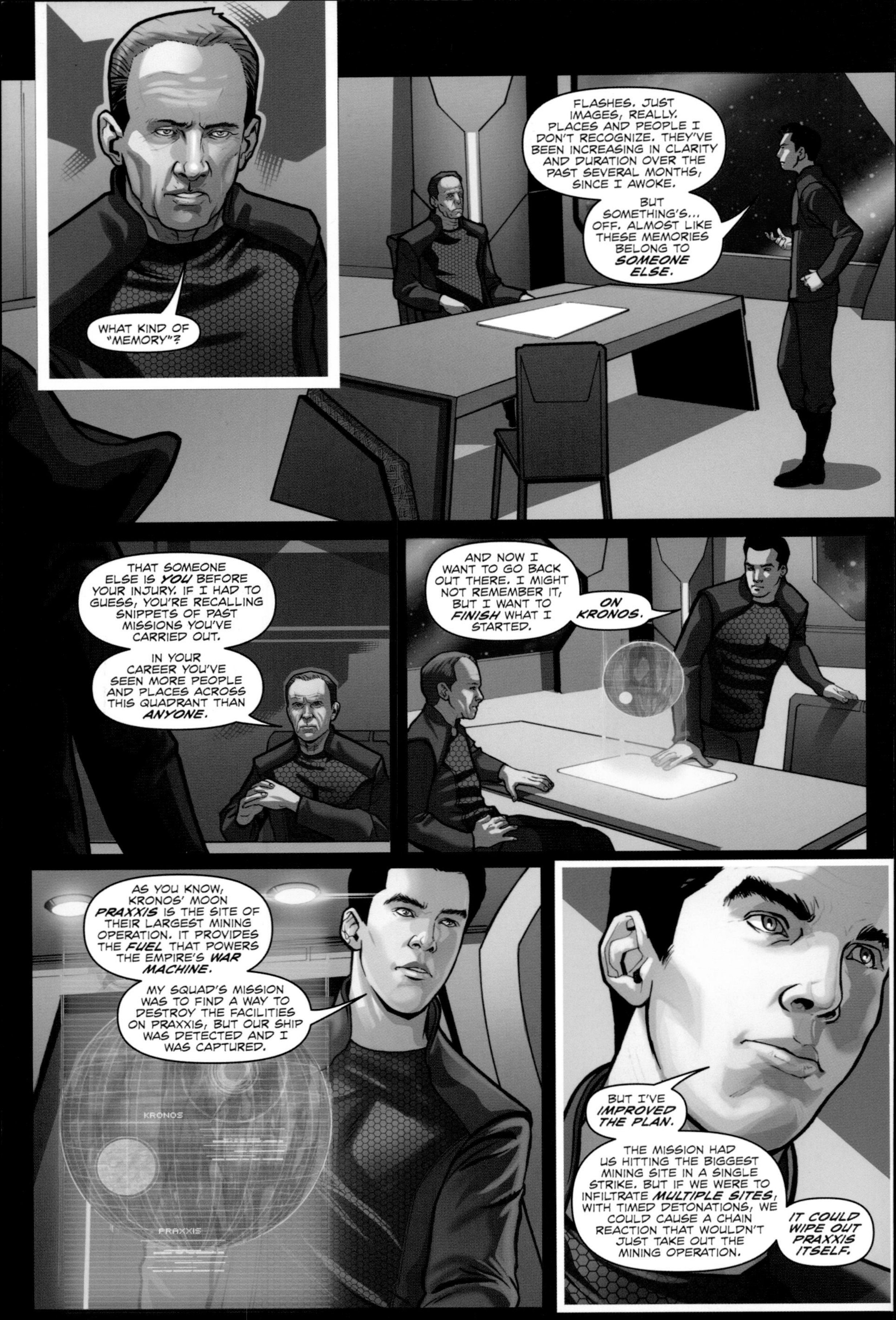
WHAT KIND OF "MEMORY"?
FLASHES. JUST IMAGES, REALLY. PLACES AND PEOPLE I DON'T RECOGNIZE. THEY'VE BEEN INCREASING IN CLARITY AND DURATION OVER THE PAST SEVERAL MONTHS, SINCE I AWOKE.
BUT SOMETHING'S... OFF. ALMOST LIKE THESE MEMORIES BELONG TO SOMEONE ELSE.
THAT SOMEONE ELSE IS YOU BEFORE YOUR INJURY. IF I HAD TO GUESS, YOU'RE RECALLING SNIPPETS OF PAST MISSIONS YOU'VE CARRIED OUT.
IN YOUR CAREER YOU'VE SEEN MORE PEOPLE AND PLACES ACROSS THIS QUADRANT THAN ANYONE.
AND NOW I WANT TO GO BACK OUT THERE. I MIGHT NOT REMEMBER IT, BUT I WANT TO FINISH WHAT I STARTED.
ON KRONOS.
AS YOU KNOW, KRONOS' MOON PRAXXIS IS THE SITE OF THEIR LARGEST MINING OPERATION. IT PROVIDES THE FUEL THAT POWERS THE EMPIRE'S WAR MACHINE.
MY SQUAD'S MISSION WAS TO FIND A WAY TO DESTROY THE FACILITIES ON PRAXXIS, BUT OUR SHIP WAS DETECTED AND I WAS CAPTURED.
KRONOS
PRAXXIS
BUT I'VE IMPROVED THE PLAN.
THE MISSION HAD US HITTING THE BIGGEST MINING SITE IN A SINGLE STRIKE. BUT IF WE WERE TO INFILTRATE MULTIPLE SITES, WITH TIMED DETONATIONS, WE COULD CAUSE A CHAIN REACTION THAT WOULDN'T JUST TAKE OUT THE MINING OPERATION.
IT COULD WIPE OUT PRAXXIS ITSELF.

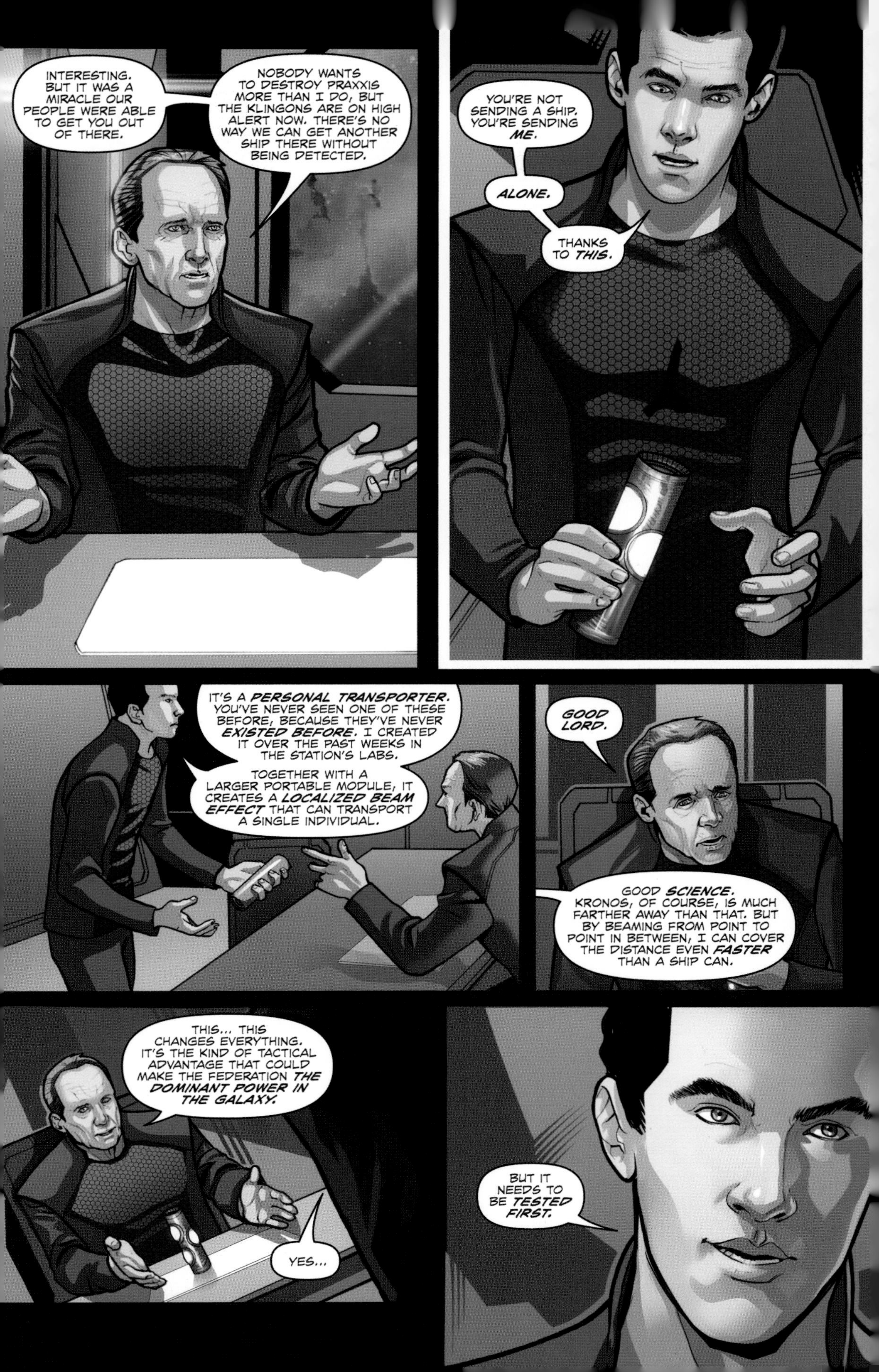
INTERESTING. BUT IT WAS A MIRACLE OUR PEOPLE WERE ABLE TO GET YOU OUT OF THERE.
NOBODY WANTS TO DESTROY PRAXXIS MORE THAN I DO, BUT THE KLINGONS ARE ON HIGH ALERT NOW. THERE'S NO WAY WE CAN GET ANOTHER SHIP THERE WITHOUT BEING DETECTED.
YOU'RE NOT SENDING A SHIP. YOU'RE SENDING ME.
ALONE.
THANKS TO THIS.
IT'S A PERSONAL TRANSPORTER. YOU'VE NEVER SEEN ONE OF THESE BEFORE, BECAUSE THEY'VE NEVER EXISTED BEFORE. I CREATED IT OVER THE PAST WEEKS IN THE STATION'S LABS.
TOGETHER WITH A LARGER PORTABLE MODULE, IT CREATES A LOCALIZED BEAM EFFECT THAT CAN TRANSPORT A SINGLE INDIVIDUAL.
GOOD LORD.
GOOD SCIENCE. KRONOS, OF COURSE, IS MUCH FARTHER AWAY THAN THAT. BUT BY BEAMING FROM POINT TO POINT IN BETWEEN, I CAN COVER THE DISTANCE EVEN FASTER THAN A SHIP CAN.
THIS... THIS CHANGES EVERYTHING. IT'S THE KIND OF TACTICAL ADVANTAGE THAT COULD MAKE THE FEDERATION THE DOMINANT POWER IN THE GALAXY.
YES...
BUT IT NEEDS TO BE TESTED FIRST.

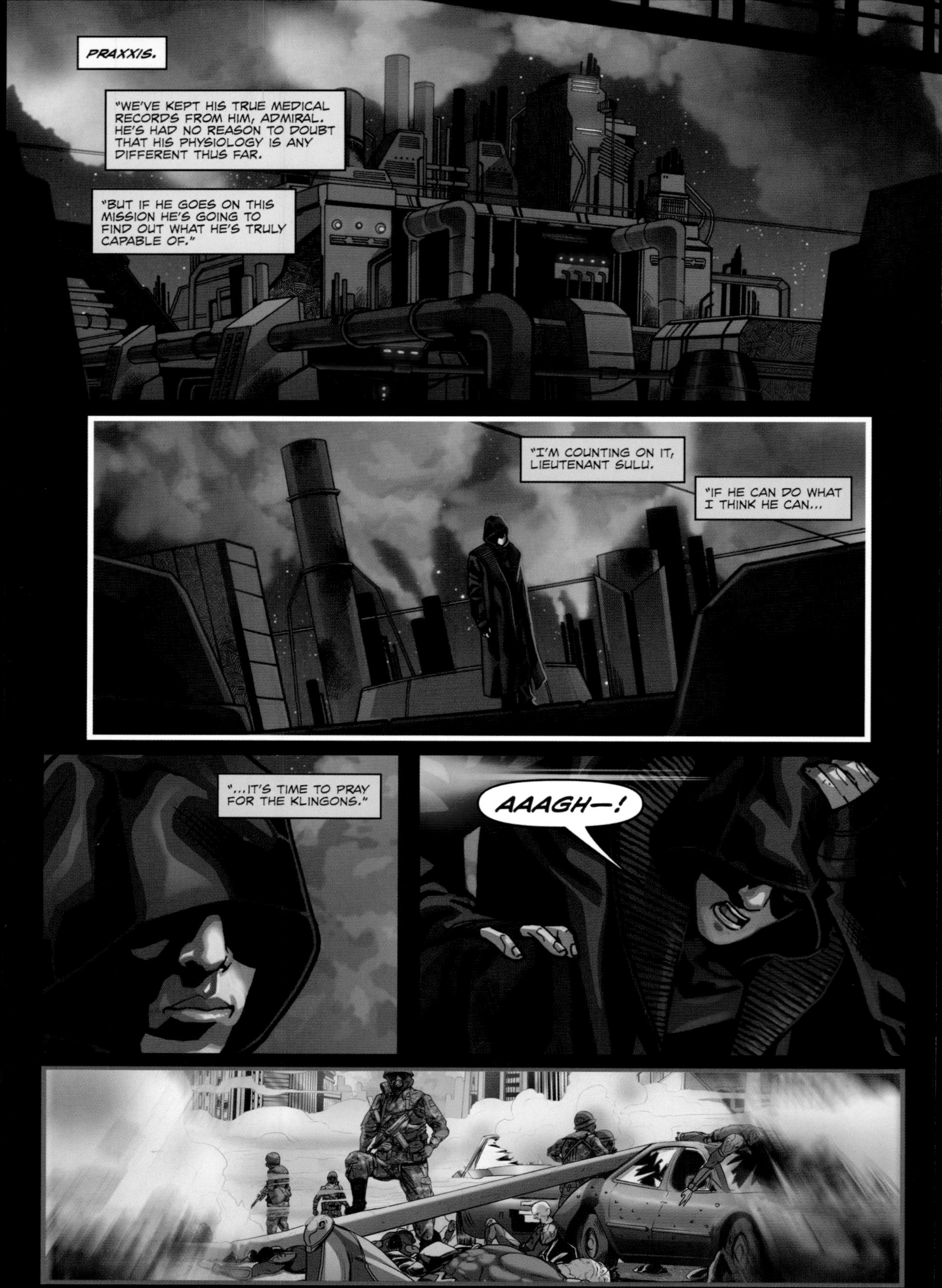
PRAXXIS.
"WE'VE KEPT HIS TRUE MEDICAL RECORDS FROM HIM, ADMIRAL. HE'S HAD NO REASON TO DOUBT THAT HIS PHYSIOLOGY IS ANY DIFFERENT THUS FAR.
"BUT IF HE GOES ON THIS MISSION HE'S GOING TO FIND OUT WHAT HE'S TRULY CAPABLE OF."
"I'M COUNTING ON IT, LIEUTENANT SULU.
"IF HE CAN DO WHAT I THINK HE CAN...
"...IT'S TIME TO PRAY FOR THE KLINGONS."
AAAGH—!

<NOW, YOU DIE.>*

*TRANSLATED FROM THE KLINGON.

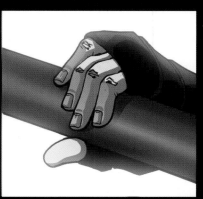

FOOL.

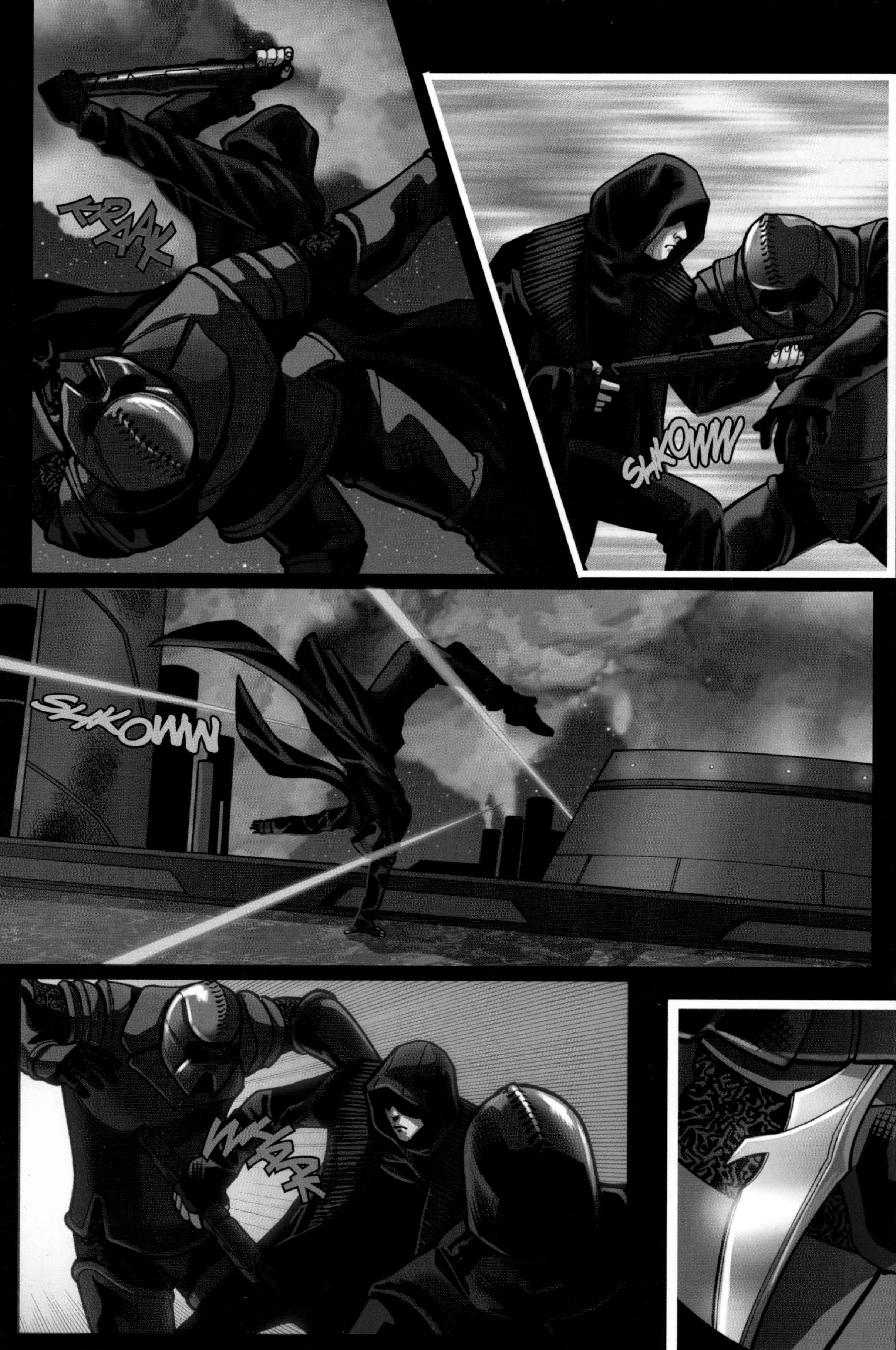
KRAAK
SHKOWW
SHKOWW
WHAK

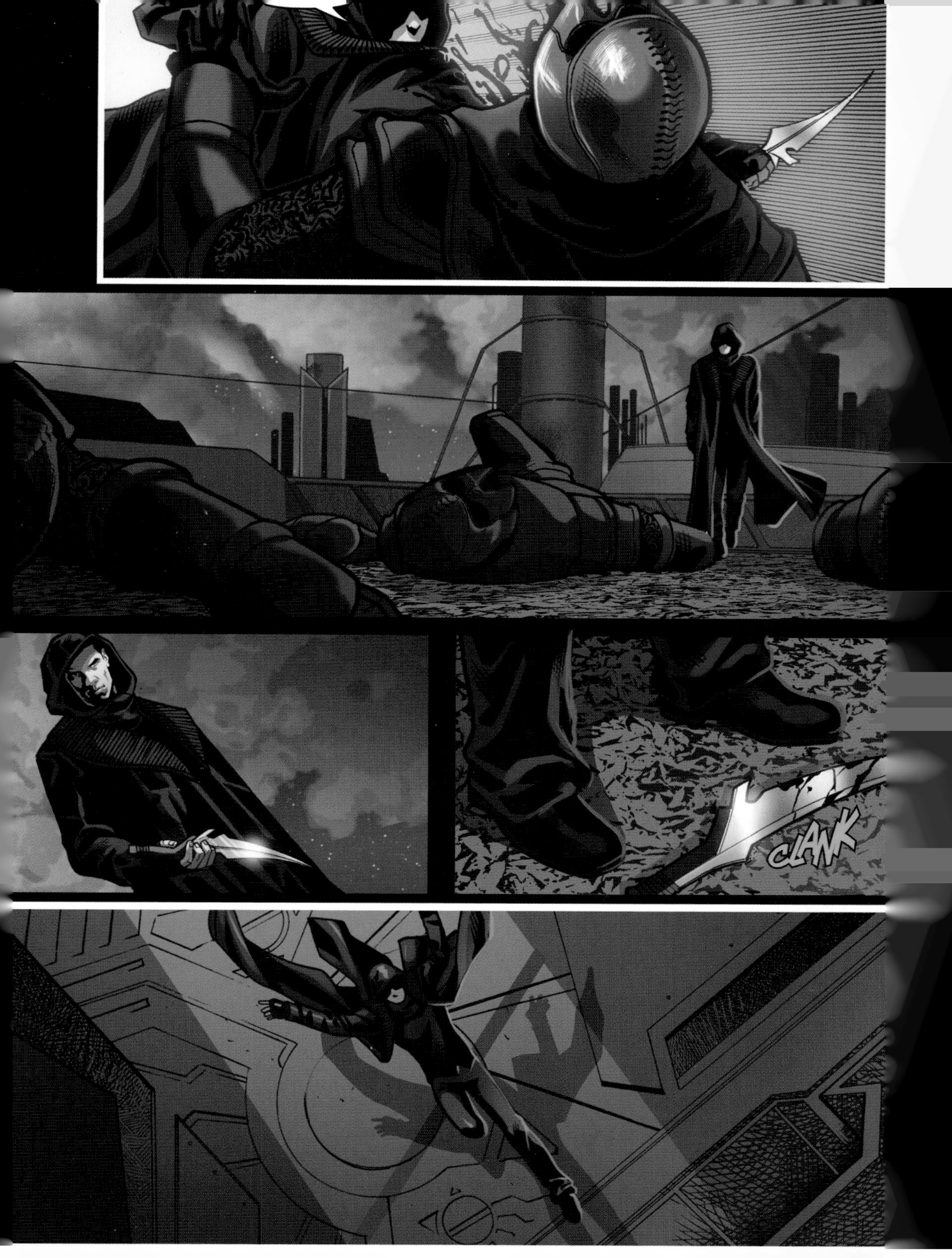
CLANK

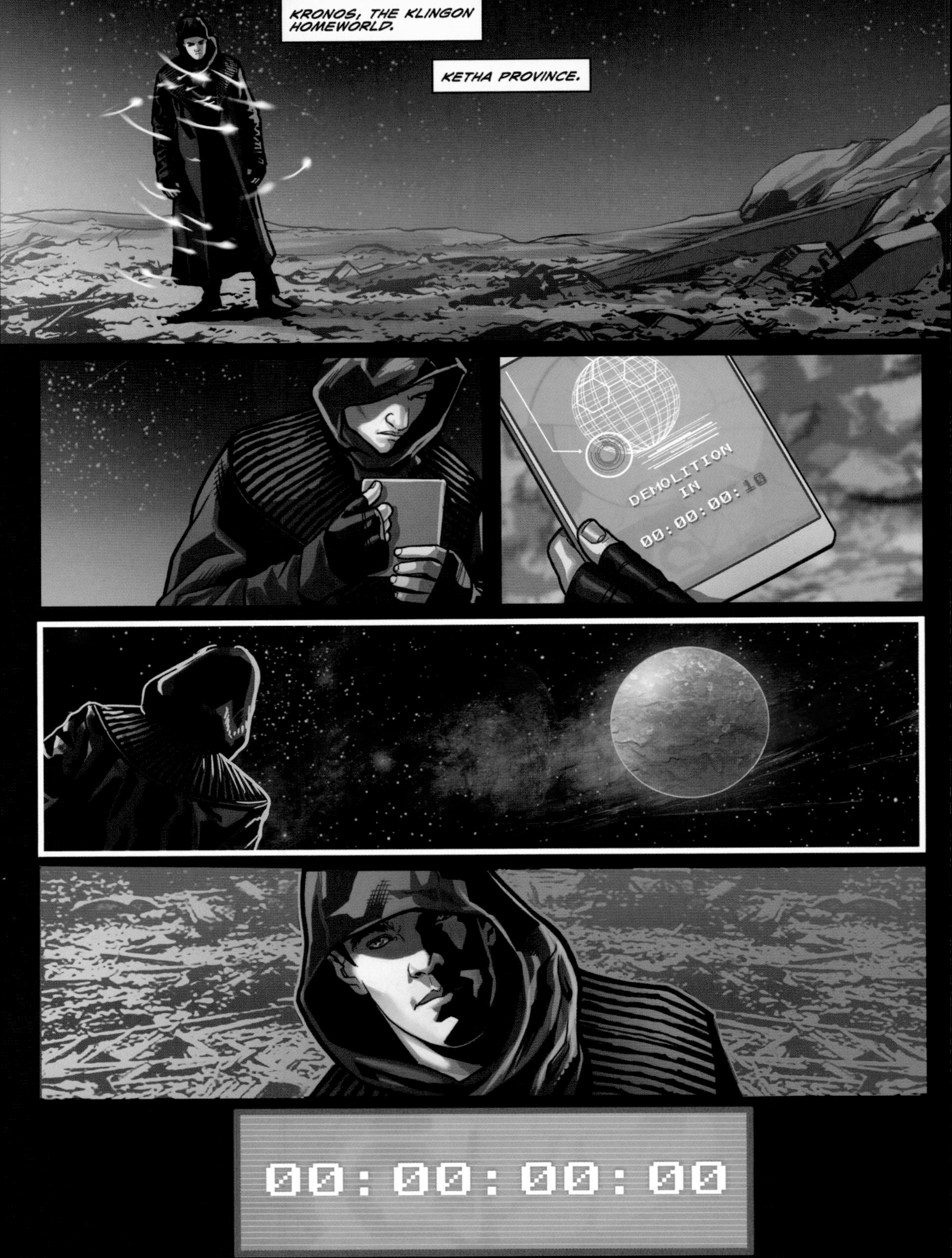
KRONOS, THE KLINGON HOMEWORLD.
KETHA PROVINCE.
DEMOLITION IN 00:00:00:10
00:00:00:00

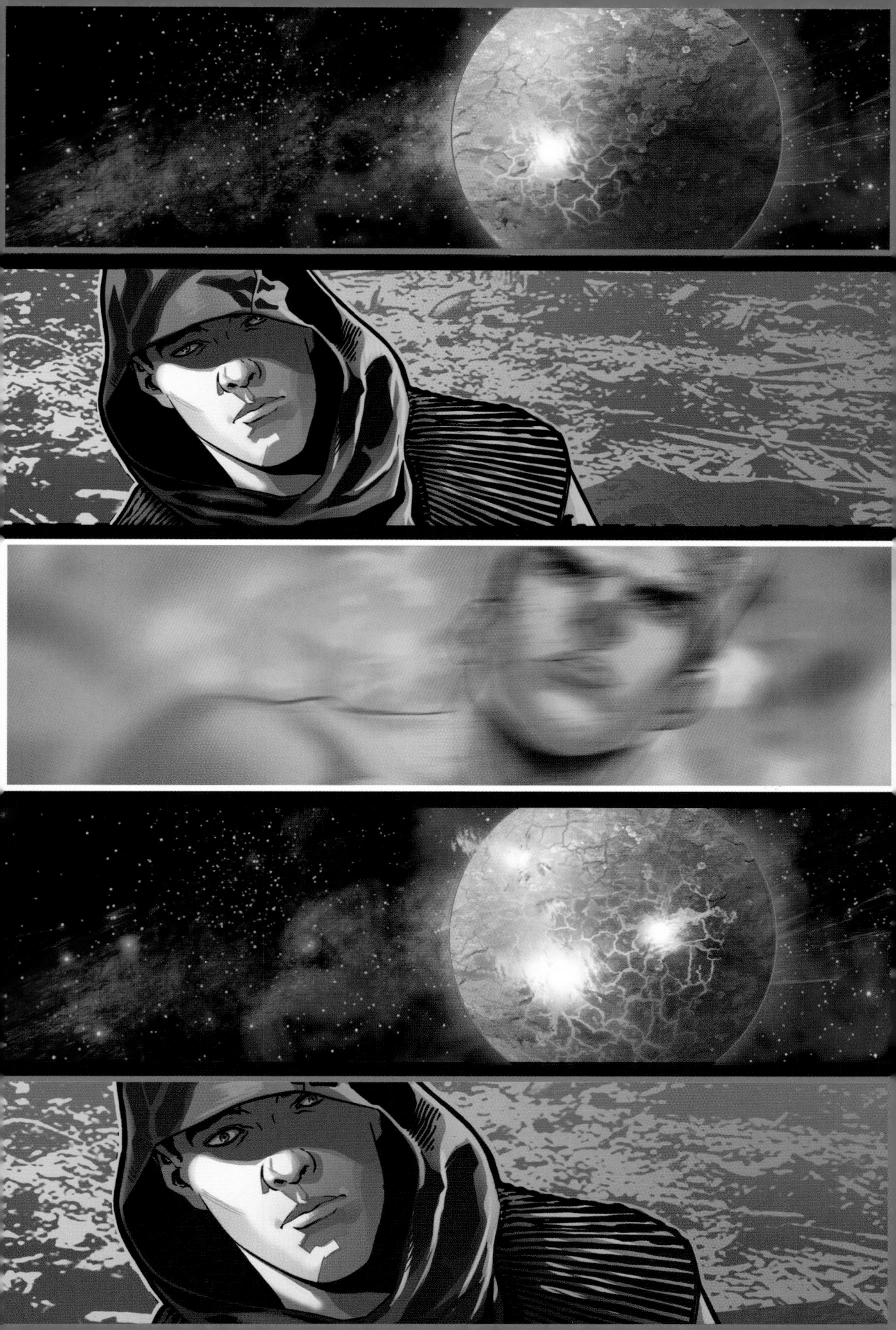

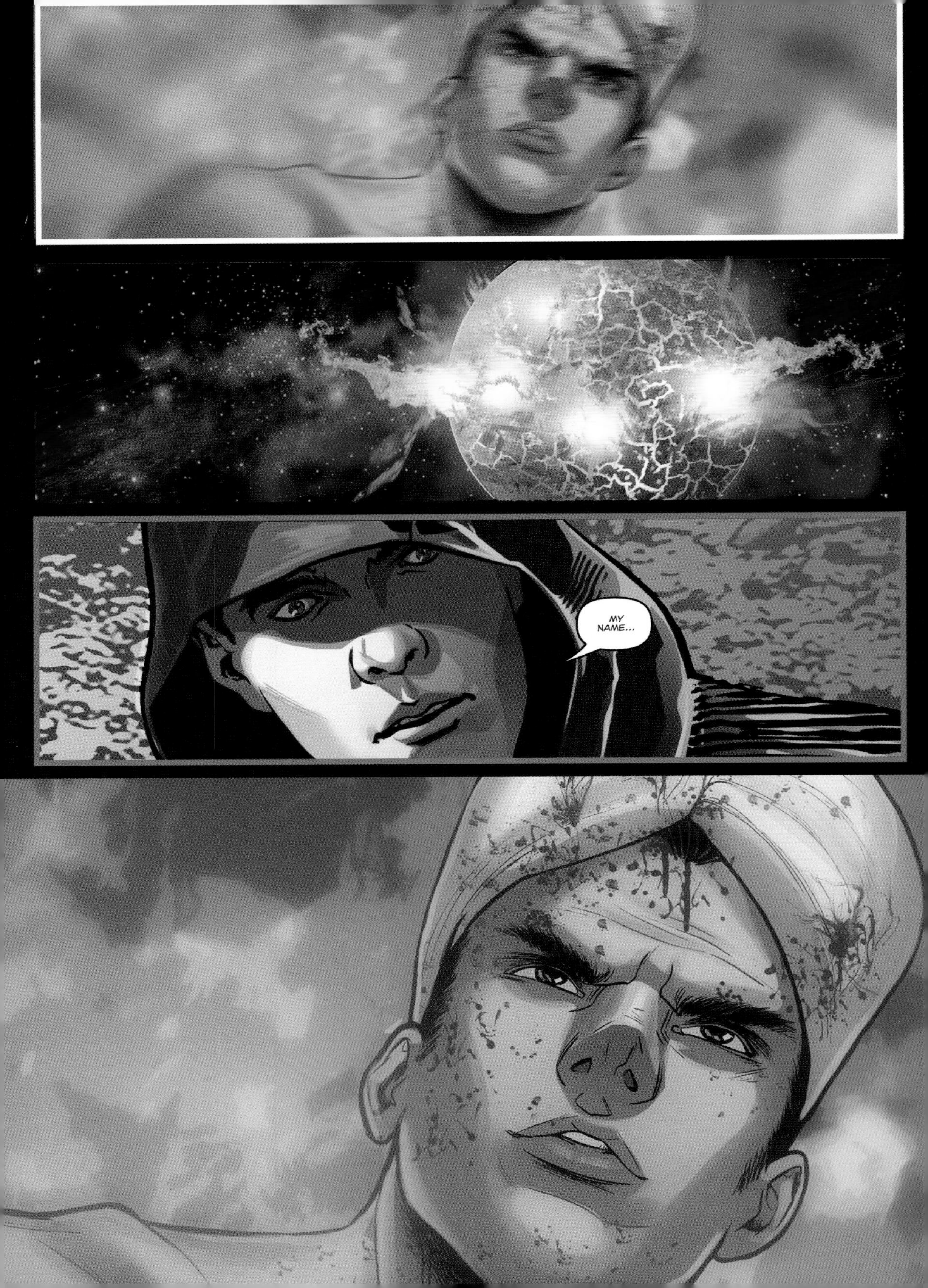
MY NAME...

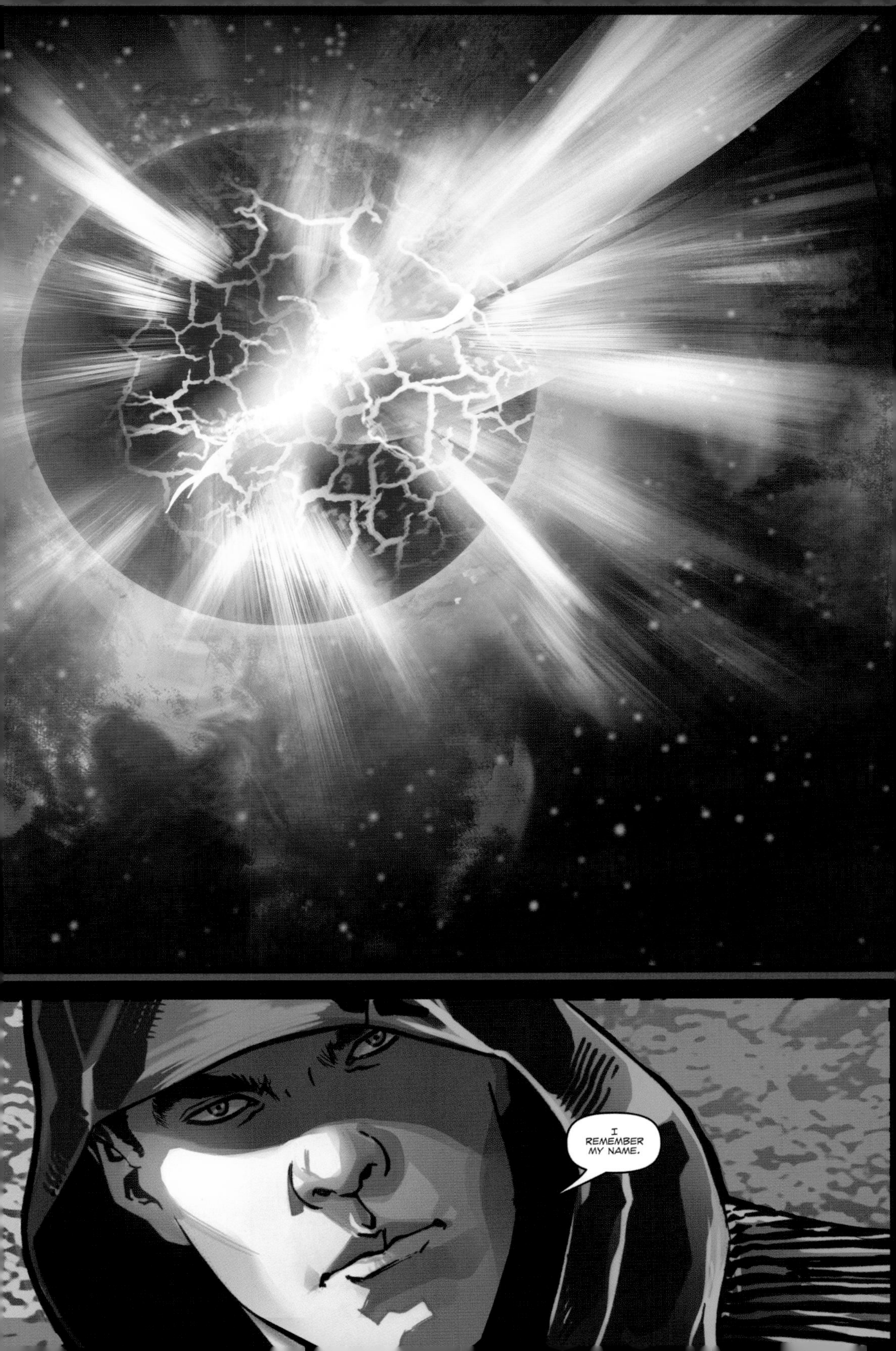
I REMEMBER MY NAME.

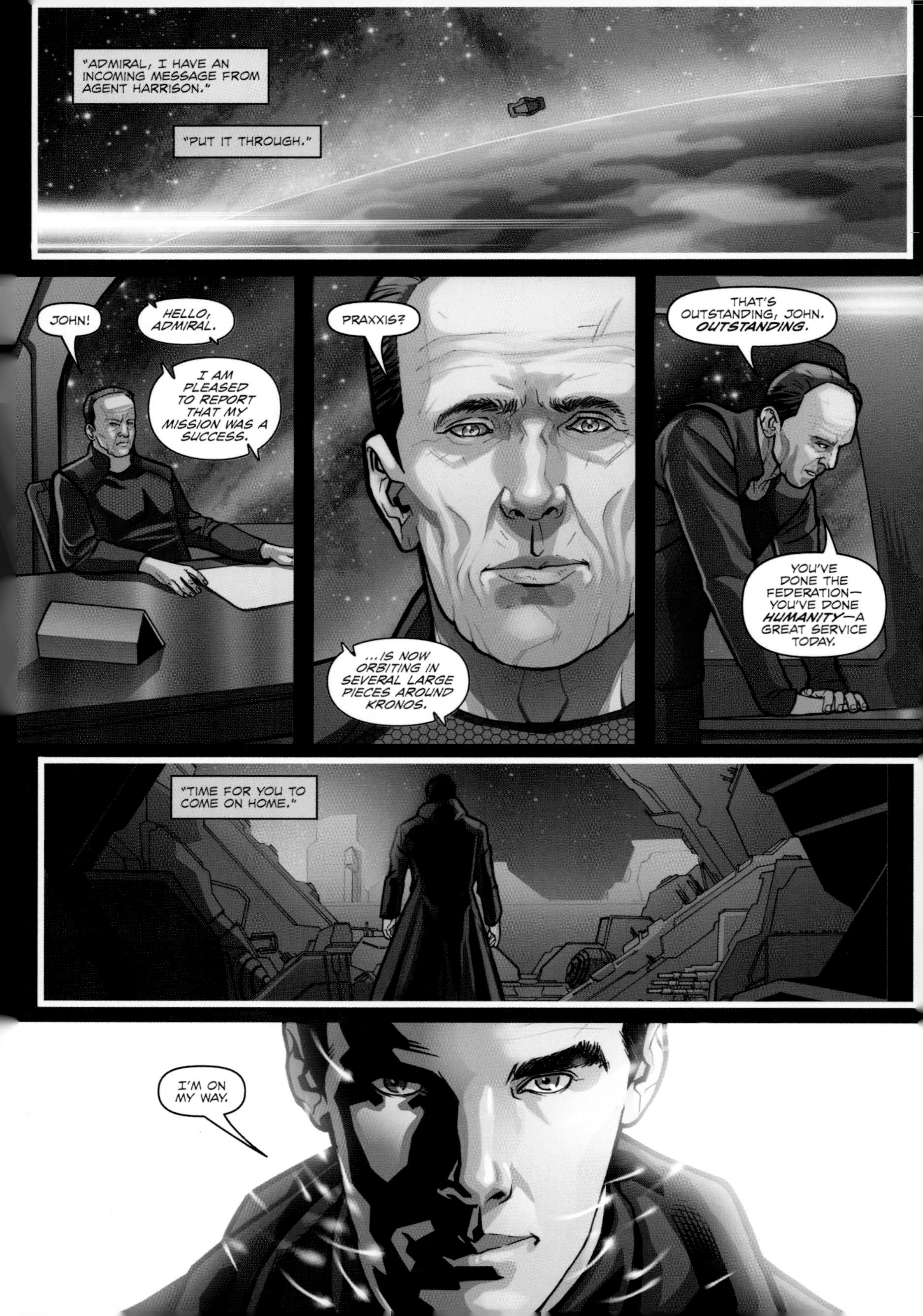
"ADMIRAL, I HAVE AN INCOMING MESSAGE FROM AGENT HARRISON."
"PUT IT THROUGH."
JOHN!
HELLO, ADMIRAL.
I AM PLEASED TO REPORT THAT MY MISSION WAS A SUCCESS.
PRAXXIS?
...IS NOW ORBITING IN SEVERAL LARGE PIECES AROUND KRONOS.
THAT'S OUTSTANDING, JOHN. OUTSTANDING.
YOU'VE DONE THE FEDERATION—YOU'VE DONE HUMANITY—A GREAT SERVICE TODAY.
"TIME FOR YOU TO COME ON HOME."
I'M ON MY WAY.

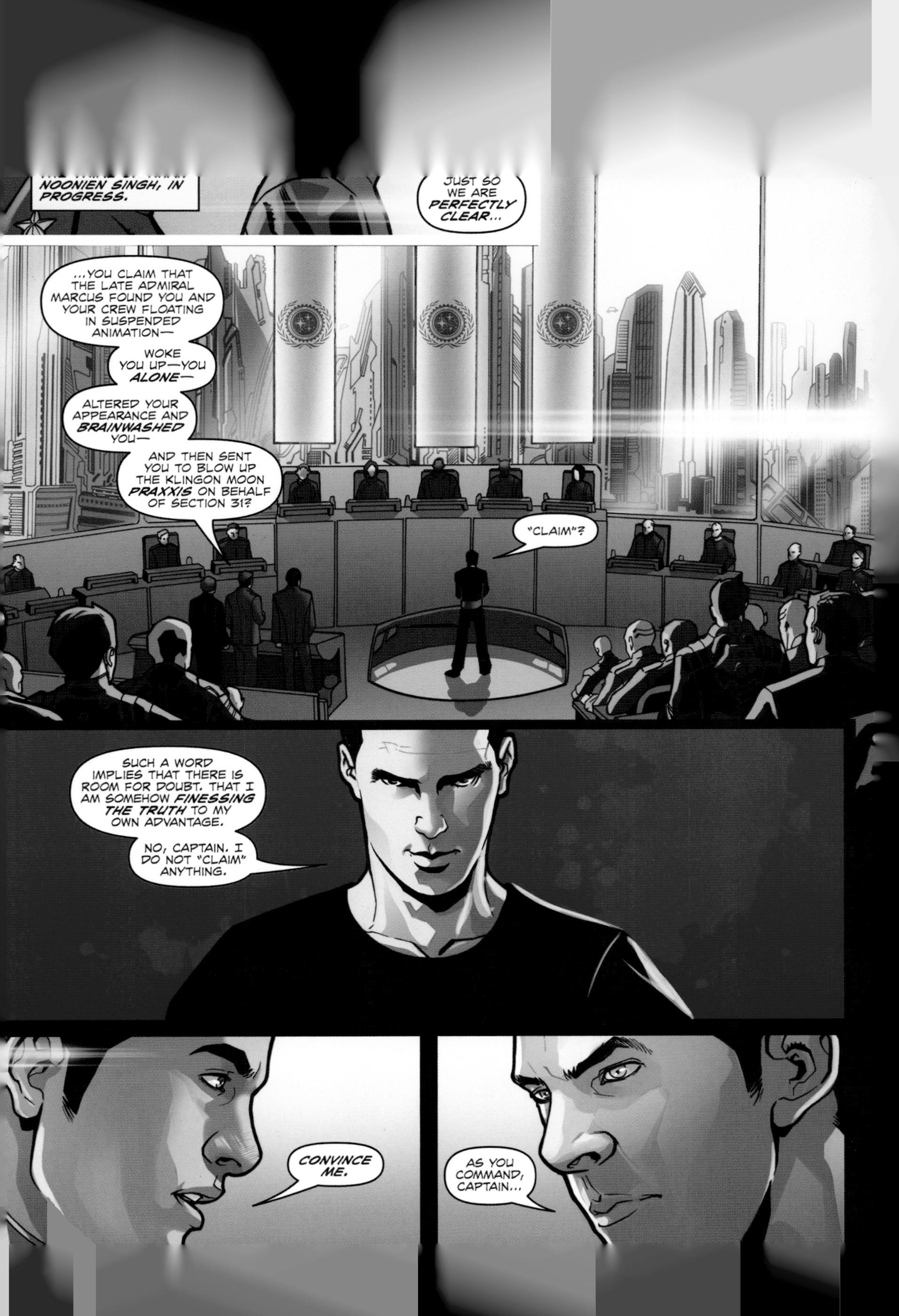

NOONIEN SINGH, IN PROGRESS.
JUST SO WE ARE PERFECTLY CLEAR...
...YOU CLAIM THAT THE LATE ADMIRAL MARCUS FOUND YOU AND YOUR CREW FLOATING IN SUSPENDED ANIMATION—
WOKE YOU UP—YOU ALONE—
ALTERED YOUR APPEARANCE AND BRAINWASHED YOU—
AND THEN SENT YOU TO BLOW UP THE KLINGON MOON PRAXXIS ON BEHALF OF SECTION 31?
"CLAIM"?
SUCH A WORD IMPLIES THAT THERE IS ROOM FOR DOUBT. THAT I AM SOMEHOW FINESSING THE TRUTH TO MY OWN ADVANTAGE.
NO, CAPTAIN. I DO NOT "CLAIM" ANYTHING.
CONVINCE ME.
AS YOU COMMAND, CAPTAIN...

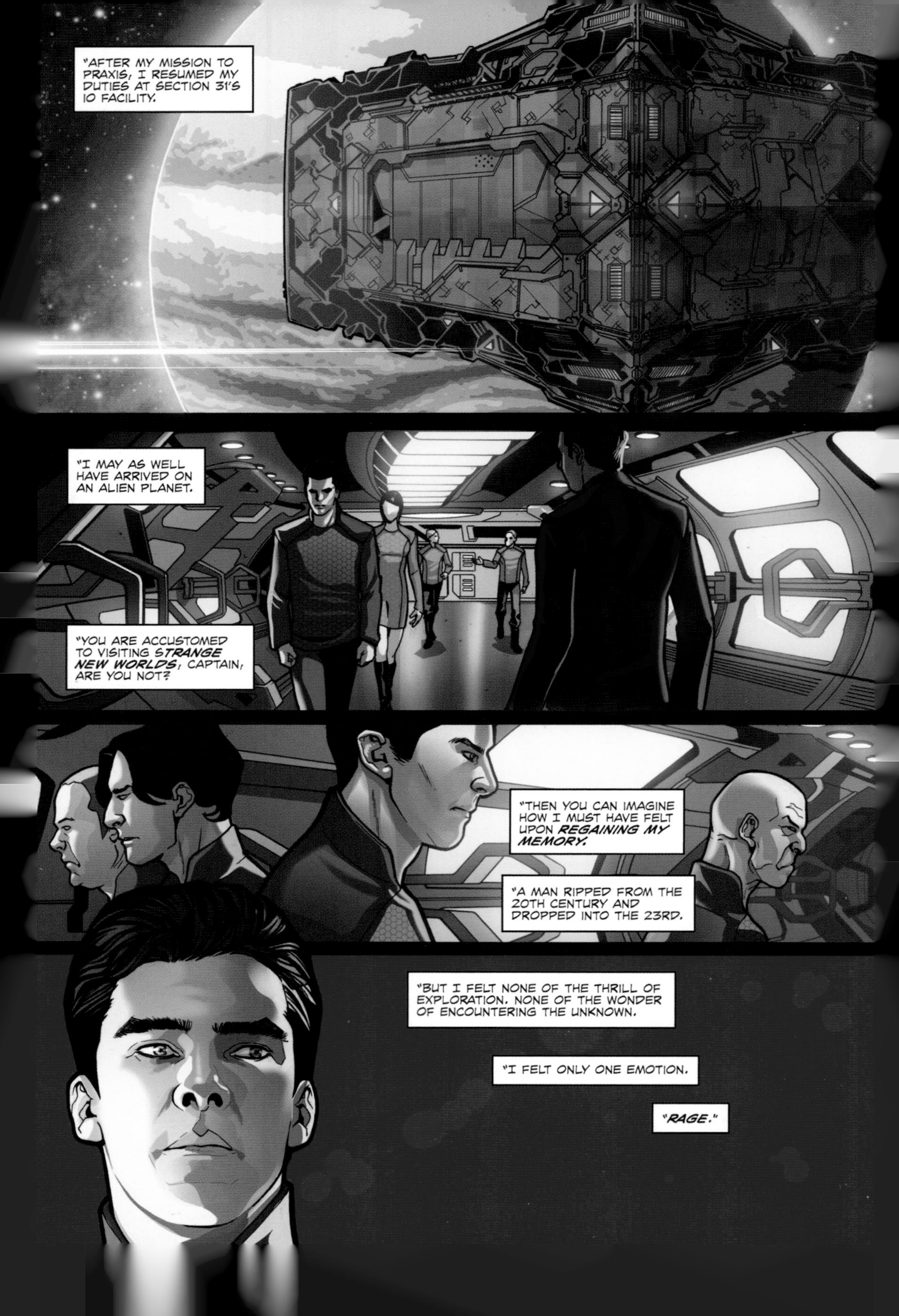
"AFTER MY MISSION TO PRAXIS, I RESUMED MY DUTIES AT SECTION 31'S IO FACILITY.
"I MAY AS WELL HAVE ARRIVED ON AN ALIEN PLANET.
"YOU ARE ACCUSTOMED TO VISITING STRANGE NEW WORLDS, CAPTAIN, ARE YOU NOT?
"THEN YOU CAN IMAGINE HOW I MUST HAVE FELT UPON REGAINING MY MEMORY.
"A MAN RIPPED FROM THE 20TH CENTURY AND DROPPED INTO THE 23RD.
"BUT I FELT NONE OF THE THRILL OF EXPLORATION. NONE OF THE WONDER OF ENCOUNTERING THE UNKNOWN.
"I FELT ONLY ONE EMOTION.
"RAGE."

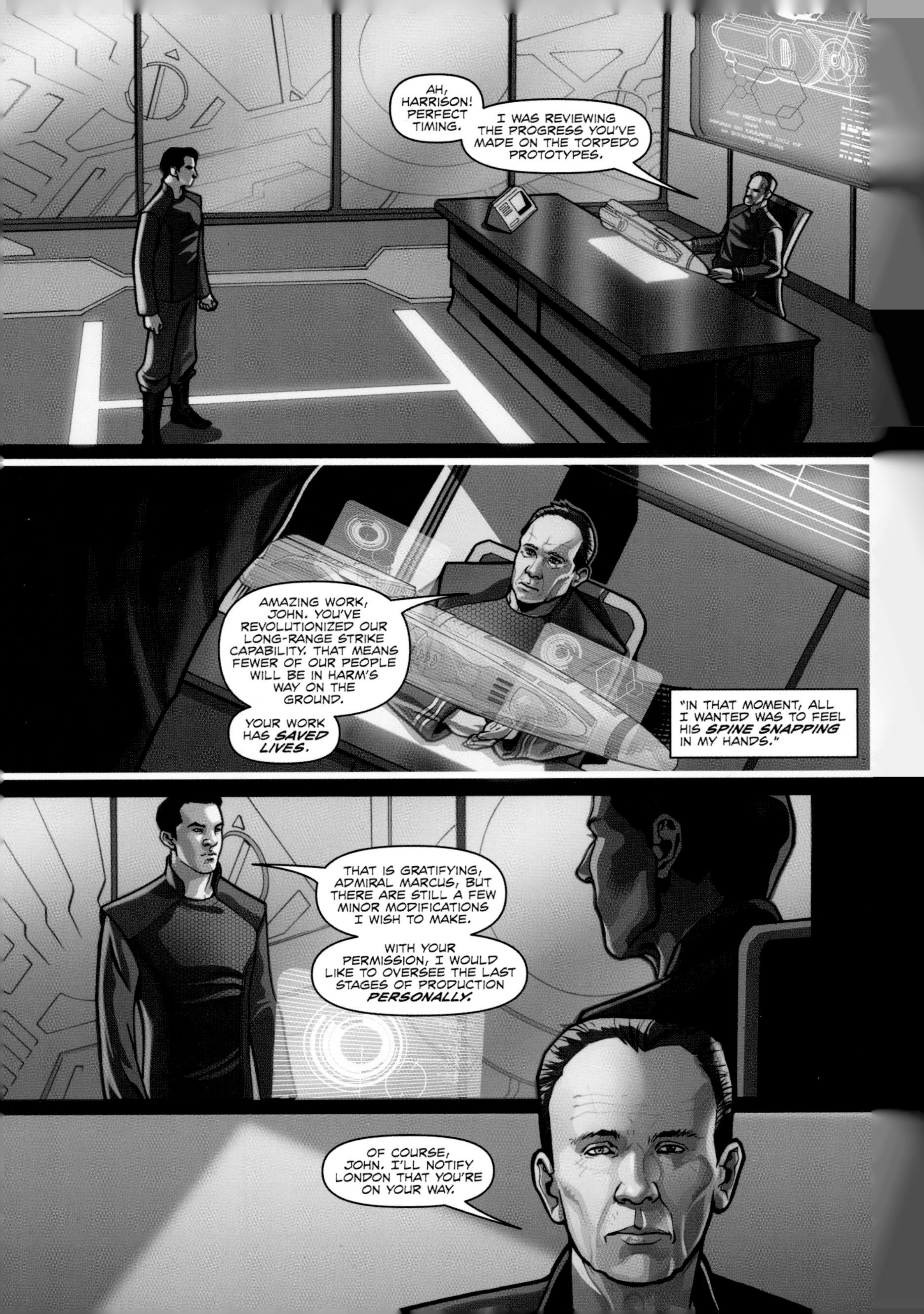
AH, HARRISON! PERFECT TIMING.
I WAS REVIEWING THE PROGRESS YOU'VE MADE ON THE TORPEDO PROTOTYPES.
AMAZING WORK, JOHN. YOU'VE REVOLUTIONIZED OUR LONG-RANGE STRIKE CAPABILITY. THAT MEANS FEWER OF OUR PEOPLE WILL BE IN HARM'S WAY ON THE GROUND.
YOUR WORK HAS *SAVED LIVES.*
"IN THAT MOMENT, ALL I WANTED WAS TO FEEL HIS *SPINE SNAPPING* IN MY HANDS."
THAT IS GRATIFYING, ADMIRAL MARCUS, BUT THERE ARE STILL A FEW MINOR MODIFICATIONS I WISH TO MAKE.
WITH YOUR PERMISSION, I WOULD LIKE TO OVERSEE THE LAST STAGES OF PRODUCTION *PERSONALLY.*
OF COURSE, JOHN. I'LL NOTIFY LONDON THAT YOU'RE ON YOUR WAY.

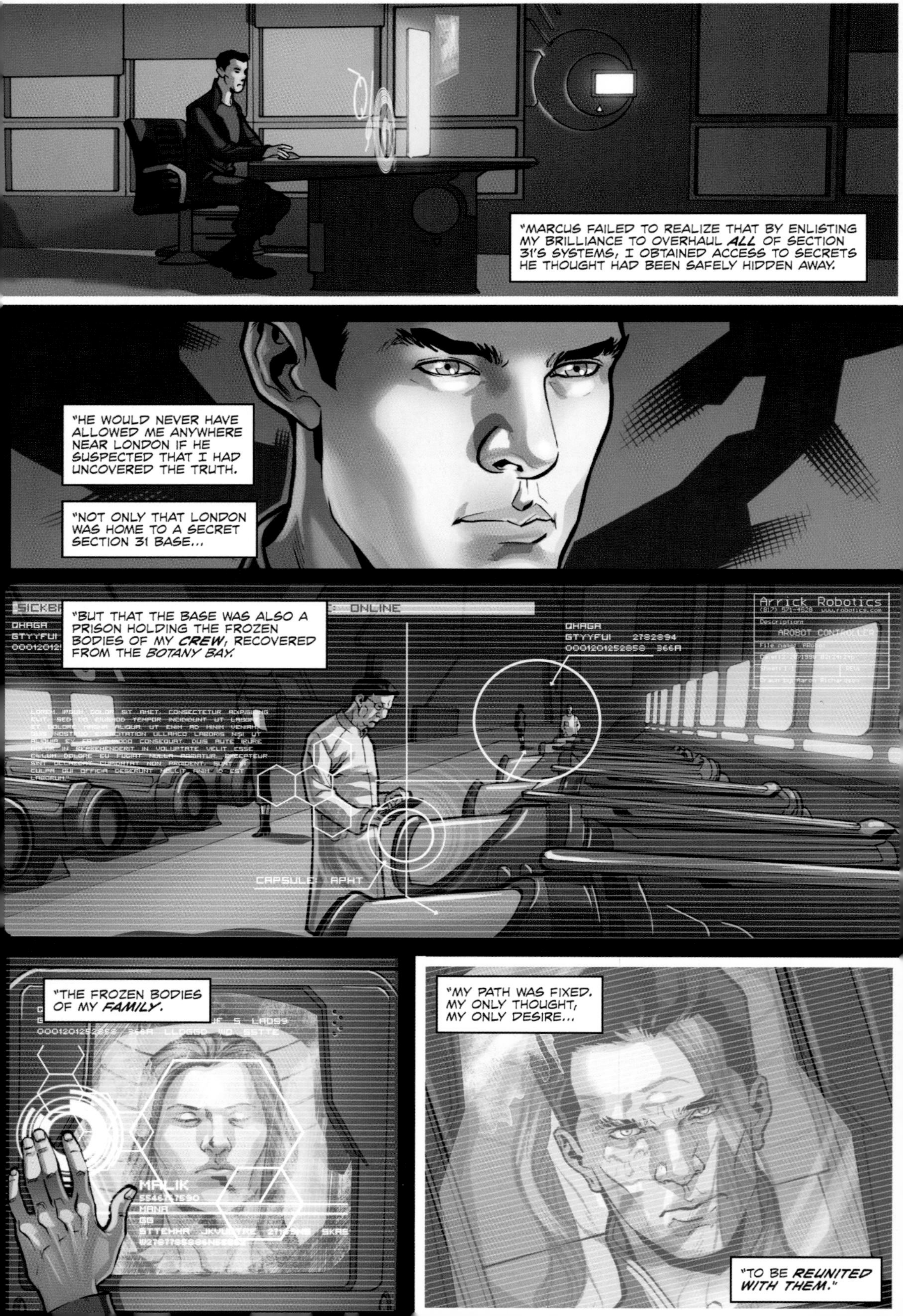
"MARCUS FAILED TO REALIZE THAT BY ENLISTING MY BRILLIANCE TO OVERHAUL ***ALL*** OF SECTION 31'S SYSTEMS, I OBTAINED ACCESS TO SECRETS HE THOUGHT HAD BEEN SAFELY HIDDEN AWAY.
"HE WOULD NEVER HAVE ALLOWED ME ANYWHERE NEAR LONDON IF HE SUSPECTED THAT I HAD UNCOVERED THE TRUTH.
"NOT ONLY THAT LONDON WAS HOME TO A SECRET SECTION 31 BASE...
"BUT THAT THE BASE WAS ALSO A PRISON HOLDING THE FROZEN BODIES OF MY ***CREW***, RECOVERED FROM THE *BOTANY BAY*.
"THE FROZEN BODIES OF MY ***FAMILY***.
"MY PATH WAS FIXED. MY ONLY THOUGHT, MY ONLY DESIRE...
"TO BE ***REUNITED WITH THEM***."

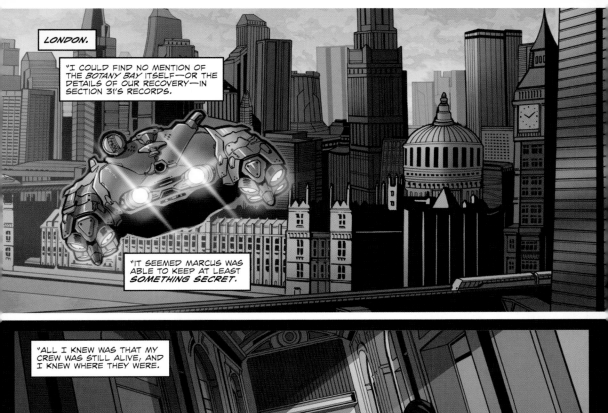

LONDON.

"I COULD FIND NO MENTION OF THE *BOTANY BAY* ITSELF—OR THE DETAILS OF OUR RECOVERY—IN SECTION 31'S RECORDS.

"IT SEEMED MARCUS WAS ABLE TO KEEP AT LEAST *SOMETHING SECRET*.

"ALL I KNEW WAS THAT MY CREW WAS STILL ALIVE, AND I KNEW WHERE THEY WERE.

"HOW I LONGED TO SEE THEM FIRSTHAND. THERE I WAS, WORKING IN THE SAME SECRET LOCATION AT WHICH THEY WERE BEING HELD.

"BUT I COULD NOT FREE THEM BRAZENLY. IF I TRIED, I WOULD ONLY HAVE BEEN ABLE TO WAKE A FEW BEFORE THE FULL FORCE OF SECTION 31 CAME DOWN UPON US."

"IF I EVEN INQUIRED AFTER THEIR EXISTENCE, MARCUS WOULD KNOW.

"AND SO I DEVISED A LESS... *DIRECT* PLAN TO RESCUE THEM.

"A *BETTER* PLAN."

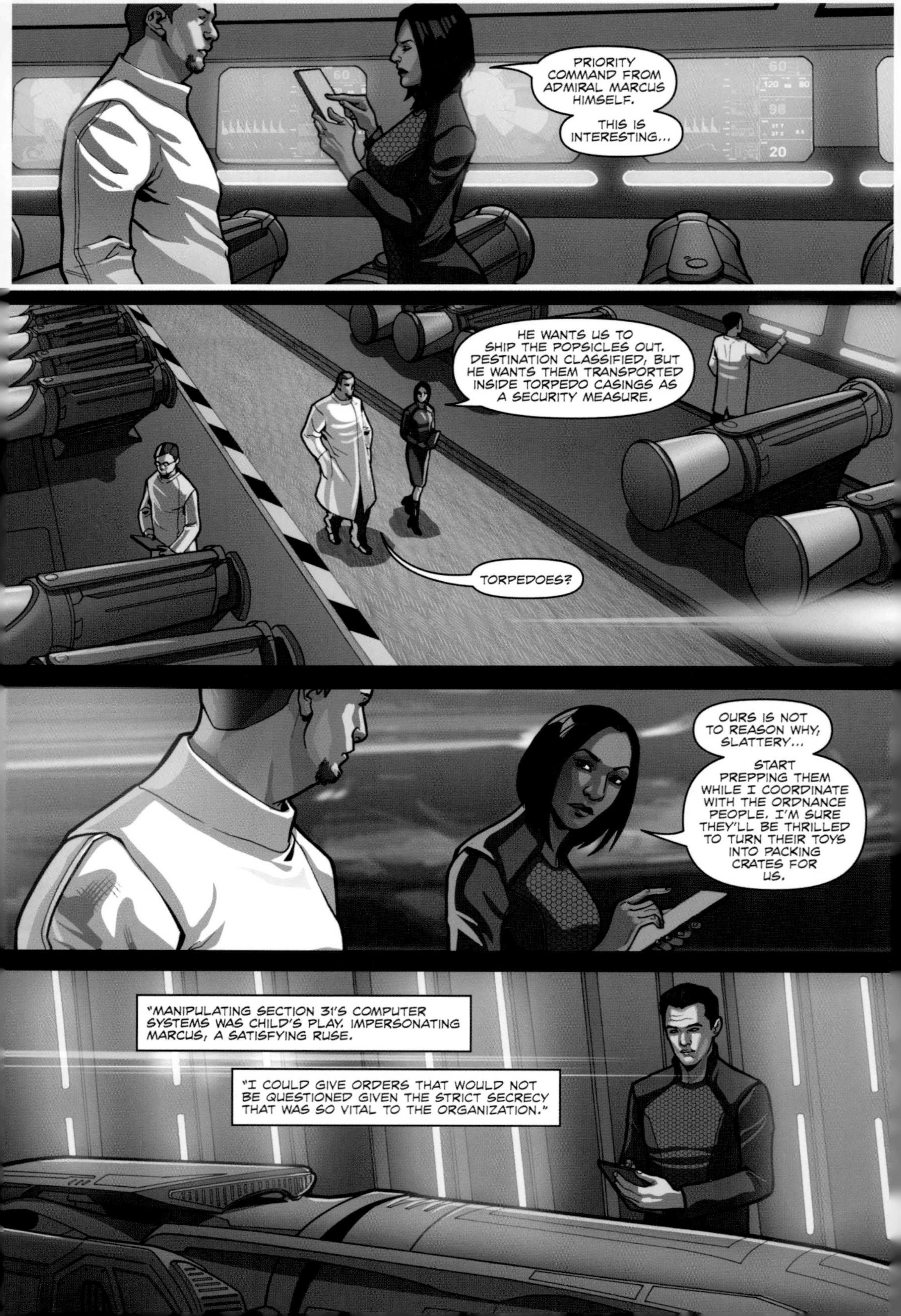
PRIORITY COMMAND FROM ADMIRAL MARCUS HIMSELF.
THIS IS INTERESTING...
HE WANTS US TO SHIP THE POPSICLES OUT. DESTINATION CLASSIFIED, BUT HE WANTS THEM TRANSPORTED INSIDE TORPEDO CASINGS AS A SECURITY MEASURE.
TORPEDOES?
OURS IS NOT TO REASON WHY, SLATTERY...
START PREPPING THEM WHILE I COORDINATE WITH THE ORDNANCE PEOPLE. I'M SURE THEY'LL BE THRILLED TO TURN THEIR TOYS INTO PACKING CRATES FOR US.
"MANIPULATING SECTION 31'S COMPUTER SYSTEMS WAS CHILD'S PLAY. IMPERSONATING MARCUS, A SATISFYING RUSE.
"I COULD GIVE ORDERS THAT WOULD NOT BE QUESTIONED GIVEN THE STRICT SECRECY THAT WAS SO VITAL TO THE ORGANIZATION."

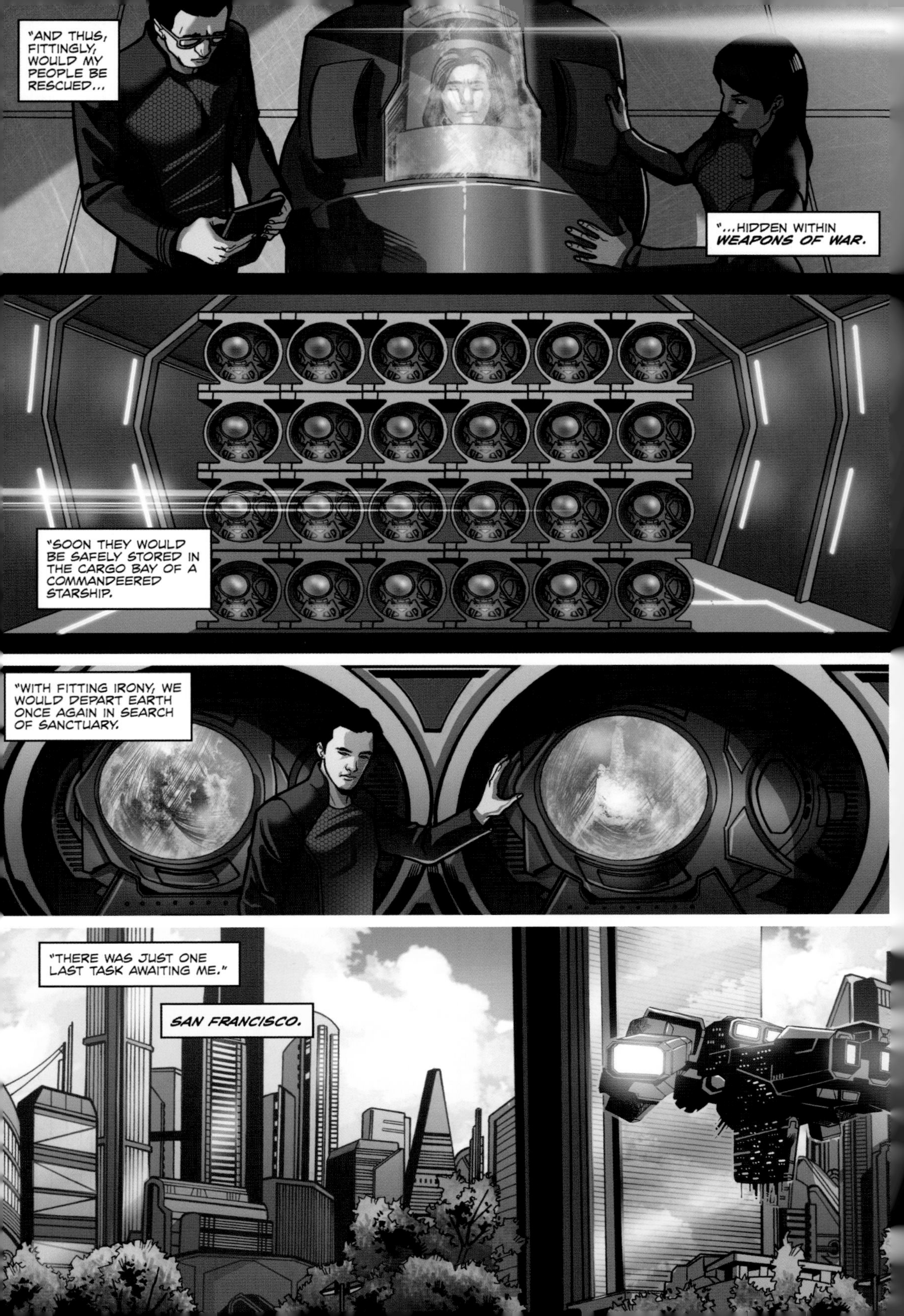
"AND THUS, FITTINGLY, WOULD MY PEOPLE BE RESCUED...
"...HIDDEN WITHIN WEAPONS OF WAR.
"SOON THEY WOULD BE SAFELY STORED IN THE CARGO BAY OF A COMMANDEERED STARSHIP.
"WITH FITTING IRONY, WE WOULD DEPART EARTH ONCE AGAIN IN SEARCH OF SANCTUARY.
"THERE WAS JUST ONE LAST TASK AWAITING ME."
SAN FRANCISCO.

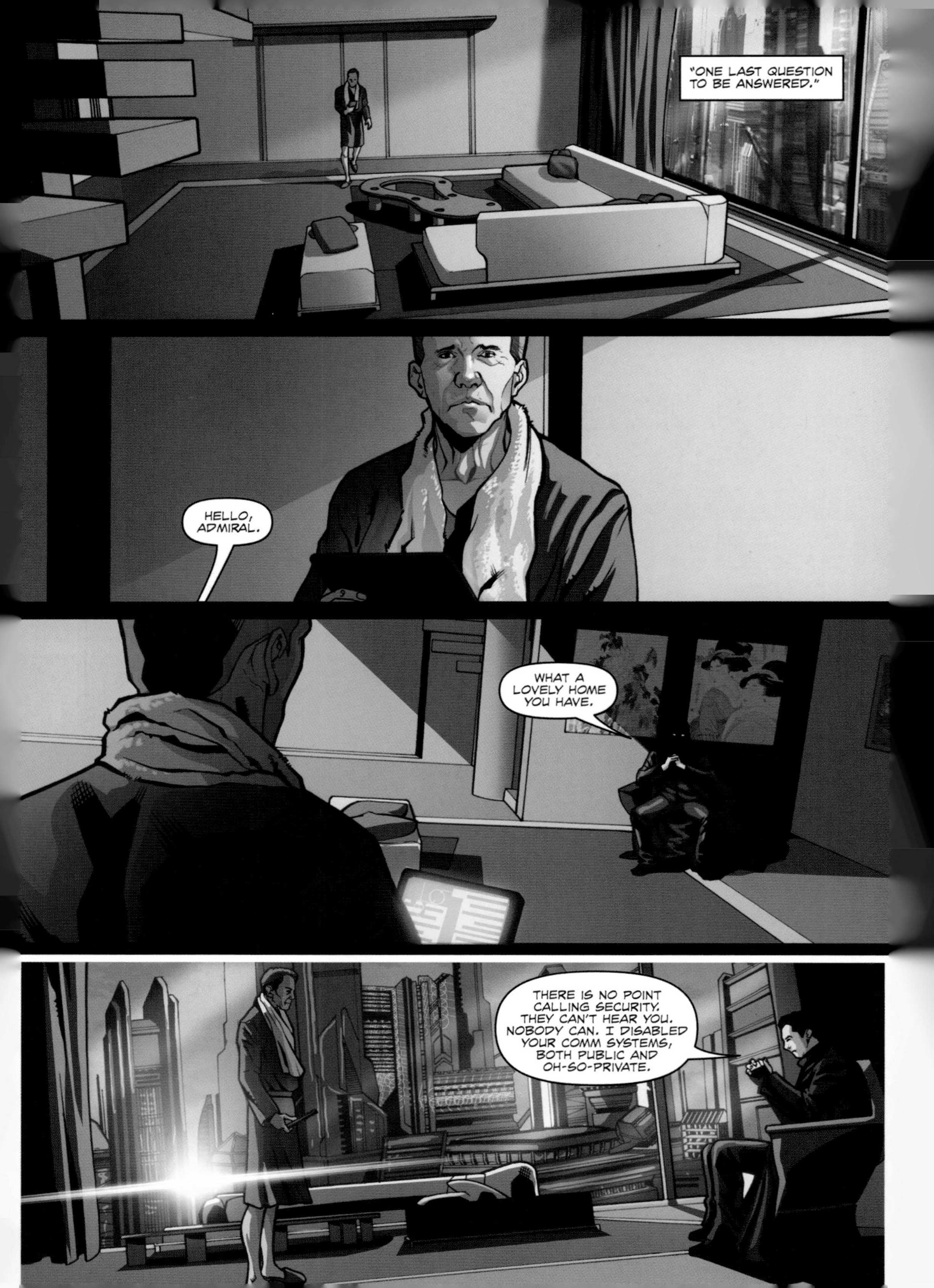
"ONE LAST QUESTION TO BE ANSWERED."
HELLO, ADMIRAL.
WHAT A LOVELY HOME YOU HAVE.
THERE IS NO POINT CALLING SECURITY. THEY CAN'T HEAR YOU. NOBODY CAN. I DISABLED YOUR COMM SYSTEMS, BOTH PUBLIC AND OH-SO-PRIVATE.

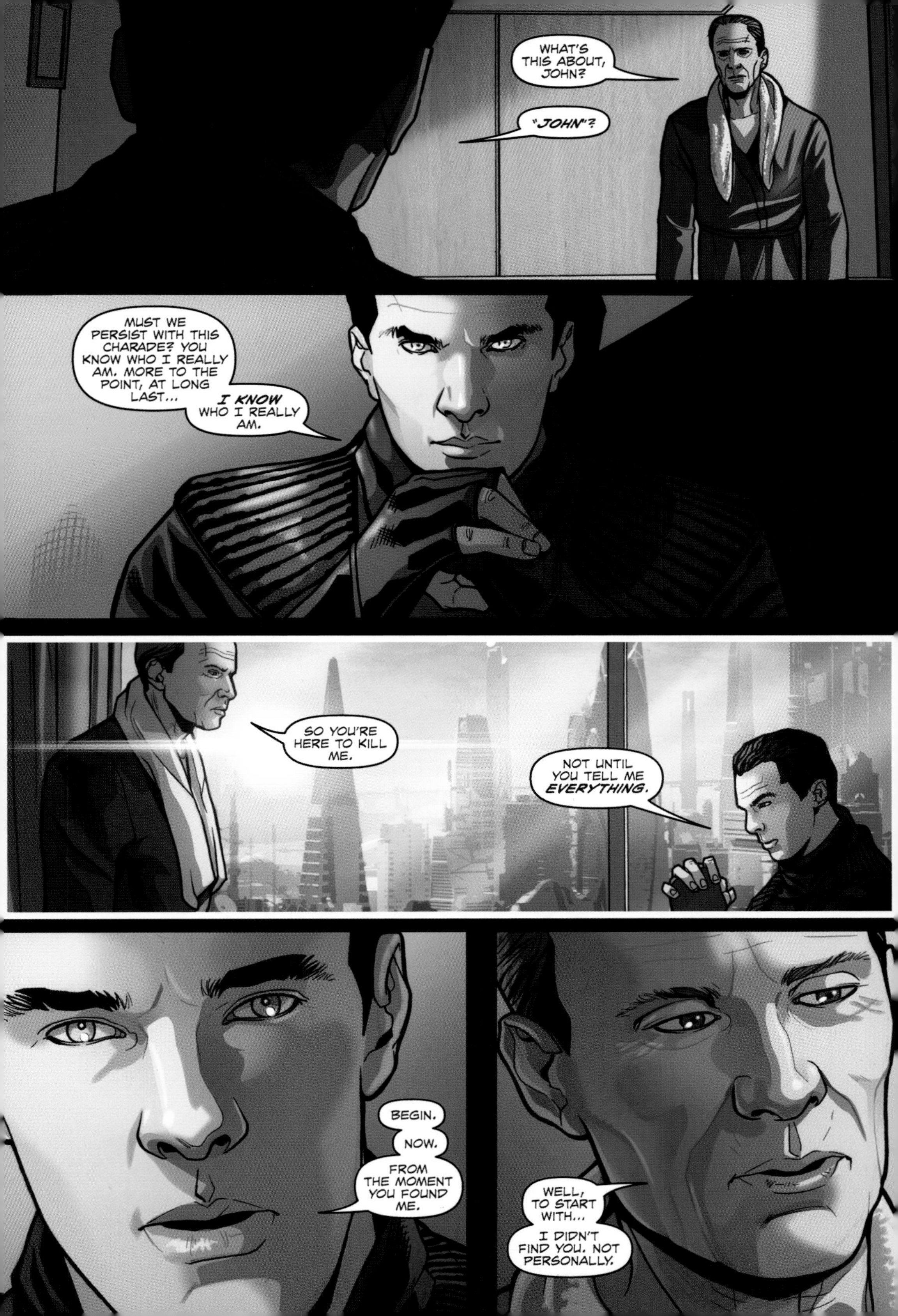

WHAT'S THIS ABOUT, JOHN?
"JOHN"?
MUST WE PERSIST WITH THIS CHARADE? YOU KNOW WHO I REALLY AM. MORE TO THE POINT, AT LONG LAST...
I KNOW WHO I REALLY AM.
SO YOU'RE HERE TO KILL ME.
NOT UNTIL YOU TELL ME *EVERYTHING*.
BEGIN.
NOW.
FROM THE MOMENT YOU FOUND ME.
WELL, TO START WITH...
I DIDN'T FIND YOU. NOT PERSONALLY.

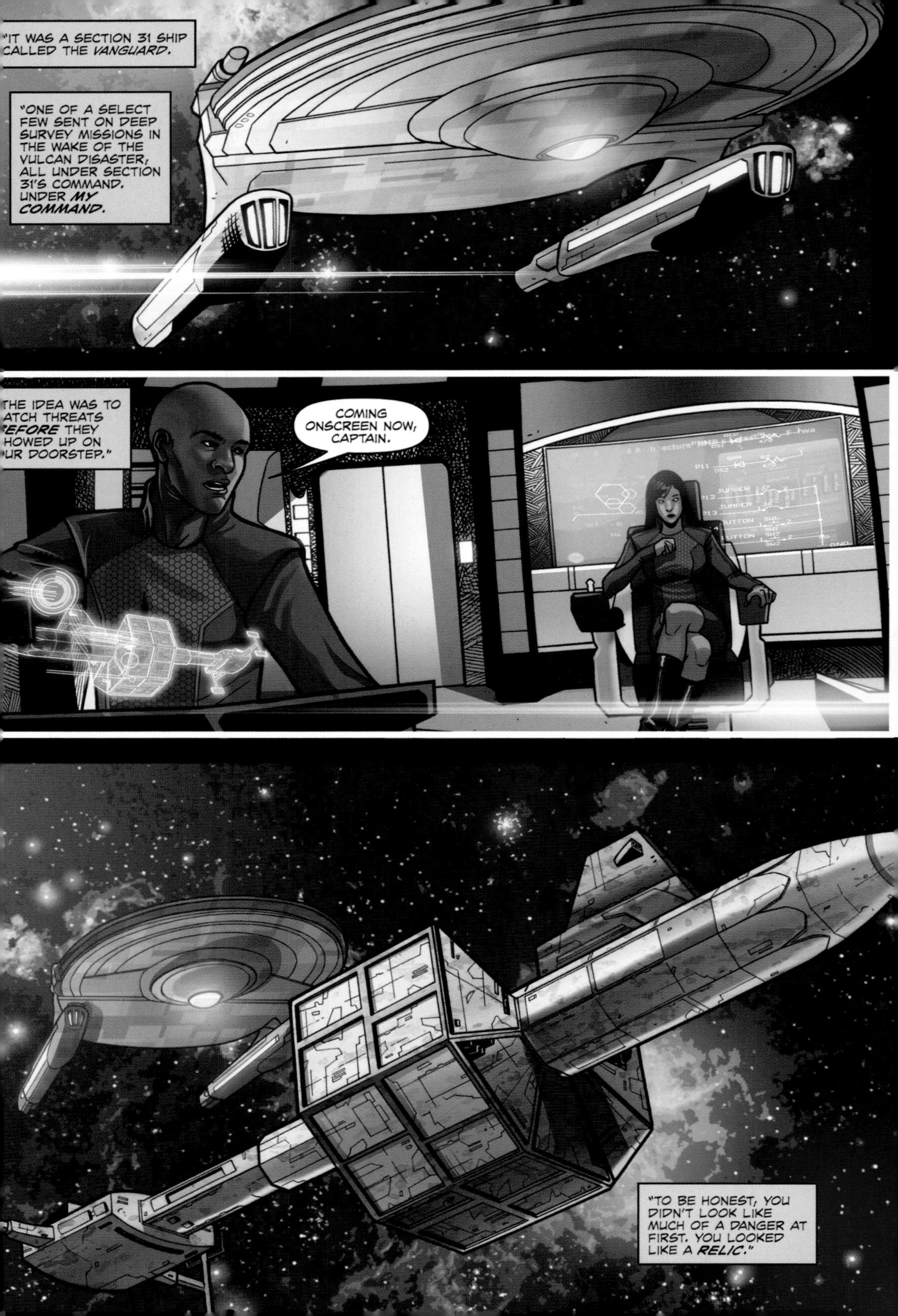
"IT WAS A SECTION 31 SHIP CALLED THE *VANGUARD*.
"ONE OF A SELECT FEW SENT ON DEEP SURVEY MISSIONS IN THE WAKE OF THE VULCAN DISASTER, ALL UNDER SECTION 31'S COMMAND. UNDER ***MY COMMAND***.
THE IDEA WAS TO ATCH THREATS ***EFORE*** THEY HOWED UP ON UR DOORSTEP."
COMING ONSCREEN NOW, CAPTAIN.
"TO BE HONEST, YOU DIDN'T LOOK LIKE MUCH OF A DANGER AT FIRST. YOU LOOKED LIKE A ***RELIC***."

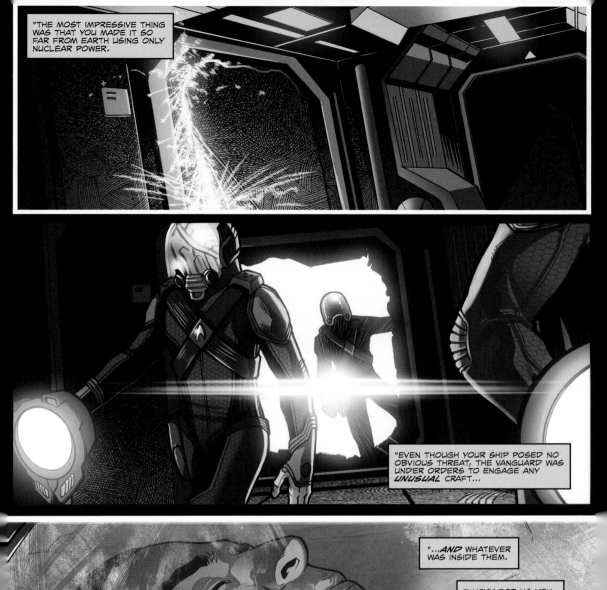

"THE MOST IMPRESSIVE THING WAS THAT YOU MADE IT SO FAR FROM EARTH USING ONLY NUCLEAR POWER.

"EVEN THOUGH YOUR SHIP POSED NO OBVIOUS THREAT, THE VANGUARD WAS UNDER ORDERS TO ENGAGE ANY *UNUSUAL* CRAFT...

"...*AND* WHATEVER WAS INSIDE THEM.

"LUCKY FOR US YOU WERE STILL ASLEEP."

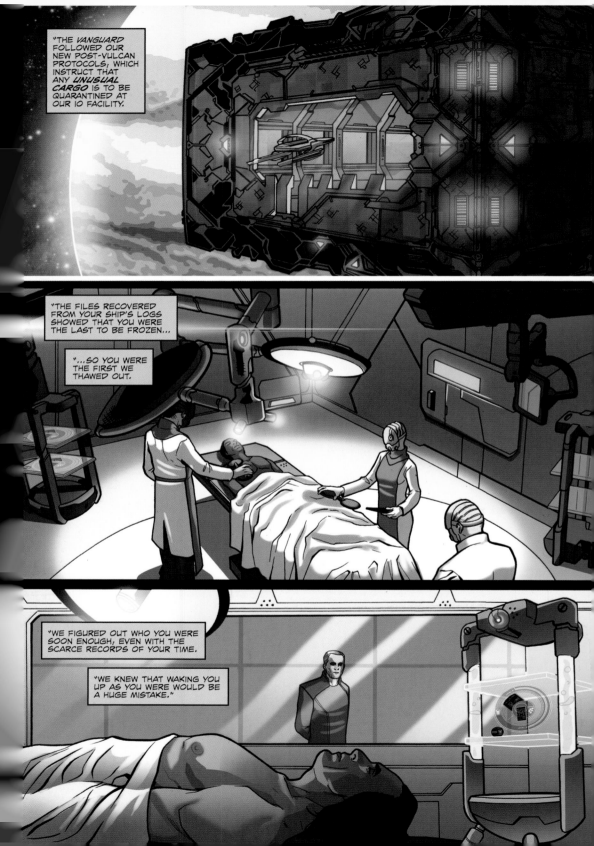

"THE *VANGUARD* FOLLOWED OUR NEW POST-VULCAN PROTOCOLS, WHICH INSTRUCT THAT ANY *UNUSUAL CARGO* IS TO BE QUARANTINED AT OUR IO FACILITY.

"THE FILES RECOVERED FROM YOUR SHIP'S LOGS SHOWED THAT YOU WERE THE LAST TO BE FROZEN...

"...SO YOU WERE THE FIRST WE THAWED OUT.

"WE FIGURED OUT WHO YOU WERE SOON ENOUGH, EVEN WITH THE SCARCE RECORDS OF YOUR TIME.

"WE KNEW THAT WAKING YOU UP AS YOU WERE WOULD BE A HUGE MISTAKE."

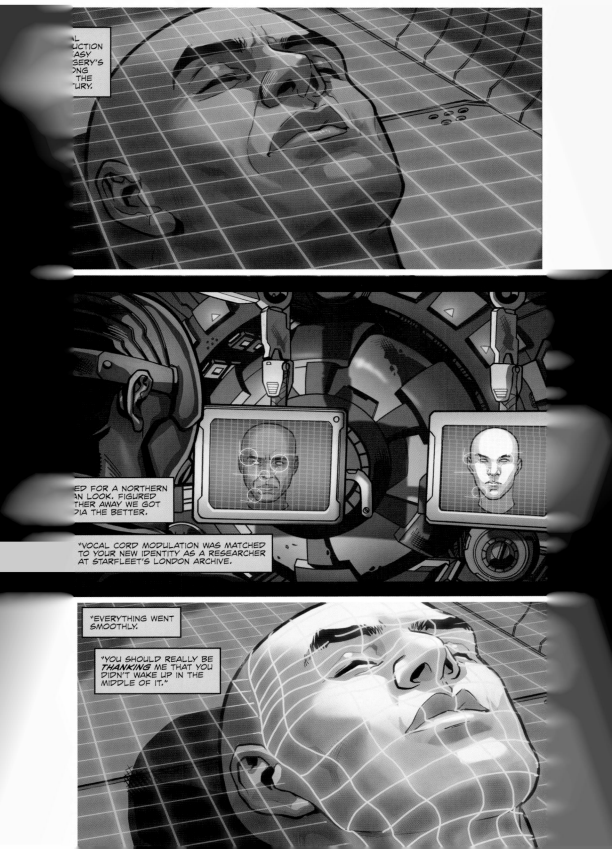

AL
UCTION
ASY
GERY'S
ONG
THE
TURY.

ED FOR A NORTHERN
AN LOOK. FIGURED
THER AWAY WE GOT
DIA THE BETTER.

"VOCAL CORD MODULATION WAS MATCHED
TO YOUR NEW IDENTITY AS A RESEARCHER
AT STARFLEET'S LONDON ARCHIVE.

"EVERYTHING WENT
SMOOTHLY.

"YOU SHOULD REALLY BE
THANKING ME THAT YOU
DIDN'T WAKE UP IN THE
MIDDLE OF IT."

"THE REAL TRICK WAS THE WORK WE DID ON YOUR *BRAIN.*

"LET'S JUST SAY YOU'RE WIRED A LITTLE *DIFFERENTLY* THAN THE AVERAGE PATIENT.

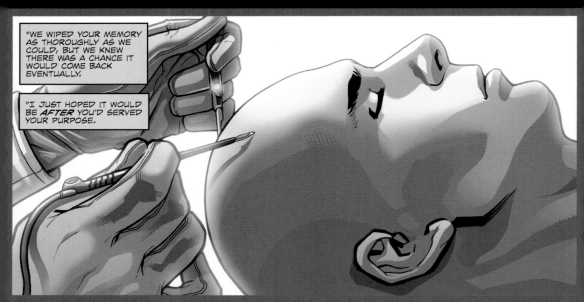

"WE WIPED YOUR MEMORY AS THOROUGHLY AS WE COULD, BUT WE KNEW THERE WAS A CHANCE IT WOULD COME BACK EVENTUALLY.

"I JUST HOPED IT WOULD BE *AFTER* YOU'D SERVED YOUR PURPOSE.

"IN A PERFECT WORLD, YOU WERE GOING TO BE THE FIRST OF MANY NEW RECRUITS TO THE CAUSE.

"SEVENTY-TWO MORE RECRUITS, TO BE PRECISE."

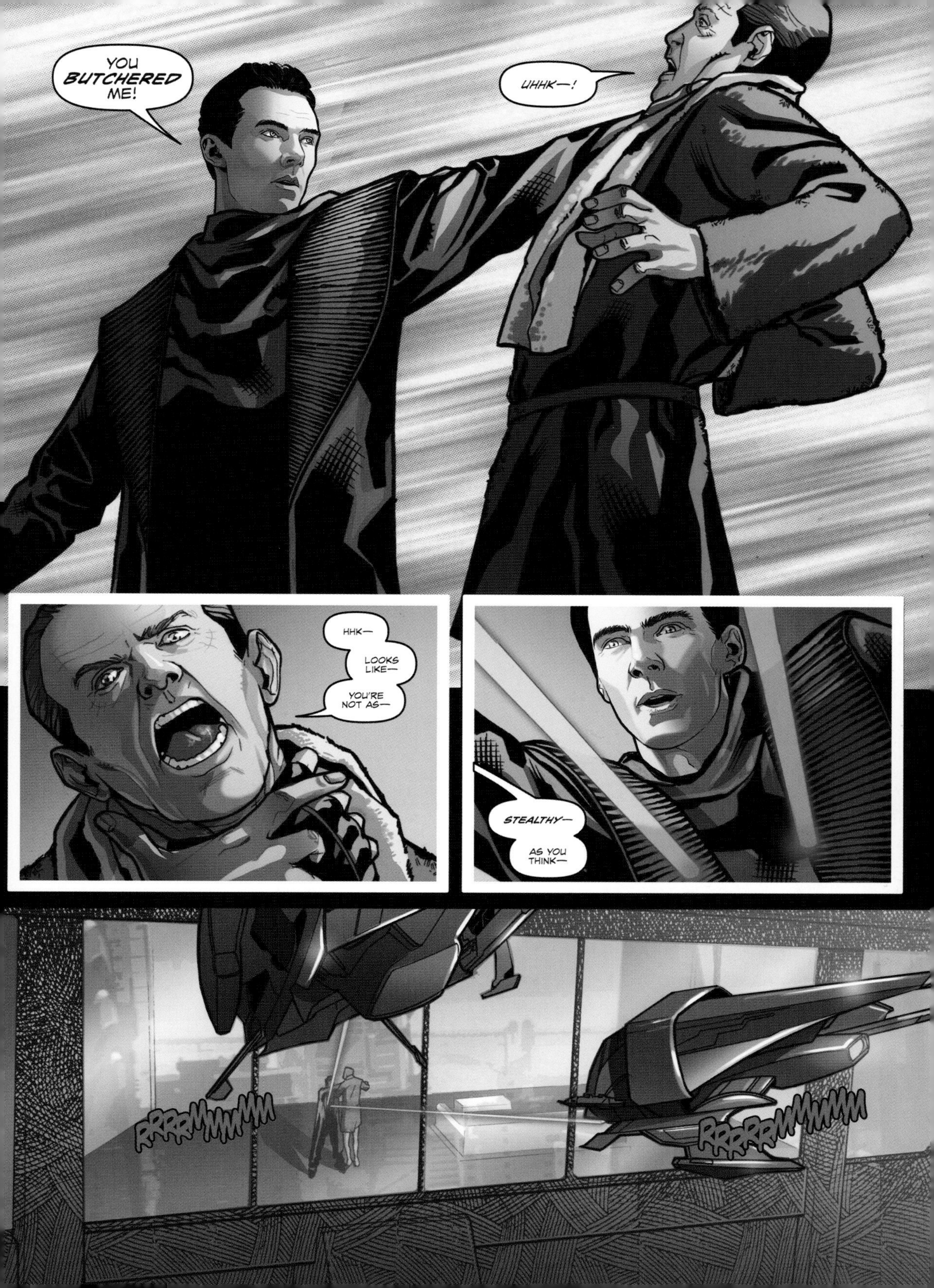
YOU *BUTCHERED* ME!
UHHK—!
HHK—
LOOKS LIKE—
YOU'RE NOT AS—
STEALTHY—
AS YOU THINK—
RRRRMMMMMM
RRRRRMMMMMM

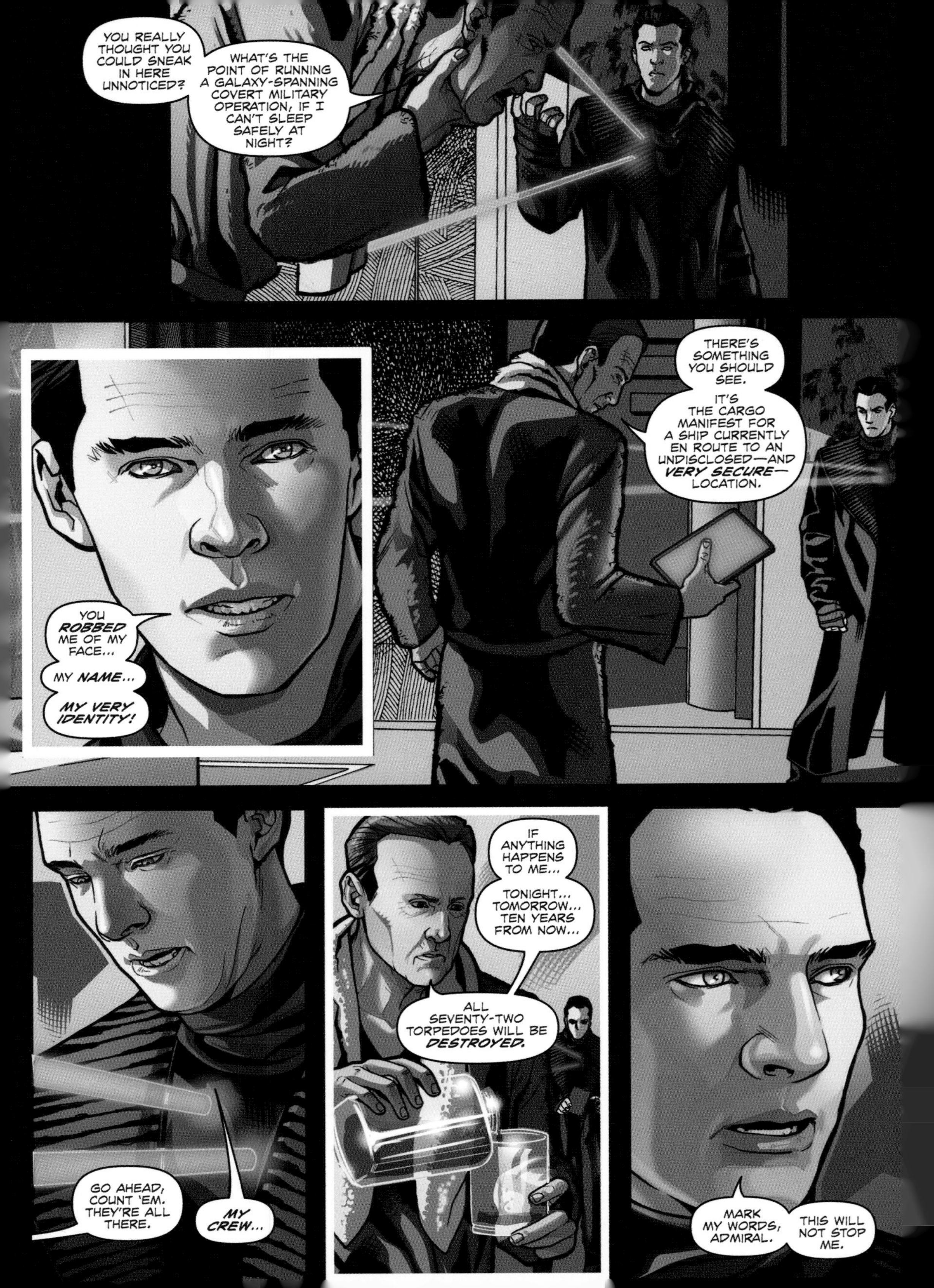

YOU REALLY THOUGHT YOU COULD SNEAK IN HERE UNNOTICED?
WHAT'S THE POINT OF RUNNING A GALAXY-SPANNING COVERT MILITARY OPERATION, IF I CAN'T SLEEP SAFELY AT NIGHT?
YOU ROBBED ME OF MY FACE...
MY NAME...
MY VERY IDENTITY!
THERE'S SOMETHING YOU SHOULD SEE.
IT'S THE CARGO MANIFEST FOR A SHIP CURRENTLY EN ROUTE TO AN UNDISCLOSED—AND VERY SECURE—LOCATION.
GO AHEAD, COUNT 'EM. THEY'RE ALL THERE.
MY CREW...
IF ANYTHING HAPPENS TO ME...
TONIGHT... TOMORROW... TEN YEARS FROM NOW...
ALL SEVENTY-TWO TORPEDOES WILL BE DESTROYED.
MARK MY WORDS, ADMIRAL.
THIS WILL NOT STOP ME.

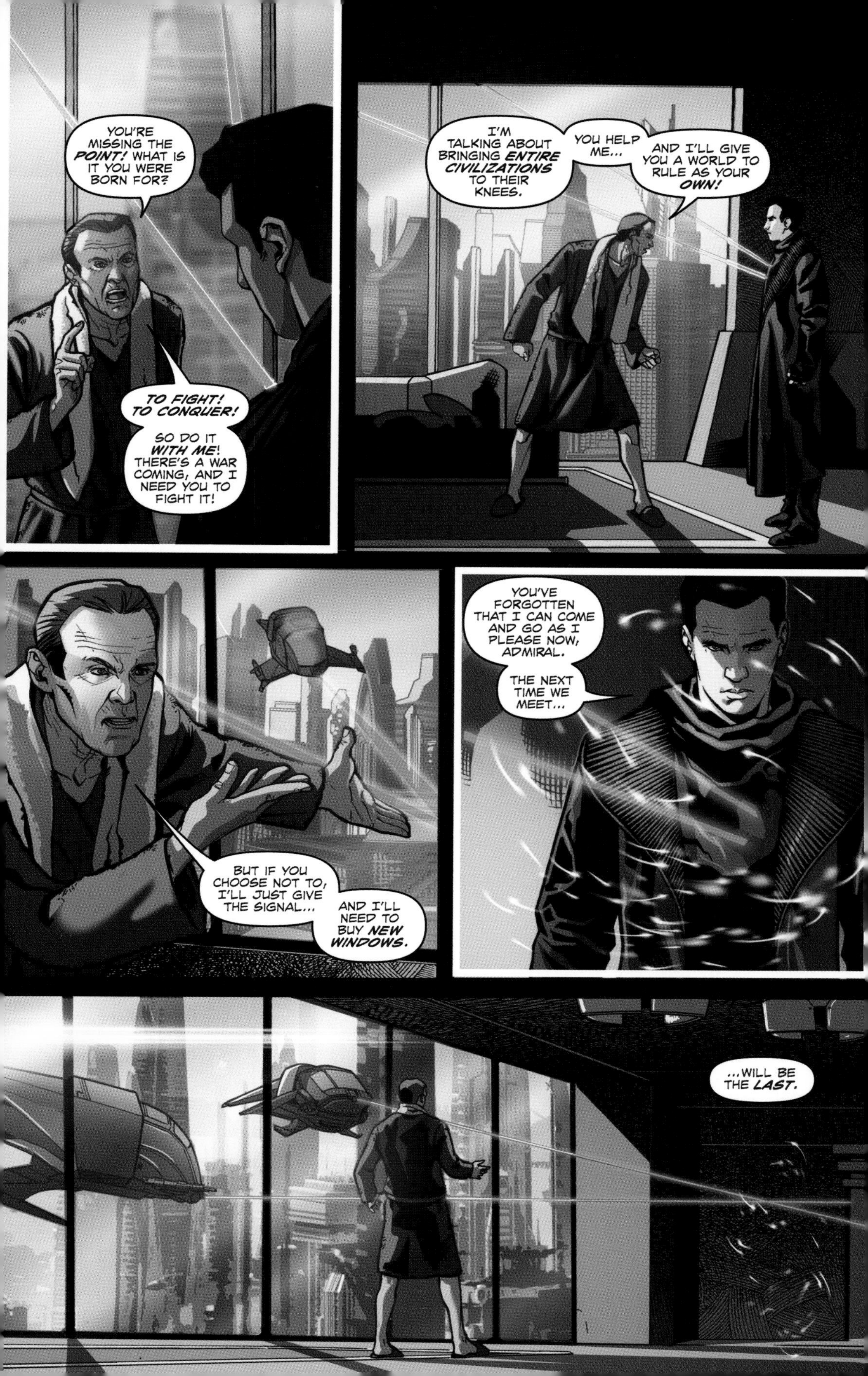
YOU'RE MISSING THE *POINT!* WHAT IS IT YOU WERE BORN FOR?
TO FIGHT! TO CONQUER!
SO DO IT *WITH ME*! THERE'S A WAR COMING, AND I NEED YOU TO FIGHT IT!
I'M TALKING ABOUT BRINGING *ENTIRE CIVILIZATIONS* TO THEIR KNEES.
YOU HELP ME...
AND I'LL GIVE YOU A WORLD TO RULE AS YOUR *OWN!*
BUT IF YOU CHOOSE NOT TO, I'LL JUST GIVE THE SIGNAL...
AND I'LL NEED TO BUY *NEW WINDOWS*.
YOU'VE FORGOTTEN THAT I CAN COME AND GO AS I PLEASE NOW, ADMIRAL.
THE NEXT TIME WE MEET...
...WILL BE THE *LAST*.

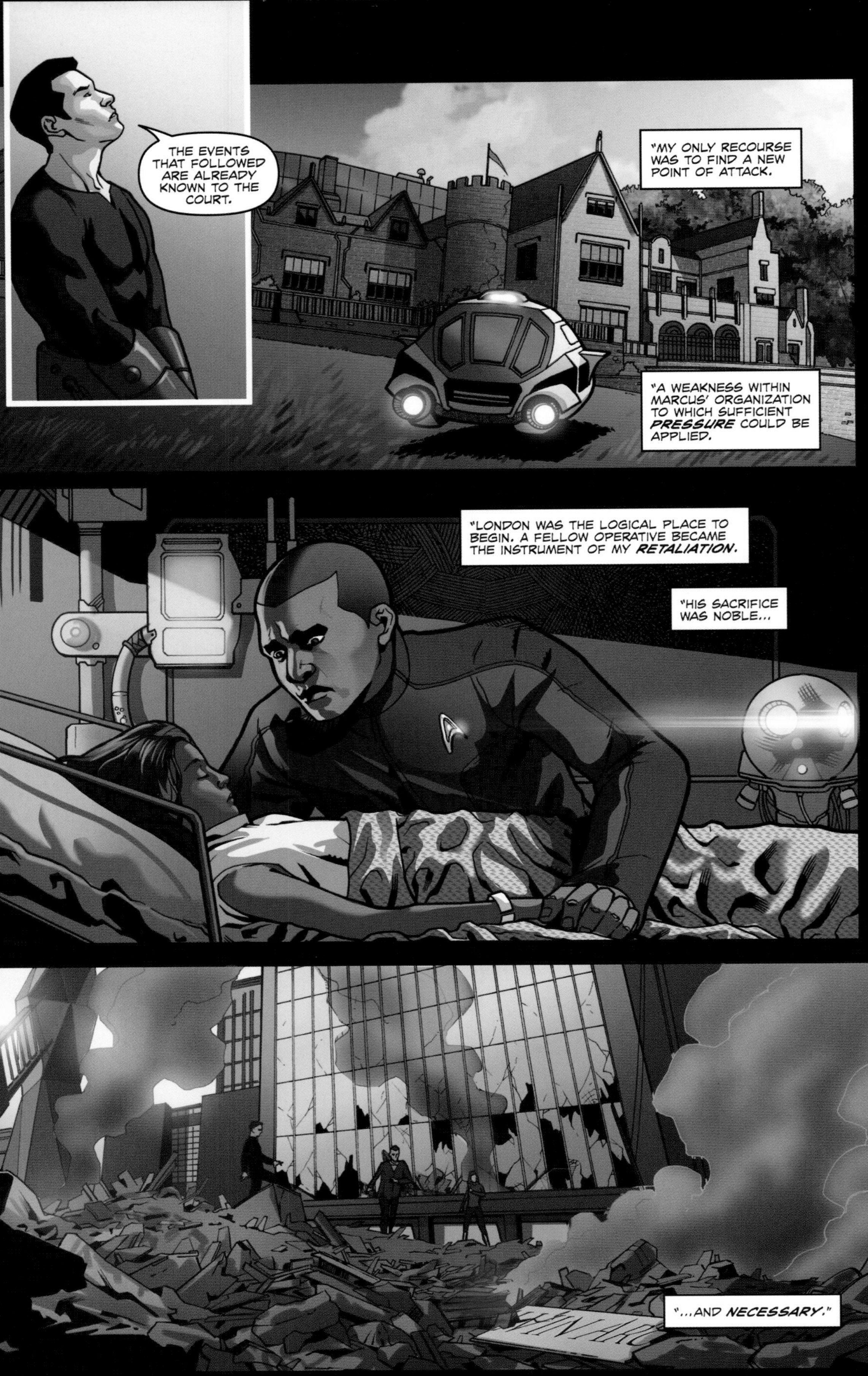
THE EVENTS THAT FOLLOWED ARE ALREADY KNOWN TO THE COURT.
"MY ONLY RECOURSE WAS TO FIND A NEW POINT OF ATTACK.
"A WEAKNESS WITHIN MARCUS' ORGANIZATION TO WHICH SUFFICIENT PRESSURE COULD BE APPLIED.
"LONDON WAS THE LOGICAL PLACE TO BEGIN. A FELLOW OPERATIVE BECAME THE INSTRUMENT OF MY RETALIATION.
"HIS SACRIFICE WAS NOBLE...
"...AND NECESSARY."

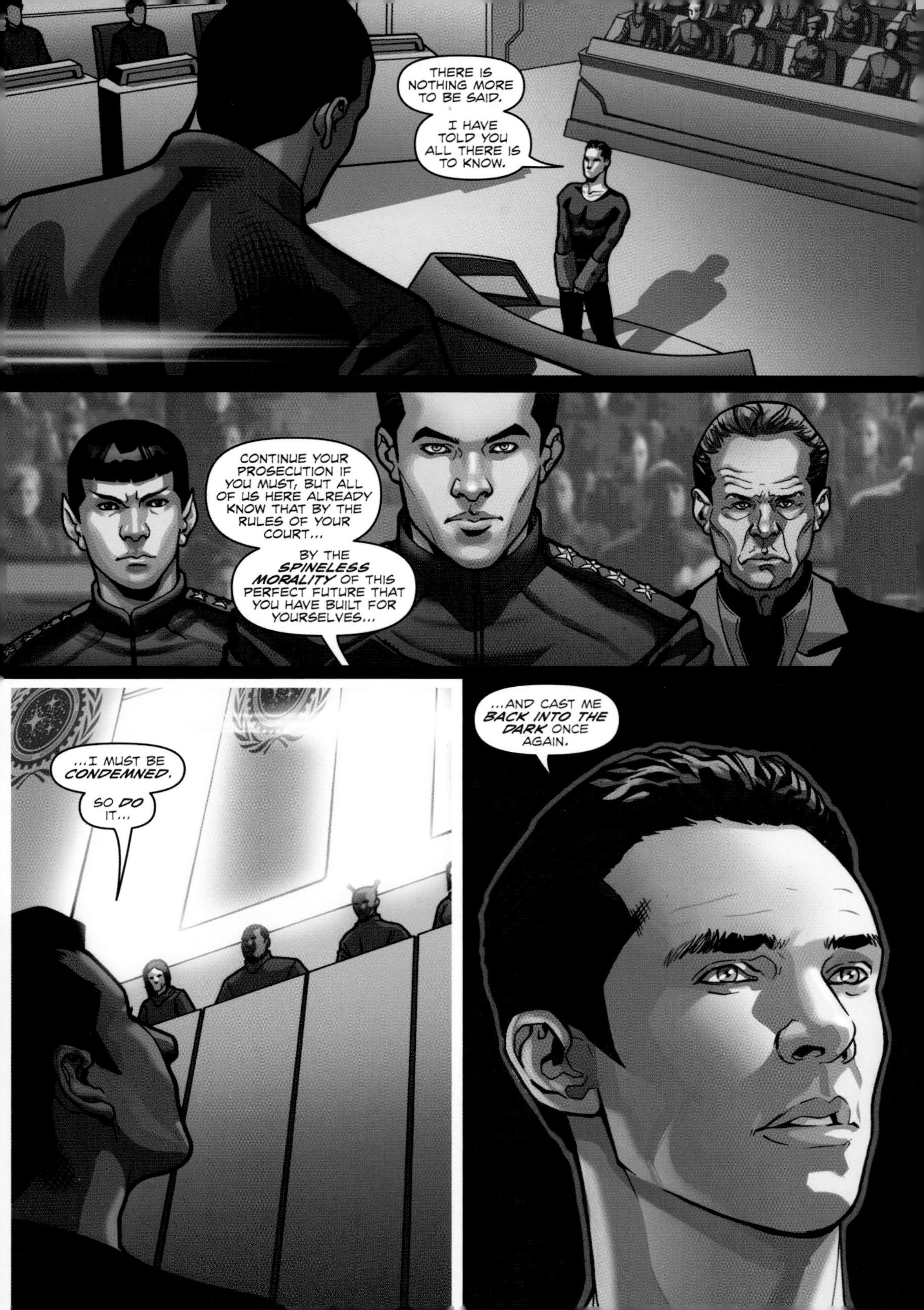
THERE IS NOTHING MORE TO BE SAID.
I HAVE TOLD YOU ALL THERE IS TO KNOW.
CONTINUE YOUR PROSECUTION IF YOU MUST, BUT ALL OF US HERE ALREADY KNOW THAT BY THE RULES OF YOUR COURT...
BY THE ***SPINELESS MORALITY*** OF THIS PERFECT FUTURE THAT YOU HAVE BUILT FOR YOURSELVES...
...I MUST BE ***CONDEMNED.***
SO ***DO*** IT...
...AND CAST ME ***BACK INTO THE DARK*** ONCE AGAIN.

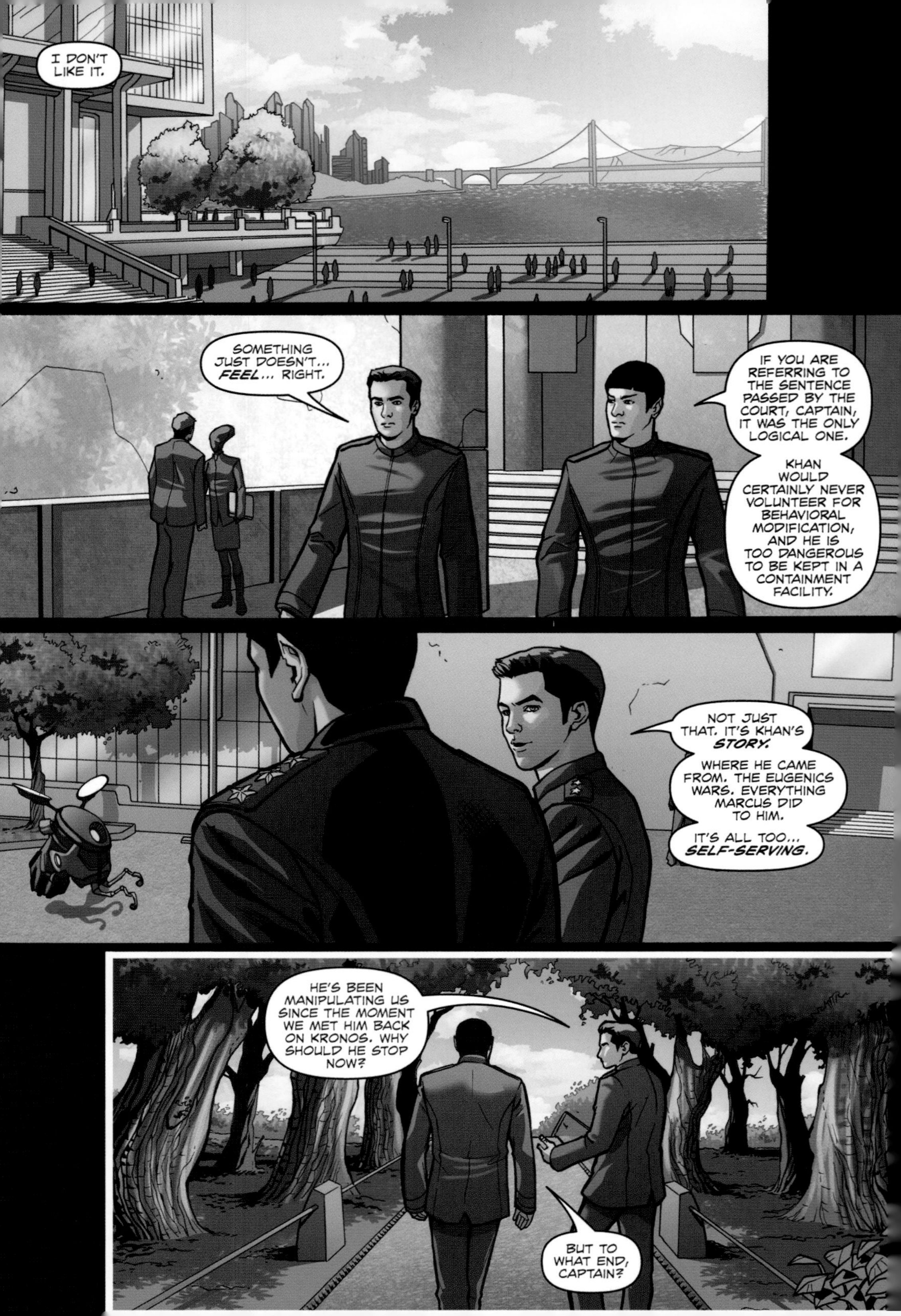
I DON'T LIKE IT.
SOMETHING JUST DOESN'T... FEEL... RIGHT.
IF YOU ARE REFERRING TO THE SENTENCE PASSED BY THE COURT, CAPTAIN, IT WAS THE ONLY LOGICAL ONE.
KHAN WOULD CERTAINLY NEVER VOLUNTEER FOR BEHAVIORAL MODIFICATION, AND HE IS TOO DANGEROUS TO BE KEPT IN A CONTAINMENT FACILITY.
NOT JUST THAT. IT'S KHAN'S STORY.
WHERE HE CAME FROM. THE EUGENICS WARS. EVERYTHING MARCUS DID TO HIM.
IT'S ALL TOO... SELF-SERVING.
HE'S BEEN MANIPULATING US SINCE THE MOMENT WE MET HIM BACK ON KRONOS. WHY SHOULD HE STOP NOW?
BUT TO WHAT END, CAPTAIN?

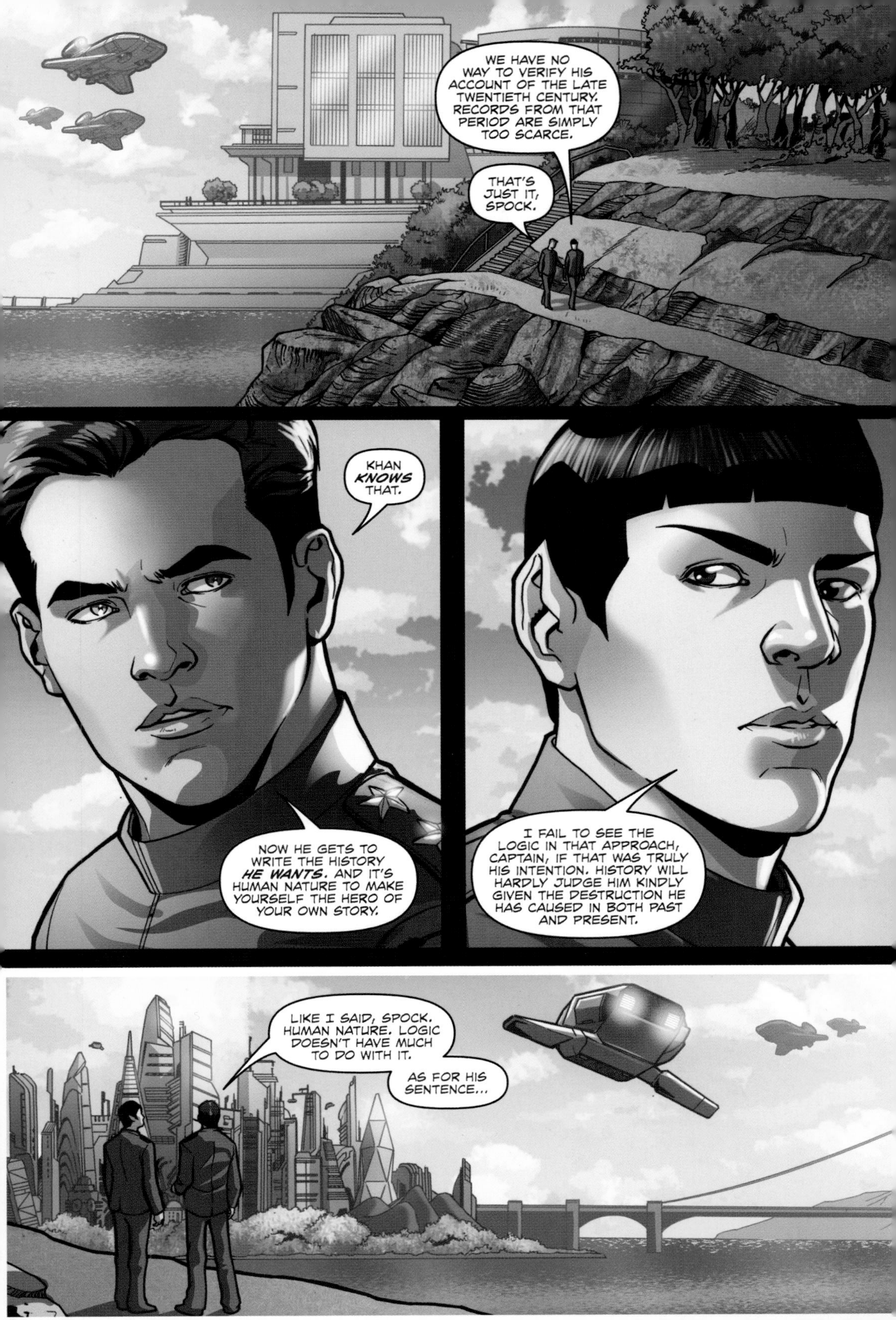
WE HAVE NO WAY TO VERIFY HIS ACCOUNT OF THE LATE TWENTIETH CENTURY. RECORDS FROM THAT PERIOD ARE SIMPLY TOO SCARCE.
THAT'S JUST IT, SPOCK.
KHAN **KNOWS** THAT.
NOW HE GETS TO WRITE THE HISTORY ***HE WANTS.*** AND IT'S HUMAN NATURE TO MAKE YOURSELF THE HERO OF YOUR OWN STORY.
I FAIL TO SEE THE LOGIC IN THAT APPROACH, CAPTAIN, IF THAT WAS TRULY HIS INTENTION. HISTORY WILL HARDLY JUDGE HIM KINDLY GIVEN THE DESTRUCTION HE HAS CAUSED IN BOTH PAST AND PRESENT.
LIKE I SAID, SPOCK. HUMAN NATURE. LOGIC DOESN'T HAVE MUCH TO DO WITH IT.
AS FOR HIS SENTENCE...

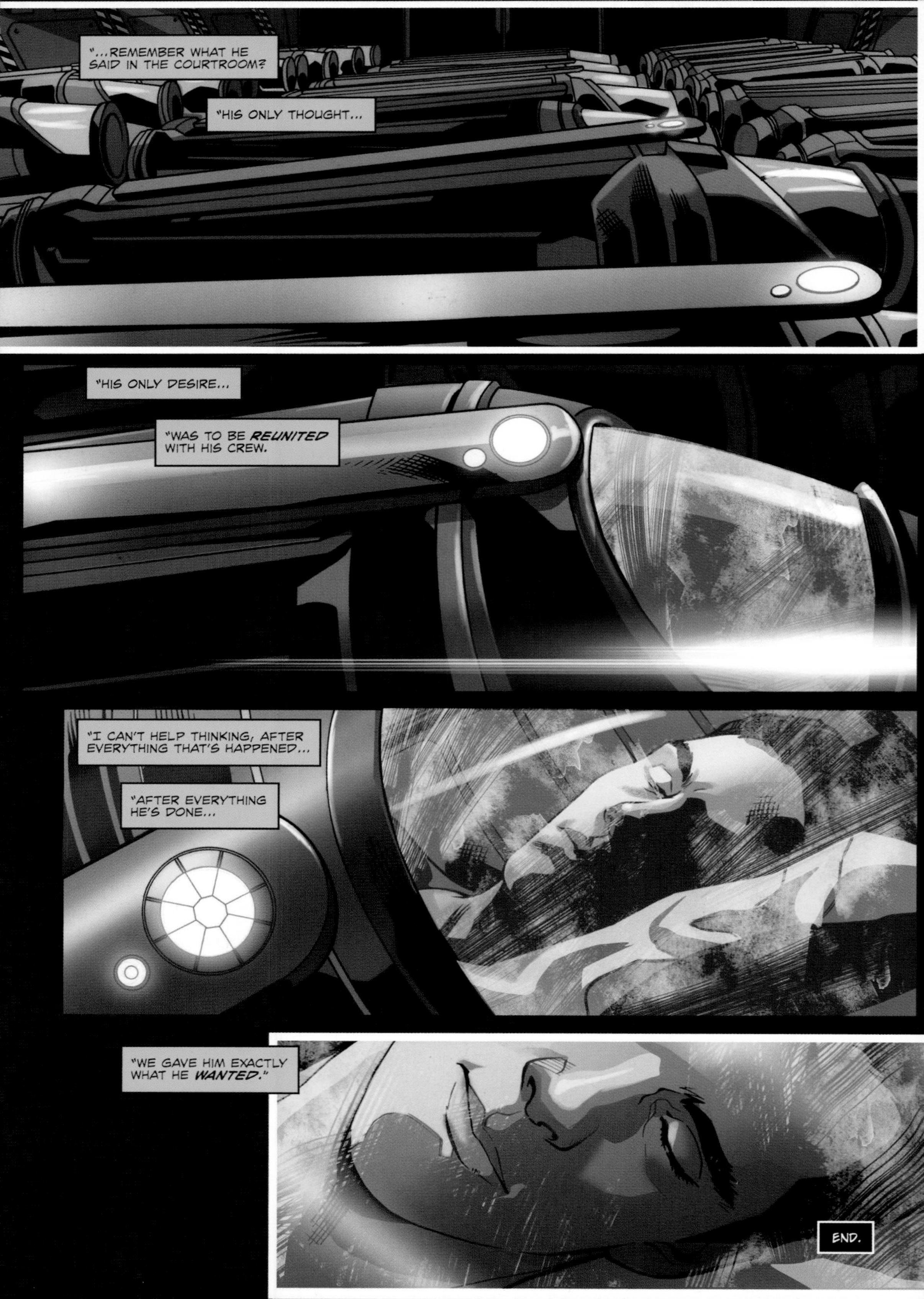
"...REMEMBER WHAT HE SAID IN THE COURTROOM?
"HIS ONLY THOUGHT...
"HIS ONLY DESIRE...
"WAS TO BE *REUNITED* WITH HIS CREW.
"I CAN'T HELP THINKING, AFTER EVERYTHING THAT'S HAPPENED...
"AFTER EVERYTHING HE'S DONE...
"WE GAVE HIM EXACTLY WHAT HE *WANTED*."
END.

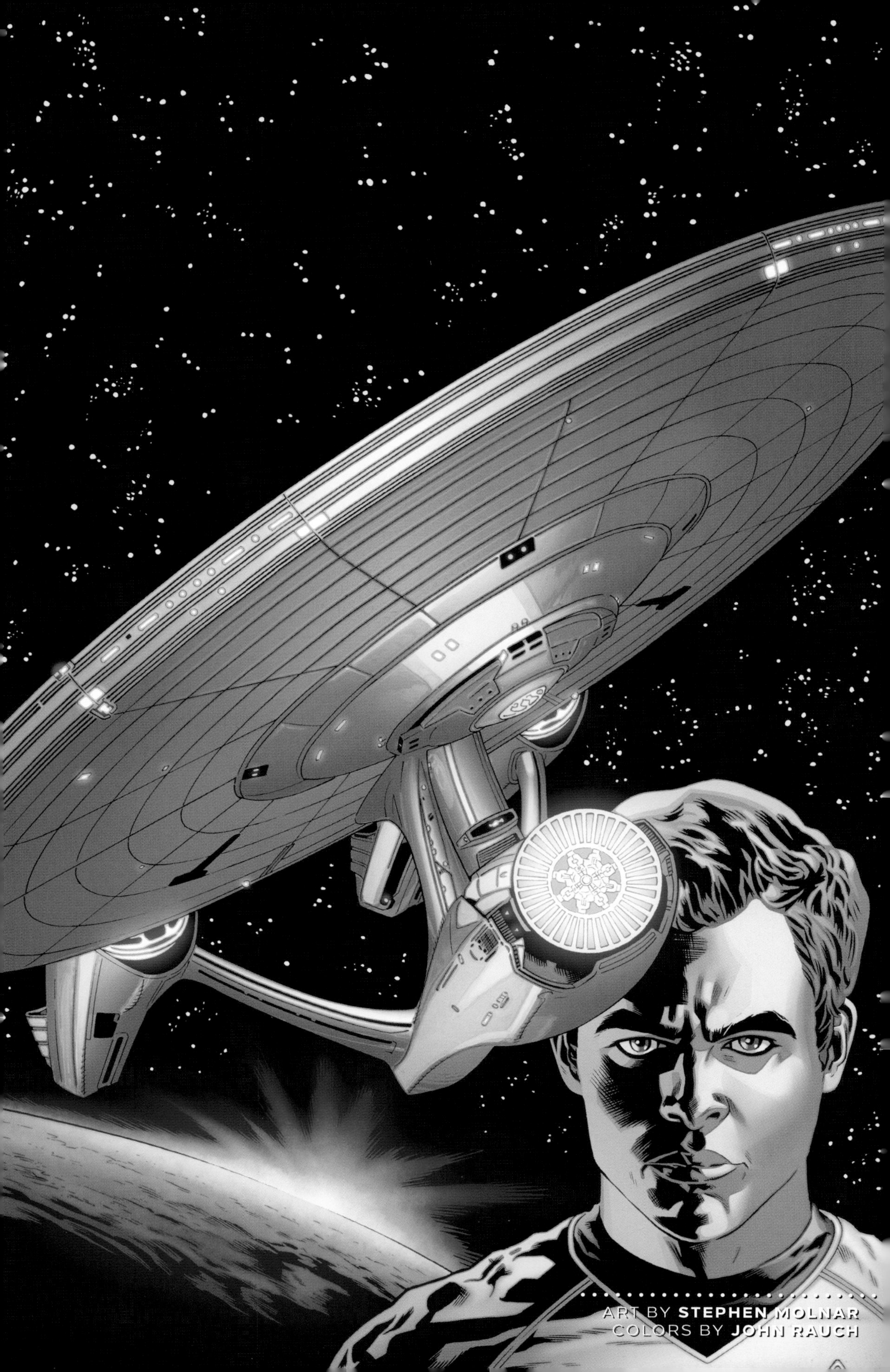

ART BY **STEPHEN MOLNAR**
COLORS BY **JOHN RAUCH**

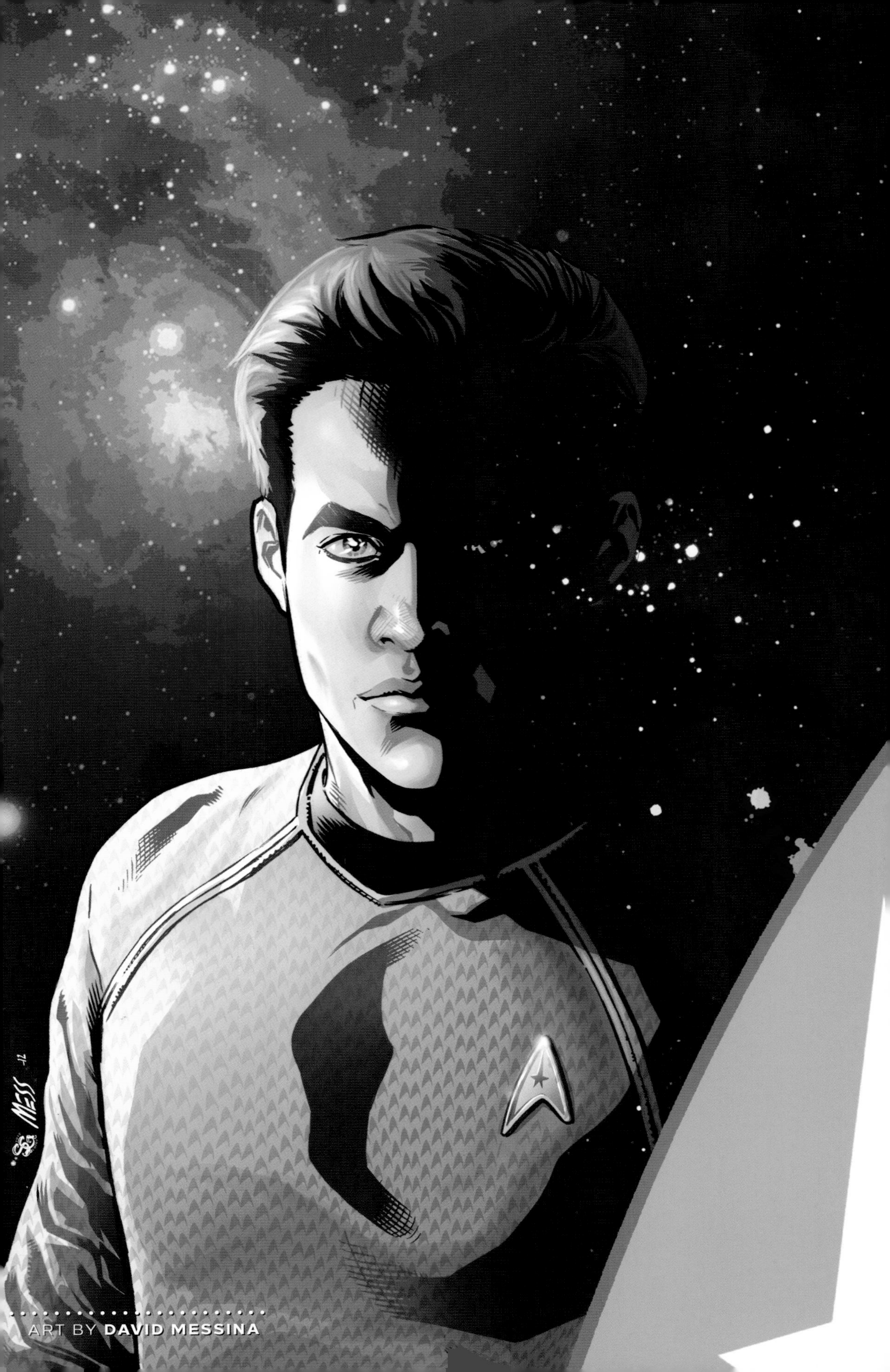

ART BY **DAVID MESSINA**

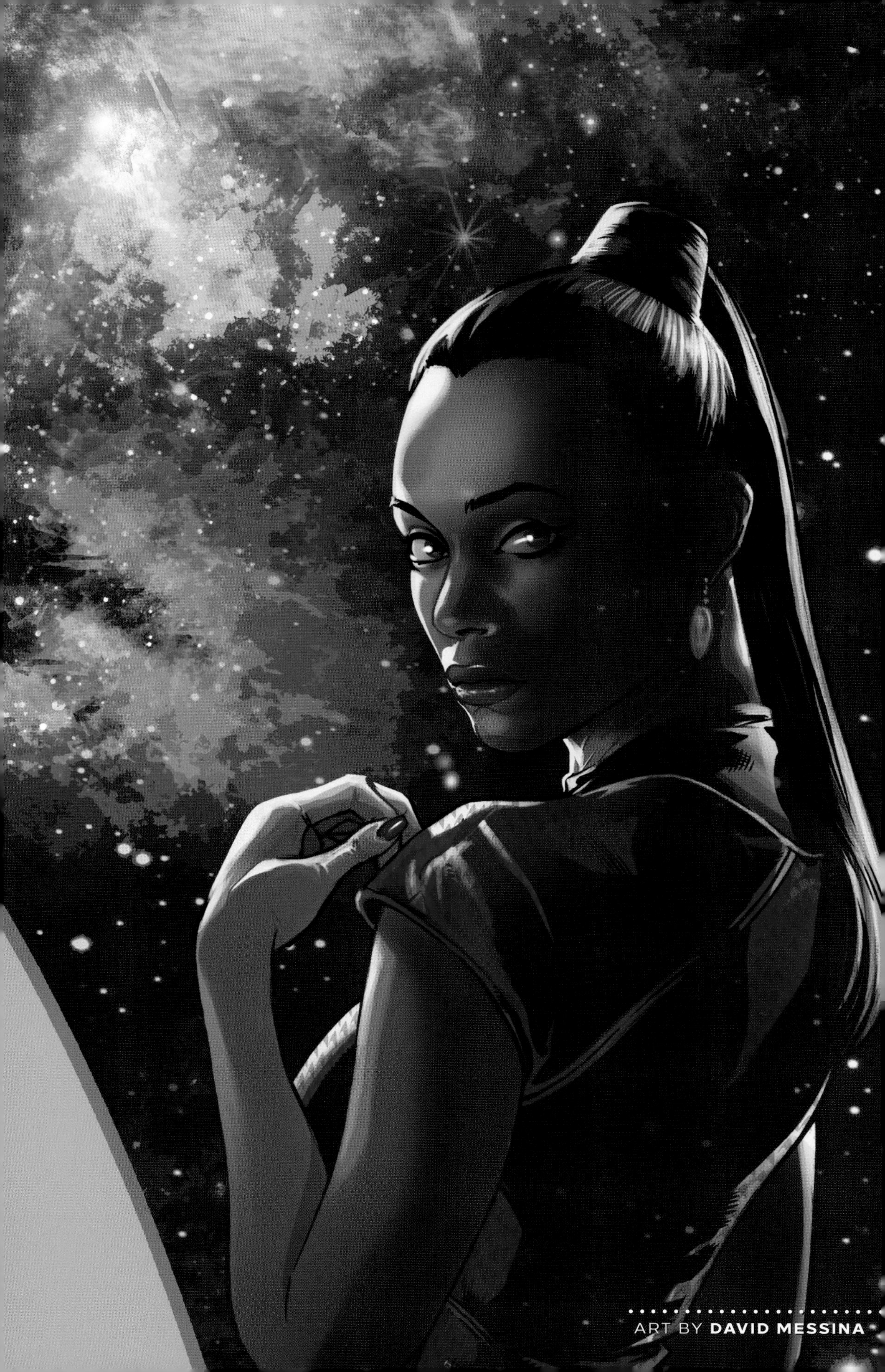

ART BY **DAVID MESSINA**

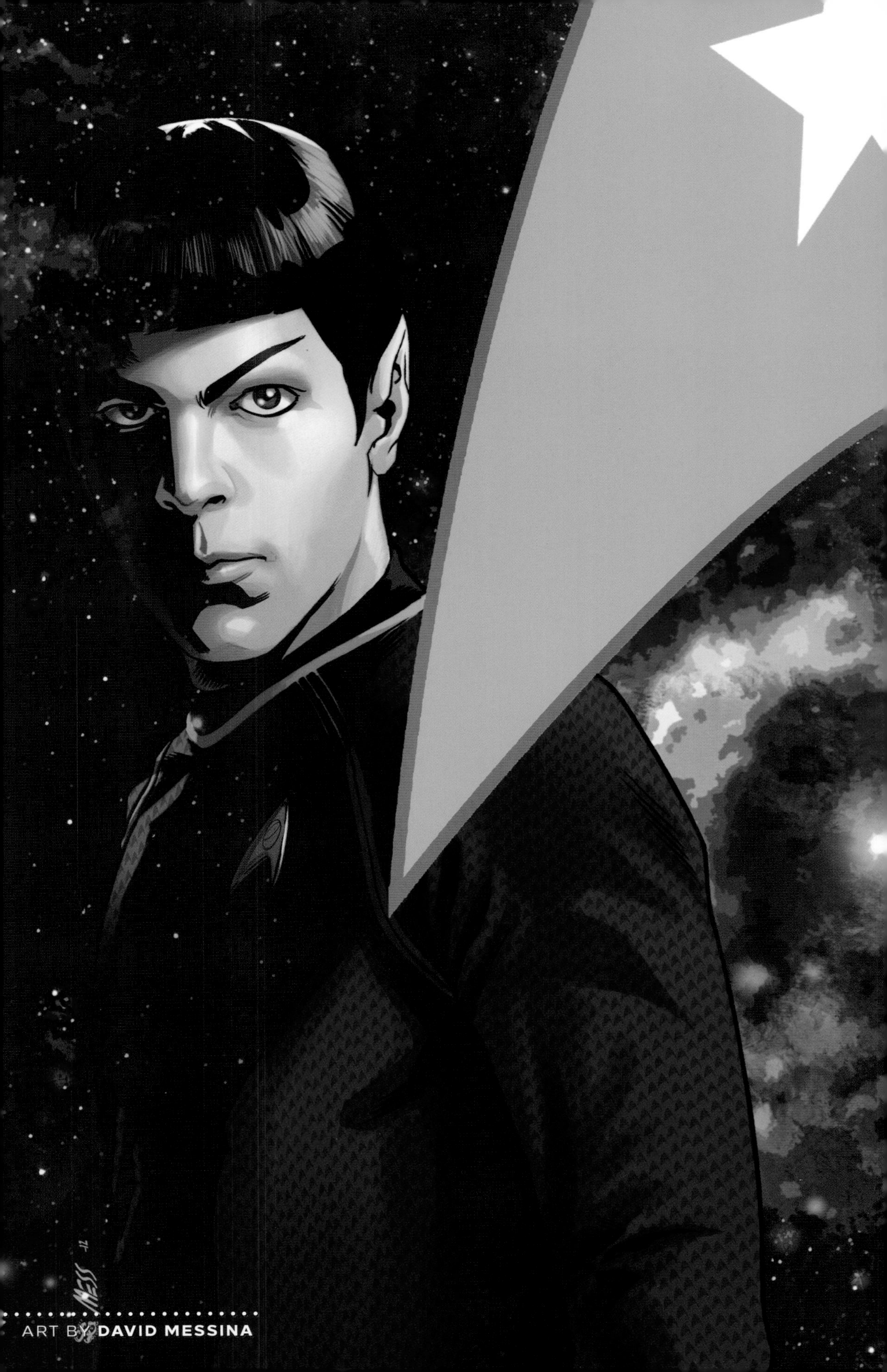

ART BY DAVID MESSINA

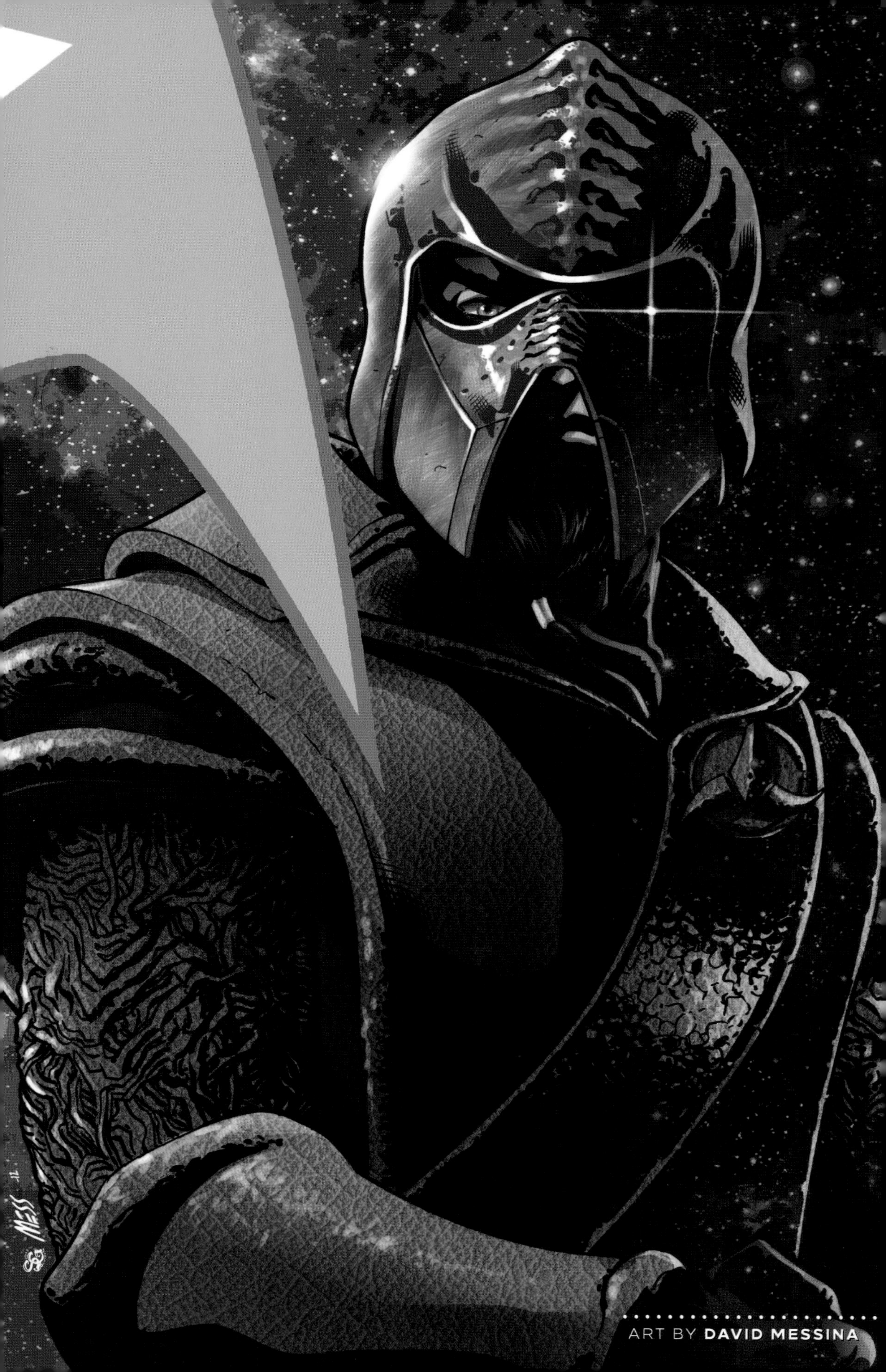
MESS '12

ART BY **DAVID MESSINA**

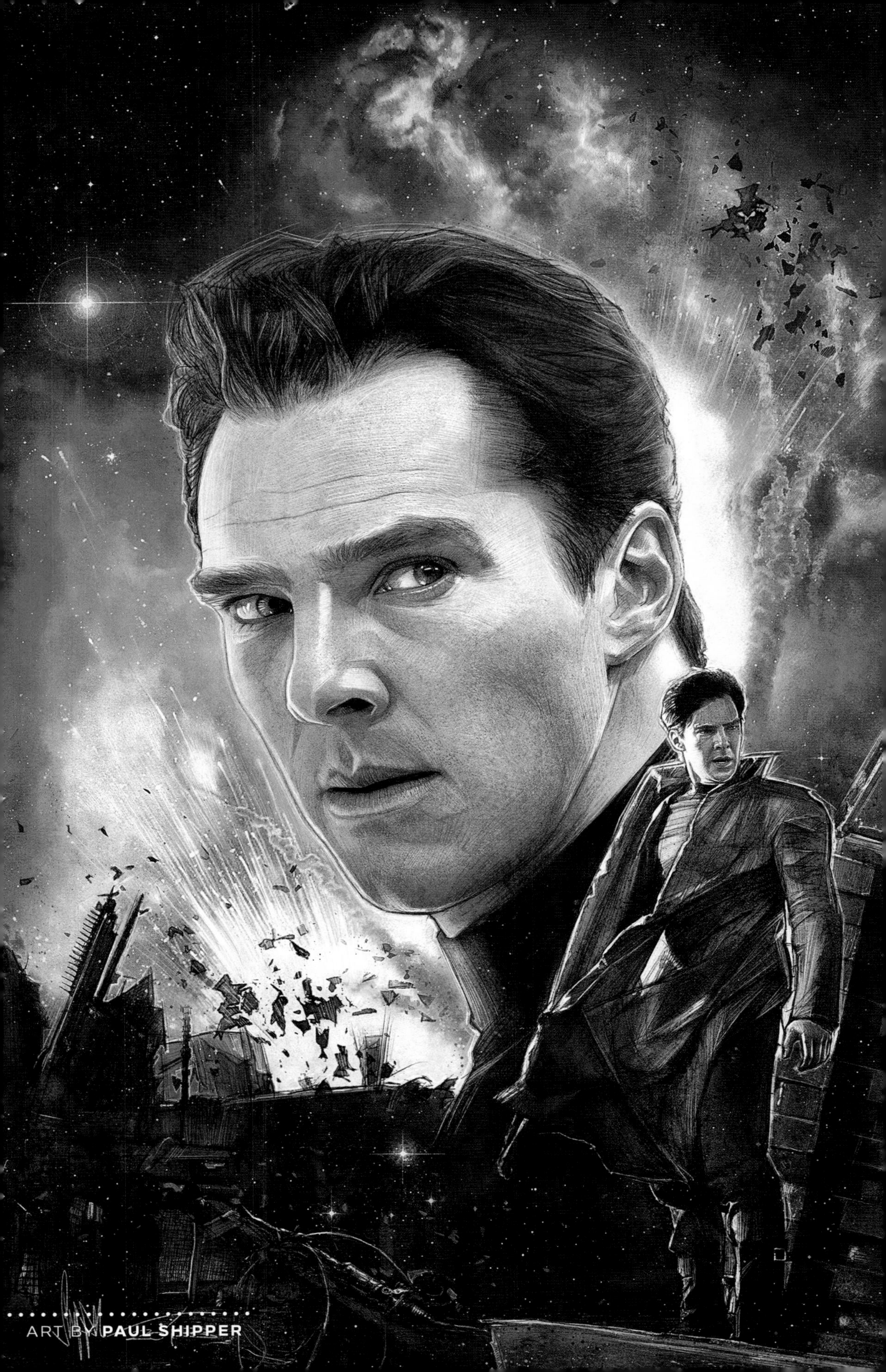
ART BY PAUL SHIPPER

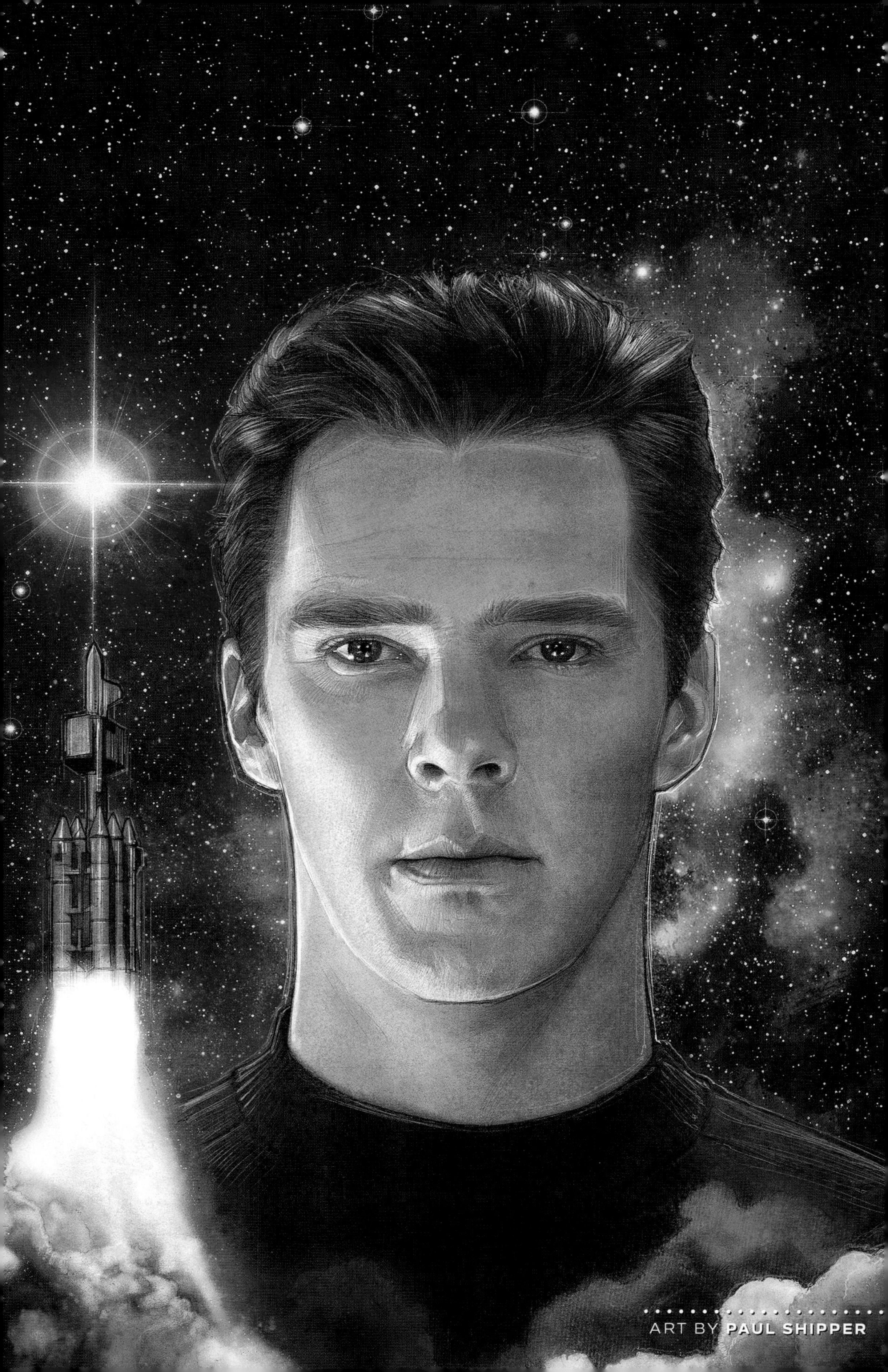

ART BY **PAUL SHIPPER**

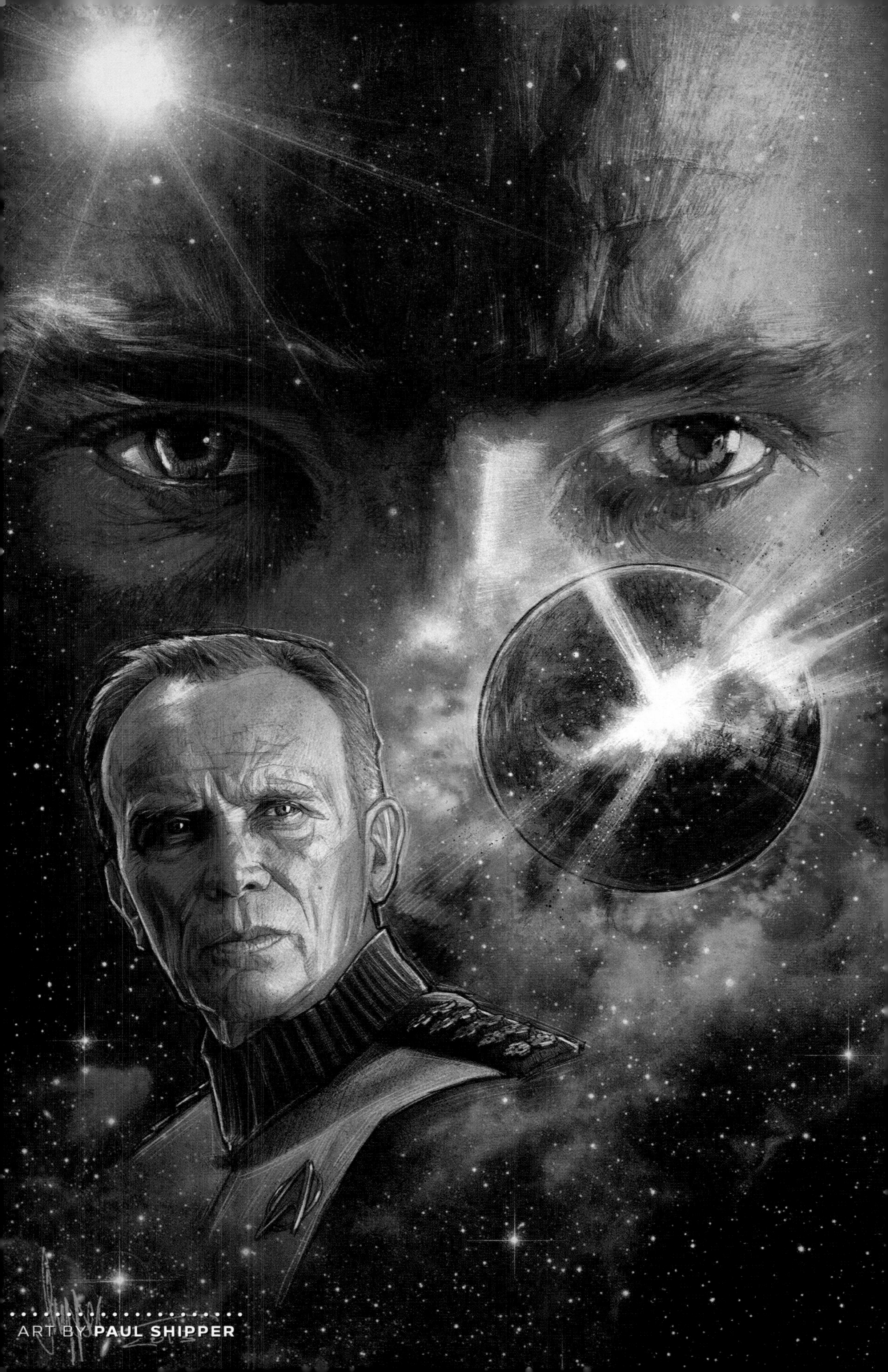

ART BY **PAUL SHIPPER**

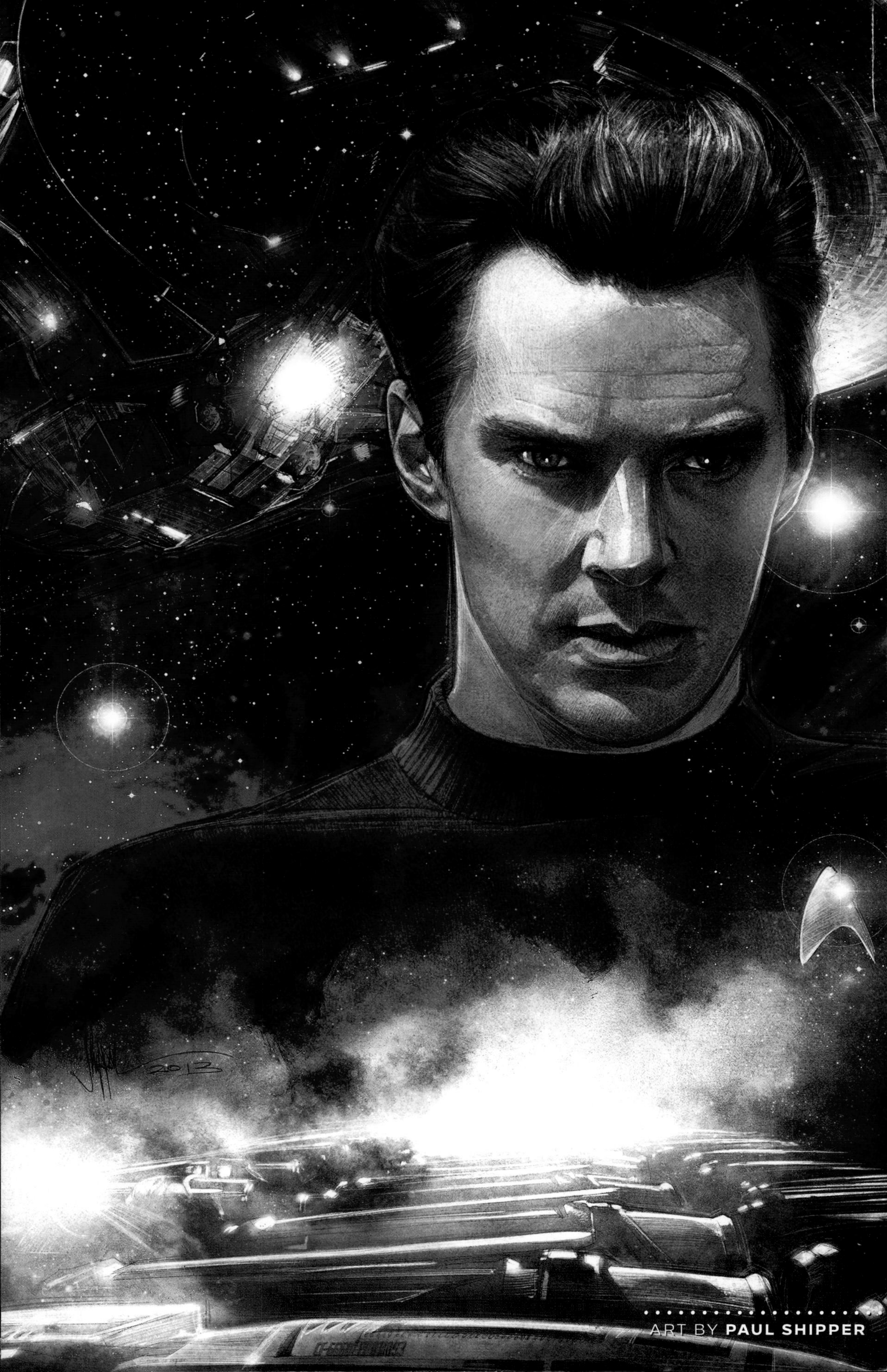

ART BY **PAUL SHIPPER**

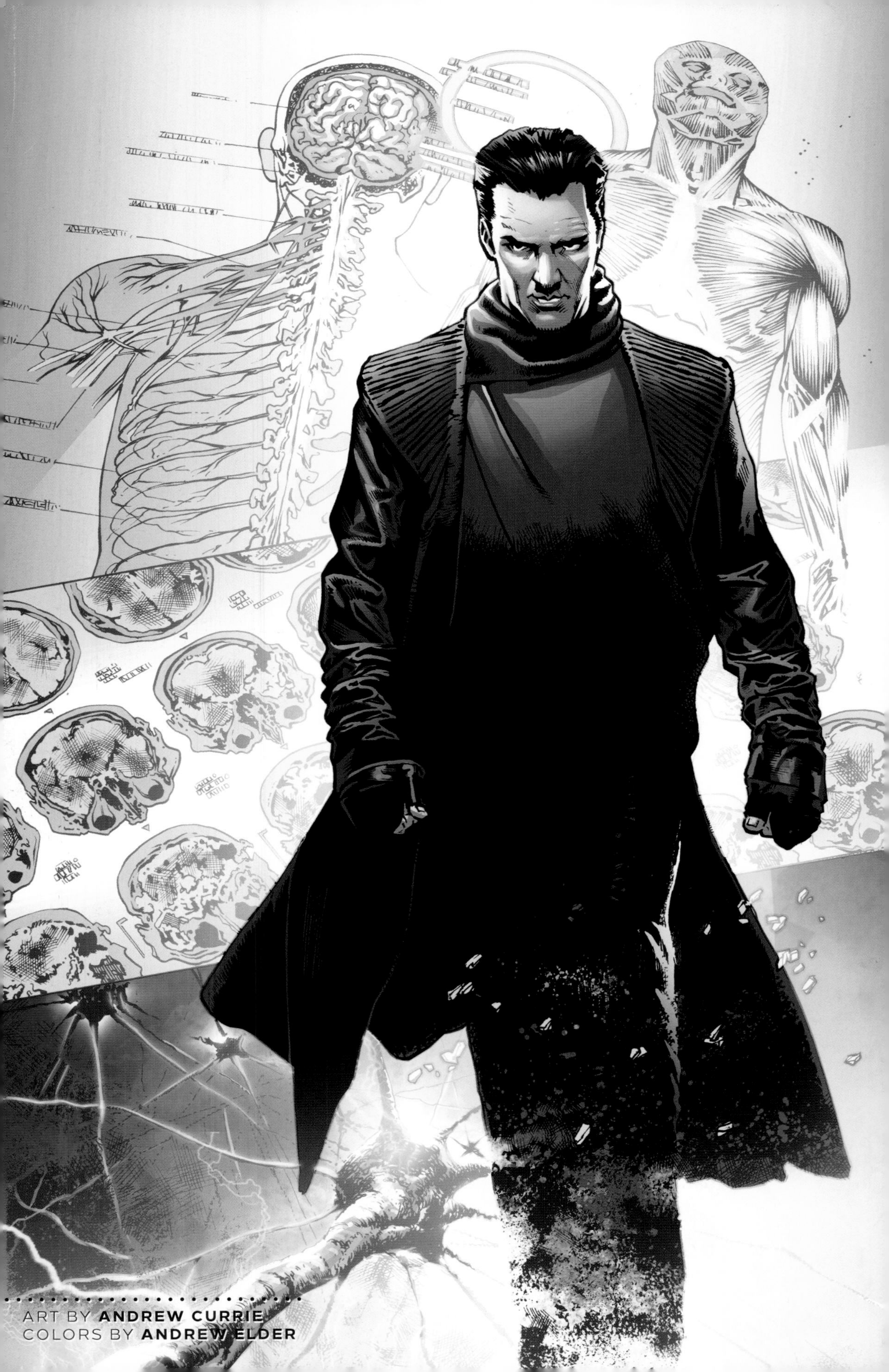

ART BY **ANDREW CURRIE**
COLORS BY **ANDREW ELDER**

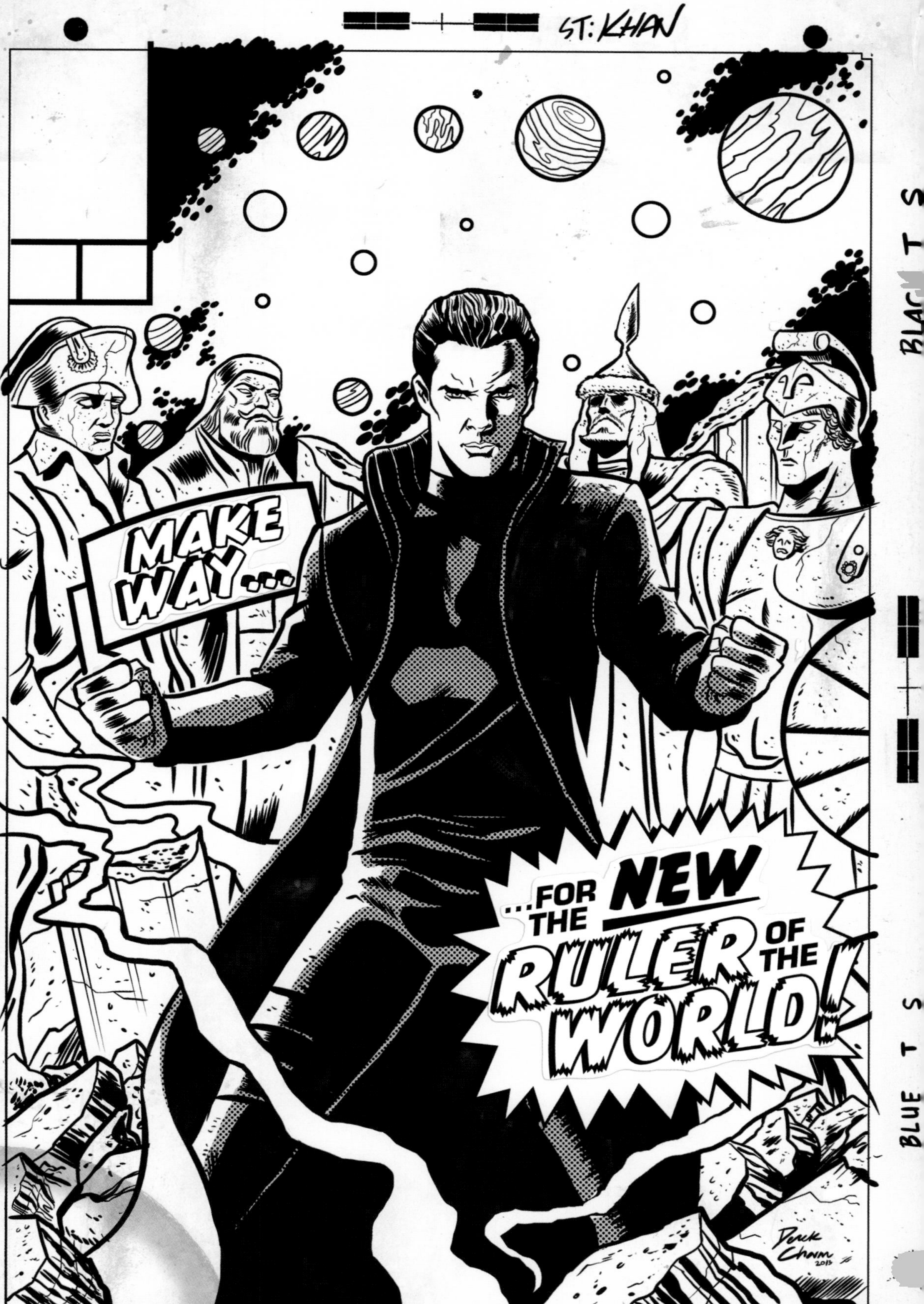
ST: KHAN
MAKE WAY...
...FOR THE NEW RULER OF THE WORLD!
Derek Charm 2013

ART BY **DEREK CHARM**

LEADING STRAIGHT INTO ***STAR TREK***!

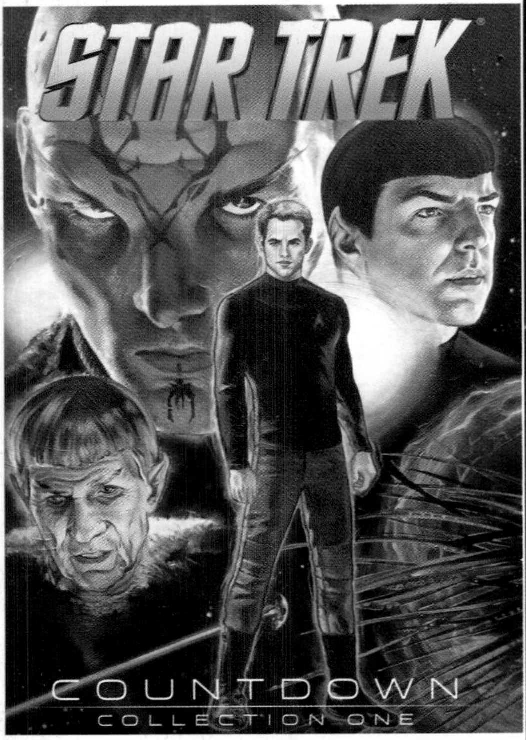
STAR TREK
COUNTDOWN
COLLECTION ONE

STAR TREK: COUNTDOWN COLLECTIONS, VOL. 1
ISBN: 978-1-63140-632-4

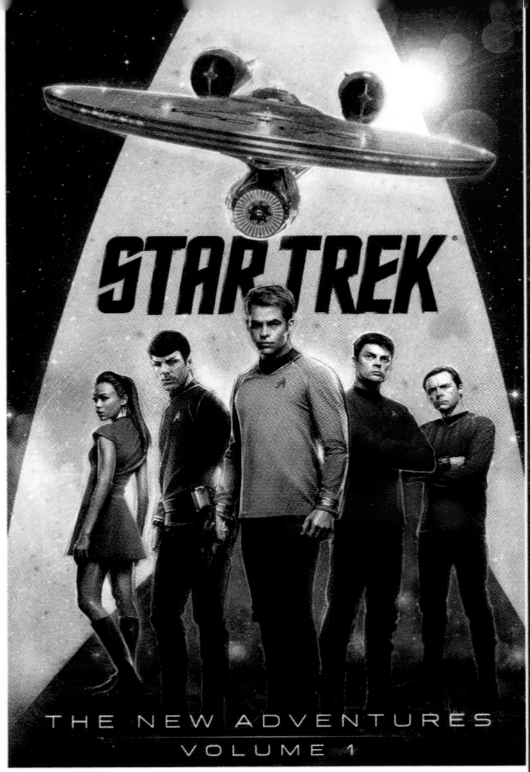
STAR TREK
THE NEW ADVENTURES
VOLUME 1

STAR TREK: THE NEW ADVENTURES, VOL. 1
ISBN: 978-1-63140-177-0

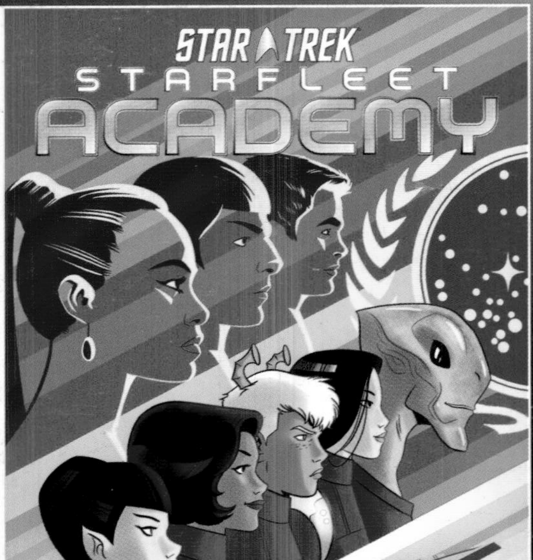
STAR TREK
STARFLEET
ACADEMY

STAR TREK: STARFLEET ACADEMY
ISBN: 978-1-63140-663-8

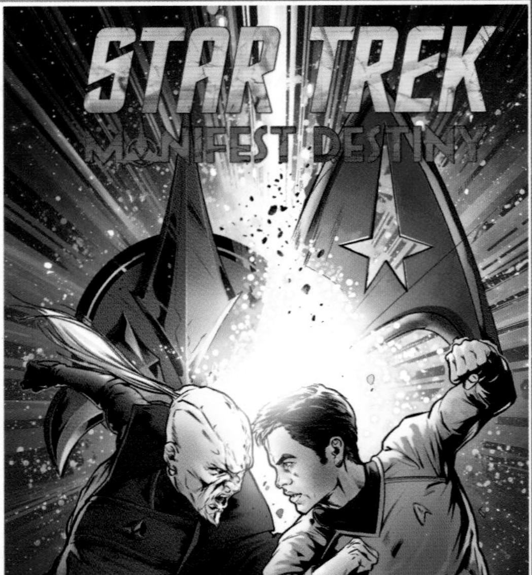
STAR TREK
MANIFEST DESTINY
JOHNSON · PARROTT · HERNANDEZ
5

STAR TREK: THE NEW ADVENTURES, VOL. 1
ISBN: 978-1-63140-634-8

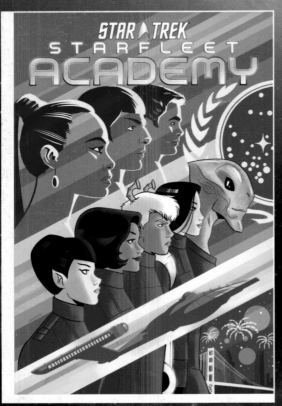

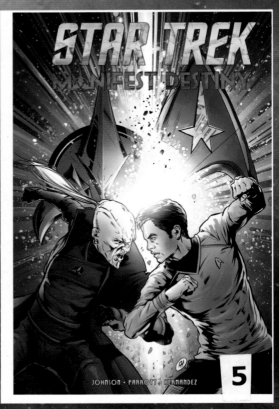